Adventures of the First Woman Mountie II

The Second Omnibus

LAURIE SCHRAMM

Adventures of the First Woman Mountie II. The Second Omnibus

An Inseparable Mountie. Book 5

An Indispensable Mountie. Book 6

An Inexorable Mountie. Book 7

An Intrepid Mountie. Book 8

Print ISBN: 978-1-7772424-8-0
ePub ISBN: 978-1-7772424-9-7

2nd printing, 2023

Laurie Schramm

DEDICATION

Dedicated to the present and past Members of the Royal Canadian Mounted Police and its forebears, the Royal North-West Mounted Police and the North-West Mounted Police.

Laurie Schramm

CONTENTS

Dedication v

Acknowledgements ix

An Inseparable Mountie. Book 5 1

An Indispensable Mountie. Book 6 167

An Inexorable Mountie. Book 7 323

An Intrepid Mountie. Book 8 483

Book 5 – 8 Summaries 645

About the Author 647

Adventures of the First Woman Mountie 649

Laurie Schramm

ACKNOWLEDGMENTS

I am extremely grateful to the growing number of friendly readers that that have provided encouragement, comments, and suggestions based on drafts of these books: Ann Marie, Victoria, Katherine, William, Al, Dawson, Jayme, Karen, and Ernie.

Special thanks also to three real-life veterans of the RCMP, all of whom have supplemented their encouragement with numerous background and factual reference materials on the Force: Chief Superintendent William Schramm (Ret.), who also kindly allowed my main character to borrow his Regimental Number, Assistant Commissioner Dawson Hovey (Ret.), and Staff Sergeant Al Lund (Ret., author of *Mounties on the Cover* and probably the world's leading authority on Mountie fiction).

Laurie Schramm

One of the inescapable encumbrances of leading an interesting life is that there have to be moments when you almost lose it.

Jimmy Buffett, American singer-songwriter
From "*A Pirate Looks at Fifty*," 1998

Laurie Schramm

An Inseparable Mountie

Adventures of the First Woman Mountie. Book 5

LAURIE SCHRAMM

Laurie Schramm

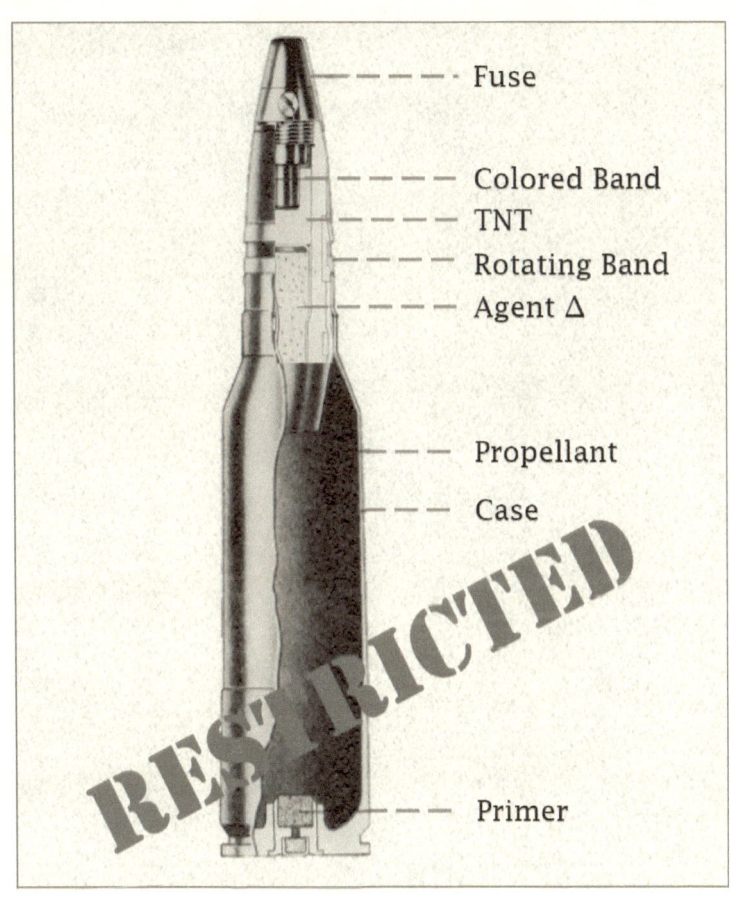

Laurie Schramm

DEDICATION

To Ember

Laurie Schramm

BOOK 5 CONTENTS

	List of Characters	9
1	Prelude. 1943	11
2	The First Clues	17
3	A Moonlight Helicopter Ride	29
4	Unusual Ordinance	39
5	The Investigation Begins	51
6	The Island	67
7	The Plot Thickens	77
8	The First Search	93
9	More Searching	107
10	Convergence	123
11	Defence	139
12	Aftermath	151
13	Epilogue	159
	Book 5 Endnotes	163

Laurie Schramm

LIST OF CHARACTERS
(IN ORDER OF APPEARANCE)

- Lieutenant Reo Saitō, Imperial Japanese Navy
- Lieutenant Boshiro Isobe, Imperial Japanese Army
- Dr. Sarah McInnes, Physician, Queen Charlotte General Hospital, BC
- Karen, Frank, and Rick, kids from a beach campfire and school-friends of Jimmy Hunter
- Jimmy Hunter, a 15-year old-resident of Masset, Queen Charlotte Islands, BC
- K'iijuu, paramedic, Queen Charlotte General Hospital, BC
- Constable James Miller, RCMP, Queen Charlotte City, BC
- Assistant Commissioner George MacLeod, RCMP Security Service
- Staff Sergeant Robert (Bob) G. Simpson, RCMP Security Service
- Captain Donald (Don) Harrison, Military Intelligence, Canadian Armed Forces
- Constable Alexandra (Alex) Houston, RCMP Security Service
- Silver, an Alaskan Malamute; and Alex's friend and companion
- George Carter, Chief of Police, Skagway, AK
- Lieutenant Sandy Moore, helicopter pilot, Maritime Command, Canadian Armed Forces
- Lieutenant Commander Rick Cook, Executive Officer ("XO"), *HMCS Huron*
- Commander Joe Nelson, Captain, *HMCS Huron*
- Ember, a cat
- Dr. Herbert (Herb) Turner, Oceanography Professor, University of Alaska
- Constable Jack McDonald, RCMP Fort McMurray, AB
- "The Scrounger," Aloysius Parker, a beachcomber, Queen Charlotte Islands, BC
- Special Agent Vivian Rule, FBI
- Deputy Director Jonathan Wheeler, FBI
- Rear-Admiral Peter White, Canadian Forces Security Branch

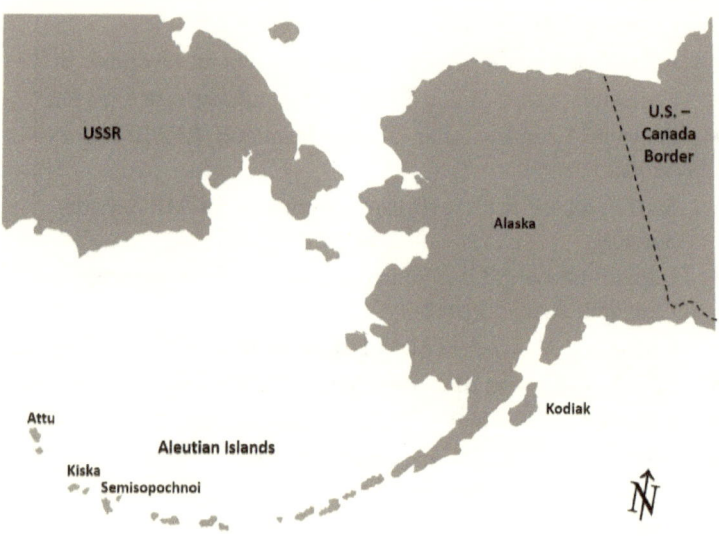

1 PRELUDE. 1943

August 15, 1943
Semisopochnoi, Aleutian Islands, Alaska,

'What a waste!' thought Lieutenant Reo Saitō, as he paused from his work sifting through piles of documents.

The Third Special Landing Force of the Imperial Japanese Army had landed on three of Alaska's Aleutian Islands the previous month[1]. Proud to have been part of the original landing, he had seen their invasion force quickly grow to nearly 7,000 personnel. In establishing bases here in the Aleutians and on Midway Island, some 1,600 miles further south, their superiors planned to support air and naval operations across the breadth of the north and central Pacific Ocean.

Although a Kaigun-daii (Naval Lieutenant) Saitō himself had been attached to assist the Imperial Japanese Army, which comprised the bulk of the invading force, and he had been assigned to Semisopochnoi Island, the most secret of the three islands. He and his colleagues had been lucky. They had been able to quickly locate and move into natural caves (old lava channels) in the volcanic Mount Cerberus. Assisted by speed and concealment, their modest force had remained undetected by the enemy.

Unfortunately, the same could not be said for the bulk of their forces, which were distributed among the other two islands, Kiska and Attu. Within only a day of their landing, an Allied patrol plane (most likely American or Canadian) had discovered their ships off Kiska Island. By

11

the next day, the enemy had discovered their force on Attu Island. Within the first week, bombers had started arriving periodically, and then submarines had come. In one attack alone, enemy submarines had torpedoed three of their destroyers in Kiska's harbour, sinking one and damaging the others. That had all been in June, 1942, just over a year ago.

The competition between their forces' efforts to establish defenses, an airfield, roads, and accommodations and the enemy's almost constant attempts to destroy them from air and sea had continued all year long. It had been a fairly even struggle, back and forth. Sometimes they would achieve a major advance, other times they would suffer a major setback. If only they had been able to complete the airfield, then the fighters could arrive that would provide the security of air cover for the remainder of their construction. After that, they would be able to seize the initiative and take the fight to the enemy.

Unfortunately, the enemy had clearly been worried about the same thing as two months earlier, on May 11, 1943, the Americans had launched their own major invasion on Attu. Despite fierce resistance, the Japanese forces were eventually overwhelmed and, facing certain defeat, mounted a final, glorious two-day banzai charge on May 29th and 30th.

While the Americans regrouped for an assault on Kiska, the Imperial General Headquarters had decided to move first and evacuate. On July 28, "Operation KE" had launched. Two cruisers and six destroyers had entered the Kiska Harbor under the cover of heavy fog. Then, a sign… the fog suddenly lifted and, having already destroyed and/or booby-trapped everything that could be of possible use to the enemy, over 5,000 troops had boarded the ships within a single afternoon and been spirited away!

Their presence on Semisopochnoi Island had not been discovered. Nevertheless, Reo's superiors had decided to evacuate it as well. With the surface ships gone, Reo and his colleagues would be taken off by submarine. It was just as well, Reo decided. Today was August 15th, and they had listened with almost magnetic fascination to the radio reports as a dawn attack at Kiska Island was underway by a huge force of Americans.

Amused by the embarrassment the Americans were going to suffer when they discovered that their huge invasion force had bravely conquered an abandoned island, Reo and his colleagues prepared for their own evacuation as, coincidentally, today was to be their day.

Now here he was, sorting through the last of their files, removing each of the confidential documents and tossing them through an open grate and into the crackling fire of a wood-burning stove. There wasn't much to destroy. Semisopochnoi Island had only been intended to be used for intelligence work and special operations support. The former had produced many files, which Reo was now destroying. The latter involved stores of special, large calibre ammunition.

Lieutenant Boshiro Isobe, Reo's friend in the army, had given him a tour of their munition stores, which were contained in long tunnels under the mountain. Along the way, Boshiro had opened a few crates.

The conventional, explosive rounds had black projectile bodies, and red-painted tips on the fuse caps indicated that the rounds had been filled and were ready for use. Coloured bands painted on the projectile bodies, just below the fuse-caps identified the payload contents, yellow or green meant high-explosive (HE), red meant shrapnel, white meant armor-piercing (AP), and combinations of colours meant combinations of contents, like yellow/green for HE-tracers.

"See here," Boshiro had said, taking a shell from its crate. "Black body means explosive, white and green band means armour-piercing tracers, and the red tip means it's filled and ready to go!"

Next, Boshiro had shown him some of the "specials," as they were called. These carried unconventional loads that were also identified by colour. The specials' projectile bodies were grey, and for these rounds blue-painted tips on the fuse caps indicated that they had been filled and were ready for use. Here again, coloured bands identified the payload contents, green meant "tear," yellow meant "blister," blue meant "choke," and red meant "vomit."

"Chemical weapons," said Reo. "I have heard of them but never seen them before."

"Now look at this one," Boshiro said, taking a shell from a different crate. Reo noticed that Boshiro was much more careful in his handling of this one. "Grey body means it's gas- or liquid-filled - a 'special.' The brown band means "nerve," and the blue tip means it's filled and ready to go!"

"A nerve weapon," whispered Reo, as a cold chill suddenly ran down

his spine. He suddenly felt afraid. "Put it away…"

Boshiro put on a brave face, but he was quick enough to carefully put the round back into its case. Then, in a low voice, he added, "In use, we would add one of these special rounds every four or five rounds, just like we often insert a tracer round after every four or five explosive rounds."

"They are small," Reo commented, surprised.

"Small but powerful. In this case, only a few special rounds are needed to kill or incapacitate dozens of enemy soldiers. These are 25 mm rounds, designed to be fired from large rapid-fire weapons like the Type 96, Kyūroku-shiki nijyūgo-miri Kōkakukijū guns. You navy types use them for anti-aircraft defenses on your ships."

Reo nodded. The ship he had arrived on had carried triple-barreled AA guns. The British called them Hotchkiss Guns.

"In the army, we normally use them against tanks and other vehicles. With high explosives, an effective firing range of four miles, and a firing rate of fire of over a hundred rounds per minute, I've seen them shred an armoured half-track in less than a minute!"

"As you can see, we have a lot of ammunition stored here." Boshiro waved his arm dramatically at the long tunnel whose sides were stacked from floor to ceiling with crates. The tunnel seemed to extend forever into the distance, under the mountain.

"And with the specials?" asked Reo.

"For use against troops in buildings and fortifications," said Boshiro. "Much more effective than flame throwers, easier to aim, vastly greater range, and…" he lowered his voice, almost to a whisper, "terrifying."

"Do you actually use these weapons?" Reo asked.

"Officially, no. In reality, yes… Trust me, you don't want to know. You don't want to see them in action."

Reo shivered again. "I believe you. I'll stick to intelligence work, thank you. Let's go." Then, another thought struck him. "If we ever have to leave this place in a hurry, you wouldn't want to leave all this behind, would you?"

"No…" said Boshiro, thoughtfully. Then he grinned. "On the other hand, destroying them would be simplicity itself. One small charge with a slow burning fuse is all we'd need. That would set off the entire armoury and probably blow the top off of this mountain we're under."

"I don't think either of us would want to be close enough to see that!"

"Maybe just close enough to see it," said Bishiro, grinning again.

"You army types always want to blow things up," Reo accused, playfully.

"You navy types always want to sink things," Bishiro countered.

Their moods restored, the two friends had left together but Reo was thinking about his visit to the munitions stores as he continued to burn the last of the sensitive documents. They would be leaving any minute now, so the army really would have to blow them all up... He definitely did not want to be anywhere nearby when that happened!

Reo had no sooner shivered with recollection than his superior had arrived to check that all of the sensitive documents had been destroyed, after which he'd been ordered to board one of the three submarines that were waiting to remove the last of their forces from Semisopochnoi Island.

It turned out that Reo was one of the last to board the last of the three submarines and he was pleased to encounter his friend Boshito again in the crowded forward torpedo room of the sub.

As the submarine pulled away from the coast and began to submerge, Reo asked his friend about the munitions.

"Just as I predicted," Boshito said, confidently. *"A series of charges spaced throughout the entire complex, all wired to a chemical fuse. The fuse is started by crushing a glass vial of copper chloride in acid. The acid eats away at a thin wire that holds back a spring-loaded striker. When the wire is eaten away, the striker hits a percussion cap at the end of the detonator. When it goes off, everything will go up! Too bad we won't get to see it."*

"I don't think I want to see it," Reo said. *"What happens if the fuse goes out or the charges don't go off?"*

"That rarely happens, but it doesn't really matter in this case. We're leaving an uninhabited island with an active volcano on it, and the enemy doesn't know we were ever here. No one will ever find it anyway."

Boshito said this so confidently that Reo dropped the topic and their conversation turned to other matters as the submarine began its journey south to their new assignment in the central Pacific, at the Tarawa Atoll, Gilbert Islands.

With all three submarines well submersed and on their way, there was no one left to see the fuse as it fizzled out...

15

2 THE FIRST CLUES

Day 1: August 20, 1977 – 34 years later.
Queen Charlotte Islands (Haida Gwaii[2]), British Columbia

Dr. Sarah McInnes was nearing the end of a long shift in the emergency ward at Queen Charlotte General Hospital. It was a modest-sized hospital that served the four thousand permanent residents of the islands plus the surge of visitors that passed through during the tourist season. The day had been long but relatively quiet, with a steady trickle of tourists and locals with minor complaints (none of which actually required emergency treatment). She was starting to think ahead to what she would do on her next few days off.

After a full week's work, it was also her turn to work a weekend, which she and her three colleagues each did once per month. Today was Saturday, and she was nearly at the end of a twelve-hour shift that ran from 07:00 – 19:00. One more day of this and she'd have a few welcome days off. Her first priority was going to be sleep, she decided.

The next patient was a girl of about fourteen years old, brought in by her parents and suffering from irritation in both eyes. While examining her, Sarah noticed that she had a runny nose, but otherwise seemed normal. When questioned, the girl said that her eyes first started to bother her while she and some friends were sitting around a campfire on the beach.

Application of a warm compress to her eyes, followed by flushing with antihistamine eye drops seemed to provide almost immediate relief, so Sarah was inclined to think that the cause of

17

the irritation was smoke from the kids' fire. Sarah explained to the girl and her parents that, although her eye irritation had responded quickly to her initial treatment, she was also going to prescribe antibiotic eye drops for her to guard against the possibility that she had a bacterial infection as well. That was all, other than a caution to phone or bring their daughter back in if her symptoms hadn't completely disappeared over the following two days.

No sooner had the girl and her parents left than two more patients showed up. Boys this time, both fifteen years old. They had bicycled to the hospital together and came in complaining of irritated eyes, just like the girl had earlier. While examining the boys, however, Sarah noticed that they both had some slight difficulty in breathing, and they also both had runny noses. When questioned, they said they had just been visiting with friends around a fire they'd built on the beach. Yes, they knew the girl that had come in earlier and were part of the same group. They also both seemed just a bit restless, prompting Sarah to wonder whether the boys had been violating a curfew or something, which could have led to some nervousness on their part. Both boys responded to the same treatment as the girl, so after observing them for a while Sarah gave them the same prescription and warnings and sent them on their way.

Sarah's last patient of her shift was more serious. She had lapsed into fighting off a wave of sleepiness, when reflections coming from red flashing lights outside caught her attention. *That's unusual*, she thought. Their single ambulance wasn't called out very often. Maybe something a little more interesting was coming her way.

Two of the hospital's five paramedics wheeled Jimmy Hunter in on a gurney. They provided a concise rundown on his vital signs and other visible symptoms, including slow pulse, contracted pupils, difficulty breathing, and irritated eyes. It was having sore eyes and trouble breathing that had made him worried enough to call for the ambulance, Jimmy explained.

As Sarah did her own quick survey of Jimmy's condition, she noticed that he was sweating despite his light clothing and the cool evening air, and either shivering or trembling. He also had a runny nose.

"Let me guess," Sarah said, "you were having a campfire with some friends on the beach and got some smoke in your eyes?"

"How did you know?" asked Jimmy, amazed.

"Three of your friends have already been in here, but none of them was in a bad shape as you are. Why is that?"

At this, Jimmy became evasive and said that maybe he'd gotten too close to the fire.

Sarah would probably have accepted this explanation except that Jimmy's evasiveness set her "spider-sense" tingling, so she tried a different approach.

"Jimmy, your friends seem fine but whatever happened to you is more serious. I can't help you get better if you won't tell me what's really been going on… OK?"

For a moment there was only the sound of Jimmy's wheezing as he clearly wrestled with whether to say any more. Finally, after a bout of strained coughing, he opened-up.

"Well, we did have a fire at the beach, but we thought it would be fun to add some things to the fire to make it burn brighter. You know?"

"Sure. What kinds of things?"

"Just bits of driftwood at first, but then we tried some other things that we'd found washed-up on the beach."

"Come on Jimmy," Sarah said, thinking this could drag out forever. "Please tell me exactly what you put on the fire. That might tell me how to help you."

There was another bout of wheezing, nose blowing and coughing. Then, "Well, some artillery shells of some kind had washed up. It was after that huge storm we had yesterday, remember?"

Sarah just nodded, not wanting to interrupt.

"Well, we found these shells, like I said, and they weren't just shells – they had big bullet-ends on them. At first, I was going to throw them into the fire, but the others were afraid that they'd explode or something, or that the bullet end would fly out and hit someone."

Sarah nodded. She thought she knew what was coming now.

"So, I got my friends to hold the shiny brass part of one of them over a log and jumped on the bullet end, and you know what? It came right out. The brass part was full of gunpowder. So that's what we put on the fire. We opened up a few more of the shells, and once in a while we'd dump one into the fire … man did that stuff burn!" Jimmy said, before being overtaken by another round of coughing.

"I can imagine," Sarah said, dryly. She had an image in her mind now, but it was far from obvious how burning nitrocellulose from artillery shells would cause any of these symptoms. *If anything*, she thought, *the nitrocellulose should have burned the most cleanly of all. That's why it had originally been known as "smokeless powder."*

Sarah was about to question him further on this point, but Jimmy immediately went into convulsions, then lost consciousness, then stopped breathing.

"Shit!" Sarah went into action.

Jimmy's breathing, at least, was easily restored. By the time Sarah got a ventilation tube down his throat and the oxygen turned-on, he'd started breathing again on his own. The nitrocellulose burning didn't make any sense to her, but she now suspected some kind of pesticide poisoning ... or maybe something worse. *That's a scary idea*, she thought, but she kept her darker suspicions to herself and put them aside for later reflection. Although their hospital was small it was modern, at least, and atropine was indicated.

Within two minutes of establishing an intravenous (IV) atropine drip, Jimmy's heart rate was increasing towards normal, and his breathing was easing considerably.

"OK... progress...," muttered Sarah, half to herself and half to her ER nurse and the two paramedics, both of whom had stayed to help. "The next hour or two will tell us whether we've chosen the right course."

"What do you think caused it?" asked K'iijuu, one of the paramedics.

"I think it was exposure to a pesticide," said Sarah. "When Jimmy is fit for more questioning, I think we'll find out that they threw some old pesticide containers on the fire along with all the other stuff they found." Then, to the ER nurse, "Let's keep him under close observation for the next two hours. Call me if his condition worsens."

"Yes, Doctor."

Sarah followed the two paramedics out of the ER, said thanks and good-night to them and then headed for her office, disturbed. Dr. Sarah McInnes loved medicine and hated lying, but she'd lied about one of the medical aspects to the nurse and paramedics. Jimmy's symptoms *could* have come from exposure to a pesticide, but she didn't really think so. Jimmy's story had triggered memories from her undergraduate university days, when she had been pursuing her first academic love: history.

She wasn't great at math, but Jimmy's case brought Sarah's two academic worlds into one simple equation. In Sarah's mind that equation came out as:

$$\left(\begin{array}{c} \text{Jimmy's} \\ \text{symptoms} \end{array} \right) + \left(\begin{array}{c} \text{Opening old} \\ \text{artillery shells} \end{array} \right) + \left(\begin{array}{c} \text{Second World} \\ \text{War history} \end{array} \right) = \left(\begin{array}{c} \text{Chemical} \\ \text{weapons} \end{array} \right)$$

Therefore, some kind of nerve agent.

"Shit!" Sarah repeated, to the otherwise empty office, then picked up the phone. "Time to call in the cavalry."

***

Sarah's call to the islands' 'one-man' RCMP detachment, in Queen Charlotte City, was taken by Constable James Miller. Despite its impressive name, Queen Charlotte City was actually a small fishing and logging village that served as a hub for the entirety of the Queen Charlotte Islands. It hosted such amenities as provincial and federal government offices, the hospital, and the RCMP Detachment.

For his part, Constable Miller made careful notes as he listened. He also had the presence of mind to ask her to keep her nerve-agent suspicion secret for the time being, and asked her to simply tell patients and family alike that the symptoms were due to something more innocent-sounding, like some kind of unknown allergic reaction. Miller promised to follow-up early the next morning with a visit to the beach where the teenagers had been exposed, when there was enough light for a thorough search, after which he would drop in at the hospital to get their names and addresses.

After hanging up the phone, Constable Miller finished making his notes. Re-reading them to make sure he hadn't missed anything he whistled softly to himself thinking, *Well, that's way above my pay grade. This one will make them sit up straight in HQ.*

Turning to the teletype machine in the small detachment office he turned it on, unleashing the hammering sound of an electromechanical typing head that transmitted a five-bit digital pulse code over a dedicated telephone line while simultaneously printing each typed character on the rolling sheet of paper in front of him. The same codes were received and translated into typed characters at an identical machine located, in this case, in the RCMP's "E" Division (i.e., British Columbia) headquarters in Surrey, just outside of Vancouver.

The telex triggered a rapid chain of events. Within minutes, the duty operator in the "E" Division radio room (which also monitored telex transmissions) immediately phoned his commanding officer (CO) at home. His CO, in turn, ordered that the original telex message be forwarded to Ottawa, attention: Assistant Commissioner George MacLeod, of the RCMP's Security Service. It was now well past 10 pm, Ottawa time, but the priority flag ensured that the "HQ" Division's radio room duty officer in Ottawa called Assistant Commissioner MacLeod at home and read-out the telex message, twice.

V
VIA WUI+
RCMP E DIV HQ

RCMP QCHARLOTTE

PRIORITY

FM: QUEEN CHARLOTTE DET.
TO: E DIV HQ
BT
CLASSIFIED SECRET

FOUR PERSONS ADMITTED QUEEN
CHARLOTTE GENERAL HOSPITAL SUFFERING
SYMPTOMS CONSISTENT WITH CONTACT
WITH NERVE AGENT. REPORTED BY ER
PHYSICIAN DR SARAH MCINNES. DR HAS
AGREED TO KEEP NERVE AGENT SUSPICIONS
SECRET FOR NOW. INVESTIGATING.
ELS.
+
RCMP E DIV HQ

RCMP QCHARLOTTE
VVV

As Assistant Commissioner MacLeod set down the phone, he poured himself a glass of Scotch Whiskey and sat down to think. *Thought before action*, was his motto, and he practised it himself on this occasion. After twenty minutes of deep thought, and his Scotch barely touched, he roused himself and made three phone calls.

The first call was to his field-operations mastermind, Staff Sergeant Robert (Bob) G. Simpson. Assistant Commissioner MacLeod briefed him on the telex, and his thoughts on how the situation should be approached. The second phone call was to his counterpart in the Military Intelligence Branch of the Canadian Armed Forces, based in Halifax, where it was by then 45 minutes past midnight local time. That call was brief, and to the point. The third call, with his counterpart's blessing, was to Captain Donald (Don) Harrison, Military Intelligence. That last call lasted an hour. Following the third call, the Assistant Commissioner went back to bed secure in the knowledge that Staff Sergeant Simpson and Captain Harrison would "get on it," and fill him in on the details later.

By the end of the third call in the chain, it was 01:45 am in Halifax. In less than three hours, Dr. Sara McInnes' news had travelled nearly three thousand miles east, up to the high echelons of the RCMP and Canadian Armed Forces and back down again to one of Canadian Military Intelligence's best field operatives. By the following day it would travel more than three thousand miles northwest to Skagway, Alaska, in which unlikely place it would reach a fast-rising field operative who, coincidentally, was also the RCMP's first woman Mountie, Constable Alexandra Houston.

***

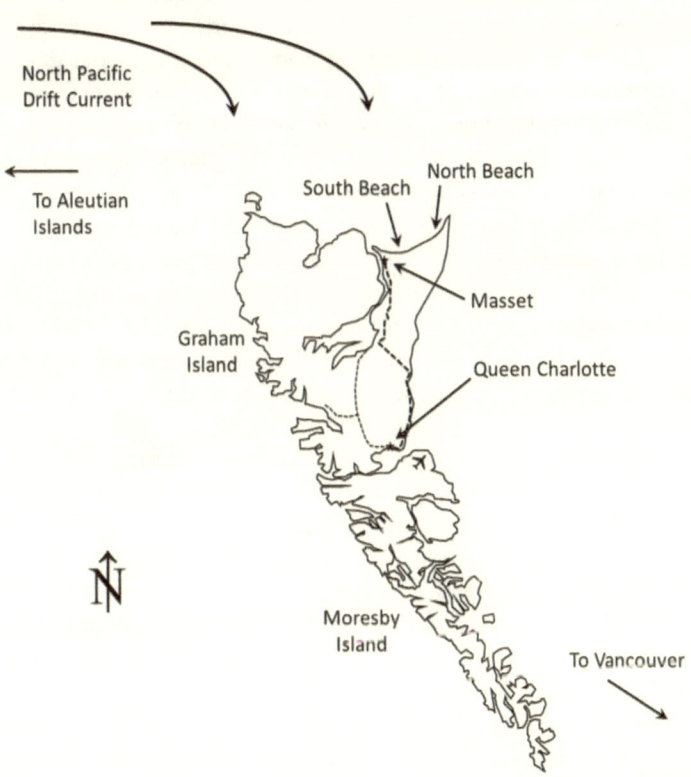

North Pacific
Drift Current

To Aleutian
Islands

South Beach

North Beach

Masset

Graham
Island

Queen Charlotte

N

Moresby
Island

To Vancouver

The Queen Charlotte Islands

Day 2: August 21, 1977.
Queen Charlotte RCMP Detachment

It was Sunday morning when Constable James Miller rose early and reflected on Dr. McInnes' call of the night before. It had been a strange call, and he didn't know whether it was more likely that the kids had been affected by some kind of dangerous chemical from the washed-up shells they'd taken apart, or that they'd been playing with cleaning chemicals of some kind. From the doctor's description it sounded more like they'd gotten into something like bleach, which he knew from his own childhood experiences (playing with things he shouldn't) caused irritated eyes, coughing, breathing trouble, and chest pains.

Oh well, he thought. He didn't really mind having to work on a Sunday as things were generally uneventful on 'the islands,' and this call was at least out of the ordinary. He planned to go to the beach the doctor specified and have a look around. Then he'd come back and visit the doctor in person to get the kids' names and addresses. Then he would see about tracking-down and interviewing each of them.

Following a quick breakfast, he filled a travel mug with coffee and headed for his highway patrol car and the 90-minute drive that would take him to Masset, near the extreme north end of Graham Island (itself the most northerly of the Queen Charlotte Islands), and then east to Agate Beach. Once there he checked each of the several vehicle-accessible firepits along the beach. He didn't have to check many before spotting one of the telltale brass shell casings lying in the sand.

There they are, he thought as he walked up to the indicated firepit. Several brass shell casings lay empty where they had been discarded after having their cordite contents dumped out. Nearby away was a single pile of projectiles, lying next to a large flat rock and a smaller, round rock with whitish score marks on it. He noticed that the projectiles had coloured tips and coloured bands on them. *That's odd*, he thought. All of the ammunition he'd ever seen had single-colour projectiles, like the lead bullets in his service revolver, or the reddish-gold coloured projectiles on high velocity rifle bullets. These were nothing like that.

He turned his attention to the large and small rocks. Presumably the artillery shells had been placed on the flat rock, with their projectile ends sticking out past the rock's edge. Then, the smaller rock was probably used to hammer the projectile out of the brass casing.

Whew, those kids were either stupid or brave, James thought, *I wouldn't have hammered on an intact artillery shell for love or money!*

Going back to his car for his camera and some evidence bags, he photographed the projectiles, casings, and the fire-pit area first, then collected all the projectiles into one bag and all of the brass casings into another bag.

As he was placing the projectiles into the bag, he noticed that a tiny amount of some kind of liquid chemical was oozing out around the coloured bands on one of them. The liquid looked harmless enough – clear and colourless. He would have put it down as a drop of water except that it had a faint, fruity odour. *Maybe they were drinking some kind of soda pop,* he thought.

It was only after he'd placed his camera and the bags in the highway patrol car and begun the drive back to Queen Charlotte City that he noticed that his eyes were feeling a bit scratchy. Almost itchy. Twenty minutes into his drive, he developed a runny nose, and by thirty minutes he noticed that it was becoming just a bit difficult to breathe. When he began to sweat and shake, the awful truth finally dawned on him.

"Shit, shit, shit…" he said out loud. Realizing too late that he must have exposed himself to the same things as had the kids on the beach, he realized that if his symptoms continued to worsen, he would no longer be able to drive.

Turning on his siren and flashing-red roof lights, he put his foot down hard on the accelerator. As the powerful engine in his police-special highway patrol car gave him full power, his complete focus was on getting to the hospital as quickly as he could without crashing into anyone or anything along the way.

Dr. Sarah McInnes was about to get another patient.

***

3 A MOONLIGHT HELICOPTER RIDE

My name is Alexandra Houston. My friends call me Alex.

In the summer of 1974, I'd been 24 years old, and feeling like my career was at a standstill. I'd studied chemistry at university and liked it, but not enough to pursue science as a career. I'd reset my sights on police work next and had joined the Metropolitan Toronto Police force ("Metro"). Although policing seemed like a better fit for me than science, my two years with Metro had mostly comprised routine administrative- and traffic duties. These assignments were important, and needed to be done by somebody, and done well. But for me, they didn't fit the Hollywood vision of policing that I had developed, and I hadn't found them to be very challenging.

They say you should be careful what you wish for.

My life soon changed drastically, beginning with an unexpected meeting. Without explanation, my Captain had sent me to go and see a Royal Canadian Mounted Police (RCMP) officer that wanted to meet me. My reaction to this was apprehension, and I wondered what I could possibly have messed-up so badly that it had caught the notice of our national police force.

That's how I first came to meet Assistant Commissioner George MacLeod. After a lengthy conversation that I belatedly realized was an interview, he told me that he had asked my Captain (his friend) to recommend one of his young officers for a special pilot project he had in mind. He wanted someone who wanted to accomplish things, someone

29

eager and tenacious, someone chomping at the bit to be allowed to do some "real" police work, and... someone female. At this point he had shed his stern "Mountie look," relaxed his entire body, chuckled, and said that my Captain had recommended the "biggest pain in the butt" in his Division - **me.**

Assistant Commissioner MacLeod had explained that the 'Force' had fallen behind the times, and that its senior leadership wanted to build a more diverse police force. "We're going to be recruiting immigrants, visible minorities, maybe even people with some kinds of disabilities as well," he said, "But we have to start somewhere, and that somewhere is by engaging women." He wanted to try a first "pilot test" with a woman, but that pilot test had to succeed as it would pave the way for an entire first troop of policewomen that would follow[3]. He had thought of using someone that had already qualified as a policewoman, and simply re-train them in the "RCMP way."

That had brought me up to full attention. "Wait a minute! Do basic training all over again?"

"Yes!" he'd replied, "that's the only way you can possibly succeed. In the old days of the Northwest Mounted Police, a person could get appointed straight into the Force, even as a commissioned officer, if they had the right political connections. No more. Now everyone starts out the same way, as a Constable, and by going through the same basic training. If you want to have any hope of being accepted, much less respected, that's how you have to begin."

So, in the fall of 1974, I went through training at the RCMP's "Depot" Division training centre in Regina, dealt with the good and the bad issues that came with being the first woman to train there, and survived to become the first woman Mountie. I hadn't intended for it to happen, really. The opportunity just came and found me.

After training, or re-training if you like, I'd been posted to Radium City, a small town in very northern Saskatchewan that, in its early days, had been a great uranium mining centre. Although my new boss, Corporal Morrison, had told me that nothing interesting ever happened around there, he'd been wrong, and I'd had to rescue him from a mine collapse, run our entire detachment single-handed while he was confined to hospital for six weeks, get rescued by a strange dog from near-death, solve a mystery, and find and catch a murderer – all in only four months!

The dog was named Silver. Investigating a mysterious series of break-ins had led me to several abandoned uranium mines. In one such mine I'd fallen through a trap and found myself hanging precariously over the sharp edge of a vertical mine shaft. Unable to get out and tiring fast, I was saved by the almost magical appearance of what I first took to be a wolf, which gave me quite a scare, but turned out to be Silver, an Alaskan Malamute. Silver somehow sensed that I was in danger, had decided to help, and with his assistance I had been able to climb up and out of the raise. To make a long story short[4], while I'd continued to investigate the case, he had attached himself to me, was eventually given to me, and we've been close friends ever since.

Sometime later I'd found myself in another surprise meeting with the same Assistant Commissioner MacLeod. Once again, a "coffee meeting" had turned into an interview and, once again, he had something new in mind for me. By this time, he'd become head of the Force's Security Service[5] and, unsurprisingly, he had some new ideas he wanted to try out by way of some experimental pilot projects. One of them involved me.

That had taken me to Ottawa in November of 1975, where I joined the Security Service. My new boss, Staff Sergeant Robert ("Call me Bob") G. Simpson, introduced me to the shady worlds of spies, counter-espionage, anarchists, and terrorists, and then sent Silver and I to Northern Alberta, undercover, to help look into a series of bomb threats directed at oil sands companies.

Our path to the oil sands was indirect, however, as Silver and I were first sent to Innisfail, Alberta, to be trained as a police dog and handler team. "If that dog is going to go everywhere with you, then we should get him trained too," I'd been told. Both Bob and Assistant Commissioner MacLeod had been interested in, and seemingly amused by, the undercover possibilities presented by the first female Mountie and her canine partner. So, in that way, Silver had officially joined the Mounties too and we were sent to Fort McMurray, undercover, to investigate the bomb threats. Our cover stories had held up just long enough for us to identify and apprehend the bomber, although not before a few more adventures. In one of those adventures I'd been able to save Silver's life, which evened up the score and reinforced the feeling I'd long had that our destinies were intertwined. That had been 1976.

In the Spring of 1977, Silver and I were sent undercover again to Nova Scotia to look into a mysterious weather station on Cape Breton Island. This had involved a lot of SCUBA diving, which was a lot of fun, and a peek inside the shadowy world of international espionage, which had at times been downright terrifying. By the end of July, the case had been wrapped-up and Silver and I had been ordered to go off on vacation and get some rest.

Throughout our adventures together I'd often wondered about Silver's origins, particularly since he was such an unusual dog. So, with the gift of free time, I decided to go explore Silver's past. That should be restful, I had thought.

I was wrong.

No sooner had we settled-in in Skagway than we were called-upon to help search for a lost Girl Guide in the region of the famous Chilkoot Trail. And no sooner had that adventure concluded, than a late-night phone call had Silver and I being whisked to the Skagway airport where we were picked up by a large military helicopter.

***

Day 3: August 22, 1977.

Silver and I were in Alaska, waiting with the Chief of Police at Skagway's airport[6], when we heard the heavy *"Thump, Thump, Thump"* sound of a large helicopter approaching. Next, we saw the approaching lights, and finally the unmistakable appearance and blasting roar of a Canadian Armed Forces Sea King[7] helicopter.

"Like I said," observed George, "not your everyday little civilian helicopter."

I just shrugged and grinned.

I had shown George the place in my truck where I stowed my red flashing light with magnetic roof-mount base and with that in place, flashing on the roof, George simply drove my truck out onto the tarmac and right over to the helicopter. When we got there a Lieutenant in a flight suit hopped out of the co-pilot's door to meet us.

"Constable Houston?" he said.

"That's me," I agreed.

"My name's Sandy. Captain Don Harrison said to look for a fiery woman with red hair, and a grey-white dog that looks like a wolf!"

"I am not a fiery woman!" I instinctively retorted. Then, having listened to what I'd just said, and hearing George burst out laughing, I grinned sheepishly. "Maybe Don knows me better than I know myself," I allowed.

Sandy laughed as well. "Hop in!"

A crewmember took my two duffel bags and a third for Silver. Over the whine of the pilot re-starting his engines, I said goodbye to George and I jumped in – followed closely by Silver.

The big helicopter took off as soon as the SAR Tech[8] signalled that I was belted-in and that Silver was reasonably secure beside me.

After that, all any of us could hear was: *"Thump, thump, thump…"*

I'd only been in a small helicopter before, so while I thought I was prepared for some noise and vibration, I was totally unprepared for the much greater noise- and vibration levels of a large military helicopter. Feeling, as much as hearing, the noise and vibration I was suddenly reminded of an expression I'd heard a pilot use once:

"A helicopter is ten thousand parts flying in close formation around an oil leak, waiting for metal fatigue to set in."

Don hadn't been very specific on the phone about exactly where we were going. Although I'd been given a helmet with boom microphone, I didn't want to bother the crew with unnecessary questions. I had a vague recollection that these Sea Kings flew from both land bases and ships, and I wondered which kind this one was. Cruising at what they later told me was 100 miles per hour, it didn't take long to find out.

Within an hour we had started to bank sharply. I could feel that we were descending and, looking out the nearest small window, all I could see was the ocean below us. Before long, we flew right past a Canadian destroyer. I was just able to make out its pennant number painted near the bow: 281. The helicopter soon made a hard turn and landed on the stern of the ship.

I say "land," but a better description would be that we were plucked out of the sky and dragged straight down to the small landing platform on the ship's stern. That's what it felt like, anyway.

After the engines had been shut down and we exited the helicopter, Lieutenant Sandy Moore explained that we had been hauled down by a "Beartrap." The navy was quite proud of their 'Beartrap,' and Sandy showed me the cable that ran from the bottom of the helicopter to the deck of the ship. He explained that, after hovering over the landing platform, the crew had lowered a line that was caught by the ship's deck crew and attached to a heavier line that was connected, in turn, to a winch below the flight deck. The heavier line was then winched up to the helicopter and secured there. After that, the pilot balanced the helicopter's lift against the pull of the ship's winch allowing the helicopter to be pulled down to just the right spot on the landing platform.

It was amazing!

Sandy explained that they could do this in almost any kind of weather, but that as a pilot he always found it disconcerting to have a cable attached to his aircraft. I found it impressive, and said so.

Shrugging, he smiled and said, "Our NATO colleagues call us the 'Crazy Canucks,' but the Beartrap lets us keep flying missions in the worst weather and seas you can possibly imagine. When the weather's so bad that there's only one helicopter left flying you can be pretty sure it's us."

By the time we'd exited the helicopter and collected our gear, we were met by the ship's Executive Officer ("XO"), Lieutenant Commander Rick Cook, who in turn took us to the bridge to meet the captain: Commander Joe Nelson.

"Welcome to *HMCS Huron*[9]," he said, offering his hand to shake.

"Thank you, Sir. It's a pleasure to be aboard." It wasn't correct protocol for me to salute him but, being a senior officer, I figured he merited a "Sir" at least.

The Captain explained that the Huron was an *Iroquois*-class destroyer, a class named to honour Canada's First Nations. It was fairly new, having been launched only six years earlier and commissioned into the Canadian Armed Forces in 1972, and she carried not just one but two of the large Sea King helicopters. I was surprised to learn that she was primarily a guided-missile destroyer and carried a full complement of mostly sea-to-air missiles.

Beyond introductions, the Captain wished us well and said that all he knew about our mission was where to pick us up and where to drop us off.

"That's more than I know. Can you at least tell me where I'm going?"

"The airport on the Queen Charlotte Islands." He added that we'd be in easy range of it in the morning. "In the meantime, the XO will show you to your quarters and arrange a bit of privacy for you."

I hadn't given any thought to privacy, but it suddenly came home to me that there weren't any women serving on Canadian combat ships yet[10]. As a woman, and a Mountie, and a dog-handler to boot, I supposed that made me a triple rarity onboard, which I assumed was the reason Silver and I were taken to the bridge to meet the Captain in the first place.

The Captain seemed to take it all in stride, however, and made a fuss over meeting Silver who, for his part, was on very good behavior and seemed quite interested in our new temporary surroundings. Based on our brief introduction, I hadn't yet detected whether the Captain had a sense of humour, but this was dispelled as the XO moved to lead us off the bridge.

"Don't forget to introduce them to the ship's mascot that I don't know about," the captain said.

I could have sworn I heard a slight chuckle from the Captain as he turned to watch the ship's helm. "Ship's Mascot?" I asked the XO as we headed down a long, narrow passageway.

It turned out that, although I was a rarity onboard the ship, Silver wasn't the only animal onboard. The second last part of the ship's tour provided by the XO was the centrally-located main galley. This turned out to also be the home of the ship's mascot, a cat named Ember.

She was well named, having a rich fur coat that was dark grey to the point of being almost black. The crew had installed a scratching tree with a comfy-looking bed on top of it. They were literally bolted to the floor and bulkhead, and the cat's bedding was nestled into a metal box that was at least three inches deep. Clearly, Ember could hole-up in her bed and ride out even the most vigorous rolling seas and storms.

There was another metal box mounted on the wall directly above the bed, with a red cross and the words "First Aid Kit" stencilled in bold letters. One of the chefs showed me how the First Aid Kit could be lowered so that it mated with the cat's bed, making it invisible.

"For use during inspection tours," said the chef with a wink.

From her elevated position of about three feet above the deck, Ember had a safe and secure view of the entire galley and it was from this commanding position that she watched our entrance.

It was only by chance that I happened to spot her as soon as we entered the galley, but it enabled me to see her rapid changes of expression as her first instinct to show disdain for me quickly changed as she spotted Silver walking right behind me. The immediately narrowed eyes and flattened ears indicated better than words that she was not amused by the presence of this canine interloper. As I instinctively walked over to say hello and offer a hand for her to sniff, she responded by baring her front claws and snapping her teeth, so I pulled back and looked questioningly at my guide.

"Ember's a bit territorial," he explained, "and seems to think the ship is hers and only on loan to the Captain and the rest of us. She's really a very sweet cat once she gets to know you though. If you give her time, she'll eventually come around to you."

After a close look and a quick sniff, taken from a safe distance, Silver, for his part, rather pointedly ignored the cat. I could tell from his manner, however, that he was alert to the possibility of a sneak attack from behind. I tried, unsuccessfully to hide my smile at this, which prompted a rather reproachful look from Silver.

They offered us food, explaining that on a warship the galley never closes, but it was late so Silver and I only had a small snack each.

We did see a different side of Ember the cat, however, before we left as a crew member that had been eating put his tray of dishes away and then walked over to visit with her. As he did, she immediately seemed to shift gears from 'queen' to 'sweetheart,' and rolled over for a belly rub...

The last part of the tour was accommodations. The XO had graciously turned over his own quarters, comprising a combined office and sleeping space. For Silver and I this was just perfect. Our duffel bags had already been delivered to the XO's quarters and the last thing he left me with was a hand-written sign that read *"Woman on Board. Privacy Please."* This, he explained, was to be attached to the outside door of the Officers' Head (bathroom) when I was using it. For Silver, he suggested that the heli-deck on the stern was probably the best place for him to "do his business," and that actually worked out surprisingly well. Other than that, Silver and I called it a night.

Even frequent travellers usually find that the first night in unfamiliar bed and surroundings make it hard to get a good sleep, but having Silver curled up with his back against the backs of my legs, as usual, was comforting. Between that and being tired from an unexpectedly full and adventurous day, I slept soundly, soothed rather than disturbed by the rocking and swaying motion of the destroyer as it cruised silently through the night.

Much later, someone would ask me if I'd felt safe being the only woman aboard a ship of 280 men. The answer is yes. I didn't expect to encounter a ship full of pirates, of course. I could also add that there shouldn't be much to fear for a woman police officer wearing a large side-arm (I was still carrying the Smith & Wesson .357 Magnum-calibre revolver that had recently[6] been given to me by Skagway's Chief of Police when I hadn't been able to take my usual service revolver into the United States. Then, there was also the fact that I was accompanied by a large police dog who looked remarkably like a wolf. Citing these facts, however, would do a disservice to the ship's crew all of whom, without exception, treated me with the utmost professionalism tempered by an easygoing friendliness.

Silver and I were, of course, the centre of attention at breakfast the following morning where we were treated to a grand meal. With no dog food on board, beyond the supply I always travelled with, Silver had to make do with eggs, bacon, sausages, and toast, all of which vanished from his "bowl" which, in reality, was a large dinner plate. About halfway through his meal, Silver looked up at me with his penetrating blue-grey eyes and an image of sheer contentment entered my mind. These uncanny mental images, that I occasionally received from Silver, never failed to surprise me.

That Silver's food vanished so promptly, was taken by the cooks as a huge compliment. While we enjoyed joking about it, I hadn't had the heart to explain to the cooks that, as a former northern sled-dog, Silver was fully capable of eating almost anything with the same relish and devotion. He certainly ate more than I did!

***

4 UNUSUAL ORDINANCE

Day 4: August 23, 1977.
Sandspit Airport, Queen Charlotte Islands

We were met by my friend and military colleague Captain Don Harrison, of the Canadian Armed Forces. I'd gotten used to seeing Don show up in different uniforms - and even wearing different rank insignia – given his job in military intelligence ("A contradiction in terms," he liked to joke), but in this case he was dressed in very casual civilian clothes. Carrying a small duffel bag, he'd come running to the helicopter as soon as it landed at Sandspit Airport, which was close to Queen Charlotte City.

Before either of us could say anything, Silver barked and rushed up to him. Standing on his hind legs, and with his forepaws on Don's chest, he proceeded to lick every part of Don's face he could get at. This was serious business, so it was a few moments before Don was able to look over at me and say, "I brought some civilian clothes, so you could change out of your uniform before getting out of the helicopter."

"Hello to you too, Don," I replied, rather archly.

I was pleased to see him blush, and even stammer ever so slightly. "Uh, well, sorry Alex. I really have missed you, but I didn't want anyone to see you getting out in uniform and I guess I didn't really think about anything else."

"That's OK Don," I replied, pleased to have been able to throw him off-guard, which didn't happen very often – this was a very self-confident guy! But I didn't entirely let him off the hook so quickly. "And how did you know what size to bring?" I asked, having raised an eyebrow enquiringly.

That threw him off again. This was going to be a record day for me.

"Uh, well, we have known each other for a while… and I have seen you…"

"Yes?"

"Well you know, I have seen you… without clothes…" He paused, then carried on, gaining poise again, "and I am a trained observer after all, so I had a pretty good idea what sizes to get," he finished much more confidently.

I know what you're thinking, but the truth is that Don and I had been shipwrecked and briefly marooned on a small island off Canada's east coast earlier the same year[11]. In order to survive, we'd had to build a fire, get out of our wet clothes, and get warmed and dried as quickly as possible, hence the revealing episode.

Anyway, Don's reminder and sweet nature brought a laugh from me, and I decided it was time to give him a break. "Thanks. If Sandy and his crew here can give me a moment of privacy, I'll change."

Turning away, I happened to look down at Silver who had been standing beside Don all this time, all the while looking attentively at us as if listening intently to our conversation. Seeing my glance, he looked straight at me with a penetrating gaze, as if to say: "I like him!"

Sandy, who had already exited and come around the helicopter, smiled, asked the rest of the crew to avert their eyes for a few minutes, and closed the helicopter's large central door so I could change. Sandy and his crew even kept straight faces during the whole thing.

Once I had changed into civilian clothes, Silver and I grabbed our own duffel bags, with Don's help, and with a good-bye to Sandy and a wave to the rest of the crew we stood back as the big helicopter lurched back in to the sky and headed back to their ship.

Don had rented a Chev Suburban four-wheel drive (4WD) sport-utility vehicle (SUV) for us. Although designed for off-road use, it had lots of room, with four doors, a large back seat, and a cavernous enclosed cargo area. As he showed off its features, I approvingly noted that there would be lots of room for the three of us and our gear.

"Thanks for coming Alex!" he said. "I'm sorry to have pulled you out of Alaska so quickly, but I'm sure glad you're here... Both of you," he added, glancing down at Silver and bending down so he could rub Silver's ears.

"Grruph," said Silver, leaning his head towards Don so he could get the most out of his ear rubs.

"No problem Don," I replied. "Duty calls... right?"

"Yes, but I know that you can refuse undercover assignments, just like I can, and I really appreciate it."

"Well, this is the kind of thing I signed up for, really. Besides, our Alaska adventure had just ended, and I like working with you, so... here we are"

If this dialog seems a bit stilted, it's because we were both carefully avoiding talking in specifics about the last time we'd worked together. As I mentioned, our paths had crossed in Nova Scotia while each of us was working on the same case, but from different angles[11]. We'd found that we worked well together, had faced near-death twice together and, almost inevitably, had become very close. Close, even to the point of dating a bit after the case was over. The dating hadn't gone badly, especially since we were always so amazingly comfortable with each other, but it had left each of us feeling a bit uncertain about whether we were ready to make commitments and take our relationship "to the next level," as they say. Before we were able to resolve anything, our jobs had separated us and taken us away to different parts of the country.

Now that we had been thrown back together, I found that I was relieved. It felt as if something that was missing had been returned. I was looking forward to working with Don on a new mission, but it was going to be... complicated. *Oh well, I guess I wouldn't have it any other way*, I thought.

Don explained that he'd rented the SUV, and a tourist cabin for us, so we would be able to accommodate Silver and also so that we could come and go fairly freely. The SUV was in case we needed to go down forestry roads or off-road and along beaches, as there weren't very many proper roads on these islands.

As we drove, Don filled me in on the high points of what little he knew so far: the kids in the hospital, the possibility they'd been exposed to some kind of chemical or biological agent, the probability that, if so, the agent had come from military munitions of some kind – probably artillery shells - and the news that the local RCMP Constable had been similarly affected while conducting a preliminary investigation. In summary: our police and military bosses were worried, and we were being sent in to figure out what was going on.

Having originally trained as a chemist before turning to police work, I tended to be wary, rather than afraid, of chemicals, but the appearance on the scene of chemical or biological weapons was a scary thought.

"It worries me too," agreed Don, "but maybe it's not as bad as it sounds. Maybe, whatever affected the kids and your Constable didn't come from the shells, and maybe it isn't something really bad. Maybe it's just some new kind of cold or flu bug that's spreading around the island."

"You don't really think that though. Do you?" I prompted.

Don sighed. "No I don't, and neither do our bosses, and that's why we're here. In any case, job number one is to find out what's been going on around here. Once we drop off your gear at the cabin we can head over to the hospital and get started."

Don had rented a modest cottage on the western edge of the village, which was perfect. We could park right beside it, it was secluded enough for us to have some privacy, it was well situated for taking Silver for walks and runs, and close to the facilities of the village itself. Leaving our luggage in the cottage to be unpacked later we headed for the hospital.

"What's our cover story?" I'd asked, while we were driving.

"I suggest we pose as CBC Reporters covering the kids' mystery illness," replied Don. "It's obviously a potential human-interest story and it will allow us to snoop around, be nosy, and ask for people's names and addresses without raising suspicion."

"Sounds like the best approach, but we'll probably need to identify ourselves properly to the ER physician that made the initial call. They have a right to know and besides, we're going to want more information than a physician would give out to news reporters."

"She's a she, and I agree. We might end up needing her help too," Don had mused.

"The real media aren't on to this story already are they?".

"Thankfully, no, but it may only be a matter of time. As far as anyone knows, we'll be the first reporters to have heard rumours and be checking them out."

Reaching the hospital, we left Silver in the SUV and introduced ourselves to Dr. McInnes. Don introduced himself as a Captain in the Army – "part of an artillery unit," he'd explained, showing her his military ID. Meanwhile I concentrated on keeping a straight face, as he seemed to have ID and uniforms for virtually every part of the military.

I'm not sure what she expected, but it clearly wasn't a military man and a Mountie woman.

"Really! A woman Mountie?" she'd exclaimed while looking at my badge.

"Yes, a Mountie. With a Red Serge coat and a large Stetson Hat – the whole 'ball of wax.'"

"Sorry, I've heard about women joining the Mounties, I've just never met one before."

"That's OK," I replied. "There aren't that many of us yet; we have about 200 women Constables out of a total force of 18 thousand, so we're still kind of a novelty. It's very helpful for undercover work though."

"I can imagine."

"Wait til you meet her dog," put in Don.

Dr. McInnes raised her eyebrows at Don's comments, but she had her priorities right and immediately took us to meet Constable James Miller, explaining that she had decided to hold him in the hospital overnight since his symptoms had been so much more severe than those of the kids.

We were soon introduced to Jim, as he asked us to call him. He seemed to be in good spirits and said that he was feeling a lot better, but foolish for not being more careful with the artillery shells he'd collected.

"So, they really are artillery shells?" I asked.

"Well, they look like it to me, but unusual ones. They are smaller than the ones I've seen before."

"How small?" asked Don.

"About like this," said Jim, making a circle with his thumb and index finger. "And another thing was strange. The projectile tips had coloured bands on them. I've never heard of shells like that before."

"The bands were put there so people could quickly identify the kind of shells they are," said Don. "That way, you could quickly distinguish star-shells from high-explosive or armor-piercing shells, for example. That kind of thing."

Something in his tone of voice made me glance at Don while he was saying this, and I could tell that there was more going on in his mind than he was relating out loud. I made a mental note to ask him about it later, although it would become all too clear later in the day.

"I'm glad you came over right away, so we could meet," said Jim. "Apparently I'm being moved later today or early tomorrow. They're sending me to a specialist over in Vancouver."

"Really!" I responded. "Any idea how long you'll be there?" I asked, looking at Jim and Dr. McInnes in turn.

"No idea," replied Jim, "but I know they're sending a replacement to keep the detachment going while I'm away. Do you know a Constable Jack McDonald from the Fort McMurray Detachment?"

"I do," I responded, raising an eyebrow and sending a knowing glance over to Don, who nodded in agreement.

"So, it's not a coincidence that he's being sent here?" asked Jim, watching Don and I closely.

"I don't think so. I think my boss is taking advantage of your injury to provide us with backup.

"Please don't be offended," I added, hastily. "Jack's had my back on two undercover assignments already, so we're used to working together, and I'm sure our bosses want to make sure that you have the time you need to make a complete recovery.'

"But…" Jim prompted.

"And my boss can be quite devious at times. I'm starting to think that he treats his cases like chess matches and likes to get all his game pieces into position before making major moves."

"My boss is the same," Don offered before Jim could reply. "I'd never thought of it that way before, but now that I think back, that's an excellent characterization of the way my boss's mind works too. It must be some kind of occupational hazard."

"So, you're not just an ordinary army officer then, are you?" asked Jim, somewhat rhetorically.

"Heaven forbid!" exclaimed Don, somewhat theatrically. "Just please don't ask me too many more questions because I'm starting to like you and I hate lying to people."

"Fair enough," said Jim, with a smile.

Offering Jim our best wishes for a speedy recovery, we returned to Dr. McInnes' office to get the names and addresses of the kids she'd treated, so we could go interview them.

"Dr. McInnes, I have one more request," said Don, when we'd made our list.

"Call me Sarah. What is it?"

"Could we get someone to drive Constable Miller's highway patrol car to someplace sheltered? Someplace where Alex and I could have a look at the shells in the trunk without being seen by anyone? I'd like to have a look at those shells and then send them off to someone that can examine them for us."

"The Emergency Entrance is completely enclosed," said Sarah after a moment's thought. "It's quiet right now, so I could ask K'iijuu, one of the paramedics, to move the ambulance outside and then drive in the car myself. If we close the big garage doors and I keep a lookout, I don't think anyone will see you."

"Great, let's do it," said Don.

While I went back to Jim's room to see about borrowing his keys, Don went off to our SUV "to get some equipment."

By the time Sarah had brought the highway patrol car to the Emergency Entrance bay, Don had returned from our rented SUV with his gear. He was wearing an Army-green backpack and carrying a fairly large, military-looking metal chest. The chest was Air Force-grey, about two feet tall by three feet wide by two feet deep, and it looked very rugged, with multiple bulky latches and heavily reinforced corners.

Setting the chest down with a "thud," Don noticed that Sarah and I were watching him very intently. "When we got the call from your boss, the first things we thought of were chemical or biological weapons of some kind, so I brought something we could use to ship out any samples we might find. From your Constable Miller's description, I think he's already found them for us."

"And paid a price for it," Sarah commented.

"I think we may find that he was very fortunate not to have been killed," said Don, shocking us both. Then, removing his backpack, he pulled out a complete body suit, made of some kind of plastic- or rubber-like material that appeared very flexible yet very sturdy at the same time. As he pulled it on, I could see that it covered all of him, over his hiking boots and clothes, and with a hood that completely covered his head. All that were exposed were an oval space around his eyes, nose, and mouth, and his wrists and hands.

"I need you two to step back inside the hospital, and let's keep Silver in the SUV for a while yet," he said. Then to Sarah: "Can these garage doors be locked?"

"Yes, they have little sliding bars that lock them shut."

Sarah and I each went to lock one of the big doors and by the time we'd returned Don had donned a full-face mask that was attached to a small, compressed-air tank hanging from a sling over one shoulder, and he was pulling large gauntlets over his hands and up over his wrists.

"OK, now you three get inside. You can watch through the Emergency doors, but don't let anyone open them until I tell you it's clear, OK?"

His voice was muffled by the face mask and the hissing of the compressed air being fed to it, but we understood him well enough, waved in acknowledgement and went to watch from inside the hospital.

We actually had a very clear view from our vantage point and I watched with absolute fascination as Don took a large sheet or tarp from his backpack and spread it out on the ground, then opened the trunk of the highway patrol car and brought out the first plastic bag. Carefully laying the bag on the tarp, he used a knife to slice the bag open, exposing the brass shell casings. These looked very ordinary to me, but he very gently moved them just enough to make them all visible, then photographed them with a camera that was itself enclosed in some kind of protective, see-through bag. When this was completed, he carefully placed all of the shells and the original bag in a new, heavier one from his backpack, and once that was sealed, he placed the whole thing into the crate.

Next came the main event: the bag with the projectiles in it. Repeating his earlier procedure, Don soon had several projectiles lying on the tarp in front of him. Whereas the shell casings had looked ordinary, the projectiles certainly did not. To my uneducated eye they seemed overly long, and they had coloured tips and also coloured bands spaced along their length.

I shivered. "They look menacing," I commented to Sarah, who simply nodded.

Just like he had done with the shells, Don photographed the projectiles then carefully placed them in another new, heavier bag from his backpack, and once it was sealed, he placed the whole thing into the crate.

These tasks completed, Don removed his heavy gloves and put them into the crate, then he closed the lid and all of the latches.

Saying "OK, you can come out now," he removed his face mask, disconnected it, unslung his air tank, removed the rest of his suit, and placed everything back into his backpack, along with the camera.

"What do you think?" I asked.

Hesitating for a moment, he glanced at Sarah.

"I can leave if you two want to talk," she offered.

"No," said Don, sighing. "You've seen the patients already, and you had the sense to sound the initial alarm. Nothing I'm going to say is going to shock you very much, and you've earned our confidence."

Glancing again towards Sarah, he sighed. "You'll have seen the coloured tips and bands. What you probably didn't see were the characters stamped on the sides."

"Characters?" said Sarah and I simultaneously.

"Yes, each projectile had some kind of characters or symbols stenciled along their sides."

"Could you read them?" I asked.

"No, but I think they were East Asian. I'm no expert, but the characters have pretty simple, curvy shapes. Korean characters usually have round shapes in them, like circles and ovals, and Chinese characters are usually a lot more complicated, so my guess is that they are Japanese. Anyway, we'll send all this stuff off and let the experts tell us for sure."

"I wonder what Japanese artillery shells would be doing here?" I mused out loud.

"I've no idea, but if they're Japanese then they're probably old. Like Second-World-War-era old. What worries me most are the coloured bands and tips. I'm no expert on artillery shells either, but those colours don't look right to me."

"How will you find out?" asked Sarah.

"I'm going to ship everything to DRES[12] – that's code for Defence Research Establishment Suffield. It's in Suffield, Alberta, and that's where we have experts on defending against chemical and biological weapons. I'm hoping they'll be able to tell us more, but there's no way to tell how long it will take them."

"Alright then," I said, "I guess we'll just have to do the best we can until then."

"Yes, but Alex, if you ever come across shells that look anything like these, keep away from them. Don't touch them, don't even breath the air near them, and for God's sake keep Silver away from them! With his nose, whatever's in those shells will hit him hard."

"Are they really that bad?"

"I think so. We'll see what we hear back from Suffield, but until then I think we need to treat them as being deadly. We've seen and heard from Doctor Sarah what happened to your Constable and the kids, and I think they were all lucky," he paused in thought. "I think it could have been a lot worse."

"OK, Don."

"Dr. Sarah, if we can borrow a phone, I need to make arrangements to get these shells to Alberta, then we'll get out of your hair for a while."

Dr. McInnes led us to a phone, and while Don made his call, I thanked her for her help and promised that Don and I would try to return later in the day to check on Constable Miller, and that we might have more questions for her at that time.

"I'm happy to do anything that will prevent more patients like the ones I've just seen," she exclaimed.

"OK, there'll be a helicopter at the airport this afternoon, so how about if we put the crate and backpack away in the SUV, and then go find and interview the kids?" said Don, returning from his phone call.

"How is it that this helicopter is magically available when you need it?" I asked Don, once we were underway in the SUV.

That brought a grin to Don's face. "The possibility that there are chemical or biological agents on the loose has your boss and mine seriously worried."

"Why? Isn't it likely that it's just a case of a few old shells from the Second World War washing-up on a beach from some kind of shipwreck or plane crash?"

"Very good," smiled Don, approvingly. "That's exactly what our bosses think is the most probable scenario. We know that the Germans developed these kinds of weapons in the First World War, and that later, during the Second World War, they and the Japanese put them into a variety of forms for possible use: mostly in bombs and artillery shells. As far as we know, the Germans never actually used them during the war, but we don't know whether the Japanese did or not."

"So, you do have an idea what was in those shells then!"

"We have a working hypothesis. Based on Dr. McInnes' report we think it's chemical – a nerve agent. We know that the Axis countries had access to three main chemical nerve agents, called GA, which we now know was tabun; GB, or sarin; and GD, or soman... and they're all really bad. Our people's testing at Suffield showed that this "G Series," of nerve agents was more toxic and faster acting, and at lower concentrations, than the phosgene or the mustard gas of the First World War."

I shuddered again. "OK, so we know why our bosses are worried, and why you were prepared with that protective suit and fancy storage crate. Why isn't this a case for one of the navy's diving units?"

"Well, for one thing you and Silver and I need to learn more about where to look, and..." he paused. "For another thing, we have no accounts of anything hinting at chemical or biological weapons ever being stored, used, or transported anywhere near the North American west coast. No unaccounted-for military or merchant shipwrecks or plane crashes either. Nothing."

"OK," I said, thinking about it. "I think I'm ready for it now. What would be worse?"

"Well our bosses have good imaginations if nothing else. What if it's more than a shipwreck or plane crash? What if there was some kind of secret base, or weapons cache of some kind, left over from the war and undiscovered until now? What if someone discovered something like that and thought it might be a good idea to sell that kind of munitions on the black market?"

"Is that likely?"

"Likely – no. Possible - who knows? We know that the Japanese forces invaded two small islands in Alaska's Aleutian Islands during the Second World War, and they were well into building fortifications and airstrips there when the Americans, with our help, found them and drove them out. What if there was a third base that no one ever found?"

"You mean there might be a whole lot more of these things lying around. Not just a few crates lying on the ocean floor."

"That's right. And there's another thing."

"What could possibly be worse than that?"

"What if there was such a base, and what if they had developed even more advanced weapons than the "G Series" nerve agents?"

"That would be worse," I agreed.

"And what if the Soviets heard about our little accidents here and came to the same conclusions as our bosses have?"

"No!"

"I hope you're right, but we have three things to watch out for: more occurrences of weapons like these artillery shells, black-market weapons dealers sniffing around, and foreign agents."

"So…"

"So, our bosses have decided to start small with us two undercover agents posing as CBC Reporters, accompanied by a very non-police or military-looking dog. But behind the scenes, we'll have priority access to almost any backup we might need, and the *HMCS Huron*, its two helicopters, and a couple of squads of the Special Service Force[13] are going to just happen to be prowling around, on exercises, between Vancouver Island and the Aleutian Islands, and…"

"And that's how you're getting the shells out to Alberta tonight isn't it?" I jumped in. "They're sending one of the Huron's helicopters in to get them, right?"

"Right again. The helicopter will fly from here to Vancouver or Victoria, and from there an air force plane will fly them to the airport at Suffield, where they'll be picked up and delivered to DRES. My crate and pack can fit in the navigator's seat of a fighter jet, so it's possible they'll arrive in Suffield by early this evening."

"Wow."

***

5 THE INVESTIGATION BEGINS

We didn't have too much trouble finding the kids that had been to the hospital. Karen, the first of Dr. McInnes' affected patients, seemed to be recovering rapidly, although she still had a runny nose. Don and I introduced ourselves as CBC reporters, and asked her about the events leading up to her affliction. We didn't learn anything more than she had already told Dr. McInnes at the hospital: she had been out at the beach with three school-friends and they had been playing with some "big bullets" they had found washed-up on the beach. She'd gone home when her eyes had started to bother her, and when her parents had become concerned, they had taken her to the hospital. When we asked her whether she'd kept any, like as a souvenir, she said "no" in a way that implied a complete lack of interest on her part. In fact, she was much more interested in Silver than her own story, so we gave her some time to pet Silver before thanking her and moving on to our next stop.

The two boys that had next gone to see Dr. McInnes turned out to be twin brothers, Frank, and Rick. Whereas Karen hadn't taken much interest in the "big bullets," Frank and Rick needed no prompting to talk about them. They were excited at the prospect of getting their names in the news, and they gave us a vivid description of their excitement at finding them, Jimmy's idea to open them, and the spectacular effects of throwing the "gunpowder," which is how they referred to the cordite contained inside, into their beach-side firepit. Their story matched the account they had given Dr. McInnes, but really didn't add anything useful. Although the boys were much more interested in the shells than Karen had been, they also said that they hadn't thought to bring any home with them. Like we'd done with Karen, we gave them the phone number at the cabin we were renting and asked them to call us if they remembered any other details later.

"What do you think?" asked Don as we were driving away from the twins' home.

"This is what people mean when they refer to 'good, old-fashioned police work.' They mean a lot of running around, asking questions, and checking into things, all of it leading to lots of dead ends and maybe one or two good leads that point to something that's actually actionable. On the plus side, the three kids seemed pretty open and honest to me, and their stories are consistent with what they told Dr. McInnes. That's a start, at least."

"Maybe our next interview will be more productive."

It was.

We found Jimmy Hunter at home in bed. Dr. McInnes had just released him from hospital that morning, along with instructions to spend his first day home resting in bed. Identifying ourselves as CBC reporters to Jimmy's parents, we assured them that we'd consulted first with Dr. McInnes, and that we'd be careful not to tire Jimmy out with our questions.

Jimmy wasn't as well recovered as his three friends had been, and I noticed that he still laboured with his breathing when he talked a lot, and that he paused, now and then, to rub his eyes or blow his nose. From Dr. McInnes' account, I expected Jimmy to be hesitant to speak with us, but some combination of the news already being out and the novelty of talking to news reporters seemed to induce him to expansiveness.

"We'd made a small fire at first, but then we got the idea of making it bigger," he began, "so we collected some driftwood that had washed up along the beach after last week's big storm."

"How did that work out?" Don asked.

"OK, but the driftwood was pretty wet, so we needed a pretty good fire just to be able to dry it enough to light up."

Then, while I was wondering how best to broach the subject of the artillery shells, Jimmy did it for me.

"Frank and Rick found some big shells, but it was my idea to open them up," said Jimmy proudly.

"What made you think of that?"

"I was in Army Cadets before we moved here to the islands. They showed us what was inside bullets, 'rounds,' when I was learning to shoot. I figured the larger shells Frank and Rick found must be artillery rounds of some kind, so that gave me the idea of getting the cordite out, so we'd have a better fire. We tried a few different ways of getting the bullet ends out, but it really wasn't all that hard."

"Has this happened before?" I asked.

"Things wash up on the beaches all the time," Jimmy said, "and sometimes we go out to see what's there, especially after big storms. When we're lucky we find coloured glass balls in old fishing nets washed up. We like those because we can sell them to the local shops that sell things to the tourists. Some of the nets come all the way from Japan, and the balls with Japanese characters on them sell for the most money."

"What about things like artillery shells?" I asked. "Do they wash up on the beaches often?"

"Not that I've ever heard. That's what got us all kind of excited to begin with."

"How many shells did you find, all told?"

"Well, Frank and Rick found the first two," said Jimmy, thinking it through. "Then, after they showed them to Karen and I, we spread out. Karen found two more, and then I found the last one: so, five, we found five."

At this, Don and I looked at each other. The kids found five, but Constable Miller only found four.

"Did you use all five in your fire?" I asked, trying to sound innocent.

"Yes... no, wait, we opened up four and burned all the cordite that was in them... Man did that stuff burn!"

"What happened to the last one?"

"Sold it!" said Jimmy, rather proudly. "Got ten bucks for it too!"

"Who would want to buy an old, washed-up artillery shell?" I asked, trying to sound matter-of-fact, but my pulse was starting to race now.

"Oh, it was The Scrounger of course. He'd come along and

watched us by the fire for a while then offered to buy the last one from us since it was still complete. We weren't interested in selling at first, but when he offered us ten bucks, we changed our minds fast."

"I can imagine," I offered. "What is a 'scrounger'?"

"The Scrounger, of course. Everybody around here knows him."

"Sorry Jimmy, we're from the mainland."

"Oh, right. I guess I didn't think of that. Well, he's what you would call a beachcomber then. He drives his boat up and down the coast looking for stray logs. Then he rounds them up and drags them to sell to the sawmills. Sometimes we see him walking along the beaches looking for stuff to sell to the tourist stores."

"Do you know where he lives?"

"Not really, around here somewhere I guess," Jimmy offered, vaguely.

Remembering our promise to keep our visit with Jimmy short, Don and I thanked Jimmy for his help, wished him a speedy recovery, and made our way out. Before leaving, we asked his parents if they'd heard about The Scrounger. They had and were clearly a bit miffed that their son had been talking to him, but they didn't seem to know exactly where he lived, mirroring their son with their response of "around here somewhere."

"We're going to have to find that fifth round," Don commented as we pulled away from Jimmy's house.

"We should probably try asking Dr. McInnes and Constable Miller first," I suggested, "so it doesn't look like we're showing too much interest."

It was getting late in the afternoon, so we decided to go back to the hospital, and then to airport to meet Don's helicopter. At the hospital, Dr. McInnes wasn't there but we were allowed in to see Constable Miller, who was quite familiar with The Scrounger.

"I'm not sure anyone around here knows his real name or where he came from," said James, "but everyone seems to know him. I've met him quite a few times, and I haven't had any real trouble from him, although I suspect that he tends to operate in the grey edge of law-abiding. He's entertaining though and is a constant source of stories about this area."

"How do we find him?" I asked.

"Like a number of other people, he's a squatter in one of the abandoned seafood canneries that are littered up and down BC's Inside Passage. In his case, he lives in an old building at Pacofi." Seeing our blank looks, he quickly continued.

"Pacofi is what people call the former Pacific Coast Fisheries cannery, which operated from the 1900s through the 1940s. It's on the east side of Moresby Island and not too far from here. It is one of the few old canneries you can actually drive to. There's an old logging road that goes most of the way. After that there's kind of a track, which you can follow, but it's rough enough that you'll need a truck or an SUV. I'll draw you a map."

As it was getting late in the afternoon, we decided we'd learned about as much done as we could for the day and headed back to the cottage Don had rented for us.

There were several individual cottages next to a small lodge, all of which were well positioned on the waterfront. As Don pulled in beside ours, we were immediately greeted by a man who had been lounging on the front deck of the cabin next door.

"Hi neighbours!" he said, walking over with his hand outstretched to shake. "Herb Turner. I thought I'd just come over right away and introduce myself."

We introduced ourselves as CBC Reporters, looking into a strange illness that had struck some kids on the island, and estimated that we'd probably only be around for a couple of days.

Herb explained that he was an oceanography professor from the University of Alaska, and that he'd rented his cottage for a week of vacationing on the islands. Although we only spoke briefly, he came across as very friendly and effusively outgoing. I think it was only because he seemed like such an extrovert that I dimly noticed that he took no notice at all of Silver. For his part, Silver seemed to be unusually aloof. While Herb was with us, Silver simply sat on the deck staring at him. *Maybe*, I thought later, *Herb didn't like dogs and Silver was able to sense it.*

By the time we got ourselves settled in our cottage, the sun was dropping ever closer to the mountains to our west and I realized that my first impressions of the island had all been rather tactical in nature. Looking again, with fresh eyes, I began to appreciate the beauty of the place. Beauty is a funny word to use in this context, because it takes work to find the very few parts of British Columbia that are not beautiful. Nevertheless, some parts are more special than others and, whether through good planning or sheer luck on Don's part, we were staying at a place that showcased the idyllic nature of the Queen Charlotte Islands. From the deck of our cottage, we had fantastic views of the ocean, which was quite sheltered at our location, with low mountains right beside us, and larger mountains in the distance, towards the horizons. Along the slopes of the mountains we could see mixtures of spruce, cedar, pine, and hemlock trees, and the constant activity of the birds that they housed, including bald eagles and ravens.

Particularly enticing to me were the tidal-flats just steps from our front door which, at low tide, provided a broad expanse of beach to walk along when tide was low. Once our gear and groceries were stowed away, all three of us went for a long walk along the beach. Silver, of course, avoided the water (as he always did) but after having been cooped-up in the SUV for significant parts of the day, he thoroughly enjoyed the freedom to run about, here and there, exploring and sniffing most everything available as we strolled along.

I found it immensely relaxing and, after about a mile I found I could set aside the stress of my recent travels and the excitement and concentration that had been devoted to the first baby steps of our new case. Only at that point did it come home to me how comforting it was to have Don by my side again and I realized, with a start, that I had missed him in the time since we'd said goodbye at the end of our first case together in Nova Scotia[11]. After that, I'd returned to Ottawa, then gone to Alaska for a short vacation (and another unexpected adventure[6]). Reflecting, I realized that we'd only been apart for six weeks. Amazing! *Maybe things between Don and I were more serious that I'd realized – or admitted to myself,* I thought.

In any case, the more we walked along the beach the more we both relaxed, and soon our previous state of warm companionship had returned. Suddenly, the whole case seemed like a tempest in a teapot. We'd found most of the odd-looking artillery shells, the people affected by them were all under medical care, and by tomorrow we'd probably be able to secure the last shell and our contribution to the affair would be over. I knew that our bosses couldn't afford to be complacent when these things arise, but it seemed like in this case, at least, they had wildly over-reacted to the possible threat.

I really should learn better than to pre-judge such things. Little did I know that I was going to be proven horribly wrong, and a near-death experience was going to teach me something about complacency and over-confidence.

***

Day 5: August 24, 1977.

After a fantastic early-morning run along the beach with Silver, we dropped by the hospital again and were fortunate to be able to visit with James once more. He seemed to be recovering well and had news for us: "I was on the phone with Division HQ in Surrey," he said, "and they told me that my temporary replacement is flying in this morning. That means I'll have time to get out of here and go meet him, and show him around the detachment, before I'm shipped out this afternoon to see a specialist in Vancouver."

We arranged to meet James and Jack at the detachment office later that morning and went off to find the local marine supply store in search of maps of the islands. Being in a traditional boating and fishing area, this turned out to be no problem at all, and we were soon equipped with a variety of land and nautical charts.

By the time we'd made our way to the local RCMP Detachment building – it was more like a converted house than a building – James had been released from hospital and Jack had arrived from the airport. Like he had with Dr. McInnes, Don introduced himself to Jack as an Artillery Captain in the Army and showed him his military ID.

"I get it," said Jack, "but I seem to recall that the last time we met you were a Captain in the Military Police... who are you really?"

"Very true..." said Don, beginning to handle it nonchalantly, but he was undermined by hearing me start to chuckle.

"Sorry," I said, as everyone turned to look my way, "but I once asked Don that exact same question."

"Well, that was then, this is now," continued Don, not missing a beat.

"Hmmm, fine by me," said Jack, sounding unconvinced.

"Look, I really am a Captain in the military but, like Alex does with the RCMP, I do intelligence work and sometimes have to pretend to be something other than the real me – just like she does – OK?"

"OK," said Jack, sounding more cheerful. "Thank you for telling me. You can count on me to keep your secret."

"I'm sorry I hesitated. You proved yourself to us when we worked together in Nova Scotia[11], it's just that old habits die hard."

"That's OK Don, I get it. We're good here."

We were interrupted at this point by the telephone ringing.

Don and I, and Silver too, sat in companionable silence while Jack took care of the call, which seemed to be from a member of the public complaining about something or other in their neighbourhood.

While we were waiting, I reflected, not for the first time, on how Jack and Don were living illustrations of how deceiving appearances could be. To my eyes, at least, Jack looked quite plain in appearance but he was a compulsive Don-Juan-type when it came to women. In basic training together, I'd learned that he had a distinct "*Love 'em and leave 'em*" style as far as women went. On the other hand, he was fun to be with, and our previous experiences working together in Alberta and in Nova Scotia had demonstrated that I could trust him. I'd learned that Jack was trying to live the story-book image of a perfect Mountie, when on duty at least, and he kept his compulsive womanizing to his off-duty hours. I'd found that I could live with that, and the two of us had developed a strong mutual respect for each other's capabilities and become friends – just friends, mind you - but friends none-the-less.

Don, on the other hand, looked like a movie star, reminded me of a young version of Rock Hudson, and his dreamy, engaging personality had almost made a lie of my cherished self-image that I'm more interested in substance than appearances. Fortunately for me, he turned out to have a heart of gold, always acted like a perfect gentleman, and had a strong character to match. As was the case with Jack, Don's strengths always seemed to complement my own. Different from Jack though, Don and I had become very close. I wasn't sure exactly what that meant yet, but there was no question Don and I had become more than just friends.

Looking down to the floor where Silver was relaxing, I could tell that, as always, he was paying close attention to everything that was going on around him. *He defies stereotyping too*, I thought. It wasn't just his wolfy appearance that belied his training and capabilities as a police dog, nor our own close friendship. In some way that I still hadn't yet figured out, he was somehow more than just a dog. Every once in a while, he displayed an uncanny ability to sense my thoughts, or my speech, and communicate with me beyond the limitations of a dog's body language and range of vocal sounds. His strange behaviour challenged my scientific training, and when we'd recently discovered his original owners[6], they too had reluctantly admitted that Silver had some kind of telepathic abilities that they didn't really understand. Although this presented another mystery that I intended to solve some day, the important thing was that he was my best friend.

Three good friends, I thought, *and each of them is so much more than they seem.*

My reverie was interrupted when Jack finished his phone call and got up from the detachment's desk to re-join us.

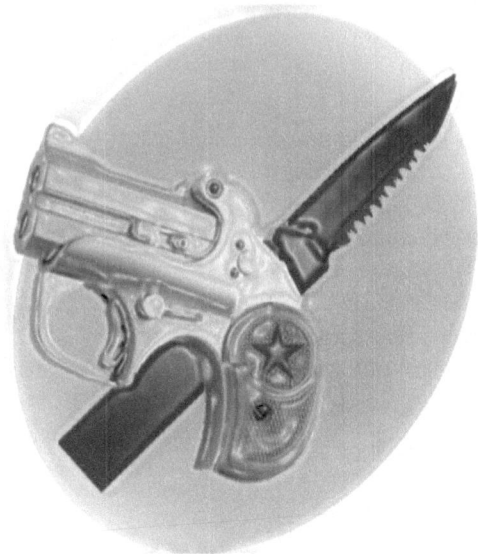

"By the way Alex, I brought your gun from the Whitehorse Detachment," he said.

"My gun!" I exclaimed, "how'd you manage to get it, and how did you get my lock-box open?"

"I couldn't. Not without your key anyway. Your boss told me you'd have left a few things in Whitehorse before you crossed into Alaska, so I flew there first from Fort McMurray. There was no spare key there, so, rather than have the box cut open they just let me bring the whole thing. It's in my duffel bag."

Once Jack had retrieved the lock-box from his luggage, I opened it up. "I've acquired a few tools over the past two years," I said, and with James, Jack, and Don looking on it felt like 'show-and-tell' time as I withdrew some familiar companions.

First out was my snub-nosed Smith & Wesson '.38 Special' revolver, which had been issued to me when I'd first gone undercover in Alberta. The snub-nose, and ammunition for it, weren't particularly remarkable, but the other items were.

Next out was a small cloth bag, containing a fancy-looking silver derringer with pink hand grips. "This is a woman's 'Mama Bear' Remington Derringer," I said, showing how its two barrels pivoted upwards for reloading, and how a cam on the hammer alternated, when fired, between the top and bottom barrels. This was issued to me by Scotty, "HQ" Division's Quartermaster, before I went out on my undercover assignment in Nova Scotia where I first met Don.

"It looks like a toy," I continued, "especially with the fancy silver plating and the pink pearl hand grips but it takes .38 Special rounds and is deadly at close range."

"I'll say it is," chimed-in Don. "She saved my life with that on Cape Breton Island earlier this year!"

"Where do you wear it?" asked James, fascinated.

"Never you mind," I said, lifting my nose in the air just a bit, which produced chuckles all around.

Finally, I drew out another cloth bag, from which I withdrew a small, rectangular metal box. It was only about five inches long and very narrow and thin. "Watch," I said, as I pressed a tiny button on one side. As soon as I did, there was a "click," and a blade hissed straight out from one end.

"A switch-blade," Jack hissed.

"Kind of," I agreed. "Except that the blade slides straight out instead of pivoting out. It's actually a small version of a military UDT knife[14] with a few modifications. Feel how light it is," I continued, reversing the knife and handing it over to him, "and the blade will cut through almost anything."

"You said it had a few modifications," he prompted, handing it back to me.

"Yes, look here," I said, turning the knife around. "The handle has been extended just enough for a ferrocerium fire-starter," I twisted and pulled on the handle's end cap, which popped-out to reveal a piece of dull grey metal protruding from the inside of the cap. "You can strike it with the knife blade to create extremely hot sparks."

"There's no sheath," James observed.

"Right," I agreed. "Something else I learned from Scotty. I just tape it to my leg. If I need to draw it, I just tear away the tape."

"Ouch," said James, Don, and Jack together.

"That's the downside," I agreed, "although I found a kind of sensitive-skin first-aid tape that sticks pretty well, even wet, tears easily by hand, and doesn't hurt too badly when pulled away. The main thing is that it actually works!" I concluded.

"Where did this stuff come from?" asked James.

"I'm not sure exactly. Scotty told me they had been confiscated during previous criminal cases and that, as an armourer, he'd kept a few of the more unusual items rather than destroy them. He issued me with special permits for each of them, so I'm covered legally, but there could be hell to pay if I ever lose any of them."

Placing everything back into the metal case and locking it, I thanked Jack again for retrieving it for me. "I doubt I'll need any of these things out here, but you never know I guess."

"Like I always say, you do the spy thing – I'm content to be a simple, ordinary policeman."

"Lucky for me you're neither simple, nor ordinary Jack, but I know what you mean. I'm just glad you're going to be around to watch our backs again!"

"It's interesting to me that all three of us have been sent here, together again," added Don.

"Grruph," said Silver, who had been nearby, intently watching the three of us.

"Sorry Silver, I should have said the four of us!"

"How much does he actually understand?" asked Jack.

"I really don't know, Jack. Not everything, but he always seems to get the gist of any conversation we have. I know it sounds crazy, but it's happened too many times to be our imagination."

With all three pairs of eyes on him, Silver simply looked up at us with those penetrating, blue-grey eyes of his and said "Grruph."

***

Leaving Jack to settle in at the detachment, we drove James to the airport for his flight to Vancouver, said our goodbyes, and then Don, Silver, and I were free to attempt to locate "The Scrounger."

The airport was at Sandspit on Moresby Island. From there, we drove south, along the coast, then turned inland for a while, and then south again. Along the way, the "road" transitioned from paved highway, to gravel road, to rougher gravel forestry road, and finally to a twinned path that reminded me of old wagon-roads. With our SUV, we didn't have any serious trouble driving over the rougher pathway, however, and the scenery was fantastic. Silver, who had adopted his favourite travelling style from my own truck, seemed to have a great time in the backseat alternating between sticking his head out the left- and right-hand windows, both of which had been rolled down for him.

The pathway took us right to the site of the old Pacific Coast Fisheries cannery on the shore of Cumshewa Inlet, where it was nicely protected from the open ocean. The cannery consisted of a couple of large buildings, several scattered houses, and a large dock area.

Getting out of the SUV, we walked around a bit to get a sense of the place. I'd expected it to be an interesting historic site, and I suppose that it is, but I was disappointed to find that it seemed more like a bunch of nondescript, weather-beaten, sagging structures standing on their last legs and they looked shaky enough that I wondered whether it was safe to even enter them.

Wandering over to the dock, we found that it was in rough shape as well. Although most of the pilings seemed to be intact and more-or-less vertical, much of the dock's surface structure had fallen away over time. If there had ever been guard railings, they were long gone, and in many places, individual planks, or even entire sections of planks were missing. *It must be passable though*, I thought, because there was a rickety-looking ramp leading down to a floating section of dock, and alongside that was tied a dull black-coloured work boat of the type that were commonly seen prowling around the West Coast islands.

"Hear that?" asked Don, referring to the faint sound of a power saw.

"Well, someone's here anyway. Let's go see who it is."

The sound of the power saw led us to a man working in one of the smaller buildings which, at some time in the past, had clearly been converted in to a workshop. The noise in the shop was much louder, or course, and we had to wait until he paused in his work and shut off the saw before we could call out to him.

"Mr. Parker?" I asked.

"Who wants to know?" came a gruff reply and, as he turned towards us, we saw a grizzled man who, although clearly an adult, could have been almost any age.

My first impression was of the countless stereotypical sailor characters in old movies. The kind that would be seen working around docks or on the decks or tramp steamers. He was even wearing a sailor's knitted-wool watch cap and had a bent-egg style briar pipe hanging out of his mouth.

He could be a deckhand on the Calypso working with Cousteau, I thought, thinking back to my early SCUBA-diving days when I'd read a lot about the ocean explorations of Jacques Yves Cousteau[15] and his crew.

We identified ourselves as CBC reporters, which didn't seem to favourable impress him at all, and explained that we were following up on reports of artillery shells being washed up on Agate Beach.

"Why ask me?" he grumbled.

"Well, two reasons," I offered. "One, you were seen at the beach that day, and we hear that you know a lot about the currents around the islands, and the kinds of things that wash up on the beaches."

My first reason got his back up, and I could see that he was formulating a sharp retort, but the second reason seemed to appeal to his ego and he exhaled sharply, seemingly letting the tension out.

"Well," he mused, scratching his chin with the stem of his pipe, "there aren't many people that have studied them like I have."

"Did you see any of these shells yourself?" asked Don.

"I may have seen some kids playing with one," he allowed.

"We're told that they actually found a few. Have you ever seen anything like them before?"

"Lots of stuff washed up on the beaches around here. Mostly on the western and northern shores. I look for logs myself – to sell to the sawmills – but I've come across my share of other stuff.

Some of it comes from the whole other side of the planet!"

"Really!" I'm not good at gushing, but I tried to sound as wide-eyed and innocent as I could. "What kinds of things could possibly come that far?"

Apparently, this was the right approach, as he warmed up considerably. "Well now, things from Japan, for example. Like, pieces of fish boxes with Japanese characters stamped on them, and sections of fishing nets, and quite a few fisherman's floats too. The local kids sometimes collect the nicer-looking floats and sell them to the souvenir and antique shops."

"Do you have any idea where the shells might have come from?"

"Could be anywhere, I suppose. Maybe they fell over the side of a navy destroyer when it was offshore on exercises or something."

"That's an idea," I said, making a conspicuous show of writing things down in my notebook.

"By the way," said Don, "we heard a rumour that you might have bought one of the shells from the kids on the beach … if so, we'd sure be interested to see it."

That got his back up again.

"Not me," he retorted angrily, "not enough profit in it for me. Maybe they sold one to someone else. Some tourist maybe."

"Oh! Well, sorry then. It's just that it would help our story if we could see one of these shells and maybe get a picture of it."

"Try the souvenir shops," he suggested. "That's where a person would take one to sell."

It didn't seem like we were going to get much out of The Scrounger for the time being, so we thanked him for his time and left.

"What do you think?" asked Don as we were driving back to town in the SUV.

"He's hiding something and he's pretty cunning. He told us some of the truth but left things out, and I don't believe his denial about buying the shell. There's no reason for the kids to have lied to us about selling it to him, so I wonder what his reason is for not admitting it to us."

"You think he's just naturally contrary?"

"I do but I also think he has, or at least had, that last shell. What do you think?"

"I agree. If the report from Suffield comes back saying what I think it's going to, then we're going to have to come back and see him again, if only to try to get that shell away from him before someone else gets hurt."

The Abandoned Cannery

Laurie Schramm

6 THE ISLAND

Damned nuisance reporters, The Scrounger thought to himself. *Well, I didn't tell them much, anyway. Too bad, really, because the real story is one for the history books! I probably could have made front-page news.* He chuckled to himself at the thought.

The Scrounger's thoughts turned to remembering. He remembered... *How long ago was it now? Must be eight weeks. Strange. It seems like just the other day that I found the island...*

***

He had found the island by accident, in his old boat, while making his way back home from a trip "up north," in which he'd been sniffing around for any wrecked boats or other salvage he could find washed up along Alaska's western shore following a particularly savage storm on the Bering Sea. With good sailing weather, and having time on his hands, he'd decided to take the opportunity to cruise around some of the Aleutian Islands, rather than simply cutting between them on his way home. In particular, he'd heard stories about the Japanese invasions of Attu and Kiska during the Second World War and he was interested in looking those islands over for anything that he might be able to salvage and sell.

Unfortunately, it had been a complete waste of time. There hadn't been anything interesting on either island. Attu was certainly littered with military equipment of all kinds, but everything in sight had been severely damaged or destroyed in what had clearly been an intense battle back in 1943. All that remained were huge pieces of rusting junk scattered around. Kiska was similar but different. All the military equipment was sitting in what looked like its original defensive positions but it had all been destroyed. Instead of a battle, in this case it had been either destroyed in advance or booby-trapped by the Japanese before they had evacuated the island. The result was the same however, as everything had been made useless and was simply rusting away.

It had taken two days to locate and search both islands. With a resigned sigh of defeat, he had turned his boat toward the mainland. He planned to use the remaining islands as breakwaters, to provide some shelter from the open sea on his way home.

As it was late in the day when he'd left Kiska, he hadn't travelled far before deciding to pull into one of the remining islands for the night. Picking a likely looking island at random, he motored close to shore in search of a convenient place to tie-up for the night. Scanning the shoreline with his binoculars, he was surprised to see what looked like pilings and the ruins of an old dock. Checking his hydrographic charts, he identified the island as Semisopochnoi Island[16]. That's odd, *he thought,* there wasn't supposed to be anything there but an old volcano called Mount Cerebrus.

Making for the old dock, The Scrounger entered the natural harbour and tied-up his boat close to the shore – at the single point where the dock looked like it might actually be somewhat intact. Continuing on foot, he found signs of a gravel road. It was mostly covered with small bushes and very young trees, but it had clearly been a well-packed road at one time, and quite wide as well. He'd followed it toward the base of Mount Cerebrus, which was about two miles to the north of the dock, and received several surprises.

In contrast to the other two islands, this one showed very little evidence of human activity along the road, just the odd tin can, crushed and rusting away by the side of the road. Spotting a bit of colour, he stooped to pick one up. He could barely make out the picture and printing on the label, but the language was unmistakably Japanese!

What were the Japanese doing here? *he'd wondered.*

Reaching the mountain, he'd discovered the second surprise: two large, rusty, steel doors stood wide open, practically inviting him to enter what appeared to be a cave inside the mountain. He hadn't thought to bring a flashlight, so he went back to his boat to retrieve a powerful portable lantern.

Returning with the lantern he'd cautiously entered the cave and found more surprises. The cave was more like a long, wide tunnel in which a wooden floor had been installed. The walls were bare except for bundles of wires running the length of the cave. As he'd continued to explore, he found that some of the wires were connected to wall switches and ceiling light fixtures, while others were connected to — he shuddered with the remembrance — explosives. Explosive charges, old and faded but still dangerous-looking, had been wired and taped into place at intervals along the full length of the cave.

They must have been planning to blow the whole place when they left, *he'd thought.* I wonder why they didn't.

Continuing to explore, but even more cautiously now, he discovered side passages. Inside some of those were living quarters.

They must have left in a hurry, *he'd thought as he gazed at beds with rumpled bedding, a kitchen with pots and pans, long dining tables with cups, plates, and cutlery on them, and even a pantry with old food cans, probably, sitting on the shelves.* I wonder if the food in those cans is still edible? Probably not, *he'd thought as he began suspect a Second World War vintage to this 'Mystery Fortress.'*

In other chambers lay crates of some kind and then, the final confirmation of his growing suspicions about the origins of the Mystery Fortress: a large chamber full of ammunition crates!

By the simple expedient of opening one of each differently sized crate he'd quickly discovered that the ammunition cache comprised mostly small arms ammunition, probably intended for pistols, rifles, and machine guns. Some crates, however, contained larger calibre ammunition that could only be for some kind of heavy, mounted weapon like an anti-aircraft or auto-cannon gun, he realized.

It's too bad that the ammunition is so old, *he'd thought,* remembering that ammunition manufacturers claim about ten years for shelf life. And that's for modern ammunition, this stuff isn't likely to still be useable after more than 30 years.

The next and last type of crate to be opened, however, brightened his outlook considerably. It turned out to be a wooden box with a sealed, inner metal liner. Prying the metal lid off, he'd discovered that the contents looked shiny and brand new. They must have sealed out air and moisture, *he'd realized.*

I should be able to sell these! *had been his next thought.*

Looking at them more closely, they weren't a size he'd ever seen before. They were about nine inches long, including both casing and projectile, and about two inches in diameter. Some kind of light auto-cannon gun maybe?

Feeling pleased that he'd finally found something he could salvage and sell he was about to move on when he noticed that some of these last types of crates had their sides painted in blue.

Opening one of the blue-painted crates revealed the same sealed metal liner and the same size and shape of ammunition, but in this case the projectiles inserted into the brass casings were differently coloured. Whereas the first crate's projectiles were all black in colour, with a white and green band and a red tip, the projectiles from the second crate were grey, with a brown band and a blue tip.

Something's different about these! *he'd thought.*

Taking stock, he'd reviewed what he'd found: some small artefacts that he might be able to sell as war souvenirs (but maybe not worth the trouble of transporting them all the way home), a bunch of old ammunition in ordinary crates (possibly no longer useable, so worthless), and two kinds of larger shells that had been carefully stored and looked as good as new. An easy choice then.

He'd decided to take away five shells of each type. Selecting one of the smaller crates of uninteresting-looking ammunition he'd dumped those shells out on the floor and then filled it with five shells each of the new-looking ones. That had provided him with one small box that he could conveniently carry back to his boat. When he got there, he'd look for a buyer and use the salvaged shells as samples. If all went well, he could easily come back for more later, as long as the Mystery Fortress remained unknown to anyone else.

That had been his plan at least. Everything would have been fine if his boat hadn't betrayed him on the way back...

The Scrounger

He'd made it most of the way home before a series of misfortunes conspired against him. No sooner was he finally just in sight of the northwest corner of the Queen Charlotte Islands than the storm that had been brewing broke out with a vengeance. Virtually simultaneously the sea, which until that point had merely been choppy with visible but unthreatening whitecaps, turned into fierce waves that quickly had the boat pounding from one wave to the next. As he was trying to match the boat's speed to the frequency of the waves, in order to avoid the punishing crashing of the bow into each new wave, Murphy's Law struck: the bilge pump failed. This was of more than usual concern because his old boat had become quite leaky even in calm water. Without the bilge pump, it took on water that much more quickly.

As his boat settled ever lower in the water, the waves continued unabated – possibly they even got a bit worse. In any case, the boat had become sluggish and more difficult to handle, while the bow got ever closer to dipping into the waves. Eventually, the inevitable happened: an unusually large wave crashed right over the bow sending water cascading all the back to the windscreen and along the way clearing everything off the front deck. That included a lifebuoy and coil of rope, a long-handled boat hook, his rubber sea-boots, and the entire crate of artillery shells. Each of these things had been tied down, including the crate, but all with utility cords that were too weak to withstand the brute force of that one huge, powerful wave.

At the time it occurred, he was too busy trying to save himself to worry about a few lost items. That came later.

He'd survived, of course, but it was a close thing. By the time he'd nursed his boat back to the dock at Pacifico, it was running very low in the water.

I guess I'll just have to go back to that island again some time, *he'd thought to himself as he tied up his boat. The last thing he'd had energy for was to plod up to his "home" and fall into bed.*

By the next morning his boat was still tied to the dock, but it was completely underwater.

***

"The Scrounger wasn't very helpful," commented Don as we drove back to town.

"No, he sure wasn't. I think we're going to need another angle on where those shells came from."

"Why don't we stop by our oceanography professor. At least he seemed happy to talk to us."

When we'd made our way back to our cabin, Don and I let Silver inside and made our way next door.

Dr. Turner was just as garrulous as he'd been on our first meeting and immediately asked us in and wanted to know how we were making out with our story on the sick kids. Explaining that their illnesses may have originated with some ammunition shells they'd found washed up on the beach, we asked whether he could help us understand the ocean currents and how they could carry things to the island shores.

"I'd be happy to help," he began, "but you need to understand that this isn't my specialty. Like all branches of science, oceanography is divided into specialties - and I'm a chemical oceanographer, not a physical oceanographer.

"But," he said, seeing our expressions of disappointment and raising his hands in the air. "That doesn't mean I can't give you the basics. Where did you say these shells were found?"

"They all seem to have shown up on the beaches in Naikoon Provincial Park. That's along the northern edge of the island, just past Masset."

"Hmmm, you wouldn't have any maps or charts, would you?"

We did, and it only took a few minutes for us to retrieve them and spread them out over his dining table.

For the next few minutes Dr. Turner went into lecture mode and explained how ocean currents work, why there are so many of them, and why sometimes change in intensity and even direction at different times of year. His explanations were delivered with much animation and hand waving, but with so much technical detail that I still found it hard to take it all in. Fortunately, he eventually ran somewhat out of steam, paused for breath and focused on our maps and charts.

"Now then" he'd said, rubbing his hands together as he pointed to the area just north of the Queen Charlotte Islands and warmed to his task. "There's a Kuroshio Current that runs northward off the coast of Japan, and there's an Oyashio Current, flows south out of the arctic. When those two currents collide, they create something called the North Pacific Drift, which is a slow but consistent warm-water current that flows towards us here in British Columbia. Once it gets near the coast, it splits into two new currents - the Alaska Current, which turns north, and the California Current, which turns south. Anything being carried by the North Pacific Drift could easily land anywhere between the northwest corner of Graham Island and the eastern tip of your Naikoon Provincial Park."

"That's a wide area," said Don, imaging it. "How far away does the current carry things?"

"Well, things like fishing gear, wood, empty bottles, and even clothes have been carried by the North Pacific Drift all the way from Japan. Some of them land on the beaches here in the islands.

If they get past the islands then they can get carried up towards Alaska or down towards Vancouver Island. But not quickly though. It's been estimated that the trip takes about two and a half years!"

"Two and a half years?"

"Well, it's a long distance and, like I said, it's considered to be a slow current."

"Is that the only way things get moved to our shores?" I'd asked.

"No, no. Heavier things can move along the bottom, especially if they are round or cylindrical, but then they're more pushed along by storm and wave action rather than being carried by the currents."

"How far away could heavier things come from then?"

"Who knows?" Dr. Turner replied. "I'm not sure anyone's even studied that, but with really big storms the turbulence can reach pretty deep water. With the fiercest storms, I'd say things from the ocean floor could get carried here from quite some distance away. They'd only be moved while the storms are active, though, so it could still take many years for things to travel any real distance."

"So again, that could be quite some distance away."

"Correct: long distances and long time-intervals."

"Thanks Doc," said Don, rising to re-fold the maps and charts. "You've given us a lot to think about."

"My pleasure. Come back any time and let me know how your story is progressing."

Promising to visit him again, Don and I took our leave and returned to our own cabin.

"What do you think?" I asked Don as we walked back.

"How do you feel about taking Silver for a walk?"

"Sure," I agreed, catching the hesitation in Don's voice. Having collected Silver and strolled along the beach for a quarter mile I wanted to bring the subject back to our recent conversation. "Any special reason for taking a walk?"

"Maybe it's just my over-active imagination, but what do you think about our Dr. Turner and The Scrounger?"

"I'm not happy with either of them," I pronounced immediately. "Everyone else we've talked to so far has struck me as being quite genuine: Dr. Sarah, the kids' parents, and the kids themselves. But we seem to be having trouble getting the truth, or at least the complete truth, out of these last two. First, The Scrounger denies buying one of the shells from the kids, and now we have both The Scrounger and Dr. Turner, each in their own way, implying that these shells, with their heavy projectiles intact, could possibly have rolled here all the way from Japan!'"

"Yes, although I'm more worried about The Scrounger, who may be in danger, than Dr. Turner, who may just have been pontificating nonsense to a couple of gullible reporters."

"And this walk?"

"I think it might be wise to treat the cabin as if it's been bugged until we know otherwise."

"What? You're kidding… aren't you?"

"Look at why we're here. You're here because your bosses are worried about public safety, and the possibilities that there are more of these shells and that they may be even more dangerous than we've seen so far. I'm here because my bosses are worried about the possibilities that there are more of these shells, that they might be much more dangerous, and that we might want to keep them away from unfriendly groups or even unfriendly nations."

"You really are worried, aren't you?"

"Well, until we hear back from the people in Suffield, I'm thinking we've had some unusual chemical or biological weapon materials show up and I'm afraid there may be more where they came from."

"And you think we're not the only ones looking for them."

"I hope we are, but it seems safer to assume that we're not."

"Soviets?" I said, remembering my own recent brush with Eastern European agents in Nova Scotia."

Well, the Cold War's still on so yes, Soviets… Americans too."

"But they're on our side!"

"Most days, yes, but they pursue their own interests, so it's best to be cautious."

"Can't you sweep?' I asked, thinking it all over.

"Sweep?"

"For bugs. Can't you sweep for bugs?"

"Oh, sure, but I don't have the equipment for it here. Maybe later, if we need to, but for now it's probably simpler to just be two boring, naïve journalists when we're in the cabin."

Still thinking about it, I asked, "how about the SUV?"

"What about it?"

"Could it be bugged too?"

"Could be, but more difficult. You need power and a recorder or a transmitter. Either way, it's harder to conceal, and I can check the vehicle over every once in a while."

"OK by me. Do you really suspect either of them?"

"Not really, it just bugs me that neither of them was as helpful as they could have been."

"I have a hard time agreeing with either of them about how far away those shells could have been. Remember the SCUBA diving I was doing as part of my cover in in Nova Scotia?"

"Right. You were looking into Red Tide phenomena and doing some dives with your friend from Dalhousie, right?"

***

Dr. Herb Turner

7 THE PLOT THICKENS

While on undercover assignment in Nova Scotia, posing as a visiting university student, I'd had to do some SCUBA diving to collect research samples and had also done some diving with university student-colleague and new friend Sharon Sanders (a biochemistry graduate student) to help with her sample collecting. We'd also done some dives together just for fun, including to see some shipwrecks. One of these, had been a shore-dive at Portuguese Cove, just south of Halifax, where the Claire Lilley had been wrecked during the Second World War.

In March 1942, the freighter Claire Lilley was approaching Halifax Harbour. It had been tracking in shallow water near the coast in order to avoid a German submarine, but in its efforts to avoid one hazard it ran into another in the form of Black Point Rock. Grounding on the rock broke the ship's back and the ship sank, along with its cargo of steel, ammunition, and bombs.

Sharon had warned me that most older shipwrecks look more like junk yards than ships, and this one was no exception. Between the original breaking of the hull when the ship grounded and three decades of the pounding of rough seas, the ship had literally been torn to shreds.

As was the case with many Nova Scotia shipwrecks, the Claire Lilley was most easily accessed by hiking down narrow pathways from a cliff, over rough terrain, to the shore. From there it was a case of gearing-up, entering the water, and swimming out in the correct direction. The cold water immediately began to work its way through my wetsuit and hit me like a shock wave. I gritted my teeth as best I could with a snorkel in my mouth, and I waited out the few minutes it took for my body heat to warm the water to something reasonable. Not comfortable, mind you, but tolerable.

We'd received detailed instructions from a local diving club and were soon swimming through a gentle swell in the greenish-blue water. When we were about a hundred yards out and correctly positioned relative to the proper landmarks on the shore, we switched from snorkels to our regulators and jackknifed down heading for the bottom. As we descended, the water colour shifted from greenish-blue to blue. Then, as we crossed the thermocline at just over 30 feet of depth, the water instantly became much colder and a much darker blue.

We found part of the wreck at a depth of 40 feet — a mish-mash of bent and torn hull and deck plates, various pieces of angular metal, and lengths of thick wire ropes, all of them heavily tarnished with corrosion. There were quite a lot of fish around, and it occurred to me to wonder whether the wreckage acted as an artificial reef for the fish.

Continuing to work our way outwards, away from shore, we followed the downward slope of the ocean floor and soon found ourselves in a large debris field at a depth of 50 feet. At this depth, there was much less light. Everything was rendered in shades of dark blue, but the visibility was still pretty good: our vertical visibility was about 25 feet, with horizontal visibility of 20 feet.

In among the wrecked pieces of the ship proper we found a few examples of its cargo, not the bombs we'd heard about but quite a few artillery shell casings partially buried in the sediment. Fascinated, I tried digging in the sediment a bit, which exposed more shells plus a sediment cloud that markedly reduced my visibility. Looking up, I caught Sharon's eyes and saw that she was pointing at her pressure gauge. Using our hands and fins to move closer together, we looked at each other's gauges. Mine read 600 psi, while hers read 900psi. Not too much air left. My dive watch showed our elapsed bottom time at 50 minutes. That was fast! Fifty minutes meant that we were nearly the limit of our no decompression interval. With time and air running low it was time to head back to the surface, so I gave the "let's go up" hand signal to her. She nodded agreement and we slowly ascended straight up.

Breaking the surface and inflating our buoyancy compensators, we made the long swim back to shore. After changing out of our suits and into warm, dry clothes I took a minute to visit with Silver, who had been lying in comfort across our two large gear bags while he waited for us. After that, we examined our treasures. Each of us had brought up a couple of the shell casings and a few screw-in primers that we'd found near them. The shell casings didn't have the projectiles mounted in them but they were full of cordite, which we emptied out while it was still wet and let the sea dilute the powder and carry it away.

We later measured the shells and found that they were 40 mm. They had probably been intended for the Bofors 40 mm gun, one of the most popular medium-weight anti-aircraft autocannons used by the western Allies in the Second World War.

***

Thinking back to my Claire Lilly dive, I remembered a few things.

"Don, remember those shells I salvaged from that shipwreck in Nova Scotia?"

"Artillery shells, right."

"Yes. There was a newspaper article about it a few years ago. The article said that sometimes, after really bad winter storms, some of those shells actually made their way to shore and were found washed up on the beach. It raised some concerns because people didn't want kids playing with them or using the cordite to make bonfires."

"That makes sense."

"Well, the shells didn't wash up all the time. Only like once in five years or so and, even then, only after really bad storms. The military used to make periodic sweeps of the beach and the wreck itself, to recover new shells that the storms released from the wreck. I never heard of anyone being affected by the shells themselves though. Anyway, in that case the wreck was only a hundred yards offshore – not very far away at all."

"So… ?"

"So, these shells we're looking for would be fairly heavy, right? A bit smaller than the ones I found, but with the projectiles still in them. So, fairly heavy. It seems to me that they must have come from reasonably close to shore, and from a reasonably shallow depth."

"Sure, even Dr. Turner didn't try to convince us that they could have come from really deep water."

"And so far, we only have reports of shells coming ashore on the one northern beach, right?"

"Right."

"OK then," I said thinking out loud. "That could narrow it down to what? Maybe up to 200 yards offshore from Agate Beach, and either due north or to the northwest. The next question is how did they get there? Could they have come from a sunken, Second World War Japanese warship?"

"That we can check with the federal Receiver of Wrecks. They have lists of all the ships reported lost on all three coasts. I have another idea too. We can check on reported Japanese military activity along the whole coast during the war. I'm pretty sure I heard about some kind of small invasion further north that was repulsed. We should look into that too."

That evening, we took a break. We'd arranged to have Dr. Sarah, K'iijuu (one of the paramedics we'd met at the hospital), and Jack join us for a bonfire and wiener-roast dinner at one of the firepits in Naikoon Provincial Park – one of the firepits on the same Agate Beach where the kids had found the shells, to be exact. We were (mostly) off-duty, however, and quickly learned why it was such a popular spot. It is a beautiful but wild location and a great spot to relax. We walked along the beach, throwing a ball at intervals for Silver to run and catch. This he really enjoyed except for the odd time when the ball landed in the water, at which point he'd run up to it and then stop and sit just beyond the water's reach and wait for one of us to come and retrieve the ball for him.

"Silver still doesn't like the water, I see," remarked Don.

"No, he sure doesn't. I found out why when we were Alaska. Remind me to tell you the story sometime," was all I'd said.

Supper was a simple affair: hot dogs cooked over the fire and served with potato salad and a few condiments that we'd purchased from a small grocery store on the drive north to the park. It seemed somehow appropriate to the beach setting, however, and we all enjoyed them, especially Silver who had lately developed an almost fanatical liking for hot dogs and regarded them as a huge treat.

Over dinner, K'iijuu - pronounced [k̲'ii](juu) – told us some stories about his Haida heritage. Some of these stories are partially illustrated in their art, such as in the frequent appearance of Raven the trickster (an embodiment of religious significance) in their famous totem poles.

After dinner, we'd chatted about a wide variety of lighthearted topics. Don and I had already found Dr. Sarah to be quick-witted and charming and, true to form, it didn't take Jack long to ingratiate himself with her. *It will be interesting to see how this turns out*, I thought, as I watched him turn on his trade-mark charm.

For the most part, though, I was content to just sit back and enjoy the breeze blowing in from the ocean, smell the salty air, and watch the waves serenely rolling in and up the beach.

***

Day 6: August 25, 1977.

Being August, the kids were still out of school on summer vacation so after breakfast we tried making the rounds of the kids' homes and were fortunate to find them all at home. For the most part our visits were all pretty uneventful, although they all seemed to enjoy visiting with Silver. We'd simply said that we were checking to see how they were recovering, whether they remembered anything more about their evening campfire, and whether they'd seen or heard anything about other shells showing up anywhere. Basically, Karen, Frank, and Rick were all healing well, didn't remember anything further, and hadn't heard of any more shells being found – not even from their other friends.

We did get a surprise, however, when we went to visit Jimmy Hunter, who was out of bed, seemed fully mobile again, and had even been out playing with his friends that afternoon. His answers to our questions matched those of the other kids, so that wasn't much help.

The surprise came when we were saying goodbye and, on impulse, I asked him one more question: "Say, you haven't heard of any boats being wrecked or grounded near the islands lately have you?"

"Not lately," Jimmy replied, his eyes lighting up. "But there were a couple of ships that hit rocks and sunk in the Inside Passage. I did a report on them for my history class last year."

"Have there been many shipwrecks then?"

"I'll say. I found a book in the library that listed a thousand shipwrecks, all here in BC[17]."

"A thousand...," I said, faintly, "all of them around here?"

"Oh, no, that's for the whole province. Up here around the Queen Charlottes and across the by the mainland, there are only about three hundred."

"That's still quite a lot," I commented. "I don't suppose you happen to know how many would have sunk around here during the Second World War?"

"I sure do," said Jimmy, his eyes shining brightly. "There were only two, and I wrote about them in my report. One was called the *Uzbekistan*. It was a Russian freighter[17] and it got lost and ran aground on Vancouver Island on its way to Seattle to pick up supplies for the war. That was in 1943.

"The second one was called the *Kvichak*. It was an American freighter[18] carrying U.S. Army supplies to Alaska, but it also lost its bearings and ran aground near the mainland directly east of here. That one was in 1941."

"And those were the only two?"

"The only two I found, anyway."

"Oh, well, thank you for the interesting history lesson."

Taking our leave, we were halfway to the road when we were brought up short by a last parting comment from Jimmy.

"We nearly had a boat sink right near us not long ago," he'd called out to us.

"Really!" I said, turning back. "When was that?"

"I don't remember exactly, but it was before school got out. Maybe three months ago."

"What happened?"

Sensing Don and my immediate interest and seriousness, Jimmy became hesitant. "It wasn't a big ship or anything, just a boat, and it didn't actually sink," he hedged. "Well, not right away anyway."

"That's OK Jimmy," I encouraged. "What can you tell us about it?"

"The *Belle* was approaching from up north somewhere and got caught in a big storm. It was just in sight of North Beach when it started taking on water. It was a pretty old boat, I guess, and she just couldn't keep up any more. Anyway, the storm got worse, and some huge waves came over the bow and washed everything off the deck."

"Then what happened?"

"Well, I guess the boat was pretty low in the water by then, but it managed to keep going and eventually made it around the tip of the island and turned south into the calmer water of the Inside Passage. From there I guess it was able to work its way down to its dock. It must have been pretty neat to see, because apparently it sunk overnight and the next morning it was lying there right on the bottom, still tied-up at its dock."

"What a great story! How did you find out about all this?"

"Oh, well, I found a red lifebuoy washed up on North Beach," then, seeing the confused looks on our faces, he clarified. "It was banged up pretty good, but it had the name *Belle* stencilled on it. When I brought him his lifebuoy back, he told me the whole story."

"Who told you the whole story?"

"The Scrounger, of course. The *Belle* was his boat."

"The Scrounger!" both Don and I said in unison.

"Right. I'd taken the lifebuoy into town and was going to leave it for him at the marine supply store. They're pretty expensive and I hoped there might be a reward for it. Anyway, when I got to the store there he was, so I just went up and asked him if he'd lost it. That's when he told me the story."

"Did you get a reward from him?"

"Sort of. He gave me a quarter and said I could go buy a Coke with it."

"That's a great story, Jimmy. Thank you," said Don, reaching into his wallet for a five-dollar bill. "Here's a better reward for you."

"Gee, thanks Mister!" was Jimmy's pleased reply, delivered with a huge smile.

When we got back to town, Don went to find a phone so he could call the Receiver of Wrecks, while I left Silver in the SUV and went to the town's library. A friendly librarian found the book Jimmy had mentioned and, sure enough, the author had listed and charted the known, recorded shipwrecks in British Columbia dating back to the 1700s – all 1,101 of them!

As Jimmy had told us, the only Second World War wreck seemed to be the one Russian freighter, and it was wrecked far to the south of us and while on its way to Seattle for supplies. So, on both counts, it was not likely of interest to us. In the area to the north and northwest of the Queen Charlotte Islands the charts only showed twelve wrecks: two sailing ships that sunk in the 1800s, three smaller ships that sunk before the Second World War, and seven smaller ships that sunk in the 1950s and '60s. There seemed to be nothing of interest for us there either, although some of the descriptions suggested that they'd make for interesting diving if we ever got some quality leisure time.

Don and I had arranged to meet at a local café that we knew had an outdoor deck, so we could keep Silver nearby while we ate. As we compared notes over lunch, we found that we'd both learned essentially the same thing. There had been no recorded shipwrecks of Second World War vintage lost to the north of the northwest of the Queen Charlotte Islands, just the American freighter to the east of us, on the mainland side of the Inside Passage, and the one Russian freighter way down south on Vancouver Island. Neither of them seemed to be candidates for carrying Japanese munitions.

"OK, that's a dead end, then," I commented. "Too bad, because I'd have liked to have had an excuse to go dive on a sunken Japanese warship!"

"We did learn something else from our young friend Jimmy though," added Don.

"Yes, The Scrounger again," I agreed. "Do you suppose the shells came from his boat in the first place?"

"I suspect so, and if he got them somewhere and lost them like that, it could explain why he bought the last surviving shell from the kids."

"But he didn't buy the empty shells," I objected.

"No, he didn't, which seems to suggest that he was only interested in live shells. That could mean he thought he could sell the shells to someone."

"OK then, but who would want to buy old Second World War vintage, live artillery shells?"

"Normally, no one. Why would you want them and why take the risk? But I'm still worried that they might have been something unusual."

"Unusual meaning valuable. So, you still think they contain some kind of chemical or biological warfare agent in them and that someone might want them, as in might want to use them?"

"Scary, huh? But yes, that's my guess. We should get a reply soon from the lab people at Suffield. Then, we'll know whether we're chasing worthless antiques or something much more sinister."

"Let's say you're right, just for the sake of argument. Who would he sell them to?"

"Some kind of international arms dealer, probably" Don muttered darkly.

"That's like fiction..." I'd started to say, and then stopped as I remembered all the other scary things that I'd been learning in my short time with the RCMP's Security Service. Changing tack, I asked "Around here?"

"No, not around here. Maybe someone in a large city like Vancouver or Toronto, but more likely someone in New York, say."

"How does a person even find someone like that?"

"Word of mouth, mostly. Someone in the black market might know someone who knows someone – that kind of thing."

"And here in the islands? It's pretty isolated here. I don't know whether the islands would even have a black market with so few people living here."

"I don't know either. Why don't we drop by the local antique store and see if the owner knows anything?"

After finishing our lunch, that's exactly what we did. Queen Charlotte City had one official souvenir shop, although the roadside gas stations and cafes in the area also had display stands filled with souvenirs. There was one dedicated antique and curio shop in town, however, and that was our next stop.

Looking around inside we discovered that, in addition to antiques and curios, the owner was also a gun collector and gun dealer.

I'll admit to having been a bit apprehensive inside the antique shop. The feel and the smell of the shop, the wall of guns at the back, plus the assortment of modern and older nautical items reminded me so strongly of the Cape Breton Nova Scotia antique shop I'd spent so much time in while on a case there earlier in the year[11]. The owner of that particular store had ultimately tried to kill me and with an effort I tried, somewhat unsuccessfully, to hold back the flood of memories.

Don must have noticed my hesitation, even if he didn't understand it, and he led the first part of the questioning once we'd found and introduced ourselves to the store's owner.

The owner had heard about the kids finding some old shells and burning the cordite from them. "Ended up in the hospital I heard," he'd remarked. "Must have been too close to the fire and got a lot of smoke and soot in their eyes and noses. Kids never learn, do they?"

Shaking our heads sympathetically, we agreed that we'd heard something like that too, and were interested in the part about the shells. Upon further questioning, the owner said "No, no one has shown up trying to sell any shells," and no, in all his years he'd never heard of large calibre shells ever showing up on the islands before.

Would he consider buying any if they did show up?

"Sure, if the price was right and if they've been emptied out so they're safe. No one around here would be crazy enough to buy old, live shells, and especially not large ones... that's what I keep telling people."

That sounded like a cue to me. "Telling people?" I'd asked.

"Well, first I get people asking if I'd buy old artillery shells and I have to explain that there's not much market around here for that kind of thing. People will buy almost anything if it's made of brass, but they won't pay very much. Then, just a few days ago, I get a phone call from someone asking if I have any old artillery shells for sale!"

"Wow. Who wanted to sell and who wanted to buy, and when did all this happen?"

"First, it was The Scrounger asking if I was in the market to buy brass shells. That was a couple of months ago. I told him the same thing I just told you – not unless they're cleaned up and cheap. He wasn't impressed and wanted to know if I knew of anyone that would want the shells intact, projectiles and all. I told him no and forgot all about it.

"Then, a few days ago I got the phone call asking specifically about loaded artillery shells. I said that I didn't have anything like that and hadn't heard of anything either. The caller wouldn't be put off that easily though and insisted on giving me a phone number to call in case anything turned up."

"Do you know who it was that called?"

"No, just a male voice. Oh, and it was a long-distance call. I remember because first the operator came on and said she was transferring a long-distance call to me, then she made the connection."

"What happened then?"

"Like I said, I'd forgotten about The Scrounger's interest, but that call reminded me. So, the next time The Scrounger came into the store I told him about it and gave him the phone number."

"You weren't interested yourself?"

"No, I deal in guns and antiques but not things that can blow up on me, and besides, I didn't like the sound of the guy on the phone. He seemed too friendly for a stranger, if you know what I mean. Overly friendly, like the way a con artist is overly nice, so you'll be too trusting. It gave me a bad feeling."

"Do you still have the phone number?"

"Sure, it's still around here ... somewhere." Stepping over to his wall-mounted telephone, he looked over the myriad of notes that were tacked to the wall before grunting in satisfaction and selecting one and bringing it over to us. "Here it is."

Thanking him, Don copied the number into his 'reporter's notebook,' and then passed the original back.

Don and I gave each other a long look, then thanked the store owner for his help and left. As we got back into the SUV and headed away, my first comment was: "Wow, the plot thickens!"

"I'll say," agreed Don. "The Scrounger's name seems to pop up at every turn, and I don't like the sound of this mystery caller."

"How would a long-distance caller even know to try phoning here about loaded artillery shells?"

"Very good question. Maybe someone heard about the accidents the kids had. The kids getting sick from the shells made the local newspaper, so it could be that. Maybe The Scrounger tried asking someone with black market connections, and word travelled through some kind of underground network."

"Well, what now?" I asked.

"Let's drop by the detachment and see whether anything has come in for us from Suffield."

Fortunately, Jack was in when we reached the detachment.

"Good timing!" he announced as we'd gone in. "Just received a telex for you marked SECRET"

As Jack handed over the flimsy teletype printout Don and I leaned in so we could read it together.

```
V
VIA WUI+
RCMP QUEEN CHARLOTTE DET.

RCMP E DIV HQ

PRIORITY

FM:  E DIV HQ
TO:  QUEEN CHARLOTTE DET.
BT
CLASSIFIED SECRET

PRIORITY MESSAGE FM CF DRES. SAMPLES
ANALYZED. CONFIRM NERVE AGENT: TABUN.
ACTIVE AGENT TOXIC EVEN IN SMALL DOSES.
RECOMMEND EXERCISE EXTREME CAUTION.
ELS.
+
RCMP QCHARLOTTE

RCMP E DIV HQ
VVV
```

"Well, now we know what Jim was exposed to," said Don. "He's lucky that he wasn't exposed to any more than he was."

"That's for sure," said Jack. "If what he got comes from just a trace of the chemical then I wouldn't like to see anyone get exposed to a full dose."

"Sounds like time for us to make some calls," said Don.

Jack waved him over to his desk so he could call in, and chatted with me while we waited for Don, who wasn't on the phone very long.

"My boss wasn't in, so I left a message. It's getting late in the evening in Halifax, so we may have to check in again in the morning."

"What did you say?" I asked.

"First, I asked them to look into that phone number we got. Then, I told them about the results from Suffield, which wasn't a surprise, really, but at least now we know for sure. Based on that, I put in a request for the navy to do a search north and northwest of the island to see if they can find any more shells."

"Won't that be like looking for needles in a haystack?" asked Jack.

"Maybe, but CFB Esquimalt isn't very far away from us and they have the west-coast part of the Fleet Diving Unit there and they also have sonar specialists based there[19]."

"Meaning?" I asked.

"Meaning that I've asked for the *HMCS Huron* to get some of the fleet divers and their latest side-scan sonar gear."

"Can they search for something as small as we're looking for?"

"They can try. They have some kind of secret new hyper-sensitive side-scan sonar that can be towed from a Zodiac. All I know is that it only works when it's towed at slow speed, and the extra sensitivity only works in shallow water – less than a hundred feet. But that should be all we need. We have a limited search area, and there's probably no point in trying to look deeper than a hundred feet anyway."

"And a single Zodiac prowling around offshore shouldn't attract too much attention?"

"Especially not if they stick a couple of large fishing poles up in to the air and make it look like they're fishing for salmon."

"OK, my turn then," I said as I moved over to Jack's desk to call my boss in Ottawa.

It wasn't quite as late in the evening in Ottawa as it was in Halifax, and my boss in the Security Service, Staff Sergeant Bob Simpson happened to be working late in the office.

His "What have you learned Alex?" took me a few minutes to recount, as I summarized what I'd learned and what I suspected.

"Sounds like our worst fears have been realized. We need to know how many of these are out there, and where they're coming from, and get to them before anyone unfriendly gets to them… if they haven't already."

"I know."

"What about this old character the kids say bought one of the shells?"

"We talked to him. He denies it, but I don't believe him, and Don and I think he's the one that actually brought them to the islands from somewhere. We're going to focus on him now, but I don't want to spook him into hiding or we may never find the source of the shells."

"Do you need anything from me?"

"Well, actually I do, but I don't think you're going to like it..." We talked for a few more minutes before I hung up and went back to Jack and Don.

"I have an idea, but neither of you are going to like it."

Neither of them liked it at all.

Laurie Schramm

8 THE FIRST SEARCH

Our next task was to see if we could learn more about the chemical nerve agent from Dr. Sarah. When we arrived at the hospital, though, we learned from K'iijuu that she was off duty and would be back the next day if we returned in the morning. Deciding there wasn't much more we could do that evening we took a break. We had dinner at the same café with the outdoor deck, so Silver could sit by us, then returned to our cabin.

As we rolled up to the cabin, our neighbour Dr. Turner was sitting out on his deck, so we went over to chat. He was his usual jovial and outgoing self and wanted to know how our big story was progressing.

We explained that we hadn't progressed very far: the kids were recovering rapidly, no new shells had been found, and it seemed like there was nothing more for us.

"No news unless it's bad news, is that it?" he'd asked.

"Pretty much," Don admitted. "We're just as interested in strong good-news stories as we are disasters, but this one isn't turning out to be very strong at all so we'll probably file what we have and be on our way before long."

Saying out good-byes, Don, and Silver and I went for another gorgeous walk along the beach.

"I think out cover story has just about run its course," I commented, when we were out of Dr. Turner's hearing.

"Yes, I think that things are going to heat-up before long anyway."

Day 7: August 26, 1977.

Sunrise found us driving to the hospital to see Dr. Sarah. She wasn't at all surprised to learn that the chemical agent that had affected her patients had been a nerve agent, since she'd successfully used atropine to treat them. Leading us to the hospital's small reference library, she hunted among the shelves for a moment and then brought down a huge book titled *Goldfrank's Toxicologic Emergencies*[20].

Finding the entry for Tabun, she gave us a running narrative as she scanned the text: "Tabun... also known as the G-agent GA... developed in 1936, in Germany, as an insecticide. It was abandoned as an insecticide because of its overwhelming human toxicity... Tabun is toxic even in minute doses... Onset of symptoms is rapid (seconds to minutes) for exposure to aerosol or vapor... delayed (minutes to hours) for dermal exposure... eye pain, dim or blurred vision, mucous secretions... cough, wheezing... localized sweating... headache, nausea, vomiting, cramps... Severe exposure can cause sudden collapse, seizures..."

"Well, that's consistent with what I saw in my patients," she said. "Tabun is about half as toxic as Sarin by inhalation, but in very low concentrations it is more irritating to the eyes. That's consistent with the kids' experiences. The number and severity of symptoms vary according to the amount of the agent absorbed and its rate of entry of it into the body. That's consistent with Constable Miller's experience, as he seems to have handled the shells more and at closer range."

"Well, at least we know for sure what we've up against now," said Don, speaking for us both.

Thanking her for her help, we left the hospital.

"Now what?" asked Don, but he knew what was coming.

"Time to go visit The Scrounger," I replied.

"Or his place, you mean. Are sure you want to be part of this? I can handle it myself you know."

"I know you can Don, but if your cover gets blown, mine goes up too. Besides, having the two of us will be better than just one, it'll be faster, more effective, and safer."

"Grruph," came a sound from the back seat.

"Right, you too, Silver. We'll need your keen ears as a lookout."

"You know," mused Don. "There was a time when I didn't believe he could follow our conversations, but we've been through so much together now that it doesn't even seem weird to me anymore."

"Grruph," said Silver.

I smiled contentedly. "Let's go see if Jack can get me a search warrant."

When we'd brought Jack up to date on everything, he'd gone to see a Justice of the Peace and obtained a search warrant for the Scrounger's place. Naturally, Jack wanted to come along with us, but I convinced him to let us try to maintain our cover identities first.

It was agreed that Don and I would first go back and try again to get The Scrounger to admit that he'd bought one of the intact shells from the kids on the beach. We all shared a feeling that he wouldn't admit anything to a uniformed police officer.

If The Scrounger wasn't there, then I'd exercise the search warrant and confiscate the shell, if we found it, before it caused injury or death to him or anyone else.

I did have to agree, however, that if we ran into any trouble, or were going to be forced to break our cover anyway, then we would call him in to join us.

***

So, Don, Silver, and I drove out to The Scrounger's place at Pacofi. As we approached the old seafood cannery, we could see that his black work boat was absent from its mooring-place at the old dock. That seemed encouraging.

"What do you think?" asked Don as we parked.

"I like the straightforward approach. If he's there, then let's see if we can squeeze anything more out of him. If he's not there, then so much the better..."

Getting out of the SUV, we casually walked up to the building in which he'd taken-up residence and simply knocked on the door. There was no answer.

Trying the door itself, we were somewhat amazed to discover it was unlocked.

"Welcome, to the simple life," commented Don. "I'm not sure anyone but shopkeepers lock their door in these islands."

"Well, that's a bonus," I commented, taking a step inside. "Mr. Parker?" I called out.

There was no reply.

"Silver... Stay... Guard," I said, emphasizing the words

carefully.

Silver made a small sound of acknowledgement and immediately laid-down and curled-up just outside the door.

"OK, in we go," I said to Don. "How about I start to the right and you start to the left?'

Don assented and we began our search. It wasn't a huge place, and we took out time. If we'd been fortunate to find no one at home, that's where our luck ended as, after the most careful search we could do without actually damaging anything, we were unable to find the shell.

"Damn," I vented.

"It was worth a try, but he's either buried it or otherwise hidden it somewhere else, or he's taken it away somewhere."

"Yes, but where?"

"Everybody calls him The Scrounger, right? His business is scavenging things and then selling them, and we already know that he was trying to sell brass shells to the antique store. My guess is that he's off finding a buyer, or maybe has already found one."

"Maybe even the one we have a phone number for."

"Right."

"OK then. What next Sherlock?"

That made Don smile. "We do seem to take turns being Sherlock and Watson, don't we? Well, it looks like we're going to have to widen our search, and that means splitting-up and going to Plans B and C, like we discussed with our bosses last night."

"I don't like the idea of splitting up, and both of our next steps seem like such long shots to me."

"I agree, but one of them was your idea in the first place. Besides," he sighed, "neither of us have come up with any better ideas. Let's collect Silver and get out of here. I don't think there's much more we can do until tomorrow when reinforcements arrive."

***

After the disaster with his old boat, things had definitely been improving, thought the Scrounger.

The phone number The Scrounger had received from the antique shop owner was a toll-free, long-distance number. The first time he had dialled it a deep, male voice answered, and the connection seemed poor. Either that, or it was coming from a long distance away.

After he'd explained about finding a cache of Japanese Second World War ammunition, the voice casually asked what kinds of ammunition. As he described the various kinds of shells he'd seen, right up to the 25 mm shells, the voice seemed remarkably disinterested, but asked what the larger shells looked like.

"There were different kinds," said The Scrounger. "They were fully loaded and all of them had the projectiles already mounted on them and everything."

The voice seemed to quickly lose interest again but sharpened when The Scrounger continued: "and another thing. They came in all different sorts of colours."

"That's right," said the voice. "They used differently coloured bands to distinguish regular explosives from armor-piercing and tracers."

"I saw that. Some of the bands were yellow, red, and green, but the tips and the bodies were different colours too."

"Different colours?" said the voice, sounding interested for the first time. "What colours?"

"Well," said The Scrounger, screwing up his face as he concentrated, "Some of the bodies were black and others were grey, and some of the tips were painted red while others were painted blue."

"That's interesting," said the voice. "I might be willing to pay for some of the coloured ones. Let me do some research and I'll call you back."

"Pay how much?"

"If they're what I think they are, I might be willing to pay you a hundred dollars each."

"Each case?"

"No, for each shell. But only for certain colours. Let me check and I'll phone you back. If they're what I think they are, how long would it take you to get me some samples?"

"A week, maybe less," said The Scrounger, cautious now and not willing to give away too much information.

"Don't say anything about this to anybody. Call me back in three days."

Three days later, The Scrounger had called back.

"I might be interested in buying some of the shells with a grey body and blue tip," said The Voice. "It doesn't matter what colour the bands are, but I'm interested in samples of each colour."

At this, The Scrounger got excited and divulged a bit more information: "I have one of that kind of shell. Do you want to buy it?"

"Just one? I thought you said you could get more."

"I can. I actually had some others, but I ran into some trouble and lost them in a storm. I can get more, but for now I just have the one. Do you still want it?"

"Yes."

"OK, where do we meet?"

"We don't. You don't know me, and I want to keep it that way. You know the cemetery that's just off the highway on the west side of town?"

"Sure."

"Wrap the shell in a bag and take it there tomorrow night. There's a big covered shelter there. Beside it is a large ships' anchor on a pedestal. Underneath one of the anchor flukes will be a plain envelope held down by a rock. Your money will be in there. Take the money and put the bag with the shell where the envelope was and leave."

"That's all?"

"That's all, don't look for me, don't look around at all – just drop off the shell, take your money and go. Don't look back. I'll be watching you from a distance."

"Fine. Then what?"

"Call me the next afternoon. If it's something I'm interested in, then we'll talk about buying more."

Feeling a bit like a spy in a movie, The Scrounger had followed the instructions, picked up his money – an envelope containing five brand new twenty-dollar bills – and then gone home.

Day 8: August 27, 1977.

Now, as instructed, The Scrounger had called the mystery

phone number again and reached what he now thought of as The Voice. "So, are you interested?" he'd asked the voice.

"I am. How many more can you get that have grey bodies and blue tips?"

"I don't know for sure," he'd replied, trying to visualize what he'd seen. "They were in wooden cases with rope handles, and I think there were fifty in each case."

"How many cases?"

"There were lots of them, but I don't know how many had the gray bodies and blue tips. The cases all the looked the same from the outside."

"Fine then. I'll pay you the same amount for as many as you can get me. If you can get fifty, I'll pay you five thousand dollars. Are they far away?"

The Scrounger's excitement had spiked sky-high at the thought of an easy five thousand dollars, but that last question brought him down to earth again and he was immediately cautious.

"Not too far away. It'll take me a day to get my boat ready, a day to go get them, and another day to get back here. I can leave on Monday and be back on Tuesday."

"That's good. Phone me when you have them and tell me how many you have. Then I'll get the money and we can do the exchange."

The Scrounger hung up the phone with an emotion that he'd carefully suppressed while talking to The Voice. *Five thousand dollars a case*, he thought to himself. The prospect of a quick trip to make some easy money seemed like a miracle, it would allow him to pay off his new boat – *The Argo* - and he was excited.

He shouldn't have been.

***

Early in the morning, Don dropped Silver and I off at the airport and then headed north to meet the navy people that were to arrive in Masset. Silver and I had no sooner entered the airport than a woman of about my own age approached us, saying "Alex Houston?"

"Yes."

"Vivian Rule, FBI. How do you do?"

"Pleased to meet you," I replied, offering my hand to shake. "I gather that we were described to you."

"Woman of about my own age with red hair, green eyes, and a large dog that looks like a wolf – yes, I didn't need any detective skills to pick you out."

Laughing, I said: "How about coffee?"

Grabbing a couple of coffees, we headed outside where Silver could stay with us, and where we could speak with reasonable privacy.

"Obviously, women are joining the Mounties now. Are there many of you yet?"

"They started with just me as a pilot project. I graduated two years ago, but they've been regularly training troops of about 30 each since then and there are about 200 of us women Constables now. That's not many in such a big country though, and women only represent 1% of the Force. What's the story in the FBI?"

"Pretty similar, really. The FBI started with two women agents[21]: myself and one other. The two of us trained in 1972. I don't know the current statistics, but I know that women represent less than 5% of the FBI."

Vivian was brunette, fairly tall, slender (but not thin), and had wonderful, large brown eyes. Her manner seemed, not so much serious as very aware and intent. *The kind of person that doesn't miss much*, was my first impression, and I immediately found myself looking forward to working with her. Her next comments only added to my first impressions.

"Is your dog a pilot project too?"

"Actually, he is. This is Silver, the most unusual looking police dog in the Force."

"Hello Silver," she'd said, bending down on one knee and offering a hand for him to sniff."

Silver had been watching her intently, and moved forward for a good sniff, after which he looked up at me with that, *I like her* expression on his face that I'd come to know so well.

Not missing a beat, Vivian had caught this exchange too. "So, do I pass?"

I laughed. "You sure do. As you can see, he's quite decisive." Then, turning serious, "How much do you know about what we're facing here?"

"Almost nothing. I was told that an Assistant Commissioner contacted our Deputy Director. That's way, way up the chain of command from me. All I was told was that you're looking for something or someone to do with some kind of serious safety and security implications, that you're doing it undercover, and that you want to be able to search in U.S. territory. I assume it's not just at sea, or else you'd be working with the Coast Guard, and that's all I was told."

"Wow. Your Deputy Director must really trust us."

"In general, I guess that's true, as far as it goes. Our two agencies have a long history of working closely together, more closely that the general public knows, but I have the feeling that our Deputy Director and your Assistant Commissioner must have some past history together too for this to be laid on so quickly and with so little information."

"You're probably right," I said, thinking about the close relationship between Assistant Commissioner MacLeod and Don's Admiral. "Well, this mission is certainly 'need to know' but there's actually quite a lot that you do need to know, so I'll share everything my partner and I have learned as soon as we're aboard the ship and have some privacy."

"Ship?"

I couldn't help but laugh. "They didn't even tell you that? Yes, a very large and noisy helicopter is on its way to pick us up and take us to a destroyer that's sailing off the coast. The ship will take us up to Alaska, and that's where our search is going to be."

We'd no sooner finished our coffees than we heard the sound of the approaching helicopter. It was the familiar navy Sea King and once it landed, out hopped the even more familiar Sandy.

"Lieutenant Sandy Moore, this is Special Agent Vivian Rule of the FBI. She's going to help us with our search."

"Pleased to meet you," he said, offering a brilliant smile and his hand to shake. "Hello to you too, Silver," he added, looking down.

"Woof, woof."

"If you three are ready, we can hop right in and get you to the ship."

The *HMCS Huron* was lurking, as I thought of it, just out of sight of the islands so it wasn't long before we saw the ship, banked sharply into position over the stern landing platform, attached ourselves to the Beartrap and landed. As we exited, yelling over the slowly diminishing whine of the huge propellers, Sandy explained the whole Beartrap thing for Vivian, who appeared suitably interested and impressed.

By the time we'd stepped to the ship's hanger and collected our gear, we were met by the ship's XO, just like when I'd landed there for the first time. The XO showed us to our temporary cabins, left Silver and I to settle in, and took Vivian to meet the Captain, and then for a tour of the ship.

When she returned, we headed for main galley to secure more coffee and give her a thorough briefing on the situation. As we entered the galley, I noticed that something had immediately caught Silver's attention. Following his gaze, I noticed that the ship's cat, Ember, was staring right back, her gaze just as penetrating and her ears laid back.

"Trouble?" asked Vivian, noticing our pause.

"Let's see. That's Ember, the ship's unofficial mascot." My concern was unjustified, however, as Silver and Ember seemed recognize each other, lower hackles, and shift to a rather pointed ignoring of each other's presence.

"They seem to have come to some kind of *détente*," remarked Vivian, dryly.

"Looks like it. They have met before. I don't think they're ever going to become friends, but at least any possible hostilities seem to have been suspended."

"Just like Nixon and Brezhnev's *détente*."

"Right," I said, laughing again. "Let's grab a table and I'll fill you in."

Settling in, I related the whole story to Vivian, including Don's involvement. At least the story as Don and I knew it, right up to having just searched The Scrounger's place unsuccessfully and Don's current excursion with the navy to try to find more of shells offshore.

"OK, I think I've got the picture. Where is it we're going?"

"Well, we're pursuing three leads right now. Don's after one. Another one is The Scrounger himself, but we're temporarily lost track of him. The third is the Aleutian Islands."

"Once the scientists at the defense research station in Alberta figured out what was in the shells, they also made a call to one of the military's historians to check on Japanese operations on our West Coast during the Second World War."

"What we in the U.S. call World War Two."

"Right. It turns out that there were a few submarine attacks here and there in these waters and that's about all. But... the Japanese did invade two of the Aleutian Islands and establish bases on them in 1942. They were eventually discovered, of course and the following year two counter-offensives were launched. The first one was by your forces on Attu, which amounted to a successful but bloody two-day battle that destroyed the installations and almost completely wiped out the Japanese forces. The second one was a joint U.S.-Canada operation on Kiska, which was also successful but bizarre in that by the time our forces landed the entire Japanese garrison had been evacuated leaving all of their installations either destroyed or bobby-trapped."

"So, you think there's something left on those islands?"

"We should probably take a look at them, but no, I don't expect to find anything there. They are too well known and your forces and ours would have thoroughly looked them over for residual threats. I doubt we could find anything that they couldn't."

"What, then?"

"Well, I got to thinking: What if there was a third island base? One that was also evacuated but no one ever discovered?"

"Hmmm," said Vivian, thinking. "Seems like a long-shot to me, although I know our forces kept tripping over small, isolated Japanese bases in the South Pacific for years after the war ended. Some of them were even still being maintained by soldiers whose communications had been cut-off and were completely unaware that the war had ended."

"Exactly, why not here as well?"

"OK, still seems like a long shot though. Boy, you talk about the FBI trusting the RCMP, your superiors must really trust you to being going along with this."

"Maybe," I'd replied, embarrassed. "But, more importantly we haven't come up with any better ideas. We know that these shells can kill, just by leaking if nothing else, and we're trying to chase down every lead – or crazy idea – that we have."

If Vivian had anything more to say on the matter it was suspended at that point by the arrival of a crew member with a package.

"Sorry to interrupt," he'd said, "but this package was delivered to the ship with instructions to give it to Lieutenant Harrison or, failing that, to you."

Thanking him, I opened to the package to find a photocopy of an old manual. Placing it between us on the table, Vivian and I opened it together. The document was titled *Japanese Ammunition*, and came from the U.S. Navy, dated 1945. The significance of the date was brought home to us as we looked at the introduction and realized that it was a bomb disposal manual.

"This should be interesting," I commented, perusing the table of contents and flipping to the section titled "Identification of Japanese Ammunition," and there it was.

"The 25 mm, Type 96 auto-cannon gun's ammunition had a shell casing that was six and a half inches long and a diameter of nearly two inches. With the projectile mounted the total length is nine inches," I read. "Each one weighs about half a pound, and each magazine held fifteen of them."

"Sounds like anti-aircraft."

"Says here that the navy used them for anti-aircraft," I agreed, "and the army used them as anti-aircraft and anti-tank guns. In both cases they were usually multiple-barreled, with either two or three barrels per gun."

"Maybe they planned to use these weapons mounted on landing craft to provide rapid-fire cover in support of a beach-head landings. By switching ammunition types, they could have done a lot of damage to fortifications, armoured vehicles, and... people."

"Does it say what they were loaded with?"

"Conventional nitrocellulose propellant in the casing and half an ounce of filling in the projectile... Ah Ha! ... Look at this. They painted the projectile bodies different colours."

There were several charts showing how to identify shells based on the type of casing and various colour codes for markings on the projectile's nose, body, and rotating bands.

"It makes sense," Vivian commented. "In the heat of battle, you'd want a quick way to identify the different kinds of contents."

"Look at all the different kinds they had!"

PROJECTILES, ARMY, COLOR SYSTEM

BODY, BLACK = "Explosive"

    TIP: Red = "Filled"

    BAND: Yellow or Green = "High Explosive"
            Red = "Shrapnel"
            White = "Armor-Piercing"
            Yellow/Green   =   "H.E.-
Tracers"
            White/Green = "A.P.-Tracers"

BODY, GRAY = "Gas or Liquid Filled"

    TIP: Blue = "Filled"

    BAND: Yellow = "Blister"
            Blue = "Choke"
            Brown = "Nerve
            Red = "Vomit"

"There we have it," I said. "The shells we saw had grey bodies, blue tips, and brown bands, and the lab analyses confirmed the active filler as the nerve agent Tabun."

"Wow, I never heard of either the Japanese or the Germans using nerve agents during World War Two."

"Me neither. Maybe they had them but didn't use them."

"So, what's our plan?"

"We'll reach the Aleutians tonight. At first light tomorrow morning, I'd like to go island-hopping from one to the other looking for any sign of a third abandoned military installation."

"Do you know how many islands there are in the Aleutians?" Vivian asked, her eyebrows raised and her eyes widening.

"Sixty-nine, I looked it up, but only fourteen are very large. I thought we could begin with the larger ones..." I paused.

"Yes?"

"There is one other minor detail. The most westerly of the islands still belong to the Soviet Union."

"What! We can't go there. The Soviets will go berserk."

"I know. I suggest we start with the most westerly of the U.S. islands, that's Attu, and work our way towards the mainland. We can worry about the Soviets if and when the time comes."

"Are any of them inhabited?"

"Apparently there are a few thousand people, most of whom live on Unalaska Island, right next to the mainland. Most of the rest seem to live on neighbouring islands in the same group, all fairly close to the mainland. If we start at the other end, with Attu, we're not likely to see many people for quite a while."

"And if we do?"

"Well, no one's going to believe that our helicopter is civilian but it's common for the military to help with search and rescue missions, so I thought we could borrow some of the ship's standard blue clothes, remove any identifying insignia, and tell anyone we meet that we're helping the Coast Guard look for signs of a ship that reportedly got into trouble and run aground on one of the islands."

We talked it around a bit more, but Vivian didn't have any better ideas to offer and agreed to go along with my plan. After that we had dinner in the mess, with Silver once again being spoiled with a gourmet dinner, and then turned in for the night.

As before, I slept soundly on the ship, being soothed rather than disturbed by the rocking and swaying motion of the destroyer as it cruised silently through the night.

9 MORE SEARCHING

After dropping Alex and Silver off at the airport to meet the FBI Agent and await the navy helicopter that was coming to pick them up, Don headed north to meet the navy people in Masset.

Arriving in Masset, Don drove directly to Canadian Forces Station (CFS) Masset[22], a small direction-finding facility used for the location and classification of enemy ships. Despite the station's somewhat covert nature, it was nevertheless quite conspicuous as its high-frequency, direction-finding technology relied on a massive circular antenna array comprising two concentric circles of ninety-foot-tall antennae, with the outer circle having a diameter of nearly nine-hundred feet.

His arrival was expected, of course, and after showing his military identification (or one of them, at least) he was admitted past the guard-house and escorted to a meeting room in a low, bunker like building. There he was introduced to the team that he'd be leading: a Petty Officer, a Boatswain, two fleet divers, and a sonar technician.

Introducing himself as a Naval Lieutenant based in Halifax, which was close to the truth, Don explained the search they were going to undertake, and with the aid of ship's charts showed them the region of seabed that they wanted to search.

"What are we looking for?" the sonar tech asked.

"Second World War vintage 25 mm auto-cannon shells," Don stated, then seeing their disbelieving looks added: "They're not your everyday shells. These ones are complete – they have their projectiles installed and we think they may be 'specials' that are loaded with a chemical nerve agent."

That got the team's attention.

"We think someone recovered them from some kind of old military installation and was bringing them here to the islands when they got caught in a storm and had them washed off the boat's deck. Several of them washed up on the beach about here," pointing to nearby Agate Beach on the chart, "and we want to know if there are any more of them out there."

"How big are these things?" asked the sonar tech.

"The shell casings were six and a half inches long, with a diameter of nearly two inches. With the projectile sticking out another two and a quarter inches, that makes the total length almost exactly nine inches."

"You realize that you're asking a lot, right?

"So I hear but I've been told it's possible."

"Possible, yes. The side-scan sonar we've brought with us is the latest thing for high-resolution searches over small areas. It's still classified Secret[23], but I can give you the essentials.

"It's basically an electro-acoustic transmitting and receiving system involving pairs of fish. One fish is just for depth control, it is towed behind the boat and is kept at a constant height above the bottom by a wire attached to a heavy chain. The other fish has the scanning transducers and fins for stability. It follows the depth-control fish, to which it is attached by a wire.

"We'll tow the two connected fish at a constant speed and at a constant height above the bottom. The transducer fish will scan a strip of the bottom with a narrow, fan-shaped beam. By making multiple passes, more and more strips will be scanned and displayed. We can tow up to three pairs of fish at a time, recording three strips of bottom at a time, to make the whole process more efficient. The maximum depth for this technique is 100 feet. Is that a problem?"

"We don't think so. We think the shells must be in shallower water than that. How about the resolution?"

"The system uses a frequency of 1.5 MHz and sends extremely short 50 microsecond pulses at a rate of 25 per second. If we go slowly, no more than four knots, and set the scanning transducer at fifteen feet above the bottom, then theoretically we can resolve objects down to three inches by three inches in size."

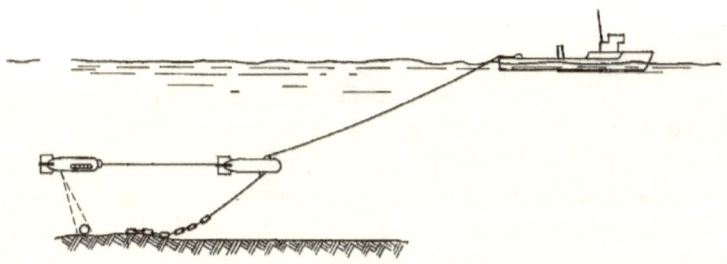

Side-Scan Sonar Device (U.S. Patent 419,759; declassified in 1980)

"So that should be enough, right?"

"It's not quite that simple. In the real world, everything will be in motion, especially the fish. With the bottom contours changing and the effect of swell on the depth-control fish, we can't maintain a perfectly constant depth for the sensing fish, and so on. I'm not saying we'd can't do it, but it will be a bit like finding a needle in a haystack. If your shells are buried in the sediment, we'll never find them, but if there are a bunch of them and some of them are sticking up from the bottom. If they're in some kind of box or crate, then we've got a decent chance."

"Well, we have to try. If you can find anything then the idea is to recover what we can. Did you bring the special containers I asked for?"

"We have them," said one of the divers.

"OK, so, the idea is to take the containers down with you, put the shells into them, and seal them. Then you'll bring them up, water and all, and we'll send them to Suffield for analysis and disposal. Remember, they might contain nerve agents, so you'll need to handle them carefully, but at least it's safer to handle them in the water than it would be in the air."

With that, they plotted their search pattern on the chart and went out. The team had actually brought two large, military Zodiacs with them, one for the divers and shipping containers, and one for the sonar tech and his six fish. It was decided that Don and the Petty Officer would accompany the sonar tech, while the Boatswain would accompany the two fleet divers.

With the two Zodiacs, they spent the entire afternoon patiently working their way through the first part of their search grid. When the sonar plot showed something interesting, they would mark the location and have the divers check it out while the boat with the sonar fish continued the sweep. By the end of the afternoon, however, all they had found were pieces of debris: bits of sunken wood, a boot, pieces of crates, empty bottles and cans, and so on. Giving up for the day, they all returned to CFS Masset, where temporary accommodations in the form of sleeping, storage, and mess tents had been erected for them. It was difficult not to be discouraged, but they had only covered a quarter of their planned search area so there was a lot of territory yet to cover.

The following day, they went out again and spent the entire day searching. By the end of the afternoon they had swept the bulk of the rest of the planned search area and only found more junk on the bottom. Feeling even more discouraged, Don and his team returned to their tents for another evening of waiting. They had now covered three-quarters of their planned search area.

I wonder how Alex and the FBI Agent are making out searching the Aleutians, Don wondered. He had mixed feeling about whether or not he wanted them to find anything.

About two hours into the morning of their third day, persistence finally paid off. Shortly after the two divers had submerged to examine the latest bottom anomaly, one of them surfaced and signalled that they had found something. Dropping an anchored buoy to mark their place in the search grid, the Petty Officer maneuvered the sonar boat next to that of the divers and tied them together.

"What have you found?" asked Don.

"Pieces of wooden crate, some lengths of rope, a boathook, a pair of shoes, and some shells," reported the diver.

"How far down, and can you tell what colours are marked on the projectile end?"

"They're at about 70 feet and there are two shells sticking right up out of the crate," he replied. "Both of them are black with red tips."

"OK, those are regular explosives, but you'll still have to be careful."

The Boatswain in the other boat handed the diver a case to put the shells in. Together, they opened the case and allowed it to flood with seawater, after which the diver took the case and dropped back down below the surface. Swimming to the bottom, he moved next to his companion, who had laid the first two shells beside a rock and was carefully searching in and around the remnants of the wooden crate. Noticing that his companion had returned he pointed down to one side of the crate, and two more projectile tips that he had exposed.

The first diver put the original two shells in the storage container, sealed it, and then used his low-pressure-accessory hose to feed compressed air into a lift bag that was attached to the container. The lift bag, once inflated, was about the size of a basketball, and had enough buoyancy to immediately begin rising up towards the surface, bringing with it the container with the two shells in it. The diver kept a hand on the tethering cable and ascended along with the lift-bag and its cargo. Once both reached the surface, the diver maintained his grip on the tether cable and swam to the Zodiac, which was only a few yards away. Reaching the Zodiac, the Boatswain grabbed the container and, with the help of the diver, was able to get it into the boat.

"This has the first two," he called over to Don. "We've found two more."

"Same colouring?"

"Exactly the same." With that, the diver accepted a second container from the Boatswain and went back down. Reaching the bottom, he found that his companion had laid the next two shells in the same location as the previous one. His companion was busy continuing his careful digging, this time into the sediment around the crate that had held the shells. Not wanting to bother him, the diver put the second two shells in the storage container, sealed it, and used another lift bag to help him bring it to the surface. Once it was safely loaded into the Zodiac, he called over to Don.

"I'm going to go down and help search, but I don't think there are any more down there."

"OK, we're going to continue with the rest of the search grid. Signal if you need anything."

The diver descended to help complete the search around the crate and the sonar-towing boat went back to re-commence their sweep. About thirty minutes later, Don noticed that the divers'

Zodiac was moving in their direction and he signalled the Petty Officer to stop and wait for them.

"We found one more shell and that's all that's there," reported one of the divers when they arrived.

"Same colouring?"

"Exactly the same."

"Five shells then," said Don, thinking. "I guess there's a kind of logic to that since the guy we're chasing found five of the specials. Maybe he took five of each kind with him, from wherever he originally found them."

"Are we done then?" asked the Petty Officer?

"We've just about completed the entire search area that we marked out. Two more hours should do it, so let's complete the rest of the sweep just to be on the safe side and then we'll head back to shore and pack up."

By noon, the complete search area had been completed and they hadn't found anything else of importance. Satisfied that they'd found what there was to find, Don called off the search and radioed the ship to come pick them all up.

The next step would be to see whether Alex had found anything in the Aleutian Islands.

***

It was a grey, overcast day as The Scrounger sailed the *Argo* north past Queen Charlotte City, heading for the open ocean and, ultimately, the Aleutian Islands. The *Argo* was 27-feet in length, entirely made of aluminum, and equipped with a 330 hp Chev 454 engine. Painted flat black and looking quite menacing, it was a perfect beachcombing boat for the West Coast waters, and this would be his first open-ocean trip in his new boat. He was looking forward to testing its handling and powerful engine, although it looked like the sea was going to be calm all day.

The Scrounger's Black Argo

As he rounded the head of Graham Island and felt the increased swell of the open ocean he relaxed and settled into his chair with one hand on the ship's wheel and another holding his traditional, chipped, ship's coffee mug. Although he kept a sharp lookout, he didn't notice the boat that quietly pulled out from the island to follow him.

Despite his early morning start, it took until noon to reach Semisopochnoi Island. This time, he knew exactly where he was going so it didn't take log to tie up, equip himself with his lantern and a crowbar, and hike to the mountain armory, as he now thought of it.

The big steel doors still stood wide open, and almost inviting, as he headed straight to the munitions stores deep inside. Finding the place where he'd originally found the 25 mm shells, he set his lantern on the floor and started opening crates.

Several hours later, he'd opened his twentieth crate and had to sit down to rest his aching back. Surveying the scattered boxes he'd opened, he felt content. Although fifteen of the boxes contained the unwanted red-tipped, black-body shells, he'd found five containing the valuable blue-tipped, grey-body ones.

Five crates at fifty shells per crate and one-hundred dollars per shell would bring him... $25,000, he thought with dreamy satisfaction. *All I have to do now is load them onto the Argo, get underway, and I'll* *soon "have it made."*

Dragging himself wearily to his feet, he was just beginning to replace the lid on the first of his five special crates when he heard a slight scuffing noise behind him. Startled, but thinking it was likely one of the Arctic Foxes that he'd seen darting among the grasses and trees outside, he was just beginning to straighten up and turn around when he heard a deep voice.

"Slowly now. No sudden moves and keep your hands where I can see them."

"Who are you?" asked The Scrounger, rising fully to his feet and peering in the direction of the voice.

"Just a scavenger, like yourself," said the voice, calmly.

"I know that voice…"

"Yes, you do," said the voice as a rather unremarkable-looking man walked into the field of light cast by the Scrounger's lantern. He was about medium age, of medium height, and medium build. He held his own lantern in one hand, while the other held a rather large and nasty-looking pistol. The pistol was pointed directly at The Scrounger.

Although his mind was whirling, The Scrounger regained his composure quite quickly. "You're the voice from the phone!" he accused.

"That's right. Since I knew when you were coming, and where you were coming from, it was a simple matter for me to watch for your boat and then follow you."

"How did you do that?" asked The Scrounger, scratching his head and momentarily forgetting the gun. "I didn't see any boats following me."

"Ah, but I don't have an ordinary boat," was the reply. "Once I saw you come up the side of the island and head northwest, I simply let you get out of sight, but not out of range of my radar."

"I never thought of that. But why are you here? I promised to bring you the shells."

"Two reasons. I wanted to find out where these things were coming from, and what else might be here."

"Well, I searched pretty thoroughly the first time I discovered this place and I didn't find anything else that was valuable looking."

"I believe you, but you never know and I wanted to be sure for myself. I'll be content just to take the special shells."

"You said you had two reasons."

"I do. I also wanted to make sure you didn't get any bright ideas about shopping around for another buyer and trying to bid the price up."

"Are there higher bidders out there?" The Scrounger asked, his nose beginning to twitch.

"Almost certainly. But you're going to sell them to me, as we agreed. Right?"

"Right. Sure, anything you say."

"We have an accord, then. Go back to what you were doing, and when you've finished putting the lids back on the boxes, you can carry them out and put them in *my* boat. I'll come along behind you to light your way and make sure you don't have a change of heart," the man concluded, still with that quiet, deep voice, now complemented with a grin that looked quite menacing in the dim light cast by the lantern.

It took only a few minutes for The Scrounger to replace the other four lids on the special crates, and he'd just lifted the first one in preparation for the journey out and down to the dock when they both heard the sound of a piece of wood breaking, followed by the sound of a woman's voice saying "Damn!"

"Freeze and don't make a sound," the man with the gun softly commanded The Scrounger.

The Scrounger began turning, to look back at the man, but then felt a sharp stab of pain on the side of his head and blacked out.

***

On board *HMCS Huron*, Vivian and I had been given ship's working uniforms to help with our new cover as search and rescue personnel. They comprised dark blue pants, royal blue shirts, and dark blue windbreakers, except that all insignia had been removed from them. The only things with any kind of identification at all were the baseball-type caps they'd given us, which were dark blue and had the ship's name and crest on them.

Following a signature ship's breakfast, which was most appreciated by Silver again, Sandy and his helicopter crew flew us out to begin searching the Aleutian Islands, beginning with the most westerly of the U.S. islands: Attu.

Attu is part of a group of five, known as the Near Islands. *Maybe the name means near to Russia*, I thought. Attu is where the big two-day battle had taken place, and it looked it. Flying low over the island, we could see rows of pilings that had once supported the docking facilities, piles of weathered wood from collapsed structures, and numerous pieces of rusty metal of all shapes and sizes lying partially covered in the tall grasses. We could still make out the remains of the original roads and even gun emplacements, but all long abandoned. We didn't bother landing on Attu, as it was clear that everything had been destroyed more than thirty years earlier.

I was surprised to learn that there were two airfields on Attu. One was obviously long abandoned and even from the air we could see that its two runways were being overtaken by nature. Sandy explained over our headsets that it was called Alexai Point Army Airfield, and that it has been abandoned following the Second World War. The second, only about four miles away, was called the Casco Cove Coast Guard Station and was apparently uninhabited but still usable, with working navigational beacons. Sandy explained that it was a restricted airfield, and that we couldn't land there without advance permission from U.S. authorities.

Continuing on, we flew over the four other Near Islands: Agattu, Alaid, Nizki and Shemya. Despite making low altitude passes over each one and inspecting each as closely was we could with binoculars, there was nothing remarkable to see.

The only inhabited island in this group appeared to be Shemya, and we did land there. The sounds and sight of our large helicopter were pretty hard to miss, so by the time that Vivian, Silver, and I had exited the helicopter and walked over to the nearest of the small dwellings there were lots of curious eyes watching us and a few adventurous souls that walked up to greet us.

We identified ourselves according to our cover story and asked if they had seen or heard anything about a boat grounding on one of the islands, or even if they'd seen or heard of any unusual ships or boats in the area recently. No one seemed aware of anything that might fit either our cover story or our real purpose in being there, so after exchanging some small talk (we learned in passing that there were about forty people living in this most isolated of places) we said we needed to get on with our search and walked back to the helicopter.

Heading east, towards the mainland, the next group of ten

islands is known as the Rat Islands. I looked them up much later, after the whole adventure was over, and discovered that Rat Islands is the English translation of the name coined for them in 1827 by the German explorer and geographer, and later Russian Admiral, Fyodor Litke. Apparently, he saw a lot of rats.

Once again, the most easterly in this group was the one that once held a sizeable Japanese force during the war: Kiska. Also, once again, it was clear from our passes over the island that there had once been a significant military presence, but all that remained now were the remnants of piers, roads, gun emplacements with mangled guns, and even bomb craters.

Continuing on, we flew over the next four of the Rat Islands: Little Kiska, Segula, Hawadax, and Kryssei. Once again multiple low altitude passes, and close inspection of each island, turned up nothing beyond the inactive volcanoes that characterized this group of islands. None of the Rat Islands seemed to be inhabited, so there was no one to land and talk to either.

By the time we had finished with Kryssei Island, it was late in the afternoon and Sandy informed us that fuel status and dropping visibility meant that we had to return to the ship for the night.

Vivian and I were tired and discouraged. We'd had remarkably good weather, with clear skies and only a light breeze, and the day had been interesting. Unfortunately, we hadn't found anything at all that was relevant to our search.

I wonder how Don's doing, was my last conscious thought as the beating drone of the helicopter lulled me to sleep. They had to wake me up when we landed.

Day two of our island searching didn't get off to as promising a start. Flying out from the ship we were sandwiched between overcast skies and a bank of fog below us. On top of that, our pilots had much more wind to contend with and despite the size and power of the Sea King, it was a rough journey.

There were five more islands to cover in the Rat Islands group: Khvostof, Davidof, Little Sitkin, Amchitka, and Semisopochnoi. Like the rest of the Rat Islands, these were all uninhabited and all uninteresting.

All that is, except the last one: Semisopochnoi.

Before we even got to the island Sandy's voice had come alive over the intercom. "Ho. We've got some activity coming up on the next island. Have a look out the starboard windows."

As he banked the helicopter, we looked out with our binoculars as directed and were able to make out what looked like two largish boats tied up by some remnant pilings sticking out of the water.

"Want to go in?" asked Sandy.

"Let's take it slow," I replied. "Can you set us down around the side of the mountain somewhere where we'll be out of sight of those boats, and then drop us quickly so no one will know for sure whether we landed or not?"

"We'll take a look," was the reply and the helicopter continued to bank to our left but now started to descend as well.

It wasn't long before the pilots had found a suitable spot to land and touched down, but with the propeller blades still whirling.

Just before we exited, Sandy's voice came on over the intercom. "We have to return to the ship for a short period. The other helicopter is down for maintenance, so we're needed for something else. Will you be OK for a few hours?"

"Sure. You know where to find us."

"Sure do. We'll give you a portable radio, so you can call if anything goes wrong."

"Great. Can we borrow a flashlight too?"

As we exited the helicopter, a crew member handed us a heavy, medium-sized backpack plus a powerful looking flashlight, and yelled to us over the noise of the engines: "This radio can reach the ship. All the instructions are printed on laminated cards inside the pack. All you have to do is follow the instructions... Good luck."

As we moved away, the helicopter lifted off and headed away.

We were on the island.

Vivian took the flashlight and I shouldered the radio pack. Together with Silver we made our way around the mountain. Although we were focused on what might lie ahead, we both noticed that we were actually on a pretty nice island. Although it was becoming overcast with ominous-looking clouds, there was only a soft breeze blowing and the sights and smells of nature were quite soothing.

A we walked along, we noticed quite a few birds of different kinds. I spotted several cormorants with orange-coloured faces, and when I pointed them out to Vivian, I discovered that she knew quite a lot about birds.

"Red-Faced Cormorants," she said, "and look there: petrels and puffins. I bet they have other ground-nesting birds around here too, it's a perfect place for them."

It wasn't just Vivian and I that noticed the local inhabitants, as Silver soon stopped rather abruptly with a fixed look on his face and his nose twitching. As I followed his gaze, I saw the face and ears of two white, thick-furred foxes. They were alert to our presence too. The two faces quickly disappeared into the long grasses and we never saw them again.

"Arctic Foxes," I said, in a low voice. "I wonder how they got here[24]."

There was no reply from Vivian, as she was peering ahead. "Look," she said, pointing ahead and to our left.

It had once been a road. It was becoming overtaken by grasses and the shoots of small bushes or trees, but it would have been wide enough for vehicles. As we approached, we could see that it went off to our right, presumably leading to the water. To our left, it led toward a bend around the mountain.

"Left, or right?" asked Vivian.

"How about left, so we can see if this leads to an entrance or cave or something?"

As Vivian nodded, I took off the radio-pack I had been wearing and placed it off the road and hopefully out of anyone else's sight, behind some large rocks.

With Vivian in the lead, we only had to go about fifty yards around the bend of the mountain… and there it was.

"Looks like you were right," commented Vivian.

"I'll be dammed. It seemed like such a long shot."

Before us lay a large, rectangular entrance to the mountain: large enough to drive a medium-sized truck into. Two big, rusty, steel doors stood wide open.

"Looks pretty human made to me," said Vivian, dryly.

"Come into my parlour, said the spider to the fly," I murmured. "Shall we?"

"Yes, let's go in, but let's go quietly – whoever's in there might not be happy to have visitors."

"Right…"

"Silver," I said, in a low voice, "we need to be quiet in here."

Silver looked up at me, gave me a brief, serious-looking glance and padded forward.

"Do you actually have conversations with him?" asked Vivian.

"You wouldn't believe it. It's a long story, ask me about it later."

As the three of us entered the mountain we immediately felt cool, damp air flowing towards us. Vivian had switched on our borrowed flashlight and, although it had a very powerful beam, it was so dark in side that we could only make out the details of things that fell within the cone of light. As she swept the beam around, we could see that we were in a large, cavern-like tunnel. Initially, at least, there was only one path forward. We had barely entered when she said "Uh Oh!"

Looking where the beam was pointing, I could see what she had spotted. "It's wired with explosives!"

"Yes, and they look very old too. Like maybe they wired the place back during the war."

"So, it's wired but they didn't blow everything up. Maybe that means there's nothing left here after all."

"Maybe, let's go see."

There were trickles of water flowing here and there on the walls and floor, but the cave/tunnel had been fitted with a rough, but serviceable wooden floor. It felt solid, too. Rather than creaking like the floor in a house, our boots barely made a sound as we crept inside.

Eventually we encountered short, side-passages that we only glanced into: living quarters with rows of bunks, complete with piles of bedding, a large but simple kitchen, with pots and pans, a mess area, with tables and chairs and even cutlery, cups, and plates, and a pantry, still stocked with old food cans.

Another short passage led to a couple of store-rooms, with a variety of fairly large wooden shipping crates: some neatly staked, others lying open, with their tops removed. A quick look confirmed that the open ones, at least, held general supplies like clothes and blankets.

Continuing along the main passage, Silver's head and ears suddenly popped-up and I could see that his gaze was focused straight ahead, with his nose and ears trying to identify something. Almost in the same motion, he sat down on his haunches and looked directly at me.

"He senses someone or something up ahead," I whispered to Vivian.

"Good boy, Silver," I said, reaching over to give him a half pat, half rub on the back of his neck. "Let's go slowly."

The passage way had developed a significant curve to it, so we couldn't see very far ahead of us as we crept forward. It was made worse by the fact that Vivian had prudently lowered the beam from our flashlight so that we could just see where we were stepping, and far enough ahead so that we wouldn't run into anything, but not much further than that.

We hadn't gone much further before the wooden floor, which up until then had seemed so sturdy and so quiet, let me down.

As I took what I thought was a careful step, the wood under my boot suddenly gave way, with a cracking sound, and my foot went right through to the stone floor underneath. It was only a drop of perhaps three inches or so, but it was enough for my foot to get stuck.

Without thinking, I involuntarily let out a soft "Damn!" and then froze as we heard two *thunk* sounds, rapid succession, come from somewhere close by.

Laurie Schramm

10 CONVERGENCE

"Hello?" said a male voice.

Vivian and I looked at each other. Both of us shrugged our shoulders. "Hello," she said.

At this, a flashlight beam softly illuminated part of the wall ahead of us. Vivian raised her beam as well, and we walked around the bend to see a medium-sized, middle-aged man standing in the passageway and holding a portable lantern.

My jaw dropped.

"Dr. Turner?" I exclaimed.

"Alex? What in the world are you doing here?"

"This is Vivian," I said, "she's with the Coast Guard looking for a boat that put out a distress call in these islands somewhere. They let me come along to cover the search as a possible story for the CBC. How about you?"

"One more question first, if I may. How did you get here?"

"A helicopter dropped us off to check on the boats we saw tied up here, then it flew off to continue searching around more of the islands."

He seemed to pause for a moment, considering. "I thought I heard a rumbling sound not long ago, that must have been it," he nodded.

"So, I take it that you're not really an oceanography professor?"

"Indeed. I'm going to save us all a lot of time by admitting that I'm not the person you thought you met." Then he pulled his large pistol from its hiding place in waistband at his back, and pointed it at us.

In the same instant Silver, who had been intently watching with his ears laid back, suddenly stiffened and began to growl. At the same time, he began to move slowly to one side of us.

"If you can't control your dog and keep him with you, then I will shoot him," he said, very calmly.

"Silver. Come here. Stay with me," I commanded.

"If you're not the Dr. Turner I met, then who are you really?"

"You can keep calling me Dr. Turner," he replied. "It's as good a name as any, it will be better for you if that's all you know. Let's just say that I'm someone that wants to take a few crates of these shells away from here before your helicopter comes back."

As he waved his lantern beam around, we could see that the cave was full of ammunition boxes and crates. Many of them had been opened, and a bunch of anti-aircraft shells lay scattered around the floor.

"Why?" I couldn't help asking.

"Always the reporter I see, but it's like I said: no more questions. If you want to get out of this alive then you need to know nothing. If you do what I say and remain ignorant of me and my purposes, then I can get what I came for and we can each go our own separate ways. If you pry into my business then I'll have to shoot you both and move the crates by myself."

He said this with such a calm determination that I didn't doubt for a moment that he was willing to do exactly what he said.

"OK, we'll do it your way then," I replied, glancing at Vivian, who nodded in return.

"Good. Next question: are either of you armed?"

I raised my eyebrows and put on an expression of surprise. "Armed? Of course not, I'm a reporter?"

Placing his lantern on the floor he stepped over to me and, holding his gun against my ribs with one hand, did a quick one-handed pat-down search with the other. Fortunately for me he either didn't notice and wasn't suspicious of the bandages I had wrapped around both of my upper legs. Seeming satisfied, he looked over towards Vivian. "How about you?"

Vivian shook her head no.

Stepping over to her, he pushed his gun against her stomach and did another quick one-handed pat-down. This time, however, he felt a bulge in one of her pockets.

Moving back a pace, he said "Take that out… carefully now."

Vivian complied, and withdrew a small, .25 calibre, semi-automatic pistol.

"Toss it to the back of the cave," he commanded.

"You said you weren't armed," he accused, when she had complied.

Vivian shrugged "It's a dangerous world out here. I really only had it for defense against wild animals like wolves."

Dr. Turner's response to this was to quickly step towards her and strike her heavily in the side of her face with his pistol. Vivian immediately dropped to her knees with both hands covering her face, and I could see blood seeping through her fingers.

"Stop!" he commanded, as he sensed more than saw me take a step towards Vivian.

"I only want to help her."

"She'll be fine. Let her deal with it herself." His voice was still an icy calm. "I'll give you that one mistake, and you've had your punishment," he continued. "if either of you cross me again, I will shoot one of you, so be warned."

Giving Vivian a moment to take a bandana from her pocket and tie it diagonally across the left side of her forehead and face, he continued: "Now, I want each of you to pick up one of these cases right here." He pointed to three wooden crates that had been stacked nearby.

Each crate had a rope handle on each end, so they were easy to pick up, but they were heavy! Remembering what it felt like to lift SCUBA-diving weight belts, I estimated my crate's weight at something like ninety pounds.

Vivian placed her flashlight on top of hers, with the beam facing forward, and Dr. Turner also picked up a crate. In his case, he held his crate one-handed, by one of its rope handles, which left his right hand free to hold his gun. His lantern, he let dangle from his gun hand. He was obviously very strong: there's no way I would have been able to carry one of those crates one-handed.

"You go in front with the light," he said to Vivian. "Alex, you go next and keep your dog under control. I'll be right behind you and will be keeping you covered with this." He waved his pistol for emphasis. "I'm a good shot, and I can fire faster than you can do anything dangerous, so behave."

As instructed, Vivian stepped towards the main tunnel, with

Silver and I behind, and Dr. Turner bringing up the rear. I was just reminding Silver to stay close to me when Vivian stumbled, bent over, dropped her crate and fell, sprawling over it.

"Are you OK?"

"Freeze!" said Dr. Turner. "Stay where you are and let her get up on her own."

"I'll be alright," said Vivian. "I'm just a bit woozy from that blow on the head."

Dr. Turner's voice was still the same icy calm: "If I were you, I'd be careful not to drop a case of old munitions again. These things have been known to go off with a very large bang."

"Give me a second, I'm just a bit shaky" said Vivian, as she retrieved the flashlight that had also fallen to the floor, but was still working, at least. As she did, she pointed the beam back towards Dr. Turner, and there was just enough light for me to see that, with her other hand, she picked something else up from the floor and slipped it into her pants pocket. Then, she pointed the flashlight forward again, hefted her crate, and starting walking forward again.

I wondered what she had picked up, and it suddenly occurred to me that her tripping and falling might not have been the accident it had first seemed.

It was slow going with the heavy crates in our arms, but we made our way into the main tunnel, trudged through the cool darkness, and eventually found ourselves exiting the mountain.

Dr. Turner let us take a five-minute rest, and then ordered us to get moving again. "Keep following the old road and it will take us down to what's left of the docks."

As we made our way along the old road, I could see that Vivian was walking awkwardly, as if she'd twisted or sprained something in her right leg. I was about to ask her if she was OK, when I realized that her twisted orientation was keeping the slight bulge in the cargo pocket of her pants out of Dr. Turner's line of sight. So, I held my tongue. Whatever she had picked up, she apparently didn't want Dr. Turner to notice.

It was a bit of a hike, but after a while we finally reached what was left of the old docks. Now it was mostly just a collection of old pilings standing up out of the water, with bits of old decking attached, or hanging from them, here and there. I was somewhat surprised to see that the boat tied-up closest to shore was The Scrounger's dull-black *Argo. Keep a straight face*, I thought to myself. I wondered where he was, but I was pretty sure that I knew what had brought him here. I hoped he was still alive, somewhere.

"Keep moving," said Dr. Turner, "Take the crates to the second boat, and put them in the stern."

Dr. Turner's boat was larger than The Scrounger's, and it was more like a touring, cabin-cruiser than a work boat. Leaving Silver on the dock, we each boarded the boat and placed our crates in the stern. We were then ordered to stand to one side so Dr. Turner could place his crate there as well.

Straightening from this, he said: "I was going to take some more of these, but these will have to do. I want to get away from here before your helicopter returns. To make that happen, you two are going to come with me. I'll drop you off a few islands down the way, and will be able to get far enough away while your colleagues waste time looking for you."

"How will they find us?" I asked.

"You'll be able to signal them. I'll leave you some matches. By the time you've collected enough wood, gotten a fire started, and then built it up enough to have a smoke signal, it will still be light enough for them to see it and come get you. By that time, I'll be long gone."

Silver, whom I'd ordered to remain on the dock began to whine.

"The dog stays behind. Dead or alive, it's up to you."

"Silver... Stay," I commanded.

Dr. Turner, still with his gun in hand, then picked up a length of utility cord and handed it to Vivian. "Tie her hands in front of her. Tie them securely, but give her about six inches of space between her hands so she'll be able to hold on to the boat and not fall all over once we're underway. Do it properly – I'm watching you."

After Vivian had tied my hands as instructed, he gave another length of cord to me, saying "Now you tie hers the same way."

Once this had been done to his satisfaction, he continued: "The two of you will stay here in the stern while I'm on the bridge running the boat. But I'll be watching you at the same time, and I'll still be able to shoot you faster than you'll be able to do anything to interfere. Understood?"

We both nodded, but as he untied the mooring lines and the boat began to drift away from the pier, Silver moaned again and crouched as if to spring into the boat.

"Silver… Stay," I repeated. "I will come back to you… I promise."

Starting the boat's powerful engine, Dr. Turner steered the boat out towards the open sea.

As the boat headed out, I had more time to think. Dr. Turner, whomever he really was, had still seemed to accept my CBC Reporter cover. I wondered whether it would do any good to break cover and tell him who Vivian and I really were. His whole manner had seemed so chillingly calm, however, even when he'd struck Vivian with his gun, that I concluded that we were better off trying to maintain our cover. I don't know whether that was a good decision or not, but it had seemed to me that if he knew who we really were, he might simply shoot us, dump us overboard, and be done with it… *Dump us overboard*, I thought, *Hmmm*.

At this point I happened to look over at Vivian, who was sitting across from me, with her back against the portside gunwale. Nodding towards Dr. Turner, who was still at the helm and seemed to be focusing on setting the correct course for the boat, she started squirming around until she was able to just barely use her fingertips to ease something out of her pant-leg cargo pocket. It was a grenade!

She held it in sight just long enough for me to recognize what it was, and then tucked it beside her leg so her body would block it from Dr. Turner's sight when he turned to look at us. She had, however, given me enough time to see that it was an old hand-grenade, somewhat like an American style grenade but smaller[25]. It looked a bit like a miniature pineapple with a stem on one end, and with a safety pin inserted into the stem and attached to the body of the grenade by a thin cord.

I didn't say anything, but I'm sure that my eyes must have been as wide as saucers.

Vivian pointedly nodded her head, first toward the grenade, and then towards the bridge. Then she, sharply turned her head to look back out behind the stern of the boat.

Then, as if to make sure that I completely understood her, she repeated the whole pantomime again and then looked directly at me, eyebrows raised as if to say "OK?"

It seemed risky, of course, but I didn't see that we had any other realistic options. Dr. Turner had revealed himself to be quite competent so far, and chillingly ruthless. I also couldn't help worrying about what had happened to The Scrounger. He wouldn't have willingly abandoned his beloved new boat, and I feared that he'd been put out of action in some way, maybe tied-up somewhere, maybe injured, or maybe dead. I was also worried about Silver, who for at least the second time in his life had been marooned on an island[26].

I'd been keeping an eye on Dr. Turner while thinking it through so I noticed when, apparently satisfied with our course, he turned towards us with a particularly malignant expression on his face.

That erased all doubts in my mind, and Vivian seemed to see it too for she glanced at him, then looked back at me with a very direct expression on her face and tilted her head to one side, as if repeating her earlier implied question.

This time, I took a deep breath, and nodded my assent. Then I carefully stood up and leaned back against the gunwale, with one foot perched where I had previously been sitting. I was ready to spring.

Vivian matched me motion for motion, except that her hands were close together, and I could see that she was holding the grenade.

Dr. Turner seemed mystified more than anything else, but not suspicious. "So much the better…" he was saying, when Vivian pulled the cord, causing the safety pin to pop out, and then tossed the grenade.

She wasn't able to properly throw it, with her hands tied together, but she did manage to get it to bounce off the deck near the bridge, and then it disappeared. Presumably, it bounced or rolled down the stairs that led to the forward cabin – underneath the bridge.

Startled, Dr. Turner exclaimed "What!" then looked towards the forward cabin, then back towards us. By that time each of us had pulled up our legs so we were standing on the benches we'd previously been sitting on, and then launched ourselves backwards, up and over the gunwales on our respective sides of the boat, and into the sea.

As I was falling into the water, I heard him swear.

Landing on my back with a smack, I immediately began to sink. I let myself sink for a while, to let the boat get further away from me then, as my lungs were beginning to ache from the lack of oxygen, I kicked my legs like mad to get to the surface.

Still kicking with both legs, I was eventually able to get my head up above water and was just drawing a couple of hasty breaths when I looked at the boat and was startled to see Dr. Turner standing right there in the stern, aiming his gun at me.

Bang! Bang!

At the same time as I heard the gun fire, I felt a bullet strike me, high up in my right leg. It was like someone had hit me there with a baseball bat. My first thought was to marvel at his ability to hit me from a rolling and swaying boat. There was no second thought, as a wave of pain, searing pain, struck and radiated up and down my leg.

Dr. Turner immediately changed position and fired two more rounds, this time in Vivian's direction. I didn't yet know whether he'd hit her or not, but he was just sighting his gun for another shot at her when the grenade went off and a cloud of splinters and debris rose up, seemingly from the middle of his boat. At this, he turned and quickly moved forward in the boat, presumably to check the damage.

My head was still filled with the pain. To make things worse, I now had my hands tied and only one leg with which to tread water. I knew I only had a second or two before I was going to sink again, so I took in the largest breath I possibly manage, and held my breath, with my jaws clenched against the pain.

***

Memory can be a funny thing. You can forget things so easily, as life progresses. Some of the old memories are lost for a while, or even forever, but sometimes they come back. Sometimes when you need them.

I suddenly remembered being a High School Senior in Ottawa. I had decided to try training to be a lifeguard, and was taking my Bronze Cross course, from the Royal Life-Saving Society. One of the things we had to practise over and over again was called drown-proofing, which basically meant sculling in-place in the water forever without, well, drowning. We'd had to practise and demonstrate drown-proofing frequently, and for increasing periods of time.

Eventually, I had discovered a trick. I found that I didn't actually have to wear out my arms and legs – I could just inflate my lungs to the maximum, hold my breath, dip my face into the water and hold a bent-over position with my upper back and shoulder blades at or near the surface of the water. In this position I didn't have to move my arms or legs, I didn't sink much, and I could just hang there for as long as I could hold my breath – which was decently long when I wasn't moving my arms or legs. When I eventually did need a breath, a little arm and hand-sculling motion was all that was needed to lift my face out of the water high enough to get some new air in. Then, I could ease back down into the water and hang there as before.

Once I'd learned this trick, I found that I could drown-proof for as long as I wanted, more than enough to out-last my stronger colleagues, and enough to satisfy my examiners. That was in a warm, calm swimming pool of course.

***

Remembering my drown-proofing trick, I used it now, hoping that as I did, Dr. Turner would conclude that he'd killed me with his shots.

Amazingly enough, it actually worked. I didn't really know whether he was even still watching me, much less thinking that I was dead or soon would be. For all I knew, he was busy trying to keep his boat from sinking.

Every time I did come up for air, his boat was further away, and the plume of smoke emanating from it was more and more impressive. After a few such cycles, I began calling out for Vivian.

It took us a while, but between calling out and kicking and sculling as best we could with our hands tied, we finally found each other. Comparing notes, we learned that we'd each been hit once, me in one leg and her in one arm.

Fortunately, I'd remembered a few more life-saving tricks. The first one I showed her was how, if we took a deep breath, pulled our shirt collars up tightly around our necks, we could hunch over, bend our heads down and inward, and blow air up and inside our shirts so that the part over our shoulder blades puffed-up like a balloon.

"There you are, an instant life-preserver," I'd said when Vivian did it the first time.

"That's all there is to it?" she'd asked, sounding amazed and disbelieving.

"Not exactly. Our wet shirts will do a pretty good job of holding the air, but they'll continually leak. So, you'll have to keep hunching over and putting more air in."

Once she had the hang of it, I asked her if she could support me while I tried something else. She agreed, and with her holding me up, I reached down with my tethered hands to undo and remove my pants. It took a few tries to get them off over my boots, but I eventually succeeded.

"What in the world do you want those for?" she'd asked, sounding like she thought I'd gone crazy.

"Two things. First watch this." I tied a knot in the cuff of each pant leg, effectively sealing it, then did up the zipper and belt, and held the waistband behind my head. Normally, you would do this holding onto one side with each hand, but with my hands tied together I just held the waistband open as well as I could. Taking a breath and kicking upwards as best I could with my legs, I lifted my pants up and over my head and brought them crashing down right in front of my face. As I did so, my pant legs partially inflated with air and sat there in the water like two limp balloons, with me still holding the waistband down, just below the water's surface. The pants didn't inflate as much as they would have if I'd had my hands free to hold them properly, but it was kind of impressive that it worked at all.

"There you go, an instant float," I said proudly. Before she could comment, however, one pant leg deflated rather quickly due to the bullet holes in it. It broke the tension though and even overcame the pain from the gunshots, briefly, as we both laughed.

"Well, half a float anyway," said Vivian.

"Hold me again, OK?" I asked, and as she took my pants from me and held on to my shirt I bent over and started pulling at the bandage on my right leg, just above my knee. It wasn't easy, and I had to go through a few cycles of surfacing for air, then bending down to pick away at the bandage. With only one leg functioning, I don't think I'd have been able to do it without her supporting me, but I did eventually manage to surface, take a large breath, and show her a tangle of bandage within which was cradled my UDT knife.

"So, you were armed too!"

"Yes. It was a good thing he didn't find this," I said as I triggered the flick-blade mechanism and released the blade. Then, with Vivian continuing to support me, I carefully cut away the ropes binding her hands. The serrated edge of the blade was incredibly sharp, so it wasn't long before the ropes parted. Then, I gave her the knife so she could do the same for me, after which I closed the knife and put it away in my button-down shirt pocket.

"Why don't you try your pants too, so we'll have better flotation?" I suggested. Vivian agreed but couldn't get her pants off with her damaged arm, so I took them off and inflated them for her.

Things became much easier after that. As Dr. Turner and his boat continued to move further and further away from us, it wasn't long before all we could see was the continuing plume of smoke from whatever was burning on the boat. As for us, we were both in pain and both bleeding, but we now had our hands free and we had makeshift flotation devices in the form of our shirts and pants.

"Now what?"

"I guess we swim back to the island. How far away do you think we are?" I asked.

"I took a quick look, just before pulling the pin on the grenade. I'd say half a mile, maybe."

"Five-hundred yards," I mused. *That's a long way to swim, but not impossible*, I thought. I had swum half-mile distances several times while training to be a lifeguard, but when I was younger, not in the ocean, and not when injured and getting desperately tired. I kept those dark thoughts to myself and tried changing the subject: "We can do it if we help each other. Nice work with that grenade by the way."

"I kept worrying that he'd find it, but I had an uneasy feeling right from the start that he was never going to let us get away alive."

"We'll never know, but I'm glad you found it and took the chance."

"Me too, and we seem to make a good team together."

"Now you're talking. Let's swim."

We were fortunate that it was late August and the ocean, where we were, was reasonably warm at about 72°F, otherwise we'd have had to worry about hypothermia along with everything else. As it was, we had enough to contend with. We used and replenished our makeshift flotation devices and, holding them in front of us, did modified breast-strokes: me with one arm and one leg, and Vivian with her legs only.

It worked though and we plodded along: lifting our heads for air, when we needed to, pausing once in a while to refill our shirt and pants flotation aids.

Repeat... repeat...

Choke and sputter with the inevitable, occasional mouthful of water instead of air.

Repeat... repeat...

Say, with inside voice, *God, when will this ever end?*

Repeat... repeat...

I tried not to think about sharks and our bleeding limbs.

We were fortunate that the island had a prominent mountain, and fortunate that we had made our getaway before we were out of sight of the 4,000-foot summit of Anvil Peak, the island's tallest mountain. Otherwise, we would almost certainly have ended-up swimming in the wrong direction. It felt like it took forever, but we did eventually make it back to the entrance to the island's harbour.

I was just trying to lift my head high enough out of the water to spot the old dock and pilings, when I saw Silver swimming determinedly toward us.

Silver! This was the dog that hated water with a passion, and avoided it like the plague, and he had seen or smelled me and swum out to help! I could hardly believe it.

It sure made a difference. Vivian and I were exhausted from everything we'd been through. Silver's appearance provided welcome muscular help, as I used one hand to grab his fur. His appearance provided a morale-boost as well.

From there, it seemed like no time before we were able to drag ourselves onto the beach and huddle there, just resting and breathing. With the giddiness of being back on dry land, it occurred to me that this wasn't the first time[11] I'd been washed up, half naked on a remote island, and wondering if I was going to survive. At least I had Silver with me again.

Our next task was first aid. The salt water had thoroughly washed our wounds, painfully so. Vivian's arm and my leg were bloody, but not bleeding very much, so we simply used my knife to cut the long sleeves from our shirts and used them to make bandages.

"I have no idea how much blood we lost," I said to Vivian, as I finished tying the bandage on her arm.

"No, but I think the bullets went right through us, or else we wouldn't be as mobile as we've been, so that's lucky."

"Rats, those bullets might have been handy to have later as evidence," was my first reaction.

"Spoken like a true police officer," laughed Vivian, "but I really think we should count our blessings that neither of us have a bullet stuck inside us."

Meanwhile, the ocean swell had increased as we had swum to shore. At the time, we'd had other things on our minds but now, sitting on the shore, we could take better account of our surroundings.

"Big storm coming," observed Vivian, looking at the horizon. Sure enough, while it was grey and overcast where we were, there were dark, ominous-looking storm clouds approaching.

"We should try radioing the ship, but I have a feeling that we're going to be spending the night right here."

We got up and headed up the road to the place where we'd left the radio-pack. As we were walking, I realized that I'd forgotten one part of my drown-proof training: I hadn't removed my boots! Neither had Vivian. Although it sure would have made the swimming easier without them, now that we were back on land, I was very glad to have them, even though they were soaking wet and squishy. Anyway, the three of us walked along the old road, with me hobbling a bit, and found the radio-pack where we had left it. Opening the pack, the first thing we found was a set of laminated instruction cards.

"You've got to hand it to the military," commented Vivian, "they know how to make emergency gear. Look at these instructions, they are literally step-by-step."

"The way I'm feeling, it's just as well," I agreed, and before long we had the antenna attached and extended, the battery – which took up most of the space and weight of the pack – attached, and had the radio switched on. It was approaching 4 pm.

***

Once Don and the sailors, divers, and sonar tech had been picked up by the *HMCS Huron*, he was naturally eager to go out and join-up with Alex and the FBI Agent. Two things in particular frustrated this ambition.

The first was the fact that one of the ships' helicopters was already out with Alex, while the other was undergoing repairs and not available for flying operations. So, they had to wait.

Finally, after more than two hours of waiting, the second Sea King helicopter arrived and was winched down to the landing platform. It was approaching 4 pm. As the big helicopter blades wound down, one of the pilots hopped out and trotted over to the marshalling area. It was Lieutenant Sandy Moore.

"Good to see you Sandy," said Don warmly. "Thanks for coming to get me."

"Always a pleasure, Sir. Great to see you too," then he hesitated, "there's just one problem. The weather in the Aleutians has been deteriorating badly, and by the time we've refuelled the meteorological people think the weather status is going to ground us."

"Aargh! For how long?"

"I don't know. We can go ask them in a minute, but the last prediction they gave us was that we'd have to wait until first light tomorrow."

"Of all the rotten luck…" Don would have expanded on his view of life at that particular point in time except that he was interrupted by a sailor who'd arrived to let him know that someone was calling for him on the ship's radio."

"Must be Alex calling from the island," said Sandy. "We left her a radio in case something like this happened."

"Well, that's something anyway," said Don, a bit of his normal good humour returning. "Can you show me to the radio room?" he asked the sailor.

"Yes Sir. Follow me please." And off they went.

"Don, we found the source of the shells in a previously unknown Japanese installation on one of the islands," said Alex, over the radio.

"That's great. Are you OK?"

"Yes, but we ran into our friend Dr. Turner. He isn't what he seemed to be, and he isn't friendly..." Alex then gave Don a very brief account of their run-in with Dr. Turner, leaving out a few details such as having been shot. "We were able to get away from him and back to the island, but he may still be out there somewhere, and he's armed and dangerous."

"Do you think he's likely to show up in the night?"

"I doubt it. His boat may have sunk by now, but even if it hasn't, he's going to have to shelter somewhere and wait out this storm that's developing, just like we are... Oh, and one more thing: The Scrounger's boat is here but we haven't seen him yet. We're going to take a look around, and then hide out in the mountain for the night. We'll be fine, and we'll see you in the morning."

Laurie Schramm

11 DEFENCE

Once we'd signed-off from our call, and dismantled and stowed the radio in it's pack, we left it on the road and walked back down to the dock area to have a look at the *Argo*. It was a sad sight, still tied to the dock but mostly under water.

"Something tells me Dr. Turner has been here," I said.

When we reached the dock, we could see that the stern of the boat was lying on the bottom, while the tip of the bow was being held just above the surface by the forward mooring line. It looked like the aft mooring line had been cut. Situated like this, most of the wheelhouse was above water, but everything else was submerged.

Vivian carefully stepped aboard, to search around and see if she could find anything we could use.

"There's not too much here," she reported after a few minutes, handing over a First Aid Kit and a flashlight. "I'll take one more look around."

After a few more minutes of searching, she appeared carrying a well worn, sailor's type sweater. "This was up by the front window, in front of the controls and ship's wheel. Everything else is under water."

"Getting cold?" I asked.

"Not yet." We were still wearing our wet clothes, but it had been a fairly hot afternoon, so we were reasonably comfortable while our clothes dried on us. "But I will be when evening sets in."

"We can use that to help us find The Scrounger. Once we get

back to the mountain, we can use this to give Silver his scent. Then we'll see if we can track him."

"You two are full of surprises, aren't you?"

"I suppose we are," I grinned.

Using the First Aid Kit, we replaced our makeshift bandages with proper ones. Both of our wounds were still bleeding, but only slowly.

"We'll have to change these bandages again later tonight," said Vivian.

I nodded.

As we made our way back up the road, we stopped to retrieve the radio-pack, and carried everything up to the mountain entrance. Placing the radio-pack on a table in the old dining area, I called Silver over and asked him to get the scent. When he'd thoroughly sniffed-over the sweater, he looked up at me, and I gave him the command for tracking.

Vivian watched in fascination as Silver went through his usual tracking routine of sniffing here and there, taking a few steps, re-checking for scents, and moving again. It all seemed pretty random, and possibly fruitless, as we worked our way forward, but as soon as we reached the main tunnel, he gave out a "Grruph," and it was obvious that he'd found the scent.

From there, Silver moved forward, not in a straight line, but continuing to take us further along the main tunnel. When we came to a side room/cave, he'd go in sniff around and then come back out and resume tracking along the main tunnel. This went on for quite a distance until we found ourselves back in the munition storage cave. Once there, Silver went back to sweeping broad swaths of the room, stopping here and there to investigate something and then, finally, leading us over to a back corner.

There, lying behind a stack of crates, was The Scrounger.

Crouching down by his head, I was able to confirm that he was still breathing.

"Mr. Parker?" I said, in a moderately loud voice, "Mr. Parker?"

He moaned a couple of times, and then his eyes cracked open just a bit, like someone waking slowly after a long slumber.

"Are you OK? Where are you hurt?"

"My head," he murmured. "That son of a bitch hit me from behind!"

"Dr. Turner you mean?"

"I don't know. He never told me his name." Then, coming more awake opened his eyes more completely and looked at me. "I know you," he said, "you're one of those nosy reporters!"

"That's right," I smiled, relieved that he seemed to be recovering, "Alex Houston. We met at your place at Pacifico a few days ago."

"How did you find me? And what are you doing here anyway?"

"I'm still chasing the story of those shells, and we saw your boat outside. We thought you might be around somewhere, and Silver led us to you."

"Smart dog," he said, struggling to sit up.

"Slowly," I advised, reaching out to help him.

After helping him to a sitting position I introduced Vivian, using her Coast Guard cover story. We decided to give him a few minutes to recover before trying to go anywhere. The Scrounger admitted that he'd originally discovered the old base and had taken some shells with him, and then lost them when everything was swept off the bow of his boat in a storm.

"How many shells did you take away?" I asked.

"Ten. Five of the black ones and five of the grey ones."

That's a relief, I thought, since we'd had gained possession of four of them and I now had a pretty good guess about the fifth – that would account for the five most dangerous ones. "What happened next?"

"Well, none of the local stores were interested, but I got referred to a buyer that was interested. I sold him the one I'd bought back from the kids and he said he'd pay a hundred dollars each if I could get more of the grey-coloured ones with the blue tips."

Vivian whistled at that. "How many did you sell him?"

"I was going to take as many cases as I could find and carry to my boat, but he must have followed me here because he showed up before I could carry any out. He pulled a gun on me, then we heard a noise and he hit me on the head with something... Next thing I knew was when you were calling my name just now."

"That noise you heard was me when my foot broke through a piece of the wood flooring out there in the tunnel. He got the drop on us too and made us carry some crates of these things out to his boat."

"What happened then?"

"We were able to get away from him and swim back here. Then we came and found you, and now here we are together," I summarized.

"So, he'll be coming back then?"

"Maybe. We did leave his boat in a bit of a mess, and it's possible that it sunk. If not, he has lots of the shells, but he might come back here anyway."

"To finish us off, you mean?"

"Maybe, but not tonight. There's a huge storm building up outside, so he'll have to take shelter somewhere for the night and I doubt he'd want to try to tackle all of us in the dark anyway. If he comes, I think it will be in the morning, but there will also be a helicopter coming for us in the morning."

"So, it might be a race then."

"Maybe."

Through all this Vivian had been partly listening to us and partly looking around the cave with her flashlight. She found The Scrounger's lantern first, and switched it on, then using its more powerful beam continued to look around. After a while, she bent over and picked something else up, turned and silently held it up to show me. She was behind The Scrounger's back at the time, so only I could see that she'd retrieved her small pistol. Once she was sure that I'd seen it, she put it out of sight in a pocket and came over to join us.

"I wonder whether we should check out the kitchen and see if we can find anything that's still fit to eat."

"After more than thirty years?" scoffed The Scrounger.

"Do you have any food on your boat?" I asked him.

"Just coffee," he said, a bit deflated.

"Let's go have a look then."

With evening and the big storm both approaching rather rapidly, it was decided that Vivian would accompany The Scrounger down to his boat, where he would check its moorings and acquire the coffee and any other food he might have on board, while Silver and I would go investigate the kitchen.

We all walked back along the main tunnel, then Silver and I

turned into the kitchen and dining area while the others continued on to the docks.

The first thing I did, when Silver and I were alone was to remove my pants and strip away the bandage on my left leg. Under that bandage had been my double-barreled derringer, stowed with the chamber under the hammer empty for safety and a single round in the other chamber. Taped in beside it were three more rounds wrapped in plastic film. I replaced my pants and placed the gun and spare ammunition in a pocket.

Taking inventory in the kitchen, my first thoughts were heat and light for the evening. The electricity was off. *There's probably a generator somewhere*, I thought, but we hadn't found it yet. The big stovetops were fuelled by compressed gas, *probably either natural gas or propane*, I thought, but all of the cylinders I could find were empty. Either they'd been used up before the evacuation or, more likely, miniature leaks over thirty-five or so years of storage had drained the tanks. There was an abundance, however, of paper and wood from packing crates in virtually every room/cave we'd seen in the complex, so the only question was ventilation.

There were metal ventilation hoods over the large stovetops but I couldn't tell what they led to, and whether the ventilation was natural or relied on electric fans. There's only one way to find out, I thought, so I placed a huge steel wok on one of the stovetops, collected some old paper and crate fragments to use for kindling, and used the ferrocerium fire-starter from my knife to start a small bonfire. Thankfully, it worked. At first the small tendrils of smoke went in several directions, but the heat from the small fire eventually directed more and more of them up and into the overhead ventilation hood and it was soon clear that the system was drawing the smoke up and away. *Must be using natural fissures in the rock*, I thought. Encouraged by this, I built the fire up a bit more and was encouraged by the warmth and the light it gave out.

Vivian and The Scrounger must have also found it to be an encouraging sight when they returned, because I could hear their exclamations from the next room/cave where I was perusing the remaining stores of cans.

"Alex?" called Vivian.

"In here. I'm checking the pantry. Come see."

Vivian and The Scrounger found me taking cans off the shelves, inspecting them, and placing them in one or the other of two piles.

"What are you doing?"

"I'm inspecting the cans. These ones," pointing to the small pile to my left, "look OK to me, but these ones," pointing to my right "don't."

"Can you eat 35-year-old canned food?"

"I think so. I remember reading news and magazine articles about people finding old cans of food and finding out that they'd lost their original colour and texture but were otherwise edible, as long as the cans had been kept cool and weren't bulging or damaged. These cans have been stored cool, dry, and away from sunlight, so I'm looking for cans that aren't dented, rusted, bulging, or leaking anything."

Vivian made a dubious-sounding noise.

"As a SCUBA diver, I've also read and heard stories of divers salvaging cans from 30-year-old shipwrecks and finding them edible, if not tasty. Some of those would have been more or less Second World War vintage cans too."

"Can you tell what's in the cans?"

"No. These wrappers are pretty faded and crumbly, and I can't read Japanese anyway. If they'd been commercial cans, they'd at least have nice pictures on them but, being military, all the labels I've seen so far only have text on them.

"If you look round while I'm doing this, there might be some sacks of rice around somewhere."

As I continued to sort cans, the others scoured the rest of the "pantry." Soon, Vivian announced her discovery of bags of rice on a pallet, and The Scrounger triumphantly announced his discovery of several cases of beer and several crates of bottles of sake.

Taking our prizes to the kitchen and laying them out on one of the counters, we used my knife to open some of the cans. They had certainly lost their original colour and texture, as they all looked like pale coloured-mush.

"Well, there's only one way figure these out," I said, taking a spoon and tasting small portions from several of the cans: "definitely tuna," I said after one, "some kind of pickled, mixed vegetables, I think," after another, "ugh, cabbage," after another, and "some kind of fruit or fruit mixture: maybe peaches or oranges in this one," after another.

"I'll go get water from the stream we saw outside," said The

Scrounger, picking up a large pot.

Vivian and I constructed a rough cooking surface by stacking small pots on each side of the fire and placing a large metal baking sheet across them. When he returned, we boiled two pots of water: one to provide safe drinking water and one for the rice. In another we heated the tuna and vegetables, and in yet another the canned fruit.

Together with the beer and sake, we actually had a pretty nice dinner, or maybe it just tasted good because we were starving. In any case, the hot food did us all a lot of good and none of us got sick from it.

Silver had rice and tuna, and water of course, and seemed quite content with his lot as well.

As we were eating, basked by the soft glow of the fire, we began to plan ahead.

"I imagine that the helicopter will leave the ship at first light and be here within a couple of hours of that," I said.

"We'll have to watch out in case your Dr. Turner comes back looking for us," offered Vivian.

"Harrumph, he's not my Dr. Turner! But I agree. Somehow, I don't see him as the type to leave loose ends hanging around. If he's alive and if his boat is still working, I think he'll be back as soon as the storm lets up."

"Why don't we just take my boat first thing n the morning and get out of here?" asked The Scrounger.

"Ah. I'm afraid we have bad news Mr. Parker: Dr. Turner seems to have holed your boat. It's resting on the bottom, still tied to the dock, but only the upper part of the wheelhouse is above water."

This prompted a significant outburst of rather sulphurous language. I wasn't surprised. This was the second boat he'd lost in the same month.

"How are we going to defend ourselves then?" asked The Scrounger, after he'd calmed down. "There's not much in here but junk."

I looked over at Vivian, who nodded. "There are a few things we haven't told you about ourselves, Mr. Parker. Vivian here is actually an FBI Agent, I'm an RCMP Constable, and Silver here is a police dog."

I thought this might be going a bit fast for him to take

everything in but to give him credit, he seemed to accept these surprises and without making the obvious comments about two of us being women in non-traditional roles.

"Call me Aloysius," he said, instead, "and tell me how that helps us."

"Well, for one thing we have a certain amount of training," began Vivian, "and for another I have this," she said, pulling out her pistol.

Up close, I could see that it was a Beretta. "How many rounds?" I asked.

"Eight: the gun will hold nine .25 calibre rounds, but I carry it with the chamber empty so it doesn't go off if I drop it."

"Me too," I said, "bringing out my double-barreled derringer. This one is a .38 Special, but I keep the first one empty so it's only holding one round. I also have four more rounds in my pocket."

"Is that what you had under that other bandage?" Vivian asked.

"Yes." Looking over to Aloysius, I explained that I'd had bandages on both of my legs, one concealing my knife and the concealing my gun and spare rounds. "We have two small-calibre guns and limited ammunition."

"So, you expected trouble?"

"No. Actually, I didn't, but each of these has saved my life at least once – as has Silver too, for that matter – so I like to have them with me when I can."

"That's still not much," commented Aloysius.

"It's worse than that. Neither of these guns is going to be much good at more than about twenty feet," I added.

"Maybe we should go back to the munitions cave and see if there's anything we can use," suggested Vivian.

"Sure, and I have another thought," I offered. "They went to a lot of trouble to build this place. It seems to me that the military mind would have wanted to have a second exit, so if they were under attack, they could use the other way out to escape and launch a counter-attack. As long as we're going to the munitions cave anyway, I think we should follow the rest of the tunnels and see if it leads to a way out."

The others agreed, so we picked up our flashlight and lantern and headed back down the main tunnel. When we reached the munitions cave, Vivian took one light and went in to scavenge.

Aloysius, Silver, and I followed the tunnel for a couple more hundred yards - I estimated the full tunnel length to be about 800 yards – until we reached its end. There we found two steel doors, smaller than the front ones. They were closed and seemed very solid and secure. We weren't able to open them, and provisionally concluded that they were locked and/or blocked from the other side.

By the time we made it back to the munitions cave, Vivian had found two more grenades, but otherwise just crate after crate of ammunition for rifles, machine guns, and anti-aircraft and anti-tank auto-cannons.

When we'd returned to the kitchen area, we discussed our options and decided that all we really needed to do was hold out where we were until Don and the helicopter arrived in the morning. We decided that we'd all sleep in the kitchen, where we could build-up the fire to provide warmth and soft lighting. We then dragged in bedding and blankets from the bunk area. The mattresses were quite thin, but we discovered that two or three of them stacked together weren't too bad. The army blankets were also thin, and coarse, but here again two or three of them stacked together were warm enough.

I made a separate bed of mattress and blankets for Silver, but he nestled up with me instead. I was glad that he did.

***

I'd set the alarm on my diving watch to wake us up well before sunrise, which gave us time to re-start the fire and heat more cans from the pantry to give us a hot breakfast. It was essentially the same menu we'd had the night before, but once again we were hungry and thankful to have anything to eat at all.

After breakfast, we went back into the tunnel to see what we could do to fortify the front doors. They were big and heavy, somewhat warped, and the hinges were very rusty, but with all three of us pushing we were able to get one door mostly closed and the other door partly closed. That left an open gap that was about three feet wide. We decided to barricade the rest, so we dragged an assortment of rocks and twisted pieces of steel to make it difficult to re-open the doors, and then set to work making a barricade on the inside that we could use to defend the three feet of open space.

We were making quite a bit of noise and raising a fair amount of dust, and that's probably why it took so long before Silver suddenly turned and stiffened, with his ears and fur up, and began to growl at the same time as we heard a deep, calm voice.

"That's all very nice, but you're just going to have to clear it all away again."

We all knew that voice.

Straightening from our tasks we turned to look behind us, and there near the entrance to the kitchen area, stood Dr. Turner with his lantern and his big, ugly pistol. The pistol, of course, was pointed directly at us.

"Dr. Turner."

"Yes, I see that we all survived our little battle on the boat." As he took a step forward, we could see that both of his legs were bandaged and bloody, and his gait was a bit unsteady.

"How did you get in here?"

"There's a path leading from the lake north of here to the backside of this mountain. The doors were easy to find, but blocked by rubble and locked from the outside. Fortunately, the lock was little more than a mass of rust, so it was easy to open.

"Now, you're going to get some more of those crates and carry them down to my boat."

He waved his gun at us again, to emphasize his point.

"I don't think so," said Vivian, raising her gun. "FBI, Dr. Turner. Drop the gun – you're under arrest."

He didn't laugh or reply, he just fired a shot in her direction and jumped backwards and to one side, putting himself in an alcove and just out of Vivian's line of fire.

Vivian fired a shot in return, as we too scrambled to find cover in alcoves on each side of our position in the tunnel: Vivian on one side, and Aloysius and Silver and me on the other side.

"We're going to need to get those doors open if we're going to get out of here," I called to Vivian.

"Leave it to me," she said. "Get as far back into that alcove as you can and fire a shot to cover me."

As I took a shot in Dr. Turner's general direction, Vivian pulled the safety pins from her two grenades and threw them both at the two big, front doors.

The delay mechanism on at least one of the grenades must have been faulty as one went off as soon as it hit one of the doors, with the second grenade going off almost immediately afterwards.

The sounds from the two explosions were deafening, but luckily, we weren't hit by shrapnel or flying debris. When the debris and most of the dust settled down, I could see that there was sunlight coming into the tunnel.

When I poked my head out for a quick look at the entrance, I heard a sharp ricochet from a shot Dr. Turner took at me, followed by the crack of a return shot from Vivian.

"I think there's enough space for us to get through," I called across. At the same time, I'd been trying to keep track of the shots fired and ammunition remaining:

Dr. Turner: two shots fired, unknown rounds left,
Vivian: two shots fired, six rounds left, and
Me: one shot fired; four rounds left.

"I'll go first," offered Aloysius, "and make sure the doors are open wide enough for us to get out. You two will have to cover me."

"OK," we both said, and with that, he scampered toward the doors. To cover him, Vivian and I took turns firing at four-second intervals in Dr. Turner's direction. I counted the pace in my head as we fired:

Bang, 1,2,3,4, Bang, 1,2,3,4, Bang, 1,2,3,4, Bang, 1,2,3,4, Bang. Five shots in all.

"It's OK," called Aloysius from the entrance, "I'm out!"

I reloaded my derringer, thinking: *only two shots left for me and three more for Vivian.*

From across the tunnel, Vivian was signalling with her hands that we should go together, and fire two shots each as we went. Nodding my head, I said "Come Silver, let's run."

The three of us sprang from our shelters and ran, crouched low, for the tunnel entrance, taking turns firing our two rounds each, this time with only a couple of seconds between each shot. We weren't aiming for Dr. Turner, just firing in his direction with the intent of keeping his head down and trying to prevent him from firing at us.

He did fire a few shots at us, but the first few went harmlessly astray, and the slow curve of the tunnel helped us to quickly get out of his line of sight. As we squeezed through the front entrance and scrambled over debris, Silver and I leapt to one side of the doors, while Vivian leapt to the other, where Aloysius was also crouched down.

In the brief silence that followed, Vivian called out to Dr. Turner: "It's not too late to put your gun down and come out with your hands up."

The response, however was a series of amazing sounds. First: the sounds of three shots and a distinct click, all in rapid succession, as Dr. Turner emptied his pistol.

Secondly, the sound of a thunderous detonation, followed by another, followed by another, followed by yet another, as the old Japanese explosives went off.

It was stunning.

Even where we were, to one side of the tunnel and with our backs to the mountain, and with our hands over our ears and me trying to envelop Silver's head with my body to protect his ears, the explosions were deafening. From the entrance to the tunnel came masses of debris, dust, and smoke.

As the sounds of the explosions subsided, we could hear the sounds of rock falling inside the complex. More and more dust and smoke came out of the entrance, and then suddenly stopped.

As we cautiously got up and stepped back from the mountain, we could see the reason for this: the entire entranceway was filled with broken rock. Looking up, we could see smoke belching out and up from the twin peaks of our mountain, Mount Cerberus.

"I don't think your friends are going to have any trouble finding us," said Vivian.

"Listen," was all I said.

"Thump, Thump, Thump, Thump."

12 AFTERMATH

This time, the big helicopter landed right near the old docks and out jumped Don and two sailors, all wearing combat fatigues and sidearms. Each of them was holding an FN C1D automatic rifle at the ready. Spotting us, they came at the run, and we trotted as best we could down to meet them.

"Are you OK?" were the first words out of Don's mouth, his eyes glued to the bloody bandage on my leg.

"I am now," I replied, "we all are, but we sure have a story to tell."

"Where's Dr. Turner?" he asked, still holding his rifle at the ready.

"He's in there. I think his body is probably crushed under the weight of the mountain. If you want to be sure, have your men take a look. You can see the main entrance behind us, and there's a rear entrance at the back. Dr. Turner somehow managed to sneak in the back and surprise us, but we held him off. He was still firing at us after we got outside the mountain, and one of his shots must have triggered some old explosives."

It was all coming out in a rush, but my adrenalin was still running high from our narrow escape. "It really was another old Japanese base from the Second World War, and they had the whole place wired to go up before they evacuated the island. I don't know why they didn't blow it up when they left, but Dr. Turner seems to have done it for them. Too bad he was inside when it happened."

Don told the two sailors to go check out both entrances, and we all just sat down right where we were and poured out the whole story.

"What a tale," marvelled Don after hearing us out. "Dr. Turner sure had us fooled, I wonder who he really was."

"We should be able to get some good fingerprints off of his boat," said Vivian. "I'm sure he'll show up in one of our databases, or perhaps one of yours."

"I'm really sorry we couldn't get to you last night," said Don. "I was willing, and so were Sandy and the crew, but we were over-ruled. The storm just kept getting worse and worse, with the wind eventually gusting to 100 knots, and then the onset of darkness made it impossible."

"I understand. We're lucky that the same storm kept Dr. Turner away too."

Don came with us to check out Dr. Turner's boat, which we found tied to some shoreline rocks, just far enough away to be out of sight from the old docks.

There was a lot of damage below the wheelhouse, but not below the waterline, as far as we could see. There was lots of evidence of the fire, whose smoke Vivian and I had seen from the water. It had clearly been large enough that it would have taken him some time to extinguish it. There was also evidence of makeshift repairs to essential parts of the decking and portions of the hull that were just above the waterline. In calm water, that is. As the storm intensified, he probably had a significant amount of water coming in from a few places where shrapnel from the grenade had punched holes in the hull. We had seen for ourselves that he had been injured in both legs, again probably from flying shrapnel from the grenade.

"Between the fire, the repairs, and his own injuries, I can see why he didn't follow us right away. He probably headed for the nearest island and took shelter to make these repairs and wait out the storm," concluded Vivian.

"Yes, and it must have taken some time to do all that," I agreed, "and then darkness and the storm would have conspired to keep him there until this morning."

Neither Vivian nor I had the equipment to dust for, or collect, fingerprints but the boat did have quite a few nautical charts, the ship's log and registration papers, plus some equipment manuals. We carefully collected all of them. Vivian later sent them to the FBI lab in Quantico, Virginia.

We also found the three crates of "special" shells sitting in the stern where we had stacked them.

"Here's the last one," said Don, emerging from the wheelhouse with the shell from the kids at the beach. He'd already told us about finding the five regular shells with the side-scan sonar and the fleet divers.

"That's a relief," I said. "If we can assume that everything in the mountain complex has been vaporized or buried then there's only these to be dealt with. What will happen to them?"

Don and Vivian looked at each other. "Since they came from American soil and are now all back on American soil, I think that's going to be up to your government to decide," he said.

"Yes," agreed Vivian. "I'll send a report from the ship, if I'm allowed, and the Agency will contact the military. I'm sure that someone will be sent to collect them."

"We'll leave a couple of people to watch over them until we get new orders," said Don.

Making out way back towards the old road and the helicopter, we were met by the armed sailors, who reported that the back doors had been blown open by the blast, and that both entrances seemed to be completely sealed with fallen rock.

"The Japanese forces did a thorough job with their explosives," commented Don. "I wonder why they didn't blow them when they left."

"I doubt we'll ever find out now."

"How about if we get you two back to the ship where the doctor can have a look at your wounds?"

As the big helicopter ferried us back to the *HMCS Huron*, I looked out window and was able to get a last look at Semisopochnoi Island as it disappeared over the horizon.

***

When the island base exploded, it was detected by seismometers in the Aleutian Islands and this, together with remote observations of the smoke and dust cloud emitted from Mount Cerebrus, led to the logical, but incorrect, interpretation that the volcano had become active. It made the news reports and may even have led researchers to begin to pay more attention to the mountain volcano, but at least there was no longer any hazard resulting from its former occupation by the Japanese Army and Navy, everything they had left behind was now well destroyed, excepting the shells from Dr. Turner's boat. All those were eventually taken away by the US Navy.

Jack was soon sent back to his regular posting at the Fort McMurray, Alberta Detachment. He had done his part. Although, in the end, we hadn't needed very much of his help, it had been reassuring to have him there and under other circumstances it could have been vital. He hadn't made any real progress with his wooing of Dr. Sarah McInnes, so he was probably just as happy to go home.

Aloysius Parker, also known as "The Scrounger," had only actually committed one offense, that of bringing live shells across the border from the U.S. without declaring them. He hadn't known about their nerve agent contents at the time, of course, but he knew that there was something different about them, because of their effects on the kids at the beach. He had fully intended to go bring more of the shells back to Canada, but bad intentions aren't illegal by themselves. In the end, and partly motivated by the help he'd given Vivian and I in defending against Dr. Turner, the Crown Prosecutor had decided not to pursue any charges against him. So, he basically got off with a warning.

It's possible the experience taught him a lesson, if not because of the prosecutor's warning then because of having been shot at and almost blown up, but you never know.

He eventually went back to retrieve his *Argo*, patched-up the hull, had the engine rebuilt, and went back to his beachcombing career.

For the rest of us, the final chapter came a few days later.

Sept. 3, 1977
Victoria, British Columbia

It was overcast, with fog and drizzle in Victoria, as Don, Vivian, Silver, and I were checked-in at the main gate of the nearby Canadian Forces Base Esquimalt. Don was dressed in his Naval Lieutenant's uniform. I wore my police tactical uniform, and was hobbling a bit with my bandaged leg. Vivian was dressed in a brown-tweed business suit and had her bandaged arm in a sling.

We were escorted to a conference room where we were shortly met by my boss, Staff Sergeant Bob Simpson, and his boss, Assistant Commissioner George MacLeod. The latter, was the man that had invited me to join the Force in the first place, and he'd demonstrated a remarkable habit of dropping in to see me and get briefed at the close of my assignments.

Moments later, we were joined by two men I had not previously met. They were a study in contrasts. The first man was extremely well dressed in a suit and overcoat, and exuded the confidence of a powerful person. I found out later that he'd been brought by a sleek, black, unmarked helicopter right to the grounds of the base. He was tall and powerfully built, with short, thick white hair, a salt-and-pepper mustache, and clear, blue eyes. He was introduced as Deputy Director Jonathan Wheeler and he gave an extremely strong handshake.

"Vivian here tells me you saved her life Constable. I'd like to offer my personal thanks, as well as that of the Bureau."

"My pleasure, Sir, but she saved my life too, and Silver's too."

"Silver?"

There were a few chuckles as he was introduced to Silver as well.

The second man was Rear-Admiral Peter White, commander of the Canadian Forces Security Branch. This was "Don's Admiral." He too exuded a sense of power but, in contrast to the Deputy Director, with the admiral it was more like the quiet confidence of someone that exercised great power, but behind the scenes and unnoticed by most people. He was slender, but wiry rather than thin, with thinning hair, and extremely sharp, piercing eyes. *Somewhat like Silver's*, I thought.

Admiral White wore a suit, but it was very understated – he could have passed for a businessman, or even a university or college professor. Like the Deputy Director though, there was iron in his handshake, and I could feel him sizing me up as we shook.

"Heard about you, Constable Houston. I'm pleased to meet you at last."

The briefing covered everything, from the first call for help through the choices our superiors made, everything Don, and Vivian, and I went through, and the follow-up activities still underway.

I learned a few things I hadn't known, and was once again reminded of chess players. I'd always tended to think of my immediate boss, Bob, that way – always thinking two- to three moves ahead of everyone else. Now, I began to perceive that the senior officers did this too, except that in their cases it was like they were simultaneously playing multiple games of chess.

Deputy Director White told us that, based on our descriptions, the FBI had tentatively identified Dr. Turner as a mid-level military *attaché* working out of the Soviet Embassy in Washington. They had a reasonable level of confidence that either the FBI or RCMP labs would be able to confirm this from the fingerprints we'd found, but there didn't seem to be much doubt.

In Washington he was known as Grigory Denisovich Ivanov but, of course, that may not have been his real name either.

"The Bureau watches all the Soviet and East-Bloc Embassy *attachés* in Washington very closely," he had explained, "because they're always intelligence agents of some kind. In this case Ivanov had suddenly disappeared, right out from under our people's noses and we had lost track of him. We were wondering what he'd gotten up to, and the timing matches well with when you first met him in the islands."

"What would the Soviets want with old chemical weapons?" I'd asked.

"Who knows? Intelligence, maybe? They have their own chemical and biological weapons programs, so they're not lacking for general knowledge or materiel but it's possible there was something special about these that tweaked their interest. More likely, the idea was to sell or provide them to others. They could feed them through an international arms dealer to any radical group that they might want to quietly support with hard-to-trace weapons. We're going to try to find out though."

"It's just as well that he died in the explosion," continued the Deputy Director. "He'd have had diplomatic immunity from prosecution, so all we'd have been able to do was expel him back to Mother Russia and have them send in someone new to start all over in his place."

I shivered. "A tough game."

"Indeed." Then, he brightened. "Anyway, it ended for the best."

"So, it's all over then."

"Not quite. We're going to do some checking into possible Soviet connections into the international arms rings. Admiral White has assigned Lieutenant Harrison here to join our team as Liaison Officer, and he'll be coming back to Washington with Vivian and me."

I tried to keep a straight face at that. This was news to me, and a flurry of new thoughts rushed in, distracting me from the meeting at hand.

The senior officers each expressed their satisfaction with the conclusion of the mission and they jointly lavished praise on Don, Vivian, and I, and we all raised our cups – of coffee, of course – in a toast to a successfully completed mission.

This, of course, prompted a fairly loud "Whoof" from Silver, which got everyone chuckling.

"Does that dog go everywhere with you?" asked the Deputy Director.

Before I could muster a reply, Assistant Commissioner MacLeod jumped in: "These two go everywhere together, and no matter what happens to them, they always seem to land on their feet, and they always manage to do it together. I think they've become inseparable."

"Hmmm," replied the Deputy Director, with a straight face, "Inseparable Mounties."

"Grruph" said Silver, his eyes shining.

I could see the obvious question about how Silver seemed to be able to follow our conversation forming on the Deputy Director's face, but the Assistant Commissioner pre-empted him by saying "It's a long story. I'll tell you about it some time over a drink."

"Make it scotch and you have a deal."

"Make it rum and I'll join you," added the admiral.

Laurie Schramm

13 EPILOGUE

With the briefing over, we all walked out of the building together and made our way to the grassy area on which the FBI helicopter had landed. Silver and I were trailing the group and, noticing this, Vivian dropped back to join us.

There was a pause, and then Vivian said, "What's the story with you and 'Rock Hudson' there?"

"What do you mean?" I asked.

"You can't fool the FBI," she said, giving me a knowing look.

I sighed. "So, Don reminds you of Rock Hudson? I had the same reaction the first time I met him too, but I don't think of him that way now that I've gotten to know him."

"And you've gotten to know him well?" she prodded.

"Yes, we've become more than just friends, but I don't know where, or even if, our relationship is going. I was hoping we'd get some personal time together so we could figure that out, and now that he's suddenly leaving, I'm starting to miss him already."

"You've got it bad, sister! But, from what I've seen of you two I think you're on the right track. Don't just let him walk away."

I'd no sooner received this advice than I looked up and noticed that the Deputy Director had already said his goodbyes and boarded the helicopter, with the Assistant Commissioner and Admiral standing to one side.

Don was already taking his first step up and into the helicopter, when he stopped, stepped back down, and turned back to look in my direction, his face uncertain.

I ran over, and threw my arms around him for a kiss that seemed both long and too short at the same time.

"I don't like being away from you," he admitted, almost sheepishly.

"Call me when you get some leave," I said. "I think we need some peace and quiet. Somewhere where we can talk about *us* for a change. Of course," I paused, "I never know where they're going to send me next either…"

"Leave that to me. I'm in intelligence after all. I'll find you."

With that, we parted, and he boarded the waiting helicopter.

As I stepped away from the whirling blades, I saw Silver sitting on his haunches, staring up at me with his, so familiar, penetrating blue-grey eyes, and I could tell what he was thinking: *I like him* !

I dropped to my knees and threw my arms around his neck in a fierce hug.

"Me too Silver. Me too."

***

… Alex and Silver return in
"An Indispensable Mountie."

Laurie Schramm

BOOK 5 ENDNOTES

1. In reality, only two (not three) of the Aleutian Islands – Kiska and Attu - were occupied by the Japanese in June 1942, during the Second World War. Attu was retaken after a two-week battle in May 1943, involving ground forces of the US Army and air support from the RCAF. In July 1943, and just before a combined US-Canadian force attacked, the Japanese destroyed and/or booby-trapped most of their weapons, equipment, and supplies on Kiska, and evacuated it without a single loss of life.

2. Long known as the Queen Charlotte Islands, they were officially renamed Haida Gwaii on June 3, 2010, under the Haida Gwaii Reconciliation Act, part of the *Kunst'aa guu - Kunst'aayah* Reconciliation Protocol between British Columbia and the Haida people.

3. In real life, a first full troop of women began training in the RCMP in 1974, graduating as full-fledged constables in 1975. However, for this fictional series, it all began with a single-woman pilot test.

4. See *An Inconvenient Mountie* (ISBN: 978-1-9994940-0-1).

5. At this point in time, it was still part of the RCMP. Years later, in 1984, the Security Service was spun-out to create the present-day Canadian Security Intelligence Service (C.S.I.S.).

6. See *An International Mountie* (ISBN: 978-1-9994940-6-3).

7. Sikorsky CH-124 Sea Kings are twin-engine, anti-submarine warfare helicopters that were used by the Canadian Armed Forces for over 50 years. They were usually housed on and deployed from destroyers and frigates of the Royal Canadian

Navy. Sea Kings were a familiar sight to people on Canada's Pacific and Atlantic coasts in the 1970s, partly because they frequently assisted with maritime search and rescue operations.

8. SAR: Search and Rescue Technician.

9. HMCS (Her Majesty's Canadian Ship) Huron, DDG 281, was an Iroquois-class (a.k.a. Tribal class) helicopter-carrying, guided-missile destroyer. She served with the Canadian Armed Forces from 1972 through 2000.

10. This was still the 1970s. Women serving on combat ships would come much later.

11. See *An Indestructible Mountie* (ISBN: 978-1-9994940-4-9).

12. Defence Research Establishment Suffield (DRES) was part of the Canadian Forces' Research and Development Branch. It was reorganized into Defence Research and Development Canada (DRDC) in 2000. DRES, now DRDC Suffield, has long been active in the development of effective defensive countermeasures against the threat of chemical and biological weapons.

13. In the 1970s and '80s the Canadian Army operated the Special Service Force (SSF), a highly mobile light infantry brigade that coupled units of 2 Combat Group with units of the Canadian Airborne Regiment. The SSF could be inserted quickly into any national or international theatre of operations, although its main roles were in support of NATO and United Nations operations. There was a different, "1st Special Service Force" that was jointly organized with the United States, during the Second World War.

14. UDT: Underwater Demolition Team.

15. Jacques-Yves Cousteau was a famous SCUBA diver and explorer, known for co-inventing the first *Aqua-Lung* regulator that enabled the modern open-circuit self-contained underwater breathing apparatus (SCUBA) and for his oceanographic research expeditions and films, most of which were supported by the *Calypso,* his ship that served a combination field laboratory and expedition/diving vessel.

16. For a brief description of Semisopochnoi Island, Alaska, see: https://en.wikipedia.org/wiki/Semisopochnoi_Island.

17. The actual book is: Fred Rogers, *"Shipwrecks of British Columbia,"* published by Douglas & McIntyre, Vancouver, 1973. Rogers' book contains a description of the wreck of the

Russian Freighter *Uzbekistan*.

18. A description of the wreck of the American Freighter *Kvichak* is given in a book by Rick James and Jacques Marc: "*Historic Shipwrecks of the Central Coast of British Columbia*," Underwater Archeological Society of British Columbia, Vancouver, 2010.

19. Canadian Forces Base (CFB) Esquimalt is Canada's principal Pacific Coast naval base. Located near Victoria, on Vancouver Island, it is home to several units including all ships of the Maritime Pacific Fleet, the Fleet Diving Unit (Pacific), and the Acoustic Data Analysis Centre.

20. First published in 1976, *Goldfrank's Toxicologic Emergencies*, by L.S. Nelson et al., is still in print and continually updated. It was published in it's 11th edition in 2019.

21. The FBI did accept its first two women as special agents in 1972. For a brief summary of their stories, see "First Women Agents: Susan Roley Malone Interview," at https://www.fbi.gov/video-repository/newss-first-women-agents-susan-roley-malone-interview/view, and "Celebrating Women Special Agents Part 2: Two Women Blaze a Trail in 1972," at https://www.fbi.gov/news/stories/celebrating-women-special-agents-part-2.

22. Canadian Forces Station Masset was originally established in 1943 as a signals-interception and long-distance-relay facility. Between 1968 and 1971 its role evolved into HFDF system to high-frequency direction finding for the location and classification of enemy ships. In more recent years, its role evolved into signals intelligence gathering.

23. High-resolution side-scan sonar was developed by the US Navy in 1958 but kept secret for until it was declassified in 1980. The principles and operation are described in U.S. Patent 4,197,591.

24. Arctic Foxes were introduced to Semisopochnoi Island for fur farming during the 1800s.

25. It was, in fact, a Japanese Second World War, Type 97, grenade, and was primarily designed for use in grenade launchers. When the safety pin was removed, a sharp blow to the stem would initiate a 4 to 5 second delay sequence before ignition.

26. See *An Inconspicuous Mountie* (ISBN: 978-1-9994940-2-5.

Laurie Schramm

An Indispensable Mountie

Adventures of the First Woman Mountie. Book 6

LAURIE SCHRAMM

Laurie Schramm

DEDICATION

To Ann Marie

Laurie Schramm

BOOK 6 CONTENTS

	List of Characters	173
1	The Mad Trapper	175
2	Kosmos 954	179
3	A Rude Awakening	187
4	Organizing	205
5	Operation Arctic Circle	213
6	The Aerial-Search Begins	223
7	The Ground-Search	243
8	Forging Ahead	255
9	Trouble	263
10	Survival	273
11	Man Hunt	289
12	Aftermath	301
13	Epilogue	307
14	Postscript	311
	Book 6 Endnotes	315

Laurie Schramm

LIST OF CHARACTERS
(IN ORDER OF APPEARANCE)

- The Stranger, a mysterious hunter and trapper
- Captain Dan Trask, RCAF, on assignment to NORAD Cheyenne Mountain Command Centre
- Constable Alexandra (Alex) Houston, RCMP
- Staff Sergeant Robert (Bob) G. Simpson, RCMP Security Service
- Assistant Commissioner George MacLeod, RCMP Security Service
- Silver, an Alaskan Malamute; and Alex's friend and companion
- Captain Donald (Don) Harrison, Military Intelligence, Canadian Forces
- Special Agent Vivian Rule, FBI
- Danny Wolki, Mayor, Interpretive Centre Guide, and Librarian, Inuvik
- Lieutenant Colonel John Stark, Adjutant from CFB Edmonton and Commanding Officer for the search and recovery mission
- Dr. Clem Goodyear, geophysicist, Geological Survey of Canada
- Corporal Wayne Robertson, Search and Rescue Technician (SAR Tech), RCAF
- Fred Warner, scientist, Atomic Energy Control Board of Canada (AECB)
- Peter Marcoux, hunter, trapper, and sled-dog musher
- Penny, a grey Siberian Husky and lead sled-dog
- Lieutenant Susan Warden, helicopter pilot, RCAF
- Sergeant Scott (Scotty) Huber, Flight Engineer, RCAF
- Jim Graham, scientist, Atomic Energy Control Board of Canada (AECB)
- Deputy Director Jonathan Wheeler, FBI
- Rear-Admiral Peter White, Canadian Forces Security Branch

Laurie Schramm

1 THE MAD TRAPPER

December 27, 1931
A cabin on the Rat River,
60 miles south of Inuvik, Northwest Territories, Canada

The stranger didn't know it yet, but he only had 21 more days to live. People actually called him 'the stranger,' as he tended to keep to himself and only spoke to people when necessary and, even then, in the fewest number of words possible and never providing an opening for more general, let alone interesting, conversation.

He had a real name, of course, but he'd previously gone by a different name in the Yukon, and possibly under yet another name before that, in the United States. In any case, no one was ever to be entirely certain of his real name

Later, he would become known in the media as 'The Mad Trapper of Rat River,' but not yet. And he almost certainly wasn't crazy, either, at least not according to those who later closely examined his behaviour[1].

His true origins were another mystery. Certainly, he had moved around different parts of the United States and Canada in his time. He was first seen in July, when he'd come to Fort McPherson to buy supplies. As the summer turned to fall, he'd show up here and there, asking directions from a roving hunting party, or to buy supplies from a trading post, but still speaking only in short sentences and always directly to the point. The trading posts were content with him because he always

175

seemed to have enough money for whatever he wanted to buy.

In this particular time and place, he was making his living as a hunter and trapper, and these activities had him ranging across more than three thousand square miles, bounded to the west by the Richardson Mountains that separated the Yukon from the Northwest Territories, to the north by Aklavik and Inuvik, to the south by Fort McPherson, and as far east into The Barrens as he cared to travel.

This area was rich in animals he could hunt, like caribou, and fur-bearing animals he could trap, like wolverine and lynx. Among the challenges, however, were the distances involved. As he identified the best places to set his trap lines, he found that, to manage them, he had to rotate among locations that were as much as 60 miles apart from each other: a long way to walk or snowshoe!

The stranger's solution to this problem, was to establish caches and camps at various locations. Whereas an open camp need not be hidden, his caches had to be carefully concealed so that he could store supplies, and even money, without risking their being stolen. In that way, he could lighten the weight of his pack which made the walking easier and left him with the ability to carry such pelts as he was able to obtain from his traplines. In one location, he had followed a wolf family's tracks to their den, which was a spacious cave in a rocky outcrop. He had shot the wolves, so he could sell the pelts, and taken over their den as one of his caches. He had just finished outfitting the last of his network of caches and had returned to his cabin on the Rat River.

People wondered not only who the stranger was, but where he was from, and what had brought him to the region. Naturally, there were rumours. Some people thought he must be on the run from the law back in the United States, although there was never any evidence to support such a view. Others thought he must have killed someone in a duel, while still others thought he'd simply come north to get away from people, and their society, and their conventions. He wouldn't have been the first person to come to far north to get away from 'civilization' and/or the 'law.' People's speculation may have been simply a way of explaining the stranger's aloofness and reticence, but they would have been fueled if anyone had occasion to examine the cabin that he'd constructed.

It was not a large cabin, perhaps eight by twelve feet on the inside and constructed of 12-inch-diameter logs. That was not unusual. The doorway was only about three feet above ground level, which wasn't all that unusual for a log cabin, because it was easier to excavate some of the soil, and lower the floor on the inside, than it was to build extra layers of logs.

What was unusual, was that the walls were reinforced with extra logs and sod to a height of 20 inches above the ground, all the way around the cabin. The reason for this became clear upon entering. Only then could a person see that the floor had been dug more than three feet below ground level, and also that holes had been bored just above the lowest level of logs, and spaced at intervals around the entire perimeter. In other words, the stranger had constructed a fortified bunker with rifle-ports. That was certainly unusual!

What was he afraid of? That someone might come after him? And why? The answers remain elusive to the present day.

It has already been pointed that the stranger did not interact smoothly or constructively with others. Only the previous week he had been engaged in a heated argument with several other local trappers, over the placement of traps. Tensions had risen, and the other trappers, possibly based on nothing more than suspicion, had accused him of interfering with their trap lines. Only words had been exchanged, however, and nothing had been resolved, with the stranger walking away muttering about individual rights and the other trappers muttering about going to the police. In fact, the others trappers did go to the police.

The Mounties arrived at the stranger's cabin the next day.

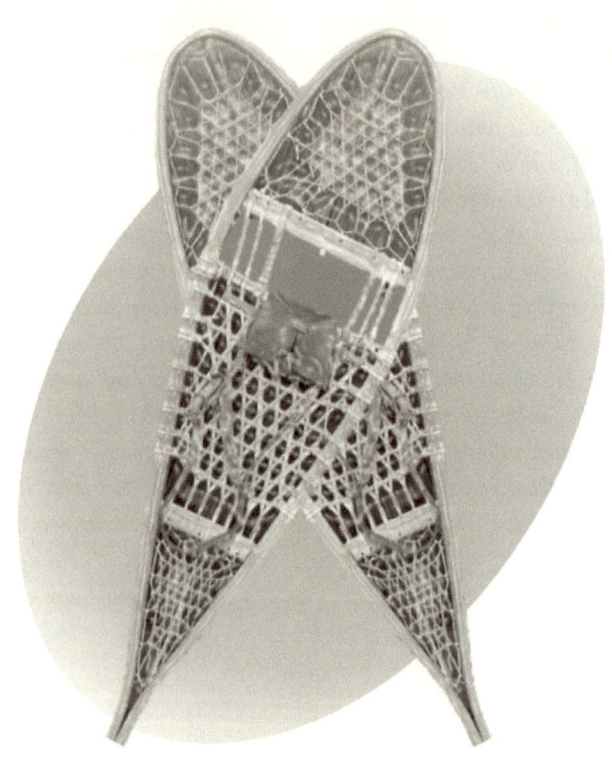

2 KOSMOS 954

A day in November, 1977
Space,
242 km (150 miles) above the earth's surface.

In the cold, blackness of space, the 400 kg, nuclear-powered satellite named KOSMOS 954 silently followed its programmed orbit over planet earth. It had been doing this for 58 days now, since its launch on September 18, 1977, and it was now in the process of following its 933rd revolution around the earth. As it did so, a highly-classified radar system scanned specific regions of the ocean below. The returning radar signals were automatically collected, processed, and transmitted to a ground station where technicians scanned them, searching for American naval vessels.

The radar system was new and unwieldy. It was large, heavy and consumed huge amounts of power. It was for these reasons that the satellite was large, heavy, and nuclear-powered. The sensitivity of the radar was not yet capable of realizing its designers' dreams: at best it could pick out the largest navy surface ships, like aircraft carriers. Unfortunately, even that was only possible with clear weather and calm-to-moderate seas. The prospect of being able to identify and track enemy naval vessels, anywhere in the world, however, was what justified building such an elaborate, and expensive spy satellite.

Unbeknownst to the satellite's original designers, and so secret that there was no security classification for it, was another spy device. This device was protected by the simple expedient of ensuring that only of a handful of people, beyond its designers, were aware of its existence, and no records of it were allowed outside of the small, innocent-looking Siberian facility in which it had been conceived, designed, and constructed. It was called Δpyr, pronounced "droog," and meaning – in this case – "sidekick."

The satellite had been modified to permit the installation of a small viewing port, to which was attached – from the inside of the satellite – a modest-sized, flat-black metal box. Δpyr drew very little power, had no data or control connections other than a single linkage to the control circuit for the radar system. When an electronic signal was generated to initiate a radar scan, a tap on the same signal line triggered Δpyr to initiate as well.

When the radar system was scanning, the device took pictures at pre-selected intervals through the special lens that had been positioned so that the camera was aimed in the same direction as the radar beam. Unlike the radar system, the camera was designed to be able to 'see' through clouds and weather, although in this case it was through the ability to record images generated by different kinds of light, from the near ultraviolet wavelengths, through the visible light spectrum, and all the way to the far infrared. Although this required a number of highly secret components, beginning with the multiple camera lenses themselves, the heart of the technology lie in the film.

To the untrained eye, the film looked like ordinary 35 mm film.

A professional photographer would notice that the film seemed to be just a bit thicker than normal 35 mm film, and for good reason. The film was made with multiple layers of photographic emulsion, each one designed to be responsive to a different band in the electromagnetic spectrum. Every time the camera took a 'picture,' it was actually taking many pictures of the same image, each one captured on a different layer of film, each one seeing something a bit different, but each one recording the same image in its own way.

The idea was that, when the satellite returned to earth, the film would be recovered, the layers of film separated and individually processed, and then each image would be reconstructed with any combination of images from the original layers. In this way, pictures could be obtained that had unprecedented clarity, unprecedented depth of field, and – and this was the critical point – completely independent of the weather and sea conditions[2].

When the system had been tested on a high-altitude spy plane, the designers had been delighted to find that its performance exceeded even their most optimistic predictions. When the Chief of the General Staff of the Soviet Armed Forces and the Chairman of the KGB were shown the test results, the project to build a satellite-capable version and get it installed into Kosmos 954 had been conceived and authorized the very same day.

This was its first space trial, and as the satellite continued on with its official secret mission, Apyr was conducting its own, doubly-secret mission.

"Click… click… click," said Apyr.

Somewhat ironically, the experimental radar system performed flawlessly and, indeed, Apyr was performing flawlessly. The satellite itself, however, was not completely under control. What began as a slight wobble, which ground control's corrective-action signals was making worse rather than better, became a not-so-slight wobble.

Kosmos 954 was beginning to wander off-course and, in faithful adherence to Murphy's Law[3], the situation soon became worse…

January 24, 1978
NORAD Cheyenne Mountain Command Centre,
Colorado Springs, Colorado, USA.

In a steel building located beneath more than a thousand feet of solid granite, Captain Dan Trask, RCAF, sat reclined in his heavy, government-style armchair, at his station in the Combat Operations Centre (COC) – the nerve centre of the North American Air Defense[4] (NORAD) Command. He was trying to stay awake.

Captain Trask looked up at the big clock on the wall. It read 00:40, meaning 40 minutes past midnight, in the civilian world. He sighed. The twelve-hour shifts were killers, and the graveyard shift from 8 pm until 8 am the next day was the worst, he reflected, and not for the first time. The unnatural hours between about 01:00 and 05:00 were the quietest and therefore the hardest. Later, the trans-Atlantic and trans-Pacific airliners would begin to cross into North American airspace and there would be something for his colleagues to watch, but for now the only thing keeping him awake was coffee and lots of it.

Captain Trask's station was in the Space Defense Centre (SDC), but there were others, arranged in tiers and each staffed by specialists of different kinds. The overall appearance was somewhat like the Mission Operation Control Room, for Gemini and Apollo rocket flights, at the Johnson Space Center in Houston, Texas. The room and its tiers of stations was dominated by a large map screen, which had a Mercator projection[5] of North America on which would be displayed the symbols and tracks objects in flight. When there was something to track, that is.

Looking around the room, his colleagues were sitting quietly at their stations. *A bunch of zombies we are*, he thought to himself, *too bad nothing interesting ever happens around here.* That was his last thought before he fell into a light doze in his chair.

Ring, ring … ring, ring, … ring, ring.

The sharp rings, and a flashing light on the panel in front of him, caused his head to snap up and his mind to accelerate back up to consciousness. Adrenalin flowing, he brought his body up from its reclining position. There were several handsets mounted at his station. He leaned forward and picked up the one with the flashing light.

"Duty Officer, Space Defense Centre, Captain Trask speaking," he said.

"This is AMOS calling. We've got a hot one for you." AMOS is an acronym for the U.S. Air Force Maui Optical System[6], which comprises a sophisticated, 1.2 m twin-telescopic-camera station located 10,000 feet up on Mount Haleakala, on the Hawaiian island of Maui. The NORAD centre had many sources of information, from the networks of ground-based radar stations that included the distant early warning (DEW) line across the northern rim of the continent, to airborne surveillance systems, satellites, and telescopes.

"What have you got?"

"Something coming at you. It's entering the atmosphere with a strong heat signature. We're sending you the coordinates now."

"Thank you. SDC out."

Reaching for another phone, Captain Trask next called the command duty officer (CDO) for the Combat Operations Centre, which on this shift was a Lieutenant-Colonel from the USAF. "Sir, the telescope on Maui has detected a sizeable object on a trajectory toward the Queen Charlotte Islands is glowing with heat as it enters the atmosphere."

"Anything from SPACETRACK, NAVSPASUR, or ADC?" asked the CDO. These were components of the Space Detection and Tracking System (SPADATS), a global system of radar, radio, and optical sensors that attempts to track all human-made objects in space. SPACETRACK was run by the U.S. Air Force, NAVSPASUR by the U.S. Navy, and ADC (Air Defence Command) by the Canadian Armed Forces.

"Computers are trying to match the coordinates now sir. One moment, please." Data from the global sensor network was all fed into the system's computers in Dahlgren, Virginia, then relayed to Captain Trask's Space Defense Centre station, among others. From there, the Cheyenne Mountain's own computers assessed the data and produced orbital correlations and predictions. Despite the massive amounts of data flowing in, the computers didn't take long.

"Got it, sir, it's number 10361, Soviet satellite: Kosmos 954[7]. We've been watching it wobble for the past two months, and it looks like it's now completely out of control and heating up on re-entry."

"Is it a nuke?"

"Yes, sir. We've been watching this one for a while. The tracking models predicted it wouldn't be coming down until April, but its orbit has been increasingly unstable. Whatever went wrong with it has gotten worse."

The CDO threw a switch on his panel, and the data from Trask's station was immediately copied to a huge, theater-like screen, so everyone in the Combat Operations Centre could see a symbol representing the satellite and coloured lines showing its projected flight zone, all laid over a map showing North America, its surrounding oceans, Greenland, Iceland, and even parts of Siberia.

"Any signs of unidentified or hostiles?" This was directed at other colleagues in the room, who were staffing other operations centres. All of the latter reported in the negative, consistent with the main display screen, which showed the positions of Kosmos 954 and a number of other, known satellites, that were orbiting over North America at that particular time.

"OK, just the satellite then. What's the current prediction?"

"Seventy seconds to complete re-entry," said Captain Trask, reading from his computer display screens. "Projected debris falling just south of Inuvik and extending in a northeast direction towards Victoria Island. There's going to be highly radioactive debris falling over pretty huge area. Mostly uninhabited though."

"OK, I'll call CINCNORAD and the Deputy CINCNORAD[8]."

Within 70 seconds, the burning Kosmos 954 began to break apart during its 2060th, and final, revolution around the earth. The re-entry took place over the Northwest Territories. "Could be worse," muttered Captain Trask. He wasn't to know how truly he had spoken.

Two minutes later the satellite exploded and vanished from all radar screens.

It was much worse.

The Daily News

Tuesday, January 24, 1978

Soviet Satellite Out Of Control
Crash Of Atomic Reactor Feared

Laurie Schramm

3 A RUDE AWAKENING

Two hours later.
Ottawa, Ontario, Canada

Ring, ring … ring, ring, … ring, ring.

Arrgh. With blurry vision I looked at the clock on my night table: 5 am. *Too early*, I thought, as I fumbled for the phone.

"Morning, Alex. Sorry to wake you." It was Staff Sergeant Robert Simpson of the Royal Canadian Mounted Police (RCMP) Security Service, my boss.

An early morning call from my boss was unprecedented, causing me to wake up fast. "Hi, Bob. What's up?"

"We need to send you up north, and fast. A Soviet spy satellite is burning up as it re-enters the earth's atmosphere, and it's doing it right now, as we speak."

"How does that affect us?"

"National security. There's something on that satellite that we need to make sure doesn't get into Soviet hands."

"I thought that all modern satellites transmit their data back to earth while they're still in orbit."

"Normally, that's true, but this one is a little different and it has something we need to make sure doesn't fall into the wrong hands."

"OK, then. Isn't this a job for the military?"

"It is, and the military is assembling a "find and retrieve" task force as we speak. But Military Intelligence wants to include an undercover team."

"In its own task force? Why?"

"There are concerns that the military may have been penetrated by Soviet agents."

"You're kidding me!" was my first response. Then, before Bob could answer, "But you're not kidding, are you?"

"I wish I was Alex. Anyway, they're having trouble figuring out who they can trust, they came up with the idea of inserting an agent of their own, and they've asked us to do the same."

"Let me guess …," I responded. All traces of sleepiness had vanished.

"Right. They're sending Captain Harrison in, and they asked for you specifically. The Assistant Commissioner has agreed, on the condition that you're willing to go. Will you do it?"

Will I do it? How many times had I been asked that question?

***

My name is Alexandra Houston. My friends call me Alex.

In the summer of 1974, I'd been 24 years old, and feeling like my career was at a standstill. I'd studied chemistry at university and liked it, but not enough to pursue science as a career. I'd reset my sights on police work next and had joined the Metropolitan Toronto Police force ("Metro"). Although policing seemed like a better fit for me than science, my two years with Metro had mostly comprised routine administrative- and traffic duties. These assignments were important, and needed to be done by somebody, and done well. But for me, they didn't fit the Hollywood vision of policing that I had developed, and I hadn't found them to be very challenging.

They say you should be careful what you wish for.

My life soon changed drastically, beginning with an unexpected meeting. Without explanation, my Captain had sent me to go and see an RCMP officer that wanted to meet me. My reaction to this was apprehension, and I wondered what I could possibly have messed-up so badly that it had caught the notice of our national police force.

That's how I first came to meet Assistant Commissioner George MacLeod. After a lengthy conversation that I belatedly realized was an interview, he told me that he had asked my Captain (his friend) to recommend one of his young officers for a special pilot project he had in mind. He wanted someone who wanted to accomplish things, someone eager and tenacious, someone chomping at the bit to be allowed to do some "real" police work, and... someone female. At this point he had shed his stern "Mountie look," relaxed his entire body, chuckled, and said that my Captain had recommended the "biggest pain in the butt" in his Division - me.

Assistant Commissioner MacLeod had explained that the "Force" had fallen behind the times and that its senior leadership wanted to build a more diverse police force. "We're going to be recruiting immigrants, visible minorities, maybe even people with some kinds of disabilities as well," he said, "But we have to start somewhere, and that somewhere is by engaging women." He wanted to try a first "pilot test" with a woman, but that pilot test had to succeed as it would pave the way for an entire first troop of policewomen that would follow. He had thought of using someone that had already qualified as a policewoman, and simply re-train them in the "RCMP way."

That had brought me up to full attention. "Wait a minute! Do basic training all over again?"

"Yes!" he'd replied, "that's the only way you can possibly succeed. In the old days of the Northwest Mounted Police, a person could get appointed straight into the Force, even as a commissioned officer, if they had the right political connections. No more. Now everyone starts out the same way, as a Constable, and by going through the same basic training. If you want to have any hope of being accepted, much less respected, that's how you have to begin."

So, that's what I'd done. I went through training at the RCMP's Depot Division training centre in Regina, dealt with the good and the bad issues that came with being the first woman to train there, and survived to become the first woman Mountie. I hadn't intended for it to happen, really. The opportunity just came and found me.

After training, or re-training if you like, I'd been posted to Radium City, a small town in northern Saskatchewan that, in its early days, had been a great uranium mining centre. Although my new boss, Corporal Morrison, had told me that nothing interesting ever happened around there, he'd been wrong, and I'd had to rescue him from a mine collapse, run our entire detachment single-handed while he was confined to hospital for six weeks, get rescued by a strange dog from near-death, solve a mystery, and find and catch a murderer[9] – all in only four months!

The dog was named Silver. Investigating a mysterious series of break-ins had led me to some unusual places, including several abandoned uranium mines. In one such mine, I'd fallen through a trap and found myself hanging precariously over the sharp edge of a raise, a kind of vertical mine shaft. Unable to get out and tiring fast, I was saved by the almost magical appearance of what I first took to be a wolf. That gave me quite a scare, but it turned out to be an Alaskan Malamute. His name is Silver. Somehow, he'd sensed that I was in danger, had decided to help, and with his assistance I had been able to climb up and out of the raise. To make a long story short[9], while I'd continued to investigate the case, he had attached himself to me, was eventually given to me, and we'd been close friends ever since.

Sometime later I'd found myself in another surprise meeting with the same Assistant Commissioner MacLeod. Once again, a "coffee meeting" had turned into an interview and, once again, he had something new in mind for me. By this time, he'd become head of the Force's Security Service[10] and, unsurprisingly, he had some ideas he wanted to try out by way of some experimental pilot projects.

"Like me?" I'd asked.

"Exactly," he'd replied. It turned out that he now wanted me to go and work for him in the Security Service. Of course, he could have just ordered me to go, but he wanted me to go willingly, and immerse myself in his new plans.

And then, just like he'd said over a year previously in Toronto, he said: "Will you do it?" and, once again, I'd said, "Yes, Sir."

That had taken me to Ottawa in November of 1975. I'd met

my new supervisor in the Security Service, Staff Sergeant Robert ("Call me Bob") G. Simpson, and been introduced to the shady worlds of spies, counter-espionage, anarchists, and terrorists.

"Surely, we don't have any of those in Canada?" I'd asked. I was wrong.

As a prelude to my first real Security Service assignment, Silver and I were sent to Innisfail, Alberta, to be trained as a police dog and handler team[11]. "If that dog is going to go everywhere with you, then we should get him trained too," Assistant Commissioner MacLeod had announced, on one of his periodic visits. Both Bob and the Assistant Commissioner had been interested in the possibilities presented by the first female 'Mountie,' especially undercover possibilities, and they were also interested in, and seemingly amused by, the notion of me having Silver along as a kind of side-kick, since he looked absolutely nothing like a police dog. That officially brought Silver into the Mounties too, and that's how my best friend became my partner.

By the time we'd had a few more adventures together[12,13,14], there was no doubt in my mind that our destinies were inter-twined.

***

"Will you do it?" Bob had asked me.

I said what I nearly always said: "Yes, Sir!"

"Good for you," was his reply. Then, he rushed on. "We think it's best to re-use your old scientist cover story."

"OK," I said. I had originally trained at Carleton University to become an analytical chemist and had resurrected part of my former life as part of a cover story on a previous case[12].

"I'll contact your old chemistry professor at Carleton and get him to 'hire' you back as a Research Associate, and tell anyone that asks that you were sent out as the university's contribution to the task force. Have you ever seen a Geiger Counter?"

"Sure, I took nuclear and radiochemistry in my third year at Carleton. There was a laboratory component, in which we learned to synthesize and test radioactive compounds. I got to use a Geiger Counter and also a scintillation counter."

"Perfect. In this case, the military will provide all the equipment you'll need."

"But, Bob…"

"Didn't I tell you? The satellite was powered by a nuclear reactor. The task force will be sweeping for radioactive debris and then collecting it up for safe disposal. They have people trained for this, but they have to search such a wide area that they're adding a few civilians to the team: civilians that know something about radiation."

"OK, but that's not all we're searching for, is it?"

"No. You only need to search for radioactive debris to the extent that it maintains your cover story. The real mission is to find and retrieve something else from the satellite… if it survives."

"And that is?"

"I can't tell you over the phone. Captain Harrison will fill you in when you meet him."

"Ah ha. The plot thickens."

"Yes. Now then, there's a C-130 Hercules[15] aircraft from the RCAF's 8 Wing warming up at Canadian Forces Base (CFB) Trenton[16]. It will pick you up at the Ottawa Uplands Airport at 10 am. Go to the government hanger about 9 am, they'll be waiting for you. The military will provide the cold-weather gear when you get up north. A CF-101B Voodoo fighter jet[17] has been sent to pick up Captain Harrison in Halifax. He'll fly out in the back seat and meet you in Yellowknife. That's a staging area. Once you're fitted out, you'll be flown north from there."

"Further north than Yellowknife? Just how far away is the search going to be?"

"The preliminary search area starts in the extreme northwest of the Northwest Territories. My understanding is that the local operations will be run out of Inuvik, which is nearly 1,100 km to the northwest of Yellowknife."

"Well, that's north all right… By the way, what's Don's cover going to be?"

"No idea. He'll have to tell you that himself…" Bob chuckled again. "That young man has more identities than anyone I've ever met before. I don't know how he keeps them all straight."

I thought I was awake, but my tired brain finally caught with what Bob had been telling me. "What about Silver?"

"What about him?" Bob said. He used a neutral tone, but I detected a note of dry humour in his voice.

"Can I bring him with me?"

"He used to be a sled dog, right?"

"Right."

"Well, we're sending you above the Arctic Circle in the coldest part of winter. It gets so cold that the helicopters can't always function, and snowmobiles tend to break down, so they're also preparing for the possibility that they may have to use dog sleds. That makes you and Silver a perfect choice."

"Some day, Bob, I'd like to learn how to be half as devious as you are!"

Bob, *the chess-player* as I thought of him, chuckled once more. "I told the military that you two are a package-deal, and the Admiral was very impressed with the work you and Silver did in the Aleutian Islands last year, so there were no arguments. They'll be ready for you both at the airport."

"OK then, I'll get up and start packing."

"One more thing Alex."

"Yes?"

"Watch your back."

After hanging up the phone, I turned to my partner and friend. "Well Silver, we're off again."

"Grruph?"

"Yes, and we're going to have to watch out for ourselves again."

"Grruph!"

"Right."

I packed an unmarked, civilian-looking version of my tactical uniform, plus a few other things into one duffle bag, and dog food and a few other things for Silver in a second duffle. Before closing them up, I added one more thing to my duffle bag: a small, lockable metal case. If anyone searched my luggage, there were a few things I didn't want found.

***

Silver and I arrived at Ottawa's Uplands Airport 9 am. We were expected, and the big C-130 Hercules aircraft was apparently ready to go, as our duffel bags were promptly whisked way and a crewmember led us straight out across the tarmac and up the big ramp at the rear of the plane.

I was given a short pre-flight briefing that mostly involved getting belted-in to an uncomfortable-looking jump-seat, and rigging a chest-harness for Silver that could be attached to the seatbelt in another jump-seat for him. A member of the aircrew gave me a set of earplugs, suggesting that I might need them. At first, I was skeptical of the need for them but once the plane took off, I quickly realized that his polite suggestion was just straight-out sensible. The noise from the plane's four engines was deafening!

We left Ottawa at 10 am, as scheduled. After a gruelling flight in which it was hard to say which was worse – the noise or the vibration – we finally landed at 2:30 pm, at CFB Edmonton. The aircrew referred to it as Namao[18].

Our stop-over at Namao included refuelling, so there was just enough time to get coffee, a snack, and a brief walk to work some of the vibration out of our bodies before taking off at 3:15 pm for Yellowknife. When we arrived in Yellowknife, at 5:30 pm, Don was there to meet us.

Wearing the uniform of an army captain, with engineering insignia, Don walked up and formally extended his arm to shake hands. "Good to see you again, Alex," he said, his voice neutral but his eyes shining. Clearly, we were to play the role of old colleagues, meeting again after some time had passed.

"Hi Don, good to see you again too," I responded, shaking his hand. It was easy to keep my tone level as I was tired from the long flight.

Silver, however, felt no need for restraint. With two sharp barks, he rushed up to Don, stood up on his hind legs and, with his forepaws on Don's chest proceeded to vigorously lick his face. It was a few moments before Don could disentangle himself from Silver and say, "Let's get your gear and I'll show you to your tent."

When my duffel bags came off the plane, we carried them to a waiting Jeep which had obviously been brought in from somewhere further south: it had a canvas top. As we installed ourselves in the Jeep, Don fired it up and we could immediately hear the roar of the Jeep's fan as both fan and heater had been set to maximum in an attempt to counter the -20° C temperature. "Good thing it's a nice day," muttered Don.

As we drove, I could see that a series of tents was being erected off to one side of the runway and taxi strips, well separated from the airport terminal and other buildings. As we got closer, I could see that a security fence had been erected around the perimeter, complete with patrolling guards. Some of the tents were what I'd expected, smaller ones that were probably for sleeping and larger ones for cooking and eating areas. Other tents, however, were huge.

"What are those for?" I asked, as we drove by.

"Those are heated, thermally-insulated maintenance tents for the helicopters we'll be using. Helicopters need a lot of maintenance at the best of times and, with the extreme cold, they'll be pushed to their limits up here. This weather is nice compared with what we'll see when we get to Inuvik."

The security fence had large, rolling gates that were wide open at the moment, so we drove on through, past several parked Hercules planes and three of the largest helicopters I'd ever seen. They were unusual-looking too, with two huge horizontally-rotating sets of propellers, instead of the one large horizontal set and a small vertically-oriented set mounted on conventional helicopters.

"Chinooks[19]," said Don, seeing my stare. "We'll be using those for the ground search."

Passing the Hercules and Chinook aircraft, and the tents that were in the process of being erected, we turned right and soon came to a cluster of accommodation and mess tents. Pulling up to one of the smaller tents, Don stopped the Jeep. "This'll be your tent for tonight."

As we entered the tent, the first two things I noticed were the sound of a heater valiantly trying to keep up with the cold, just like in the Jeep, and the fact that the tent was made up with two cots.

As I raised a questioning eyebrow, Don explained: "You'll be bunking with another woman. The Americans are sending a physicist to join the team. She'll be joining one of the ground-search teams and operating a hand-held gamma-ray spectrometer, just like you and I will. All we know, so far, is that she's a woman, she's expected in later tonight, and she'll be bunking in here with you. Silver can either sleep in here with you or outside the tent.

Before I could say a word, Don held up a hand and rushed on. "Let's go for a walk and I'll answer as many more of your questions as I can."

Back in the Jeep, Don drove us outside the compound and stopped at an open space between it and the permanent airport buildings. A short walk took us to a small hill that, although quite low, gave us a clear view of the surrounding landscape.

"Welcome to the Barrens[20]," he said. The Barrens, I knew, consist of a relatively treeless plain made slightly more interesting by frequent rock (granite) outcrops and countless streams and lakes. The ground is called permafrost because, even in summer, the earth is frozen below a depth of a couple of inches.

"It looks... peaceful," I offered, looking out over the snow-covered plain.

"It is, really," said Don. "If we were here in summer, when everything isn't completely covered in snow, you'd see a gently rolling plain – not as flat as the prairies of Saskatchewan and Alberta - covered with grasses, moss, and lichen. There aren't a lot of people up here, but there are lots of caribou, muskox, foxes, and bears. When we're up flying around, you'll probably see lots of caribou and muskox."

"So, what's really going on?"

"OK. Sorry for all the secrecy but our bosses are really worried. First of all, I'm posing as an engineer from an Engineer Support Regiment based in Gagetown."

This, I knew, was in New Brunswick. "You picked Gagetown because it's so far away, hoping no one will suspect you?"

"That's the idea. You, as you know, are a chemist from Carleton University, just like when we were in Nova Scotia[12] together, except this time its your nuclear and radiochemistry training that qualifies you."

"And..."

"Maybe I should start at the beginning," said Don, pausing to marshal his thoughts. "Apparently, the Soviets launched a radar ocean reconnaissance satellite - *Upravlenniye Sputnik Aktivny* - last September. It's called Kosmos 954. At first, it followed a typical orbit, but by November, U.S. intelligence noticed that something was going wrong. It had begun to wobble, and then its orbit became somewhat erratic."

"Bob said it was a spy satellite."

"That's right. It used a powerful, side-looking radar to monitor the movements of large U.S. warships, like aircraft carriers."

"They can use radar to identify ships from space?"

"Sometimes... we think. No one in the west has actually seen one up close, but U.S. Intelligence estimates that they have a high probability of detecting aircraft carriers in good weather and moderate seas, and a reasonable probably of detecting destroyers and frigates in excellent weather and calm seas. Apparently, they can't detect anything in rainstorms or high seas."

"OK, so a spy satellite has fallen out of orbit and burned-up on re-entry with the debris being scattered over the Northwest Territories. Right?"

"Right."

"So why is there such a big search for the debris? And why by the military? And what are Silver and I doing here?"

"Two reasons. The official reason is that the satellite was powered by enriched uranium in a 3 kW nuclear reactor. Normally the reactor would have been ejected into a disposal, or 'cemetery' orbit at an altitude of about 1,000 km. Then, all the short- and medium-life isotopes would decay - iodine-131, strontium-90, and cesium-137 - before the reactor falls to earth 500 to 600 years later. Of course, even then it would still have the unused, enriched uranium fuel in it. The uranium lasts almost forever…"

"Right, uranium-235 has a half-life of over 700 million years," I interjected.

"How do you know that?"

"I studied nuclear- and radiochemistry in university," I explained. "But my memory isn't that good. I looked it up before going to the airport."

"Right," said Don, sounding amused. "Anyway, with the reactor ejected, the idea was that the rest of the satellite would burn-up on re-entry into the earth's atmosphere, and everything would be more or less OK."

"But something went wrong?" I prompted.

"Probably a few things went wrong. The Soviets lost control of the satellite, it began to wobble and veer off course, then it started coming down, and it failed to eject the reactor before coming in."

"How big is – was – this thing?"

"U.S. Intelligence thinks that the Buk reactor weighed 130 kg, and the entire satellite may have weighed close to 400 kg."

"Wow, that's huge! And the fuel?"

"No one seems to know for sure, but it's estimated that the reactor core contained 30 to 50 kg of enriched uranium fuel. The Soviets aren't saying much, but they claim that the reactor was only fueled with non-enriched uranium, that there is no risk of the reactor going critical or of any other risk of explosion and that, in any case, the core was ejected into cemetery orbit before the satellite re-entered the atmosphere. They do admit that there is a risk that some fragments may have fallen to Earth, but nothing serious."

"How much of that do you believe?"

"Not much. We already know that the satellite exploded on re-entry, and no one is much inclined to believe the rest."

"Ok," I said trying to take it all in. "The reactor core would have been heavily shielded with metal. Would it have survived intact?"

"No one seems to know. That's why it was supposed to have been ejected. Some or all of the reactor, or the core, may have broken up along the way."

"So, some of the debris is probably highly radioactive."

"Right."

"Wow." Don didn't continue right away, so I prompted him: "What's the other reason?"

"Mmmm?"

"When you started explaining all this, you said there were two reasons we're here."

"Your memory isn't bad at all," Don observed.

I just looked at him and raised an eyebrow.

"I was going to get to that eventually. Let's walk a bit."

Trying make it look like we were just chatting while I took Silver for a walk, we slowly trudged through the snow across the empty field as Don continued the story.

"There was something else on that satellite: a new kind of camera with high power lenses and a powered drive mechanism for the film."

"A motor-drive," I said. "Right, I have one for my Nikon 35 mm camera. What's so special about that?"

"It's not the power drive, it's the lens and the film. The lens involves something called 'catadioptric optics' which, to ordinary people like you and me means it's made with a combination of mirrors and lenses. Apparently, this enables a really long focal length plus the ability to focus different kinds of light, including infra-red and ultra-violet. In addition to a new kind of lens, we think that they were testing some new kind of film that allows them to simultaneously create multiple images of a single view, each one based on a different kind of light: infra-red, visible, ultra-violet – the whole spectrum. I don't understand how it all works, but the idea is to be able to take high-resolution pictures through any kind of weather: clouds, rain, fog, even snow."

"OK. Sounds pretty neat, actually. What's the big deal?"

"Normally, the Soviets use satellite-mounted cameras to locate and monitor ballistic missile launching sites in the U.S., but after all these years they pretty much know where they all are now anyway. The concern is that when the satellite went off course, its camera may have recorded something we really didn't want them to see…"

"Like what?"

"Like two exploration drilling rigs that were being set up in the high arctic. It's a Canadian-U.S. effort to drill deep, looking for oil and natural gas. Ever since the 1973 energy crisis, both countries – but especially the U.S. - have been looking for new oil resources that could help achieve energy independence."

"OK, that sounds normal."

"Well, what isn't normal is that those drilling rigs are located in disputed territory in the Arctic. They were going to be disguised, so that any satellites or aircraft that happened to fly over them wouldn't notice anything unusual, but when Kosmos 954 went off course, it happened to fly over them just when things were being set-up. The camouflage wasn't in place yet, so everything was exposed."

"Isn't it kind of weird for spy agencies to be interested in things like petroleum?"

"Well, it's unusual, but we've seen this kind of thing happen a few times in recent years. My bosses think that some countries are instructing their foreign intelligence services to focus less on things military and more on things that could help them grow their economies. In this case, if valuable petroleum or mineral resources are discovered in disputed territory, and if only one side knows about them, then they'll be able to focus their negotiating efforts. They could bargain harder for some territories, or offer to trade areas they know are less valuable for ones that are more valuable. Or, if push comes to shove, they might just take the risk of sending in troops to annex a disputed territory and then defy the rest of the world to do anything about it."

"Would the Soviets do that?"

"They might, if the stakes were high enough. They'd hardly be the first country to try something like that. Remember how the English, French, and Spanish came over and carved up North America between them?"

"Yes, but that's ancient history."

"Well, history repeats itself I guess."

"OK then, who knows about this camera thing?"

"In this place? Just you and me for now. Even the search commander hasn't been told. As far as anyone here knows, you and I are just technical specialists that were sent in to use gamma-ray spectrometers as part of the searches. There'll be three planes doing high altitude searches for radioactivity, then three helicopters going out with teams to check the 'hits' on the ground. You'll go with one, I'll go with another."

"What about the third team?"

"The Americans are sending someone up to join us, they'll go with team three."

"Who'll that be?"

"I don't know. The woman that will be bunking with you. She's a physicist and knows how to use a gamma-ray spectrometer. When someone like that shows up, we'll know who it is."

As we walked around, out in the middle of nowhere, Don explained how the search was going to work. Basically, people and equipment were being flown in, by Hercules aircraft, from Nuclear Accident Support Teams[21] (NAST) at RCAF bases across Canada, and the arctic clothing and tents, and so on, was already available from the airbase at Namao.

"There's heavy communications traffic along the diplomatic channels, of course," Don added. The U.S. has offered any necessary assistance. The U.S. Air Force is sending up a U-2[22] to survey at high altitude for any traces of uranium or its fission products, but they think that everything from the satellite has probably already fallen to Earth. Meanwhile, all of the other NATO countries are being kept informed of the situation."

Don explained that some of the equipment and supplies would be held in readiness at Namao and the rest ferried up to Yellowknife, where we were, then on to the temporary base being set up at Inuvik.

Once that was done, three Hercules aircraft would be made available for aerial search patterns. If no nuclear material from Kosmos was detected at high altitude by the U-2 aircraft, then a lower-altitude search would be conducted by the Hercules aircraft, each of them equipped with a full-size gamma-ray spectrometer – the latest experimental model that had been developed by the Geological Survey of Canada for aerial exploration for uranium deposits. The Geological Survey was sending specialists to run the big gamma-ray spectrometers, and Don, the American woman, and I would simply go on the first flight to learn how the search was being carried out, and how any 'hits' were being detected and recorded. If the reactor core was still intact, it should be relatively easy to detect from the aircraft.

Once the first Hercules search patterns had been flown, teams would then have to be sent out to investigate the 'hits' and identify and secure any radioactive materials that were found. This would be done with three of the RCAF's big, twin-bladed Chinook helicopters, each of which would carry a scientist with a hand-held gamma-ray spectrometer (that was us), a scientist from the Atomic Energy Control Board of Canada (AECB) to handle the lead-lined containers for the debris, plus a snowmobile and a dog-sled team, and two survivalists – one from the Army and a local resident.

"Survivalists?" At this point, I'd interrupted Don in his explanations.

"Yes," he explained. "We're going out into some of the harshest and most unforgiving territory in Canada and we're doing it in the coldest part of winter. We can't rely on snowmobiles and we can't predict how well the helicopters will perform, so we'll do what the locals do.

"No local hunter would take a chance out in the tundra with only a snowmobile. Even snowmobile-borne hunters that are great mechanics usually travel in company with another hunter and a dog team. They can so easily have a mechanical breakdown, get hit by a huge whiteout-storm, run out of fuel, or run out of food – or all of those at the same time. The dog team won't break down, the dog sled is easily reparable, and if the worst happens the dogs can provide food."

"Really? Eat the dogs? No!"

"Well, yes. You know very well that desperate people have even been known to resort to cannibalism, even in Canada[23]."

"Don, let's be really clear about this right now. No one's going to eat Silver while I'm alive!"

"I know, I know... Look, we're going to be working pre-planned search grids, and carry radios, Arctic survival gear, and even radar reflectors so that if anything happens to one team the other two teams will immediately switch to search-and-rescue mode, with every other asset in Canada made available to us, on a priority-one basis, to be shuttled up here via Edmonton. If a team gets lost or storm-bound they'll be rescued within 24 hours, even in the worst conditions. We'll also have the military and local survivalists, who know how to survive in these conditions."

"Ok then, just so we're clear."

"I don't mean there aren't any risks Alex. It's been judged too risky to use snowmobiles, for example. But we've prepared for every contingency we can... Well, except for one I guess...."

"What's that?"

I was a bit shocked to see that, at his point, Don actually paused and looked around, as if to be absolutely sure no one could see or hear us.

"Our bosses are worried that the Soviets may have infiltrated agents into the search teams."

"My boss, Bob, mentioned that. But how... and why?" Then I answered one of my own questions: "OK, I can guess why: they'll want to make sure that if we find this secret fancy camera of theirs, they can grab it away from us."

"Or destroy it, right. As to the 'how,' I don't know, it's not my area of expertise. All I know is that there's this huge cat-and-mouse game going on around the world, where every country seems to be trying to get secret agents embedded into the military and intelligence agencies of every other country. It's like the world's gone crazy. Maybe it was always this way, and I just never realized it before, I don't know. Anyway, its possible that the Soviets have penetrated our operation before it was ever launched. That's part of the reason that you and I are going to be attached to two of the helicopter/ground teams."

"What about the third team?"

"I don't know. I guess our bosses are hoping two of us will be enough."

"So, our real mission is to find and recover the camera while watching out for a Soviet spy among us."

"Right."

"Oh, great. I suddenly feel like my back is exposed."

"Keep thinking that way, it could keep you alive. I'm sorry,

Alex. I even asked that you not be assigned to this mission..."

"What? You don't think I can handle it?" I could feel the pitch of my voice rise, and even feel the roots of my red hair stiffen. In the time we known each other, Don had more than once accused me of having a fiery temper.

"Easy Alex. Of course not... it's just that... well..."

"Come on Don, out with it. We've been through enough together by now that you can just tell me straight-up."

I happened to be looking into Don's eyes when I said this and I was surprised to see his eyes widen, then narrow, then soften in rapid sequence.

"All right. You win. I don't want you to be here. I don't want you to get hurt. I've... fallen in love with you."

"Oh, Don," I felt my own eyes softening and started laughing. "And this..." I opened my arms and swept them around. "You decided this was the best time and place to tell me?" I leaned forward to reach out for him but he surprised me by taking a step back.

"Not here, we can't risk anyone seeing us... I'm sorry, Alex, I was going to tell you at the end of our last mission, but then they hustled me onto that helicopter in Victoria and I didn't get a chance. Then I couldn't call you because I couldn't get a secure phone line and I didn't want to tell you by phone anyway. Then, as soon as that mission ended, I was sent up here.... Anyway, on this mission, we have to simply be colleagues from different organizations that happen to have met before – let's call it SCUBA diving in Nova Scotia where we met in real life. Nothing else. Nothing... deeper. It's for your own safety – both of ours. This mission could turn to life and death in an instant. Anyway... now you know the worst."

The worst and the best. I thought about it for a moment. It was left-brain time. I mentally wound my emotions down and tucked them away in a corner of my mind – for now, anyway. As I did, I glanced over at Silver, who was sitting on his haunches watching us both intently. He looked somehow... amused... Silver never missed much. Then, I turned back to look at Don.

"Sorry. You're right of course, it's just that this is all coming a bit fast. I appreciate your concern – thank you, by the way – but this is my job too, and I want to do it. Besides, if you're going to go on with this then I'd rather be here with you than off in an office somewhere not knowing what's going on."

Don sighed, then straightened up, looked around the cold, barren landscape, took a deep breath and said: "I knew you'd come no matter what, and I'm glad you're here, but I'd have prevented it if I could have."

"I know, Don. Thanks."

"I guess we should be getting back. You know the deep stuff now. We'll review all the search protocols and meet the rest of the teams once the American woman shows up and we have the dog teams and guides, and the rest of the equipment in place."

With that, he started walking back towards camp.

I let him go about three paces before calling out softly: "Don."

He turned.

"I love you too."

"Grruph!" said Silver.

"I hate this," said Don.

"We'll survive it, and we'll have a long talk when it's all over. OK?"

"OK," he smiled and started walking again.

"Come on Silver," let's go find some warmth and some food.

"Grruph!" said Silver.

As the three of us walked back to camp. I reviewed everything Don had told me. I was afraid. Don had described a multi-layered disaster scenario and it scared the hell out of me. But... deep down, I felt really happy. Here we were in the Barrens, not all that far from the Arctic Circle, deep into winter, about to go looking for potentially lethal radioactive debris from a nuclear-powered satellite, all the while watching our backs for fear of Soviet secret agents, and all I felt was happy. I didn't know whether to laugh or cry, and my next thought was of an old Hollywood Movie.

"Don... Silver!" I called out. Both of them turned to face me.

"I think this is the beginning of a beautiful – three-way - friendship!"

Don started chuckling, and I swear that, in Silver's eyes, I could see him chuckling too.

4 ORGANIZING

When we reached the Jeep, Don drove us for a quick look around downtown Yellowknife. As we were driving back to the airport, we saw a truly massive, four-engine cargo jet descending for a landing. As it passed over us, I could see that it was painted military grey and carried U.S. Air Force markings.

"C-141 Starlifter," said Don, "The Americans are loaning us some of the equipment and personnel we'll need. I'll bet that our physicist is on that plane too."

"Let's go see," I suggested.

By the time we drove onto the airport site and over to the military camp, the huge Starlifter had landed and was being guided to a spot near where the Hercules aircraft were parked. What a sight! When seen up close, it was hard to believe that any of these monstrous planes could lift into the air and fly.

Once the Starlifter was in place, its huge back doors opened up, almost gull-wing style, and a series of tractors lined up to begin pulling things out of the back. Meanwhile, a personnel door opened up near the front of the plane. Unlike large commercial aircraft, the Starlifter had forward and aft doors set low in the fuselage so that, once opened an internally-mounted set of stairs could be extended out and down to the ground. Once this was done, a crew member stepped out to make sure everything was in order. Satisfied, the crew member ducked back inside the plane and several men and women carrying coats, backpacks and duffle bags disembarked.

At the end of the line was a woman I recognized. I gave Don a gentle elbow in the ribs. When he turned to me in surprise I nodded meaningfully towards the woman at the rear of the line.

"The plot thickens," I murmured.

"Interesting," was all he said.

As Don, Silver, and I walked closer to the plane, the woman at the end of the line spotted us, broke away from the column of other passengers, and headed our way. Coming right up to us, she dropped her gear on the tarmac, put out her hand to shake, and said "Hi! We've never met before, but my name's Vivian Rule. I'm a physicist with the U.S. Geological Survey.

For appearances sake, we introduced ourselves all around and walked back to the Jeep. Silver and I crawled into the back so Vivian could sit in the front-passenger seat. As Don started the Jeep moving, I leaned forward over the bags that had been crammed into the back with us and said: "Vivian! It's great to see you again[14]. I didn't realize that the FBI's in on this too?"

"Oh yes, the Bureau was probably called at about the same time as the RCMP[24]. When I was called in for a briefing with our Deputy Director, everything had already been set-up with Don's Admiral and your Assistant Commissioner. He said a third agent was needed, and they seem to have decided that we three make a good team."

"Grruph?"

"Sorry Silver, we **four** make a good team, but I don't think anyone else would believe how much of a team member you really are."

"Grruph!"

"Anyway, I was asked whether I was willing to volunteer and here I am."

"Well I'm glad you're here Vivian. This could turn out to be a tougher assignment than our last one."

"That's a scary thought," she said, "we were both lucky to come out of that one alive."

It was difficult to talk in the Jeep as a commercial jetliner was taxiing past us, so rather than trying to yell over the noise I sat back in my seat to wait for a better time.

***

Vivian was brunette, fairly tall, slender, and had wonderful, large brown eyes. Her manner usually seemed, not so much serious as very aware and intent. The kind of person that doesn't miss much, had been my first impression when meeting her for the first time, which I realized with a shock had only been five months earlier. Our backgrounds were stunningly similar. A couple of years older than me, Vivian had been part of a pilot project to introduce women into the FBI. Whereas I had been alone in the RCMP's first such project, Vivian had been one of two women selected to become the first female FBI agents. Just like with the RCMP, the FBI had been quick to appreciate the unusual potential for a woman to serve in an undercover role, at least until the public became used to the idea of women agents. Five months earlier we had been matched up when an investigation Don and I were conducting required us to be able to work on both sides of the Canada-U.S. border. That had led to several brushes with near-death for Vivian and I, and we had discovered - the hard way — that we worked well together. Apparently, our bosses had noticed too.

As our Jeep trundled its way towards our tent, Silver had been watching my face intently, and looked at me with that, *I like her too* expression his face that I'd come to know so well. I just leaned over, put my arms around his neck, and sighed. Somehow, with Silver, Don, and Vivian around, I began to feel a bit less afraid.

I shouldn't have.

***

It was getting late by the time we'd stowed Vivian's gear in our tent. Don explained that the mess tent wasn't yet set up to serve much more than coffee and snacks, so we left Silver in the tent and drove into town to have dinner at the Explorer Hotel.

Over dinner, we kept our conversation to topics that were aligned with our cover stories, but that gave us lots to talk about.

"Isn't the business with the satellite crashing and the possibility of radiation supposed to be secret?" I'd asked.

"Yes," said Don, chuckling, "but you'll be hard pressed to find anyone in Yellowknife that doesn't know about the search.

"You can't bring a mass of people and aircraft and equipment into a small town without people getting nosy and rumours spreading, and even though Yellowknife is the capital of the Northwest Territories, it's still a small town in most ways.

"Just before you landed, Alex, the editor of the local newspaper, the *Yellowknifer*, approached me in town and told me that several townspeople had seen a flaming light in the sky last night, heading northeast. Some thought it was a meteorite, others thought it might be an aircraft on fire, others thought it might be a spaceship landing. They described it as a bright red, flaming object with a tail of bright lights that reminded them of fireworks. After that, they all went to bed, but by mid-day today there was a constant influx of military cargo aircraft, then the helicopters, then a big military camp gets set up at the airport." At this point the editor looked me straight in the eyes and said, "Now then, soldier, you're not going to try to pretend that nothing's going on, or that it's only an exercise, are you?"

"What did you tell him?" I asked.

"I told him that I was only an engineer, and that all I knew was that we were going to be sent out to search for something. He nodded his head, as if that was obvious, and then dropped the next bombshell on me.

"What if I was to tell you," he went on, "that I got a phone call this morning from an American reporter asking if a Russian satellite had come down near here. Then at lunchtime, I got a call from the BBC in London, asking whether a satellite had crashed here and weren't we worried about nuclear fallout?

"I just stuck to my story about being an uninformed engineer sent to do a job that hadn't been explained to me yet, but what the hell, it's only been eight hours and the town already knows almost as much as I do about the whole thing!

"Also, it sounds like things are going to get worse. According to the editor, a horde of international news types are likely to descend on us at some point, although if that happens the Air Force will send some kind of liaison officer up to deal with them. The government doesn't want a *War of the Worlds*-type panic scenario[25] on their hands."

I didn't know whether to be amused or horrified, but Vivian immediately started chuckling. "Well, it seems like we can discuss the technical stuff pretty openly then."

So, that's what we did over dinner. Don opened a case he'd

brought with him and handed out printed descriptions of the large gamma-ray spectrometers that would be flown in the Hercules aircraft, and the manuals for the hand-held units that we would be using on the ground. These, we'd be able to study the next day.

After dinner, we were all pretty tired so Don drove us back to camp, showed us where his tent was, and then dropped Vivian and I off at ours. I thought I'd be too wound-up to be able to sleep, but having spent almost the full day flying in noisy, vibrating aircraft my body had other ideas and, with Silver curled up against the back of my legs, I dropped off into a deep sleep almost immediately.

***

January 25, 1978
Day 2

When we rose in the morning, it was still pitch black. Yellowknife only gets about six and a half hours of daylight in late January, so sunrise wouldn't be until 09:30 and then it would begin to set again by 4 pm in the afternoon. The good news, was that the army had worked late into the night to get the mess tent into full operation so we were able to meet Don there for breakfast.

I suppose I shouldn't have been surprised by the reception Silver received, but I was. Far from being upset by Silver's presence with me, or banning him from the mess tent – which I half expected them to do - the cooks seemed to welcome Silver as an interesting change to their routine and they fussed over him outrageously. When I mentioned that he'd be serving as one of our sled dogs when the search got underway, they simply nodded understandingly and served him a good-sized plate of eggs, bacon, sausages, and toast.

I'd seen something like this happen the year before, when Silver and I had found ourselves spending the night on a Canadian destroyer off the B.C. coast. The navy cooks had been just as flexible and accommodating – and interested – in Silver, and now we were finding that the army cooks were cut from the same cloth. I wondered whether it was some kind of men-love-big-dogs thing or the professionalism of our military people, and suspected that it was a combination of the two. In any case, Silver looked up at me with his penetrating blue-grey eyes and sent me a mental image of sheer contentment, then focused his attention on the feast in front of him. Just like with the navy, that Silver's food vanished so promptly, was taken by the cooks as a huge compliment. He certainly ate more than I did!

After breakfast, we took a stroll around the camp, which by now had a security-perimeter-fence and MP guards stationed at large rolling gates. Another large tent – actually it was several large tents connected together – that had sprung up overnight was already full of supplies.

Here, in one corner of the tent, we were issued our hand-held gamma-ray spectrometers, which we would keep with us at almost all times over the next several days. Another corner of the tent was fitted out with tables and chairs, and it was there that Vivian and I were issued Arctic clothing. Each of us had arrived with nondescript tactical clothes and winter coats and boots, and I had brought with me two sets of polypropylene long-underwear – tops and bottoms – which were the latest thing in functional but lightweight and comfortable winter underwear. I'd used them while winter camping with friends and found them to be fantastically better than the older cotton type.

The military-issue Arctic clothing began bottom up, with large, white-nylon mukluks. These were basically large outer boots with inner, fur-lined booties. Next, came Army-green quilted pants and parka, a green wool cap, and a pair of large, white, padded mittens connected by a string.

"Idiot mitts!" I exclaimed involuntarily. "That's what everyone called them in Ontario, when we were kids. The string was a mother's way of reducing the number of winter mitts her kids lost. The string would go inside and up one parka sleeve, behind a kid's back, then down and out the other sleeve. When they weren't being worn the mitts would hang down below a kid's hands."

Vivian had never seen such things before, but Don had. "That's what we called them too," agreed Don, "but in this case it's a lot more serious. Losing mitts could mean losing hands to frostbite, but the mitts are so bulky that you'll find you're constantly having to take them off to do anything dextrous – hence the string."

The Army Quartermaster Sergeant that was issuing us the clothes insisted that we try them on to make sure that they fit properly. He started with me.

"I gather that I'm not making a fashion statement?" I asked, in response to Don's laughter once I had put all the layers on.

"With all that padding and the fur-lined hood, you look like an abominable snow woman[26]," he said, still chuckling.

"Don't listen to him ma'am," said the Sergeant, "this suit will protect you down to -50° Celsius, that's -58° Fahrenheit for our American friends," he said looking at Vivian and having correctly interpreted her accent.

"When we get back to our tents, I'll give each of you a pair of silk gloves that I brought to wear inside the mitts," said Don, more serious now.

"That's a good addition," agreed the Sergeant, "There's a huge risk of frostbite out there, so try not to expose your skin to the cold at all when you're out in the field. I'll give you some wool gloves that you can wear under the mitts. If you need to do something requiring dexterity, do it with just the gloves on – not with bare skin. The Captain's silk gloves will be even better, but take the wool ones too so you have a spare in case you lose a glove out there."

Thanking the Sergeant, we left, with Vivian and I each carrying two large duffel bags that our gear had been packed into, and Don carrying the three hand-held spectrometers and a case of extra batteries for them.

I'd naïvely expected that we'd dump all the new gear in our tent and have time for another look around Yellowknife, but it wasn't to be. Instead, we gathered up all of our gear and delivered it to a C-130 Hercules for loading. It took a while for them to fully load the plane with other people and supplies, and then we were in the air again, flying northwest to Inuvik.

It took us about two and a half hours to fly the 1,100 km northwest to Inuvik. As we did, we crossed the Arctic Circle, marking the first time I'd been this far north. For most of the flight there was nothing to see, but as we made a slow descent into Inuvik the sky cleared and I had a good view of the gently rolling tundra. As I continued to gaze out my window and take in the quiet beauty of the area, I saw several caribou making their way across a frozen lake. I could see that it was difficult for them, as they had to contend with deep snow, requiring them to periodically lunge up and forward, like a runner running hurdles. *It must be exhausting for them*, I thought, watching in fascination and wondering how anything could survive in these conditions. Eventually, they found a stretch they could walk on - either the snow cover had become thinner, or the snow crust was finally strong enough to support their weight. This made me feel a bit better.

Soon, the caribou were out of sight and the plane banked and roared downward to make a solid-feeling landing at Inuvik's small airport.

We had arrived.

RCAF C-130 Hercules

5 OPERATION ARCTIC CIRCLE

Inuvik is in far northern part of Canada's Northwest Territories, it is about 200 km north of the Arctic Circle, about 1,100 km north-northwest of Yellowknife, the territorial capital, and about 1,960 km northwest of Edmonton, Alberta.

We flew there in a C-130 Hercules, and I was surprised to learn that Inuvik had a long enough runway for such a giant aircraft. Don explained, however, that there was a DEW Line[27] radar station and a Navy signals-intercept facility[28] nearby, so the runway had been made long enough to accommodate cargo aircraft. "Besides," Don added, "the C-130 was designed to be able to take-off and land on the shortest possible runways – with a normal load it needs about 5,000 feet."

"How long is the Inuvik runway?" I'd asked.

One of the air-crew had overheard me on the on-board intercom to which we were all connected, and he jumped-in with more information. "The Captain is right ma'am. The Inuvik runway is 6,000 feet long, and with our current loading we need 5,000 feet, so we have room to spare. If we were fully loaded, we'd weigh 155,000 pounds, and at that weight we'd need 6,300 feet. Since the runway isn't quite that long, all the flights up here will be at less than our maximum loading."

This time, when our bags had been off-loaded from the plane, there was an Army Corporal with a 15-passenger van waiting for us. This was a lot less cramped, and much warmer, than the Jeep we been driven around in at the Yellowknife camp, and we gratefully loaded ourselves in. The temperature was now -20° C, so no one stayed outside any longer than they had too, although I noticed that Silver seemed perfectly comfortable.

Just like I'd seen on arrival in Yellowknife, here too a series of tents was being erected off to one side of the airstrip, well separated from the small airport terminal and other buildings. This too, had a security fence around its perimeter, with patrolling guards. Now that I knew what to look for, I could easily distinguish the maintenance, mess, and accommodation tents. It was a busy scene. As the Hercules plane that had brought us in was being unloaded, we could hear the roar of another one taking off while another one, in the air, was clearly circling as it waited for a landing window. On the ground, pallets loaded with crates secured with cargo netting were everywhere.

Off to one side, a Hercules was being loaded with some very bulky looking equipment. I found out later that this was the first of the large, airborne gamma-ray spectrometers being loaded for installation.

Pulling up to two of the smaller tents, the Corporal indicated the one that Vivian and I would be using, and the one for Don, and then helped us with our duffel bags. As we were carrying our bags to the tents, we could hear the thumping sound of a helicopter approaching.

Stopping to listen and look, I couldn't at first see the helicopter. After a minute or two, I discovered why. It wasn't one helicopter but three. Three of the huge Chinook helicopters, flying in formation, approached the landing strip then one-by-one flew the length of the strip and landed in front of the huge maintenance tents. It was an amazing sight.

"Those are the Chinooks for the ground search," confirmed Don. "We'll be riding in those the day after tomorrow."

Entering the tent, we were once again greeted by the sound of a propane heater valiantly trying to keep up with the cold, and once again the tent was made-up with two cots.

"I overheard someone refer to these as '10-Man Arctic Bell' tents," I said, "and I'm trying to imagine how you'd fit ten large adults into one of these."

"Cozy," was all Vivian said, with two cots, a low stove and chimney arrangement, and a place for Silver to curl-up, there was still room for one person to stand-up straight near the door, and not much else.

This was confirmed as Don said "Knock, knock" and entered.

"I brought this for Silver to curl-up on," he said, arranging an arctic sleeping bag on the floor by my cot. With that in place, there was just enough room for him to sit on the floor for a visit with us.

He explained that a few more people were expected to arrive in the next hour or two, so we'd have time to get a drive into town and sight-see a bit. Then, there'd be a mid-afternoon briefing with the Commanding Officer (CO), then dinner, a free evening, and the next day we'd take a ride on a C-130 Hercules and watch the first test of one of the airborne gamma-ray spectrometers.

So, while Don went off to confer with his military colleagues, the same Corporal drove us into town, where Vivian and I took Silver for a walk around. One of the first buildings we came to was a cultural centre and, leaving Silver to wait outside, we went in. It was a modest-size building, and the inside looked like part museum and part library.

"Oh, my," said Vivian as we entered.

There was no mistaking what had caught her attention. Just inside the doorway was a stuffed polar bear, standing on its hind legs with its front legs up and its teeth bared. It must have been close to nine feet.

Vivian and were just standing there, looking up at the bear's expression when we heard a voice behind us.

"Welcome to Inuvik! From the look of your parkas, you must have come in on that big Air Force plane that just landed."

"We did," I answered. "My name is Alex and this is Vivian."

"Danny Wolki," he replied, shaking our hands. "Are you part of the search for the big meteorite?"

"You know about that already?" asked Vivian.

"It's all over town. I actually saw it streak across the sky two nights ago. It looked like a comet to me. Like a ball of fire with a tail. Yesterday, the rumours started that there was something odd about it and that the military would be coming up to try to find it and have a look at it. By the afternoon, big planes started coming in and the Army started putting up tents by the airstrip, and now more planes and people have been coming in today."

I detected a questioning tone in his voice. "Sounds like you know about as much about all this as we do. We're not military, we're scientists along for the ride. If the Air Force can find

215

whatever came down from space, then we want to be the first to have a look at it."

"Your accent sounds American," said Danny, looking at Vivian (when she'd said 'already' it sounded like 'orreddy').

"That's right, I'm with the U.S. Geological Survey, and I grew up in Boston," Vivian answered, confidently, and with a bright smile.

"Interesting… well, you seem to be my only visitors so far toda. Can I tell you a bit about Inuvik?"

I responded quickly with a "Yes, please," wanting to change the subject away from the purpose of our search.

Needing no further encouragement, Danny launched into a summary of the town and its history. Although he must have told the story countless times, he had an enthusiastic and engaging manner, and seemed to genuinely appreciate the opportunity to share.

He explained that the name Inuvik means 'Place of People' in Inuvialuktun, that the region is the homeland of the Inuvialuit and Gwich'in peoples[29] and that, for a very long time their principal interactions had been among these two peoples – who were traditional enemies – and to some extent with the Inuit to the west, and the Dene First Nation to the south. Eventually, there was contact with European Explorers searching for a northwest passage to the Pacific Ocean (1700s and 1800s), then came fur traders and whalers (1800s and early 1900s). Over time, trading posts and settlements grew up, and whaling captains started basing their winter whaling headquarters in the region, but there wasn't much development at the site of present-day Inuvik itself until a railhead was established in northern Alberta, in the 1920s, and bush planes opened up access from the south to the far north in the 1930s. Then, 1954 brought a military presence, with the DEW Line radar stations, and right after that construction of Inuvik began.

"You mean, you just built a town? From scratch?" asked Vivian.

"Well, it wasn't me. I was just a kid then. It was my parents' generation, but yes, there wasn't an actual settlement here until modern times. The town itself was built between 1955 and 1960. Due to the permafrost, everything had to be built on piles or thick gravel pads. From 1960 onwards, the town grew, and then grew again after oil and gas were discovered in around 1970. The population is about 3,000 now, and most of the residents here are still Inuvialuit."

"That must have been exciting," I offered, remembering my own exposure to the effects of the oil boom in Alberta.

"Well, it was exciting at first, and up here our 'boom' was going pretty well until this past Spring, when the 'bust' came."

"Bust?"

"Yes. The federal government imposed a ten-year moratorium on Mackenzie Valley pipeline development, and we've lost 500 people from the town already because the oil- and service companies immediately shut their offices and moved out."

"Wow. Are people angry?"

"It all depends on who you ask. Many people here were excited about the economic boom, but the Aboriginal Communities were concerned about the environmental and social impacts, about not having been consulted, and about still not having their land claims settled. The Berger Report tackled those issues head-on, leading to the moratorium[30]. If you're asking me, personally, I'm not happy with the federal government and the way they handled things, but I agree with the reasons for the moratorium. The way I see it, the oil and gas will still be there waiting for us when all the other issues get sorted out, and we can develop it then and have our 'boom' back."

"Sounds like a pretty mature view of things to me."

"Well, part of being mayor means listening to everyone's point of view. That's the easy part," he chuckled. "The hard part is trying to keep everyone more or less equally unhappy."

"You're the Mayor too?" I asked.

He nodded, "Mayor, interpretive centre guide, librarian, and a few other things. You see, everything's connected. The DEW-Line radar station brought more people in from the south, trapper families moved into the towns to live, and, eventually, the descendants of the original inhabitants realized that they were losing their language and culture. In the 1960s, a movement began to seek greater sovereignty over their traditional lands, and a continuation – and even restoration – of their languages and traditions. I got caught up in it all, got involved in the interpretative centre and library, and then got talked into becoming mayor."

As we continued chatting, Danny showed us around the centre and library. Eventually, after showing due appreciation for the centre and his history lesson, we took our leave so we could stroll around the town a bit, but not before promising to go back and spend some more time there before leaving Inuvik.

As we left the Interpretive Centre, Silver magically appeared by our sides and accompanied us as we walked around some of the town. It was fascinating. We'd already noticed that most buildings were raised-up on piles, but now we could see that, like other communities in the far north, the buildings were connected by long, narrow, above-ground boxes called utilidors, which contained the pipes for water, steam, and sewage. Although the scene was unusual, with the buildings raised and inter-connected by the utilidors, it was otherwise a pretty typical looking town, with all the usual buildings, stores, and residences.

The one place I didn't want to get too close to, was the RCMP Building. Inuvik was the location of one of three Sub-Divisions in the Northwest Territories, with the "G" Division headquarters located in the Yellowknife. Housing, as it did, a Sub-Division office, there was a sizeable RCMP presence in Inuvik. I hoped I wouldn't encounter anyone who knew me, but the Force was like that: you could run into a colleague from training or an earlier posting anywhere in the country.

Stopping well short of the RCMP Building, and satisfied with our walk, we turned around, found a phone to call for the Army shuttle, and returned to camp. We hadn't been back long before it was time for the briefing. Leaving Silver behind, Don led us over to a tent that had been set up like an operations centre, to meet the officer that would command the overall search mission. We'd no sooner entered the tent, and I was taking in the scene of several men, wearing different uniforms, huddled together near a wall covered in maps, than one of them – an Air Force officer, looked over at us and walked over. Lieutenant Colonel John Stark introduced himself as the adjutant from CFB Edmonton, and explained that he'd been assigned on-scene command, which meant that he'd be in charge of the search. Like us, he and his command centre had been airlifted up to Inuvik that same day.

Calling the briefing to order, Lt./Col. Stark introduced himself to the group and then had everyone else stand and introduce themselves in turn, but by groups: first his own operations team, then the Hercules crews, Chinook crews, and the six Search and Rescue Technicians (SAR Techs) that would accompany the Hercules and Chinook teams. The latter six, he explained, were experts in Arctic survival and would ensure the search teams could survive crashes or delays out in the Barrens. That covered the military personnel.

Next, came introductions of the three scientist/operators of the big gamma-ray spectrometers that were being mounted in the Hercules aircraft (two from the Geological Survey of Canada, and one from the U.S. Geological Survey), the three scientist/operators of the small hand-held gamma-ray spectrometers that would travel in the Chinook helicopters (Don, Vivian, and me), and finally three AECB scientists who would take charge of any radioactive debris that we found.

"OK. Welcome to Operation Arctic Circle[31]," he said, after all of the introductions had been made.

I found the rest of the briefing rather lengthy, probably because a lot of the logistical details didn't affect me, but the gist of it was as follows: the next day there would be one Hercules flight to test out one of the big gamma-ray spectrometers. Apparently, they had never been used for this purpose before. While that was happening the other two big spectrometers would be mounted in two more Hercules aircraft. Assuming all that was successful, then the next day would mark the beginning of the search patterns with all three Hercules aircraft.

At this point he had turned to a stand holding a corkboard to which a large map had been pinned.

"Computer models have been used to designate the most probable area for the search, some 120,000 square kilometres," explained Colonel Stark. Then he pointed to an outline that had been hand-drawn onto the map.

"The computer modellers think that the satellite probably disintegrated in the sky over a straight course 1,000 km long, depositing everything from metre-long pieces of scrap metal, down to tiny particles. Any or all of them could be highly radioactive. Drawn on the map is an outline of the initial search area." It looked a bit like the profile of a revolver[32].

Colonel Stark then went on to describe the search plan. Basically, the three planes would fly a grid search of the marked area. Subject to how well the spectrometers worked, the Hercules aircraft would fly, three abreast, at an altitude of 1,000 feet along their search patterns. Weather permitting, the plan was for the aircraft to take-off for a 10-hour mission. When the three Hercules returned, the raw data from the completed mission would be analyzed on the ground. As soon as the data was processed, and if 'hits' were identified, then any or all of the three Chinook helicopters and their teams would take-off and try to locate and recover whatever radioactive components had triggered the hits.

"This is going to be a challenge," said Colonel Stark, in summing up. "You're going to have to stay alert to keep on course, so the operators can do their jobs properly and we don't miss anything important. It will be interesting at first, but that will soon turn to monotony. That's when I'm counting on you to remain vigilant... and there's another problem." He paused for effect.

"I'm told that these computer models are not very reliable. So, be alert to the possibility that we may find debris scattered over a larger area. If that happens, we'll have to expand the search grids."

After taking questions from the audience, for which the answers were almost inevitably "We'll see," he dismissed us.

Although Colonel Stark looked stern, and a bit worried, his unmistakeable Newfoundland accent somehow put me at ease. He seemed like the epitome of the professional military officer and, fortunately for us all, the events of the next few days would prove my first impression to be correct.

Once again, the mess tent was still in the process of being made operational, virtually everyone took the shuttles into town and spread out among the available restaurants for dinner. I was looking forward to this. I'd had my first taste of fresh Arctic Char the previous evening in Yellowknife, and I was hoping to try another new experience at dinner that night. That turned out to be Caribou steak, which was excellent. I saved some to take back to Silver, whom I'd had to leave behind.

When we returned to camp, I made time for an evening walk with Silver and then once again made it an early night. I hadn't realized how tiring long, back-to-back plane flights could be and dropped off almost immediately.

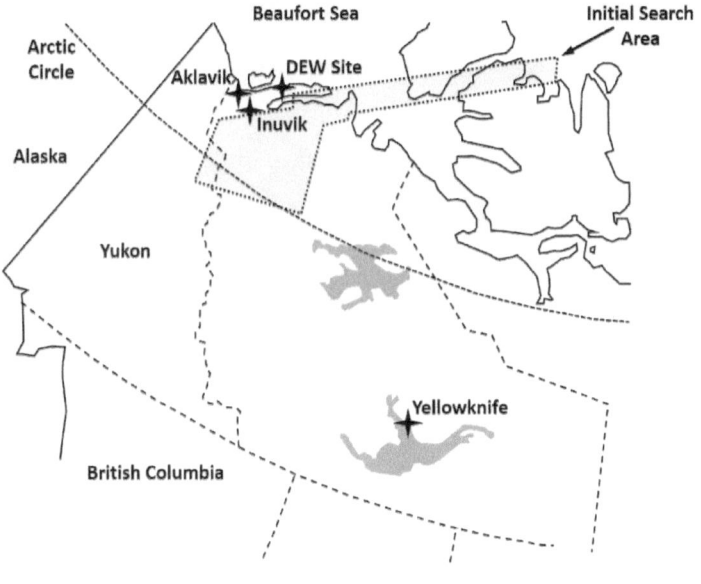

Laurie Schramm

6 THE AERIAL-SEARCH BEGINS

January 26, 1978
Day 3

The next morning was bright and clear but colder: a cold-front had swept in, reducing the daytime temperature to -30 °C. If that wasn't bad enough, the cold was worse, of course, with the wind chill. The pilots were happy with the clear skies, however, and as we got ready to board the first spectrometer-mounted Hercules, we were introduced to its father – literally.

Dr. Clem Goodyear was a geophysicist from the Geological Survey of Canada. Medium height, and wiry, he seemed to have boundless energy and came across as more like the stereotype of an old-time prospector than a geophysicist. *With that shaggy beard and those rough clothes, he could fit in to any mining town in Northern Canada,* I thought to myself.

We were also joined on this flight by one of the SAR Techs, who identified himself as Corporal Wayne Robertson. Wayne explained that his job was to help keep us safe, and he inspected each of us to make sure that we were wearing the complete Arctic clothing ensemble before we got on the plane. One of the rules of flying in the Arctic, he explained was to make sure every person was wearing the gear they might need for survival in the event of a forced landing or crash. Don chimed in at this point, explaining that in the event of a survival situation, Cpl. Robertson would effectively out-rank everyone else and would be in charge of keeping us alive.

For his part, Wayne immediately showed us that he meant business by insisting that Clem put on all of his gear before boarding. Clem, who had brought his winter gear in a duffle bag, thinking that would be sufficient, resisted, but Wayne politely yet firmly refused to let him on the plane, saying: "Unless you can guarantee me that you can find that bag, and quickly, in a crash, then you need to be wearing the gear. Once we're in the air, the pilots will keep the cabin temperature cool, and you can open everything up, but all of us will have to keep the gear on."

While Clem donned his gear, Wayne told us a few sobering stories about people that had flown without the right gear, or who had the right gear packed away but were unable to retrieve it following a crash landing. *One thing about the military*, I thought to myself, *they always have gruesome real-life stories to illustrate the importance of following their safety rules.*

It was a subdued group that finally boarded the plane.

Once we were up in the air, and heading for the beginning of our search vector, Clem brightened up considerably and was eager to show us his 'baby.' It was named 'GRS-1,' and was a gamma-ray spectrometer that he'd designed and built himself. It was intended for airborne prospecting for uranium minerals. Unstrapping himself from his seat, and leading us forward in the cavernous cargo bay of the Hercules, he gave us a guided tour.

GRS-1 was big: five feet high, three feet wide, and ten feet long. Although large, and heavy, it easily fit into the cavernous interior of the C-130 aircraft. At one end of the machine was an operator's console, which included a computer and data display and recording devices. Clem showed us how the mini-computer, display, chart recorder, magnetic-tape recorder, and power inverter, were all rack-mounted and equipped with castors so the whole thing could be wheeled into any large aircraft. It wasn't just large, it was heavy. Clem explained that GRS-1 weighed over 1,000 pounds!

Clem was in his element now, and continued with his briefing: "Data from the spectrometer is fed into the mini-computer, which can calculate the functions, based on almost any algebraic function we want to apply to the counts. It will then display one of them on a cathode-ray-tube (CRT) display and up to six of them on this 6-channel strip chart recorder. These profiles are run in real-time during the flight, allowing the operator – in this case, me - to look for 'hits,' which can then be relayed to the pilots, who can provide the coordinates of our position at that point in time[33]."

"Sounds easy," said Don, with a completely straight face.

GRS-1

"It is, except that we don't know what functions will best eliminate the natural radioactivity background. Maybe it will be easy, and the peaks we need will just rise up out of the background noise, or maybe not. That's what we need to figure out today, and we'll just do it by trial and error – I hope."

"What is it that you're actually detecting with the GRS?" I wondered out loud.

"Signal peaks at specific energy levels that correspond to nuclear fission products," he replied. "Take Lanthanum, for example. A signal peak at 1.59 meV shows the presence of nuclear fission product Lanthanum-140."

"Great, so then you just look for the peaks?" I asked.

"Not exactly, the peaks are usually buried in the background, which comes from the natural radiation from potassium, uranium, and thorium in the rocks we'll be flying over."

"So, the trick will be to eliminate the background," put in Don, not wanting to be outdone.

"That's right, and I don't know how to do that yet. I designed the GRS-1 for uranium exploration and geological mapping, not to search for fission products. Also, it's new technology, and I don't really have much experience with it yet. We're going to have to learn as we go."

Further discussion was halted by the roar of the Hercules' engines and, in any case, we had to strap ourselves in for take-off.

The plan was to fly at an altitude of 1,000 feet, right down the centre of the predicted fallout zone. Once one of the pilots announced that we were at cruising altitude and had reached the southwest end of the initial search zone, we all huddled around Clem and his spectrometer, eager to see whether it would work.

In a way, it worked too well. The raw data was all sent to the reel-to-reel magnetic tape recorder, which would be analyzed when we were back on the ground. We were all more focused on the chart recorder, which Clem had set to trace the signal from a single energy level that would correspond to one of uranium's radioactive decay products. The recorder traced a continuing series of peaks, all of which looked more or less the same except that, every once in a while, there would be a larger peak. Wayne called the larger peaks 'anomalies.' The good news was that the spectrometer was picking up activity, lots of it.

After this had been going on for a while, Clem turned to the mini-computer and had it print the full energy spectrum corresponding to a single point in time during our flight. This he had printed on the dot-matrix printer that was mounted beside the chart recorder. The spectrum showed a wide range of peaks and valleys, some of which were easily distinguishable from the others. Having looked the spectrum over carefully, Clem explained that we were getting readings from rock outcrops that contained natural uranium minerals and that, since the rocks contained uranium, they also contained other radioactive metals that would have been created by the decay of some of the uranium over time.

"What does that mean?" asked Vivian.

"It means that we should be prospecting for uranium up here instead of looking for pieces of a nuclear-powered satellite. If we were doing the search in southern Alberta, say, then any radioactive debris from the satellite would stick out like crazy on the chart recorder, or show a smaller number of very clear peaks on the energy spectrum graph. As it is, we're getting so much signal from the natural minerals that sending search teams to the locations of the strongest signals would just lead them to a huge number of natural radium or uranium deposits."

"So, this isn't going to work then?" asked Don.

"Not necessarily," said Clem, thinking it through. "We'll keep collecting the data from the planned flight. Then, when we're back on the group, I'll go to work on the raw data. Maybe I can find a way to subtract out the background from the natural minerals. The problem is that I have no idea where they are or how they are distributed in this area, so I have no real reference point. I'll have to go more by trial and error."

So, that was a let-down. There wasn't much to do after that but look out the windows at the broad expanse of the tundra below us which, to be fair, was quite a sight. The broad expanse of undulating, snow-covered ground was made more interesting by rocky outcrops, clusters of brave-looking trees, and the occasional appearance of a herd of caribou or muskox. I even spotted what looked like two wolves trailing one of the herds.

Although Clem had probably collected enough data after an hour or two, he continued to collect data for a total of six hours before deciding that it was pointless to continue and signalled this to the pilots. By the time we landed back at the base, we'd been up in the air for ten hours and still didn't know whether we'd learned anything useful.

Tired after a long day of flying, I had mixed feelings about going for a walk with Silver, whom I'd left behind at the camp. I told myself that it would be good for me to get some exercise after sitting for so long, however, and I felt a bit guilty about having left Silver behind for the day, which tipped the scales in favour of going for the walk. Vivian just wanted to curl-up on her cot for a quick nap before supper, so it was only Don that joined us in a stroll around the camp.

The sun had gone down already, and it was getting colder so, although we had stripped off our extra layer of lined pants, we kept everything else on. The wind had picked-up as well so, although we had our hoods up and had to turn and face each other to talk, the combination of the winds and our hoods – plus the fact that there were very few other people in sight - meant that we could talk without being overheard.

"What do you think?" I asked, as we strolled along.

"Well, for one thing I hope Clem finds a way to recognize the right signals from that spectrometer of his, or we'll have to do a ground search that could take forever."

"Is there no other way?"

"See those Twin Otters[34] over there?" he said, pointing to one side.

I hadn't noticed them when we landed, but they were unmistakable now. Parked to one side of the maintenance tents were three twin-engine airplanes, each of them painted in the bright yellow with red-stripe that denoted the Air Force's search and rescue aircraft. They were immediately recognizable as Twin Otters, one of the most famous of Canada's 'bush planes.'

"While we were up in the air today, there were three Twin Otters flying low over the highest probably debris trajectory from the computer models. Their mission was to try and spot anything large that might have come down."

"And?"

"Nothing, they came up this morning, refuelled and started search right after we left and only returned a few minutes ago. They didn't spot a thing. The current thinking is that the satellite burned-up on re-entry and that none of the surviving fragments are likely to be larger than about two feet across."

"Not easy to find then."

"Visually? No. But even tiny pieces could be highly radioactive."

"That brings us back to the spectrometers then," I concluded. When Don just nodded, I changed tack. "Any ideas about who might be a foreign agent?"

"None at all. Someone could be impersonating one of the scientists, it's been tried before. That's more difficult with the military personnel, or even the local people, because there's a greater chance that people are known by their comrades. Anyone could be a mole though."

"Great." Since there wasn't much more to say, we just walked until it seemed like a good time to return for supper.

This time, we had supper in the big mess tent, which was now in full operation. The food wasn't gourmet, but it was good, hot, and plentiful. Sitting with Vivian and Wayne, and a few of the others we mostly talked about where people were from, and their day-jobs, and other light chatter. The mood wasn't exactly sombre, but no one seemed to have had a very successful day. I managed to get a good-sized doggie-bag from the cooks and took it back to our tent for Silver.

It was later in the evening, and we were back in the mess tent having coffee, when Clem walked in excitedly, waving a double handful of chart recordings in the air, saying "I've got it!"

That got an immediate rise out of the other two geophysicists, who beat us to the table where Clem started laying out his charts. "Look here," he said, pointing to two of the chart recordings. "Most of the fission products are showing most of their gamma activity at less than 1.0 meV – right?" There were nods of agreement from the others.

"OK. Now, the gamma activity coming from the naturally occurring radioactive minerals in the rocks is more consistent across a broader range of energies. Yes?" More nods, all of us could see what was coming now.

"So, what we need to do is take the average count rate in the lower part of the energy spectrum and divide it by the average count rate in the higher part of the energy spectrum. If we do that…" He brushed the chart recordings to one side, and spread out a new chart. "See what we get!"

The computer-generated chart still had a wavy trace, but it was much less noisy, and now a peak in the signal stood-out unmistakeably from the background. "When we're flying the search pattern tomorrow, we can have the output from the computer split into two identical signals. We send the original spectra to magnetic tape, with no signal processing at all. That gives us the original data, which we can use for further analysis when we're back on the ground. In parallel, we have the computer average the signals in the low and high energy ranges, and divide one by the other. That will reduce the signals from the naturally-occurring minerals in the rock, but not the signals from satellite debris. As the plane flies along, all we have to do is watch the chart-recorder pen as the chart paper rolls by. If we see a signal spike on the chart-paper, then we have a 'hit.' When that happens, we get on the intercom to the pilots, who give us the position coordinates. We can write the coordinates beside the spike on the chart, and go back to watching for more. I think we'll still get some false hits, but hopefully not too many."

With Clem's new theory in mind, I think we all went to bed with a renewed sense of optimism that night. It would take two more days for us to find out whether he was right.

***

January 27, 1978
Day 4

I didn't have to get up early the next day, since there was no need to accompany the three Hercules that would be flying the first proper aerial search. Sleeping-in was another matter however, as the roar of the three massive planes taking off at 5 am must have woken all but the deepest of sleepers in the camp.

Instead, after breakfast, Don, Vivian, and I were taken to an area in one corner of the camp that had been set up for the dog teams. Colonel Stark, looking wider awake than any of the rest of us, was there to meet us and introduced us to the companions we would have on the Chinook flights. Each helicopter would have its own team of pilot, co-pilot and flight engineer, plus a SAR Tech, a scientist from the AECB, one of Don, Vivian, or I, and a guide/musher that would handle the dog team. Having been introduced, we divided up into three teams.

In my group, was Corporal Wayne Robertson, whom I'd already met. The AECB scientist was a cheerful-sounding fellow named Fred Warner. Our guide/musher was Peter Marcoux, who explained that he had grown up in nearby Tuktoyaktuk, was of Inuvialuit heritage, and was a part-time hunter, trapper, and competitive dog-musher in races like Alaska's famous Iditarod[35]. He added that his father and grandfather had passed-on their knowledge of the land, and how to survive in it.

Wayne and Peter then showed us our transportation: a rugged-looking snowmobile with a sled attached to the back, and a dogsled. Two people would ride on the snowmobile, with a few supplies, shovels, and the containers for the debris we hoped to find. One person would ride in the dogsled, which would be driven by Peter.

The sled looked unusual to me. Seeing my expression, Peter explained that it was called a basket-sled, or *qamutivialuk*. It had runners with elegant, highly curved front ends and which were attached to vertical posts at the back. Between the curved front ends and rear posts, there was a side rail on each side. Completing the frame was a row of cross-slats, raised above the runners, that extended the full length from front to back. This assembly created what was essentially a basket of slats and rails. Peter said it was a traditional design of the sort that was favoured during the fur-trade-era of the early 1900s.

Next to be introduced, were the dogs, but before walking over to the makeshift kennel area Peter asked to be introduced to my dog. Upon being introduced to Silver, Peter knelt in front of him so Silver could get a good sniff, and then their eyes met. After a lengthy gaze into Silver's eyes, Peter turned to me. "He's been a sled-dog, hasn't he?"

"How did you know?"

"I've been watching him ever since you two walked over here. He sees things and he isn't surprised by them. He knows what the sled is for and, although he's never once looked directly at the other dogs, he knows they are there and he knows that they're part of a team. Watch him when we walk into the pen and he'll immediately go up to Penny, the lead dog."

Sure enough, as we all walked over to the pens and stepped inside, Silver made a beeline for a grey Siberian Husky, slowed his pace as he got closer, then stopped about five feet away and stretched out his front paws, lowering his head in a dog's bow. After watching him for a moment the husky, who had gotten to her feet at Silver's approach, walked over to him and gave him a sniff. She must have been satisfied, because after that Silver rose and they did that circular sort of dance you often see dogs complete, in which they go around each other sniffing at each other's bellies and rear-ends, and so on.

"Told you," said Peter, with a satisfied-looking smile. "Once a sled-dog, always a sled-dog. Come on, and I'll introduce the whole team."

Peter's pen contained thirteen dogs, including Penny. With a group of strangers advancing to meet them, some were friendly, some aloof, and some a bit growly, but all looked to be in prime physical condition.

"How many dogs do you normally use?" I asked.

"It depends," said Peter. "More dogs can pull more weight but with more dogs you have to carry more food. In our case, we only plan to be out for hours at a time but the sled will be loaded, so I had planned on fourteen."

"So, you're missing one?"

"Yes, we accidentally crossed a trapline when we were out running yesterday, and one of the dogs – Angel – stepped into a trap."

"Will she be OK?"

"The jaws of the trap broke her leg, but the vet says she'll be fine. It will just take some time before she can run again. I was going to just go with the thirteen dogs, but we can put Silver in if you want." He looked at me rather shrewdly then. "You didn't bring him all the way up here just to leave him behind in the camp, did you?"

"No, you're right. I've never seen him in harness, but I was told that he used to be a good lead dog. As long as he's OK with it, let's give him a try."

Among our group, it was agreed that when we were out searching, Fred would ride on the snowmobile with Wayne driving, while I would ride in the dogsled with Peter mushing. The rest of our gear would be distributed between the snowmobile sled and the dogsled, while spare gear and extra shielded containers for satellite debris would remain with the helicopter.

With that settled, the rest of the group retreated to the warmth of the camp, while Peter suggested I stay and we would see whether Silver would fit in with the dog team.

As Peter laid out the traces, he explained how it would be set-up. There was a long, central towline, called a 'gangline.' To this were attached the dog harnesses, in pairs, with one dog on each side. Peter called the names of what turned out to be the two largest of the dogs, both of whom promptly got up, padded over to us and positioned themselves by the first two harnesses in front of the sled.

"They seem very well trained," I remarked in surprise.

"Trained, yes, but they also love to run as part of the team, and they tend to get quite protective of their accustomed places on the team. These two are called 'wheel dogs,' and they have to be strong enough to take more than their share of the sled's weight on start-up.

By the time Peter had tied the wheel dogs in, most of the rest of the dogs had sauntered over and were standing near what I assumed were their accustomed places.

The next eight dogs were tied into their harnesses, leaving four to go.

"Let's try putting Silver in the second pair of harnesses," said Peter. "These are called 'swing dogs.' Their job is to make sure that when the lead dogs make a turn, the rest of the team doesn't try to take a short-cut, but follows in the lead dogs' tracks. That helps keep us on the trail. If Silver's done this before, he'll know what to do when the time comes."

It didn't work out that way, though. No sooner had Peter and I called Silver over to be tied in, the second-last dog pushed his way in and resolutely stood over the harness, clearly expecting to be tied in.

Chuckling, Peter said, "As you can see, some of the dogs get quite protective of their customary place in the team. Let's let him keep his spot, and we'll try Silver in Angel's place, beside Penny.

"I always thought there was only one lead dog on a team."

"The lead position can have one or two dogs, even three if we wanted to. Some mushers prefer one, some prefer two. I like to do whatever works best for the team. Some lead dogs really need to be number one, and tying a second lead dog just creates trouble. On the other hand, two lead dogs that work well together can't be beaten. Two lead dogs working together are better at route-finding, better at steering, better at keeping the gangline tight, and better at maintaining discipline among the rest of the team… Let's give it a try and see what happens between Silver and Penny. Want to come for the ride?"

I sure did.

The sled had several animal hides piled on it, and since I was so well dressed in my Arctic gear, Peter suggested I just sit on top of them, with my back next to the upright poles that he would be holding on to while mushing. When Penny and Silver had been tied in, he went to the back and called out "Let's go!"

"Aren't you supposed to say 'Mush?' I asked, turning to face Peter as much as I could, as the sled jolted forward.

He chuckled again, "They'll respond to 'mush' all right, but I'm a simple person. I've always preferred to just say 'Let's go'"

And that was it. It was a rough ride at first, as the team pulled the sled over the rough roads of the camp, but once we got out onto fresh snow, the ride improved a lot – except for the occasional bump when the sled struck a rock or tree branch hidden under the snow. When we got to deeper snow, however, it was very smooth going. Every once in a while, Peter would call out a command, like 'gee' – for turn right - and 'haw' – for turn left, and the front four dogs would carve out a smooth arc for the rest of the team and sled to follow.

After a few turns, and seemingly satisfied with the team's performance, Peter just let them run.

It was glorious. We weren't moving all that fast, but it was a clear, sunny day with no wind, the sled was gliding over the snow, and the barking of the dogs made it clear that they were enjoying themselves.

Eventually, Peter called out "Come gee!" which apparently meant that they should make a 180-degree turn to the right. I guessed that this was another test for Silver, who was on the right-hand side. If so, I think he passed, as Penny matched him stride for stride, and the swing dogs strained to their left while turning, so that the whole team, and then our sled, made a graceful 180-degree turn.

At this point, Peter called "Whoa!" and, when the sled halted, stepped up beside me and pulled his hood back a bit.

"That was wonderful!" I said.

Peter grinned. "If you liked that, maybe you'd like to try mushing the sled yourself."

"Sure!"

Peter, showed me where to stand on the footboards and how to release the snow-hook, which was kind of like an anchor for the snow, when the sled was stopped. Then he climbed into the sled, where I had been, and said "Take it away, Alex."

Standing at the back of the sled, I yelled "Mush!" and then immediately found myself sitting in the snow. Not being prepared for the jolt of the sled starting to move, it had been pulled right out from under me!

Peter seemed to have been ready for this, as he immediately called "Whoa!" and came back to help me up.

"Are you OK?" he asked.

"Embarrassed, but OK, I guess. That sled gives quite a kick!"

"Don't worry about it," he replied. "My grandfather used to say that making mistakes is how we learn. Would you rather ride on the sled and have me drive?"

"Oh, no. Not after that. I'd like to try it again, if it's OK with you."

Peter made a waving motion with his hand, and simply got back onto the sled.

With all the dogs watching me, I got back into position at the back of the sled. I took a much firmer grip this time, and called out "Mush!" As the sled lurched forward, I was able to maintain my position and start looking ahead. After a few experimental turns, I was able to get the sled onto its previous track, which increased our speed quite a bit. Then, tightening my grip again, I called out "Haw!" as was able to hang-on as the sled turned out of the track and back onto fresh snow. As it did, the sled leaned dangerously to one side. Throwing my weight the other way, to counteract that, I was able to keep the sled from tipping over, but just barely. As I did so, I noticed that Peter had continued to sit upright on the sled: he had deliberately held his position leaving it completely up to me to keep the sled on its runners. Another test, I assumed.

After letting the sled run for a while, curving a few turns this way and that, I called a halt so Peter and I could change places.

"That was great! Thank you," I said.

"Maybe we can find time for you to practice again sometime, and see if we can make a musher out of you before you leave."

"I'd love that!" I replied. "How do you think Silver is doing?"

"He fits in seamlessly, and I can tell that he and Penny like each other. They make a good team. You can tell he likes it too – just look at him."

Silver was watching us from his position at the front, and as I looked directly at him, I could sense his thoughts: "*I like this.*"

Peter must have sensed my body relax as I locked my gaze on Silver, or maybe he sensed that we were sharing our thoughts because he looked at me rather shrewdly for a moment, but didn't comment further.

Having switched places, Peter got the team moving, and this time gave them their head and let them pick the route and the speed back to camp.

The sled-ride back was, once again, amazing.

When we reached camp, I went to greet Silver and knelt-down

beside him to see how he was feeling. He had a very satisfied look in his eyes and, while Peter undid the harness, Silver and I shared a long gaze into each other eyes.

It is good to run, he was thinking.

Peter seemed to be focusing on what he was doing, but when he had freed Silver and started to undo Penny's harness, he made a comment that showed he didn't miss much.

"You have the gift, don't you?' he asked.

"What do you mean?" I responded, instinctively cautious.

Peter was silent until he'd freed Penny, then turned to look at me. "Another thing I learned from my grandfather is a lot of stories about the old days. Stories that have been handed down through the generations... One of those stories tells of a time at the dawn of human evolution, when a wolf was a friend and brother of the first man. That wolf was said to have had intelligence, intuition, and the ability to communicate with humans as well as other wolves."

"Do you believe in these stories?" I asked.

"Well," Peter responded, "I think that I'm a pretty well-educated, rational person, but I've also spent a lot of time out on the land and some of the things I've experienced make me think about the old stories and wonder about things. Watching you two, makes me wonder about things."

"Now you sound like me," I said, thoughtfully. "I was trained as a scientist, but I've heard your grandfather's story too, and I've had some experiences with Silver that make me wonder... I don't understand this at all, but there have been too many times where Silver and I seem to be able to share our thoughts for me to discount them... Would you do me a favour and not tell anyone about this? If it's a gift, then I don't understand it, but I'm sure grateful for it..."

"Hah!" Peter laughed. "Who would believe me?" Then he sobered, and said "You can count on me."

"Grruph!" said Silver, looking directly at Peter.

"*You* can count on me too, Silver," said Peter, gravely.

Feeling like we'd made a friend, I thanked Peter again for the sledding-lesson, and Silver and I walked back to the main part of camp to see what the others were up to.

In the mess tent, Vivian and I were having lunch when a woman lieutenant that I recognized as being one of the Chinook helicopter pilots came over to join us. Susan Warden was her name, and she wanted to meet us partly because there were so few women in camp. She seemed nice enough, and the three of us had an enjoyable chat over lunch. I discovered later that she was one of the pilots on the Chinook to which I was assigned.

In the afternoon, Don, Vivian, and I were issued with hand-held gamma-ray spectrometers, which we took to the mess tent so we could spread them out on the tables and look them over. We'd already studied the manuals for these units, which were much more sophisticated than Geiger-Counters.

Each unit came in a leather carrying case and weighed about 18 pounds. This didn't impress either Vivian or I, who were not looking forward to wandering around in the Barrens with our big bulky Arctic clothing on plus the additional weight of the spectrometers.

The main components of the spectrometers were an electronics box, which weighed 10 pounds, connected by a cable to a large aluminum cylinder that was 5 inches in diameter and 14 inches long and weighed the remaining 8 pounds. The cylinder contained a high-voltage (1,000 V!) power supply and a sodium-iodide detector crystal coupled to a high-gain photomultiplier tube. In use, the aluminum cylinder would be hand-held, and the electronics box would hang from a shoulder strap.

Every gamma ray from a radioisotope would be detected by the electronics as a short voltage pulse, and the pulses would be counted over preselected time intervals. The greater the gamma ray energy, the greater the voltage change, or size of the pulse, allowing the electronics to sort the number of pulses, or counts, by energy level. Being designed for prospecting, the units were set to count in three energy ranges that were characteristic for potassium, uranium, and thorium. In our case, we weren't prospecting and we were going to be looking for pieces of highly radioactive material, so we would use a fourth option that was provided by the spectrometers: the total count setting, which simply added-up all the pulses received over the complete energy range for which the units were capable.

There were a couple of other simplifications that we could use, which a professional geochemical survey team would not. In prospecting, a person would go relatively slowly, allowing the spectrometer to accumulate count-rates for a selected time period, which would maximize the unit's sensitivity. We would simply set our instruments to continuous display. Also, since the gamma ray intensities vary with distance, it would normally be important to hold the detectors at a consistent height above the ground. We decided that we would try to hold ours at approximately 1-metre above the ground as we walked, but the exact height wouldn't be critical for our purposes, and it was really just to make our results comparable when we reported findings and compared notes on them later.

Each of our kits came with a calibration sample, whose label identified it as a small sample of barium-133 isotope. These, we held in front of the detector cylinders and verified that the instruments gave the correct reading when set to the proper channel and a long counting interval. With that completed, we reset the units to the simplified settings I have already described, and we were ready to go.

We noticed, with interest, that the manuals said the instruments were for operation between temperatures of -10 and +50 °C. We were going to be testing their ability to operate at -30 to -40 °C, or worse! Another consequence of the low temperatures we'd be facing would be battery life. Part of the reason the spectrometers were so heavy was that they were powered by 12 D-cell flashlight batteries. These were stated to be capable of powering the units for "over 40 hours of continuous operation," but we had no idea how long they'd hold up at the temperatures we'd be experiencing. Obviously, we'd have to bring cases of spare batteries with us in the helicopters.

While most of us were gathered in the mess tent for supper, the three Hercules landed and disgorged the geophysicists. They burst into the mess tent, headed for the far corner where there was a computer station set up, and immediately covered a large table with their armloads of notes, strip-chart recordings, and magnetic tapes. Too excited to eat, they immediately dove-in, comparing their charts and the corresponding map coordinates. A map had been pinned to a large corkboard on a vertical stand, like the one in the CO's operations centre. This map also, had a hand-drawn outline of the gun-shaped, initial search zone. We stayed away for a while, so they could focus on what they were doing, but after an hour of overhearing bits and pieces of their discussions, which seem to range from triumphs, to disappointments, to arguments over interpretations. Finally, when the discussions died down, Don, Vivian, and I went over to see how it was all going.

When we did, Clem Goodyear noticed our approach and waved us over to the map.

"How'd you make out Clem?" Don asked.

"Pretty well, I think. We think we've isolated some hits that aren't due to natural elements in the local rocks. I had time to run a few other comparisons through the computer while we were flying back here, and we all agree." He looked over at the other two geophysicists, who nodded their agreement.

"We're on the right track. Here is the part that we flew over today," he continued, pointing to a shaded area within the outline of the search zone. Next, he walked us over another large corkboard on a vertical stand, to which a topographic map had been pinned. It had a much-enlarged outline drawn on it, within which had been placed differently coloured pins.

"This is the area from today's search. The pins mark the spots where we think the hits are. What we did was to divide the hits into three categories and give each a colour: the red pins mark hits we're really sure about, yellow for hits we're pretty sure about, and green for hits we're not sure about."

As we crowed closer to the topo map for a closer look, I could see that, although the green pins were scattered all over the searched zone, the red and yellow ones seemed to occur in clusters that followed a shallow, wavy curve across the map.

"What's next?" I asked.

"We'll go through all this with the CO after we get something to eat, then give him our recommendations for the ground search. By tomorrow morning, each helicopter team will be assigned an area to search and we'll see what you actually find. Meanwhile, we'll fly another zone tomorrow in the three Hercules. When we're all back tomorrow night, we'll compare our hits with what you actually find, if anything, then we can recalibrate what we're doing."

"You sound like you're not sure we'll even find anything," observed Vivian.

"To tell you the truth, I'm not sure this is going to work," replied Clem, rubbing his face and looking suddenly tired. "We have two problems, one is distinguishing real hits from the background, as you know. The second problem, is the accuracy of the navigation. There aren't many geographic navigational aids, and compasses are notoriously unreliable around here. The position data we get from the pilots comes from the Omega[36] which isn't very accurate for this kind of work, so our hit coordinates could be off by as much as 2 kilometres in any direction. That means you'll have to scramble around a bit when you're searching. Even if there really are pieces of satellite out there, unless they're really hot you may not be able to find them."

Thanking Clem, we left so they could get on with their work. Although it was only 6 pm, the sun had almost completely set as we left the mess tent. I had taken some food with me for Silver, and said I'd meet the others in Vivian's and my tent after feeding Silver and taking him for a walk.

Although it was fairly dark when Silver and I went for our walk, the camp was well lit, so we basically walked the camp. As we walked toward the aircraft maintenance tents, the three Hercules stood silently, like giants waiting for their time to fly again. I didn't see the Chinook helicopters, and assumed that they must be parked inside the tents.

Continuing to walk the camp's perimeter took us behind the maintenance tents, and I was surprised to encounter a pool of aviation fuel lying by the fence. *Must have been a spill*, I thought. Given the extreme cold and the barren nature of the snow-covered field, it wasn't a fire hazard, so I didn't give it any more thought until we had walked up behind one of the tents itself. At that point, I smelled gasoline. *Another spill?* I thought to myself. I supposed that one of the last tasks of the day must have been fuelling up the various aircraft and ground vehicles. Shivering from the cold, I decided I didn't envy the ground crews their work and Silver and I headed back to our tent for a visit with the others and an early sleep.

The plan was for us to depart in the Chinooks at 9 am the next morning, which would give us an hour to fly – in darkness - to our first search area, then we'd gear-up during the morning twilight and begin searching in earnest as daylight came, at 11:30. That would give us only five hours of daylight visibility plus, at most, another hour of twilight before having to halt for the day and fly back to camp – again, in darkness.

I was looking forward to getting on with it.

RCAF CH-147 Chinook

Laurie Schramm

7 THE GROUND-SEARCH

January 28, 1978
Day 5

First thing in the morning, being ever conscious of my real mission, I had opened the small metal case from my duffel bag and extracted my double-barreled derringer and compact, modified UDT knife that had been issued to me before I went on an undercover assignment to Nova Scotia[12].

Was it really only a year ago? I thought, remembering. That was when I'd first met Don. *So many things have happened since then.*

Rummaging around in my duffel bag I found my roll of 'sensitive-skin' first-aid tape and began using it to tape the gun and knife to my thighs, one on each.

"Are you still wearing those things?" asked Vivian, having looked up from her own preparations. Vivian, I knew preferred somewhat heavier-duty armament and I was sure she'd have something secreted in her clothing somewhere.

"I sure am," I replied, winding the tape around my gun and one leg. "They've helped save my life, and Silver's, and Don's before now... yours too, now that I think of it."

"Oh, I'm not complaining," said Vivian, sounding amused, "it's only that you still strike me as a kind of female James Bond."

"Could be worse. At least James Bond always survives his cases." Having finished wrapping the gun so it looked like a lumpy bandage on one leg, I'd begun taping my knife to the other leg.

When we went to assemble for our first ground-search, all three Chinook helicopters had been moved outside the maintenance tents and were sitting with their side and back doors open. As we got out of the shuttles and grabbed our gear, we could hear the whooshing hiss of propane heaters pumping hot air into the aircraft. *A futile gesture*, I thought, although I was pretty sure that the aircraft would warm-up quickly once the big rear cargo doors were closed. One surprise was that each helicopter was equipped with skis. Looking closely, I could see that the skis were designed a bit like a person's over-boots in that the wheels were still mounted and sat nestled in a hollow space in the centre of each ski. *Neat*, I thought.

As we divided up into out three groups, the Chinooks' flight engineers came over and introduced themselves. For our group it was a cheerful-looking, red-haired Sergeant Scott Huber. "Everyone calls me Scotty," he said, displaying a huge smile.

"Let me guess, you're a *Star Trek* fan," I responded, impulsively.

"Yes, ma'am."

"Do all engineers want to be called Scotty these days?" I asked, semi-seriously.

"Only the good ones, ma'am."

Laughing, and with a request to call me Alex, rather than Ma'am, we went aboard so he could show me where to stow my gear.

Besides my Arctic clothing, the only other gear I had to contend with was a medium-sized daypack, and the heavy leather case containing the gamma-ray spectrometer. Giving a wave to Don and Vivian, who were getting ready to board the other two helicopters, I went to see if I could help the others.

Fred was supervising the loading of several drums that I took to be the lead-lined containers that would be used for any radioactive debris that we found. Each canister was about the size of a standard garbage can. Wayne was supervising the loading of the snowmobile and its sled. As both of them seemed to have all the help they could use, I went to help Peter with his dogs.

Greeting Peter, I saw that his dogsled was already loaded. He welcomed my help with the dogs, although I doubted that he needed it. As he called them one by one, he put their harness on, and led them up the ramp into the helicopter, past where the sleds and snowmobile were being secured, and along to a point where each harness could be attached to a strap from the wall. After observing how he was doing it, I chipped in and we alternated taking the rest of the dogs in, saving only Penny and Silver, who would be tied in next to our own seats.

When all of the big gear was secured, the large rear cargo door was raised up and closed. A few minutes later, Scotty came over to where we were clustered and said we were ready to go.

Although large, the interior of the Chinook wasn't nearly as large as that of a Hercules, and it's lower ceiling probably made it feel more cramped that it really was. It was more than large enough for our team and our gear, however, and we strapped in to the fold-down seats that lined each wall. These had us sitting near the front of the helicopter, with our backs to the walls, facing each other across the cabin. Penny and Silver were each attached by their harnesses to a short lead that allowed them some freedom of movement, so that they could sit on their seats or the floor, as they preferred.

Having secured a lead to Silver's harness, I was about to take my own seat when I noticed a sign taped to the wall above my seat. It read:

BUCKLE UP!

A HELICOPTER CONSISTS OF 10,000 PARTS FLYING IN CLOSE FORMATION AROUND AN OIL LEAK, WAITING FOR METAL FATIGUE TO SET IN.

It was obviously meant as a bit of military-aviation humour but, somehow, I didn't find it very amusing or reassuring when I was about to take my first flight in such a huge helicopter.

Although it was cold, still around -30 °C, there was very little wind and the skies were clear. As the three helicopters took off, the sun was just beginning to appear on the horizon, and the day was beginning to look more cheerful, so that helped lift my spirits and I was looking forward to our search.

With our backs to the walls, there was no opportunity for sight-seeing, so most of our team just sat in a kind of early-morning doze as the Chinook rattled and roared towards the starting coordinates for our first search. After about an hour, when we must have been close to our destination, instead of descending the helicopter suddenly banked sharply to the left and we could hear the sound of the engines and rotor blades increase as if the pilot had suddenly applied full throttle. As soon as the helicopter had stabilized on its new flight path, Susan, the pilot that I'd met earlier, came on the intercom to inform us that one of the other helicopters was in trouble, and that we were going to try to assist them.

We couldn't have been far away as it was only about fifteen minutes before the roar of the engines eased and we descended, turned in a half-circle, and landed. As we disembarked, we were in for a shock. The Chinook we'd come to assist wasn't simply having trouble – it had crashed!

Telling us to stay put, and well away from the crash site while they checked for hazards like spilled fuel, Scotty and Wayne ran over to check things out. This gave us a few moments to take in what was lying before us. Whatever had gone wrong, the helicopter had come down hard. It was leaning sharply to one side, and part of the nose was crumpled against an outcrop of rock. The forward cabin door, on the side that was tilted upwards, had been opened but there was no other sign of activity.

Having carefully circled the wreck, Scotty ran back to us while Wayne seemed to be checking to see if the rear cargo door could be opened.

"Some people are injured. We're going to need help," said Scotty, on his way into the Chinook in which we had arrived. Almost immediately, we heard the whirr of the cargo door being lowered, after which he emerged from the rear carrying a ladder. Fred immediately went to help with the ladder, while Peter and I followed along.

When we reached the crashed Chinook, Scotty positioned the ladder by the open door and climbed up, followed by Fred and Wayne. Almost immediately, the first figures started coming out. The first two were the AECB scientist and local guide/musher, who were obviously mobile, but wobbly. Wayne asked Peter and I to help them over to the third Chinook, that had just landed, and which would keep its engines running so it could serve as a kind of warm refuge. I took the unresisting arm of the AECB scientist, whose name I couldn't remember and, seeing that he was still in shock, didn't ask him any questions about the crash. Peter had a little more on his plate, having taken the arm of the other guide/musher and was constantly having to reassure him that his dogs would be looked after.

When Peter and I returned to the crash site four people, two on each end, were carefully maneuvering a loaded stretcher out of the door and down the ladder. It was the SAR Tech from the other helicopter. He was conscious, but seemed to have been bandaged with splints along most of the length of his body. It took four of us, Peter and I plus Wayne and Scotty, to carry the stretcher and it was hard work trying not to jostle the patient while tramping through the snow. Wayne explained that the port side of the helicopter, where the SAR Tech had been seated, had come down hard on a rocky outcrop, like the one that jutted up by the nose of the helicopter, and that they suspected fractures to his ribs and or hips. I listened to this with my heart in my mouth, as the fourth passenger – Don – was still in the wreck and must have been sitting on the port side as well.

"Is Don Harrison OK?" I asked, as we tramped along.

"I think so," replied Wayne. "They're looking at him now, and he's conscious. That's a good thing. He's in pain though. My guess is that he'll come out on a stretcher as well and have to be checked over for fractures."

Although worried for Don, I had my hands full bearing my share of the stretcher, which was probably just as well as it kept my mind occupied while the professionals tended to Don and the others.

Sure enough, by the time we had made out way back to the crash, another loaded stretcher was sticking out of the door, waiting to be lowered down the ladder.

This time, I made sure that I was positioned at one of the stretcher poles by Don's head.

"How badly are you hurt?" I asked, as we took up the load and started along the well-worn path that led to the warm, idling Chinook.

"Not sure," said Don, trying to smile through clenched teeth. "I don't think anything's broken but everything from my ribs to my hips hurts like hell!"

"What happened, anyway?"

"I don't know. We were flying along and then all of a sudden, the engines started running rough and then stalled. I think the pilot must have tried to autorotate us down, but something must have gone wrong with that too because all of a sudden we just dropped and then hit the ground – hard!"

Reaching the idling Chinook, fresh hands took the stretcher from us and we were sent back with two empty stretchers for more casualties. Back at the crash site, the dogs were being unloaded. Apparently, half of the dogs had been tethered on each side of the aircraft and, once again, those on the starboard side were shaken up but OK, but six out of seven of those on the port side were suspected of having fractured ribs.

Peter immediately took charge of the eight healthy dogs and led them away. The other six dogs were taken out, two dogs to a stretcher. These weren't splinted so much as bandaged and immobilized right onto the stretchers, and they seemed to know that people were trying to help them as each one of them lay quiet and subdued on their stretchers, watching us with wide eyes. One of the pilots from our Chinook had now joined Wayne, Scotty, and I as stretcher bearers, and off we went with the first two injured dogs. With two dogs on them, the stretchers were slightly heavier than they had been with humans so it was still hard work, although we now had a very well-trodden path to follow in the snow. After three such round-trips, we had all the dogs accounted for. That left the two pilots and flight engineer.

Wayne climbed up into the crashed Chinook and, when he returned explained that the cockpit was in really rough shape, having been crushed from two sides by the rocky outcrop it had hit. As a result, the other engineer had been working all this time to extract the two pilots but they were being brought out momentarily.

Sure enough, a loaded stretcher was soon pushed through the helicopter's door and brought down the ladder. This one carried the co-pilot, who had been sitting on the starboard side, and who seemed to have just his legs splinted. Wayne explained that the co-pilot had remained conscious just long enough to explain that both legs were broken and then passed-out. When we had delivered him to the waiting hands at the idling Chinook, we were told we could stand down as the last stretcher was being brought along behind us.

Looking back, I could see the stretcher being brought along, and was watching it closely as I was joined by Vivian, who had been helping with the patients inside the idling helicopter all along.

"What's up?" she asked, seeing the look on my face.

"I don't know, they're walking faster with that one than we did with ours and its bouncing more. I don't think that's a very good... uh-oh... I'm afraid that the other pilot didn't survive." As the stretcher party came close, we could see that it bore a body that had been covered head-to-toe with a blanket.

Despite the shock and the sadness of a sudden death, everyone carried on and it wasn't long before the Chinook that had been loaded with the injured was ready to leave. I had just enough time to say good-bye to Don before the shaken-up but uninjured people from the downed helicopter also boarded and they all departed for Inuvik.

Scotty explained that an accident investigation team was being dispatched from CFB Edmonton and would likely be on the scene by the next morning. It would be their job to figure out what had caused the crash.

Wayne, meanwhile, had received instructions from the CO that we were to go ahead and do as much of our planned search for the day as visibility would allow. Knowing how tired we all were, Wayne insisted that we first have a hot lunch.

For me, sitting in the warm comfort of the helicopter cabin, with my Arctic parka wide open, the first – and best – part of lunch was the large mug of steaming coffee that Scotty brought me.

***

One thing about the military, they know how to remain focused on a mission. It wasn't long before we'd resumed our flight to the beginning of the day's planned search area, offloaded the snow mobile and secured two lead-lined drums onto its sled, and set up the dogsled with all fourteen dogs, including Silver, tied into place.

The pilots had put us down on the estimated coordinates of one of the hits from the Hercules' searches. Now, we had to find it.

I had already taken out my portable gamma-ray spectrometer. Switching it on, I pointed the large detector tube away from me and slightly downwards, and walked a large circle around the helicopter. I'd started with a high sensitivity measuring range, and was more than three-quarters of the way around and starting to feel discouraged, when all of a sudden, the display jumped from background readings to off-scale. Just to be sure I walked another complete circuit, and then turned to the others.

"Something out that way," I said, pointing.

Fred mounted up behind Wayne on the snowmobile, and Peter took the dogsled with me sitting in front of him, in the basket part of the sled. We found that I could continue to point the detector cylinder as we went, which allowed me to switch measuring ranges as needed and make course corrections by simply pointing this way or that. Peter translated my hand gestures into commands for the dog team, while the snowmobile followed.

As we continued, the readings became larger and larger until at one point, a few hundred metres from the helicopter, they peaked and began to decline. At this, I waved one hand in a circular motion and Peter turned us around and backtracked until I motioned for a halt. Climbing out of the sled, I found that I could tramp through the snow without snowshoes and followed the readings on foot, going slowly now, with the spectrometer counting with 10 second sampling times for greater accuracy.

As I got closer, I had to pay more attention to the readings themselves. A conversion chart had been included with my kit, that allowed me to estimate the gamma-radiation exposure – in units called röntgens[37], symbol 'R' - corresponding to a particular count rate. The same chart showed some examples of important exposure levels. In this case, I was able to walk right up to the source of my readings, at which point my reading was 10 mR, meaning 10 milli-röntgen, that is, 10 one-thousandths of a röntgen. This is about the same exposure as one would receive from a single chest X-ray so, while you wouldn't want to get one every day, an occasional one is not thought to be harmful.

Seeing me stop, Fred came over, looked at my display and went back to the snowmobile to get one of the lead-lined drums and a shovel. Returning with them, he carefully used the shovel to remove a layer of snow and had me check it with the spectrometer. Nothing. The next shovelful of snow, however, gave a positive reading and he slowly tipped the shovel this way and that, shedding snow, until we could see the cause: a greyish-white, frost-covered piece of twisted metal. The whole thing was two- to three- inches in diameter. I followed Fred as he walked over to the drum and opened it, exposing a garbage-bag-lined interior.

"Hold the shovel over the drum for a moment, would you please?" he asked.

When I did, he withdrew a pen from inside his parka and, without extending the ball-point, used it to scrape the frost away from a small portion of the object. The exposed metal surface was heavily charred.

"There we go," he said, with satisfaction. "Our first recovery."

"Any idea what it is?" I asked.

"None whatsoever," he replied cheerfully, "except that it's from the satellite and it was somewhere near the reactor core, but not close. Otherwise, it would be much hotter than this."

Reaching into his parka again he withdrew a small camera and took a picture of our finding, then said "OK, you can drop it in the barrel now."

I dropped it in, he put the lid on, I re-swept the area to make sure there were no more pieces, and that was it. Our first ground search had taken an hour and a half. At this rate, and including flying time, our pilots estimated that we could investigate two more of our assigned hits, so we packed everything back into the Chinook and took off. The next two hit locations were disappointing. The next one began in similar fashion to the first, I got a reading right away and established a direction. We were able to follow it with the snowmobile and dogsled, although the readings were weaker than at the first location. When we arrived at the location of the maximum reading, shoveling into the snow produced only a patch of rocky outcrop. Somewhere in that rock was a radioactive mineral. Switching channels on my spectrometer, I took readings at the standard energy-level settings used for uranium prospecting, one each for the isotopes potassium-40, bismuth-214, and thallium-208. These I recorded in my note-book, in case they would be of any use to the geophysicists back at camp.

When we landed at the third hit location, we found absolutely nothing: no signal to home-in on whatsoever, even though we must have travelled at least 3 kilometres in every major direction: north, east, south, and west. The decision on what to do next was taken out of our hands by the onset of twilight, making it time to begin the flight back to camp.

It was a long, sober ride back. Sitting there buckled into my helicopter seat I had little else to do but take stock of the day. On the plus side, we had proven that the aerial- and ground search techniques worked, although all of our efforts so far had only produced one odd little piece of scorched, twisted metal.

On the negative side, one helicopter had crashed, killing one of the pilots and injuring Don, the other pilot, one of the SAR Techs, and six of the dogs. The third helicopter had been turned into a flying ambulance, which took it out of the day's search, but that was OK, we weren't in all that much of a hurry.

I don't sleep well on airplanes, and all the things that interfere with sleeping on an airplane were magnified in the noisy, vibrating environment of the helicopter. On top of that, I was worried about Don, and trying to figure out how I was going to maximize my time with him without blowing my cover. So, it shows how exhausted I must have been that I immediately fell asleep.

When we returned to camp, things were pretty quiet, considering. Fred and I reported our findings to the CO, and I made a copy of my notes to give to the three geophysicists when they landed from the day's Hercules flights.

I had expected to be summoned to a briefing on the day's events, but learned that with so many teams coming and going at different times of day, everyone would simply be briefed as they reported in to the command centre.

Colonel Stark told us that the preliminary assessment was that the helicopter crash was due to a combination of metal fatigue and the extremely cold weather. This made me think of the sign that had been jokingly posted to the wall inside the helicopter I'd flown in. It was not an encouraging thought and, for the first time, it occurred to me that I could die on this mission. The Colonel said that it would be some time before the exact cause could be established. He'd requested a replacement Chinook, and another guide/musher and dog-team, but he clearly wasn't optimistic that either would arrive for another day or two. In the meantime, we would carry on the search as best we could with the three Hercules and the two Chinooks.

By this time, I was starving, but my priority was to go to the hospital. When I mentioned this to the Colonel, he immediately assigned a soldier to drive me, and anyone else that wanted to go, to the hospital.

Fred said he'd like to go, and when I went to drop off Silver and my gear at my tent, Vivian said she'd like to go as well.

As the three of us piled into a military shuttle van, I was surprised and pleased to see that a big thermos of coffee and a bag of sandwiches had been supplied by the mess tent. I suspected the

Colonel's hand in this, and wondered how he found the time to worry about little things like us being fed. I actually asked him about that much later, and his reply was one that could just as easily have come from the mouth of my own boss at the time: "We have a saying about leadership: *Look after your people, and they will look after you.*"

When we reached the hospital, Fred, Vivian, and I went to see the SAR Tech but found that he had been heavily sedated and was fast asleep. The ward nurse told us that although none of his injuries were life-threatening, he had multiple fractures and wouldn't be going anywhere for a few weeks. When we went to see the injured pilot, he was also asleep, under sedation, and his situation was essentially the same.

Don, fortunately, was another matter. As we entered his room, we were met with an "About time you folks got around to paying me a visit. I've been lying here waiting all day!"

"How are you feeling?" Vivian and I asked, simultaneously.

"Well enough to get out of here, but they won't let me go yet. The doctors say that my ribs are so badly bruised they can't figure out why they can't find any fractures in them, and they X-rayed me twice in the attempt! Apparently, they did find some hairline fractures in my pelvis, which is why I'm laid-up here."

"Are they going to have to operate?" asked Fred.

"They say that the fractures are 'stable' and there's no sign of internal bleeding, so for now they're holding me for observation."

Don knew as much as we did about the others, so we spent some time answering his flurry of questions about how the search had gone. His reaction to the search was quite different than mine, in that he hadn't expected us to find much of anything that day, even if all three teams had been out on the ground. The fact that we'd found one piece of confirmed satellite debris made the day a success, he said.

When I told him that another helicopter was on order and that the two remaining ones would go out again the next day, his response was "Situation normal."

I must have looked surprised, because he looked at me and added: "We have a saying in the Canadian Forces: *Do what you can, with what you have, now.*"

I was getting a lot of 'sayings' that day, but this latest one, from Don, I've always quite liked.

We'd have stayed and visited longer, but the ward nurse was keeping a watchful eye on things, and came to shoo us out so Don could rest.

It was hard playing the role of only a caring colleague, but I decided that seeing the brightness of his eyes and hearing the banter in his voice would have to suffice for the moment.

8 FORGING AHEAD

January 29, 1978
Day 6

The next day was Sunday, but it certainly wasn't a day of rest for any of us. It was another clear day but colder, we were down to -35 °C now, and the wind was beginning to pick up. Under those conditions, when bare flesh touched something metal, it stuck to it. Vivian discovered this first-hand, and learned something all Canadians know: that it is not an enjoyable experience.

As we took our places in the remaining two Chinooks, the three Hercules aircraft were already up in the air and well into their day's search pattern. We too, had our new sets of search coordinates and the two helicopters went their separate ways.

Vivian and the second helicopter team had a day that was similar to our first day of searching. They found several good hits, a few areas in which the radiation seemed to be due solely to natural minerals in the rocks, and a couple of blanks. The hits came, once again, from bits of twisted metal, all of which were placed into one of the lead-lined drums. Our instructions were to locate and remove any debris reading more than 0.5 mR, and most of what they found ranged from 1 to 10 mR.

Our team had pretty similar success in the morning, having found several more low-level hits, another mineral source, and one blank. One of the pieces of debris we found actually looked like something that could have come from a satellite. Although not highly radioactive, and therefore not from very near the reactor, it did have several pieces of twisted metal attached to a squished cannister, all of it well charred. The whole thing was about two and a half feet long and barely fit into Fred's lead-lined drum.

255

"Any idea what this used to be part of?" I asked Fred.

"Hard to say. I'd guess it was either part of the propulsion unit or maybe part of the radar unit."

When we stopped for lunch, the mood was still subdued, but we felt like we were making progress. The afternoon turned out to be a bit more exciting. After collecting another small piece of debris at one location, we had quite a different experience at the next.

Peter and I had the lead and had just stopped for me to get out and continue on foot when I signalled for Fred to come up and join me.

"Something interesting?" he asked.

"Different anyway, I'm already reading 50 mR and I don't think we're close to it yet."

"Hang on a minute and I'll get some markers."

Our plan had been that we wouldn't approach anything highly radioactive without wearing full radiation suits. Instead, we were to map out a circle around the item and mark it with flags.

When Fred returned from the snowmobile, he was carrying a bunch of four-foot poles and a handful of bright, fluorescent-orange streamers. Starting where I was standing, he used a mallet to pound one pole into the ground, and then attached a streamer to it.

"OK, see if you can find another spot five- or six feet away with the same reading, without it going higher."

Moving to my left, I walked a few feet. The reading dropped, so I went another four- or five feet and then turned right and walked slowly until my spectrometer read 50 mR again. At that point Fred pounded in another pole and streamer.

We repeated this twice more and then stood back. We had now marked out a rectangle that was roughly 7 feet across.

"Well, depending how deeply it's buried, that piece might be quite hot," remarked Fred, quite casually.

At the next location, I encountered another moderately high reading, and we repeated the same procedure with the poles and streamers. The only difference was that for this second hit, we ended up placing eight poles and streamers around an oval-shaped area that was about 20 feet across.

The next day, one of our teams would go out wearing full radiation suits, find the debris and contain it. Ultimately, all of the recovered debris, large or small, and whether highly- or only slightly radioactive, would be shipped to AECL's Whiteshell Laboratories[38], in Pinawa, Manitoba - near Winnipeg - for analysis and eventual disposal.

Having found debris that was radioactive enough for us to flag it rather than collect it, there was another change to our routine when we landed back at Inuvik. Upon landing, our Chinook taxied over to a very large tent that had been set up for radiation screening. In it, NAST soldiers wearing yellow radiation suits, gas masks, and hand-held Geiger Counters checked over every one of us for radiation, even the flight crew, before allowing any of us onto the rest of the camp. We were a little tired and grumpy about it, but it really was a reasonable precaution, so we had no good cause for complaint.

After supper, Fred, Vivian, and I went into town again to see our colleagues in the hospital. The injured SAR Tech and pilot were awake this time, in quite good spirits, and seemed resigned to being confined to the hospital for some time to come.

Don was in good spirits, and a lot less pale than he'd been the previous day. The ward nurse told us that additional X-rays had been taken, without finding anything, and that his injuries seemed to be miraculously mild, considering what he'd been through.

For his part, Don was 'chomping at the bit' to get out, especially as there was some hope of being released the following day.

"No flying around in planes or helicopter for a few more days yet, though" the nurse cautioned.

"Looks like I'll be confined to camp for a while, but at least I'll be up and around," was Don's summary.

I was looking forward to Don getting out of the hospital for another reason. It was still really hard playing the role of casual colleague, particularly with him being injured. With him returned to camp, I hoped to be able to find the odd secluded moment in which we could really talk. It wasn't that I mistrusted Fred or the hospital staff. Fred, in particular, seemed to be on the level, had done more than his share of helping at the crash site, and had come with Vivian and I both days to check on our injured colleagues. It was the risk that he or someone else might notice my attachment to Don and mention it to someone else in casual conversation later on.

Anyway, without more to discuss at the hospital, and with

fatigue setting in, we all headed back to camp. I don't know about our other colleagues, but once Vivian and I got back to our tent we collapsed onto our cots and I fell asleep almost immediately, with Silver curled up at my feet.

January 30, 1978
Day 7

Another day. At breakfast, Colonel Stark came around to each of the tables where people from the Chinook teams were eating. He had two messages. One was that we were still down to two operational Chinooks, and the other was a warning not to push ourselves too hard that day.

"This will be your third day of ground searching, and you're going to really feel the tiredness in all those muscles you're not used to using," he warned. "Factor in the effects of the cold and the flying, and it will be easy to make mistakes, so I want you to be extra careful out there."

His words reminded me of the time I had been on downhill-skiing trips. *It was always day three*, I remembered, that the effects of high altitude and overworking little-used muscles came together to produce exhaustion.

On this occasion, it was the other Chinook team that got the call to go after the two hot items that Fred and I had found and flagged the previous day. Before taking off, Vivian and Jim Graham, the AECB scientist from her group donned full radiation suits. Sealed into their bright yellow suits, with their boot covers on, they looked like science-fiction astronauts. When they donned their gas masks and pulled their hoods over them, they looked more like space invaders.

It turned out to be a good thing they had the suits. We discovered later that, in both cases, the debris was buried under a thick layer of snow and ice. It was thought that both must have been thermally hot enough to melt snow when they hit, so that the melted snow re-froze into a covering layer of ice after cooling. In both cases, they'd needed ice axes to chop out the debris. They were hot in terms of radioactivity too. One registered 6 röntgens, enough to give even a nuclear industry worker their allowable dose for an entire year. The other one gave a reading of 100, enough to cause radiation sickness. That one had been plucked out with long tongs, and from behind a lead-lined shield.

Fred's opinion was that both must have come from somewhere close to the satellite's reactor core. Now I better understood why scientists and engineers had been selected to operate the hand-held, gamma-ray spectrometers and the lead-lined drums. The job called for more than just reading instrument dials and following instructions, it called for people that would understand the science and the risks well enough to take appropriate precautions, and be neither too complacent nor too afraid.

As far as additional ground searching went, both ground-search teams found more debris at additional locations during the day. Some fragments were tiny, some looked like clusters of tangled metal, and occasionally a large number of small fragments would be found at a single location. A few of the larger pieces looked almost recognizable: looked like a squashed cylinder, and several

Vivian and Her Radiation Suit

looked like they might have been pieces of antennae. All were logged and placed in the lead-lined drums for others to study later.

Once, when flying from one hit site to another, I noticed that my spectrometer started beeping with radiation counts.

"Hey, Fred, look at this," I said, showing him the display, which as showing readings in the low milli-röntgen range.

"Must have been too weak to be picked up by Hercules flights," he concluded. "Let's ask the pilots to circle and see if we can find it."

As our Chinook reduced altitude and circled, we pinpointed the location and, having landed and found it, discovered several small pieces of debris, which Fred collected and secured.

We also made a careful note of the location so the geophysicists would later be able to go back to their tapes from the Hercules flights and see if they could learn anything useful that might guide future searches.

There was one amusing incident after both Chinooks had landed back at camp after the day's searching. All of us were scanned in the radiation-screening tent, and Fred must have had some fragments from a hit rub off because his clothing lit up the Geiger Counters, causing his pants to be confiscated. This wasn't a problem, but it caused much amusement and teasing at supper.

The camp included a medical tent, even though Inuvik had a real hospital that was only a short drive away. That's where I found Don, who had been released from hospital but still confined to bed. He was hoping to be mobile soon, but had been given stern warnings that there was to be no riding in airplanes, helicopters, or even jeeps and trucks in the near future. I quietly filled him in on the day's events and left to let him rest.

At supper, there was news. The geophysicists had been analyzing the differences between Hercules hits that led to us finding satellite debris versus those that didn't, and had adjusted their computer processing routines accordingly. Clem reported that, as a result, he was confident that almost all of the future hits passed on to the ground-teams would result in positive debris-finding. That would make our searches more efficient.

The other encouraging news was that the locations of the debris actually found were starting to provide something of a pattern, so that the search area itself could be refined somewhat.

Although both of these advances were good news, the harsh

reality was that it was still expected that debris was scattered over approximately a hundred square kilometres. That meant a lot more flying, for everyone.

There were also two pieces of not-so-good news. One was that the replacement Chinook helicopter had arrived, but that having reached Inuvik, one rotor was refusing to turn. It was in one of the maintenance hangers being disassembled, but we were told that a Chinook has five transmissions and three hydraulic systems, so diagnosing and fixing mechanical problems can be time-consuming. Scotty, our Sergeant-engineer, explained that this kind of thing was to be expected.

"In this kind of cold, the Chinooks are being pushed to their limits. If it gets much colder, the rubber seals can deform and the oil can freeze solid. Then, we might have a bit of a problem," he concluded.

His remarks fit in rather well with the next bit of bad news, I thought, which was that there was an Arctic high-pressure area front approaching. It was going to get even colder. No one was ready to give up, however. For the time being, at least, both Hercules and Chinook searches were expected to continue.

Another Search

Above image based on an AECB photograph[39].

9 TROUBLE

January 31, 1978
Day 8

As predicted, it had become much colder. The new weather front had caused the temperature to drop further. It was now -45 °C.

I was just finishing breakfast in the mess tent when Scotty walked in looking like a thundercloud.

"What's wrong?" I asked, after he'd poured himself a cup of hot coffee and taken a seat beside me.

"The replacement Chinook is still not operational," he replied, shaking his head. "These machines have been flying every day, in harsher conditions than they were designed for. Eventually, something has to give, but this particular one seems to be cursed. All of the mechanics and flight-engineers are pitching-in to help when we can, but every day ends with the aircraft ready to fly, and every morning begins with a new problem."

"What's today's problem?" I asked, more out of politeness than any expectation of understanding the answer.

"A dead battery! I can't believe it, and neither can the crew's flight engineer; he says he installed a new one only a week ago... Cold weather plays havoc with batteries, just like everything else, but this is ridiculous."

I must have murmured something sympathetic, but my 'spider-sense' was tingling. So far, I'd seen no evidence of a Soviet agent at work, and neither had Vivian. On the other hand, I couldn't help wondering whether it was just that we didn't know what we should be watching for.

As the moment passed, Scotty and I discussed the upcoming search-flights and then went to load-up. This was to be the last day of the Hercules flights. The recovered satellite debris had been found to track more or less down the centre of the projected area, so it had been decided that the 'initial' search zone had been the correct one to search. The three Hercules were expected to be able to complete the last few grid blocks of the search by the end of the day. The ground searches, however, were expected to take at least two more days.

The morning's searching turned up more radioactive 'junk,' as I now thought of it. Mostly small, twisted, torn, or crumpled bits of charred metal, all of them ranging in size from about 50 cm at their largest, down to about 1 mm at their smallest. Those emitting sufficiently low radiation for us to approach, Fred collected and placed in his lead-lined drums. The large emitters we ringed with poles bearing the bright, fluorescent-orange streamers, and left them for more careful collection the next day.

One difference from previous days' searching was the effects of the enhanced cold. For one thing, the pilots stopped switching the engines off when we went out to search for the hits. In the most secluded locations, we faced the -45 °C temperature plus 30-knot winds, making it effectively -70 °C with the wind chill. Back in camp, if a helicopter engine was allowed to fully cool, then it could take three hours for propane heaters to warm the engines and transmissions enough to be able to start up. Out in the barrens, each helicopter carried one such heater and enough propane for one such start, and that was reserved for emergencies. Even with the engines idling while we searched, they consumed a lot of fuel, so our search-day was going to be short.

For us searchers, the increased cold and wind meant that if frostbite was a hazard before, it was an extreme hazard now.

After landing at our second hit site of the morning, we had zeroed in on the hit and I was about to get off of the dogsled when my spectrometer-display suddenly shifted to read 'L' for 'low batteries' and then went blank. I had been replacing the batteries every second evening, but as the weather turned colder, even brand-new batteries were lasting for shorter and shorter periods of time.

I had brought a spare set of batteries with me, and had been keeping them warm in an inner pocket of my parka, but even a simple task like replacing batteries was a trial in the extreme cold. Between having to use my thin, inner gloves, which was both awkward and cold, and the reluctance of anything metal to move or flex, it took far longer than usual to replace the batteries and resume detecting.

Having resumed the search, we located another piece of satellite debris. This one was unusually large, measuring perhaps eight inches by six inches, by four inches. It looked like a squashed box with gear wheels inside.

"What do you think that used to be?" I asked Fred.

"Search me. Something mechanical, obviously." Fred seemed particularly interested in it and, since it was only giving me very low radiation readings, he was able to hold it in his hands. Turning it one way and then another, he examined it from various angles and then set it down on the blade of the shovel and stepped back to take some pictures of it.

When he took up his camera, which had been slung from a strap around his neck, the cold struck again and his camera almost immediately jammed. When he tried to force the film advance, we could both hear the sound of metal breaking inside the camera body.

"Damn," was Fred's comment. "That was my personal camera too and I have holiday pictures on this roll of film!"

Laughing, I said that I was sure that if AECB wouldn't replace his camera, then the military probably would.

Although he was upset, he recovered quickly, shrugged, and re-slung his camera then dropped the mechanism in a lead-lined drum, and we all headed back to the Chinook.

Everything we were doing had slowed down in the cold, and we were just discussing whether to break for lunch or do one more search when the pilots received a radio message from the other helicopter.

Apparently, the other team had also found something interesting and, as they weren't far away from us, Fred's AECB counterpart, Jim Graham , wanted us to join them so the two of them could consult on it. Everyone was agreeable to this and, I think, eager to see what they had found. I know I certainly was.

Having made the short flight and landed near the other team, Fred, Wayne, Peter and I went over to see the latest find while our aircrew remained behind.

Vivian and the others were standing beside one of the lead-lined drums and, as we approached, I could see that lying on the blade of a shovel was another charred mechanism of similar size to the one we had just found, perhaps a bit larger. It also had a tube projecting just slightly from one side. When Fred brushed away the charring, we could see what looked like broken glass.

"Looks like some kind of readout port," said Fred.

"Or viewing port, or even a lens maybe?" I offered, remembering Fred's recently broken camera.

"Could be," was all Fred said.

As I happened to look Vivian's way at that moment, she gave me a significant look.

Having looked the thing over, Fred put it back in the drum and we gathered in the back of our Chinook, which was still warm with the engines idling, and had lunch together with some people sitting on the stowed snowmobile, sled, or dogsled. The other Chinook had been shut down for some reason, *maybe to save fuel*, I thought.

After an amiable lunch, Vivian and the others walked back to their helicopter to begin their afternoon searches. We didn't leave right away, however. Susan came on the intercom to say that we'd wait a bit to make sure that the other helicopter was able to start up successfully. It was only because of this, and the fact that I wasn't strapped in yet, that I was able to look out the window by my seat and see the unusual sight of the big rotor blades vibrating and giving every impression of being in the process of turning, without actually doing more than wobble. It had previously been explained to me that the rotors were synchronized, so that one couldn't run into the other, so neither set of rotor blades actually moved very far.

Following some radio chatter, Scotty hopped out from our aircraft and made his way over to the other, to see if he could help. Obviously, something had gone sufficiently wrong that both engineers were needed, whether to consult or to make repairs. There was nothing for the rest of us to do, so we simply waited and tried to rest.

Peter commented that there was a big storm coming.

"How do you know?" I asked.

"My grandfather would tell you that the ability to forecast weather changes is a gift that has been handed down from generation to generation in my family, going way back. With my modern education, I would tell you that I watch the skies very closely, that I can feel the relative humidity changing, and that I have an unusual sensitivity to pressure changes."

"Which do you believe?"

"Both, of course," he said, with a wink.

"What kind of storm?"

"Well, it can't get too much colder by the thermometer, but the wind's going to pick up and there'll be a whiteout."

"How soon?"

"Hard to say, but if we can get going soon, we should have time for one more search and then we'll need to retreat to the camp and wait the storm out."

That sounded like bad news but, again, all we could do for the moment was wait. That was another thing I was learning from the military: you took every available opportunity to rest because you never knew when the action might start up again.

My problem, was that I found myself unable to rest, or even relax. Watching the other helicopter just sitting there, I found myself counting up all the other things that had gone wrong on this mission. First one of the helicopters has a mechanical breakdown, then its replacement has mechanical problems – twice - and now the one Vivian was on was in trouble. Each time, the air force people took it in stride and made comments about the effects of the cold weather, and the difficulty of keeping such complex machines flying, even in good weather. These were experienced people, and everything they said made perfect sense, and yet... it felt wrong and I felt my spider-sense tingling, like I was missing something. The more I thought about it, the more I wondered if there was a pattern to it all.

Finally, since I hadn't been able to relax anyway, I went up to the cockpit and asked Susan if she'd like to join me for a quick stroll before we got the OK to take off.

She looked at me in surprise at first, then looked again and I saw her eyes narrow, and she nodded yes, said a few words to the other pilot and started unbuckling. As we casually walked along, seemingly aimlessly, I told her a little bit about me, a few of my suspicions, and what I wanted her to do. She naturally thought I was crazy, so I had to do some fast talking but, in the end, she agreed to at least consider my request. It didn't leave me feeling comfortable, but felt that I'd pushed her as far as I could and that I would have to hope for the best.

It was probably about half an hour, all told, before two figures emerged from the other helicopter and trudged over to us, carrying one of the lead-lined drums between them. It was Vivian and Jim Graham, the other AECB Scientist.

As they climbed aboard, Wayne helped Jim stow the drum and Vivian explained that there was something wrong in one or more of the transmissions and the two engineers were going to work on it while the rest of us went on with our search. Rather than sitting around doing nothing, Vivian and Jim had asked if they could accompany us, and Jim had wanted to bring an extra lead-lined drum along "just in case." She also explained that the plan was for us to do two more searches, and if the problem hadn't been fixed by then, we would return and pick-up everyone and return to camp, leaving the helicopter to be repaired at a later time.

As Vivian was explaining all this, the back ramp of the other Chinook had been lowered, and two figures emerged dragging a snowmobile sled. When they reached our helicopter, they removed our portable propane tank and heater, explaining that they were going to use the heaters to warm up the transmissions before disassembling things.

As the two engineers made their way back, our pilots revved up our engines and we took off to fly to our next search location, which was to the northwest. The direction was important because of the things that happened next. We were already in the northwest part of the overall search area, and the days' searches had been taking us northward. Our next hit location was even further north so that we were northeast of Inuvik but at the extreme north edge of the overall search area. Having found and recovered another piece of uninteresting looking, medium 'hot' debris, we had just loaded one of the lead-lined drums and the snowmobile and its sled into the Chinook, when Fred stopped us.

"Wait for a minute," he said, in a more authoritative tone of voice than he had ever used before.

Surprise, more than anything else, caused Vivian, Wayne, Peter, and I to stop and look at him questioningly.

"There's no need for us to search any further."

"What do you mean?" asked Vivian.

"I mean the search stops here. We have what we came for."

"What do you mean, 'what we came for?', there's still more

debris to recover. Isn't there?" she asked.

"I'm sure there is, but that's not important now. I have what I came for and it's time for me to leave."

"That mechanism you were so interested in?" I asked.

"That's right, and now that we've found it, my work here is done and I'm taking it with me."

"Where can you possibly go?" asked Vivian, sweeping her arm to indicate the vast expanse of the Barrens.

"Here's what's going to happen," Fred explained, patiently. "The mechanism and I are going to fly to a pick-up location, where I'll meet up with some friends of mine. Then, my friends and I will take the mechanism home. You four will stay here. I'll leave you a survival pack, and by tomorrow, your friends will come and find you, so you can go home too."

"That's crazy," said Vivian. "Who are you really, and what are you up to, and what makes you think we're all just going to let you take the helicopter and fly away leaving us out here in the middle of nowhere... There are seven of us and only one of you."

"You might want to reconsider your math," said Fred, with a smirk. His face had changed completely now.

Fred had been a model colleague, cheerful, interested in everything, caring, and always helpful, but the friendly, easy-going Fred was gone, and I now saw his behaviour through a new lens. This was a colder, harsher Fred.

Raising his voice, he called out: "Everything OK Jim?"

"Ready when you are," came a reply from inside the Chinook.

"Jim is one of my friends too," Fred explained, "and right now he's holding a gun on our two pilots to make sure that they're going to do what we want. As for the rest of you..."

Crack!

The sound seemed to come from nowhere and, in the fog of shock, I saw a rapid sequence play out:

A hole appeared in the pocket of Fred's parka, where he had clearly been holding a pistol, and a wisp of smoke came out.

Vivian screamed, dropped the gun she must have pulled from the pocket of her own parka, and dropped to her knees.

I saw the bright red of blood splotches appear against the brilliant white of the snow.

The sled dogs, startled by the sound of the gunshot started to bark, but could do little more as they were all still tied into their harnesses and the dogsled.

Meanwhile, my own body was in motion, even before I realized it, as I instinctively went to help Vivian who, I discovered was bleeding from her right hand.

"Stop!" commanded Fred, pointing a heavy-looking pistol at me.

"But she's hurt," I pleaded.

"First, I want you to very carefully pick up that pistol and, holding it by the barrel, toss it over to me. Then, you can help your friend."

With his gun aimed at me, and at such close range that he could hardly miss no matter what I might do, I did as he said and then turned my attention to Vivian and her hand.

As I pulled off her outer mitten and inner glove, and wrapped a handkerchief around her hand to stop the bleeding, Vivian was raging at Fred. "You're Russians, both of you!" she accused.

"Maybe," replied Fred in a softer voice now that he had asserted control. Keeping a close eye on Wayne and Peter, he continued: "This is not like a detective novel, where the master sleuth gets the bad guy to tell his life story and incriminate himself before the tables are turned and the detective wins everything... and while we're on the topic of people who are something different than they seemed to be, I don't suppose you'd like to tell us who you really are, why you were carrying a gun, and why you were so willing and able to use it?"

Silence.

"No, I didn't think so. Well, it doesn't matter. We suspected there would be one or more agents on the search teams, but we had no way of knowing who or how many." He paused then, and looked at her in a penetrating way. "Interesting. From your accent, I'm going to guess that you're American, either FBI or CIA. But, as I said, you don't need to admit anything because it doesn't really matter. All my friend Jim and I want now is to..."

Crack! Crack!

He was amazingly quick. In mid-sentence, he had shifted his aim just that little bit from me to Wayne, who had seen his opportunity and lunged forward. Fred had been faster, however, and judging from the way Wayne had dropped, one of the shots had hit something vital. Peter had been a bit further away, and had followed, an instant after he saw Wayne lunge. Fred's second shot had caught him in one leg, as evidenced by the rapidly growing pool of blood in the snow.

As Fred took a step back, and Peter was holding his injured leg, I first went to check on Wayne, but as I carefully rolled him over onto his back, I could see that the bullet hole was just about in line with his heart. Only, it wasn't 'just about' at all, the bullet must have actually punctured his heart. As I opened his outer parka, and his inner sweater, I could see a large flow of blood welling up, then Wayne lifted one arm and opened his mouth, as if to say something, but I never learned what it was because he was only able to make a gurgling sound before he died right there in front of us.

Leaving Wayne, I got up very slowly and wearily went to check on Peter who was grimacing with pain but was able to show me that the bullet had only grazed his leg. There was a fair amount of pain and bleeding, but nothing worse. Unwrapping a bandanna from around his neck, he passed it to me so I could bandage his leg.

"Any more heroes?" asked Fred. "No? Then you two," he motioned to Peter and I, "go untie the dogs and turn them loose. Then you, Peter, are going to make sure they run off."

"How…" Peter began.

"Don't give me that. You're a musher, you'll know how to do it. So, don't waste time arguing with me, just cut them loose and make sure they all leave."

"How do we know you won't just shoot us anyway?" I asked.

"Because I'm a professional. I'm perfectly willing to kill when it's necessary, as you've just seen, but only when it's necessary. Besides, you don't have any choice but to hope that I'm telling you the truth, do you?"

Well, he had us there. There wasn't anything anyone could do for poor Wayne anymore, and Vivian was OK for the moment, cradling her wounded hand inside her parka. So, Peter and I got to our feet and trudged over to untie the dogs. Peter was hobbling, but at least he was mobile.

Most of the dogs were eager enough to run off when released, but the better trained ones, Penny and Silver and the two swing dogs, were unwilling to leave us.

We looked up at Fred, who sighed rather theatrically. "Do I need to shoot another of you, or should I start shooting the dogs too?"

Peter and I exchanged a look and then he took Penny's head in his hands, aa I did with Silver and, each in our own way, told them to lead the swing dogs away from us. I don't know quite how Peter did it because I was focused on Silver. Looking deeply into his eyes, my voice said "Silver, go!" while in my mind I tried to project: *Go away with the other dogs, but bring them back later.*

I'd never before attempted to give Silver such a detailed command, but I didn't see that I had any better options that to try. Silver, for his part, gave me that penetrating look he was so good at, then moved forward to give me a lick from chin to nose, and then turned away. Silver and Penny, standing side by side, approached the other two dogs and barked, growled, and snapped at them until they started running the way the other dogs had gone, followed by Penny and Silver.

"Impressive, very impressive!" said Fred. "You two certainly know your way around dogs. I was sure I'd have to shoot a couple of them."

After that, with Fred covering us with his gun and giving us orders, we located the survival pack and dragged it out of the helicopter. I insisted on bringing the helicopter's First Aid kit as well, but that was the only other concession Fred was willing to make.

Waving us to stand back, he then strode up the ramp that was the rear door and raised it as the engines wound up and the big blades of the Chinook began to turn. Then, leaving the three of us sitting tiredly on the dogsled, they simply flew away.

We were completely alone at that point. If you want to try feeling cold and alone on the Barrens, try it in winter, with a storm coming in, and no means of transport at hand. Even with all my Arctic clothing on I felt a chill run up my back. Shaking my head, to get focused, I turned to Peter.

"How long before the storm hits?"

10 SURVIVAL

"Wind's picking up..." Peter paused to consider. "The storm will hit in an hour, no more."

He said it in a tone of absolute certainty, and I wasn't the least bit inclined to doubt him. I'd already seen and learned enough for that.

"So, you think we should find a place to lie low and ride out the storm then?"

He nodded, then pointed off in the distance, in the direction the helicopter had gone. "See that hill over there?"

There was only one hill to be seen anywhere around us, as we seemed to be on the surface of a frozen lake.

"That will be a rock outcrop. If we make for that, we can survey the terrain again from the summit. If we don't see anything better, then we can make a shelter in the lee of the outcrop."

As Vivian and I nodded our agreement to this, Peter put his fingers to his lips and gave a shrill whistle. Then, "Listen," was all he said.

I listened, but I didn't hear anything but the wind... and then I did hear something. Very faint it was, then louder, then... "The dogs! It's the dogs," I exclaimed.

Peter just smiled, and soon we could not only hear them but see them running towards us across the frozen plain. The first batch of dogs ran right up to Peter, followed by more, and more, and then there were Silver and Penny, at the rear, like shepherds driving their flock.

Silver was so excited that he bowled me right over, and I just lay there in the snow, flat on my back welcoming him, accepting his licks, and hugging him to me.

"I guess the dogs came back," said Peter, with a quiet smile.

"What, all of them?"

"Every last one, we have a full team again."

"That's great Peter, because we're going to need them tomorrow."

"You're going to want to go after those two, aren't you?"

That caught me by surprise. Again. "How did you know?"

"Just a feeling. There's something about you that you've been holding back, isn't there? Just like you've been doing, Vivian?"

"Yes, Fred wasn't far off. We're both policewomen."

"Let's talk about it later. We should get the dogs tied in and find ourselves a place to shelter."

It didn't take us long to get the dogsled set up. While we were crossing the frozen lake, Peter had both Vivian and I sit in the sled itself and we made pretty good time. Just before we reached the shore, Peter called a halt and, taking an axe from the sled went and chopped a number of large pieces of ice from the lake. These he loaded into the sled in front of Vivian.

Beyond the shore, the snow cover was deeper, and Peter and I took turns mushing or walking behind the sled. Our pace was now somewhat slower, with the dogs having to break trail as we went, but the snow behind the sled was well packed, so the walking part wasn't too hard.

By the time we reached the outcrop, there was no point in climbing to the top to look around as the visibility was dropping rapidly as the storm front approached. Instead, I untied the dogs while Peter took the shovel, the one we'd been using to dig for satellite debris, and started digging snow away from the side of the outcrop. He hadn't dug away much snow before Penny and Silver started barking.

At this, Peter stopped digging in surprise and, moving quickly to the dogsled, removed a long, slender fur case that had been stowed along one side. I didn't initially realize what it was. It looked familiar somehow. If it wasn't for the fur... Then I had it.

"You have a rifle!" I exclaimed, in amazement.

"Of course," Peter replied, as he extracted a hunting rifle. "I wouldn't willingly travel the Barrens this time of year without one."

"Too bad it was tucked away when Fred and Jim pulled their guns on us."

"Maybe, maybe not. Two people with pistols can shoot more people, faster, than one with a rifle and besides, we have a better chance of survival with it here with us now, than if it had been taken away from us."

"I suppose so," I conceded.

"Let's go see what all the fuss is about, but stay behind me. They may have cornered something that bites."

Silver and Penny were not far away, and they both stopped barking when they saw us approaching. Instead, they alternated looking at us, and looking rather pointedly at the side of the outcrop.

Peter carefully approached the side of the outcrop, then returned and handed me his rifle. "Looks like they've found an animal den of some kind. Wolves, maybe. I can see an entrance but no tracks, so I don't think its in use. I'm going to get the shovel and see if we can expand the entrance and find out how big it is."

"Good work, Silver," I praised. "You and Penny may have found us a den for the night!"

"Grruph!"

Returning with the shovel, Peter dug away at the snow for a while, then backed away a bit and said "Come see."

The rock jutted out from the broad side of the outcrop, creating a kind of sheltered nook that hadn't been obvious until the snow was removed. What Peter had exposed wasn't just a nook, it harboured a small cave-like entrance.

Retreating to the dogsled once more, Peter dug out a large flashlight. With this in hand, he returned to the entrance, laid down on the snow and scrambled his way in. He was gone for what seemed like quite a while, and then finally shuffled his way back out, head first, and said: "Penny and Silver have just saved us a lot of work. It's not a den, it's a cave, quite a large one, and someone has used it before."

"Is it safe?" asked Vivian.

"I think so. It's very old, and whomever used it before made some improvements. We're lucky that the entrance is downwind from the storm and, even better, there's an opening of some kind high up near the entrance, and I could feel fresh air coming in from somewhere at the back. With a little work, we should be able to adjust the air flow and use a stove."

"Do we have a stove?" I asked.

"A little one, but it'll do."

With Vivian's help, we dragged the dogsled up alongside the outcrop and near the cave entrance. Then, Vivian crawled in with Peter's flashlight. With her inside, Peter and I unloaded the dogsled itself. Peter had food for the dogs, which he left there, but the survival pack and Peter's stove and furs we passed in to Vivian. Outside the cave, Peter used the shovel to build a wall of snow on each side of the cave entrance, to help deflect more of the oncoming storm, to provide some shelter for the dogs and, he explained to provide shelter from the wind for anyone needing to heed the call of nature.

That brought some winter camping memories back. I'd discovered some years earlier that women are at a severe disadvantage, compared to men, when it comes to heeding the call of nature in the middle of freezing-cold nowhere!

Finally, Peter put his rifle back into it's fur case and carefully placed it on the ground along one of the walls he had just built, saying: "If I bring it inside the cave, it will warm up and moisture from the air will condense inside the rifle's mechanism. Then, when I take it back outside, the film of condensed water will freeze and the rifle may not work when I need it," he said, seeing me watching him.

I'm not sure I would have thought of that, I thought.

With those things completed, we both crawled into the cave. Upon entering it for the first time, and peering around in the dim light cast by Peter's flashlight, my first impression was surprise at how large it seemed. Although not tall, the cave consisted of a large chamber, and it looked like there was a second one at the furthest point away from me.

As I pushed back my hood and took off my woollen toque, I could hear a hissing sound. Vivian had found a gasoline-fuelled Coleman-type lantern in Peter's 'stove' box, and had just pumped it up and got it started. That provided much more light, and I could now see that someone had actually brought timber beams in from somewhere, to shore up parts of the cave's ceiling. Several had nails projecting from them, which would be handy for hanging up our parkas.

Next out was Peter's stove. Since Vivian had been basically

working one-handed, I took over getting the stove going. This too, was a Coleman-type single-burner unit. This type ran on most kinds of liquid fuel once pressurized by a tiny hand pump, and was very similar to the stoves I had used when winter camping. Whereas my friends and I had used white-camping gas[40] on our trips, the smell made it obvious that this one ran on gasoline.

Gasoline! that got me thinking. *What is it that the smell of gasoline reminds me of?* I wondered.

"What?" said Vivian, seeing my expression.

"I'm trying to remember something. Ask me again after I re-bandage your hand and Peter's leg, OK?"

Vivian agreed, and Peter said, "OK, but first I'm going to go get that ice so we can melt it." As he went out, I noticed that Silver had quietly slipped in and was lying on one of the furs.

The helicopter's First Aid kit was well stocked, and I was able to clean and properly bandage Vivian's hand and give her something for the pain.

"How are you feeling?" I asked.

"Not bad, but I don't think I've ever felt this cold in my life!"

"You'll feel better with a hot drink."

The good news was that the bullet had gone right through her hand and, despite the swelling she was able to flex her hand and fingers well enough that I didn't think any of the bones or tendons had been seriously damaged.

By the time I had finished with Vivian, Peter arrived with a cloth bag full of ice, and I was amused to notice Penny slink quietly into the cave with him, just like Silver had done with me.

Once we had some ice melting in a pot on the stove, I was finally able to persuade Peter to lie still long enough for me to look at his leg wound. After exposing and cleaning it, it still just looked like a nasty flesh wound, which was fortunate, so I only had to put on a proper bandage and give him something for the pain.

The cave by itself was much warmer than being outside exposed to the elements and now, between the stove and the lantern, it was warming up even more.

When entering the cave, you had to crawl or scramble up a slight incline to the big open chamber. Peter showed us how someone had dug out a section of rock to create a cooking area down at the level of the entrance, and to one side of it. Someone had done this, he explained, so that warm air from the stove would circulate upwards into the cave, while cold air was drawn down to the stove.

As the only uninjured one, I took over the making of hot water for tea or coffee of whatever I could find in the helicopter's emergency survival pack. Other than the hissing of the lantern and stove, it was quiet in the cave while I did this and I didn't think anything of it until I had made a pot of tea and turned to pass out the cups. When I did, I found Peter and Vivian looking at me expectantly.

"What?" I asked.

"I think this might be a good time for you two to tell me what's going on," said Peter.

"And I'd like to know what's going on in that devious mind of yours," said Vivian.

I tried to look innocent, but failed, so I sighed and said, "OK, let's start by re-introducing ourselves. You're right, Vivian is a friend and colleague. Fred got it almost right, out there." I paused and nodded to Vivian.

"My name really is Vivian Rule, and I really am American..." she paused, "but I'm not a scientist with the U.S. Geological Survey, I'm an FBI agent." She looked meaningfully over at me.

"And my name really is Alexandra Houston – Alex – and I really was trained as a scientist a long time ago, but I'm actually a policewoman now."

"A Mountie, in fact, right?" said Peter.

I nodded.

"I had a feeling you were hiding something, but I didn't get the sense of anything bad, just... hidden. I heard the Mounties had begun to admit women now, and Inuvialuit, First Nations and Métis people too. It's about time." He paused in thought for a moment, then, "OK, tell me about the Russians."

Vivian explained that our bosses had been concerned that there might be one or more Soviet agents hidden among the search teams, watching out for the secret camera – if it survived – and planning to either recover it or at least make sure no one else did.

"Fred and Jim," said Peter musingly. "Did you suspect them?"

"I didn't," I said.

"Me neither," supplied Vivian. "Some detectives we are.... Speaking of which," she added, looking at me narrowly, "how about telling us what else we've missed?"

"Ok. I might be wrong, but here's how I think the pieces fit together. The smell of the gasoline from the lantern and stove reminded me of the last time I smelled gasoline. It was back in camp when Silver and I were walking by one of the helicopter-maintenance tents. At the time I thought it was just spilled fuel, or mechanics working on a turbine, but if that were true it should have been jet fuel I smelled, not gasoline.

"It was the very next day that one of the helicopters had some kind of catastrophic failure and crashed because it couldn't even autorotate down. Well, you may think I'm crazy, but I think someone drained most of the jet fuel out of that helicopter and replaced it with gasoline."

"What would that do?" asked Vivian.

"Gasoline has a lower density than jet fuel[41], which is more like kerosene. So, the gasoline would float on the jet fuel. The pilots wouldn't notice anything at first because their gauges would show that the fuel tanks were full, and they would start up normally and fly on jet fuel at first. After a while, however, they would run out of the jet fuel from the bottoms of the tanks and start burning gasoline."

"OK, why would someone put gasoline in a turbine-engine helicopter, won't it burn too?" asked Vivian.

"Sure, but I remember Scotty explaining to me that the fuel isn't just burned in the engines, it's also used as a hydraulic fluid and to lubricate some of the moving parts. Gasoline boils at a lower temperature than jet fuel. If it boiled off inside the hydraulic system – Scotty called it a fueldraulic system – it could have cut-off most or all of the fuel flow, or the air flow, causing the engines to stall. Then, if the same kind of thing happened in drive shaft transmissions, which are interconnected, it might have interfered with the helicopter's ability to autorotate. Then, bang, the helicopter comes down hard."

"If you're right, that's a pretty ingenious way to bring down a helicopter and make it look like an accident," said Peter, "and it worked. Everyone thinks it was just a combination of the cold and metal fatigue. But you still haven't explained why."

"Well, let's call that accident number one," I said. "After that, we were down to two search helicopters. I think that's because there were only two foreign agents, and they were determined that one of them had to be part of any search team that might have

Laurie Schramm

found the camera.

"Naturally, as we got on with our searching, a replacement helicopter was brought in, hence accident number two. I have no idea whether the one rotor refusing to turn was sabotage or just a lucky accident, but it sure wouldn't have been hard to short out the battery. Once again, we're down to the two search teams, and there's another delay keeping the third one grounded.

"Then we come to today. Vivian's Chinook just happens to experience trouble after the camera has been found and our team has been called over for a consultation. I have no idea how it was done, but I'll bet you that Jim found a way to make sure that engine doesn't get started – that's accident number three - and I'll also bet you that by now they've discovered that their radio isn't working either. Meanwhile, our two foreign agents have found the camera, teamed up together, and reduced our numbers - step by 'lucky' step.

"Finally, this afternoon, we fly off to resume searching and the two of them hijack the helicopter and get rid of the rest of us. Now they've whittled our entire force down to one helicopter, the two pilots, and the two of them."

"When did you figure all this out?"

"It was the dead battery. A brand-new battery suddenly dying gave me that uneasy feeling that there was more going on than met the eye. Then, this morning, Fred seemed unusually interested in the mechanical-box thing that we found, and Jim was so interested in the one Vivian's team found that they called us over so Fred and Jim could consult, then their helicopter wouldn't start. Remember, Peter, when we were just siting there waiting for news. That's when the pieces started falling into place in my mind."

"I wondered about that box Jim was so interested in, and whether it was the camera, so I was starting to suspect Jim, but that was as far as I got," said Vivian.

"That's why you were so ready, and so quick, with your gun," I said. "Mine was still taped to my leg inside two layers of pants."

"You have a gun too?" asked Peter.

"A little one. It's a double-barreled derringer. Deadly at close range though."

"So that's it then?" asked Peter, "they've won?"

"Not yet," I replied, taking a sip of my hot tea. The cave was becoming much more comfortable now, as the temperature had probably risen to at least zero °C.

"It seemed to me that, if I was right, then Jim would find some pretext for coming over to join our team for the next search. Then the two of them would be able to pick their time and place, hijack the helicopter, get rid of most of us, and fly to wherever they expect to be picked up by their friends.

"So… remember when I went and asked Susan to join me in a stroll while we waited?"

"I do," said Peter, "I thought you were just restless."

"I was very restless. Anyway, I got her out of earshot of everyone else and made her promise me that if they happened to get hijacked, would they find a way to ground the helicopter, like by faking an instrument malfunction forcing them to fly VFR[42] rather than IFR, for example. That way, when your storm hit, they'd have had to land and wait it out. Just like us."

"How did you get her to agree?"

"I did have to do some rather fast talking, but I was only asking her to take action if they got hijacked, which must have seemed like such a remote possibility that she agreed to talk to the other pilot.

"Anyway, by then our time was up, you and Jim came over from the other helicopter, and there wasn't time for anyone to do anything else."

"I think I'm going to regret asking this," said Peter, "but why delay them, why not just let them go?"

"I thought a delay might create an opportunity. Maybe Scotty and the others would get their helicopter repaired and come after us. Maybe radio silence from us would prompt a search from the CO, either with the replacement Chinook or even the Hercules."

"Those sound a lot like long shots to me," mused Vivian. "I wouldn't be surprised if Jim found a way to make sure that helicopter doesn't get fixed any time soon."

"You want to go after them. Don't you?" said Peter. "You had that in mind when you talked to Susan."

"Yes."

Peter's face showed his surprise and disbelief. "But why?"

I could tell he wasn't going to go anywhere without knowing. So, I told him why. Then, before he could argue, I went on: "Look, we're here and mostly OK. Right? And the dogs all came back. And they were flying towards the storm so it would have hit them sooner than it did us. So. Let's assume that Susan did her part and they're on the ground somewhere within what, maybe 30 minutes flying time from here?"

I was on a roll now, so I kept on to the end: "If they're grounded like we are, waiting out the storm, and with no heater on board, they're not likely to be able to get the engines and transmissions running any time soon, so what will they do?"

"They'll take the snowmobile and make a run for it, just the two of them," said Vivian.

"That's what I think."

"So, Peter, given where we are, is there anything nearby that you'd have selected in advance as a possible rendezvous point if you were planning this?"

"The nearest community to us is Tuk – Tuktoyaktuk - which is just west of here. Inuvik and Aklavik, are further away, to the southwest. If you wanted an easy to find place with few people around, there's an old DEW Line radar station right beside Tuk[43]. It's about a hundred miles from here, but how would they know we were going to end up around here at all?"

"They wouldn't," said Vivian, "but they'd have been tracking the satellite just like us, and they'd have their own computer projection for the fallout pattern, and they'd have chosen several likely pickup points. I'll bet one of them has a radio transmitter with them. It wouldn't have to be very large, just enough to be able to send a signal saying they're ready to be picked up and which of the predetermined locations they're heading for. Can they be picked up at this place called Tuk?"

"Sure, they can. The harbour is frozen over this time of year, but Tuk is right on the edge of the Beaufort Sea. The Russians could have one of their icebreaking-research ships sitting at the edge of the icepack and fly a helicopter in to get them. But…"

"Yes?"

"You both know that a snowmobile can travel faster than a dogsled, right? Even if the helicopter is grounded, we may not be able to catch them."

"I know Peter," I said gently, "but I'd like to try. We'll never pull it off without you though. Compasses don't work well this close to the North pole, and I'd probably end up going in circles."

Peter looked over at Vivian and raised his eyebrows questioningly.

"Well, I'd certainly never make it alone, so don't put me in charge. I don't even understand how people can live up here in this cold. But, if you're asking me if I want to go chase them, and you're willing to guide us, then damn right I want to go. At least we'll know we tried everything we could."

"All right then," he said, "we can try. In that case, I suggest we make an early start tomorrow. They won't be able to find their way in the dark but we can. I should be able to keep us heading in the right general direction, and the dogs will avoid any of the really obvious hazards. With luck, we can gain at least fifty miles before they can attempt the snowmobile. Then we can re-evaluate."

With that settled, we were ready to eat and we raided the meals in the helicopter's survival pack. These were designed to be eaten cold or hot, but with a pot of boiling water on the stove we were able to heat them. Being cold, tired, and hungry, those emergency meals tasted wonderful! Although, we probably could have been fed almost anything and thought it tasted wonderful.

Once we'd eaten, I crawled outside with Peter to help him feed the dogs. I'd already watched him give the dogs pieces of frozen fish to eat as snacks when on the trail, but main meals were more substantial. From a box on the dogsled, he brought out several bags of frozen food, which we carried into the cave to be heated in the pot on the stove. While this was underway, he explained that most mushers develop their own recipe for sled dog food. In his case he took commercial dog food, and added either lard or fat, plus water. Once the bags had been heated through, we took them back outside and poured them into several stainless-steel bowls. Peter called the dogs in, several at a time and watched carefully to make sure that the food was divided up properly so each dog received a fair share.

With that done, we crawled back into the cave. This left the entire evening for us to relax as best we could. The cave had become relatively comfortable by then, as long as we kept most of our Arctic clothing on. We were all tired, of course, but still too wound up to be able to go to sleep right away so we lounged on the furs from the dogsled and chatted about everything and nothing. While we were doing this, one more thing happened that isn't so much related to my adventure as it is to my perceptions of it. Here is what happened.

Having had their dinner outside, Silver and Penny had once again slipped into the cave with us, but only after letting it be known to the other dogs, with much snarling and snapping, that this was a privilege reserved for them alone. While Vivian, Peter and I were chatting and lounging, the two dogs thoroughly explored the cave, as evidenced by much prowling around, with their noses practically touching the ground, accompanied by the kind of deep sniffing dogs exhibit when they are examining new smells. I was only peripherally observing this until Silver started pawing at something with both forepaws. As this was somewhat unusual behaviour for him, I got up and went over to where he was, at the far back of the cave.

"What have you found Silver?" I asked.

He immediately sat down on his haunches, and lightly pawed at a portion of the cave's wall. At first, I thought it he must have been attracted to something that had splashed onto the wall and then dried, but then I noticed a crack in the rock.

"Peter, may I borrow your flashlight for a moment, please?"

Peter brought it over and then, curious himself, sat down to watch.

Under the flashlight's illumination, I could see that there was a pattern to the crack: it looked oblong, and kind of like a jagged oval perhaps ten inches by four inches, more or less. "I think there might be something behind this piece of wall," I said. I had previously extracted my UDT knife to help with the pouches of emergency meals and then placed it in the cargo pocket of my outer pants. With the knife, I was able to work the oblong piece of rock, bit by bit, out of its niche in the wall.

By this time, Vivian had come over to watch as well, so we all watched in fascination as the piece of rock finally came away, revealing a hole in the wall. Even in the light from the flashlight, it just looked like a black hole.

"Rats," said Vivian, in disappointment. "I thought for a moment you might have uncovered a cache of northern gold or something."

"Hang on a second," I said, feeling around inside the hole with one hand. "It goes back about a foot and... I can feel cloth." There was just enough head space for me to dig my fingers into the cloth and drag out what turned out to be something wrapped in a musty smelling piece of cloth.

"Maybe it's a treasure map," said Vivian, not willing to give up on the notion of treasure.

We all got up and went over by the lantern, so we could conserve the flashlight batteries, and I carefully unwrapped the cloth. First, there was a row of tallow candles.

"Made from the fat of caribou or muskox," grunted Peter. "That's what the dogs smelled." Taking one, he crossed over to the stove and lit one, which he then brought back to where Vivian and I were sitting.

By that time, I had set the rest of the candles aside and was exploring the next item, which was something rectangular and wrapped in oilskin. Inside the oilskin were a small pile of money and a book."

"Here's your treasure," I said, spreading out the money. It comprised eight small gold nuggets, some dark, heavily tarnished coins, and some paper money. I handed the 'loot' over to Vivian to examine and opened up the book.

Except, it wasn't a book, it was a journal. On the inside cover, the initials A.J. were inscribed in pencil. As I flipped through the first few pages of the journal, it became clear that it wasn't a daily journal but more of an event journal with just-legible, printed, pencil notations.

"There's about a thousand dollars in both Canadian and American money here," said Vivian, "and look at the coins."

Peter had taken a few of the nickels and quarters and was rubbing them on his sleeve so he could read the dates. "The Canadian coins all seem to have King George the fifth on them, and the dates go from the 1920s all the way up to…"

"1931, I bet," I supplied.

Peter looked up at me, "1931."

"This book seems to be kind of a trapper's journal. A lot of the notations seem to refer to trap lines, where they were set, and the numbers and kinds of animals caught, that kind of thing. The journal starts off in July 1930 and ends six months later, in December 1931."

"So, we're staying the night here courtesy of a trapper with initials A.J." said Vivian.

"Yesss…" a little bell was going off somewhere in the back of my mind.

"You're getting that thoughtful look again," said Vivian, "care to share."

"Yes… Peter, where is Rat River?"

"Rat River? It's south of here, maybe 70 miles or so. Why?"

"Let me tell you a story…. A stranger showed up in the Rat River area in the summer of 1931. He mostly kept to himself, but established trap lines in the area and started hunting and trapping. He built a cabin on the Rat River, but had several caches of supplies in various places, that were found later."

"Later?" asked Vivian.

"He died, not long after. Around Christmas time, the RCMP received complaints from other trappers that the stranger had been interfering with their trap lines. Two constables went to see him to ask him about the complaints, and to see if he had a valid trapping licence. The stranger refused to talk to them through, so they left.

"When a larger patrol went to his cabin, this time with a search warrant, the stranger actually shot one of them, right through the door of his cabin. That triggered a firefight, during which the injured constable was able to escape, and the patrol withdrew.

"After this, a larger party was sent, but this time to arrest the stranger. By this time the temperature had dropped to -45 °C, just like we had here today. There was another firefight, and again the RCMP had to withdraw. Four days later, yet another party was sent out, but by this time, the stranger had escaped and it took three or four days of searching just to find his trail. When the trackers did find his camp, the stranger immediately fired upon them, and a third firefight ensued, during which one of the Constables was shot dead.

"What followed, was a month-long chase, culminating in a fourth gun-battle in which, they discovered later, the stranger was hit multiple times. After a number of fierce exchanges of gunfire, the stranger was eventually no longer shooting back.

"They found him lying dead in the snow, having succumbed to multiple bullet wounds."

"They called him the 'Mad Trapper of Rat River' – I remember hearing the story," said Peter. "People knew him as Albert Johnson, but it was assumed that he'd made the name up and no one was ever sure what his real name was."

"That's right, so his initials would have been written in his journal as 'A.J.' There's an exhibit on him at the RCMP Museum in Regina[44]. I remember looking at the artifacts and reading the story when I was in training there.

"If this cave was one of his trapline shelters then the whole chase and gunfights would have been not very long after the last entry in this journal[45]."

"Well, whatever else he may have been and done, he sure did us a favour with this cave," offered Vivian.

"That's true," agreed Peter, "and I doubt we'd ever have found it without Penny and Silver's help."

After that, we settled in for the night as best we could. The temperature in the cave was probably only a few degrees below freezing by then. In addition to the protruding nails, there was a clothesline strung between two wooden timbers, along one wall, so we were able to hang up any clothing we weren't wearing, even our woollen toques and mittens, so they wouldn't be full of frost in the morning.

Each of us had one of Peter's furs which, doubled up, provided some insulation and cushioning from the rock floor of the cave. Our outer parkas we used like blankets. Other than that, we slept in our clothes with even our mukluk liners still on our feet. Silver curled up with his back against the backs of my legs, as he so often did.

Although I was worried about Don, and about Don worrying about me, I was getting drowsy and was lulled to sleep by the moving shadows cast by the quietly dancing candle flame.

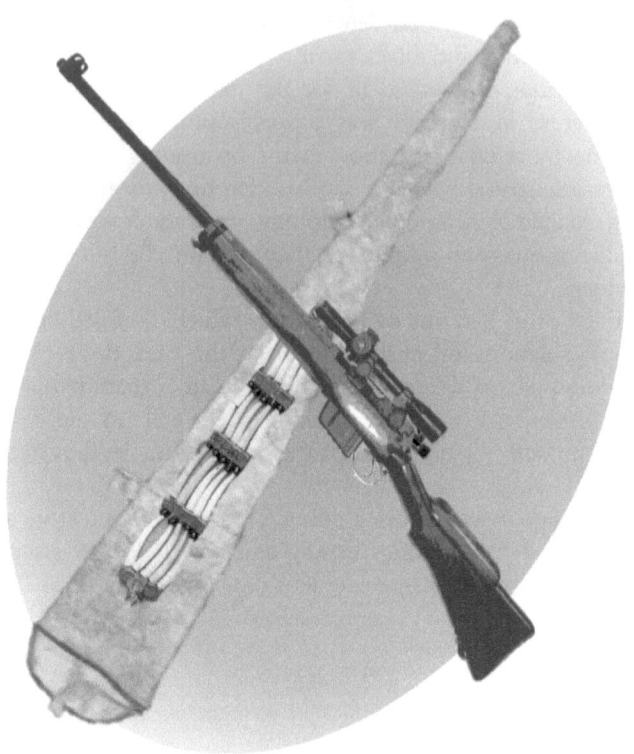

11 MAN HUNT

February 1, 1978
Day 9

When Peter woke us at 4:30 am, he had already relighted the lantern, put water on the stove to heat, and gone outside to check on the dogs and the weather.

"I see you have a notebook too," I observed when I'd moved to sit beside him near the stove.

"Oh yes, and a few modern conveniences." Lying on a piece of fur beside him were a mercury thermometer and a long, thin metal tube into which the thermometer could be screwed for storage and protection. It was exactly like the ones I'd used for field sampling and testing during one of my summer jobs as a university chemistry student.... It seemed like a long time ago.

Lying beside the thermometer was a small, precision altimeter/barometer of the kind used by mountaineers to determine altitude. Whereas a mountaineer would assume that the barometric pressure was constant while ascending or descending a mountain, so that pressure changes could be interpreted in terms of altitudes, Peter was clearly using it the other way around: assuming that altitude was constant so pressure changes could be interpreted in terms of weather changes.

"Storm's lifted, the wind's gone, and the temperature is rising," he said, as he entered the morning's readings. "By the time we get started I think it'll be approaching -15 °C, thirty degrees warmer than yesterday, and a good temperature for sledding."

"What's a good temperature for sledding?" said a drowsy-sounding Vivian, who had yet to arise.

"Fifteen below Celsius" I repeated.

"Plus five degrees Fahrenheit," Vivian translated. "Back home, no one would consider that a good temperature for anything other than staying indoors!"

Armed with a reasonable night's sleep and another hot meal, it didn't take long to repack the sled and hitch the dogs. Although technically morning, it was pitch dark but the clear sky was absolutely full of stars, and then a show of Northern Lights 'switched on.' That got Vivian's attention, as she had never seen them before, and we paused for a moment to take in the spectacle of moving green lights. Even so, we were on our way again before 6 am.

At first, we were travelling across fresh snow, which slowed us down, but at least there was no longer a headwind. Peter estimated our pace at 8 mph. Later, we crossed a series of frozen lakes upon which the winds had left only a thin covering of snow. On the lakes, both Vivian and I rode on the sled, with Peter on the runners, and Peter estimated our lake-crossing pace at 10 miles per hour, or perhaps a bit more.

As we were about to begin the crossing of one of those lakes, we disturbed a small flock of ptarmigans. I'd seen ptarmigans before in the Rocky Mountains, in their mottled brown and grey plumage, but these were pure white and almost invisible against the snow in their white winter plumage. If they hadn't been startled into motion, we'd never have seen them.

"Food," said Peter. "There's still life out here in the Barrens, but it's often well hidden."

We stopped for a break at the edge of another of the lakes, in the early morning twilight. This allowed Vivian and I to stand up and stretch, while Peter checked the dogs and gave them each a snack of frozen fish. At that point, the sun was just beginning to rise and I could see a couple of animals – caribou or muskox - off in the distance. When he returned, Peter caught me staring at the pristine panorama that was slowly being revealed by the rising sun.

"You're starting to like it here. Aren't you?" he asked.

"I am. I've been to a lot of places, and I've snowshoebackpacked in the winter, but this is a whole new world. Here we are trying to survive, hoping we can track down and stop two killers, and yet... it's not the barren wasteland I've heard people call it. It has a magic of its own."

Peter must have felt that words were unnecessary because, with a quite smile, he simply joined me for a moment, drinking in the quiet beauty of our surroundings.

"How are the dogs doing?" I eventually remembered to ask.

"Very well. This is a good temperature for them, and they're enjoying the run."

"How far can they go?"

"In rough country, they can cover 100 miles a day sledding in conditions like this."

After our rest, it was back to business and sledded our way over tundra, frozen lakes, and even a few hills. Peter called a halt at the top of one such hill, and took out a pair of very old binoculars, with which he scanned the horizon ahead of us.

Grunting in satisfaction, he motioned to Vivian and I, saying "Come have a look."

He didn't comment further when he handed me the binoculars, so I wasn't sure what to look for. The sun was well up in the sky by then, however, and we had a clear view of everything in front of us. Scanning the horizon, I first noticed a couple of muskox digging in the snow near a few isolated trees, and I thought he was thinking about going after them for food.

"Look more to your right," he said.

As I did so, I gasped. "The helicopter!" We hadn't been heading straight for it, but would have no trouble reaching it now.

By noon, we had reached the helicopter and were met by Susan and the other pilot, a Lieutenant named George. Moving into the relative warmth of the main body of the helicopter, they explained what had happened since the previous day.

"Once we were up in the air, they ordered us to fly to Tuk," Susan explained. "They both had guns on us, so we didn't have much choice but to look up the new heading on our maps and try to fly in the right direction."

"What do you mean 'try'?" asked Vivian.

"Well, they out-smarted them selves a bit. The guy named Jim seems to know a lot about machinery but not electronics. When he wanted to disable our radio, he shot into anything that had radio frequency dials so, although he did put the radio out of commission, he also took out our ability to receive navigation signals. The compass is no good this close to the north pole, so our only navigation tools were dead reckoning and our ability to spot landmarks on the ground, as we tried to find our way."

"Until the storm hit."

"Right. We could see it coming, but they ordered us to keep going. When it hit, we lost all visibility almost immediately, however and we had to land. We hit hard too, since we couldn't see the ground. We were lucky not to have come down on one of those rocky outcrops."

"Where are they now?" I asked.

"We spent the night huddled up in here, then they unloaded the snowmobile, took out maps, and headed off to the west. You only missed them by thirty minutes."

"Thirty minutes!" Vivian and I both exclaimed.

"Well done, Peter! You got us here in record time." Indeed, we had covered 60 miles by dogsled and actually found the Chinook. So far, at least, we had been fortunate.

"What now?" asked Susan.

"We keep going," I replied. "That is if Peter and Vivian here are still game for it."

"We're not likely to catch them," warned Peter. "They should be able to make 20 miles per hour on the snowmobile once they figure out that they should abandon the sled. We can't travel that fast by dogsled."

"What if I stay here?" asked Vivian.

"What? No. We can't just abandon you now, after having come so far together."

"Nice sentiment Alex, and I appreciate it. But look at it logically. You and Peter can go faster without my weight on the sled. Right Peter?"

He nodded.

"And I'll be safe here with you two, right?" she asked, looking at the pilots.

"Yes. With clear weather, the Hercules will be up looking for both Chinooks right now, and both should have their emergency locator transmitters activated – our is, we checked. If the replacement Chinook is finally flying then they'll come pick us up. If not, the one of the Hercules will do an airdrop to keep us supplied while they figure something else out. All we have to do is stay put."

There you go then," said Vivian.

"Peter?" I asked, turning to him.

"We can try," he replied. "With less weight on the sled and the fact that we can ride on their snowmobile track, we should be able to pick up our pace to 15 miles per hour. If they're inexperienced drivers or have mechanical troubles, or hit something, then we might be able to catch them – just. Otherwise…"

"How will you catch them?" asked Susan. "They're both armed."

"We'll have to figure that out when we get there. Peter has a rifle, and Silver has experience taking down an armed suspect, although I wouldn't like to put him up against two armed suspects."

"You have your gun?" asked Vivian.

"In my pocket," I looked at the others. "It's only a two-shot derringer though, so it's not likely to be much help against these two. Peter, I don't have to tell you that this is going to be dangerous. I'm willing to go alone if you'll loan me the sled and your team."

Peter didn't reply directly, but instead turned to face the pilots. "How much further is it to Tuk and the DEW Line station? Forty miles?" They nodded. "Then we'd better get moving."

So that was that. With a few hugs and goodbyes, Peter and I took the dogsled and headed west, riding on the clear path that had been broken for us by the escaping snowmobile.

After about two hours, 30 miles out, we came across the sled from the snowmobile, lying abandoned in the track. It still had some duffel bags with food and clothing plus one of the lead-lined drums tied down to it, but the drum was empty. They had obviously decided to lighten their load, and were probably worried about how few hours of daylight were left to them.

"They've done a good job of wayfinding," remarked Peter, "they're heading straight for Tuk."

Resuming the chase, we'd probably gone another 10 miles and had stopped to give the dogs a break when I noticed Peter looking at several hills that were just ahead of us, perhaps 100 yards distant.

"Trying to decide which way to go"" I guessed.

"No, I was just wondering whether your two agents are smart

enough to stop and look behind them."

I had wondered about that myself, but hoped that Fred and Jim were too focused on getting to their rendezvous point. As I looked at the hills with new eyes, Peter went to dig out his binoculars, and then stopped suddenly, as a shot rang out.

Crack!

The sound, which seemed to come from our left, was sharp and spurred both Peter and I back into position on the sled. The dogs were already alert to the new sound, and Peter's "Let's go!" command had an unmistakeable tone of urgency to it. As a result, the dogs pulled hard. Peter immediately took us to one of the hills on the right, as a second shot rang out.

I don't know where either of the first two shots went, as we only heard the sounds. A hundred yards is a long shot for a pistol, even in the hands of a skilled shooter and under good conditions. I didn't doubt the skilled shooter part, and anxiously held my breath until we rounded one of the hills and had some cover. As we jumped from the sled, Peter handed me his binoculars, took up his rifle case plus the shovel, and the two of us cautiously scrambled up the hill.

When we were just shy of the summit, Peter used the shovel to throw up a good-sized mound of snow right at the top. Then he carved a bit of a wall out of the part that faced us and then, reversing the shovel, used the handle to poke a hole in it.

"Still have your gun?" he asked.

"Sure, but I'll never hit anything at this range."

"What calibre is it, and how many rounds do you have?"

"It's a .38 Special," I said, taking it out to show him, "and I keep the first barrel empty, so it's only holding one round. I have four more in my pocket."

"That's fine. It will sound like your service revolver. They'll have to worry about you getting a lucky shot, and they'll have to assume that you have at least six or twelve rounds with you. Do me a favour and use the binoculars to watch that hill for any sign of movement from either of Fred or Jim. The next time they take a shot, you should be able to see at least the top of a head. When you do that, fire a shot into the air. It doesn't matter where you aim, I just want them to hear it."

"What are you going to do?"

"I'll try to draw a shot. Then, when they fire, and you respond,

I'll circle over to the next hill. When I get there, I'll give a whistle. When you hear the whistle, fire another shot, and I'll try for the next hill, which should take me beside them and a bit behind. When you hear me fire a shot, you can call for them to surrender."

"And then?"

"You're the policewoman. I know you won't shoot at them without giving them a chance to surrender, so go ahead and try. Just keep out of sight. If they answer with bullets, then I'll try to disable them. Time's on our side now, not theirs. I think they're too professional to panic, but they can't afford to let us pin them down for more than an hour or they'll start to lose the light and never make it to Tuk."

As he was saying this, Peter had taken up his rifle and placed his fur hat on the end of the barrel. I agreed to give it a try, and used the binoculars to watch the other hill for motion as Peter used the rifle to raise his hat so that it should have been just visible above his snow wall.

Nothing happened, and I was just about to make a comment when he moved the hat a bit, side to side.

Crack!

They'd seen the hat alright, and I had just managed to spot a bit of movement near the top of the hill we'd identified as the one harbouring Fred and Jim. So far, so good.

With a grim smile, Peter retrieved his hat and scrambled back down the side of the hill, leaving me to maintain my vigil. I almost immediately spotted another movement and fired a shot in their general direction.

I thought that might surprise them, and indeed there was complete silence until some minutes later when I heard a whistle. I fired off another shot. With two rounds gone, I had only three left. I belatedly realized that I should have asked Peter how much ammunition he had.

Maintaining my vigil, I wasn't surprised that there were no signs of movement and I wondered whether Fred and Jim were aware that someone might be trying to sneak around them. I assumed the answer was yes. A few minutes later I head a loud crack as a bullet from Peter's rifle broke the sound barrier, followed quickly by the thump of the muzzle blast from the rifle itself.

All I could think of was to fire off a shot to remind them that they were facing two armed opponents. Then, without exposing myself, I called out as loudly as I could, identifying myself as a police officer and calling for them to surrender. The only apparent result of my order to surrender was an exchange of gunfire between the two hills. Fred and Jim must have retreated a bit down and sideways, as I couldn't make out any motion through the binoculars. I don't know whether Peter was slightly exposed or not, but I assumed so, since there were two pistol shots in rapid succession, then the louder rifle shot, then a pause, then the cycle repeated itself.

The next shot came from Peter, and was accompanied by a metallic clang. *He's shooting at the snowmobile!* I realized, in surprise.

This triggered more pistol shots as Peter fired off two more rounds that were accompanied by the metallic clanging sounds.

Almost immediately, I saw motion on the far side of Fred and Jim's hill, and I immediately fired another shot myself. They must have thought to try to get around us, but my shot dissuaded them.

Then, I head Fred's voice. "OK, we surrender. We're coming out. Don't shoot!"

Watching through the binoculars, I saw Fred emerge from one side the hill with his hands in the air.

Time slowed down.

Peter appeared, with his rifle still raised and pointing in Fred's direction.

But where was Jim?

"Peter! Get back," I yelled, as I fired another shot, but it was too late. He had shown himself too soon.

Crack!

That must have been Jim.

Crack-boom! That was Peter, returning fire.

I thought, for a moment, that maybe it would all be OK. That Jim had missed Peter, but Peter had hit him, and Fred would surrender.

Wrong!

Peter collapsed into the snow and Fred retreated to the cover of the hill.

I had only one round left.

Working my way back down the side of my hill, I freed Silver from the traces and the two of us cautiously worked our way around the two hills to our right. I was determined to check on Peter.

There were no further shots fired as I did this, and when I finally reached the far side of the far hill, I carefully poked my head out for a quick look. I could see Peter lying in the snow. Perhaps 50 yards away, I could see someone else lying in the snow: that was Jim, and not far away I could see and hear Fred trying to start the snowmobile.

I decided to risk going to Peter's side, and as I gently rolled him over onto his back, the depression he left in the snow was full of bright red blood.

"Jim's down. Just Fred left," he said.

"Don't try to talk, just lie still," I said, as I fumbled with his parka and the underlying layers of clothing he had on, trying to get to the source of the bleeding.

I heard the roar of the snowmobile engine as Fred got it started, and gunned the engine as he made yet another getaway.

"Don't worry about him," Peter said, his teeth clenched in pain. "I was shooting at the gas tank, not the engine. He'll only get a few miles before it dies on him."

"The hell with him!" I said angrily. "I need to get you bandaged up, and the dogs and I will get you to a doctor in Tuk."

"It's too late for that now," said Peter, almost in a whisper now. "Do something for me?"

"Anything."

"Look after Penny, will you?"

"Of course, but look, we'll get you fixed up and you can look after her yourself. OK?"

But he just gave a sigh, and then died in my arms....

With my eyes so full of tears I could barely see, I reached for his fur hat and placed it gently over his face. Then I wiped my eyes clear. This wasn't the time for tears. That would come later.

I suddenly felt very old, as I wearily got to my feet and picked up Peter's rifle. It had one more round left in it.

Silver was close by my side as I tramped over to check on Jim. As we neared him, I motioned for Silver to swing over to one side so we could come at him from different angles. We'd done this so many times before that he understood immediately and was gone in a flash. Then, cradling the rifle in my arms I approached Jim, who hadn't seemed to move since he'd fallen.

My caution was unnecessary: Jim was dead.

Sighing, I left him where he was and returned to the dogsled with Silver.

There was going to be one more chase.

When we reached the dogsled, I left Silver out of the traces. There was less reason to hurry now, and Penny and the remaining dogs were going to be more than enough for the chase. Besides, I wanted Silver to be free when we caught up with Fred. As I placed Peter's rifle with easy reach on the sled, I looked at my watch. Amazing! The whole episode at these hills had taken only twenty minutes. It had felt like hours.

I choked a bit when yelling out Peter's customary "Let's go!" command, but Penny got the idea and drove us forward.

I stopped, for a moment, when we reached Peter, and released Penny from the traces so she could go to him. The three of us knelt there for a moment, at Peter's side: Penny, Silver, and I.

I tried to explain to Penny what had happened, but I'm sure she only heard the tone of my voice. Silver, however, moved in front of her and they stared at each other for a few moments, and I think some kind of communication passed between them, but I don't know what.

I didn't think Penny would come with us, when I rose up, but she did, and she followed us back to the sled and allowed herself to be tied back in.

"Let's go!" I commanded again and the dogs, hearing a new resolve in my voice, launched themselves so forcefully ahead that I was nearly thrown off the sled's runners.

Once again, the snowmobile had left us a perfect trail to follow and we set an even faster pace with the lighter sled. With uncanny accuracy, Peter had called it right about the snowmobile too: we'd only gone about four miles before I could see it sitting idle on the path ahead of us. As I brought the dogsled abreast of the snowmobile, the only sign of Fred was the snowshoe tracks leading off from the snowmobile in the direction of another hill.

Unbelievable! The man never quits. I thought.

Fred couldn't be far away, and now the tables were turned: I could move much more quickly by dogsled than he could on snowshoes!

Commanding the dogs to get moving again, I signalled to Silver and he once again sped off to the side so that we'd be able to converge on Fred from different directions. I guessed that we'd see him when we came around the next hill.

I was wrong, but not by much. The tracks led to another hill, and he was just beyond that one.

It was after 4 pm when we finally caught up to Fred. The sun had just set, and he was lying face down in the snow when I stopped the sled, slung the rifle over my shoulder and took out my derringer. I had only one round left in each, and I suspected one last trick from Fred.

Fred, however, had no more tricks to play. He wasn't playing possum, he was dead. He must have been hit by one or more of Peter's bullets and had finally succumbed.

I just stood there in the snow looking at him as Silver came over to join me.

The wind was picking up again and little snow drifts were starting to form around Fred's body.

I thought of everything we'd been through. So many people killed, so many people and dogs injured. My friends Don and Vivian had both been injured, but they would recover. My new friend Peter would never travel these lands again.

I remembered the words of my former boss, Corporal Mike Morrison, after I'd finally proven myself at our little detachment in Northern Saskatchewan. "A Mountie always gets *her* man!" he'd said, at the end of a difficult case, and I'd felt very proud in that moment.

Well, this Mountie had gotten her two men this time, but they were both beyond the law now. I felt no pride this time, only sadness.

Silver must have felt my emotions, because he raised his head and gave a howl of the sort that his wolfly ancestors might have given. He had the mood right.

I was still standing there, trying to sort out my thoughts when I heard a new sound, the unmistakable sound of a jet fighter approaching...

Looking toward the sound, I was intime to see a speck in the sky separate into two specks that quickly resolved themselves into two fighters: a pair of CF-104 Starfighters, flying low.

They screamed over me, made a hard turn, circled around and swept over me a second time. This time, the trailing fighter tipped its wings at me, first to one side, then to the other, to make sure I knew that I had been sighted. Then, they roared away.

Fifteen minutes later, I heard the '*thump, thump, thumping*' sounds of a large helicopter approaching. They must have been already in the air, doing their own search. Somehow, I knew Don would be on the helicopter and I simply walked back to the sled to wait with the dogs.

12 AFTERMATH

The first person out of the big Chinook helicopter was Don, of course, who got a friendly greeting from Silver but was a bit disconcerted to be met with a warning growl from Penny. Undeterred, he made a beeline for me, stumbled right up on top of my snowshoes, and put his arms around me.

Neither of us said anything for quite a while.

"Aren't you supposed to be confined to quarters, or confined to base, or something?" I asked, when we were disentangled.

"Technically I suppose, but I think I'll be forgiven."

"Seriously, are you well enough to be out here?"

"Now that I'm with you, I am!"

That was all I was likely to get out of him, for the time being, so I pointed the way to where Fred lay in the snow. Walking over to him, we found the secret camera in a canvas bag Fred had slung over his shoulder, and I told Don that Fred and Jim had been trying to reach the DEW Line station.

"Fred would have made it if it hadn't been for you," Don said. "He was only 2 miles from Tuk."

"Whatever else he was, Fred was very brave, and very persistent. He very nearly succeeded."

"Very skilled too. Vivian filled me in on what you've been up to since yesterday morning. If you hadn't figured out what they were up to, they'd be on their way home with the camera right now."

"Just lucky, I guess."

Don snorted.

Others had jumped out of the helicopter to help get the dogs and sled stowed inside. Then Fred's body was carried to the helicopter and we boarded as well, along with Silver and Penny.

Vivian was there too, so we were tearfully reunited as well.

Back in the camp at Inuvik, we had a large meal in the mess tent and recounted stories of the past several days.

Don explained that the warmer weather had made it easier to repair the grounded helicopters.

The CO dropped by to congratulate us, and to explain that replacements for us had arrived, so that the final phase of the ground searches could be completed. With the secret camera recovered, and the two Soviet Agents dead, Don, Vivian, and I were released from further searching. He had only been briefed by Don that morning on the real mission in which we three had been engaged. "I'm only the CO around here, nobody tells me anything," he complained, in a long-suffering tone of voice.

He also told us that it was estimated that, ultimately, only about one percent of the satellite was likely to be recovered, but the Canadian Forces were determined to remove as much of the radioactive debris as possible.

After that, it all caught up with Vivian and I, and we were packed off for a good night's sleep.

The best part was just being warm again.

.***

February 2, 1978
Day 10
Yellowknife, Northwest Territories.

Early in the morning, Don, Vivian, and I had packed up and flown to Yellowknife for a debriefing with our bosses. Actually, it was mostly our bosses' bosses. When we were ushered into a meeting room at the RCMP building in Yellowknife, we were met by my immediate boss, Staff Sergeant Robert (Bob) G. Simpson, and his boss, Assistant Commissioner George MacLeod. The latter, was the man that had invited me to join the Force in the first place, and he had an uncanny habit of dropping in to see me at the close of my assignments.

Also in the room, were two other men whom I'd met only once before. Even out of uniform, there was no mistaking Rear-Admiral Peter White, commander of the Canadian Forces Security Branch, and the man I always thought of as 'Don's Admiral.' Wiry, with thinning hair, and extremely sharp, piercing eyes, this was a man that exercised great power, but he did it behind the scenes; unnoticed by most people. The other man also wore a suit but, unlike the Admiral's, this suit exuded raw power and confidence. Tall and powerfully built, with short, thick white hair, a salt-and-pepper mustache, and clear, blue eyes, this was Vivian's boss' boss, FBI Deputy Director Jonathan Wheeler.

Greetings were brief, as we had all met before. The debriefing covered everything, from the first calls for help; the choices our superiors made; everything Don, and Vivian, and I went through; and the follow-up activities still underway.

Based on the search results, the military's assessment was that Kosmos 954, and its reactor, must have almost completely burned up on re-entry leaving mostly just small, charred bits and pieces to settle down from the upper atmosphere. The debris, radioactive and nonradioactive alike, were thought to have been pushed by the northerly winds such that they settled along almost precisely the area projected by the computer models.

Subject to the last several ground searches, it looked like the debris-search objectives would all be met. All radioactive debris identified by the Hercules search aircraft would soon have been picked up, all of the local communities were considered to be safe, as was the local environment. Whatever was leftover from the searches was confidently predicted to fall within acceptable parameters and, in any case, having radiation levels that were virtually indistinguishable from background radiation from the local rock formations.

As far as our secret mission went, between us, and with the benefit of hindsight, we were able to paint a pretty clear picture of Fred and Jim's actions by which they had managed to ensure that only two helicopters were engaged in the ground search, so that one or the other of them would be on hand if the camera were found. At the same time, they'd very efficiently and effectively sequenced the various accidents so as to reduce the numbers of people bit by bit, until they were eventually down to the two of them plus the two helicopter pilots. Even if some of it came down to luck, it was judged that Fred and Jim had been thoughtful and skilled agents.

Our bosses suspected that Fred and Jim may have been worried about Don all along. Although he was undercover, with a plausible cover story, he did fit a common stereotype in that he was large, male, and in the military. Whether this was a factor in the disabling of the first helicopter will probably never be known. My boss, Bob, said he suspected that they may have felt that they got a lucky – for them - bonus when accident #1 not only grounded the helicopter but put Don out of commission for a while too.

Fortunately for Vivian and I, Fred and Jim hadn't seemed to worry too much about two slender women scientists. At least, not until Vivian pulled a gun on Fred that is.

I learned a few things too. Apparently the third AECB scientist was thought to be genuine, had finally been released from hospital and was participating in the final stages of the search. The two Russians had adopted the identities of real AECB scientists, and military intelligence was still trying to discover the whereabouts of the real scientists and how the switch had been managed. Admiral White and Deputy Director Wheeler were of the opinion that the scientists were most likely still alive and would eventually be found 'tucked away' somewhere.

There had, in fact, been a Russian research-icebreaker lurking in the Beaufort Sea, just at the edge of the ice-pack. It had been under constant Canadian and American surveillance, however, such that the two fighter jets had been scrambled immediately when the ship's helicopter crossed into Canadian airspace. Apparently, the Russian helicopter had snuck in low, trying to avoid our radar, which would have worked had it not been for the active surveillance. By the time the fighter jets had caught up to it, the helicopter had overflown the DEW Line station and was flying in outward radial sweeps, looking for the two agents. Don estimated that it would only have been a matter of a few more minutes before the helicopter would have found Fred. It was that close.

As it turned out, the jets had been in time and, once they had forced the helicopter to retreat, it had returned to the ship which, in turn, promptly sailed away. Admiral White said that the ship would remain under active surveillance for a few more days, mostly just to see where it would head next.

Meanwhile, the secret camera was already being examined by someone, somewhere, and I never heard anything more about it.

I've always wondered whether any useful technology or images were ever recovered from it. Even if there were, I doubt whether it was worth the human cost that had been paid: five dead, including Peter, Jim, and Wayne, five others injured, some seriously, and 6 dogs injured.

The senior officers, however, seemed well satisfied that we'd kept the camera out of Soviet hands and offered praise to Don, and Vivian, and I. We all raised our cups – of coffee – in a toast to another successfully completed mission. As the senior officers had other things to discuss, the rest of us were dismissed and we found ourselves with enough time to go for a stronger drink before Vivian would be flying home with her Deputy Director in their FBI jet.

.***

Additional observations from Staff Sergeant Bob Simpson:

With the departure of Alex, Don, and Vivian, there were just the three of us left in the conference room. Deputy Director Wheeler, as usual, got in the first words:

"Thank you for your kind words to Vivian, and I'm sure your boy Don did a great job out there, but it was your girl Alex that put it all together. Not many people would have remembered smelling the gasoline and figuring out the trick of substituting it for most of the jet fuel in the helicopter."

"Woman," murmured Assistant Commissioner Macleod.

"What's that?"

"Woman. Our woman Alex."

"Yes, yes, your woman Alex." Undeterred, the Deputy Director continued. "The point I'm trying to make is that not many people would have figured out the fuel switching trick, nor figured out *in time* that the sequence of 'accidents' weren't accidents at all. This is the second time she's pulled something like this off and I have to say I'm very impressed."

"Yes, she seems to be becoming quite indispensable," put in Admiral White, "*an indispensable Mountie*, wouldn't you say?"

.

"What I'm try to say," said the Deputy Director, rushing on, "is that she was the key to figuring out who the agents were, the key to stopping them, and she probably saved my agent's life, again. So, I want to express my thanks and the thanks of the Bureau. We can't give her any kind of official commendation, but I hope you'll accept our thanks and make sure she's looked after."

"Gracious of you to say so, Jonathan, and I agree with you entirely. We'll look after her, never fear."

The conversation then turned to a few other matters, after which the Deputy Director said his goodbyes and left to collect Vivian and fly home to Washington.

That left just the Admiral, the Assistant Commissioner, and myself. By unspoken agreement, rank and titles were then left aside and it was just us three old warhorses.

"They say no one's indispensable, George, but your woman Alex sure comes close!"

"You're wrong you know, Peter" said Assistant Commissioner MacLeod, in a low voice. "She actually is."

"What?"

"We all tell ourselves that no one's indispensable, and usually we're just talking to ourselves. Telling ourselves that we don't have to carry the entire world on our shoulders. Reminding ourselves to stay humble – keep our big egos in check – but every once in a while, if you're lucky, you come across that one-in-a-thousand, one-in-a million, person that has that extra ability. The astronauts call it having 'the right stuff.' I don't know what to call it, or how to measure it, but I know it when I see it and I'm grateful."

"An indispensable Mountie then? Maybe you're right at that. Let's drink to it," said Admiral White, reaching into his briefcase for a bottle. Rum, of course. We drank it from our coffee cups.

13 EPILOGUE

Don, Vivian, and I had gone to one of the downtown Yellowknife bars for a drink before Vivian had to leave. As we walked there, Vivian asked what I was planning to do with Penny.

"I don't know yet," I responded. "I promised Peter that I would look after her, but my job has me travelling so much that I'm not sure I should try to keep her with me. I was thinking that I might take Silver and her back to visit Ross and Sally Peake in Alaska. They're the ones that train sled-dogs, and it's at their place that Silver was born and raised[12]. They'd be good to her, and let her run with a sled-team like she's used to.

"But, I'm not sure," I sighed. "Maybe I'll try keeping her with Silver and I first and see how it goes.

The bar was crowded, and we had been forced to sit on stools at the bar itself. When our drinks arrived, I raised my head to take a sip of mine, and that's when I happened to look at the wall behind the bartender for the first time.

I must have frozen in place as I took in the large painting that hung there. It depicted a snowy northern scene, twilight was setting in, and the Northern Lights were visible in the sky. In the foreground was a body, lying in the snow. Standing nearby and looking reflectively at the body was a Mountie on snowshoes. To one side, a sled-dog had raised his head to howl into the cold winter air.

"Oh, my God…," I whispered.

"What's the matter?" asked Don, following my stare.

"Like the painting?" said the bartender, who had noticed my stare and walked over.

"Do you know what that is?" I asked, still staring at it.

"Sure do. It was painted in the 1930s by a famous artist[46], and it shows the final scene in the story of '*The Mad Trapper of Rat River.*' Seems he'd shot a Mountie and tried to escape, which led to a manhunt that took more than 40 days.

"It was the dead of winter, and they had to battle the cold and the rough terrain as they chased him all the way through the mountains and into the Yukon. Along the way, he shot and killed another Mountie in a firefight, but they just kept on chasing him. They didn't know it at the time, but during the last gunfight, he'd taken a lot of bullets from the posse. When the Mounties finally caught up to him, he was lying dead in the snow. They way I heard it, as his dog howled to the moon, the Mountie gazed down at the trapper thinking that he was now beyond the law, and that's what the painting is called: '*Beyond the Law.*'"

"My God!" I said again. But I was thinking:

That's exactly how it was. Fred lying there in the snow, dead. Me thinking Fred was beyond the law, and Silver raised his head and howled like a wolf... I've just re-enacted a piece of Mountie history... What an adventure! But who would ever believe it?

Photo of *'Beyond the Law,'* a painting by Sanford Fisher (1965) from the collection of C/Supt. W. Schramm (RCMP, Ret.). Fisher's painting is an interpretation of the original painting of the same name by Franz Johnston[46] (1933).

Laurie Schramm

14 POSTSCRIPT

May 30, 1978
Dark Water Lake, Northwest Territories
87 km (54 miles) south of Aklavik

Counterintuitively, although the computer models had done a good job of predicting the trajectories and ultimate fate of the small and tiny pieces of satellite debris, this was not the case for one large piece, which comprised most of the reactor's core. The core's heavy shielding had protected it for most of the re-entry, and then it had been ejected from the rest of the disintegrating satellite, so that its final descent to earth was along a slightly different trajectory from the rest of the debris. The remainder of the satellite had been blasted into millions of pieces, fragments, and fine particles, many of which had been found by the search.

The surviving portion of Kosmos 954's reactor core, comprising some 20 kg of the original 30 kg of uranium, had landed near the centre of Dark Water Lake and immediately melted enough underlying ice for it to drop 4 feet (1.2 m). With surface temperatures hovering at about -40 °C, it only took a week for the water to re-freeze around it and all the way back up to the surface of the lake.

Now, nearly four months after the surviving parts of the satellite had fallen to the earth, spring had finally arrived in the north. As the month of May had advanced, most of the rivers and some of the lakes in the northern half of the Northwest Territories had thawed, and for the past several days the ice was finally thawing around – and under - the surviving bulk of the reactor core.

As the last of the ice melted, it released its grip on the core, which quickly dropped to the bottom of the lake.

It was never found.

… Alex and Silver return in
An Inexorable Mountie.

Laurie Schramm

BOOK 6 ENDNOTES

1. According to the official 1933 RCMP report, there was a man in the area who went by the name of Albert Johnson (although his real name was unknown). However, the RCMP discerned no evidence of insanity and, to contrary, found him to be "an extremely shrewd and resolute man, capable of quick thought and action. A tough and desperate character." See: "The Case of 'Albert Johnson'" in *Report of the Royal Canadian Mounted Police for the Year Ended September 30, 1932*, Dominion of Canada, Ottawa, 1933.

2. Regardless of whether a system like this was ever developed in real life, advances in improved optical and imaging systems for surveillance satellites were vigorously pursued by the United States and the Soviet Union during the 1970s, as they strove to overcome the challenges of distance resolution, imaging through clouds, fog, and rain, and getting data back to earth quickly. See, for example: S.B. Johnson, "The History and Historiography of National Security Space," Chapter 15 in *Critical Issues in the History of Spaceflight*, S.J. Dick and R.D. Launius (Eds.), NASA, Washington, 2006, pp. 481-548.

3. An adage, one form of which states that: "*Anything that can go wrong, will go wrong.*" The name 'Murphy's Law' may have originated from mathematician Augustus De Morgan, who in

1866 wrote: "*whatever can happen will happen.*"

4. The North American Aerospace Defense Command (NORAD) is a joint initiative of Canada and the United States. Its mission is to defend North America against an air or space attack. Its headquarters is located at Peterson Air Force Base in Colorado Springs, Colorado, and its alternate command centre is deep inside the famous Cheyenne Mountain Complex, nearby.

5. Mercator projection is a form of map projection in which the meridians are equally spaced, parallel vertical lines, and the latitudes are parallel horizontal straight lines that are spaced farther and farther apart as their distance from the equator increases. Mercator projection charts are commonly used for navigation.

6. Originally established in the 1950s, by 1969 the AMOS facility had 1.2m twin-telescopic cameras for tracking missile launches and satellite surveillance. One telescope was used for tracking, and the other for special observations. At the time, these were among the world's largest astronomical telescopes.

7. Kosmos 954 was a Soviet, nuclear-powered spy satellite that developed operating problems, re-entered on January 24, 1978, and mostly disintegrated. Radioactive debris crashed over a wide area, mostly in the Northwest Territories. This triggered a massive, real-life Canada-U.S. operation search and recovery exercise called *Operation Morning Light*. For more information, see:

   ➢ B. Aikman, "Operation Morning Light," Ch. 10 in *Canadian Arctic Operations, 1941-2015. Lessons Learned, Lost, and Relearned*, Lajeunesse, A. and Lackenbauer, P.W. (Eds.), The Gregg Centre for the Study of War & Society, University of New Brunswick, 2017, pp. 245-269.

   ➢ L. Heaps, *Operation Morning Light: Terror in Our Skies*, Paddington Press, 1978.

8. The Commander in Chief, North American Air Defense Command (CINCNORAD), and the Deputy CINCNORAD

positions were periodically rotated, and always so that one was from the United States and the other from Canada.

9. See *An Inconvenient Mountie* (ISBN: 978-1-9994940-0-1).

10. At this point in time, it was still part of the RCMP. Years later, in 1984, the Security Service was spun-out to create the present-day Canadian Security Intelligence Service (CSIS).

11. See *An Inconspicuous Mountie* (ISBN: 978-1-9994940-2-5).

12. See *An Indestructible Mountie* (ISBN: 978-1-9994940-4-9).

13. See *An International Mountie* (ISBN: 978-1-9994940-6-3).

14. See *An Inseparable Mountie* (ISBN: 978-1-7772424-0-4).

15. The RCAF's C-130H Hercules are four-engine-turboprop, tactical-transport aircraft. Designed to operate from low quality, short airstrips, they have been used for everything from troop and equipment transport, to search and rescue, and even air-to-air refueling operations.

16. Canadian Forces Base Trenton, located in southern Ontario, is home to 8 Wing: which provides tactical transportation worldwide and supports search and rescue operations over central and northern Canada.

17. The McDonnell CF-101B Voodoo was a supersonic, all-weather-interceptor jet fighter. They were a variant of the US F-101 aircraft, and the 'B' designation referred to the dual-seat version.

18. Although CFB Edmonton is close to the city of Edmonton, it is also just south of the hamlet of Namao and was formerly called RCAF Station Namao. For many years, the base continued to be referred to by its older, short-form name: Namao.

19. The Boeing CH-147 Chinook was a twin-engine, tandem-rotor, heavy-lift helicopter used by the RCAF beginning in 1974. The Canadian model, also known as the Super C, was similar to the American CH-47C, but included a power hoist above the crew door and a flight engineer station in the rear cabin. Newer models are still in active service at the time of writing.

20. Also called the 'Barren Lands' or 'Barren Grounds,' the Barrens comprise a wide expanse of tundra (subarctic prairie) ranging from the eastern Northwest Territories to Hudson Bay in western Nunavut.

21. Nuclear Accident Support Teams (NASTs) are teams of scientists, technicians, and engineers drawn from operational units of the Canadian Armed Forces. Their function is to be able to assemble and deploy quickly to any kind of radiological incident. The United States has a similar capability, named Nuclear Emergency Support Team (NEST), which operates under the U.S. Department of Energy.

22. Lockheed U-2 ultra-high-altitude, all-weather reconnaissance jet operated by the USAF and/or CIA.

23. In the winter of 1972, a bush plane crashed in the Canadian Arctic killing the two passengers and severely injuring the pilot. The pilot was reported to have been forced to resort to eating meat from one of the dead passengers in order to survive the 31 days until he was rescued.

24. In the United States, the FBI is responsible for the prevention and neutralization of non- military nuclear threats.

25. On October 30, 1938, CBS broadcast a live radio drama called *The War of the Worlds* to audiences in the US and Canada. Orson Welles performed as the narrator of H.G. Wells' 1898 novel of the same name which, as a Halloween stunt, was adapted to make it seem like it was happening live and in real-life in 1939. The show was presented as if it were a typical evening of radio programming that was interrupted by a periodic series of news bulletins, through which the H.G. Wells story was brought to life. For the first half-hour, the show was broadcast without any commercials, adding to the sense of realism. The program famously tricked some listeners into panic, believing that a Martian invasion was actually taking place, although subsequent research suggests that the number of panic-stricken listeners was actually quite small.

26. The 'Abominable Snowman', or Yeti is a character from

folklore. The concept of a high-mountain dwelling, creature of super-human size originated in the Himalayas, but an Arctic counterpart of the same name - and/or similar ones named Nuk-luk, and Sasquatch - appear in Canadian mythology as well.

27. The DEW Line (Distant Early Warning Line), was a Cold-War-network of radar stations that was set up in the 1950s to watch for Soviet military aircraft. Located in the Arctic, the radar stations were located from Alaska, across Northern Canada, to Greenland, and Iceland. It was set up to detect incoming Soviet bombers during the Cold War, and provide early warning of any sea-and-land invasion.

28. Canadian Forces Station (CFS) Inuvik was a signals intercept facility located near the Village of Inuvik. Originally named Naval Radio Station (NRS) Inuvik in 1961, it was briefly commissioned HMCS Inuvik in 1963, and then renamed CFS Inuvik in 1966). Its purpose was mainly Arctic communications research, but its high-frequency, direction-finding (HF/DF) antenna array was also used to support search and rescue missions in the region.

29. The Inuvialuit are Inuit people that traditionally live in Canada's Western-Arctic. The Gwich'in are First Nations people that traditionally live in the northwestern Canadian Arctic and Alaska.

30. In response to concerns expressed by the Mackenzie Valley area Aboriginal communities, the federal government appointed Justice Thomas Berger to conduct an inquiry into the proposed Mackenzie Valley pipelines and their potential environmental, social, and economic impacts. Released on May 9, 1977, the 'Berger Report' recommended a ten-year moratorium on pipeline construction to allow for additional impact studies and to give the affected Aboriginal communities time to settle their land claims. The moratorium was lifted earlier than recommended, however, by 2000 the land claims of the local Inuvialuit, Gwich'in, and Sahtu peoples had been

settled.

31. In real life, the mission to find and retrieve debris from the fallen Kosmos 954 satellite was a joint Canada-U.S. Mission, and it was code-named Operation Morning Light.

32. The drawing of the initial search area is representative but, for this story, it has been moved about 1,100 km (690 miles) north-northwest of where the real-life search for Kosmos 954 actually took place.

33. For a detailed explanation of the more complex methodologies used in the real-life search, see Bristow, Q., "The Application of Airborne Gamma-Ray Spectrometry in the Search for Radioactive Debris from the Russian Satellite Cosmos 954 (Operation 'Morning Light')," In "Current Research, Part B," Geological Survey Paper 78-1 B, Geological Survey of Canada, Ottawa, 1978, pp. 151-162.

34. The de Havilland DHC-6 Twin Otter is a Canadian short takeoff and landing aircraft developed in the 1960s and still in production (now by Viking Air). Easily switched from wheeled-, to float- or ski landing gear, they are ubiquitous in Canada's more northern and remote regions.

35. Although dog teams originally played critical roles in Alaska's and Northern Canada's evolution, snowmobiles (the 'iron dogs') had almost completely replaced them by the 1960s. The 'Iditarod' was conceived as way to celebrate Alaskan history. A first, two-heat, race was held on part of the Iditarod Trail in 1967 and 1969 (there was a lack of snow in 1968). After completion of the entire trail, all the way from Anchorage to Nome, Alaska, the first full-length *Iditarod Trail Sled Dog Race®* was held in 1973.

36. The Omega radio-navigation system was a network of satellite- and ground-based transmitters that sent out very-low-frequency (VLF) radio signals. It was operated from 1971 to 1997, at which time it was abandoned in favour of the present-day Global-Positioning-System (GPS).

37. The röntgen (R), is an older unit of exposure to gamma rays

and not exactly comparable to modern units of radiation quantity absorbed, such as the sievert (Sv). For practical purposes, with gamma-rays, 1 Sv is approximately equal to 100 R.

38. AECL's Whiteshell Laboratories, in Pinawa, Manitoba (near Winnipeg) were established in 1963 as research laboratories, focused on Canada's heavy-water-moderated nuclear reactor technology. At the time of this story the facility was fully active. In the present day, it is closed and in the process of being decommissioned.

39. Image based on: Library and Archives Canada, "Aerial view of Cape Dorset," Atomic Energy Control Board (AECB) collection, Accession number 1985-178 NPC, Mikan-4073498.

40. White-camping gas is a liquid petroleum fuel designed for camping stoves and lanterns. It is designed to be clean-burning and non-clogging. In North America, it is often referred to as 'Coleman Fuel' in reference to Coleman™ Camp Fuel – a popular brand.

41. The density of gasoline is approximately 0.73 g/cm^3 at 0 C (increasing to about 0.79 g/cm^3 at -30 C). The density of Jet A fuel is lower, at about 0.83 g/cm^3 at 0 C (increasing to about 0.85 g/cm^3 at -30 C). The density of Jet B fuel is very slightly less than the Jet A (e.g., 0.84 g/cm3 at -30 C).

42. Flying under VFR (visual flight rules), refers to circumstances under which a pilot has good visibility in front of and around the aircraft. Flying under IFR (instrument flight rules), refers to flying on the aircraft's instruments, and using electronic navigational aids, in which case the aircraft can fly in poor visibility, such as in clouds.

43. The DEW Line site beside Tuktoyaktuk, NT, is designated BAR-3. It was one of several intermediate auxiliary and intermediate stations that were spaced between the six main stations of the DEW Line. In this case, BAR-3 funnelled data to the nearest main station, which was at Barter Island, Alaska (BAR). BAR-3 was transitioned into the more modern North

Warning System (NWS) in 1990.

44. Now the RCMP Heritage Centre.

45. In real life, the man known as Albert Johnson was found dead, after a lengthy pursuit, on February 17, 1932. It was found that he had prepared several well-hidden caches of supplies in the area of his trap lines. A reference to the official RCMP report on the Albert Johnson case is provided above in endnote #1. Another good reference is: T.E.G. Shaw, "Man Hunt in the Arctic," *RCMP Quarterly*, **1960**, *26(2)* October, pp. 103-113.

46. The original oil painting, *'Beyond the Law,'* was painted in 1933 by Group of Seven artist Franz Johnston. It is on display in the RCMP Heritage Centre in Regina, Saskatchewan.

An Inexorable Mountie

Adventures of the First
Woman Mountie. Book 7

LAURIE SCHRAMM

Laurie Schramm

Photo courtesy of VIA Rail Canada (Resource ID 1520).

Laurie Schramm

DEDICATION

To Cleo

BOOK 7 CONTENTS

	List of Characters	331
1	Prelude: A Robbery	333
2	A Cross-Canada Venture	341
3	Ontario Interlude	357
4	The Canadian	363
5	Crossing Northern Ontario	377
6	The Prairies	391
7	Alberta	397
8	Red Pass	411
9	Showdown	419
10	Escape	429
11	The Chase is On	439
12	The Tipping Point	451
13	Loose Ends	463
14	Epilogue	469
	Book 7 Endnotes	479

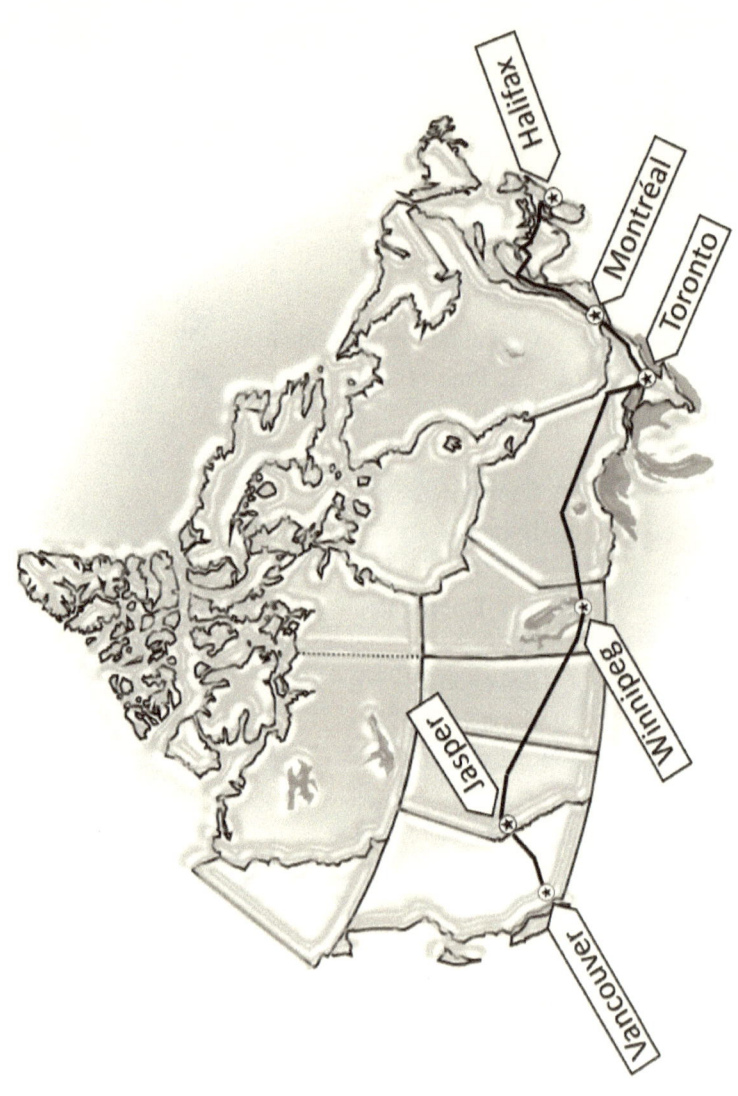

LIST OF CHARACTERS
(IN ORDER OF APPEARANCE)

- Jonathan (Jon) Hope, a thief
- Slim and Jess Peters, brother thieves
- Constable Alexandra (Alex) Houston, RCMP
- Silver, an Alaskan Malamute. Alex's friend and companion
- Constable Jack McDonald, RCMP
- Assistant Commissioner George MacLeod, RCMP
- Staff Sergeant Robert (Bob) G. Simpson, RCMP
- Oliver Risk, American Businessman
- Jonathan (Nathan) Risk, United Church Minister
- François Boucher, VIA Rail Conductor
- Colonel James Peters, retired Canadian Army Veteran
- Hannah Peters, daughter of Colonel Peters
- Benjamin (Ben) Shaw, a bit of a mystery
- Cleo, an orange, black, and white Calico Cat
- Émile Cournoyer, VIA Rail Attendant

1 PRELUDE: A ROBBERY

August 2, 1920
Canada's Rocky Mountains,
Somewhere on the British Columbia side

"Are you ready Jon?"

Jonathon (Jon) Hope was a young man of average height and slender build. He was unremarkable, in fact, except possibly for his youth and his bright, clear eyes. He didn't look like a con-man, cheater, or thief but he was, unquestionably, all three.

"Yes, I think it's time," he replied. "Are you ready to ride?" he asked his two companions, Slim and Jess Peters, who were busily tying their axes to the saddles on their horses. When they were finished, all three men mounted up.

"Ready boss. Let's go," replied Jess. Jess and Slim were brothers. Jess was the talkative one, while Slim, for his part, simply nodded.

It was a small gang. If, that is, a group of three men could be called a gang. Whereas a discerning observer might have found fault with the men's rough appearances, it would have been difficult indeed to find fault with their horses. These latter were uniformly fine specimens of their species. Young, healthy, and strong looking, these were horses that had been well cared for. They could be counted on to maintain sure footing, speed, and endurance – all qualities that would shortly be needed.

The three men rode into the nearby forest and disappeared into the first game trail they encountered.

***

Train number 63[1] of the Canadian Pacific Railroad had just exited from one of the many tunnels and snow sheds that protected its journey through the Rocky Mountains, and was now in an open clearing. It would have made a fine sight, comprising as it did one of the grand steam locomotives of the pre-diesel era, its tender (to provide its fuel and water), two passenger cars, a baggage car, an express car, and the ubiquitous red caboose (or crew car). Now that it was clear of the latest tunnel, the train slowly gained speed as it purposefully rolled along its track, in parallel with a rocky stream that was flush with meltwater from the glaciers and snowfields that lie high above. As the train began to gain altitude, the engineer looked ahead to the next patch of forest, swore loudly, and opened the steam valve to throttle back the engine.

Up ahead, at the entrance to the forest, a large tree had fallen and was lying diagonally across the tracks. As the train began to slow, the engineer began applying the steam brake. The fireman, who had by now seen the fallen tree, pulled the whistle cord with sharp tugs so that the locomotive's throaty steam whistle would produce a succession of short blasts. This was their standard method of alerting the conductor, and the two trainmen at the back of the train, that something — usually people or livestock - was on the track. In this case it also served as a warning to two armed guards in the express car that there might be more to this obstruction than met the eye.

There was only the one tree lying on the rails, and the pointed shape of the end combined with the similarly pointed shape of the stump suggested that it had been felled by beavers. The trainmen had seen things like this before and were prepared. Within a matter of minutes, one end of a heavy chain had been attached to the bottom of the tree, with the other end being attached to a standing tree of the forest fringe that was several yards away from the tracks. One end of another heavy chain was then attached to the top of the fallen tree, with the other end attached to the 'cow-catcher' at the front of the locomotive, which had been inched forward for this purpose. Then, with the train in reverse, the second chain straightened out and pulled the tree more or less parallel to the tracks.

As the train continued to reverse, the first chain straightened out, which pulled the bottom of the tree away from the tracks. When this was done, the tree lay diagonally away from, and sufficiently clear of the tracks. After that, it was simply a matter of untying the chains, stowing them away, and re-boarding the train.

As the engineer shifted the locomotive back to forward gear and opened the throttle, the train slowly resumed its entrance into the forest and the crew began to relax.

That was a mistake.

Whether the train's crew was tired, inattentive, or both will never be known.

Perhaps it was simply the nearness of the forest that now bordered the train's right of way – providing a false sense of security.

Perhaps the shadows cast by the tall trees prevented anyone from seeing what came next.

Crouched low, Jess darted out of the forest and climbed up the steps at the rear of the locomotive. By the time the train's engineer and fireman turned and realized they had company, Jess was pointing two double-action U.S. Army Colt .45 revolvers[2] at them. To the crew they simply looked big, dark, and menacing.

"Keep your hands where I can see them, please," said Jess, "and stop the train – NOW!"

Although spoken politely, there was no mistaking his seriousness.

At this point, only the locomotive and the first few cars were actually in the forest. The rest of the cars were still in the clearing.

When the engineer had complied and the train came to a full stop, Jess told them to "keep the steam up and stand quietly where you are for a minute." Taking out his pocket watch, Jess waited for exactly four minutes, then said "OK, start the train moving again."

This time, he waited until the train had proceeded up the track for about two miles. Given the steep slope, the train was still moving quite slowly despite having travelled the two miles, at which point Jess simply said: "Good day," jumped off the locomotive and disappeared into the forest.

It took a moment for the engineer and fireman to recover from this latest surprise, after which they promptly stopped the train again and went to find the conductor. All three men realized that the train was being robbed, and now they even knew how it was being done. Following a quick discussion, it was agreed that they would reverse the train and retrace the two miles they had just travelled.

There was no reason to hurry.

***

While Jess had been busy in the locomotive, his partners had not been idle.

As soon as the train had been stopped, Jon and Slim had boarded it and hunched down over the link-and-pin coupling between the express car and the baggage car. The pin didn't want to come free but Slim had brought a crowbar with him, which he applied effectively. Despite the stuck coupling pin, this had only taken a little over three minutes. By four minutes, they had jumped off the train and were running to their next positions.

When the train restarted its ascent into the forest, the express car and the caboose were left standing alone at the edge of the clearing. By this time, Slim had taken up his position in front of the express car's big sliding door, while Jon had boarded the caboose to check for railway personnel. Finding two crew members in the caboose, Jon kept them in place at gunpoint. Like Jess, Jon had produced two large Colt double-action .45s. As the next few minutes ticked by, the two frightened crew members must have wondered what the stranger was waiting for. They soon found out, however, as a large, double explosion rang out.

At the express car, there was no attempt to order the guards that must certainly be present to open the big sliding door. Instead, Slim had simply dropped the crowbar he had been carrying and, taking several sticks of dynamite from a bag slung over his shoulder, affixed them along the lower edge of the door. He then lit the fuses and ran to take cover around the end of the car. He had just covered his ears with both hands when there was a double, thundering roar from the exploding dynamite.

The big, sliding door, being held in place only by its rollers along the top and double latches secured from the inside, was completely destroyed by the blasts. Splinters from the door were still falling from the sky as Slim ran back to the gaping doorway with, again, two large revolves drawn. Pointing and waving with his guns, he ordered the two shell-

shocked guards to drop their rifles – which, in fact they had already done – and jump out of the car. Slim herded them to the caboose, and ordered them to join the two trainmen that were already being watched by Jon.

With Jon watching the four men in the caboose Slim returned to the express car, spent only a few minutes there, then jumped and once again took position to one side and put both hands over his ears.

Things were happening so quickly that the four captives in the caboose had only just realized what was coming next, when three explosions rang out in rapid succession.

When the dust settled, Slim re-boarded the express car carrying his crowbar. Moments later, canvas bags began to sail through the air, out the door, and down onto the ground beside the track. There were 13 bags in all, and a careful observer would have noticed that the bags were moderately heavy – about 10 pounds each - of which some made clinking sounds when they struck the ground, while others did not. The former were nine bags containing $5 and $10 gold coins from the Canadian Mint in Ottawa, while the latter were four mail sacks containing Dominion of Canada paper currency.

Once again, the process only took a few minutes after which Slim jumped down from the express car, placed two fingers into his mouth and gave a sharp whistle. This was a signal for the gang's three horses to come out of the forest and join them, which they did. Slim's whistle was also the signal for Jon to go and help load the horses, which he did after first leaving the men in the caboose with stern instructions to "stay put."

With Slim and Jon working together it took several more minutes to distribute the bags among the three horses and to tie Jess' horse behind that of Jon. After that, they picked up the guards' rifles, mounted up and rode off into the forest. As soon as they were out of sight, they made a sharp turn onto a game trail, rode just far enough to be out of sight of the tracks, then dismounted and prepared to wait.

It wasn't long before the rest of the train made its way slowly down the track, and the crew reconnected the cars. As the gang's leader, Jon, had predicted, the train then simply resumed its original journey up through the forest. Not being equipped to chase or deal with three heavily armed robbers, the crew had decided to continue to the next town where they could report the robbery and let the authorities deal with it.

When the train had passed them for the last time, Jon and Slim rode back down the game trail and then brazenly followed the path of the train — right up the tracks. Two miles ahead, they encountered a man sitting on one of the rails.

"Any trouble?" said Jess.

"None. You?" replied Jon.

"Nope," said Jess. Slim just gave a quiet smile.

Untying his horse, Jess mounted up and the three men rode off. Once again, they simply followed the tracks, but this time going the other way — heading west.

The gang hadn't bothered to wear masks because they were unknown in Canada and were planning to promptly leave the country. They were, in fact, headed for Vancouver where they would board a steamship heading south to the United States.

The whole episode took place so quickly and smoothly that it had either been meticulously planned and practiced, or they had done this before, or both. In only 45 minutes' time, the three men had stolen $44,000 comprising just over a thousand ounces of gold coins, worth $24,000, and paper currency comprising twelve thousand 25¢, $1, $2, and $5 bills worth $20,000.

Not everything went completely smoothly, however. Shortly after the three men entered the train tunnel, several shots rang out in the darkness.

One mile further along the track, a single man, on a single horse, rode out of the tunnel.

Knowing that an alert would be put out to watch for people trying to sell gold coins — which had become rare since the beginning of the 1914 world war - Jon planned to hide that part of the loot until it was safe to come back for it. Which might be never, he reflected, as he now had $20,000 in currency, which seemed like more than enough — especially since he no longer had to share it.

As for his former partners, Jon was reminded of a saying of his fellow American Benjamin Franklin[3]:

"Three may keep a secret, if two of them are dead."

The Daily News

Tuesday, August 3, 1920

Daring Train Robbery
Thieves Strike in Mountain Pass

Laurie Schramm

2 A CROSS-CANADA VENTURE

Day 1
May 26, 1978
Halifax, Nova Scotia
At the CN Rail Station

"All Aboard!"

Silver and I had been waiting to board VIA Rail's *Ocean* train at the Halifax South End Station. The progress of history was very much in evidence here. First, there was the station itself. This was Halifax's third train station, built in 1922 to replace its immediate predecessor the North Street station, which had been essentially destroyed in the Halifax Explosion of 1917[4]. Beside the station was the classic Hotel Nova Scotian and not far away was Halifax's famous Pier 21.

The current station reminded me of a museum to the age of steam locomotion. Its ornate, white-limestone exterior had an imposing sequence of tall columns. Passing through these into the station, you just had to stop and stare at the sheer size and grandeur of the Ticket Lobby, with its immense, arched ceiling and its huge expanse of information, ticketing, and baggage wickets plus benched seating areas, and innumerable side arches and doorways leading who knows where.

This would be a security nightmare, I thought to myself, imagining what it would look like in peak holiday season. So many people could be crowded into so much space, with so many entrances and exits. I remember thinking: *Looking for someone in here could be like looking for a needle in a haystack.*

The station was the eastern terminus for Canada's cross-country VIA Rail passenger trains, what the train people called a 'stub-end terminal.' Here, incoming trains would disembark their passengers and baggage, then locomotives and rail cars would be turned around on a turntable in preparation for their next departure.

When Silver and I had checked in and made our way to the departure area, the past and present came together in striking contrast. We were standing in the train shed, which was another massive structure – essentially a big roof that provided cover from the weather for the trains and passengers alike as they got on with the business of embarking and disembarking. This was no ordinary roof, however. It extended for some 1,500 feet south over the tracks and was supported by large, strong-looking steel pillars and cross-braces, all of them in a kind of dirty black. In addition to the feeling of space, the train shed felt dark and dirty, which it wasn't really, and damp, which it was – this was Halifax after all – and it felt old, which it certainly was. I say all this to underscore the contrast between the station we were in and the train we were about to board.

The train, in contrast, looked clean, modern, and new. It wasn't really all that modern and new. The Canadian government had just created VIA Rail as a Crown Corporation (meaning government owned) the year before and it had only been in the current year that the whole project had fully come together: a single, integrated passenger rail service that would span almost the full breadth of Canada. The locomotives and rail cars had all been acquired from the Canadian National (CN) and Canadian Pacific (CP) railways but had been cleaned-up and painted-over with the new VIA Rail livery, so that they looked new. Not only that, standing there in the literal shadow of the historic Halifax train station made them look almost futuristic.

It felt different to be in uniform for this trip. Granted, it was only my tactical uniform with a dark blue police-baseball cap, not the formal, red-serge tunic for which Mounties are famous. But so much of my work lately had been under-cover that being in uniform at all had become somewhat uncommon for me. Even Silver was wearing a police-service-dog vest.

Between me being a woman and Silver an Alaskan Malamute that looked remarkably like a large wolf, neither of us looked like most people's image of a Mountie. The same could not be said, however, for my colleague, Constable Jack McDonald.

Jack was tall, square-jawed, and handsome with an easy, outgoing disposition. If anything, he looked like the stereotypical Hollywood Mountie. Although he wasn't wearing his red serge, Stetson hat, and high boots, he did have on his yellow-banded forage cap, brown serge jacket with brown leather Sam Browne belt and holster, yellow striped pants and short boots. Even in his working ('Service Order') uniform, he wouldn't have looked out of place on a movie- or recruiting poster.

I don't want to give you the wrong impression, I liked Jack, and still do. We met in basic training[5] and had trained in the same troop together. Although he had a fearsome, and well-earned reputation as a womanizer, he had always treated me as a colleague – professionally and with respect. In the years since graduating, of the whole troop, it was Jack whose path I'd crossed most often. We'd worked well together on some dangerous assignments, and I'd learned that I could depend on him[6,7,8].

Perhaps I should back up a bit and tell you some of my story.

My name is Alexandra Houston. My friends call me Alex. Four years previously, in the summer of 1974, I'd been 24 years old, and feeling like my career was at a standstill. I'd studied chemistry at university and liked it, but not enough to pursue science as a career. I'd reset my sights on police work next, and had joined the Metropolitan Toronto Police force (Metro). Although policing seemed like a better fit for me than science, my two years with Metro had mostly comprised routine administrative- and traffic duties. These assignments were important, and needed to be done by somebody, and done well. But for me, they didn't fit the Hollywood vision of policing that I had developed, and I hadn't found them to be very challenging.

They say you should be careful what you wish for.

My life changed drastically with an unexpected meeting. Without explanation, my Captain had sent me to go and see a very senior Royal

Canadian Mounted Police (RCMP) officer. My reaction to this was apprehension, and I wondered what I could possibly have messed-up so badly that it had caught the notice of our national police force.

That's how I first came to meet Assistant Commissioner George MacLeod. After a lengthy conversation that I belatedly realized was an interview, he told me that he had asked my Captain (his friend) to recommend one of his young officers for a special pilot project he had in mind. He wanted someone who wanted to accomplish things, someone eager and tenacious, someone chomping at the bit to be allowed to do some 'real' police work, and... someone female. At this point he had shed his stern 'Mountie look,' relaxed his entire body, chuckled, and said that my Captain had recommended the "biggest pain in the butt" in his Division - me.

Assistant Commissioner MacLeod had explained that the 'Force' had fallen behind the times, and that its senior leadership wanted to build a more diverse police force. "We're going to be recruiting immigrants, visible minorities, maybe even people with some kinds of disabilities as well," he said, "But we have to start somewhere, and that somewhere is by engaging women." He wanted to try a first 'pilot test' with a woman, but that pilot test had to succeed as it would pave the way for an entire first troop of policewomen that would follow. He had thought of using someone that had already qualified as a policewoman, and simply re-train them in the 'RCMP way.'

That had brought me up to full attention. "Wait a minute! Do basic training all over again?"

"Yes!" he'd replied, "that's the only way you can possibly succeed. In the old days of the Northwest Mounted Police, a person could get appointed straight into the Force, even as a commissioned officer, if they had the right political connections. No more. Now everyone starts out the same way, as a Constable, and by going through the same basic training. If you want to have any hope of being accepted, much less respected, that's how you have to begin."

So, in the fall of 1974, I went through training at the RCMP's 'Depot' Division training centre in Regina, dealt with the good and the bad issues that came with being the first woman to train there, and survived to become the first woman Mountie. I hadn't intended for it to happen, really. The opportunity just came and found me.

After training, or re-training if you like, I'd been posted to Radium City, a small town in very northern Saskatchewan that, in its early days, had been a great uranium mining centre. Although my new boss, Corporal Morrison, had told me that nothing interesting ever happened around there, he'd been wrong, and I'd had to rescue him from a mine collapse, run our entire detachment single-handed while he was confined to hospital for six weeks, get rescued by a strange dog from near-death, solve a mystery, and find and catch a murderer – all in only four months!

The dog was named Silver. Investigating a mysterious series of break-ins had led me to some unusual places, including several abandoned uranium mines. In one such mine I'd fallen through a trap and found myself hanging precariously over the sharp edge of a vertical mine shaft. Unable to get out and tiring fast, I was saved by the almost magical appearance of what I first took to be a wolf, which gave me quite a scare, but turned out to be Silver, an Alaskan Malamute. Silver somehow sensed that I was in danger, had decided to help, and with his assistance I had been able to climb up and out of the raise. To make a long story short[5], while I'd continued to investigate the case, he had attached himself to me, was eventually given to me, and we'd been close friends ever since.

Sometime later I'd found myself in another surprise meeting with the same Assistant Commissioner MacLeod. Once again, a "coffee meeting" had turned into an interview and, once again, he had something new in mind for me. By this time, he'd become head of the Force's Security Service[9] and, unsurprisingly, he had some new ideas he wanted to try out by way of some experimental pilot projects. One of them involved me.

That had taken me to Ottawa, where I joined the Security Service. My new boss, Staff Sergeant Robert (Bob) Simpson, introduced me to the shady worlds of spies, counter-espionage, anarchists, and terrorists.

As a prelude to my first real Security Service assignment, Silver and I were sent to Innisfail, Alberta, to be trained as a police dog and handler team[6]. "If that dog is going to go everywhere with you, then we should get him trained too," Assistant Commissioner MacLeod had announced, on one of his periodic visits. Both Bob and the Assistant Commissioner had been interested in the possibilities presented by the first female 'Mountie,' especially undercover possibilities, and they were also interested in, and seemingly amused by, the notion of me having

345

Silver along as a kind of side-kick, since he looked absolutely nothing like a police dog. That officially brought Silver into the Mounties too, and that's how my best friend became my partner.

Since then, we've had more hair-raising adventures together[7,8,10,11], and our destinies were firmly inter-twined.

***

"All Aboard!" the conductor repeated.

Silver and I moved toward the train, which was called *The Ocean*. There were a few seniors ahead of us, being helped onboard. As we waited, an elderly man in front of us turned, looked at me and my uniform, then Silver and his police-service-dog vest, and said "You're a real policewoman?"

"Yes, Sir," I replied.

"Huh! What will they think of next?" I must have looked a bit put out, because he quickly followed-up with "No offense intended. My name's Oliver Risk and this is my son Nathan."

"How do you do? My name's Alex Houston, and this is my partner Silver." I looked at Oliver Risk with interest because I thought that I knew who he was but had never seen him in person before. He was of medium height with silvery-grey hair, which receded back from an expanse of forehead, bushy grey eyebrows topping heavy jowls and a boxer's slightly flattened nose. His manner seemed a bit grumpy to me, possibly even surly, and I noticed that Silver rather pointedly ignored him completely, which was never a positive sign.

His son, Nathan Risk, provided quite a contrast to his father. The first thing I noticed was his wide, innocent-looking, blue eyes, and his infectious smile. These were well complimented by a full head of blonde hair that gave him something of the appearance of a California surfer. The next most striking thing about Nathan's appearance was that his clothes proclaimed his profession. He was wearing a white clerical collar with a blue shirt. Clearly a pastor or minister in a Protestant religion.

My thoughts were interrupted by Nathan taking his father's arm and saying: "Come on Dad, it's the 1970s now. Things are changing. Let's get on the train and get settled."

"I see you're still getting the same reaction from people," said my colleague Jack, who had been standing just behind me.

"Not as often as I used to," I replied. "I don't mind, as long as people are polite, and it still helps when I'm working undercover."

As Oliver and Nathan disappeared up the steps and into the train, we found ourselves face to face with the conductor, who gave us a casual salute and said "Good afternoon. Looks like you officers are on duty. Is there some kind of trouble?"

"No trouble," I said, "I'm Constable Houston, this is my colleague Constable McDonald, and this is my partner Silver. When you have a spare moment, we can explain why we're here."

"François Boucher," he said, offering his hand to shake – even to Silver, who promptly raised one paw for him. "I did hear something about you already," he paused and thought for a moment. "We'll be leaving at 1 pm exactly. Why don't you come see me after the 2:30 stop at Truro, eh? I'll have an hour free then."

"Sounds great, thank you," I replied.

"My office is in the first sleeping car behind the dining car. Look for a sign saying 'Conductor' on the door."

Saying "OK," we boarded the train and set off in search of our roomettes.

The train comprised several different kinds of cars. Behind the locomotive was a diesel-powered, generator-boiler car (to provide battery-electrical power and steam heating to the rest of the train), followed by a baggage car. Next came a dome car that had passenger seats on the upper level, a dining room on the main level, plus a kitchen, snack bar and lounge. Behind that was a dedicated dining car, with its own kitchen, followed by two sleeping cars, and then a regular passenger car. Bringing up the rear of the train was another dome car, this one with passenger seats on the upper level, and four roomettes, a bar and a panoramic lounge at the very end.

Jack and I each had our own two-person roomette in the second sleeping car. Just ahead of us, I noticed Oliver and his son Nathan going into their roomette, which was only a couple of doors down from us.

In their day-time configuration, the roomettes had two comfortable armchairs and a small private washroom. In their night-time configuration two single beds folded down to replace the chairs.

We agreed to allow some time to stow our carry-on bags and then meet for coffee in the forward dome car, which was called the

'Skyline.'

There wasn't much to unpack so, while Silver curled up on the floor, I mostly sat in one of the armchairs and looked contentedly out the large picture-window. There wasn't much to see while the train was standing in the rail yard, but I was greatly looking forward to watching the scenery as we made our way across the country. *The Ocean* would take us from Halifax to Montréal, then a corridor train would take us from Montréal to Toronto, and finally *The Canadian* would take us from Toronto to Vancouver – all-in-all, a distance of more than 4,400 km.

When the train jolted forward to begin the journey, it shook me out of my reverie and Silver and I went in search of a table in the Skyline Car. While we waited for Jack, I ordered two cups of coffee, which the attendant promptly delivered along with a bowl of water for Silver.

Jack and I knew each other well enough that we mostly just sipped our coffees and watched the scenery pass by. I liked the ocean views the best, beginning with the protected waters of the Bedford Basin.

Our first stop, Truro, was one of many brief stops which only allowed the few minutes needed for a few passengers to get on or off. If we wanted to get off, we were told not to stray beyond the platform or, after a single brief warning, the train would leave without us. Neither of us got up from our table and, sure enough, it was only a few minutes before the train was moving again. That made it time for us to visit the conductor.

We had no trouble finding him. One of the doors on the first sleeping car had a brass plate with the word 'Conductor' engraved in it. Just underneath that was a holder into which one could slide temporary nameplates. It held a black plastic nameplate with white letters giving the current conductor's name: François Boucher. The door was open, and we found François waiting and ready for us.

His office appeared to be a converted 3-person roomette. There was a small desk and chair, a small side-table, and two visitor chairs. Where there would normally have been an upper bunk, a basket shelf had been installed along the full length of the wall. This was filled with an assortment of boxes. *Files and supplies*, I guessed.

"Come in. Take a seat," said François, with a large smile and waving expansively. "Not as comfortable as the chairs in your roomettes I'm afraid, but at least they fit into this little office, eh?"

There was, in fact, room for Jack and I to sit down, but not much else. I was about to ask Silver to wait in the corridor, but he was way ahead of me, squeezing himself in and laying on the floor at our feet with his body resting partly across Jack and my boots.

François was quick. He had correctly interpreted the expression on my face and Silver's quick movements. "That's a smart dog you have there, eh? He doesn't want to miss a thing that one, and if you close the door for privacy he won't be left outside."

"You're right about both," I confirmed, "but I don't think we need to close the door. It doesn't matter if we're overheard."

Our preliminaries were interrupted by Silver himself, however. He had no sooner settled himself in front of Jack and I than his head went up and he scrambled to his feet, clearly sniffing and heading for where François was seated.

"Silver…" I cautioned.

"It's OK," said François immediately. "He smells the cat, eh?"

"The cat?"

"I have a cat named Cleo. She's not here right now but Silver has caught her scent. Come see." He motioned for us to stand up and look over his desk and, sure enough, there on the floor beside his office chair was a comfortable-looking cat bed and one of those double-bowls for water and cat food.

After thoroughly sniffing around the cat's bed Silver came back, gave an unamused snort, and lay back down in front of Jack and I.

"Sorry about that," I said.

"*Pas de quoi*[12]," said François with a broad smile. "She's a railway cat, eh? She prowls the whole train. Sometimes she sleeps in the generator-boiler car where it's warm. Sooner or later, you'll see her. If you spot an orange, black, and white calico cat that looks like she owns the train – that's Cleo.

"I'll try to make sure Silver doesn't give her any trouble," I promised.

"Don't worry, she's fast and she's acrobatic. The most he'll be able to do is make her jump, but he'll never catch her." Then, looking pointedly at Jack and I, he returned to our previous topic. "I was told about you. I'm supposed to help you if I can. You're here to look over security, eh? Anything I should be worried about?"

"No. Not at all. There's going to be a group of VIPs travelling this route later this year. Our job is travel with you and observe. Then we'll pass our notes up the line, and others will finalize the security arrangements for the VIP trip."

"OK. What are you supposed to observe?"

"Everything and anything," began Jack, who ran down a list of things we wanted to observe like the various stops, the facilities and terrain near the stops, the ease with which someone could slip onto the train unnoticed, and so on.

"That should keep you busy," commented François thoughtfully. "Let me show you something." He pulled out a copy of the train schedule covering the portion from Halifax to Montréal. "See here we have two 15 minutes stops, at Moncton and Sainte-Foy, plus 14 stops that are just long enough to get the odd passenger on or off, then 9 other places where we only stop if a passenger at the stop waves us down or if a passenger on the train comes and asks me. Plus, we can be stopped in many places to wait for a freight train to pass us."

We must have looked a bit disconcerted at this, because François chuckled and said: "Don't worry. Once you've watched a few of each kind of stop, they all look pretty much the same after that. Besides, if you have any questions about anything, come and see me."

"Thank you," said Jack, "that's great."

"Will you only be our conductor as far as Montréal?" I asked.

"Normally that would be the case, yes. But in this case, the answer is no..." He paused for effect. "I won't be with you on the corridor train between Montréal and Toronto, but we'll be together again on *The Canadian*, all the way to Vancouver. Very unusual, that is. But, it's the company's idea of being helpful – so you don't have to keep explaining yourself over and over when you change trains, eh?"

"That's great," I said, "I hope you don't mind?"

"Mind? I've been in a rut, eh? Travelling with *The Atlantic* back and forth, back and forth. This will make for some adventure. I'm going to enjoy it." He punctuated this with another brilliant smile, then: "So, if you don't have questions for me right now, how about if I take you on a tour of the whole train, eh?"

We said that would be great, and François took us to the dome car at the rear of the train, then we backtracked and went all the way to the front. The only locked door we encountered was that of the baggage car. As we passed through it, François recommended we leave Silver there as the next passageways would be very noisy. Leaving Silver, the three of us continued forward.

'Noisy' turned out to be an understatement, particularly as we walked along the narrow corridor that led to the front of the locomotive. Once we reached the cab, however, it was reasonably quiet and we were introduced to the engineer and shown the fantastic view that he had of the scenery and the rails and signals that lie ahead. The scenery changed to rivers and forests as we passed from Nova Scotia into New Brunswick.

François indicated that he wanted to remain up front and speak with the engineer so, after a last long look through the forward windows, Jack and I said our 'thank-yous' and headed back to collect Silver at the baggage car and return to our roomettes.

We hadn't been back to our roomettes for long before the train stopped in Moncton, New Brunswick. At 15 minutes, this was one of the longer stops so Silver and I went for a walk along the length of the train, pausing only to watch some baggage being loaded and unloaded for a few minutes. I took out my notebook and made a few notes on how easy it would be for someone to slip onto the train at such stops.

It certainly didn't look like it would be difficult for a stranger to slip on or off the train at any crowded station stop. The trick would be for someone to find a place to hide on the train itself, unless they could get a *bona fide* passenger to hide them in one of the larger roomettes.

Neither Silver nor I sensed anything concerning, although I thought that he looked a bit longingly at a snowshoe hare that had paused at the side of the railway property.

When the "all Aboard" call came, at 5:35 pm, we simply boarded the baggage car and walked back to our roomette via the inside corridor. It was already almost time for supper.

As we walked, I noticed that it wasn't very crowded on the train. Family vacations wouldn't begin for several more weeks yet, after schools recessed for the summer in mid-June. University students were out for the summer semester, however, and the passenger car was about half-full of university age students travelling coach class, meaning that they only had upright seats for the whole trip, although they could get up and walk around of course, or go to the bar and dining areas. Seeing the students brought back memories for me. As a university student, I had travelled that way myself once, from Saskatoon to Toronto and had found the trip exciting but exhausting - due to lack of sleep. I was glad I had a roomette this time.

Once again, Oliver and Nathan Risk were ahead of us when Silver and I entered the Dining Car. They were sitting alone. Nathan seemed to be doing all the talking, while Oliver simply stared out the window, seeming not to pay much attention to either his son or the scenery, which was shifting from lakes and farms into mostly forests and rivers.

I wasn't sure whether the staff would let Silver come with me to the dining section, but the attendant took it in stride and seated us as if it were an everyday occurrence. She did seat us at a table at one end of the dining section, commenting that it was to minimize any potential problems for people with allergies, but that was no problem for us. Another attendant simply removed one chair from our table so Silver could sit or lie down beside me. Not only were we able to eat together, but the staff made quite a fuss over Silver and the lady chef obviously appreciated the opportunity to prepare something out of the ordinary, as she came out first to meet us and make some suggestions. We had experienced something like this on a previous case[13], in which we travelled, twice, in a Canadian

Navy Destroyer. There, the Navy chefs had made extravagant efforts to feed Silver in royal style. I certainly appreciated their efforts and I think Silver did too although, as a former sled dog, he could probably have eaten just about anything. Once again, I was contentedly enjoying the scenery pass by when Jack came to join us.

"I could get used to this kind of duty," he said, taking his seat across from me.

"Me too," I agreed. "I still find myself appreciating how nice it is to be warm again."

"You were up to something north of the Arctic Circle earlier this year, weren't you? Something to do with that Soviet satellite that crashed up there?"

"Yes, to both questions. Let's order our meals, then I'll tell you all about it." After the attendant took our orders and brought us coffee, I related my previous big assignment, in which I'd posed as a university scientist so I could join a team of specialists in their search for radioactive debris from a fallen Soviet spy satellite[11]. My underlying mission had been to watch out for Soviet agents that might also be on the team looking for a piece of secret new technology that might have survived. As we ate dinner, I related the story while trying to casually observe the other people that came into the dining car. This wasn't too difficult a task as I was facing the entire dining section, and only six other people came in to eat. Of those, only three struck me as being out of the ordinary.

The first two were an elderly man and a young woman who came and sat two tables ahead of us and on the same side of the train, which put them in the middle of the dining section and on the opposite side from Oliver and Nathan Risk. I knew who the man was: Colonel James Peters, a retired veteran of the Canadian Army with distinguished service in both the Second World War and the Korean Conflict.

He was the type of person that's hard to miss: tall and solidly built, ruggedly handsome with a square jaw and piercing blue eyes. He was showing his age a bit now, with greying hair, receding at the temples. *He must be about 75*, I thought, but he still retained the overtly military bearing of his former career, and still seemed to be quite fit and mobile.

I later learned from François that the young woman with him was his daughter, Hannah Peters. She certainly didn't look much like him. She was slender, almost willowy in build, of medium height, and had long, drab-blonde hair, and brown eyes that seemed to me to have a melancholy look. I guessed that she was probably about 18 years old. The two of them seemed to pass their dinner in companionable discussion, and the Colonel's quiet smiles, with their hint of mischievousness, made me think that the two of them were probably quite close. Unfortunately, I was too far away to hear anything.

The third person that caught my attention was another young man that I overheard asking specifically for the table that was just ahead of mine but on the other side of the train. When the attendant tried to seat him, he ignored the first seat proffered and sat himself so that he was facing towards the majority of the other tables. I would have put this down to a simple desire to face the same way that the train was heading - as some people find it uncomfortable to have their back to the direction of travel – except that, as dinner progressed, he seemed to be closely watching Oliver and Nathan Risk. Certainly, he spared an occasional glance at the scenery rolling by to one side, and also for the pretty Hannah sitting across the aisle and one table further ahead, but his gaze would always come back to rest on the Risks.

It seemed to me that Oliver Risk, in particular, was the focus of the young man's attention. Whenever Oliver spoke to his son – which wasn't very often – the younger man paid close attention, although I doubted that he was sitting close enough to overhear anything. I found out later, from François, that his name was Benjamin Shaw, that he was travelling alone, and that he was booked to travel with us all the way to Vancouver, as were the Risks, as were the Peters.

The plot thickens! I thought.

Silver

Laurie Schramm

3 ONTARIO INTERLUDE

Day 2
May 27, 1978
Sainte-Foy, Québec

I awoke to the rising sun at 5 am. During the night, the train had continued to make its way through New Brunswick and would have crossed into the province of Québec shortly after midnight. The next brief stop would be in Sainte-Foy, a small city near the provincial capital: Québec City, so I had a bit of time to lounge in bed watching the scenery before getting dressed. I wanted to take Silver for another walk around the train when it stopped.

We had just enough time to make a complete circuit of the train. Passengers weren't allowed to walk around the far side of the train, but with Silver and I in uniform, no one bothered us. I didn't spot anything new or noteworthy on our circuit, but I made a show of writing notes in my notebook anyway, and then a sharp "All Aboard!" signaled that it was time for us to get back on the train.

Jack joined Silver and I for breakfast in the dining car and, since for a few minutes we were the only passengers dining, we were able to quietly 'talk shop.'

"How was your evening?" I asked Jack, knowing that he had planned to change into civilian clothes and spent some time in each of the coach, coffee shop, and bar sections of the train.

"Not bad," he replied. "There was a little excitement just before

357

midnight when one of the passengers in the bar got pretty rowdy, and you could see that some of the others were worried he might turn violent. He was loud and obnoxious more than anything else though, so I just sat back and kept an eye on him. When we stopped in Campbellton, the CN Police[14] came on board and arrested him. There was a laugh-or-cry moment, when the man's wife tried to intervene. When that didn't work, she followed them all off the train, yelling and screaming at them the whole time. I suspect she may have had too much to drink as well.

Other than that, the main passenger car was like one big party. It was noisy too, but that was because a couple of the kids had brought guitars with them, and there was a lot of singing going on."

"I remember it being the same when I travelled in 'coach' as a teenager one summer. I gather they were better behaved than your drunk though?"

"Oh, sure. They seemed like a pretty good bunch, just having fun."

"I don't doubt it," I said, suddenly feeling a bit old.

"When I left, they were going strong and planning to party through the whole night," Jack continued. "No sign of anyone of special interest." That meant he hadn't seen Oliver Risk or the Colonel.

For my part, I had left Silver behind, changed in to civilian clothes, and spent time in each of the upper-deck vista domes and other small lounge areas. "The domes were quiet," I reported. "It was sightseers until sunset, and then it seemed to be people in coach class that wanted to find a quiet place to sleep for the night. I didn't see anyone of special interest either, so it looks like they kept to their roomettes."

After breakfast, the three of us took an inside stroll along the full length of the train and back, returning to our roomettes to re-pack our carry-on bags as the train crossed the St. Laurence River prior to pulling into the station at Montréal. Arriving at 10:15 am put us only a few minutes late, leaving us time to walk around the station.

While I had the opportunity, I stopped at the first pay phone I encountered and placed a collect call to my boss, Staff Sergeant Bob Simpson in Ottawa. He wasn't there, but I left a message with a duty officer providing a brief description of Benjamin Shaw and asking for any information they could find on him.

Silver and I then boarded the corridor train that was scheduled to depart for Toronto at 11 am. The corridor trains, being mostly for commuters and not travelling overnight, only had coach cars so we took a spot at one end of the car where two bench seats faced each other, with a table in-between them. I sat on the side facing the length of the car, but positioned myself so I could watch people as they entered, and we settled in.

Within minutes I was treated to an interesting procession. First came Oliver and Nathan Risk, the former looking a bit grumpy – again – and walking slowly. Nathan Risk, again wearing his clerical collar, had a supportive hold on one of his father's arms, and a sunny expression on his face. He held a thick book in his other hand, just like he'd had when we first met, and it dawned on me that it was probably a bible - part of his standard equipment.

Behind the Risks were a cluster of business people, all of them wearing suits, looking very focused, and carrying briefcases. Next, came the Peters. Once again, the Colonel exuded a purposeful military bearing that contrasted sharply with the carefree, fluid movements of his daughter Hannah. I noticed with interest that the Colonel again chose seats that were somewhat behind, and across the aisle from, the Risks.

Next came another cluster of business people and briefcases, followed by Jack. Silver was lying on the bench seat across from me, so when Jack turned to join us, I quietly patted the seat beside me. That gave him the same view down the length of the car, and I leaned towards him and whispered: "All parties of interest are further up the car. Do you want to place a bet on whether our mystery person sits behind them?"

I never found out what Jack thought because I'd no sooner whispered the words when Benjamin Shaw stopped right beside us and carefully scanned the disposition of the car ahead of us. After a moment's hesitation he took a seat facing forward that was on the same side of the car as the Risks but behind both the Risks and the Peters. If I'd had any doubts the day before about his presence on the train being coincidental, there were no doubts any longer and I was glad that I'd put the request for information through to my boss before boarding.

The trip from Montréal to Toronto was relatively short, being scheduled for five and a half hours. We very quickly passed from

Québec into Ontario, and people mostly sat in their seats and looked out the windows or, in the case of the business-people, read newspapers or read and scribbled notes on important-looking files. There was a service counter in our car, from which people acquired lunch or snacks, but not in any particular pattern that I could discern. Near the mid-point of our trip there was a brief stop at the Kingston Station, but Silver and I were virtually the only ones to take advantage of the opportunity to stretch our legs and, in his case, heed the call of nature.

As the journey unfolded, I tried to inconspicuously keep an eye on the Risks, Peters, and Benjamin Shaw but, from my vantage point at least, it was a re-run of the previous evening's action. Oliver Risk seemed to moodily look out the window, Nathan Risk seemed immersed in reading his book or bible, the Colonel and his daughter gave every appearance of two people enjoying a father-daughter vacation, while Benjamin reminded me of a hawk watching its prey. The one difference from the previous evening was that Benjamin seemed to be more frequently distracted by the presence of Hannah Peters.

This is starting to feel like a movie drama, I thought.

We arrived in Toronto at 4:30 pm and disembarked into Union Station. This is another classic structure, reminiscent of Halifax's train station but much larger! Jack and I collected our checked bags and walked across the street to the Royal York Hotel, where we'd be staying for the night. The Royal York was another experience in living history. Built by the Canadian Pacific Railway Company (CP) in 1929, it is one of Canada's more than twenty historic, grand 'railway hotels' which, whether built by CN or CP, stretch from St. John's, Newfoundland to Victoria, British Columbia. The first sensations I had when entering the hotel were the early-20th century architecture and décor, the size of everything, and the quiet. Despite the number of people going about their business on the expansive first floor, once the doors swung shut behind us the sounds of the busy downtown were sealed out and a hush descended around us.

While we were checking in, we asked the concierge if there might be a chance of getting a reservation in the revolving restaurant of the CN Tower, which was only a few blocks away. He said he'd see what he could do and would call us.

Although the hotel was a classic – in other words: very old – it had gone through several renovations in the previous six years and our rooms were quite modern, but still furnished and decorated to match the hotel's long-standing character. Here too, the rooms were extremely comfortable looking, and extremely quiet.

I had no sooner dropped my bags on the floor and looked around my room than the phone rang. It was Jack calling to say that the concierge had phoned, and we could have a table for two if we could get to the tower by 5:30, otherwise they were fully booked for the evening. Jack said the concierge had also cautioned that, unless we were on official duty, Silver wouldn't be allowed in. Agreeing to go right away, I changed into casual clothes, put a bowl of water out for Silver and left him to wait in the room while I went down to the lobby to meet Jack.

Reaching the lobby, I found that Jack was there ahead of me and sitting in a large leather easy chair: the comfortable type that is both mentally and physically difficult to get out of. As I approached, I expected him to get up right away but he surprised me by just sitting and looking at me. When I was close enough, he used a very soft voice to say: "Take a moment, and then casually glance over to your right."

Hesitating as I took this in, I slowly turned to my left and swept my gaze around the whole lobby area, as if taking in the architecture. As my gaze came nearly full circle, I saw what Jack had. About thirty feet away, three people were just meeting, and then walked out of the lobby together as if heading for a night on the town. It was Nathan Risk, with no clerical collar this time, Hannah Peters, and Benjamin Shaw.

"Looks like the young people are getting acquainted," said Jack.

"Young people!" I said, "you're making me feel old." I was about to turn 28 that summer, and not at all prepared to think of myself as being old. I estimated that Jack was four or five years younger than me as he had joined the Force within a year of graduating from high school, whereas I had gone to university and then spent two years with the Toronto City Police before joining the Force.

Chuckling, Jack levered himself out of his chair and said: "Want to try following them?"

"No. I think we should lie low. Let's go out on the town ourselves."

As I mentioned, the CN Tower was only a few blocks from our hotel and a pleasant stroll took us to the tower and the elevator that whisked us to the top. I was looking forward to the view. Construction of the tower had just begun when I left Toronto to join the Force, and I hadn't been back to Toronto since it was completed and opened in 1976.

Our table was right beside the expansive glass windows, and we had to tear our eyes away from the scenery to look at the menus and decide what to order. The backs of the menus explained that the CN Tower was the world's tallest free-standing structure (at that time), and the equivalent of a 147-story building, standing 457 m (1,500 ft) to its roof, and 553 m (1,815 ft) to the top of its antenna spire.

Luckily for us, it was a clear evening and as our dinner progressed it made a complete revolution. Since the tower stood about four blocks from the shore of Lake Ontario, we had great views of the lake and shoreline for about half of the time, and of the mass of downtown high-rises for the other half. Beyond sight-seeing, we avoided talking about work and just had a nice, relaxing dinner.

It was still nice outside after dinner and I wanted to go collect Silver for a stroll along the waterfront. Jack wanted to come too, so we went back to the hotel for Silver and then took a long walk along the lakeshore. Being a Saturday night, there were plenty of people out for walks, going to waterside bars and restaurants, and taking harbour cruises.

For a few moments here and there, it was easy to forget that we were on a mission but the mission - a mission within a mission, really – was never very far from our thoughts.

The next morning we'd be boarding another train, and I remember wondering whether it was all going to be just a big waste of time.

It wasn't.

4 *THE CANADIAN*

Day 3
May 28, 1978
Toronto, Ontario

It was a windy and rainy Sunday in downtown Toronto when Silver and I took an early morning walk along the lakeshore. There was no message from my boss, Bob, yet but I knew that it could take some time for them to get the information I asked for.

After checking out of the hotel and meeting up with Jack, we walked across the street, checked in with VIA Rail, and boarded *The Canadian* for its 09:45 departure.

The train pulled out of Union Station on schedule. I noticed that it had a few more cars than we'd had on *The Ocean*, but our car seemed to have the same passengers as before, and with their roomettes in the same corresponding positions.

Not long after leaving the outskirts of Toronto the weather improved just as we began to cross the Canadian Shield, with its lakes and forests. As we continued along, rocky outcrops began to appear more and more frequently, and I knew that as we approached Northern Ontario, we'd be seeing more and more rock. Although there were periods of heavy forest, these only made for a greater contrast when everything opened up as we crossed various waterways on old-looking railway bridges.

It's not uncommon for people to fall into habits like sitting in the same seats for school or university classes, and a similar thing had happened for many of the passengers when we were on *The Ocean* train. Things started to change on *The Canadian*, however. When Silver and I went to the dining car for lunch, we were again seated at one extreme end of the section, but this time some of the other passengers changed their seating arrangements. Oliver Risk and the Colonel were nowhere to be seen, and Hannah had initially sat down alone. She was soon joined, however, by Nathan and Benjamin, who came in together and were already in the midst of some kind of religious debate. Nathan was clearly back 'on duty,' wearing his clerical collar. As the three young people were sitting at the table right next to us, I could see that the book Nathan carried around when 'on duty,' was in fact a bible.

They're starting to get to know each other, I thought.

When Jack came to join us, sitting across the table from me and with his back to the next table he raised his eyebrows, signifying that he had also noticed the change in pattern. I nodded in turn, and settled in to listen and observe. I had no trouble overhearing, but the direction of the conversation threw me at first.

Nathan was saying to Benjamin: "Look Ben, I know it would be convenient, but no one gets to see God. The Bible says '*No one has ever seen God,*' John 4:12, and '*No man has seen or can see God,*' Timothy 6:16."

"That can't be right though," argued Ben. "Adam and Eve saw God, right? And in Genesis it says that God appeared to Abraham while he was sitting near his tent at Mamre, right? And in Exodus it says that God spoke to Moses, right?"

"That's right, how did you know?"

"I was dragged to a lot of Sunday-School Classes and they gave us tests. Since I was stuck in them anyway, I did the work and won some prizes for scripture knowledge. But you didn't answer my question."

"I think we're both right. God spoke to a very few people for specific reasons, but I think the general teaching is that no one should expect to be able to see God just because they want to."

"OK, but…"

As the debate continued, Jack raised his eyebrows and we shared a glance. Taking out my pen, I wrote a few words on a paper napkin and passed it across the table. *I think the boys are starting to compete for Hannah's affections*, it said.

Jack's eyes widened in understanding, then he nodded and

passed the napkin back. Nathan and Ben's argument wasn't the least bit interrupted by the arrival of their food and they continued their verbal game throughout lunch. I had a clear view of Hannah's face during this time, and noted that she seemed bored, only half-listening as she ate and watched the rolling scenery out the window. I decided that I would look for an opportunity to engage her in casual conversation as soon as I could.

As it turned out, the opportunity dropped into my lap a few hours later. I'd been sitting with Silver in the Skyline Car, which was one of two dome cars on the train. We'd been up there for a while already: even Silver had been interestedly looking out the dome windows as the changing scenery rolled past. The observation levels in both dome cars tended to be full during daylight hours, and when Hanna came up the stairs looking for a seat, almost everything was already occupied.

Catching her eye, I waved her over and asked Silver to move from the double seat he'd been sprawled across to sit beside me. The freed-up seats faced mine and Silver's, separated by a small table. With a huge sigh, she flopped down on the seat facing me and dropped her huge purse on the seat beside her.

"Thank you," she said, "my name's Hannah."

"Pleased to meet you Hannah, my name is Alex and this is Silver."

"I saw you and your dog in the dining car on the train from Halifax, are you going to Vancouver as well? You're a Mountie, right? And a dog handler? Are you on duty?"

That was the most words I'd ever heard her say, but I didn't want to dampen her willingness to talk, so I tried to answer all of her questions.

"It's because you're on duty that they let a dog into the dining room, right?"

"That's right, and it's a real treat for Silver because the chef is spoiling him rotten."

She chuckled. "Can I pet him?"

"Let's find out. Try extending your hand so he can give it a good sniff, and look into his eyes."

That wasn't the answer she was expecting, so when she got up to reach over, it was a very tentative hand that she extended. Silver stretched his nose out a bit and gave it a good sniff.

"Now what?" she asked.

"Look at his body language. Does he look like he'd be OK with a friendly pet?"

"I think so," she said hesitantly, "I'm not sure."

"Trust me, if he didn't want you to get closer, you'd know. Go ahead, just do everything slowly so you don't surprise him."

Reaching her hand out further, she gave him a cautious rub behind one ear and her eyes opened wide. "He's leaning in to my hand."

"That's because you picked a good spot. He'd have been fine if you just patted him on the head, but he loves having his ears rubbed."

Sitting contentedly back in her seat, she smiled. It was the first time I'd seen her smile and the change from her usual melancholy was startling. Silver must have thought so too, because he immediately got up, switched seats, and laid down beside her, with his head on her leg.

"Looks like you've made a friend," I said, as she went back to rubbing behind one of his ears.

"I guess so," she said, sounding surprised. "I thought police dogs were trained to be vicious?"

"Not vicious, just trained to respond appropriately to different circumstances."

Sensing an opportunity, I decided to try a little gentle probing. "Is that your father you're travelling with?"

"The Colonel? Yes. We're doing a father-daughter trip across the country." She must have seen the look of surprise on my face, and added: "Yes, everyone calls him Colonel – it's who he is and what he is."

"Well, it sounds like a nice idea to me. Aren't you interested?"

"Oh, yes. I wasn't at first because it came up so suddenly and he wasn't very nice about it. Last week, from out of nowhere he said we'd should do a cross-Canada train trip together and we'd be driving to Halifax and leaving on Wednesday... Just like that. As if he was giving order to one of his soldiers. Anyway, now that we're here, I'm actually enjoying it, so it turned out to be a good idea after all."

"How about the two admirers you seem to have attracted?"

That brought a blush to her cheeks. "Boys!" she said, dismissively. "Nathan and his dad are doing the same thing: a father-son cross-Canada trip to celebrate his graduation from divinity college."

Interesting coincidences, I thought. I knew the most likely reason that Oliver Risk was taking the trip. Now I had some insight into the reason for the timing, although I didn't expect it to help me much. I was tempted to risk prying a bit more, but was forestalled by a sharp voice coming from the stairwell.

"Hannah!"

"Oops, that's the Colonel bellowing. Have to run. Thanks for letting me pet Silver," she said, rising and picking up her purse.

"You're welcome. It was nice to meet you."

She leaned over while making her way around Silver and out into the aisle. "I don't think I'm supposed to be talking to you actually. Dad doesn't approve of women in the military and I'm pretty sure he feels the same way about women in the police."

"I'll try not to corrupt you too much," I whispered.

That prompted a giggle as she waved and went to join her father.

I decided to leave the dome level as well, and when the train pulled into the station for a half hour stop at Capreol, Ontario – which is near Sudbury - we took the opportunity to take a stroll around the train and the station. In both cases, I let Silver roam and sniff around as he pleased, while I scribbled inconsequential notes in my notebook.

At the baggage car, we went in and I had Silver search for explosives. I didn't expect there to be any, but I wondered how long it would take him to search the car when it contained so many pieces of luggage, each with their own set of scents. It took longer than I expected.

While we were in the station, I also took a few minutes to use a pay-phone to call my boyfriend Don who, fortunately, was at home in Halifax. Don was a Captain in Military Intelligence. We had met on a particularly hazardous assignment[7] and had since shared several others together[8,11]. Each shared assignment seemed to draw us closer together, although it had remained a long-distance relationship since I was based out of Ottawa.

It was nearly 6 pm when the train left Capreol: dinnertime.

When I went to see if Jack was ready for dinner, he wasn't feeling very hungry. "I spent some time looking over the food and bar preparation areas and talking to the staff there. I'm no health inspector, but everything looked proper to me and I made notes on their routines. While I was there, the chef and bartender insisted on feeding me samples, though, so I'm doing fine."

So, it was just Silver and I taking our accustomed places in the dining car. After a few minutes, Oliver entered and took his customary table, followed a few minutes later by the Colonel, who did the same. It was some time later, and most of us early diners were well into our entrées, when the three young people arrived – together.

Their voices preceded them, and even before seeing any of them I could hear Nathan's voice. "But Matthew said: '*whosoever shall smite thee on the right cheek, turn to him the other also,*' chapter 5, verse 39."

"Very noble," sneered Ben, "but in Exodus it says: '*and if any mischief follow, then thou shalt give life for life, eye for eye, tooth for tooth, hand for hand, foot for foot, burning for burning, wound for wound, stripe for stripe.*'"

That brought them to a halt, right beside my table, as Hannah exclaimed: "*Eewww,* how horrible. You shouldn't need a bible to tell you that's wrong."

Ben just angrily stared at both of them, and I could feel the tension rising between the three of them. The tension was broken, however by the one person I thought might be the most dogmatic: Nathan. "I can't tell you what the right answers are Ben. All I can do is give you some alternate perspectives. In the end, you have to make up your own mind what to believe."

That took the wind out of Ben's sails, as he was clearly expecting a rebuke, or at least an argument. Whatever his reply was, it was lost as the three of them moved along. Nathan went further ahead to join his father. Hannah, for her part, seemed to hesitate, then made a show of inviting Ben to sit with her and her father, the Colonel.

I tried to hide a smile. Ben was either trying to shake Nathan's faith or win the war of words. I suspected both, having now seen his temper flash. I couldn't tell whether Nathan was Pollyanna-like naïve or very smart, but either way he was proving to be up to the challenge of sparring with Ben.

There were no further episodes or outbursts during dinner.

Hannah and Ben seemed to engaged in casual conversation with her father while, further up the car, Nathan seemed to eat in silence while his father, Oliver Risk, simply ate and moodily stared out the window again.

Silver and I, for our part, had a great dinner. Each day's menu had several options to choose from and I was pleasantly surprised to find that the dining car meals were consistently very good. The dining car chef had once again created a 'daily special' for Silver, which he promptly devoured. Besides keeping a weather-eye on the travelers ahead of me and having lots of scenery to enjoy, François even dropped by for a friendly chat and a cup of coffee when we were finishing up. While I had his attention, I asked about how easy it would be for someone to stop the train.

"Simple," he replied. "Anyone can stand by the tracks and raise their arms above their head to indicate danger ahead, or they can wave a red flag, or at night wave a red light toward the train. But the train doesn't stop right away, eh? It can take a mile before it stops."

"How about from inside the train?"

"Well, someone can pull one of the emergency-brake handles in the cars. When that happens, it releases pressure in the brake lines, which puts the brakes on. Even then, the engineer can use an override control to keep the brakes off until they find a safe place to bring the train to a stop."

"Have you had people try to stop the train before?"

"Oh sure. Sometimes it's a drunk in the bar, or a crazy person on the tracks, but not often. The company gets upset, and the penalties are stiff, eh?"

"Hmmm," I said, scribbling in my notebook.

"Don't worry," he said, "it's very unlikely to happen."

Later in the evening, Silver and I were sitting in the upper level of the rear dome car when I saw François come up the stairs with a worried expression on his face.

Uh oh, I thought. Sure enough, he saw us and came straight over.

"Could I talk to you for a moment please?" he said, with a tip of his head indicating that we go somewhere else.

"Of course," I replied, and we followed him down the stairs and forward several cars until we reached his office. This time, he closed the office door when we were inside.

"One of the passengers is complaining that their roomette has been broken into."

"Really? How and when?"

"They say it must have been while they were in the Skyline Dome Car, where they went to wait while the attendant set up their sleeping berths for the night."

"They?"

"Mr. Risk and his son."

"Ah... and what was taken?"

"That's the crazy thing. Nothing was taken, eh?"

"How do they know their room was broken into then? Were things broken, stuff scattered around?"

"Nothing like that. Apparently when they returned to their roomette, they noticed that a few things had been moved from where they left them."

"Could it have been the attendant cleaning up?"

"No. Some of the things that were moved were files and documents in Mr. Risk's briefcase, and they swear that things were rearranged in their carry-on luggage."

"And the attendant?"

"Has been with the company for years. I knew him way back when we worked for CN, long before VIA Rail was created."

"Hmmm... and which of the Risks came to tell you about it?"

"The younger one, Nathan Risk. He was very upset. Why?"

"Just curious. What did Oliver Risk have to say?"

"He was mostly angry that the roomettes can't be locked from the outside. I told him that I can put any valuables he might have in a safe until we reach Vancouver, but he says they don't have anything valuable with them."

I considered this for moment, then, "OK. It doesn't sound like much of a crime has been committed, then. What would you like me to do?"

"I'd like to reassure them that we are taking this seriously. Would you come and talk to them; take a look at the roomette?"

"Sure. Lead the way."

François led us to our sleeping car and knocked on the door, which was opened by Oliver Risk.

"Now what?" he said.

"Would you please show Constable Houston the things that

were rearranged?"

Oliver Risk wasn't in an accommodating mood. "Why?" he growled, "I told you nothing was taken. We just want our privacy, that's all. If you want to do something constructive, put a lock on this door."

"Hi Mr. Risk," I tried. "We're very sorry to bother you, but the Conductor is very distressed about this, and he's asked me to take a look. I don't know whether there's anything we can do to help or not, but would you please just show us what was moved? It will only take a moment and then we'll leave."

Oliver hesitated a moment, and then seemed to judge that it would be the fastest way to get rid of us. "Come in then, if you must," he said ungraciously, and then showed me things in their carry-on bags that weren't in their usual positions and papers in his briefcase that weren't out of place, exactly, but not as neatly arranged as usual – as if someone had taken papers out, looked them over, and then hurriedly stuffed them back into their folders."

"And nothing was actually taken?" I asked.

"No. That's what I keep saying. Just some snoopy-drawers looking for valuables, but they didn't get anything."

"All right. Thank you," I said. "In that case, I don't think you'll be disturbed again. If we have a thief onboard, they'll go try someone else next time – if there is a next time. In the meantime, please let the conductor or I know if you remember anything missing. Good night."

"Good night!" he said, grudgingly.

As I made to leave the roomette, I happened to turn my head and look back as Oliver was bent over, closing up his briefcase. Reflected in the window I could see that there was a smirk on Oliver's face that he thought no one would be able to see.

There IS something to find, but it hasn't been found yet, I thought.

Motioning to François, I went and opened the door to my roomette. He was scandalized at the thought of being seen in a single woman's roomette but agreed to stand in the open doorway.

"Could I have a word with the attendant from this car?"

"Of course, come to my office in five minutes, eh?"

When Silver and I appeared at François' office at the appointed time, Émile Cournoyer, the attendant for our car was sitting in one of the chairs. We had previously met when he changed over my roomette, so I launched straight in. "Did you see the things that the Risks' say were rearranged?"

"Of course, but I didn't do anything or take anything."

"The things they say were moved, were they like that when you set up the berths for the night."

I didn't mean for it to be a trick question, and I don't think Émile even realized the trap as he simply answered that he didn't open any baggage or the briefcase, so there was no way for him to know.

"So, we don't know whether the intruder came before or after you then," I said.

"After," he said, positively. "The briefcase was in the right place, but the order of the two bags had been reversed. When I did the room, the black bag was to the left of the brown bag, but when François called me back to the room later, the black bag was on the right."

"You're sure?"

"Very sure."

"That's helpful, thank you. And did you see anyone or anything unusual in the car after you did the Risk's roomette?"

"No nothing at all… just the nun."

"The nun?"

"Yes. I'd just come out of doing one of the other rooms, when I saw a nun walking towards the end of the car."

"What did she look like?"

"Her back was facing me, so I couldn't see her face, but she was wearing a full black habit with one of those little caps on her head."

"Is that all you noticed about her?"

"Yes… no, wait. She was tall for a nun. Six feet at least."

François then asked Émile a few questions but it all came back to the same thing, he had seen the back of an unusually tall nun walking out of the sleeping car at about the right time, and no one else until later, when several of the passengers began returning to their roomettes.

François thanked him and Émile left to return to his duties. When he was gone, I noticed that François had a quiet smile on his face.

"What?" I asked.

"You are going to ask me about the nuns on the train, eh?"

"Yes, of course. Can you give me a list of names and whether they are travelling coach, or in berths or roomettes?"

"Certainly." His smile broadened. "There are no nuns on the train!"

"What? Are you sure?"

"Well, certainly there are none wearing formal habit. I have been up and down the full length of this train many times since we left Toronto. A nun in full habit I would have noticed. A six-foot-tall nun would stand out, eh?"

"So. Someone in disguise then… I think Silver and I will take a stroll along the train…" I saw the look in François' eyes. "No, I believe you. I'm not looking for nuns, I'm going to look for a discarded nun's habit. Would you ask the attendants to do the same, especially in the public washroom and shower areas?"

"Of course."

"Shoes too," I reflected. "Especially elevator shoes."

That prompted another chuckle. "I'll tell everyone right now."

Thanking him, Silver and I went to the rear of the Park Dome Car, at the back of the train, and slowly walked forward. As we went, I tried to glance at trash cans and the like without being too obvious about it. Along the way, we encountered Jack and I'd taken him aside and filled him in on what had happened.

Moving along, I got a shock in one of the upper-and lower-berth combinations that the railway called 'sections.' By day, these comprised open-plan, facing bench seats. In the evening, an attendant would arrange the two seats together and cover them with a mattress to make a lower berth. Above that, an upper berth would be hinged down from above. The evening arrangements would then be completed by attaching a short ladder to the upper berth, and attaching heavy curtains to each bunk for privacy.

In the car I was walking through, some of the sections had been set up for the night, while others were still in their seating configuration. As I passed one of the made-up sections, I noticed that the upper berth had a big lump under the blankets. It was the size lump that a balled-up nun's habit could make, and the section was unoccupied at the time, so I pulled up the top of the blankets to see what was underneath.

"*EEEAAAARRRRIR!*"

I was so startled that my subconscious immediately took over. As I let go of the blanket and pulled my arm back, a blur of orange, black, and white flew off the berth and vanished down towards the far end of the sleeper car.

"Silver!" I called, sharply, as I sensed him tensing to spring forward. "Stay! Let the cat go."

"*Eerrrr*," he said, fighting down his instinct to chase the cat.

We had just met the conductor's cat, Cleo.

When my heart rate came down from hyper to just elevated, Silver and I continued our prowl through the rest of the train. It took a while, and when we finally reached the baggage car, the door was securely locked and didn't seem to have been tampered with. It had been a long shot, but I still felt discouraged. I had no further clues, no discarded disguise, and I hadn't seen any nuns either.

When Jack and I met up later on, I told him about our episode with Cleo the cat. Jack, of course, thought it was hilarious and didn't try to hide his grin as he related the news of his own scan of the train. Basically, he hadn't noticed anything out of the ordinary either.

We decided there wasn't anything more to be done for the time being, and said good night.

An hour later, I was in my bunk and still trying to get to sleep when there was a knock on the door. It was François. When I unlocked and opened the door, he refused to come in but he had a mischievous twinkle in his eyes. "We found something!" he said, raising a double armload of tangled black cloth."

"The nun's habit!" I exclaimed, as quietly as I could. "Where did you find it?"

"When the train stopped at Gogama, one of the attendants noticed something fluttering in the wind near the back of the Park Car. He called me and we went to have a closer look. Someone must have thrown it out a window further up the train, and instead of blowing away it got caught on one of the handholds bolted to the side of the car. It's where you climb up when you need to replace a burned-out bulb from the lights that face backwards along the track. So another train doesn't run into us in the night eh? It got caught there and wrapped around so tight, the wind couldn't dislodge it. Took us a while to get it off, but here it is."

"Can I hang onto it for a while?" I asked.

"You can have it. It's just garbage to us eh?" François handed over the habit, along with a plastic bag he'd thought to bring along, and I gave it a quick look-over to see if there were any identifying labels or markings. There weren't, and I stuffed the habit into the bag and thanked François for finding a good clue.

There's a pattern here, I thought.

Laurie Schramm

5 CROSSING NORTHERN ONTARIO

Day 4
May 29, 1978

Once again, I awoke to the rising sun at 5 am. During the night, the train had continued to make its way through Northern Ontario. The sky was clear, and I knew that we would be in store for a cheerful morning of alternating forest and waterway views.

After getting dressed, I took advantage of the next brief stop to give Silver a chance to heed the call of nature. This turned out to be a five-minute stop at Longlac a small, appropriately named town on the shore of Long Lake. Then, it was on to breakfast. This being our second day on *The Canadian*, and the fourth day for those of us that had embarked in Halifax, most people had settled into vacation mode. As a result, there were very few people in the dining car for breakfast.

While I was eating breakfast, François joined me for a few minutes and had a cup of coffee for himself. I told him about our meeting with his cat, Cleo, the previous day, which amused him greatly.

"She pops up now and again, eh? You'll probably see her again before the trip is over." Then he turned serious and asked: "What do you think about the break-in? There's some kind of intrigue going on, I think. Maybe something that involves the police?"

I could tell that it worried him, and I wasn't surprised that he might be starting to suspect Jack and I of having an ulterior motive for being on the train."

"Maybe," I said, noncommittally. "Jack and I will try to keep an eye out for trouble and will let you know if we see anything that could affect the safety or security of your passengers."

That seemed to satisfy him for the moment, and our discussion shifted to less weighty matters. Somehow, we discovered that we shared an interest in SCUBA diving, he having grown up diving in quarries in Québec and having originally planned to go to university and become a fisheries biologist. He never got away from the railroad once he'd started working summer jobs there, which then led to full-time railroading, and then promotions led to becoming a locomotive engineer and, finally, a conductor. "It's in the blood now. That and being part of a huge family of colleagues, and the travel...," he sighed. "I won't leave it now until retirement time comes and they push me out, eh?"

After breakfast, I decided to take a chance and see if there was any available space on the upper viewing deck of the Park Dome Car at the rear of the train. Surprisingly, it wasn't very crowded. *People must be sleeping-in this morning,* I thought. It was easy to lose track of days on the train. For those of us that had taken *The Ocean* train leaving Halifax at 1 pm on Friday and taken the most efficient connections from Montréal to Toronto and boarded *The Canadian,* it was now our fourth day of travel.

Although there were quite a few seats available, I noticed Nathan sitting alone and, sensing an opportunity, I made a beeline for him.

As we approached, it became obvious that he wasn't exactly sitting alone. Curled up in his lap was the conductor's cat, Cleo.

"May we join you?" I asked, when we were close enough.

"Of course," he said, looking up and waving in the direction of the seats facing his.

Motioning for Silver to jump up on the seat beside me I said, warningly, "Leave the cat alone, Silver."

"*Eerrrr?*" he said, doing his best to look innocent.

"I've never seen such a well-behaved dog before," said Nathan, continuing to pet Cleo, who hadn't moved but was clearly watching Silver with untrusting eyes. "He really listens to you, doesn't he?"

"Most of the time, yes. We've become very close over the past few years.

"My name's Alex, and this is Silver."

"How do you do? My name's Nathan." Then he pointedly looked at my uniform, then directly into my eyes… "I guess neither of us has to identify our profession."

Despite his direct gaze, I found his manner to be unusually open and unoffending. *Innocent, almost,* I thought. "I guess not," I smiled.

"And both of us chose professions so we could help people, right?"

"Well, yes, but in my case, I also wanted something that would involve adventure."

"Do you get much adventure? I would have thought that policing is mostly just routine these days. Catching people speeding, handing out parking tickets, that kind of thing?"

"It was like that at first, but these last few years I've had enough scary adventures to make me realize that I should be careful what I wish for," I said, somewhat ruefully. But I wanted to try to steer the conversation back to him. "What about you? Are you actually on duty too?"

"Kind of," he replied. "I just graduated from the Atlantic School of Theology."

My face must have looked blank with lack of recognition, so he came to my rescue.

"It's a divinity college. They're affiliated with Saint Mary's University in Halifax."

"Ah," my eyes lit up. "I've been to Halifax several times. Silver and I used to walk by Saint Mary's on the way to Point Pleasant Park and the harbor!"

"Right. Having graduated, I was just ordained in the church, but haven't been assigned to a congregation yet. My dad surprised me by coming up to Halifax to help celebrate. He drove up from New York, took the ferry from Bangor, Maine, and showed up out of the blue. He insisted on taking me on a cross-country, father-and-son vacation as a kind of graduation present… To get back to your question, the clerical collar isn't required but I've been experimenting with wearing it when I'm trying to be 'on duty' and leaving it aside when I need a break and some personal time."

"How is it working out?"

"Actually, it's working out pretty well," his eyes lit up, and he flashed a brilliant smile. "With the collar on, people naturally assume I'm on duty, and they just assume that it's OK to come up and start a conversation with me. I thought that they'd first want to know what religion I follow, but for most people it doesn't seem to matter that much."

"Because they mostly just want someone to talk to?" I ventured.

"Exactly!" He gave me another big smile. "It's amazing how complete strangers will come and start a conversation when I'm wearing the collar. It seems to make it socially acceptable, even though I might be a complete stranger. It's like it gives them advance permission, and even a promise that I'll listen to them – which I will, of course."

"I imagine that it also gives you a chance to practice your religious knowledge," I added, looking meaningfully at the bible he had laid on the table between us.

"Not very often, actually. Most of the conversations aren't about religion at all, and I've even had some people tell me flat out that they're agnostics, or even atheists, but somehow they still hope to get a sympathetic ear."

"And you provide it?"

"Of course! It can be hard through. Some of the situations people find themselves in, or get themselves into, are heart-rending. After they leave, I sometimes feel like crawling off somewhere to take the collar off and have a good cry."

"I can image," I said. "I get that sometimes too."

"Of course you must, in your job too… I'm sorry, I should have realized that right off."

"It's OK," I replied. "I only meant that I understand what it's like." Then, sensing an opening, "But you must get the religious questions too. I couldn't help overhearing parts of a discussion about the meaning of biblical quotations with another young man in the dining car."

"Ah, with Ben. Yes. I'm sorry if it disturbed your meal. Ben is a very intense fellow, and he gets easily worked up. He's been challenging me with contradictions in the bible."

"Don't you mind? It must be a bit disconcerting to be challenged that way?"

"Not at all. I don't take it personally…" He paused as if thinking about what he'd just said. "OK, I mostly don't take it personally..." Another huge smile. "I enjoy the discussions, they're very good practise for me: they make me think and re-evaluate my own thoughts. Besides... it's become something of a competition."

"Really?"

"Yes. In fact, he ran out of challenges after our first few arguments, so now he's secretly reading the bible looking for new things to challenge me on!"

I had to smile at that. "So, you're actually making him read the bible?"

He just smiled back at me and knowingly placed an extended finger alongside his nose.

"Do you think he's likely to 'get religion' as they say?"

"Maybe not," he replied, with a shrug, "who knows? Sometimes the fiercest critics can become the most fervent converts. Anything is possible."

He paused in thought for a moment, then continued. "But, in Ben's case, I can't escape the feeling that there's something underneath it all that's grating on him. There's an anger there that he hasn't resolved, and I suspect it has nothing much to do with religion... or lack of religion even... In any case, I'm doing the little bit that I can." The latter thought was accompanied by another of his broad smiles.

I looked at him, with new eyes. "If you don't mind me saying so, I think you're going to be very good at your profession."

"I hope so," he said, but he sounded pleased. "You seem to be pretty good at yours too, if you don't mind me saying so. You've gotten me to go through this whole thing about getting people to open up and listening to them, while you've been doing it to me the whole time. And you've made me feel better too. I was sitting here feeling a bit melancholy until now."

"Thank you, and you're welcome," I replied doing my best to give him a bright smile in return.

That created a slightly awkward silence that was quickly broken by Cleo the cat, who suddenly decided that it was time to move along. Standing up and stretching, she very slowly walked across Nathan's lap, looking warily at Silver the whole time.

Just as she was preparing to jump into the aisle, I said "Silver," in warning. As the cat made her jump and trotted off, Silver, who had been watching Cleo closely, said "*Eerrrr,*" and looked up at me with his own version of a wide-eyed, innocent expression. It reminded me so much of Nathan's innocent expressions that I actually giggled.

I was saved from further embarrassment by Nathan's rising to his feet, and saying that he needed to go check on his father.

"It was nice meeting you," I said.

"You too!" He gave me another dazzling smile, and a friendly nod. "See you around."

I continued, for a while, to sit in the dome section, with Silver's head in my lap and watching the unending sequences of lakes and forests go by. As other passengers came and went, a few others struck up conversations when they sat across from us. In succession, I met a couple of university student friends travelling to take up summer jobs in tourist hotspots like Jasper and Banff, then a youngish tourist couple from Germany on their first visit to Canada, then a late-middle-aged Newfoundland couple travelling with us as far as Edmonton. From there, they explained, they would be renting a car to drive north to Fort McMurray to visit their two sons, both of whom had moved there to get jobs in the booming oil sands industry.

I explained that, two years earlier, I had spent some time on assignment in Fort McMurray[6]. This information triggered a torrent of questions about the oil sands industry, Fort McMurray, and Alberta in general, and I was kept busy answering questions for at least an hour. They seemed like such a nice couple, that I found that I didn't mind in the least.

By this time, the dome section had completely filled up with passengers and, when there was a lull in the conversation, I decided it was a good time to release our seats so others could enjoy the unfolding panoramas so I said goodbye and wished them well with the rest of their trip.

Strolling forward along the train, we encountered Jack sitting alone in the coffee shop and joined him for a while, during which I related my earlier conversation with Nathan.

"It all sounds consistent with what we've already observed," judged Jack, when I was done. "It seems like all we have to do is stake you out somewhere beside an empty seat and people practically line up to talk to you." He seemed amused by the notion.

I decided to take him seriously this time. "In that case, maybe I'll try the other dome after lunch. I'd like to have a try at Ben."

The train hadn't stopped for quite a while that morning and, looking at our watches, we saw that the next stop would be in Sioux Lookout. If we arrived on schedule, we'd be there for half an hour, and we decided that would be a good opportunity for a walk around the train - partly to be consistent with our role as observers of security details, but mostly to get some exercise and fresh air.

After Sioux Lookout, we had lunch, after which Silver and I took a stroll down the full length of the train, hoping for an opportunity to meet Ben in person. He was nowhere to be seen, however, so I gave up and found a double seat on upper deck of the Skyline Dome car. Watching the scenery, I was noticing that the many lakes and forests were becoming interspaced with broad expanses of bare rock – evidence of the Canadian Shield – when I heard a perky voice say "Hi." It was Hannah.

Smiling, I waved toward the facing seats, which had just been vacated, and said "Hi yourself." As she took a seat, Silver immediately abandoned me to go across and sit beside Hannah, where he contentedly allowed himself to be petted. Over the past few years, I'd found Silver's instincts to be uncannily perceptive. *If he thinks she's OK, then she probably is,* I thought.

Hannah didn't seem to be after anything more than someone to talk to, and it occurred to me that it might be that she wanted someone female to talk to. I tried testing this theory a bit. "How are you doing with the two boys?"

"You were right, I think they are trying to compete for me," she said, leaning forward conspiratorially. "It was fun at first, but it's become boring now." She sighed. "Nathan's really nice – almost too good to be true – you know?"

I nodded. I felt a bit that way myself. "And the other one?"

"Ben? He's interesting, and that sense of darkness he has about him was intriguing at first, but he has these flashes of anger that worry me sometimes." She bit her lip, thoughtfully.

"What's he doing on the train, do you know?"

"Oh. Yes. He's a university student, somewhere, and he's kind of like the rest of us - travelling across Canada to see the country. He says he plans to look for a job when we get to Vancouver."

We chatted further, while half watching the scenery go by, but I didn't really learn anything more. When our conversation tapered off, we both got up so others could take our places and watch the views, and we went our separate ways. As we did, I reflected that

I'd learned a bit about Ben, but it didn't seem like I'd learned anything useful. *Oh well.*

As we continued west, toward Winnipeg, there were so many lakes and waterways that we crossed a seemingly endless number of bridges, which was always interesting. Some of railway stations in the towns along the way were right beside lakes, like the one at Minaki, Ontario, where we stopped for a couple of minutes to pick up some passengers.

We didn't go to the dining car that evening. Like many passengers, we had decided to wait for Winnipeg, which was one of the longer station-stops.

Although we arrived in Winnipeg a bit late, at 8 pm, we still had an hour and half before departing so most passengers took the opportunity to disembark and wander around the downtown area. Jack and Silver and I went off in search of a restaurant with an outdoor terrace, so Silver could sit with us. We were very close to the national historic site called The Forks, so we walked there and found several nice places to eat nearby. After a nice dinner, it was a short stroll to the shore of the Red River, and we had a nice walk along what, in later years, would be developed as The Forks Riverwalk.

Before heading back to the train, I found a pay-phone and tried calling my boss in Ottawa. He wasn't in and there were still no messages for me. *Oh well, the wheels turn slowly*, I thought. While I was at the phone, I also put in a call to my boyfriend Don to let him know where I was. We didn't exchange much real news, but it was good just to hear his voice.

The train departed on schedule at 9:30 pm, and I had just sat down in my roomette and was wondering what to do next when there was a knock on my door. It was François.

"There's been another break-in! Can you come?" He sounded affronted that such things should be happening on his train.

"What, again? The same room?"

"No! No, it was the Colonel's room this time, and it's a mess."

So, I got up and followed him down the corridor, with Silver trailing behind. The Colonel and Hannah were standing just outside the open door to their roomette. The Colonel looked angry, and Hannah looked pale and shocked. When everyone stood aside so I could peer in, I saw that François had spoken the literal truth: it was indeed a mess.

It was also a study on contrasts. The roomette had been made up while we were all off the train in Winnipeg, and the two berths had their sheets, blankets, and pillows neatly, even perfectly in place, even down to the little packages of chocolate bar on each pillow.

Their carry-on bags, and what I assumed was the Colonel's briefcase, however, were lying open as if they had been simply cast aside, and clothes, books, and papers were scattered across the lower berth. Some had fallen, or been cast, onto the floor.

As I looked around, I could hear fragments of the Colonel giving François a piece of his mind, "…in all my years… how the railway can let this kind of thing happen… in this day and age… having paid your goddam exorbitant fares… the least you could have done…" and so on.

I tried to tune out the Colonel, look at everything, and think. No one could doubt that there'd been a break-in this time, and if Oliver Risk was who I thought he was, and given that I knew exactly who the Colonel was, there was no way that this was some random intrusion. *But why be so obvious this time?* I wondered. *To send a message? Or because the intruder was in a great hurry?* I suspected the latter.

As I considered, the sounds of the Colonel berating François broke into my thoughts, to be quickly interrupted by the sound of Jack's voice asking what was the matter.

"Ah, Constable, I'm so glad you're here!" François had leapt at Jack's arrival like it was a life-buoy, and gave him a quick summary of what had happened.

I moved out of the way so Jack could squeeze in and take a look. While he did that, I stepped over to Hannah and asked if she was feeling OK.

"Oh, yes, I'm fine. It's just the shock, you know? You read about things like this in detective stories but you never expect them to happen to you. Do you?"

"Well, you hope not, that's for sure… Can I ask you and your dad a few questions?"

"I'll answer any questions you have," said the Colonel, who had overheard and was either feeling protective of Hannah, or else in need of asserting some control over the situation.

I decided to play along. "Thank you, Sir," and fed him a short-list of initial questions:

"Who discovered the break-in?"	The Colonel and Hannah.
"When?"	When they boarded the train.
"Was anything damaged?"	No.
"Is anything missing?"	No.
"Did they see or hear anyone?"	No.

Meanwhile, Jack had come out of the roomette and gave me a questioning look. I shook my head to indicate that I hadn't learned anything useful from the Peters.

We had just asked them to tell François, or one of us, if they discovered or remembered anything new, and were about to leave when I thought of one more question. "Is there anything in your room that shouldn't be there?"

"No," said the Colonel, more as an instinctive reaction than anything I thought, but Hannah had a puzzled look on her face and went back into the roomette and looked around again.

She was back almost immediately carrying a tie. "I didn't really think of it until you asked, but this doesn't belong here."

It was a clip-on tie. The kind with a permanently tied knot that can be quickly clipped or unclipped from a dress shirt with all the buttons done up.

The tie was in VIA Rail colours.

François was outraged and, before the Colonel could start in on him again, he was full of indignation, with promises of swift investigation, and dark insinuations about punishment for the guilty party, whomever that might be. He promised to immediately interview all of the train's staff in an effort to uncover the culprit.

It was his train and we still didn't have much of a crime on our hands so we left him to it. Before taking our leave, however, I asked if I could hold onto the tie for a while and went back to my roomette to get a plastic bag in which to preserve it.

It was after 11pm, and the train had just made a brief stop at Portage la Prairie, when François found Jack and I sitting at a table having a cup of late-night coffee. He was still visibly upset.

"Nothing! Not a damn thing eh?" he pronounced, as he sat

down with us.

"I take it that no one broke down and confessed?" asked Jack.

"Everyone denies everything. No one saw or heard anything," he sighed. "Now that I've had time to think about it, I can't believe it was one of the crew." Seeing our expressions, he hurried on: "It's not stubborn loyalty. The railroad's like a family, eh? We've worked together a long time... we look after each other... there's no reason to do something like this."

"Well, for what it's worth, I don't think it's member of the crew either," I offered.

"You don't?"

"No. I think it's the same person that searched the Risks' roomette last night. Whomever it is, I think they're looking for something specific."

"Specific? Like what?"

"I don't know for sure. Something small. Maybe some kind of documents, since even the file folders in briefcases have been rifled."

"What about the tie then?"

"Remember how last night's villain was disguised as a nun? Well I suspect that tonight's villain was disguised as a VIA Rail attendant. There was a crew change in Winnipeg, right? So, if a VIA Rail employee on the train saw another employee that they didn't recognize, wouldn't they just assume that it was someone from the other crew?"

"Probably, yes... no, I'm sure they would, because the crew that left are based in Toronto and they'll be working back on an eastbound train. They would all know each other, but not necessarily the crew that is based in Winnipeg. Whew, I feel much better now, eh?"

I found it interesting that François was more worried about the possibility of a crew member going bad than he was about the break-ins themselves, but I supposed that it was only natural. When François left, we were alone in the dining area. In a low voice, I asked Jack what he thought about it all.

"Well, if the break-ins aren't a coincidence, then I think you're right about them being the work of one person, using different disguises. I also think that if our mystery person hasn't found what they're looking for then they'll try again. Not getting caught either time will have boosted their confidence too. Where do you think they'll strike next?"

"I think the baggage car might be a target. Other than that, the only connection I've noted so far is through the three young people. Maybe Ben's roomette will be the next target, or maybe Ben is our mystery person."

"You don't like him, do you?"

That startled me. "No, I don't, but I'm trying to keep an open mind... Is it that obvious?"

"No, I don't think so. It's just that I know you pretty well now and I can sense that his attitude grates on you."

"Well, it does, but thanks for pointing it out. I'll try to keep my thoughts from showing... If you were going to try the baggage car, when would you make your attempt?"

Jack paused in thought for a moment, then brought out his copy of the railway timetable. "Once we cross into Saskatchewan, the main stops are in Melville, Saskatoon, and Biggar. We're scheduled to leave Biggar at 1:40 pm. After that, we'll only stop for advance requests until tomorrow night when we reach Edmonton at 8:50. The best odds of breaking into the baggage car without being caught should be between Biggar and Edmonton. That's how I'd do it."

"I agree," I said. "Want to take turns watching the baggage car?"

"You're a bit too noticeable. How about if I do it. I'll dress in plain clothes and ask François if I can borrow some kind of worker's jacket and maybe a hat or toque, and then I'll plant myself in the café part of the Skyline Dome car where I'll have a clear view of the door to the baggage car."

I agreed to this, and we walked back to our roomettes together.

That night, I was sitting up in bed, with Silver curled up beside me, watching the stars in the sky and the occasional light of civilization flash by, wondering what the next day would be like. Between the connections that were forming between some of the people I was watching and the sequence of break-ins, I was starting to feel the anticipation that comes when you shift from data gathering to hunting, and I remember thinking that the next day would probably be interesting.

I had no idea.

Laurie Schramm

6 THE PRAIRIES

Day 5
May 30, 1978
Crossing into Saskatchewan

I'd slept well, having come to appreciate the gentle rolling of the train and having gotten used to the dim thudding of the wheels on the tracks below. The day began quietly enough. Once again, there were only a few early-birds in the dining car for breakfast. I had a leisurely meal while enjoying the change in scenery. Heading west from Winnipeg, we progressively left behind most of the forests and lakes in favour of the prairies. While some people thought of the prairies as 'flat and boring,' I always found it interesting with the huge skies and the unending patchwork of fields, towns, and rivers. Later in the summer it would be even better: when the different crops began to bloom there would be brilliant, contrasting colours. Like fields of golden yellow canola next to fields of soft blue flax. The peaceful looking, wide-open spaces put me in a reflective mood that was only broken by brief visits from Jack and François.

There was a scheduled one-hour stop at Saskatoon just before lunchtime, and Silver and I got off to do one of our routine walks around the whole train, take a few notes, and make a call to my boss in Ottawa. I actually got him on the line this time. He didn't have any solid information on Benjamin (Ben) Shaw yet, but when I briefly described the patterns Jack and I had observed he offered a couple of thoughts on the kind of person that might be watching the Risks and Peters families. His thoughts were interesting, but didn't really change anything. I left him with one more request: would he please have someone check all of the car rental agencies in Edson, Hinton, and Jasper for any reservations booked for the next few days in the names of Risk, Peters, or Shaw. I said that I expected to be able to call from Edmonton when we arrived at about 11 pm that evening. I also made a few other requests while I was at it.

Once we had re-boarded it was lunchtime, so Silver and I went and took our accustomed table in the dining car. This time the young people were seated at the table right beside us. Hannah flashed us a smile and a wave when she came in, and I was about to initiate a conversation with her when the two young men arrived.

As they came in, they were arguing – again.

"We only have to look out for our own sins," Nathan was saying. "That's how we will be judged. The Bible says: *'Fathers shall not be put to death for their children, nor children put to death for their fathers; each is to die for his own sin,'* Deuteronomy 24:16. And both Jeremiah and Ezekiel talk about how people will only die for their own sins."

Ben pounced on this with unusual heat, however. "Ah ha! But the Bible clearly says that children have to be punished for their parents' sins. How about the book of Exodus where it talks about God punishing the children for the sins of the parents?"

Nathan took a breath in preparation to answer this, but he didn't get a chance as Ben rushed on. "And Jeremiah talks about God taking vengeance on people because their ancestors forsook him. Right?" Ben's tone and body language suggested that this particular argument was more than academic, and more than competition for a girl's attention.

This is what Ben has been leading up to all along with these arguments, I thought.

Ben seemed to win this round, too, as Nathan merely replied "I don't know what to tell you Ben. I think it's the difference between things God has done himself, and the things he wants us to do. Like when chain-smoking parents tell their kids not to smoke. Sort of 'Do what I say, not what I do.' You know?"

"Yes, I know all right!" said Ben, sounding angry as he got up again and marched out of the car.

Nathan gave a huge sigh. "I don't think I'm helping him."

At this, Hannah actually unbent a little and placed a consoling hand on his shoulder. "All you can do is try Nathan." She seemed to be looking at him with new eyes. "You really do care, don't you?"

"Of course I do, but I don't seem to be able to find the right words to help him."

"I think you may be helping him more than you know," she replied, thoughtfully. "I don't think this is about religion or faith at all. I think he's trying to work through some kind of personal issues, and I think you're helping him by just giving him a way to talk things out."

"That's a kind thought, Hannah. Thank you."

I thought Hanna was probably right. With Ben having stormed off Nathan and Hanna settled into a friendly discussion of some kind that I couldn't clearly overhear, and then they were joined by the Colonel who didn't seem to be as disapproving of Nathan as he clearly was of Ben. Their three-way conversation must have turned religious at some point, as Nathan opened up his bible to look up some kind of quote or passage.

After lunch, the views leading west of Saskatoon continued to be mostly farms on slowly undulating terrain, with the occasional river and town. There was a short stop at the town of Biggar, and then we continued making our way across the rest of the prairies to Alberta.

At this point I was curious to see what Jack's stakeout looked like, so Silver and I walked the length of the train as far as the baggage car. When we turned back, at the front end of the Skyline Dome car, we were in the coffee shop and there at the furthest table from the front of the car was what appeared to be an engineer or mechanic-type railway worker of some kind. As we walked by his table, I looked at him out of the corners of my eyes and saw what I was supposed to see: a tired-looking fellow wearing a grease-stained beige-leather jacket and one of those black-and-white-striped engineer's caps, and huddled over his coffee cup as if it was the most important thing in the world.

I didn't want to draw any attention to Jack, or even appear to recognize him, so I kept my body and head pointed straight ahead and walked the rest of the way through the car. It was hard to keep a straight face, but I managed.

After lunch, Silver and I took a casual stroll along the rest of the train. There was no sign of Oliver Risk or the Colonel, but I spotted Ben in the bar, alone and drinking. At the rear of the train, I noticed Nathan and Hannah sitting together in the upper section of the Park Dome Car. The rest of the upper section was full, as usual, so Silver and I just continued on and tried our luck with the upper section of the Skyline Dome Car. I was glad I did, because a pair of seats had opened up at the very front of the dome, facing forward.

We now had two of the very best viewing seats on the train and we spend the next two hours with a panoramic view of the approaching scenery. The best view came just west of Wainwright, Alberta, as we approached and then crossed the Fabyan Trestle Bridge. This is a turn-of-the-century style bridge that crossed a broad, shallow valley with Battle River at the bottom. Opened in 1909, it was only about 60 m high but it was nearly a kilometer long! From my vantage point high up on the train, it looked like a long curtain of rust-coloured iron, with what must have been at least fifty double sets of pylons individually anchored in concrete footings. When I mentioned it to François later, he told me that when it was built, it was the largest railway structure in Canada.

Although I always went for the first seating at dinner, this time everyone else seemed to have the same idea as the dining car almost immediately filled, nearly to capacity. Partly for that reason, it was noisy too, so I had no hope of overhearing any interesting conversations. I did notice Oliver and Nathan Risk enter and get seated by themselves, soon followed by Hannah, who joined them. I noticed with some amusement that Ben was seated well past Hannah and the Risks, and facing away from them. *He won't be watching them at dinner this time*, I thought. I didn't spot the Colonel, and assumed that he either ate later or in the coffee shop, if at all.

From 5:30 pm onwards there were no more stops until we reached Edmonton at around 10 pm. The train had no sooner come to a halt in the station than Jack stopped at my open door with a bundle under his arm. I could see that it was the engineer/mechanic-type jacket he'd been wearing all afternoon.

"Any luck?" I asked.

He grimaced. "Nothing but a painfully full bladder. I only had one cup of coffee the whole time but it was more than I had room for."

I smiled, trying hard not to laugh out loud. "We've got three hours in the station here, how about coming for a walk?"

"Sure, let me give the jacket and hat back to François and I'll meet you on the platform."

While we waited for Jack, Silver and I walked along the outside of the train, watched the baggage handlers load and unload bags from the baggage car, then back. When he joined us, we wandered around the station for a while, then went in search of a payphone.

When I called my boss' number I didn't expect him to be in the office but I hoped the duty officer would have a message for me. He did.

"Got your notebook handy?" he asked, "it's a long one."

I told him when I was ready, and the next few minutes were spent writing as he read the message to me. Jack was standing beside me, watching to make sure I wouldn't be overheard, so he got to hear the whole message as I read it back to the duty officer. When he confirmed that I had it all, I thanked him and hung up.

"Well, no messages for me for days and now it all comes at once. We now know who Ben is, and we already knew about the Colonel..."

"And there's no doubt now about who Oliver Risk is," supplied Jack.

"I guess not," I added. "We'll have to have a chat with François in the morning."

Laurie Schramm

7 ALBERTA

Day 6
May 31, 1978

It was midnight when the train pulled out of Edmonton, and it felt like I'd just gotten to sleep when I awoke to knocking on my door. It was François.

"I thought you should know. Someone's broken into the baggage car, eh? Everything looks OK, but I thought you'd like to know."

"OK, have you told Jack?"

"Yes. He's getting dressed."

"Give me a moment and we'll come too."

It was only when I was dressing that I realized that the train wasn't moving. A look out the window confirmed that we were stopped at a small town somewhere. It was 1:30 am.

It was only a few minutes before we were all ready, and François led us to the baggage car. There were scratches and large dents on both the doorframe, near the lock, and the aluminum-clad door itself. It looked like the door had been forced with something like a crowbar.

"One of the attendants noticed when we stopped here in Evansburg to pick up a passenger, eh? He came and got me, and we took a look around but it doesn't look like anything is missing. Who breaks into a place and doesn't take anything?"

"Maybe they were interrupted before they could do anything

more," I said, but that wasn't my first thought. As we stood there, looking at the luggage sitting in the racks I happened to make eye contact with Jack. We were both thinking the same thing.

"Could you help us find the bags belonging to the Risks please?"

That brought a shrewd gleam into François' eyes. "I had a feeling you were on the train to do more than just assess security. That kind of thing has been done many times before, and not much changes on the railroads, eh?"

"I'm sorry François. We weren't able to tell you everything unless there was an emergency."

"That's OK," he said, "it's made things interesting, with the missing nun and the phantom attendant. Something to tell the grandchildren one day."

As he was speaking, he led the way to the racks of luggage that were destined for Vancouver, and the three of us set about pulling the bags out and checking the name tags. We found two bags bearing tags marked for Oliver and Nathan. It was an anticlimax, though, as they seemed to be perfectly intact. Although each bag was locked with a small padlock, the locks were intact and showed no signs of tampering.

"Huh," said Jack, sitting back on his heels after inspecting the locks. "These little locks are the easiest things to the world to open. Nothing like the work that went into prying the car door open. Either our intruder had the keys or they didn't get as far as the bags."

"Maybe they were after something else," I said. "Let's see if we can find the Peters' bags."

"I saw them when we were looking for these ones," said Jack. "Hang on a moment."

It only took a couple of minutes for him to work backwards and find the Peters' bags. Again, there were two. At first sight, they too seemed undisturbed... except that neither of them had locks securing the wrap-around zippers that sealed the bags shut.

"Either they're very trusting people, or the locks have been removed. Do you have a flashlight I can borrow?" I asked François.

"But of course." He went to the end of the car, where there was a heavy-duty-looking flashlight secured in spring-clips beside the door to the generator-boiler car. Bringing it back, he handed it to me.

With the aid of the flashlight, I tried looking in the corners, nooks, and crannies of the car, not finding anything helpful until I tried looking at the racks we'd just cleared of their luggage. There, lying on the floor near the wall were two broken locks.

"Our intruder seems to have wanted a look at the Peters' luggage," I said, pocketing the locks. "Let's take a look."

Placing them on the floor, Jack and I each opened one up. Both appeared to be full, but the contents were in disarray, as if they'd been taken out and then simply stuffed back in.

"Well, either the Risks are both messy packers or these have been searched," said Jack.

"Yes, and look here," The inside lining of the top of the Colonel's bag came away when I touched it. "The lining has been slit open with a knife."

"Same with this one," said Jack, "prodding gently at the lining of Hannah's. I think our intruder has been looking for documents."

"Yes," I agreed… *Or a map,* I thought. "François, would you be willing to help us with a little deception?"

"What do you have in mind?" he asked.

"Would you be willing to pretend that all you found was the broken door, you came and got us, and we all looked together but there was no other apparent damage, and it didn't look like anything was stolen tonight?"

"But that is exactly what has happened. Where is the pretend?"

"I'd like for us to put all these bags back into the racks, and pretend that we didn't notice that these two bags have no locks."

A smile crept into onto François' face. "And those two little locks you found could have belonged to anyone, heh? Could have been lying there for months for all anyone knows."

"Exactly, and if the Peters come to you in the morning complaining that their luggage has been disturbed?"

"I will be my usual helpful self, eh? We will inspect the luggage together. I will be very shocked and conciliatory, and we will do lots of paperwork, of course!"

"Actually, I doubt they'll even come and talk to you about it. So you might not have to pretend anything, OK?"

"*D'accord,* as long as you come back one day and tell me what it was all about, OK?"

Jack and I nodded our agreement.

"One more request?" I asked of François.

He looked at me expectantly.

"If anyone asks you to let them off at one of the next stops, just do everything as you would normally do it and then tell us about it at breakfast. We'll be in the dining car early; about 5:30."

He raised his eyebrows, as if to ask questions, then thought better of it, nodded, and simply said, "Let's clean up then, eh?"

I didn't feel able to tell him that I'd received a message informing me that, while none of our people of interest had booked rental vehicles in Edson, there was one booking in Hinton, and another one in Jasper.

We put all the luggage back into place and left, with François pulling the damaged car door closed as best he could.

***

When the train pulled into the small station at Edson, Alberta, it was 3:10 am, only slightly behind schedule. Only one passenger disembarked at the station, then waited for a few minutes while his checked luggage was retrieved. Only a few blocks away, the Yellowhead Highway had split into separate one-way sections as it crossed through the town. In between the two lanes were a variety of services, conveniently placed so that drivers going in either direction could pull over for food, gas, or shopping. Among the amenities were a cluster of medium-sized motels. It was toward these that Ben walked, backpack on his back, and his carry-on and checked bags in each hand.

At this time of night, there was only the occasional semi-trailer truck or other vehicle travelling the highway.

Within four blocks he was standing where he had a good view of four motels. Choosing the nearest motel, he walked into the lobby, which was empty. Looking around, he found the small alcove, close to the elevators, where several luggage carts sat empty — waiting for the next guests to arrive or depart.

Selecting a cart, he placed his backpack and bags on it and wheeled it into the corridor. The large rubber-shod wheels were silent as he pushed the cart down the corridor, following the Fire Exit signs to find the back door leading to the rear parking lot.

Stooping to remove a long, thin piece of metal from his backpack, he left everything else on the cart, by the door. Then, he picked up the door stop that lay just inside the door and put it in his pocket. Finally, carefully testing first to made sure that it did not lock behind him, he went outside and crossed the parking lot, heading for the other motels.

Not liking the looks of the first motel he came to, which had outfitted its parking lot with an array of high-intensity lights, he passed it by. He also walked past the next motel for the same reason. The next motel however, had lighting in its parking lot but there were a few corners, at the extreme ends of its lot, that were not well lit. He headed for one of those.

Now to choose a car. He was looking for a car with manual door locks, but more than that, he was looking for something common. He knew that the most popular passenger car sold in 1977 and 1978 was the Chevrolet Impala, or its upscale model, the Chevrolet Caprice. The most common vehicle colours of the 1970s were green, beige, yellow, or gold.

Wouldn't you know it, *he thought to himself,* no Impalas in sight.

There was, however, a mud-covered beige Ford F100 half-ton truck sitting there. Pickup trucks, he knew, were as common in Alberta as cars were in Ontario. Oh well, when in Alberta…, *he thought.*

Taking a quick look around, to make sure no one seemed to be watching, he took out two tools. The wooden doorstop that he'd stolen from the motel he pushed in-between the driver-side door and roof to create a slight opening. Into this he inserted the long, thin piece of metal he'd retrieved from his backpack. This was a 'Slim Jim,' a thin piece of metal nearly two feet long with a hook shape cut into one end. It was the kind of tool a tow-truck would carry for helping motorists that have locked their keys inside their vehicle. By its very nature, it was also the kind of tool thieves could use to enter a locked vehicle.

Working the hooked end down and over towards the locking knob near the bottom of the window, he maneuvered the tool back and forth, trying to get the hook to catch the flared top of locking knob. It took half a dozen tries before he finally caught to top of the knob with the hook. Then, with a careful upwards pull, the knob came up, and the door was unlocked.

Withdrawing the Slim Jim, he opened the door, at which point the doorstop fell to the ground. He kicked it under the truck. Entering the truck, he carefully shut the door so the dome light would turn off, and slid across the bench seat to the passenger side.

Reaching into his jacket, he then removed his next two tools: a Swiss-Army-style pocketknife and a small flashlight. Twisting so he was lying with his torso underneath the steering column, with his head facing up, he turned his flashlight on and held it between his teeth. Thus armed, he navigated through the various coils of wire until he'd located the three main bundles of wires: two leading to controls like signal lights and windshield wipers, and a third that connected the ignition switch to the battery and starter that lie on the other side of the engine firewall. Pulling aside this latter bundle, he looked at the wire colours.

One of the wires he identified as bringing power directly from the battery system. Using his knife, he cut it and stripped some of the plastic insulation back from the end of the segment that led from the firewall. Another of the wires he identified as the one that normally received power with the ignition key in the 'On' position. This he cut, exposed the metal on one end, and connected to one of the red wires. The dashboard lights and radio immediately turned on. So far, so good, he thought, reaching to switch off the radio.

Next, he identified the starter wire that normally received power with the ignition key in the 'Start' position. This he cut, then exposed the metal on the end leading to the engine compartment. Holding this wire carefully, he touched it momentarily to the battery wire. The engine started. Reaching over to the floor pedals, he pushed the gas pedal once to rev the engine – to make sure it didn't stall – then tucked the bare wire out of the way and levered himself out from under the steering column.

Now the engine was running but the steering wheel was still locked. With the screwdriver blade of his knife he pried off the metal keyhole plate, then jiggled the blade around inside the lock cylinder until the lock-spring came free.

With this, he was able to ease the truck out of the lot, drive back to the first motel to pick up his backpack and bags, and he was ready to go.

It was 4 am. With luck, it would be at least another two hours before the theft of the truck was noticed, maybe more. He estimated that it would take almost an hour to drive to Hinton. Another hour's driving

after that should put him in Jasper by 6 am.
The train was scheduled to arrive in Jasper at 6:30.

Plenty of time, *Ben thought.*

***

The train's next stop was at the town of Hinton; arriving at 4 am.
This time, two passengers disembarked and collected their luggage.

Like Edson, the town had many of its businesses located along the
length of the highway. Unlike Edson, however, the highway did not split
into one-way lanes, and there was no particular cluster of services. As a
result, the services stretched along the full length of the portion of the
highway that ran through the town.

Using a pay phone to call for a taxi, they sat down to wait as the
train pulled out of the station, heading for the Rocky Mountains. Its
next stop would be Jasper.

When the taxi arrived, they asked it to take them to the nearest
place they could eat, which turned out to be a 24-hour truck-stop at the
edge of town. They took their time over breakfast, because the automotive
dealership from which they had booked a rental car didn't open until 8
am.

Unfortunately, the car rental company was at the easternmost edge of
town, nearly a mile away. Not wanting to carry their luggage that far, at
7:30 they used the truck-stop's pay phone to call for another taxi to take
them to the dealership. They were sitting with their luggage outside the
door of the dealership when the service manager arrived to open up at
7:45, and the manager took pity on them and let them in right away.
As a result, by 8 am they had completed the paperwork, and were
stowing their luggage in a two-tone eggshell-white and brown Dodge
Aspen.

It would take about an hour to drive to Jasper, which should have
them there by 9 am.

As they pulled onto the highway and out of town, heading for Jasper
National Park, Hannah Peters resumed her conversation with the
Colonel: trying to understand why he had been so determined to get off

the train early and make the trip through the mountains by car instead.

They didn't notice the mud-covered, beige pickup truck that was about half a mile behind them.

***

Having had only two-and-a-half hours' sleep, it was a struggle to get up and get to the dining car, and I arrived feeling grumpy and desperate for coffee. I didn't have the Hollywood-stereotypical cop's love for doughnuts, but countless long shifts, and especially long night-shifts, had addicted me to strong, black coffee. On the flip side, once Silver and I were seated in the dining car and I'd had my first half-cup, I was starting to feel human again. This was fortunate, because it was then that Jack joined us, followed in short order by François.

François' expression showed plainly that he had news for us.

"How did you sleep, eh?"

"Hardly at all," I said, still a bit grumpily.

"Great," said Jack, brightly. Looking at his face, I could see that it was true. He looked as bright-eyed and bushy-tailed as ever, making me feel uncharitably jealous.

I couldn't fool Jack though. Once glance at me told him what I was thinking, and he tried to soften the blow. "Don't worry, it always hits me on the second day. Tomorrow morning I'll feel like hell."

"Promise?" I asked, feeling just a little bit better.

Our morning banter was cut short at this point by François, who couldn't contain his news any longer.

"We had one passenger make us stop in Edson so he could get off!"

"It was Ben Shaw, right?"

François' jaw dropped. "How did you know?"

"Just a lucky guess. I'll tell you why in a moment. Did anyone get off in Hinton?"

"Suddenly, I have the feeling you know that one too," said François, but he answered anyway. "It was the Colonel and his daughter."

"And they all took their luggage with them?"

"Yes, but that's not unusual. Passengers can get off wherever they like, and then re-book themselves to continue on a later train… Of course, they don't usually interrupt their trips at small towns like these, it's usually at big centres like Edmonton, or tourist spots like Jasper."

"OK, here's the thing. I think the Peters are following someone, and I think Ben is doing the same thing."

"Ah, *je comprends*. And neither party wants the other to know what they are up to, eh?"

"Right."

"And let me guess who it is that they're following…"

"Don't say it out loud." I interrupted. "But, I know what you're thinking, and yes that's who they're following."

"And you are following them too?"

"Yes. Don't ask why just yet. If you-know-who gets off in Jasper, then we will be doing the same. If that happens, can you arrange for us to be able to get off the other side of the train from the other passengers."

"So nobody sees you, right? It's no problem. Just come to the baggage car. I'll meet you at the broken door. If you want to get off, we'll get your bags and I'll let you out on the side away from the station, and I'll have one of the attendants help you carry your bags. If you walk forward, none of the passengers will be able to see you when you cross in front of the engine."

"That would be great, thank you François."

He chuckled. "Like I said, a story for the grandchildren, eh?"

"Would you like to be in one more thing?" I asked.

"*Bien sûr!*"

I noticed that bits of his mother-tongue slipped into conversation when he was excited. "Give us a few minutes to eat and then you can watch Silver do his stuff, OK?"

"OK."

Twenty minutes later, we'd eaten breakfast, François was back with us, and we all went to my roomette. Taking the VIA Rail tie from the plastic bag I'd stored it in, I showed it to Silver and let him give it a good sniff. Then, I asked him to track, and stood back.

Silver first went forward along the car's corridor, sniffing along the floor and back and forth from side to side, including at the various compartment doors. As he neared the forward end of the car, he sniffed around in the communal shower area, along the berth sections, and inside each of the two shared bathrooms. When he reached the door at the end of the car he stopped and looked at me.

"Let's try the other way," I said, and motioned for Silver to search in the other direction. This time, he walked slowly along the corridor until he neared our roomette, at which point he slowed down and went back to his thorough tracking routine.

He went like this for less than twenty feet before he stopped by one of the roomette doors, gave the door jam and sill a more thorough investigation, and then promptly sat down on his haunches and gave me his '*Found it!*' gaze.

"That is the roomette of Benjamin Shaw," exclaimed François.

"Yes. Let's try one more experiment, shall we?"

Retracing our steps, I went back to my roomette and exchanged the VIA tie for the rescued nun's habit. Once again, I let Silver have a really good sniff of it, then asked him to track the scent.

I didn't specify a direction to search this time, and Silver looked up at me for confirmation and then headed off on his own. There was no careful sniffing around everywhere this time, however, as he promptly walked straight to Ben's roomette and sat down.

As I was congratulating Silver and rewarding him with a few dog treats, François was still busy being amazed.

"He must have been the one that broke into the Risks' roomette and also the Peters'!"

"Yes, and almost certainly the baggage car as well," added Jack.

We asked if we could look inside the roomette, and François motioned his assent.

With the roomette being empty, the door wasn't locked, so I pushed it open. The lower berth was a mess of rumpled sheets, blankets, and towels.

"It hasn't been cleaned yet, eh?" said François.

"That's perfect for us," I replied, looking around more carefully this time. There wasn't anything hidden in the covers or under the mattress of the lower berth, nor for the upper berth. The small waste basket, however, was full. Spreading out the blankets on the lower berth, I dumped the waste basket contents on top and spread them out.

Apart from the gross stuff: soiled Kleenexes and mostly empty junk food wrappers, there was a wad of letter-size papers that had been rolled up and stuffed into the basket. That looked promising.

Clearing some space, I rolled out the papers. There were six of them, each of them bearing newspaper clippings that had been glued into place, with hand-written notations on the dates and names of the newspapers from which the clippings had come.

I looked up at Jack, who was standing beside me, and we exchanged a look and a nod.

"Here François, you may as well see what we've found but don't touch them, OK?"

As Jack made room, François came forward into the roomette and looked with interest at the newspaper headings. "Don't read them out loud," I cautioned.

When he looked up, wide-eyed, I touched my index finger to my lips and added, "Remember, don't ask us anymore and don't say anything to anyone – not for a day or two anyway, after that it won't matter."

"So you'll be getting off at Jasper," he asked, his eyes still wide.

I looked at my watch. It was 8:30, the train was running two hours late. We'd be stopping in Jasper very soon. "We'll meet you at the baggage car in a few minutes. We'll be able to tell you then."

As François hustled off to prepare for the next stop, I carefully gathered up the pages, handling them by the edges as much as I could, to avoid covering them with my fingerprints. I still had the nun's habit with me, so I used it to hold the papers and went back to my roomette to store them in bags and repack my carry-on bags. Jack went to do the same.

When we all met again at the baggage car door, François raised his eyebrows and said: "Mr. Risk and his son, the minister, told me they've suddenly decided to get off here and explore the mountains for a few days. We're just searching for their bags now. I suppose that means you're wanting to get off as well?"

I nodded. "Yes. Could you do one last thing and delay finding the Risks bags for ten minutes?"

Nodding his head, he slyly placed an extended index finger alongside his nose. He was enjoying his role in our intrigue.

"Thank you for all your help, and I won't forget to phone you later and tell you what it was all about – for your grandchildren!" I barely caught myself from adding "eh?," as I was afraid he might be insulted, but I couldn't help smiling to myself. François had been a helpful and enjoyable travel companion of sorts.

With the help of one of the attendants, who had appeared with a kind of wheelbarrow-for-luggage that had a huge front wheel, we got our checked bags and made our way around the far side of the train from the station platform and crossed in front of the locomotive. The attendant had no trouble pushing the wheelbarrow, with its large front wheel, over the rails and soon we were out of anyone's sight, skirting the far side of the train station.

When we reached the front corner of the station, the engine started in a nondescript-looking station wagon that had been waiting in the parking lot. It drove directly to us, and when the driver's window was rolled down, it revealed a uniformed RCMP Constable.

The constable identified himself, and got out to open the back of the station wagon for our luggage.

When we were all in pace in the car, he said that the Detachment was on the far side of town, and that they had everything ready that we'd asked for.

Now it's going to get interesting, I thought.

Photo courtesy of VIA Rail Canada (Resource ID 386).

Laurie Schramm

8 RED PASS

Just before approaching the town of Jasper, we had been treated to a gorgeous sunrise that spread a pink hue over the east-facing slopes of the mountains. At 9 am, it was fully daylight as Jack and Silver and I parked a block away from the car rental company that my boss, Bob's team had discovered held a reservation for a Mr. James Peters, also known as the Colonel.

For our part, we were sitting in the same station wagon that had been used to pick us up from the train station, which turned out to be an unmarked police car. There were two more constables in a marked, highway patrol car, on standby too, but they were well out of sight, having positioned themselves at the outskirts of town – on the southwest side, where the Yellowhead Highway intersects the Columbia Icefields Parkway. We would stay in touch with them by radio.

Our position was on a connecting street, close to the junction, so that from my position in the passenger seat I had a clear view across to the street to the rental agency and its car lot.

We also knew the kind of vehicle that had been reserved – a full-size car - but not the exact make, model, or colour. I hoped to learn those details by watching through binoculars.

We only had to wait about ten minutes before Oliver and Nathan Risk showed up by taxi. As they got out, I was surprised to see that they had quite a few bags with them. In addition to their

411

carry-on bags and Oliver Risk's briefcase, were three larger bags and a good-sized backpack.

After a few minutes in the agency, they emerged and made their way to the car lot. As they loaded their bags and then pulled away, I had binoculars in one hand and the police radio microphone in the other so I could relay descriptions. These would be noted by the highway patrol car outside of town and also the radio room operator in the Jasper Detachment.

"Persons of interest numbers one and two, Oliver Risk and Nathan Risk, driving a late-model Chev Caprice, two-tone light blue with white trim, Alberta licence number…"

Almost immediately, a car that had been parked about a block away, and on the same side of the road as the car rental agency, pulled away from the curb. It was driving in the same direction as the Risks. As the car passed us, I could see the Colonel and Hannah in the front seat, and radioed this in as well.

"Persons of interest numbers three and four, James Peters and Hannah Peters, driving a late-model Dodge Aspen, two-tone white or beige with brown trim, Alberta licence number…"

"Look there," said Jack, pointing further down the block.

There, about another block behind the spot where the Peters had been parked, a pickup truck had pulled away from the curve and was driving in the same direction as the Peters and the Risks.

I whistled as the truck approached and then passed us. It was Ben Shaw.

"This is like watching a scene from a TV or movie drama," I said to Jack, then went back to my radio reporting.

"Person of interest number five, Benjamin Shaw, driving a late-model Ford pickup truck, possibly beige in colour but covered in mud. Licence plate obscured by mud. Pickup truck is suspected to be stolen, possibly in Edson."

My last sight through the binoculars was of all three vehicles heading southwest on the main street, which the street signs all informed them would lead to the Yellowhead Highway once they were out of town. Since we thought we knew where they were going, we didn't bother trying to follow them. The highway patrol car would already be in motion to a predetermined location, near what we thought would be the second-most-likely place for the Risks to be heading.

Our plan was for Jack, Silver, and I to now drive directly to what we thought would be the first-most-likely place for the Risks to be heading, which was deep into the mountains, some 71 km (44 miles) away.

Jack is a more aggressive driver than I am, which is what we needed right now. He had already started the car and we pulled out, keeping well behind Ben. After only two blocks Jack took a hard, left-hand turn and accelerated as I switched on the small, magnetic-base, red-light flasher that was sitting in the front dash, nestled up against the front window. I didn't throw the flashing light outside and up onto the roof, because we only wanted vehicles that were directly in front of us to see it. Whereas the convoy of vehicles ahead of us had remained on the main street/highway, we were now on Hazel Avenue, going southeast, but only for two more blocks at which point we turned right onto the Yellowhead Highway. Here, the highway was clear, and the engine roared as Jack opened it up full throttle.

With us now travelling at least twice the speed of the others, we expected to reach the main highway junction ahead of them even though it was only about a kilometer ahead. I had my binoculars out again, watching for the upcoming cross-road.

"There they are," I said, as we approached the junction. "The Risks are about two blocks away."

Jack didn't slow down, as we had the right-of-way through the intersection. By the time the Risks reached the stop sign, then made their right-hand turn to follow, we were well ahead of them and still moving fast.

Although it was hardly a time for sight-seeing, we were now travelling through some of the most beautiful scenery in Canada. First, we passed the road to the Jasper Sky Tram, with the partially-snow-clad summit of Whistler Mountain visible above and behind it. Another 25 km (15 miles) brought us to the British Columbia border, and about the same distance again brought us into Mount Robson Provincial Park.

That it was a very clear day was obvious from the fact that we had an unusually great view of the summit of Mount Robson itself, which is quite often obscured by clouds. This brought a fleeting reminiscence of some great backpacking trips, before I forced my mind back to the business at hand.

Our drive next took us along the Fraser River and the 12 km-long (7 mile) Moose Lake, near the end of which was Red Pass – our destination. The highway patrol car was already there, waiting for us.

At the place where we stopped, there was room for a vehicle to pull over, off the highway to the right, and then a mountain rising rapidly beside that. To the left of the highway, there was also a broad shoulder. Down the embankment on that side was a shallow but fairly fast flowing stream – an offshoot of the Fraser River. Across the stream was a rising embankment, beside which ran a set of railway tracks. To the left of the tracks, was another rapidly rising mountain. A short distance ahead of us was the opening to a train tunnel. This was one of the classic Rocky Mountain train tunnels, built in the 1800s and looking like an ageing concrete doorway with an inky black mouth. To the right of the entrance, a gravel and scrub-brush slope descended to meet the running stream. On the left side of the entrance, the terrain was also gravel and scrub-brush for a distance of twenty or thirty feet, then solid forest all the way up the mountainside until rock and gravel made their appearance high up, above the tree-line.

We decided that Jack and I would stakeout this area, while the other two constables would position themselves out of sight near the other end of the train tunnel, a couple of miles away. Jack and I found a trail leading into the right-hand mountain and backed our car into it, making sure it was far enough in so that it wouldn't easily be seen from the highway. It was a tight fit, but we were able to squeeze out of the car, after which Jack, Silver, and I walked back to the highway, across it, and across the stream.

Between the stream and the tracks there were several dense clumps of trees that looked like good vantage points from which we could both hide and observe. Jack chose a spot with the best overall view of the area, taking the risk of possibly not being able to hear much. Silver and I took a position that was as close to the mouth of the tunnel as I thought we could risk. Then, we settled in as best we could. We didn't expect to have long to wait.

I had brought the binoculars with me, and so had the best view of what came next.

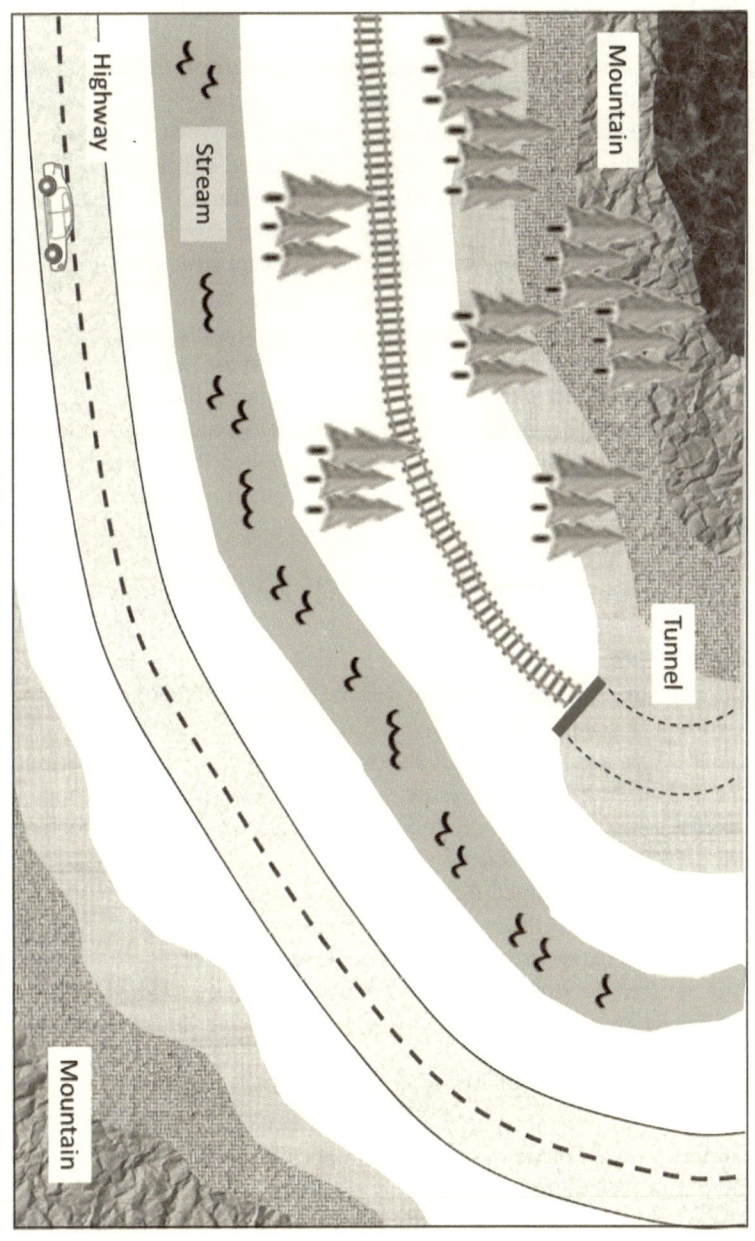

Oliver and Nathan Risk, upon reaching Red Pass, pulled off the highway and parked their car on the shoulder. As they got out, Oliver in particular took a hard look down the highway in both directions. Seeming satisfied, he opened the trunk of the car and extracted the aluminum-frame backpack. Reaching in, he withdrew a folding shovel and a rucksack, the latter of which he passed to Nathan, who was no longer wearing his clerical collar. He did have his bible with him, however, which he placed into the rucksack.

Shouldering their packs, and with Nathan carrying the shovel, Oliver led the way. They crossed the highway, stream, and railway tracks, then approached the tunnel entrance. At this point Oliver took a careful look at the old, concrete-framed tunnel entrance.

"Things look a bit different than they used to," he said.

They were so close to my position that I had little trouble watching and listening, and I kept a hand on Silver so he would know to remain still. I thought that, by then, I had a pretty good idea of what was going to happen next, but there were still some surprises.

"Hand me your bible, Nathan," said Oliver, with his hand out.

Nathan seemed to be as surprised at this as I was, but he took off his rucksack, withdrew and handed over the bible that had never been far from his hands over the previous six days.

With a pocket knife, Oliver carefully slit the stitching of the bible's soft leather cover all the way around the edges, front and back. Handing the bible back to Nathan he said: "Remember I always told you that if anything happened to me, you should look inside your bible? This is why."

"A map!" exclaimed Nathan.

Sure enough, Oliver held open the leather bible cover and they looked at what was drawn on its reverse side. I couldn't see what was written or drawn there, of course, but they studied it for a while. Then Oliver looked around again, as if recalibrating his bearings.

"This way," he said. "Bring your pack."

I was able to observe the two of them scramble up the steep slope on the left side of the train tunnel's concrete opening. When they reached the top of the concrete frame, Oliver stood with his shoes placed right against the frame's top-left corner and said: "Read off the paces."

"Twenty-five left from the edge, keeping to the same elevation as the top of the tunnel... OK, now ten paces to your right, straight up the slope... OK, now..."

I couldn't hear the rest, nor see them anymore. They couldn't have gone much further, though, because a few minutes later I could hear the sounds of digging as they used the shovel to excavate gravel and dirt. The digging sounds went on for a while, until the shovel made a kind of 'clunk' sound. They had struck something.

I could hear the voices of the two of them talking for a while, but couldn't make out any of what they were saying.

Things went completely quiet after that, and after fifteen minutes I was trying to decide whether to risk changing my position or not, when the two of them came back into my line of sight. They had their packs on and were very carefully making their way back down the gravel and scrub-bush covered slope. I judged that their caution was due to their packs being heavier than they were used to. I found out later that Oliver's backpack had become 30 pounds heavier, while the weight of Nathan's had increased by 60 pounds. The shovel, they had simply discarded.

When the two of them reached the clearing in front of the tunnel, they stopped and took their packs off for a few moments rest. Despite the lighter pack, it was Oliver that had tired the most easily, and when he'd recovered his breath he said, "OK, let's get moving again."

As they were about to hoist their packs, they were stopped by a commanding voice coming from the direction of the tunnel:

"Just leave the packs where they are!"

9 SHOWDOWN

When the Peters reached the area of the train tunnel, the Colonel noted the Risks' rental car parked beside the road and kept driving for a few hundred yards before stopping and making a U-turn on the highway. Doubling back, he drove until just before the tunnel entrance and clearing, and parked beside the highway.

Instructing Hannah to remain in the car, he took something from his carry-on bag in the back seat and walked beside the highway towards the clearing. When he rounded the corner, Hannah immediately got out of the car and followed him.

As she walked along the side of the mountain, she came up to the clearing and rounded the corner by the entrance to the train tunnel just in time to hear the Colonel's voice, saying "Just leave the packs where they are!"

✳✳✳

My hidden vantage point had turned out to be almost perfect. I saw Oliver and Nathan Risk come down the mountain and stop for their brief rest. I saw the Colonel step forward from the shadow of the train tunnel, with a large automatic pistol in his hand. *Probably a military .45 calibre,* I thought.

I also saw Hannah come around the corner in time to be able to take in the whole scene for herself as well.

The brief silence was broken not by the Risks, who stood there

419

for a moment, scowling, but by Hannah.

"Dad, what's going on? Why do you have a gun? And what are Nathan and his dad doing here?"

"I told you to stay in the car!" the Colonel barked. "Now that you're here, stay where you are and don't interfere...." While saying this, he hadn't taken his eyes away from Oliver and Nathan, nor had his gun – which was pointed at them – wavered at all.

"Who the hell are you?" asked Oliver.

"Just someone with an interest in the gold, that's all... take your gun out and toss it over to me."

Oliver visibly hesitated.

"Don't try to bluff me. You wouldn't have come here without a gun. I want it now!"

Then, as Oliver reluctantly reached into his jacket pocket, the Colonel spoke sharply and warningly: "Carefully now. I'll start by shooting your son if I have to."

Continuing to scowl, Oliver carefully withdrew a revolver from his jacket and carefully tossed it over to the Colonel.

"OK, now back away from the packs."

When they did so, the Colonel called out to his daughter. "Hannah, now that you're here anyway, come and take one of these packs."

As Hannah stood frozen in place, the Colonel moved quickly to pick up Oliver's gun and put it in his own pocket. With his gun hand covering the Risks, he used his free hand to experimentally heft the two packs. Finding what appeared to be the heaviest one, he grabbed one of the shoulder straps and one-handed it up and onto one shoulder.

"Who are you, anyway?" croaked Oliver Risk.

"Why Jon, I'm surprised you don't remember me. After all these years, I certainly still remember you!"

As Oliver just stood there, looking confused, the Colonel continued. "No? Let me give you another hint. We were partners once upon a time. You had the brains and I had the dynamite. Does that help?"

"Slim?" said Oliver, disbelievingly. "But you can't be..." his voice trailed off.

"Why not, because I'm dead? Because you killed my brother and me inside that tunnel 58 years ago? Well, you shot both of us in there all right, and then took the gold and rode off, leaving us to die. Except that I didn't die. I don't know why.

"I was unconscious at first. When I came to, you were gone. I crawled over to my brother, who was alive but in bad shape. As I lay there holding my brother in my arms while he died, I wanted to join him. But I didn't die, and when they came and found us still lying there together, they took my brother and buried him somewhere while I ended up under guard in a hospital, until I was well enough to go to jail.

"Meanwhile you had taken off with the loot... Hannah, get over here. What are you doing?" he asked, without taking his eyes off of the Risks.

Hannah hadn't moved. "Dad! What is all this? What are you doing?"

"I'll explain it all to you later. For now, just come and get the rucksack and we'll leave. No one will get hurt... no one besides Jon - or Oliver - there, that is, and I'll tell you all about it after we've left."

Reluctantly, Hannah went over and picked up the rucksack, then walked over to the front of the train tunnel and stopped again. Still hesitant, she took off the pack and put it back down on the ground, then stood there staring at her father.

"Now what?" demanded the Colonel.

"This feels wrong Dad. Like stealing. What's in these packs? What has any of this got to do with us? And why are you threatening these people?"

"I said I'll tell you about it later. Now do as I say. Lift that pack up, and let's get out of here!"

"No, Dad. I don't know what's in here that's so important to you, or why everyone seems to have guns, but we can't just steal stuff from Nathan and his father."

"Hannah, I'm telling you for the last time. Bring that pack over here or I'll take it away myself and leave you here."

"Dad!"

"I mean it. Make your choice. You're either with me or you're with them!"

Hannah just continued to stand there, but visibly shaking now. It was obvious that strong emotions and uncertainties were swirling inside her.

"Hannah can just stand still where she is," said a new voice.

***

Ben, who had been following the Peters, kept going when he saw the Colonel make a U-turn. He continued past them and drive on for another mile, then made his own U-turn and drove slowly back. By the time he had a clear view of the Peter's car, the Colonel was already walking away and Hannah was just getting out, in contravention of her father's instructions.

Ben slowed down.

Only when Hannah turned the mountain's corner, and went out of sight, did Ben pick up speed, driving until he reached the Peters' car, then pulled his pickup truck in behind it. Exiting the truck and closing its door very quietly, Ben jogged ahead to the edge of the mountain that Hannah had disappeared behind.

Crouching low, he peered around the corner and was just in time to hear the Colonel identify himself as a former partner of Oliver and pocket the latter's gun. When the Colonel demanded for the second time that Hannah pick up a pack and help him, Ben took his cue.

"Hannah can just stand still where she is," said Ben.

Even the Colonel was startled into turning his head, just as Ben quickly darted forward to reach Hannah and grab her arm. In his other hand he held a gun, too.

I think everyone except Jack and I were surprised to see Ben appear. Of the rest, Hannah was the first speak up.

"Ben! What are you doing here? What's going on?"

"I think I'm here for the same reason your father is, and it's not to see the sights," said Ben. "I'll tell you about it later, if you want, but for now, just stand here quietly with me…. Well, Colonel? How about tossing both guns over here?"

As they stared at each other, the Colonel spoke. "Look son, let me give you some military advice. Number one, that little revolver of yours has nowhere near the destructive power of my army .45.

"Number two, I'm a better shot that you are, so while you may or may not be able to hit me, I most certainly will not miss hitting you.

"Number three, if you shoot or otherwise hurt Hannah, I will put all seven rounds into you.

"Number four, even if you manage to hit me, it will take several shots to take down a man of my size and determination, whereas I will most certainly shoot you dead.

"So, my advice to you is to toss your little gun over to me, and you can walk away from this and live to fight another day. Now that's sound tactical advice, but it's entirely up to you. What do you say?"

"I want to know what happened to the loot," said Ben, angrily and with Hannah positioned in front of him as a shield.

"Don't ask me," said the Colonel calmly. "Ask him," he motioned with his gun towards Oliver.

"You know him as Oliver Risk. I knew him as Jon Hope the outlaw and leader of our little gang. I was a member, and so was my brother Jess. We stopped a train and robbed it, right over there," he pointed along the tracks, a short distance away.

"After the robbery, the three of us each took part of the loot and rode into the tunnel, planning to come out the other side and make our way to the coast. From there we were going to take a liner down the U.S. to San Francisco, to hide out.

"But Jon tricked us. When we entered the tunnel, our eyes were still adjusting to the darkness when he shot us down, just inside the entrance there. Then the bastard left us for dead, except I pulled through.

"It took me a long, long time to recover, serve my time in jail, serve in a couple of wars, and then, finally, I got my life's wish: I found out where he was hiding in the States, and the name he'd assumed: Oliver Risk."

The Colonel paused a moment, as if remembering.

"But he took all the loot. Like I said, after getting shot I was unconscious for a while. Maybe that and the blood are why he thought I was dead. Anyway, he didn't take our horses. Maybe he thought it would be too conspicuous, I don't know. Whatever the reason, part of it was in gold coins. The gold was too heavy for him and his horse to carry, so he hid it around here somewhere.

"The rest of the loot was paper money. He must have taken with him. As near as I can tell, he spent the money over the years, went into debt, and came back here to get the gold...

"Now. How did you find out about it? And who the hell are you anyway?"

Somewhat reluctantly, Ben picked up the tale from there.

"There weren't three people in the gang back then, there were four. My father was Robert Shaw, the fourth member, and what they called 'the man on the inside.'

"It was my father that that tipped off the others about the train's route and schedule, the express car's contents, and the fact that a particular run had less than the usual number of guards and no alarms installed.

"And my father got cheated too. Jon Hope high-tailed it for the U.S. without ever handing over my father's share of the loot, and my father died just around the time he finally tracked him down.

"He knew all about you though. Before he died, he told me all about the robbery, and the gang, and the loot. Because he worked for the bank, he knew that the gold coins had never surfaced, and he knew that only one horse had been ridden away, so he figured that the paper money was gone but that coins must have been hidden around here somewhere.

"He knew, through the bank, that some of the paper money had been spent in the southern U.S., and in little bits at a time, although that knowledge hadn't helped the police to track him down. He also knew that your brother hadn't survived, of course, but he followed your career closely. So closely that he even knew about your efforts to find Jon Hope, including that you found him and turned his secretary into a double agent."

There was a pause as he looked closely at the Colonel's face.

"I see that surprises you. Here's another surprise. You were paying his secretary to keep you informed about Jon Hope's business travels, which is how you knew exactly when and how he was going to come back to Canada and then all the way across the country to this place. What you didn't know, is that my dad bribed the same secretary into becoming a triple agent. Every time he sent you a report on Jon Hope's travel plans, he sent the same information to my dad and got paid all over again for the same information.

"My dad died recently, but not before the last report came in.

424

The one about his plans to come to Canada and come all the way west. His train ticket was good all the way to Vancouver, but I figured – just like you did – that his real plan was to get off the train and find his way here.

"I didn't know where he'd hidden the loot, so I just followed you while you followed him.... So, you see, my father found him by following you, and I found the loot by following you. Satisfied?"

"I remember your father," the Colonel said, reflectively. "He seemed like a good man. The authorities thought there must have been an inside man on the job, and they tried to make me give him up. Even promised me a lighter sentence. But I never did..."

He shook himself out of his reminiscences. "Look, I have no grudge against you, and now you know that you should have no grudge against me, otherwise your father would have gone to jail like I did. How about if you take the other pack that's lying there and walk away. Hannah and I will do the same with this one and we can go our separate ways."

"What about those two?" asked Ben, nodding towards Oliver Risk (a.k.a. Jon Hope) and his son.

"If it wasn't for Hannah being here, I'd say let's just kill them both and move along, but she'd never forgive me for that and I guess I don't have anything against the reverend there. We could each shoot Jon in a leg though. At least he'd spend the rest of his life in misery that way."

No one said anything for a moment, but Ben's gun slowly moved to point toward Oliver (Jon), and likewise did the Colonel's gun.

Time to step in, I thought. I hoped I knew what I was doing.

"That's a horrible choice you offered Hannah a moment ago, you know," I said as Silver and I stepped out from the small cluster of trees behind which we'd been hiding. My service revolver was pointed towards both the Colonel and Ben, but I was speaking to the Colonel.

"On the one hand, she loves you and feels a duty to you as her father; on the other hand, she has correctly sensed that something very wrong is going on here. Making things worse for her are the feelings she's obviously developed for Nathan there, and maybe even for Ben."

"And you think you know what's going on?" The big .45 revolver was pointing at me now.

"Yes, I think I do. If you drop that gun I'll explain."

His gun didn't waver until Silver, without needing to be told, started shifting himself sideways so he'd be able to come at the Colonel from the side if he needed to.

The Colonel was experienced enough to immediately recognize a flanking maneuvre, of course. "Keep that dog away from me or I'll kill him," he barked.

"Colonel, that's a police dog doing his job. If you shoot at him, you will be shot yourself."

"By you?" he said, disbelievingly.

"Without hesitation. I hope you can believe that. But before you decide, let me give you some police advice, just like the military advice you offered earlier for Ben over there.

"Point number one, my revolver doesn't have quite as much destructive power as yours does, but it's more than enough to seriously wound or kill you.

"Point number two: mine's fully loaded and I don't think Ben's a killer, so I really only have one target to worry about: you." I hoped I was right about Ben.

"Point number three, I might not be a better shot than you are, but at this range, it won't matter much.

"Point number four: just like you said, even if you manage to hit me, it will take several shots to take me down, meaning that I'll get a couple of shots in too.

"Point number five, there's Silver to consider. He's faced men with guns before, and he's even been shot before. He won't hurt you unless I ask him to, but I need to warn you that he and I aren't just partners, we're close friends. What that means is that if you shoot me, he will attack you. Even if I ask him not to, he will attack you. Of course, he won't kill you... but Jack might."

"Jack?" he quickly glanced around, warily.

"Yes, my colleague, Constable Jack McDonald." I waved vaguely over my shoulder towards another clump of trees, behind me. A quick glance confirmed that Jack had been listening closely, and had taken his cue and stepped out from the trees, immediately dropped to one knee, and shouldered a rifle.

"Drop the gun Colonel," he ordered.

"So. That makes six reasons," I continued. "Any one of them

by themselves might not be convincing, but take them all together... I think that sound military strategy would call for a surrender in this case. Wouldn't you?"

He hesitated.

"At this point, you may be thinking that Mounties won't shoot first. That's generally true, and we might just let you get the first shot off. But what then? If you shoot one of us, the other will certainly shoot you, and despite what you might think from Mountie fiction, we're not trained to shoot to wound."

Still the Colonel hesitated, and it felt like a frozen moment in time.

Perhaps it was because no one was speaking, but I suddenly heard a new sound layered over the background sounds of the running stream beside us. It took me a moment to figure out what the sound was. It sounded faintly mechanical. Something about it made me glance towards the tunnel entrance. Then I saw the light.

Oh no!

The others must have seen the direction of my glance, or perhaps the expression on my face, but before any of us could do anything, nothing could take precedence over the locomotive's five-chime horn.

I actually went and looked it up later. Under Transport Canada regulations, Canada's train locomotives must be equipped with a dual-tone horn located in an unobstructed location near the front of the roof, facing the direction of travel, and capable of producing a soft 'normal' sound, and a loud 'emergency' sound. Well, the locomotive's engineer must have seen us near the mouth of the tunnel, because they had pulled the cord for the emergency sound.

A five-chime locomotive horn under emergency air pressure is designed to get people's attention, and has to be at least 96 decibels at a distance of 30 metres (100 feet) away. For us, standing within about 10 metres (30 feet) of the emerging locomotive it was deafening – like standing next to a jackhammer.

It certainly made me jump!

The problem with the train was that Jack, Silver, and I were on the 'stream' side of the tracks, while everyone else was on the 'mountain' side. And, of course, it had to be a freight train. It had three locomotives and more than sixty cars, giving it a total length of something like one-and-a-half kilometres (nearly a mile). Coming, as it was, out of a tunnel, it was moving fairly slowly too.

I thought I heard gunshots, but there was nothing we could do but wait.

10 ESCAPE

On the 'mountain' side of the tracks the Colonel, of course, was the first to unfreeze. Boldly striding forward, he moved closer to Ben and Hannah, took careful aim, and shot Ben in his gun arm.

The force of the high-calibre slug spun Ben nearly 45 degrees to one side and dropped him to his knees. It also caused him to drop the gun he was holding, and to release Hannah so he could press his other hand against his bleeding arm.

Sprinting the last few yards, the Colonel swiftly picked up Ben's gun, pocketed it, and used his own gun to deliver a punishing blow to Ben's head. Stunned, Ben dropped like a stone.

Ignoring him, the Colonel reached over and took Hanna's arm.

"No time to debate this, Hannah. You need to come with me now, and I promise I'll explain everything later – right?"

"I don't understand any of this," she said, shakily.

"Just pick up that pack, like I told you, and follow me." As Hannah tentatively made to go and pick up the rucksack, the Colonel strode over to where Oliver (a.k.a. Jon) and Nathan were still standing.

"All right you two. Hannah and I are leaving with the gold, and you two are going to stay right here, yes?"

Nathan's response was to open his bible, as if to cite some passage that would make the Colonel change his mind.

The Colonel looked at him in disbelief and disdain. "Freeze. Don't make any moves at all!"

Before Nathan could decide what to do next, Oliver tried to take advantage of the distraction and lunged at the Colonel, as if trying to get at the gun he was holding. If that was his intention, he had badly miscalculated as he was too far away. Before he could even get close, the Colonel simply aimed and fired, bringing Oliver down into a collapsed heap, holding the leg where he'd been hit.

Nathan's reaction was instantaneous. Dropping the bible, he went to help his father.

Still angry at Oliver's foolish attempt, the Colonel's first impulse was to raise his left hand as if to physically attack Nathan, but then his professional instincts took over and, realizing that Nathan wasn't a serious threat, simply snarled "Look after your father."

Stepping over to Hannah, he went to help her finish putting on the rucksack, but she backed away as if afraid of him. "Look Dad, I don't care what you did when you were young, but you know better now. You've hurt these people – we have to stay here and help them."

"Help them!" the Colonel was incredulous. "Jon there is lucky I didn't kill him, and Ben there got what he deserves for trying to interfere with me!"

"No, Dad. It's wrong… You go if you want, but I'm going to stay here and help them."

"Hannah, I told you to come or I'd leave you here. Decide now!"

But Hannah had already made her decision. Visibly shaking, but standing her ground, she said, defiantly, "Go then. I'm staying here to help them."

The Colonel stared at her for a moment, then came to a decision. "Fine then. Have it your own way." The larger backpack was still on one shoulder. Switching his gun to his left hand, and keeping a close eye on the Risks, he slipped the other strap up and over his right shoulder. Then, switching his gun over again, he picked up the rucksack in his left hand and jogged toward the mountainside path that the Risks had descended earlier.

As Hannah ran to help Nathan and his father, the Colonel began climbing the mountain and disappeared into the forest.

By this time, Nathan had made a quick inspection of his father and discovered that Oliver's leg was bleeding from a point on his front thigh, and another on the back side.

"Looks like the bullet went straight through," he said to both his father and Hannah, who had rushed over. "That's a good sign. We just have to stop the bleeding." Stripping off his light jacket and taking out a pocketknife, he cut each jacket sleeve off and tied them together. Then, he rolled-up the rest of the jacket and wrapped it around his father's injured leg as a makeshift bandage. Using the tied jacket sleeves like a strap, he wrapped it around the jacket and tied it in place. Then, he looked Hannah straight in the eyes. "Would you do something for me?" he asked.

It all took place in about five minutes, after which the train had passed them by, on its way east.

***

Once the train had passed, Silver and I crossed the tracks, followed, not far behind, by Jack. I was closest to Ben, so I ran to where he lay, while Jack ran over to Oliver and Hannah.

Ben was barely conscious and lying in a pool of blood, his eyes unfocused. His pulse was strong though, and as I checked him over it seemed like the blood was all coming from his right arm. I gave him a full pat-down anyway, looking for weapons, but only found a pocketknife.

Turning my focus back to his injury, I had a bandanna in one pocket, which I took out and tied around his arm to slow the bleeding. As I tied the bandanna, Ben seemed to come out of his stupor and I could see the exact moment when his mind cleared and the pain hit.

"He shot me and then he hit me," said Ben, in a shaky voice.

"Who did?"

"The Colonel."

"OK, just sit here quietly for a moment while I go check on the others, then we'll radio in for some help."

By the time I had walked over to Jack, he had just checked over Nathan's first aid work.

"Looks like the bullet went right through. Mr. Risk looks a bit shaky and is pain, but I don't think the bullet did more than graze the bone as it went past, so he should be OK."

"How many shots did you hear?" I asked Jack.

He thought for a moment. "Sounded like two. Large calibre."

"Me too," I agreed.

Stepping back a couple of feet, I looked pointedly at Oliver and Hannah. "Where's the gun?"

Silence.

"If you want our help, you need to tell me where the gun is… and where are the Colonel and Nathan?"

"Dad has a gun. Ben and Mr. Risk both had guns too, but dad has them as well." Hannah then related what had happened on their side of the freight train, finishing up with: "…and then Nathan asked me to look after his father while he went after Dad and the gold."

"That's crazy," Jack exclaimed. "Your father has already shot two people and is on the run with stolen gold and, according to you, he has three guns with him. What does Nathan think he's going to be able to do?"

"I don't know," said Hannah, breaking into tears now. "But he does have a gun. I saw him take it out of his bible and put it in his pocket before he left," she said, pointing vaguely to one side.

There, lying open but upside down on the ground, was Nathan's bible. When I went over to pick it up and turned it over in my hands, the bible was half open. The right-hand pages had been hollowed out in the approximate shape of a gun.

My jaw dropped in surprise. *Nathan had a gun?* I thought.

"Look at this, Jack."

"Must be a small one. About the size of a derringer, wouldn't you say?"

I nodded. It looked exactly right for a derringer. I knew, because I sometimes carried one myself, when working undercover. "OK, so he's armed, but he's probably only got two rounds – he'll be hopelessly outgunned."

Suddenly, we heard the *Crack!* of a gunshot.

"What was that," cried Hannah.

"One of them took a shot," said Jack.

"You'll stop them, won't you?" asked Hannah, still sniffling from shock and stress. "You won't let Dad hurt him?"

"We'll certainly do our best, Hannah. But first, we need to look after Mr. Risk and Ben. Then, we'll see what we can do."

Leaving Silver and I to keep an eye on things, Jack ran down to the highway and our unmarked police car to radio for the highway patrol car, which was still at the other stakeout position at the far end of the tunnel, to come help. The he ran back, bringing with him the police car's first aid kit.

As we cleaned and properly bandaged Oliver Risk's leg and Ben's arm, we verified that, in both cases, the slugs had gone right through. We couldn't, however, judge how much internal damage the slugs had done along the way. By then, Ben had regained consciousness, and both he and Hannah wanted to know how we had known to be there.

Since we had a few minutes before help arrived, I told them some more of the story.

"As you both know now, right about here, back in 1920, three men robbed a train: Jon Hope – also known as Oliver Risk, Slim Peters, - also known as Colonel James Peters, and Slim's brother Jess.

"I'm told that the robbery went like clockwork, and that the three men robbed the train of $44,000 in only 45 minutes. Of the loot, $20,000 was in banknotes, and the other $24,000 was in gold coins.

"That was a lot of money back in 1920. In today's dollars, the paper currency would be worth about $66,000, with inflation. But the gold is worth a lot more now that it was back then, about $220,000."

At this point there was an audible gasp from Ben, but if he had a question, he was pre-empted by Hannah.

"Who cares about a robbery that happened nearly sixty years ago?" she asked.

"Actually quite a few people care, really," I continued. "In the first place, very little of the loot was ever recovered. You already know that some of the paper money had been spent in the southern U.S., and in little bits at a time. It's assumed that more of the paper currency was spent in other places, also in relatively small amounts at a time, that was never identified with the train robbery.

"The gold, on the other hand, was in the form of Dominion of Canada, George V, $5 and $10 coins issued between 1912 and 1914. Now, the interesting thing about the coins is that partway through 1914, Canada was preparing for the First World War and it stopped selling gold coins and began hoarding gold instead. That made the coins fairly rare by 1920, and anyone trying to sell more than a couple of them would look suspicious to the banks, who were on the alert. If any of the rare coins had shown up, they would certainly have been noticed.

"Now, we had no way of knowing for sure, but the Force always thought that the gold was hidden away somewhere: either where it was originally hidden or somewhere else. Jon Hope had ambushed his partners in the tunnel there, presumably under the cover of the darkness, and left them for dead. He also left their horses behind, probably thinking they'd be too conspicuous, but that left him with a problem: his horse couldn't carry him plus all the loot. It was thought that he hid the gold, which would have weighed 90 pounds, and took the currency, which would have weighed only 40 pounds, and which would have been easier to spend if he was careful. And it seems he was very careful.

"Of course, as we found out today, the gold was buried just up there, in the side of this mountain, and if it was all here it will be in 9 or 10 bags, in those two packs that the Colonel took.

"Anyway, getting back to 'who cares,' the Bank of Canada would still like to have the gold recovered, which is reason number one, and they want the thieves caught and tried, which is reason number two."

"Isn't there some kind of statute of limitations on that sort of thing?" asked Ben.

"You may be thinking of American law. In Canada, there is no statute of limitations under the Criminal Code for indictable offenses like major theft, and don't forget murder.

"So, reason number three is murder. Now Jon, that is, Oliver here, might not realize this, being American, but we in Canada take murder very seriously and – just like they say in all the Mountie novels and movies – once we're on a murderer's trail we never give up. There's been an outstanding warrant for the arrest of Jonathan Hope for 58 years now."

"I thought you said you were checking out security on the train for a VIP trip that was coming up," said Hannah.

"That's actually quite true. Jack and Silver and I have been diligently making notes on security strengths and weaknesses along this whole trip. But we've had another mission too. To explain that,

I need to go back to your father's story.

"As you heard, your father recovered from the ambush and was caught and hospitalized. After spending a year recovering from two near-fatal gunshot wounds, he was tried, convicted and sentenced to 15 years. It was a high sentence because the gang had used dynamite in the robbery, and he was the dynamite expert. He was released in 1928, after having served seven years of his sentence, but he immediately joined another gang, got caught robbing a bank – using dynamite again – and people in the bank got shot, so his next sentence was higher: 20 years. He served eight years of that sentence, then was then paroled in 1938."

This started Hannah sobbing again, although she kept listening, despite the imagery of having placed both hands over her ears.

"After his second release from jail, your father seemed to finally decide to 'go straight' and you probably know most of the rest. Using his proper first name, James, he enlisted in the army - specializing in demolitions, of course. He served in the Second World War from 1939 to 1945, got married in 1946, then served in the Korean war from 1950 to 1953, and retired in 1954. From there, he went into a civilian demolition business. You, Hannah, were born in 1960, and your father retired again in 1968.

"Your father knew that Jon had gotten away, and it seems he tried hard to find him, although we don't know whether that was a long-term thing or a recent thing. Meanwhile my boss, or at least my boss and his predecessors, had been trying to locate Jonathan Hope as well. With the help of the FBI, they finally located him, but only recently.

"It turns out that Jonathan Hope used some or all of the stolen money to became Oliver Risk and establish himself as a businessman in the southern United States. He married late in life, but his wife died young, leaving him to raise their only son, Nathan Risk. He seems to have done fairly well in business, but his business began to falter in the 1970s, leaving it near bankruptcy earlier this year. On top of that, the FBI discovered that he had been siphoning-off company funds for many years. So, this year, finding himself in desperate need of money again, and possibly worried that his company's bankruptcy would expose his fraudulent activities, he decided to come back for the gold.... Any comment Mr. Hope?"

"No," was all he said.

"Well, Nathan had been studying at a divinity college in Halifax. When he graduated and was ordained in the church, he phoned and told Nathan that he wanted to celebrate by driving up to Canada and taking him on a father-son trip across Canada. He 'always wanted to see Canada,' he said to him…"

"How the hell did you know that?" spoke up Jon (Oliver), in spite of himself.

"The FBI were already investigating you for fraud, and they had a wiretap on your phone. They passed on the details to us, so we knew which train you were going to take and when. Unfortunately, this was all very recent, so we didn't have a current photo of you yet, only a description. That's why, I didn't know who you were until we met as we boarded the train in Halifax. There was only one elderly man travelling with a newly minted minister."

"How did Dad find him then?" Hannah asked.

"We don't know. It's possible he maintained some underworld connections. We think he probably used private detectives but, in any case, he finally located Jon in the U.S., going under the name Oliver Risk. Figuring that Oliver would probably return for the gold one day, he managed to meet Oliver's executive secretary, and arranged to secretly pay him to pass on advance details every time Jon (Oliver) went on a trip. It paid off this year, when Oliver asked his secretary to book a trip to Canada. The secretary promptly informed the Colonel of the trip and its itinerary, which is how he ended up on this same train ride across Canada. We know all this, because the FBI had wiretaps on the secretary's office phone and also his personal phone."

"How did you find out?" asked Jon (Oliver).

"Once my boss knew that Jon Hope had become Oliver Risk, and had learned that both Oliver and the Colonel had tickets booked on the same train trip across Canada, he was sure he knew where that would lead, so he sent Jack, Silver, and I to keep an eye on you."

"Were you watching me then, too?" asked Ben.

"No, not at first. But it didn't take long to discover that, while the Colonel was keeping an eye on the Risks, you were always there watching the Risks too. At first, I didn't know whether you were also watching the Colonel, or maybe just watching a pretty girl in the form of Hannah here, but over time it seemed like you were watching all of them. I asked my boss to try to find out who you were, but it took them a long time. It was only late in the evening, when we were in Edmonton, that I received a message saying that our people had made a connection between you and your father, and between him and the train robbery. That gave us a possible reason for your interest.

"Then there were the break-ins. I was pretty sure that they were the work of the same person but in different disguises. The VIA Rail people found the nun's habit you threw out the window, because it got caught on a projection from the Park Dome Car and was noticed hanging there at the next station stop. That was just bad luck. Your only real mistake was dropping the VIA Rail Tie when we were stopped in Winnipeg.

"I kept both of them, and later asked Silver to track the scent. I expected him to lead me to Hannah, whom I suspected might be in league with her father.

"I was wrong, though. Silver led me to your room, Ben. Your disguises were perfect, but they couldn't fool Silver because he tracks people by their scent. Of course, by that time, you'd abruptly left the train."

"How did you know that the gold would be hidden here?" asked Hannah.

"We didn't, but we knew where the train robbery occurred, and the most likely places to hide the loot would have been near one or the other of the entrances to this train tunnel. That's why there's a police car at the other end: we had two people at each entrance."

"So this was all about revenge?" asked Hannah, looking disdainfully at Ben."

"Revenge and money. My father knew all about money. Those packs hold 1,200 $10 coins and 2,400 $5 coins. They are all George V coins, minted between 1912 and 1914. In today's dollars, the gold value is over $217,000, but they're also very rare, so they're worth more than that to collectors. Anyone possessing them would be instantly wealthy, and for life."

"And Dad's a fanatical coin collector!" breathed Hannah.

"Really? Well, then he knows their value too."

At this point, we were interrupted by the sound of a wailing siren and the approach of the highway patrol car that had been stationed at the far end of the tunnel. Given that we were an hour's drive from the nearest small hospital, which was in Jasper, the two constables agreed to take Oliver and Ben by police car, rather than wait for an ambulance to come all the way out and back, which would have doubled the time needed to get the two injured people there. Hannah wanted to go with them, which was just as well since Jack, Silver, and I had other things to do.

Oliver Risk (Jon Hope) was arrested on the outstanding warrant, with more charges to follow. We had to arrest Ben too, of course, for threatening people with a restricted weapon, the theft of the truck, and the three earlier break-ins on the train. Oliver was placed in the back of the unmarked station wagon, lying on some folded blankets with his hands cuffed in front of him, then one constable sat with a handcuffed Ben in the back seat, while the other constable drove, with Hannah in the front passenger seat.

Tossing the magnetic-base, flashing-red light up on the roof, and with the siren actuated, they took off for Jasper leaving us with the marked-highway-patrol car and a promise to radio in for extra backup for us.

Then it was time for us to track down the Colonel and see if we could prevent Nathan from any further foolishness.

11 THE CHASE IS ON

Before trading cars, Jack and I had pulled all of our luggage out of the station-wagon to make room for Oliver (Jon) to be put in the back. As we put them in the trunk of the highway patrol car, I pulled a daypack out of one of my bags and stuffed in a light jacket, flashlight, and two large bottles of water that I'd purchased in Jasper. The Jasper Detachment had also loaned us two handheld, Motorola MX300, VHF police radios. They were bulky and heavy, weighing nearly a kilogram (2 pounds), I was going to need one, so I attached the radio to the front of one shoulder strap and the microphone to the other strap.

When I was ready, we looked across the stream and tracks to the mountainside.

"Which way do you think" asked Jack.

"I think the Colonel's crazy to run at all... but if it was me, I'd look for game trails and try to make my way west, following the train tunnel from above, then drop down to the highway at the other end. He may have been up there watching the others being taken away, in which case he'll probably guess that it's just you, Silver, and I that he has to worry about for the next hour until we get backup. He's probably too smart to come back for his rental car, so maybe he'll pretend to be a tourist backpacker and try hitch-hiking?"

"Sounds reasonable. How about if you go see if Silver can find their scent and I'll wait here? Once you're sure which way they're

439

going, radio me and I'll pace you from the highway with the car."

"Agreed. Come Silver. Time to hunt."

"*Grruph!*"

After Silver and I had re-crossed the highway, stream, and railroad tracks, I checked my watch as we looked up at the mountain beside and above the railway tunnel: it was just about 1 pm and the Colonel had about an hour's lead on us.

Spotting Nathan's bible on the ground, I picked it up. Crouching down on one knee, I took Silver's face in my hands and looked deeply into his eyes. "Remember Nathan, Silver? Track Nathan…" and I gave him the bible to sniff. Although the leather cover/map had been cut away, it was still wrapped around the bible and should have been a good source of scent, I thought, given that it was seldom out of Nathan's hands.

Silver gave it several careful sniffs, then went into tracking mode. Without hesitation went over to the exact spot where Nathan had been tending to his father, sniffed around as if to confirm his scent, then went straight to where the rucksack had originally been lying and did the same thing. Seemingly satisfied, he straightened up, gave me a very direct look, and then started making his way to the side of the tunnel and the faint path leading up the mountainside.

Following him, I had no trouble making out footprints here and there, where there were patches of dirt and shale dust in among the rock and scrub brush.

I don't know whether Silver was following the main overlay of scents at first, or whether he could pick out Nathan's scent from the others, but he led me quite directly to the spot where Oliver and Nathan had been digging. There was a rough hole, perhaps two to three feet below grade, several piles of rubble that had been excavated, and the collapsible shovel that I had watched Oliver take from his backpack some two hours earlier. Off to one side, and barely visible among the rock, brush, and grasses were two axes and a prybar, all very old-looking, with the metal parts heavily rusted and pitted. *The original tools from the train robbery*, I thought.

At this point, Silver circled the whole area, then zig-zagged slightly east and mostly uphill. Just when I'd become convinced that the trail was going to actually lead us to the east, we encountered a game trail that crossed our path. It looked well and recently used, with noticeable piles of fresh-looking mule deer droppings, and it seemed to extend for some distance to our right and to our left, before disappearing into the trees in each direction. Silver went a few feet to the right, sniffing carefully, then returned and went a few feet to the left, sniffing again, then lifted his head and looked meaningfully to the back to the right, as if to say "*That way.*"

"Find Nathan," was all I said, and he resumed tracking, heading west and into the trees. As I followed, I turned my radio on and said: "Jack? 10-23[15], heading west."

"10-4[16] Alex. I'll parallel you and advance 150 metres. Let me know if he changes direction."

"OK, I'm going 10-7[17]." That was to let him know that I'd be switching off the radio for a while. I wasn't worried about eavesdroppers, being on a restricted tactical frequency in the middle of the mountains, but I didn't want any radio messages or static to alert the Colonel to my presence if we got close to them.

Motioning for Silver to continue, we advanced.

I didn't actually expect to catch either the Colonel or Nathan on the trail. Although the Colonel would have had his own problems trying to find his way along while being weighted down with heavy packs, Silver and I could only advance at a pace that allowed Silver to keep following the scent. This took a lot of zig-zagging, sweeping in arcs, and occasionally going in complete circles so that, although he never lost the scent for long, we only advanced slowly.

After about 30 minutes of tracking, Silver found several places of interest in a small clearing. Looking closely at the spots that most attracted Silver's attention, I could see scuff marks on the ground, and places where the grasses and low brush had been compressed, by the rucksack.

Turning my radio back on, I called Jack. "Our 10-20[18] is about half a mile, and I think we've found where they stopped for a break. I can see where he put the packs when he set them down."

"10-4," crackled Jack's voice over the radio. "Heading?"

"West, as we thought. Unless something changes, let's meet at the west end of the tunnel."

"10-4. Out."

As Silver continued tracking, there came a time when I heard a train horn give a succession of short blasts.

It took us another 30 minutes to reach a junction with a trail branch heading down the slope. It was 2 pm. Silver very decisively followed the downward branch and we quickly emerged from the forest. Looking down, I could see that we had passed the tunnel opening by about 30 metres (30 yards). Directly below us, railroad tracks emerged from the tunnel. Close beside the track was the same rippling stream as before but, at this end of the tunnel, the highway was much further away from the stream. Pulled over onto the shoulder of the highway was the highway patrol car. Of the Colonel and Nathan, there was no sign.

I motioned for Silver to continue tracking and he led directly along the new path, which took us through several switch-backs as it led down the steep slope, then we were finally on clear, level ground again. At this point Silver angled vaguely westward and almost diagonally toward the tracks. When we reached the tracks, he carefully sniffed his way along one side of the track, then retraced his steps, still sniffing, then he sat down on his haunches – right beside the track- and stared at me.

The scent trail had ended.

Suddenly, I knew what they had done

Damn!

***

The Colonel had climbed the mountain slope as quickly as he could, found the spot where Oliver and Nathan had dug up the gold, and paused to look down. From this vantage point he could see Oliver (Jon), Hannah, and the two police constables, but there was no sign of Nathan.

Damn! *he thought.*

Anger and frustration dominated his emotions, but he was still too much the soldier to let emotion get in the way of strategy and tactics. He would have to keep going and make the assumption that Nathan was in pursuit. Taking one of the smaller caliber guns from his pocket, he fired a shot, vaguely aiming back the way he had come. He had no expectation of hitting Nathan, if he was really back there, just of forcing him to take cover and then proceed slowly, if at all.

There was a slight indication of a trail leading up the mountain slope. He followed it until it intersected a game trail, one branch of which led west. That was the direction he wanted to go. Eventually, he came to a small clearing and decided to take a brief rest. Placing the rucksack on the ground, he also shed the external-frame backpack he'd been wearing.

Allowing himself only a few minutes, he took up the backpack and looked hard at the rucksack. In order to make better time, he decided to abandon the latter. Continuing west, he forced himself to a faster pace.

Before long, there was a junction with a well-worn trail leading down the slope. Heading down, he soon emerged from the forest. There, down and to his right, was a set of railroad tracks and the western end of the tunnel. Next to the tracks was the stream and, further away, was the highway.

Being careful not to trip, he moved down the slope as quickly as possible then jogged to the tracks. He was about to cross the tracks, thinking to ford the stream and try hitchhiking on the highway when he heard a soft mechanical sound echoing from the tunnel.

Smiling grimly, he changed direction and jogged along the side of the tracks, moving away from the tunnel and towards the place where the clearing turned to dense forest.

The sounds of the approaching train were getting louder, and he could just see some light from the locomotive's powerful headlights being reflected along one tunnel wall as he dug out from his pocket a red bandanna.

What a day to have picked a red one, *he thought as he began waving it over his head, just as the locomotive emerged from the tunnel.*

***

The engineer and conductor of the freight train were seated, one on each side, looking ahead as the locomotive emerged from the train tunnel. As a result, they both spotted the figure waving a red flag at the same time.

'Something wrong up ahead," said the conductor.

Nodding, the engineer jerked the cord for the train's horn so it gave a succession of short blasts – a warning that the train was preparing to stop.

***

As soon as he heard the horn blasts from the train, the Colonel stopped waving his bandanna and tucked it back into his pocket. Crouched low, he ran to the forest fringe and hid behind the nearest trees.

***

As the engineer, carefully applied the brakes, looking ahead for any kind of obstruction, the conductor, on whose side the figure had been waving at them was looking hard at the trees.

"Bastard," he muttered. "Looks like some tourist backpacker thought it would be fun to give us a scare. As soon as you hit the whistle, he stopped waving and ran into the forest. Better go slow for a while, just in case, eh?"

The engineer just nodded. Being less sure that it was just a prank, she was intent on slowing the train while straining her eyes looking for any signs of trouble ahead.

The locomotive was soon deep into the forest so even had they looked back, neither the conductor nor the engineer would have seen the backpack-wearing figure jump onto one of the passing freight cars.

***

Nathan, for his part, had reacted instinctively to give chase to the Colonel. As a result, he hadn't given any thought to what he hoped to accomplish nor how to go about it.

Like the Colonel before him, he started to climb the mountain slope and hadn't gone far before a shot rang out and he actually heard the slug hit a nearby tree. That caused him to halt, and even freeze in place, before deciding to carry on. He had learned caution from this, however, so he moved as stealthily as he could. He too came across the spot where Oliver and Nathan had dug up the gold, and passed on. Sparing only a brief glance down to where Oliver (Jon), Hannah, and the two police constables were, he kept moving.

There was a slight trail, with the occasional footprint, leading up the mountain slope, which he followed. When it intersected the game trail, he didn't know whether to head east or west, but took a chance on right and was soon rewarded with more footprints. Further confirmation came *when he reached the clearing at which the Colonel had stopped for his brief rest.*

The rucksack was lying right there.

Although he didn't need a rest, he did stop to inspect the rucksack. Hefting it, experimentally, he then set it back down. Feels like about forty pounds, *he thought. Looking inside, he found four leather bags, each weighing about 10 pounds. The bags were full of gold coins!*

He must have had to lighten the load. So he dropped it! *Thought Nathan.*

Encouraged, he shouldered the rucksack and continued his stealthy pursuit. When he came to the junction with the trail leading down-slope, he stopped to look around. There was the train tunnel, there the tracks, the stream, and the highway, and... THERE!.... *there was the Colonel! He was standing by the tracks near the edge of the forest... but what was he doing?*

Being careful not to move, Nathan watched and listened. Then, he heard the echoing sound of the train in the tunnel. Looking back toward the forest, he saw the Colonel waving some kind of red flag over his head. Shortly after that he heard the train give a series of short blasts.

Nathan's eyes widened. You clever bastard! *he thought, as he realized what the Colonel was going to do next.*

Sure enough, as the train began to slow, and the three locomotives at its head disappeared into the trees, the Colonel popped out of the trees and ran up to the tracks watching for his chance to jump up on a passing car.

Nathan wasn't watching any longer though, he was running as fast as he could down the mountain trail.

He too was going to catch that train!

***

I had Silver search along each side of the tracks, all the way to the edge of the forest, but after each pass he just looked up at me as if to say: "*Gone.*"

Jack was standing beside the highway patrol car as Silver and I made our way up to join him.

"The train," I said. It was both a statement and a question.

Jack nodded. "A freight train. I saw the back end of it vanish into the forest before I could even get out of the car."

"Did you see anything else"

He shrugged. "Only the signal light shining back at me from the rear of the caboose," he said, ruefully. "How about you?"

"Silver followed the trail just fine. I didn't see either of them, or hear any more shots, but I heard three short toots from the train's horn.... The scent trail ended right beside the tracks, so I think one of them must have flagged the train down and hopped on."

"Both of them, you think?"

"I suppose so, otherwise Silver would have scented something."

"Hmmm. They would both have been on the other side of the train, so I wouldn't have seen them either way. What do you want to do?"

"That's the question, isn't it? Do we have a highway map?"

We did. Jack found one in the glove compartment of the police car. He spread it out on the hood of the car so we could look at it together."

"Looks like the tracks go to Kamloops," said Jack.

"Kamloops..."

"What are you thinking Alex?"

"I'm trying to put myself in the Colonel's shoes. I'm wondering what he would be thinking. If it were me, I think I'd try doubling back to see if I could convince Hannah to get away with me. But, in his case, I think he's too angry with her for that. I think he's more likely to try to make his escape, set himself up somewhere we can't find him, and maybe try to reconnect with Hannah sometime later."

"In that case," reasoned Jack, thoughtfully, "if it were me, I'd ride the freight all the way to Kamloops, then..."

"That's the question, isn't it?... Do you still have a train schedule with you? I left mine behind."

He did. Retrieving it from his carry-on bag, he spread it out on the hood of the car, on top of the map."

The next two VIA Rail 'on request' stops were Blue River and Clearwater, then a scheduled stop at Kamloops, the latter scheduled for 6:30 pm.

"It's nearly 2:30 now..." I started, then stopped.

"What?"

"He could just get off anywhere, but his style is strategy, remember? And he has time to think now that he's hiding on the train. What if he got off at Kamloops then re-boarded the VIA train?"

"If he still has his ticket, they'd have to let him back on," Jack reasoned. "And it's too soon to have rebooked his roomette, so he'd even get his room back."

"Yes, and if he rode all the way to Vancouver, he'd have a bigger city to hide out in. One with stores for coin collectors! If he only sold one coin at one store, he'd get over $200 for it. Sell another one at another store and he'd get another $200, all without raising any suspicions... and if the stores re-sold them to collectors, the Bank of Canada would never hear about it, and neither would we."

"Makes sense to me, but they'll never believe it," said Jack.

"Who?"

"Our bosses. They'll never believe it. They'll want to do ground searches everywhere that freight train stops or even slows down, and especially in every town or city along the way."

"My boss would believe it..." I reflected. "It's the way he thinks too – the way he'd do it himself. But I agree with you that others will see it differently. Tell you what. Let's radio it all in, tell them we're pursuing a lead in Kamloops, and ask them to pass it all along to Bob in Ottawa. That way, he'll know where we're headed and he or someone else can decide what else they want done."

"Is there time?"

"Let's see." We consulted the VIA Rail schedule again. "If it was on schedule, the VIA train would have passed through here around 11, but we were two hours behind at Jasper, so they probably passed through here about 1. The next two 'on request' stops are Blue River and Clearwater, then a scheduled stop at Kamloops at 6:30 pm. Let's call it 8:30 if they're still running two hours late."

"In that case, the freight train was about an hour behind them. The freight train gets priority over the passenger train so, somewhere up ahead, I bet the VIA train has to pull onto a side track and let the freight train pass it. If that takes half an hour, then the VIA train should get into Kamloops around 9 pm."

"And the Colonel could be there waiting for it!" finished Jack.

"Yes, and maybe with Nathan right behind him. I wish I knew

what was going on in that boy's head!"

"You talked to him more than I did. What do you think?"

"I don't know. Could be that he wants to strike back at the Colonel for shooting his father, could be his way of trying to help Hannah. He seems so innocent sometimes. Maybe he's a bit of a Boy Scout trying to catch the bad guy."

"Let's hope not. He could catch a bullet," said Jack, darkly, then shook himself. "Let's see what we can do." Drawing his finger along the map he counted off the distances. "Looks like a little over 220 km to Clearwater, then another 125 km to Kamloops. The speed limit's 90 km/hr in the parks, then slower in the towns but higher on the highway outside the parks. Let's say four hours overall. We'll have to stop for gas along the way, but we can grab take-out food to eat as we go. Even with lights and siren all the way, we're probably still looking at four and a half hours."

I looked at my watch. "It's 4 o'clock now. If we're lucky, we can make the Kamloops railway station by, say 8:30 – it's going to be close!"

"Let's do it!" said Jack. "You've been doing all the work for the past hour, let me drive the first shift while you rest, and then we can switch when we stop for gas or food, OK?"

"OK!"

Once we were settled in, with Jack driving the highway patrol car, we hit the first snag in our plan. I couldn't reach a radio room in any detachment, ahead of us or behind us. I only had to look around to determine why. Unlike low frequency ham radios, which could bounce a signal off the ionosphere and practically 'skip ahead' great distances, our very-high-frequency, VHF, radios required line-of sight. Deep down in valleys and surrounded on all side by towering mountains, we weren't going to be able to reach a detachment radio room until we got clear of the mountains.

"We're not going to be able to call this in until we get clear of these mountains, they're blocking the signal." I looked again at the highway map. There was no RCMP Detachment in Blue River, but there was one in Clearwater. We'd have to wait until we could get a signal through to them. Even so, it would take some time for them to relay the information to Jasper – which probably wouldn't be anything beyond informative – and to my boss Bob in Ottawa. It would be late evening in Ottawa by then. Even if it was decided to initiate a ground search, I doubted that anything would begin until the next morning.

"I think we're on our own again," I said to Jack, having summarized my thoughts.

Jack, as always, took it in stride. "Oh well, at least Jasper will know we didn't steal their highway patrol car," he joked. "You know, this is the fourth assignment I've been asked to help you out on, and I've been enjoying it. I'm still not cut out for the cloak-and-dagger stuff you always seem to get into, but they're exciting sometimes. I think they're growing on me."

"I'm glad Jack, because I'd have died several times over by now if you hadn't been around when I've gotten into trouble."

"All part of the job," he grinned, but I could tell he was pleased.

I had a lot more time to think, as we raced along the highway, but there were so many unknowns that I'm not sure that it did me any good.

Laurie Schramm

12 THE TIPPING POINT

Colonel James Peters (Ret'd.) had a lot of time to think as he sat at the end of an older-style grain car. His somewhat random choice had been a fortunate one as the inward sloping end-wall of the car created a small space at the end where he could sit, directly above the rearmost wheels.

He now regretted his stubborn insistence on taking the gold and running, especially since it had led to his arguing with and abandoning his daughter Hannah. Sixty years of obsessing on Jon's betrayal and being cheated out of his share of the robbery loot had just been too much to overcome, he thought. But, decades of military life had taught him that there was no point dwelling on what was past. You just had to pick yourself up and keep moving.

But moving where? That was the question now.

He had the gold. Fine. The police would be searching the Mount Robson area by now, probably with roadblocks along the highway, and they'd be organizing searches of the nearby towns. He should be able to hide out in Vancouver long enough to sell a few of the coins, spreading them out among several coin dealers, then he could buy an old car for cash and drive somewhere. If he drove south, he could look for a quiet place to cross the border into Washington State, giving him two more big cities in which to sell off more of the coins: Seattle and Spokane.

He had no worries for Hannah's safety. Fortunately, he hadn't told her of his real reasons for wanting to take the train trip and, although she now knew about some of his disreputable past, her standing up to

451

him as she did would ensure that there were no legal repercussions for her to deal with.

Later, he could get a message to her so she'd know that he was safe... and to tell her that he was proud of her.

If only her mother could have seen the way she stood up to me, *he thought with fierce pride,* she'd have been proud too.

He'd have to watch out for the kid, Nathan, though. He hadn't had time to watch carefully, but if Nathan had been able to jump the train as well, then he would have to deal with that one last loose end...

***

The Reverend Nathan Risk was also thinking, as he sat at the end of another grain car closer to the end of the train. He was also reliving his previous hour's actions and questioning the wisdom of his impulsive decision to set off in pursuit of the Colonel.

Why had he done it? To get back at the Colonel for shooting his father? Some kind of vigilante-justice instinct? He wasn't sure.

It probably didn't even impress Hannah, *he thought.*

So, now what? Like the Colonel, he assumed that the police would be busy helping the injured and searching the highways and local towns.

They'd never guess he jumped the freight train, *he thought,* so maybe it's up to me now...

***

The freight train accelerated as it continued its journey south and it didn't even slow as it passed through Blue River. Continuing south and then turning west, it passed through Clearwater, again without stopping. It did slow down a bit, however, as it passed through Clearwater, and both the Colonel and Nathan were treated to the unbelievable sight of passing The Canadian *which stood on a separate set of tracks just outside of the town. Both of them immediately realized what that meant. This was the same VIA Rail train they had left in Alberta, the Colonel in Hinton, and Nathan and his father in Jasper. Clearly,* The Canadian *was running late and had been pulled over to let the higher-priority freight train pass it by.*

At this time, a well-placed observer, had there been one, would have seen the Colonel and Nathan do the exact same things: each pulled a timetable from his pocket and, consulting the schedule, realized that the next stop was Kamloops. Since the VIA Rail train was running late, it would be a quick stop — just enough to deal with embarking and disembarking passengers. That could be an advantage.

Who would ever expect me to get back on the original train? *thought the Colonel.*

Who would ever expect the Colonel to get back on the original train? *thought Nathan. Then he set his jaw firmly.* I guess I'll have to see this thing through...

***

The freight train finally slowed to a crawl as it entered the rail yards that precede the station on the north side of Kamloops. As it advanced, the Colonel looked around and, seeing no one around, jumped down from the grain car on which he had been riding. He checked his watch. It was 8:35 pm. So far, so good.

Hoping to look like a backpacking European tourist that had taken a wrong turn, he hitched his backpack up a little high on his back and walked purposefully towards the station. No one accosted him, he entered the station and made his way to the first available washroom to clean himself up as best he could. After that, he took a seat in the station's coffee shop and settled himself to wait.

It wasn't long.

***

The Colonel hadn't been accosted when he jumped off the freight train, but he had been seen. Nathan had been watching closely from his position close to the rear of the train, and had a clear view of the Colonel's exit. He also correctly interpreted the Colonel's attempt to look like a backpacking tourist and judged that he was unlikely to risk attracting suspicion by furtively looking around. Indeed, the Colonel adopted a very purposeful-looking stride in the direction of the station.

Nevertheless, Nathan took the precaution of jumping from his grain car to the opposite side of the track and walking along that side while the rest of the train continued past him, all the while blocking the view of anyone on the station side. When the caboose passed him by, its red rear signal light glowing in the evening twilight, he crossed the tracks.

Not wanting to risk confronting the Colonel in the station, where there might be a large number of innocent passengers and staff, he chose a bench in the station's parking lot from which he could wait for The Canadian *and also make sure that the Colonel didn't double-back and come out of the station.*

He didn't have long to wait, either.

***

At 8:50 pm, running two hours behind schedule, The Canadian *rolled into the station. Passengers wanting to stroll around the station were warned that the stop would be brief, so they should remain on the platform. Any passengers that chose to do so might have been mildly surprised to see that the front few cars had been disconnected from the train and were being pulled away to make room for an additional car, which was shunted in and then everything re-connected.*

As soon as the few disembarking passengers had left the platform area, the Colonel went up to board the train.

François was surprised to see him, but this was far from the first time that a passenger had disembarked from a train and then wanted to re-embark from a different station. He was a bit miffed not to have been informed in advance, of course, but then this has hardly the first time that had happened either. As a long-serving railway man, he had learned to take such things in stride and, as the Colonel's ticket was still valid and his roomette had not yet been re-assigned, he had no real reason for complaint. It was only after the Colonel had boarded that it occurred to him to wonder what had become of the Colonel's daughter, Hannah.

Whereas experience and instinct had enabled François to maintain a nonchalant professional demeanor in the face of the Colonel's surprise appearance, it took concentrated effort on his part to deal with the surprise, a few minutes later, of seeing Nathan show up seeking to board and re-establish himself in his former roomette. François was up to the challenge, however, and soon Nathan was on the train and heading for his sleeping car.

It belatedly occurred to him, that each of these latest two passengers had acquired a backpack somewhere along the way, and that neither of them seemed to have any of their former checked or carry-on baggage with them.

There's a connection there, he thought to himself, and it occurred to him to wonder whether these strange goings-on were connected to the two Mounties that had been on the train.

Shaking himself from these distracting thoughts, he checked his pocket watch, took a careful look along the train in each direction to ensure that all was in order, and called out "All Aboard!"

He was just about to pick up the small step stool that was always placed by the steps leading up to the train, when he sighted two more passengers – and a large dog that looked like a wolf – waving frantically to him from the far edge of the platform.

"Sacré bleu!"

***

Jack had turned off the siren a few blocks away from the train station, so as not to give any advance warning of our arrival. Pulling into a spot near the entrance we got out, grabbed our carry-on bags and ran through the station. We stopped on the platform side just in time to hear the "All Aboard" call. Not wanting to be easily seen, we stayed where we were and began waving at François, trying to attract his attention.

When he spotted us, his jaw dropped in surprise, but he was quick enough to stride over to us.

"François, did the Colonel get back on the train?" I asked.

"*Mai oui*, but just a moment ago, and the young reverend too!"

"OK, at least we haven't lost them. Are they in their same roomettes as before?"

"Yes, the same, why?"

"Because they're on the far side of the train. If they're hiding in their roomettes, they won't see us…"

"You wish to board, yes? The train leaves now."

"Yes, we do, but is there somewhere else we can stay? Somewhere they won't see us. We can explain later."

François thought for the briefest moment, then his eyes widened. He clearly had an idea. *"D'accord!"* was all he said. "Come with me."

François led us toward the front of the train, and up and into the car directly behind the baggage car that had been broken into. The door of this new car was locked and, when we went in, we found ourselves in a very unusual kind of car.

"We added a second baggage car, eh? so we have a locking door again. It was the easiest way – the car was just sitting here and we didn't have to move any of the baggage but it's secure again.

"You can see that this car is different. It's an older style that has a conductor's office and crew quarters. Since it's an extra car, the crew quarters are empty. There are berths and a communal washroom, but it's not fancy, eh? Not what you're used to."

It was a question.

"This will be great. Thank you!" I assured him.

He seemed pleased. "I can have food delivered here from the dining car. I'll bring you a menu…" Then, he seemed to remember his other responsibilities. "Will there be trouble?"

"I think so. There's been fighting, shooting even, and the Colonel is trying to escape, and he's armed. We would have asked you to stop the train while we wait for help, but he'd know if there was an unusual delay – especially after hearing you call the 'All Aboard' – and we don't want him to panic and try taking hostages."

As I was speaking, my words were underscored by the slight lurch of the train getting underway.

"Yes, I see," he said, seeming to notice for the first time the rifle that Jack had brought with him. "What do you want me to do?"

I looked at Jack for confirmation. When we were able to get radio reception, we had provided a summary of the situation to the radio room duty officer in the Kamloops Detachment and asked that it be relayed on to my boss in Ottawa. We hadn't stated any plans beyond following the Colonel and saying that we would advise further if and when we located him.

Jack just nodded.

I took a breath. "OK. What's the next stop?"

"Ashcroft, but only if someone requests it. That's four hours away"

"Four hours, so we have some time. What we'd like you to do is to come up with some excuse to quietly ask people to leave the sleeping car that has the Colonel's roomette. They can go anywhere else: the dining car, dome cars, coffee shop, anywhere but their sleeping car. Can you do that?"

He thought for a moment. "I can throw the breakers for that car. It will put them on low-power emergency lighting in the corridor, but the power will be off in the roomettes... I can tell them that we need to have someone check each room to find out where the short-circuit is... I'll offer them free drinks in the bar and the dining room while we're checking."

"That should work. Let us know when everyone's out, OK?"

"I will. It will take a while, though, and the emergency power is a battery system, so it only lasts so long, eh?"

There wasn't much for us to do but sit and wait while François set about his task. Silver was happy with the opportunity to get a bowl of water and a chance to rest. For my part, still feeling the effects of having spent over an hour tramping around the mountain when we were tracking the Colonel, I took the opportunity to get a shower and a clean shirt.

It took an hour, but François finally reappeared bearing news, a thermos of coffee, and a plate of sandwiches.

"Thought you might be hungry, eh?" he said, setting them down on a table in the vacant conductor's office.

"How did you make out with the passengers?" asked Jack.

"Not bad. I decided to move everyone forward, so I cleared out the Park Car too. Most people took it well enough and are in the dining room or the bar enjoying their free drinks. The reverend didn't want to go, but I finally persuaded him out. He insisted on taking his backpack with him, though, and he insisted in sitting in the Park Car. He's the only one there. I think he's watching to see if the Colonel emerges, eh?"

"And the Colonel?" I asked.

"A bit of a tense moment there..." he said, scratching his chin. "Heard me talking to the other passengers, eh? And stuck his head out the door to see what was up... I told him what I told everyone else, but in his case, I made it sound like more of a request than an order. I was sure he'd refuse.

"And he did refuse. He said he was staying put, wasn't

interested in any damn-fool nonsense, didn't need any light, and didn't want to be disturbed. I put on my meek, conciliatory face, didn't argue with him, apologized for the disturbance, and left, eh?"

I breathed a sigh of relief. "Well done, François, that was quick thinking, and brilliant to think of clearing out the Park Car as well. But we've got to get Nathan out of there too. Would you please try one more time and try any excuse you can think of to get him up here with us?"

He agreed, and went off to try again.

A few minutes later, François was back with Nathan in tow.

"Hi Nathan," I said. "We need to talk."

I motioned for him to sit down with us.

"How did you know?" he asked.

"That you were here? We were tracking you and the Colonel. Silver lost the scent at the tracks on the far side of the train tunnel. We figured that both of you must have jumped the freight train. There are others looking for you elsewhere, by now, but we thought the Colonel might be brazen enough to get back on the original train, and it seemed like wherever he was, you might not be too far behind. We got on just as the train was pulling out of the station, and the conductor confirmed that both of you were on the train. So, here we all are." I paused for a moment.

"I assume you've been following him with some idea of getting even for shooting your father?"

"I guess so…" said Nathan, looking and sounding more confused than his usual innocent-appearing self. "At first, I just reacted, then I was angry. I had a lot of time to cool down on the freight train though. After that, it was mostly that I didn't want him to get away with it all. I was thinking that maybe I could slip off at the next station and call the police, you know?"

I looked at him. "Well, Constable McDonald and I are here now. Why don't you give me the gun, Nathan?"

He started. "You know about that?"

"I saw the cut-out in your bible."

"That was dad's idea. He's the one that gave me the bible. He was always worried about me, and how my work would put me into contact with all kinds of people. He insisted that I should have some way to defend myself if I got into a bad situation. Growing up in the States everyone has a gun, so I didn't think much about it before now."

"Well, handguns are restricted weapons in Canada. You shouldn't have brought it into the country, and you shouldn't have it with you now. At least you haven't shot or threatened anyone with it... or have you?"

"No," he said. "I'm not even sure that I could, you know."

"I know... why don't you give it to me, and let us deal with the Colonel? OK?"

Nathan hesitated for a moment, but I could see the decision in his eyes even before he grimaced, reached into a pocket and brought it out.

"Here. Careful, it's loaded."

It was an older-style Remington derringer, double barreled, and loaded in both barrels. "Thank you," I said, unloading it and placing the gun and both rounds into a pocket. "I have a very similar one that I carry myself sometimes."

I smiled.

"What's in the pack, Nathan?"

He surprised me by giving me one of his familiar, brilliant, wide-eyed, innocent-looking smiles. "Gold!" he said. "It's full of gold coins. I found it on the trail. I figured that the Colonel dropped it so he could make better time, and I just kind of picked it up and brought it along... I guess you'd better take that too," he said, rather reluctantly. "It doesn't actually belong to me, you know."

I smiled again. "Well done, Nathan. You stay here and hang on to it for me for now, OK? I'm pretty sure there'll be a reward for this."

"What are you going to do?"

"I'm going to go talk to the Colonel. See if I can get him to come to his senses and give himself up. If that doesn't work, we'll keep him bottled up in his roomette until we get to Vancouver and we can get some help."

"But he's dangerous!"

"Thank you, Nathan... but so am I."

Most of the passengers had become used to seeing Jack, Silver, and I in uniform on the train, so I don't think we caused a stir as we made our way to the back of the train although the rifle Jack was carrying should have looked conspicuous to anyone paying attention. Mostly, people seemed to be chatting away quite animatedly. The normal social barriers to conversing with strangers had come down for those used to seeing each other day after day on the train, and the free drinks had probably helped lower them even further.

When we reached the last sleeper car, Jack stationed himself at the front, while Silver and I passed along, aiming for the Colonel's roomette. When I reached it, I turned to make sure Jack was watching and ready, which he was.

I raised a hand and pointed towards the Colonel's roomette. Jack nodded and patted the rifle he was holding. No one would be getting between him and the rest of the train and, thanks to François' quick thinking, there was no one near or behind us.

I didn't like having Silver with me, but I thought I might need him. I compromised by stationing Silver at the end of the sleeping car with instructions to 'guard.'

I decided, and hoped, that we'd isolated the Colonel about as well as we possibly could under the circumstances.

Now for the hard part, I thought.

Stepping up to the door of the Colonel's roomette, I took up a position well to the side – in case he became rattled enough to try shooting through the door – reached over and knocked.

"Go away!" was the response.

"Colonel, it's Constable Houston of the RCMP."

Silence.

"Remember me… Alex?"

Silence… then, "I remember you."

"Can we just talk for a moment. Please?"

"I'm not coming out, and you're not coming in… You know I'm armed right?"

"I know. No one's going to rush you, and you can stay where you are. I just want to talk, OK?"

"How did you find me?"

"You remember my partner, Silver? He's a tracking dog. We

followed your trail around the mountain, then Silver lost the scent where the tracks came out at the other end of the tunnel. It seemed likely that you jumped the freight train that went through – that must have seemed like a gift from heaven to you. There was no way to tell what you'd do after that, but with all your experience in military strategy, it occurred to me that you might figure that no one would ever expect you to get back on the same VIA train you'd been on before. There'll be police looking everywhere else for you by now, but I decided to take a chance and see if you were here."

"And now here we are... Is Hannah OK?"

"She's fine. She went back to Jasper with two other Constables, Oliver Risk, and Ben Shaw. I think she's feeling pretty mixed-up and upset about you though."

"I've really messed things up this time. I'm not sorry I shot Jon, or Oliver as you know him, he had it – and worse – coming to him. That fool Ben should have had more sense too. I never wanted to hurt Hannah, though. She probably despises me now."

"I kind of doubt that, you know. I talked to her a bit on the train, and I think she has a pretty good head on her shoulders. She handled herself pretty well when all the violence broke out too. I can't pretend that she'll approve of some of the things you've done but, in my job, I have to study people pretty closely and I was paying attention to her reactions after the train had passed and you were gone..."

"And?"

"And she was focused on two things: helping us look after the two injured people and worrying about what was going to happen to you."

There was a long moan from inside the roomette.

"Colonel?"

"What?" The belligerence was gone now; replaced by despair.

"From what I know of your background you've done some bad things and also some good things in your life, some heroic things even. Maybe when Hannah looks back on it all the two will kind of cancel out. You know?"

Silence... then, another groan. At least he was hesitating.

"Look, you got your revenge on your former partner. You're not going to be able to keep the loot, but the others aren't going to get it either…. Why not call it a day before your legacy gets tarnished any further? You'll be able to talk to Hannah when things calm down… explain your side of the story."

"She'll never listen."

"Never is a very long time. Give the girl some credit. I know she still cares for you. I think she'll give you a chance."

More silence…

"Why not leave the guns behind and come out? Give her a chance, and a chance for a future."

"All right…" he said, after another long pause. "Give me a minute, will you?"

"Sure Colonel. Take your time… I'll be here when you're ready."

Looking back toward Jack, I raised a hand with my palm facing him, to let him know that we were at a critical juncture.

Seconds went by… then minutes…

"Colonel?… Are you OK in there? Do you need anything?"

Blam! The almost deafening blast of a .45 calibre gun going off in a confined space.

Damn! I thought. "Get François and a key!" I yelled to Jack, who turned and ran towards the front of the train, looking for the conductor.

But there's no rush now, I thought, looking at the still-closed roomette door as I leaned back against the outer wall of the corridor.

The Colonel would never be in a hurry again.

13 LOOSE ENDS

When François came and unlocked the roomette door for us, we found the Colonel half-lying with his back upright in one corner of the lower berth, beside the window. His .45 pistol had fallen to one side, and he looked peaceful, if you disregarded the layer of blood on both walls behind his head. When we went to check his pulse there was none, then his body crumpled forward revealing horror.

Part of the back of his head was partly gone, shot away as the slug he'd fired through the palate - the inner roof of his mouth - travelled up, through his brain, and then out again through the upper-rear of his skull.

I still get nightmares sometimes.

It could have been worse. We found all three guns. He could have tried to shoot his way out, and or take hostages.

Even after we evacuated the rail car, he could easily have shot me, then Silver, then who knows? Jack would have taken him down, of course, but Nathan could have been another casualty had he been brave – but foolish – enough to try to rush in.

But none of that happened because, in the end, although he was too stubborn to surrender, in his own way he tried to avoid more bloodshed for Hannah's sake. I know that, because he'd spent those last few minutes, when I was waiting for him to make his final decision, writing a last note. He was holding it in his other hand when we found him.

Laurie Schramm

My Dear Hannah, it began.

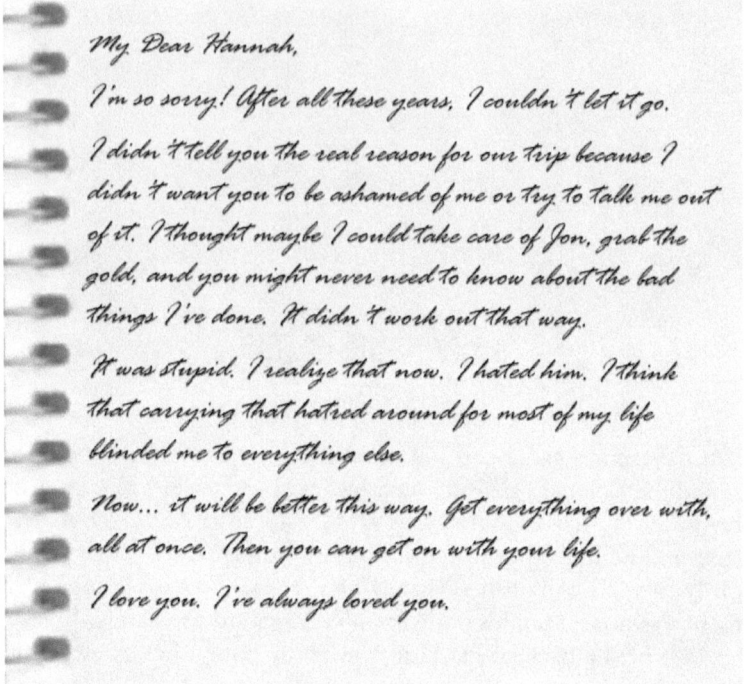

> My Dear Hannah,
>
> I'm so sorry! After all these years, I couldn't let it go.
>
> I didn't tell you the real reason for our trip because I didn't want you to be ashamed of me or try to talk me out of it. I thought maybe I could take care of Jon, grab the gold, and you might never need to know about the bad things I've done. It didn't work out that way.
>
> It was stupid. I realize that now. I hated him. I think that carrying that hatred around for most of my life blinded me to everything else.
>
> Now… it will be better this way. Get everything over with, all at once. Then you can get on with your life.
>
> I love you. I've always loved you.

With François' agreement, we moved the Colonel's shrouded body up to the mostly empty baggage car. We did the same with the confiscated guns and the two packs of the gold, so we could keep them secure. François then locked the Colonel's roomette from the outside, with his special key.

During all the action, the train had passed through Ashcroft, without stopping, and we were travelling through the Fraser Canyon towards Hell's Gate when François and Nathan found Jack and I collecting our thoughts and letting the adrenaline fade away, as we sat at a table in the crew quarters of the baggage car. The views from the train were spectacular, I suppose, particularly those from high up on the train bridge when we crossed the Fraser River, but we were no longer in the mood for it.

"Everything is settling down back there," said François. "Except for the young reverend here, so I thought I should bring him up here. OK?"

464

"Thank you, François, you're been great.... Hello Nathan, how are you feeling?"

"Oh, me? I'm OK. I guess I'm worrying about Hannah and my father..." He stopped abruptly, as he belatedly realized the order in which those words had come out.

"We understand. You know, you took some crazy risks, and really should have stayed put with your father and the others, but I'd like to say thank you. It was your scent that Silver was familiar with, and I think it was you that he was able to follow over to the mountain to the other side of the tunnel. If you hadn't followed the Colonel, we might never have been able to discover how he got away. If he'd made it to Vancouver, we might never have found him again either."

"We might never have found the gold you recovered either," added Jack. "Someone might have come across it years from now, or not. Even if it was later found, it might not have been by someone honest enough to turn it in."

"What will happen to me now?" asked Nathan.

"I think your future's pretty much up to you. Don't you?"

"You mean you're not going to arrest me?"

I glanced at Jack. "Well, you brought a restricted weapon into the country but you turned it in, you found some of the stolen gold and you turned that in, and you helped us catch a fleeing criminal that was armed and dangerous. I have to report it all to my boss, but I really don't think you have anything to worry about."

"That's a relief," he sighed. "I guess I'll have to try to find a way to get back to Jasper then."

"Yes, I think there are at least two people there that will be glad to see you."

"Will dad be arrested?"

"It's already happened. There was still a warrant out for his arrest from the original robbery. Whether the Crown Prosecutor decides to take it to trial though is another matter. Given your father's age, and the recovery of the gold, and everything else that's happened, I really don't know. I think that both your dad and Hannah are going to need your support right now though."

The train's next stop was at Boston Bar, and this time I asked François if I could use the radio phone in his office. Even though it was after midnight our time, so after 3 am Ottawa time, I dialed my boss' home number, woke him up, and gave him the whole story.

After that, there was nothing to do but try to get some sleep. We arrived in Vancouver on schedule, at 8 am, the next day.

Day 7
June 1, 1978

Colleagues from the Vancouver Sub-Division and the coroner's office met us at the station in Vancouver, and we signed over the backpacks full of gold and the confiscated handguns.

My boss had cleared us to go back to Jasper so we could type-up and file our reports related to Oliver Risk (Jon Hope) and Ben Shaw. Knowing that Nathan would be desperate to get to Jasper as well, we offered him a ride with us.

After a bit of work, we found a taxi driver with a van that was willing to take us from Vancouver to Kamloops, which took 4 hours. From there we retrieved the Highway Patrol Car we had left at the train station and drove ourselves the rest of the way to Jasper. It took five hours to drive nonstop to Jasper, as we had to obey the speed limit this time. It was pretty surreal driving through Red Pass, as we drove through Mount Robson Provincial Park, but otherwise a pleasant trip.

Ben Shaw had been treated and released from hospital, but was being held in the cells at the local detachment pending a court appearance the next day. Oliver Risk (Jon Hope) was still in hospital, undergoing observation to make sure his wounds had not been dangerously infected. Although it was late when we finally reached the hospital, they allowed us to see him in his room.

Nodding to the constable that was keeping an eye on Oliver's room, we let Nathan go in first. His cautious entry became jubilant, though, when he discovered that his father was awake and looking well, and that Hannah had been there keeping him company.

On the other hand, we had to tell Hannah what had happened to her father. Such duty is part of a police officer's life, and always a horrible duty to have to discharge. Fortunately, Nathan was there to help comfort her, so at least she wasn't alone with her grief.

Saying our goodbyes, we eventually left the three of them there and went to find motel rooms for the night.

"At least some good came out of all of this," I said, as we drove away.

"You mean Nathan and Hannah finding each other? You're a romantic, Alex," said Jack.

That sounded like the proverbial pot calling the kettle black, but all I said was: "Guilty as charged, Jack."

Days 8 and 9
June 2-3, 1978

We spent most of the next morning at the Jasper Detachment. Having returned the Highway Patrol Car, it took a while to type out our reports. I had brought the Colonel's handwritten note to Hannah with me and, although the original had to be kept as evidence for a while, I was able to make a photocopy to give to her.

The detachment had a vehicle that needed to be returned to their divisional headquarters in Edmonton, so they killed two birds with one stone by offering it to us so we could get there as well. After another visit to Hannah and the Risks, it took the rest of the day to reach Edmonton.

The next day, we flew out by commercial airline. We were on the same flight to Toronto, after which Jack changed to a plane for Halifax, while Silver and I took a flight to Ottawa.

Laurie Schramm

468

14 EPILOGUE

Days 10 and 11
June 4-5, 1978

A few things happened fairly quickly after that. Between the shooting in Red Pass, the subsequent chase and capture in the Fraser Canyon area and, of course, the whole story of the stolen gold, we caused a brief media sensation. There was even a feature article being written for *Macleans* magazine.

We'd unintentionally upset the Officer in Charge (i/c) of the Kamloops Detachment, who handled the media questions well enough and managed to take most of the credit. But I could tell from the TV footage my boss had videotaped, that there was some simmering resentment that the case had been resolved by Jack, Silver, and I, rather than his own officers.

I was still part of the Security Service at the time, and based in Ottawa, while Jack was posted to a detachment in small-town Nova Scotia at the time. As a result, some members of the media were able to find Jack and I when we were briefly back in Jasper, and the Kamloops people weren't able to completely manage the news. That the Officer i/c took it a step further and complained about me within the Force, I was about to find out!

June 4 was a Sunday, but my boss, Staff Sergeant Robert (Bob) G. Simpson, wanted me to run through the whole adventure from start to finish with him, which we did at his house.

Bob seemed well satisfied, once I'd finished my story.

"They put up wanted posters with a very good sketch of him at the time. The trainmen had heard his partner call him 'Jon,' but no one knew his full name, where he'd come form, or where he'd gone."

Bob said that the Force had always suspected that he'd gone to hide out in the southern U.S., because that's where some of the stolen money had turned up, but neither the Force nor the FBI had been able to find the source of stolen bills. It was only because the FBI was investigating Oliver Risk for fraud, nearly sixty years later, that it was discovered that Oliver Risk was actually Jonathan Hope. It had taken all that time to finally track him down.

Slim Peters, later the Colonel, they'd quietly watched for all those years and Bob told me the 'untold' story of how they discovered when the Colonel had identified American Businessman Oliver Risk as the former Jon Hope. The original investigators in the Force had suspected the involvement of an 'inside man' with the gang, and even that it might be Ben's father, Robert Shaw, but the Colonel had refused to identify him and there was no hard evidence against him so nothing more could be done at the time.

When he discovered Oliver Risk's planned trip to Canada, Bob was immediately suspicious, and when he learned about the coincidence of the Risk's itinerary and that of the Peters, he was sure that 'the game was afoot' and decided to send me to keep an eye on them all, backed up by Jack.

"Kind of a long shot, though, after all those years. Don't you think?" I asked.

Bob smiled his 'Cheshire Cat' smile, that I'd gotten to know so well. "Nothing ventured, nothing gained, but I had a feeling..."

When Bob has 'a feeling,' criminals should cringe, I thought.

My world seemed to turn on its head the next morning, when Silver and I walked into the office, however.

"Come on!" said Bob as soon as he saw me, "The Assistant Commissioner wants us in his office ASAP."

Uh-oh, I thought.

"What's up?" I asked, hastening to keep up as he strode down the hallway to Assistant Commissioner George MacLeod's office.

"I think we're about to find out," he said, as we were waved directly into the Assistant Commissioner's office.

It had been Assistant Commissioner George MacLeod that had talked me into leaving the Metropolitan Toronto Police Force for the RCMP four years earlier, and when I had graduated from training, he had been the one to make sure I was assigned to remote, small-town policing at first. When Silver had come into my life, he had been the one to see the potential for the first woman graduate and a dog, that looked nothing like a conventional police dog, to work undercover. When he had assumed command of the RCMP Security Service, he had asked me to transfer there as well, which is how I'd come to work for Bob for previous three years. In all that time, I'd developed an immense respect for the Assistant Commissioner but, in all honesty, I was still a bit afraid of him too.

Perhaps part of it was the 'parade-ground' voice that he seemed to be able to switch on or off at will, and which – at full volume – rivaled even that of the Depot Division Sergeant-Major from my training days.

He used it now.

"HOUSTON!"

At times like this, one doesn't get asked to take a chair and relax. One comes to rigid attention a few paces from the front of the desk, calls out "Yes, Sir!" and waits for the axe to fall. I tried not to flinch physically, but I sure did mentally.

"I have a telex here from the Officer i/c Kamloops Detachment, demanding your head."

Uh-oh, now I thought I knew what was coming.

Waving the telex form in the air, the Assistant Commissioner continued: "He says that, with a known criminal and gunman on the train you jumped on yourself and played some kind of damn-fool game to apprehend him that put countless passengers and crew at risk, when what you should have done is stopped the train and waited for the ERT[19] to arrive and deal with it."

He paused and looked at me, but it was a rhetorical pause, and I knew better than to say anything, yet.

"Now then," he said, ratcheting the volume down just a little. "What have you got to say for yourself? No, Staff-Sergeant, don't bother trying to jump to her defense - I want to hear it first-hand."

"Well Sir, he's correct, as far as it goes... but it would have taken at least two hours to call-up the nearest ERT team and get them all the way from Kelowna to Kamloops. Long before that, the Colonel would have realized that he'd been found and he was too good a military strategist to have just sat there waiting while we had reinforcements on the way. I was afraid that he would judge that his best bet was to brazen it out, take hostages even, and bulldoze his way out, even if it meant ultimately going down in a blaze of glory. As a military veteran of two wars, and well-armed as he was, he had the experience for it. I was also afraid that he'd have had time to realize that he'd already made a few mistakes and that desperation might be clouding his judgement.

"On the other hand, I judged that if we could let the train proceed and evacuate the entire train car, that I might be able to talk him down - get him to think about the legacy he'd be leaving his daughter – and that maybe he'd come around to being sensible and surrendering. At that point, I was only risking my own life – and that of Silver's."

It was only then that I realized that, instead of lying by my side, which would have been normal protocol, Silver had been sitting on his haunches, looking directly at the Assistant Commissioner, and listening. He was acting as if he were on trial too!

The Assistant Commissioner just sat there for a moment, looking at me without speaking, but I avoided flinching again, held his gaze, and shut up. I'd said my piece. Finally, he shifted in his chair and shifted into a very quiet tone.

"So, you didn't know about the dynamite then?"
"No Sir."
"But you suspected it, didn't you?"
I shifted my shoulders just a little bit and tried to put some life into my voice. "Yes, I suspected it... he'd worked with explosives his whole life. I thought it might have seemed natural for him to have brought along a stick or two of dynamite. That's partly why I didn't try to send Silver away. He's trained to detect explosives, and I hoped that if the Colonel had dynamite with him and reached for it, that Silver might give me an extra second or two of warning."
"And you would have too, wouldn't you?" said the Commissioner, looking directly at Silver for the first time.
"*Grruph!*" answered Silver. He might not know all the words, but Silver had an uncanny ability to follow the rough sense of my

conversations, as the Assistant Commissioner well knew.

He smiled then, the Assistant Commissioner, and his penetrating gaze came back to me as he rose from his chair, tore the telex form in half and dropped it into his wastepaper basket. "That will about do for the Officer i/c's complaints," he said.

"Sir?"

"Look. Bob filled me in, and I've already had a chat with a few other people. You were on the spot. You knew the circumstances and the psychology. You assessed the risks. You came up with a plan, and you, your colleagues, and the VIA Rail conductor, carried it off. Too bad the Colonel decided to end it all, but no one else got hurt. Perhaps it's all for the best. I don't really give a damn about the recovered gold, but let's call that icing on the cake. The important thing is that... You. Did Well!" and he actually, very seriously, saluted me!

Before I could think of anything to say, he went on.

"Do you remember our first meeting back in 1974, when my friend, your Captain, on the Metro Toronto force recommended you, and I asked you to join us instead?"

"Yes, Sir."

"Well, I have to go to Toronto now and meet with him in person for two reasons. One: to tell him that he did us a big favour, because you're the best thing that has happened to the Force in many years – and if either of you ever tells anyone what I just said I'll have your spurs[20]. Understand?"

"Yes Sir," Bob and I both said, in perfect unison.

"The second reason I'm going to Toronto – and I want you to come with me - is because I want to see the look in your old Captain's eyes when he sees your Corporal's stripes."

At that he reached over to his desk and picked up a shiny new pair of gold laced corporal's stripes, the formal kind that go on a red serge, and held them out. "Bob, I think you should be the one to present these."

"Yes, Sir!" said Bob for the second time.

As he did so, my mind started functioning again. "But Jack was part of it all too, and I only have four years' service," I said.

"Yes, Constable McDonald did a good job on this assignment.

He'll get a Commissioner's Commendation for it. As for the years' service, it's the quality of the service not the time, and we gave you credit for your time on the Metro Toronto police force. There's lots of precedent for that. But, at the end of the day, it was up to the Commissioner. It was actually his idea, although I completely agree with him, and I'm certainly not going to tell you that the Commissioner said "Promote her! And for God's sake keep her away from office jobs. Put her back out in the field where she belongs!"

Jack did get his commendation, and was both surprised and well pleased with it.

Bob and I, together, wrote an official letter to VIA Rail Canada, commending François for his assistance through the railway parts of the case, and I heard from him later that he received a nice pat on the back from the company in consequence.

A few days later, Silver and I drove to Toronto for the Colonel's funeral. We were mostly there to support Hannah. Funerals are for the living, I've always felt. But we also wanted to pay our respects to the part of the Colonel that had been a highly decorated military veteran whose service had included two overseas wars.

It was a grey day, and I had time to reflect, as we stood there in the rain, me in my seldom-worn red serge, and Silver wearing his RCMP mini-shabrack[21] dog jacket with its yellow stripe around the border and the famous yellow 'MP' brand in the lower back corner on each side. He'd been awarded that for 'outstanding service while on duty' several years earlier[6].

I don't know how the balance of the Colonel's life should be added up, but he put his life on the line for our country many times over, and that seemed to outweigh the other things he'd done as I looked at his coffin, draped with the Canadian flag, with his many medals resting on top.

Sometime later, the Bank of Canada confirmed that – amazingly – every single gold coin was accounted for. All 1,200 of them, comprising 400 $10 coins and 800 $5 coins. Needless to say, the bank was happy to get the gold back, although they had long since written it off. They did pay Nathan a reward for his role in recovering some of the horde, and they even presented him with one of the original $10 coins as a souvenir. A very nice touch, I think.

Sometime after that, Silver and I attended another ceremony. We'd been invited to Nathan and Hannah's wedding. The last I heard he'd received his congregation assignment and they were living in an outport community on the Labrador coast. The Newfoundlanders and Labradorians would be amused by his wide-eyed innocence, and they would love his infectious smile, I thought.

I do love a happy ending.

Laurie Schramm

… Alex and Silver return in
An Intrepid Mountie.

Laurie Schramm

BOOK 7 ENDNOTES

1. This part of the story was inspired by a real-life train robbery on August 2, 1920, in which CPR train No. 63 was stopped in the Rocky Mountains and robbed by three men. *See* Robert Collins, "Canada's Last Great Train Robbery," *Maclean's Magazine*, 15 February 1958, https://archive.macleans.ca/article/1958/2/15/canadas-last-great-train-robbery.

2. Colt 'Model 1902' double-action revolvers were produced in 1902 for the U.S. Army. They were actually Model 1878 revolvers fitted with 6-inch barrels and chambered to fire .45 calibre rounds. The 'double-action' feature meant that the trigger was used to both cock and discharge the revolver.

3. The source for this quote is: Richard Saunders, *Poor Richard's Almanack*, 1735, published by Benjamin Franklin, Philadelphia. The almanac was actually written by Benjamin Franklin and was published for many years under the pseudonyms 'Poor Richard' and/or 'Richard Saunders.'

4. On December 6, 1917 two cargo ships collided in the Narrows, which connected the Bedford Basin with the rest of the Halifax Harbour. One of the ships, the *SS Mont-Blanc*, was carrying high explosives. When a fire that broke out on the *Mont-Blanc* reached the high explosives there was a massive

explosion that destroyed most of Halifax's North End, killing some 2,000 people and injuring approximately 9,000 more.

5. See *An Inconvenient Mountie* (ISBN: 978-1-9994940-0-1).
6. See *An Inconspicuous Mountie* (ISBN: 978-1-9994940-2-5).
7. See *An Indestructible Mountie* (ISBN: 978-1-9994940-4-9).
8. See *An Inseparable Mountie* (ISBN: 978-1-7772424-0-4).
9. At this point in time, it was still part of the RCMP Years later, in 1984, the Security Service was spun-out to create the present-day Canadian Security Intelligence Service (C.S.I.S.).
10. See *An International Mountie* (ISBN: 978-1-9994940-6-3).
11. See *An Indispensable Mountie* (ISBN: 978-1-7772424-2-8).
12. French for "don't worry about it," or "it's not worth fussing about," a shortened version of *"Il n'y a pas de quoi."*
13. See *An Inseparable Mountie* (ISBN: 978-1-7772424-0-4).
14. The Canadian National Railways Police (CN Police) carry out dedicated policing focused on CN infrastructure. Its members are granted the powers of police constables under Canada's *Railway Safety Act*.
15. "At Scene."
16. "Message Received."
17. "Temporarily Out of Service."
18. "Location."
19. The RCMP first established Emergency Response Teams (ERTs) in 1977, beginning with ERTs based in 31 locations across the country.
20. Meaning "I'll have you fired."
21. Dating back to at least the 18th century, the shabrack (or shabraque) was originally a large cloth placed over, or under, the saddles of European cavalry. At some point it became traditional to add a border of contrasting colour, and to display a crest or other symbol in the lower-rear corner. The RCMP shabrack, which is placed under the saddle, seems to have originated in 1887, at about the same time as "MP" was registered as the horse brand of the North West Mounted

Police. It is black with yellow trim and displays the MP brand, topped by the Royal Crown, displayed (also in yellow) in the lower-rear corner on each side.

Laurie Schramm

An Intrepid Mountie

Adventures of the First Woman Mountie. Book 8

LAURIE SCHRAMM

Laurie Schramm

DEDICATION

To Staff Sergeant Al Lund (RCMP, Ret.), author of *Mounties on the Cover* and probably the world's leading authority on Mountie fiction.

Laurie Schramm

BOOK 8 CONTENTS

	List of Characters	489
1	First Prelude: The Major	491
2	Second Prelude: The Activists	499
3	Another Protest Movement	507
4	The Actress	533
5	The Activists Continue	545
6	Calm Before the Storm	555
7	The Call of the North Atlantic	583
8	Confrontation	599
9	The Chase	609
10	Epilogue	629
	Book 8 Endnotes	637

Laurie Schramm

LIST OF CHARACTERS
(IN ORDER OF APPEARANCE)

- Major David Jones, U.S. Army Special Forces
- Michael (Mickey) Webb, Captain of the *MV Ocean Saviour*
- Corporal Alexandra (Alex) Houston, RCMP
- Silver, an Alaskan Malamute. Alex's friend and partner
- Arne Kristiansen, President, International Alliance for Animal Protection (IAAP)
- Staff Sergeant Robert (Bob) G. Simpson, RCMP
- Special Agent Vivian Rule, FBI
- Ginger Brandt, Canadian TV and film actress
- Sam Hynes, a sailor on the *MV Ocean Saviour*
- George O'Dell, tour boat operator, Bay Bulls, NF
- Jimmy O'Dell, George's son
- Lieutenant Commander Jon Stanford, Captain of the *CCGS John A. Macdonald.*
- Sergeant Al Donaldson, RCMP, St. Anthony Detachment
- Constable Nick Ross, RCMP, St. Anthony Detachment
- James MacDonald, a young fisherman from St. John's, NF

CIDG Strike Force Patch

1 FIRST PRELUDE: THE MAJOR

January 2, 1964
Buon Enao,
A small village in South Vietnam's Central Highlands.

Although it was the day after New Year's Day, it was still hot at 90°F. At least it was the dry season. As the sun settled into dusk, the relative silence of the jungle was broken by the sound of an approaching helicopter. The sound became louder and louder as it appeared over the top of the surrounding jungle. Visible now, it was an older model 'Huey.'

The first Hueys were properly named Bell UH-1 Iroquois, and had been used extensively by the American military in Vietnam since 1960. The nickname "Huey" came from the original designation as HU-1. Despite its redesignation (in 1962) to UH-1, the nickname had stuck. This particular Huey was fitted out as a 'Cobra,' that is, a gunship. Both of the large sliding doors were latched open and onto each side had been bolted a swivel-mount (called a pintle) bearing an M60 7.62mm machine gun. The U.S. Army had deployed thousands of Hueys during the Vietnam War, so they were a common sight.

This particular Huey bore the common U.S. Army olive drab, except for the nose, which was covered with a flat-black antiglare paint. The paint on this particular Huey was well faded, and it carried no identifying markings. It was, however, expected.

Close to the village of Buon Enao was a fortified camp of the U.S. Army Special Forces. It was laid out in the shape of a square, with a defensive berm around the entire circumference and twin .30 calibre machine guns placed at each corner and halfway along each side. Inside the camp were barracks and other buildings, most of them occupied by members of the Civilian Irregular Defense Group[1] (CIDG). Although the camp was commanded by a Vietnamese Special Forces Commander, it was a U.S. Special Forces Captain - the local military 'advisor' - that was waiting at a clearing just outside the fortified berm.

Having circled the camp and seen nothing of concern, the helicopter descended diagonally towards the clearing and landed. As the rotor blades slowed, the waiting captain could see that the machine gun positions at each door were unmanned, and that the Cobra carried only a single pilot. As the main rotor slowed to a lazy crawl, the pilot climbed down from the left-hand pilot's door and walked across the clearing. The pilot wore a green beret and was dressed in a U.S. Army Special Forces uniform that bore a major's golden oak leaves but no unit patches. "Captain?" he said, extending a hand when he was close enough.

"Yes. Major Jones, I presume." The two men shook hands. It was clear that Jones was not the pilot's real name.

"You have the Deer Guns?" asked the pilot.

"Right here," said the captain, pointing to three medium-size wooden crates. When they'd walked over, he lifted the lid from one of the crates. Inside were packed styrofoam boxes, each containing a small, clumsy-looking pistol, three cartridges, and a cartoon-picture sheet of instructions on how to load and fire the gun.

As both men knew, the Deer Guns were disposable CIA assassination pistols[2], designed to be provided to South Vietnamese guerrillas - such as the CIDG — for use against North Vietnamese soldiers. The idea was that they would kill the enemy soldiers, dispose of the pistol, and arm themselves with the victim's more powerful (and expensive) arms and other equipment.

"This is all of them?" asked the pilot.

"Yes, 150 of them were shipped here last year for field testing but by the time they arrived we were already providing the Yards[3] with much better weapons, so these were never used. This is all of them. Seems like a shame to destroy them all, but the directive from MACV[4] was very

clear...." He paused, then said "You know I'm going to need some kind of receipt, right?"

"No problem," said the pilot, taking a folded piece of paper from his pocket. The paper was actually a three-sheet form with carbon paper between each form. It had already been filled in for materiel disposal, specifying the type and quantity of pistols. Taking out a ballpoint pen, the pilot signed the form as Major Davy Jones, U.S. Army Special Forces.

"Davy Jones?" said the captain with a smirk.

"It's as good a name as any, and this form will cover your ass."

"Sounds good to me. Do you want one of the copies?"

The pilot snorted. "Not likely, I'd just have to burn it. If you'll give me a hand with these crates, I'll give you your reward."

It only took a few minutes to carry the three 60-pound crates to the helicopter and stow them at the rear of the cabin. Then the pilot opened the right-hand door and extracted three large bottles of French Brandy.

"Here you are. One bottle for each crate, as agreed."

"Thank you major," said the captain, cradling the bottles under one arm. "I assume you're not really going to destroy the guns?"

The pilot just looked at him for a moment; long enough for the captain to decide that he wasn't going to get an answer. But he did.

"I'll tell you this much. These guns will never be seen in Vietnam again."

CIA Deer Gun (1962-64)

May 3, 1970
Kent State University
Kent, Ohio, U.S.A.

A shadowy figure joined the hundreds of students and other protesters as they gathered for a second day of protests against the escalation of the Vietnam War.

Although the President had promised to end the war, in seeming contradiction, just two days earlier he had sent U.S. troops to invade Cambodia, from which North Vietnamese troops had been launching attacks on the South. The very next day, hundreds of students had gathered on the university's Commons to speak out against the war. With the onset of night, peaceful assembly and speeches had been marred by incidents of violence between protesters and police. The mayor's decision to close the city's bars infuriated additional people, and the size and spread of the crowd increased. Eventually, the police resorted to using tear gas to break up the crowds.

Now, on day two, a state of emergency had been declared and the Ohio National Guard was reportedly on its way. Nevertheless, hundreds of students and other protesters had once again descended on the university campus. As evening approached, tempers again frayed and skirmishes began to erupt. The shadowy figure had thick, long hair, wore aviator-style sunglasses, and was dressed to fit in with the crowd, with a tie-dyed t-shirt sporting a carved wooden peace symbol, faded jeans and dirty sneakers. As such, he bore little resemblance to the U.S. Special Forces persona that he had adopted while working in South Vietnam.

As he wove his way through the crowd his senses were alert to the emotions around him. He was searching for a cluster of people that might be angry enough to cause some real trouble.

Like all major U.S. campuses, Kent State had a Reserve Officers' Training Corps (ROTC) building, and it was there that he found what he was looking for. A large cluster of protesters near the building were yelling, screaming, and throwing rocks and beer bottles at the police. As he skirted around this cluster, he could see that the police, for their part, were preparing to respond with tear gas. The time is just about right, he thought.

Moving even further to one side, he was able to make his way around the crowd and around the building. Although the back doors were locked, he had no trouble using a knife to force open one of the large, multipaned ground-floor windows and enter the building. Being a Saturday evening, the interior of the building was deserted and he was able to quickly roam the hallways peering into each room until he found what he was looking for. One of the large rooms had clearly been dedicated to assembling and storing promotional pamphlets for the ROTC Program. Various pamphlets were piled on large work tables, along with portfolio covers into which they would be inserted, and in two corners of the room were piled boxes of heavyweight paper waiting to be printed. As luck would have it, this room had windows that faced out of the front of the building. Perfect, *he thought.*

Moving to one of the piles of boxes, he cut one open and began removing handfuls of paper, which he tore into strips and used to make a large pile. Then, striding to the nearest table he picked up one of the wooden chairs, raised it high over his head and brought it down with a crash onto the edge of the table. The table was strong, having been made of thick oak, whereas the chair was old enough that the dowels holding it together had long lost most of their integrity. The chair splintered into pieces. Gathering up the pieces, he used them to make a teepee-shape over his pile of shredded paper. From his back pocket he took a hip flask of the kind that was popularly used to carry bourbon. It was full, but not with bourbon. The flask contained 'white gas' camp fuel.

Emptying the entire flask onto the pile of shredded paper, he took out a box of wooden matches, lighted one and gently tossed it to the edge of the pile, then quickly stepped back. Almost instantaneously there was a loud "whoosh" sound and a blaze of intense flame. Without waiting for the wood to ignite, which would happen momentarily, he walked calmly back down the hallways, pausing only to step into the men's restroom, where he used soap, water, and paper towel to remove any fingerprints from the hip flask and then threw everything into the trash.

By the time he had exited the building and made his way around the edge of the crowd, which was still protesting in front of the building, he could see through two of the front windows a reddish glow that evidenced a growing fire.

He waited a few moments, for the glow to increase, then yelled out: "Look, someone's burning down the ROTC. Let's help them."

Almost immediately, the crowd surged and he could hear the crashing sounds of bottles and rocks being thrown through the ROTC Building's windows. This, of course, caused an inrush of fresh air that fanned the flames, which almost immediately engulfed much of the ground floor room in which the fire had been originally been set.

By the time the National Guard arrived, later that evening, the university's ROTC Building was fully ablaze, the police were again using tear gas in an attempt to break up the crowds but, undeterred, the cheering from hundreds of protesters drowned out even the sounds of the sirens from the approaching fire trucks.

By this time, the silent figure was long gone. As he calmly strode across the campus, he removed his peace sign and dropped it into a trash can, disposed of his sunglasses at another trash can, and then removed and discarded his wig just before leaving the campus altogether, for the moment.

Despite the presence of the National Guard and officers from several police forces, and notwithstanding the efforts of the university to ban further mass gatherings, several thousand people turned up at the

Commons the next morning. As the crowd gathered, the same shadowy figure from the previous day joined in. Had anyone looked closely, it would have been difficult to identify him as such, as he now wore a differently coloured and styled wig, John Lennon-style sunglasses, an open-neck Hawaiian-style shirt, and a necklace bearing a peace medallion.

As various people took turns making brief speeches through a megaphone, the Ohio National Guard attempted to halt the speeches. This was met with derision, anger, and rock throwing. After a brief interlude, the national guard attempted to disperse the crowd. This time, rock throwing was met with tear gas, which was ineffective due to wind. The guards next tried fixing bayonets on the rifles and advancing towards the crowd. This was somewhat effective in moving the crowd back, but as the crowd retreated the advancing guards, for some reason, took a slightly different route and found themselves blocked by a large fence. As the protesters kept moving around, the guards decide they had achieved their purpose in clearing the Commons and began to make their way back. As they did so, large groups of the protesters followed them, still throwing rocks and tear gas canisters.

With the protesters now advancing, and the guardsmen looking nervous, the figure in the Hawaiian shirt moved near the front of the crowd, took out a small pistol that had been tucked into his waistband, and fired at a sergeant, grazing the side of one leg[5]. In response, the sergeant began firing his pistol into the crowd, followed by nearly thirty other guardsmen who immediately shouldered and fired their rifles at the students.

By this time, the figure in the Hawaiian shirt had already faded to the back. Just before leaving the crowd he used his shirt to wipe any fingerprints off of the gun, then simply dropped it on the ground and walked out of the crowd and away. When he passed Taylor Hall, he turned left, walking between it and Prentice Hall. Between the two buildings, largely screened from most people's sight, he removed his wig, peace-medallion necklace, and sunglasses. Next, he did the same with his Hawaiian Shirt, revealing a simple but differently coloured t-shirt. The Hawaiian Shirt he carried crumpled up in one hand.

Emerging from between the two buildings and calmly striding across the campus, he dropped the necklace and sunglasses into a trash can, then the wig into another trash can. The Hawaiian Shirt, he discarded at yet another trash as he continued to walk back towards the Commons.

The man was satisfied with his performance. He had judged the timing perfectly and baited the national guard into firing indiscriminately into the crowd. There were bound to have been at least a few casualties. The point was to create an event that would horrify America and catalyze angry, possibly violent protests across the country.

He succeeded. The guards' bullets had struck 13 students, three of whom were shot in the back, and four of whom died. The shootings at Kent State led to protests and strikes at universities across the United States, not to mention a protest demonstration by a hundred thousand people in Washington, D.C., itself - fuelled by chants like "Four Dead in Ohio[6]" and "They Can't Kill Us All."

His masters' hopes of bringing an early end to the war, however, failed. Notwithstanding the massive and wide-ranging protests that were precipitated by the Kent State events, the war continued for several more years[7].

In the aftermath of the four days of demonstrations, the FBI discovered a small, single-shot pistol lying on the university grounds where the students had made their last stand. A few members of the FBI had heard rumours of such guns being made for the CIA, this was the first physical example they'd actually encountered.

It would not be the last....

2 SECOND PRELUDE: THE ACTIVISTS

"Before the turn of the century… riots were spontaneous and practically leaderless. They were not the offspring of sobering thought or calculating mind, but were the sudden outbursts of passion. The leaders of these mobs were characterized as the most angry and least discreet members of the mob. [Later], though, a change in the nature of the mob took place… [and] professional agitators were part and parcel of [these events][8]."

March, 1978
'The Front,'
100 miles southeast of Labrador

Captain Michael (Mickey) Webb stood on the bridge with his feet slightly spread out for stability. An experienced sailor, this was all he needed to do to maintain his balance, so he was easily able to use both hands to hold and focus the binoculars through which he was peering ahead in the dawn's first light.

The water is certainly choppy enough, *he thought, as the* MV Ocean Saviour *relentlessly pushed its way towards the icepack off the coast of Labrador. Although stable in the water it was not a gentle ride, particularly since the originally fitted external stabilizers had been removed. In fact, when the former marine meteorological and oceanographic research ship had been purchased by the Ocean Saviour Foundation, a number of ice-strengthening modifications had been made. To the pre-existing double hull, an ice belt had been added – a very thick layer of structurally supported steel at the lower part of the bow. This and the double hull were intended to provide a buffer in case of a collision with ice (or another ship).*

This was not to say that the ship was an icebreaker, but rather that it was capable of Arctic or Antarctic operations "where ice regimes permit," as the ship's certification papers read. This official language meant that it was fully capable of ramming its way through seasonal and even Second-Year Ice, but not the much heavier Multi-Year Ice. As it was, the modifications had cost upwards of a million dollars, not considering the original purchase price.

The ship itself was the flagship of the Ocean Saviour Foundation. Not that this designation meant a lot, considering that the rest of the 'fleet' consisted of small Zodiac™ boats, but it was a recognizable symbol of the society and its cause and its supporters hoped it would be the first of many such ships. The 500 gross-ton ship measured 184 ft (56 m) in length, was classed as a Research/Survey Vessel, carried a crew complement of up to 35 and was capable of 18 knots (33 km/h).

The Ocean Saviour travelled the world. Their most recent voyages had been to the waters between California and Hawaii, where they had harassed Russian whaling ships with such tactics[9] as using Zodiac[10] boats to prevent the whalers from firing their harpoon cannons, getting close enough to obtain graphic film recordings of the whale killings, especially those of undersized whales, and even boarding some whaling ships to distribute anti-whaling materials to the crews.

Now on the opposite side of the continent, their current mission was to interrupt the annual commercial seal hunt off Canada's East Coast. Such hunts occur in two main areas: one in 'the Gulf' meaning the southern Gulf of St. Lawrence (between Newfoundland and the Magdalen Islands), and the other in "the Front" meaning the area southeast of Labrador and northeast of Newfoundland. Right now, they were at the Front, where about half a million seals were reportedly gathered on 60 square miles (155 km²) of pack ice. Here, when the pack ice was available, the female harp seals had gathered to give birth and nurse their pups.

"There they are," said Captain Webb to the helmsman. "Come right, 10 degrees. Half ahead."

Before long, the seals were visible to the naked eye, and the captain called out "Slow ahead. Prepare to strike the ice."

That last command caused a flurry of action as the warning was broadcast throughout the entire ship and crew members scurried around making preparations.

Meanwhile, the slowing ship continued its approach.

After about five minutes of this, the captain decided they had more than enough momentum and ordered "Slow astern."

As the single propeller stopped and then began thrashing the water in reverse, the ship's bow struck and was driven well up onto a huge ice floe carrying a large number of seals. At this point, rope ladders were dropped from each side of the bow and a dozen young men and women scrambled down and onto the ice. Each of them had strapped to their back a portable sprayer of the type commonly used for spraying weeds in a lawn or garden. As they approached, the seals continued to lie on the ice, taking at best only a cursory interest in the newcomers.

Each protester slipped the sprayer off their back, placed the tank vertically on the ice, and pressurized it by hand-pumping. Grasping the spray wand with one hand, the other was used to twist its nozzle to a desired spray pattern. Then, using one hand to lift and carry the tank and the other hand to aim the spray, they stepped around the seals, searching out the 'whitecoats.' These were six- to twelve-day old harp seal pups, highly prized for their pure-white fur. Each whitecoat was sprayed with the contents of the tank: a nontoxic green dye. When the tank pressure fell off, the protester would stop, pump the pressure back up, and continue spraying.

The idea was that the brightly-coloured, indelible dye would eliminate the commercial value of the whitecoats' fur, thereby saving them from death at the hands of the sealers. Accompanying the protesters were several reporters and photographers from CBC, NBC, The New York Times, *and* Der Stern. *These were busily filming and photographing the event. It was because of the media that green dye had been chosen. In earlier protests, red dye had been used, but the resulting photographs didn't look sufficiently different from photographs of bloody pups being killed by the sealers, hence the change to green.*

Before long, the sounds of five short blasts from the ship's horn were heard. This is a nautical signal for danger, in this case meaning that the whaling ships – and probably police – were approaching. By this time many hundreds of pups had been sprayed, so everyone quite contentedly stopped what they were doing and made their way back to the ship. When everyone was back aboard, the captain ordered "Full astern," and the ship backed off the ice.

As the sealers continued to approach the ice pack, the Ocean Saviour *moved diagonally away and accelerated to full speed, heading for port. Captain Mickey Webb was well satisfied. They had saved hundreds of baby seals and, more importantly, should receive a wave of useful publicity when the media stories, photos, and documentary footage were broadcast by the media. One of the reporters had already been overheard planning to do a feature 'David and Goliath' type story on the youthful idealists taking on the grizzled, money-grubbing sealers. He didn't expect much in the way of retaliation. Beyond revoking permits, there was little that the Canadian government could do to them.*

A Saturday in March, 1978
Toronto, Ontario

The demonstration's beginning was orderly enough. Several hundred people, mostly women, had gathered in front of the two curved towers that housed City Hall – one of Toronto's most famous landmarks. The women were there to show their support for women's rights[11], and to hear from various speakers on the topic.

Some of the speeches were broad in nature. One speaker, for example, railed against the nonsensical idea that women could (and should) find fulfillment only through childrearing and homemaking. "It's 1978," the speaker called out. "We shouldn't have to still be having this conversation in this day and age."

Other speeches were more focused. One of the speakers related the plight of women workers at a Southern Ontario manufacturing plant, in which working conditions had become so bad that they had just staged a walkout in protest[12] and were still out on strike. The speaker listed the women's working conditions, which included operating dangerous equipment, virtually intolerable heat (in the summer), cold (in the winter), and harassment from male supervisors, all for less pay than male maintenance workers in the same plant, no benefits, and no job security.

As the speeches progressed, the size of the crowd grew. Mostly they were women but there was a sizeable number of men as well. They came from all kinds of backgrounds and circumstances. There were university and college students, of course, but also office workers, factory workers, part-time workers, and others.

Woven into the speeches were attempts to rally the people in attendance with calls to action. Meanwhile, volunteers circulated through the crowd handing out placards to carry and wave. The placards carried slogans like **"Yes It's Time**," and "**Equity – Now!**"

Following the speeches, one of the organizers explained that their main objective was to achieve gender equity in Ontario's Labour Laws, so it was provincial politicians that needed convincing. Accordingly, everyone was asked to march – in solidarity – to the Provincial Legislature and let their voices be heard.

By this time the crowd was sufficiently roused that they

503

marched *en masse*, chanting and waving their placards as they marched from City Hall to University Ave. Once there, they spilled out over the sidewalk to fill the entirety of the two northbound lanes leading to Queen's Park (about 25 minutes away).

As news of the march spread, more people joined and what had started as a few hundred became a few thousand. One of the later additions to the crowd was a grey-haired, rather matronly-appearing woman complete with granny-style glasses, full-length skirt, and even a shawl. Although one could have been forgiven for assuming her to be someone's grandmother, a careful observer would have noticed that she seemed remarkably nimble, and that she was able to navigate within the moving crowd with surprising ease.

When the demonstrators reached the south lawn of the Ontario Legislature, they stopped. This was their ultimate destination. It was also where they met a large police presence: the riot squad and 200 additional police officers.

At first, the crowd contented themselves with chanting and waving their placards. For a moment, there was a feeling of optimism as the Minister for Labour came out to address the crowd with a bullhorn. As the Minister spoke, it quickly became clear that he was unacquainted with the issues, spoke in condescending platitudes, and asked everyone to quietly go home where they belonged.

If he expected meek compliance, he had greatly underestimated the demonstrators who immediately became angry again, some of whom began lobbing rocks and beer cans over the front wall of riot shields and into the deeper layers of police officers. At this, some of the police officers visibly began preparations to return fire with tear gas canisters.

Near, but not quite at the front of the line of demonstrators the grey-haired woman judged that the time for escalation was just about right. Reaching into her oversized purse, which resembled a messenger bag in size and shape, she withdrew a glass beer-bottle that had a wick extending beyond a tightly fitted cork stopper. Using a powerful underhand throw, she unobtrusively lobbed it into the back ranks of the police cordon.

Even to the people standing near her, it appeared that she was simply throwing a beer bottle. This was because it wasn't an ordinary Molotov Cocktail, and she hadn't had to light the wick before throwing it. Inside the bottle, besides the fuel mixture of gasoline and motor oil, had been placed a certain amount of concentrated sulfuric acid. The wick, for its part, had been treated with a mixture of crystallized potassium chlorate and sugar. These features made the fuel self-igniting[13] once the bottle was broken.

Indeed, when the bottle smashed on the concrete roadway near the back of the police ranks, there was an immediate burst of purple-tinged flame followed by a cloud of smoke and burning droplets of fuel that spread out in all directions.

Several of the police officers already had their gas masks on and immediately sent four canisters of tear gas flying out and into the middle of the crowd of protesters.

By this time, the woman had already slithered to a new position near, but not quite at, the front of the demonstrators. Reaching into her purse, she withdrew another beer-bottle and again used an underhand throw to lob it into the ranks of the police cordon. When the bottle smashed on the ground, another burst of purple-tinged flame erupted spraying burning fuel in all directions, accompanied by another cloud of smoke. Here again, several nearby police officers responded by tossing tear gas canisters into the crowd which, predictably, triggered more rock and bottle throwing by the demonstrators.

The grey-haired woman, who had already taken up a third position near the front of the protestors reached once again into her bag and this time withdrew a small, ugly-looking pistol. Aiming from the hip and being careful to maintain a line-of-sight between the protestors that were immediately in front of her, she shot into the police ranks.

"They're shooting at us!" she yelled, in as a high-pitched voice as she could.

This caused some people to hurl more debris, including some of the landed tear gas canisters, into the police ranks, while others tried to stampede in virtually every direction only to find themselves running into other people.

The police incident commander had the presence of mind to yell "Hold Your Fire!" and almost all of the officers were able to hear and respond to this command – barely – although another volley of tear gas cannisters was fired into the crowd and a couple of officers discharged their firearms without really aiming at anything.

As confusion, smoke and tear gas swelled in both the police and demonstrators' ranks, the grey-haired woman nimbly slipped diagonally to the back and one side of the crowd. As soon as she reached the edge of the crowd, however, she slowed to a pace more befitting of an elderly woman, adopted a slightly hunched walking style, and calmly walked across the grounds and onto University Avenue heading south, back towards City Hall.

Somewhat before reaching Queen Street, she turned left and proceeded between the courthouse and Osgoode Hall, then past the fountain at Nathan Phillips Square, and finally entered the City Hall Branch of the Toronto Public Library. Strolling through the library she found an unoccupied, well-screened corner between the tall rows of shelving, and turned the now-empty purse inside out so that it now clearly appeared to be what it really was – a common messenger-style shoulder bag. Looking around to make sure she was unobserved, she removed her granny-style glasses, grey wig, and shawl, all of which went into the bag. The back of her floor-length dress had a continuous seam secured with Velcro strips, so that it was only the work of a moment to pull it open from each side and slip out of the sleeves. This too went into the bag.

Now fully revealed for what he really was, a middle-aged man, he walked to the men's washroom, where he washed off the makeup he had been wearing to smooth out his cheeks and chin.

Exiting the washroom, and library, he simply walked away. As he did so, it occurred to him to wonder whether the people that had hired him wanted the protesters to win or lose their struggle.... He shrugged his shoulders. It didn't matter.

A *Toronto Star* headline the next day read "Police Fire into Crowd of Mothers and Grandmothers."

3 ANOTHER PROTEST MOVEMENT

> "The better part of valour is discretion; in the which better part I have saved my life."
>
> Sir John Falstaff, In *Henry IV, Part One*, Act V, Scene 4, W. Shakespeare, 1597

July 9, 1978
Ottawa, Ontario

The street was crowded as I turned onto Wellington Street, heading east.

Very crowded for a Sunday! I thought.

The people were mostly young – in their twenties for the most part. There were also quite a few older teenagers, of the 16 to 19 sort and there were also some upper-middle aged people – in their 40s and 50s. It was the people that weren't there that caught my attention.

What I didn't see many of, were families with small children, people in their early teens, people in their thirties, or seniors – or tourists, even. This struck me as an interesting demographic mix, or absence if you like, for a summer afternoon in Ottawa, the nation's capital. There were some tourists about, of course, but their presence was dwarfed by the others.

The crowd seemed to be heading towards the Parliament

Buildings, whose grounds are on the north side of the street, so I stayed on the south side of the street so I could avoid being caught-up in the press of people. That was the other thing about the crowd, they weren't out for a casual afternoon stroll. They were heading somewhere specific, and were moving purposefully enough to suggest that they were on a schedule.

Sure enough, as the people passed the westernmost of the main parliament buildings – named, appropriately enough, the West Block - they turned onto the Parliament Grounds, and dispersed across the broad lawns that lie between the Centennial Flame, which was quite close to the street, and the main Parliament Building, Centre Block, the one with the tall Peace Tower at its front. Although the front lawns were huge, they were about half covered with people, as the crowd I had been paralleling joined an even larger crowd that was already there.

Looking back down the street behind me, there were many more people coming our way as well.

"This is going to be a big one!" I said to Silver, my friend and partner.

Perhaps I should back up a bit and tell you some of my story.

My name is Corporal Alexandra Houston. My friends call me Alex. Four years previously, in the summer of 1974, I'd been 24 years old, and feeling like my career was at a standstill. I'd studied chemistry at university and liked it, but not enough to pursue science as a career. I'd reset my sights on police work next and had joined the Metropolitan Toronto Police force (Metro). Although policing seemed like a better fit for me than science, my two years with Metro had mostly comprised routine administrative- and traffic duties. These assignments were important, and needed to be done by somebody, and done well. But for me, they didn't fit the Hollywood vision of policing that I had developed, and I hadn't found them to be very challenging.

They say you should be careful what you wish for.

At about the same time, Assistant Commissioner George MacLeod of the Royal Canadian Mounted Police (RCMP) had been looking for an existing police officer, with one of Canada's provincial or municipal police forces, for a special pilot project he had in mind. He wanted someone who wanted to accomplish things, someone eager and tenacious, someone chomping at the bit to be allowed to do some 'real' police work, and... someone female. My Captain had recommended the "biggest pain in the butt" in his Division - me.

When we first met, Assistant Commissioner MacLeod explained that the 'Force' wanted to begin engaging women as regular Members. As the RCMP training centre at 'Depot Division' was under his command, this task had been given to him and he wanted to first try a 'pilot test' with a woman. But, he emphasized, that pilot test had to succeed as it would pave the way for an entire first troop of policewomen that would follow. He had thought of using someone that had already qualified as a policewoman, and simply re-train them in the 'RCMP way.'

I had not been enthusiastic about doing basic training all over again, but I did. In the fall of 1974, I went through training at 'Depot' Division in Regina, dealt with the good and the bad issues that came with being the first woman to train there, and survived to become the first woman Mountie. I hadn't intended for it to happen, really. The opportunity just came and found me.

After training, or re-training if you like, I'd been posted to Radium City, a small town in very northern Saskatchewan that, in its early days, had been a great uranium mining centre. Although my new boss, Corporal Morrison, had told me that nothing interesting ever happened around there, he'd been wrong, and I'd had to rescue him from a mine collapse, run our entire detachment single-handed while he was confined to hospital for six weeks, get rescued by a strange dog from near-death, solve a mystery, and find and catch a murderer – all in only four months!

The dog was named Silver. Investigating a mysterious series of break-ins had led me to some unusual places, including several abandoned uranium mines. In one such mine I'd fallen through a trap and found myself hanging precariously over the sharp edge of a vertical mine shaft. Unable to get out and tiring fast, I was saved by the almost magical appearance of what I first took to be a wolf, which gave me quite a scare, but turned out to be Silver, an Alaskan Malamute. Silver somehow sensed that I was in danger, had decided to help, and with his assistance

I had been able to climb up and out of the raise. To make a long story short[14], while I'd continued to investigate the case, he had attached himself to me, was eventually given to me, and we'd been close friends ever since.

Sometime later I'd found myself in another surprise meeting with the same Assistant Commissioner MacLeod. Once again, he had something new in mind for me. By this time, he'd become head of the Force's Security Service[15] and, unsurprisingly, he had some new ideas he wanted to try out by way of some experimental pilot projects. One of them involved me.

That had taken me to Ottawa, where I joined the Security Service. My new boss, Staff Sergeant Robert (Bob) Simpson, introduced me to the shady worlds of spies, counter-espionage, anarchists, and terrorists.

As a prelude to my first real Security Service assignment, Silver and I were sent to Innisfail, Alberta, to be trained as a police dog and handler team[16]. "If that dog is going to go everywhere with you, then we should get him trained too," Assistant Commissioner MacLeod had announced, on one of his periodic visits. Both Bob and the Assistant Commissioner had been interested in the possibilities presented by the first female 'Mountie,' especially undercover possibilities, and they were also interested in, and seemingly amused by, the notion of me having Silver along as a kind of side-kick, since he looked absolutely nothing like a police dog. That officially brought Silver into the Mounties too, and that's how my best friend became my partner.

Since then, we've had more hair-raising adventures together[17-21] and our destinies have been firmly inter-twined.

***

Now, on this sunny Sunday afternoon Silver and I crossed the street at the next intersection. I was wearing civilian clothes, including an Ottawa Rough Riders[22] cap, baggy shorts, lightweight hiking boots, and a small daypack. I was trying to look like a slightly older version of the university student that I once was. A graduate student and/or teaching assistant, perhaps.

Since we weren't in uniform, Silver had to be on a leash - which he tolerated, but not before giving me some pointedly martyred looks from time to time.

Silver's Version

I don't mind the broad leather collar that Alex had made for me not long after we'd first met. I do not, however, like the leash, especially since Alex knows me well enough to know that I never stray far from her without good reason.

There are times, however, when she insists that it is a necessary custom and I trust her judgement, although I always make sure that she understands my feelings in the matter. To be fair, the leash isn't imposed very often.

As we crossed the busy street to where most of the people were gathering, my senses went from being pleasantly distracted to overloaded. There were so many people of different sizes, shapes and expressions, and even more scents.

Some of the people were carrying banners and signs. The signs that humans make are still something of a mystery to me. I have learned a few of their symbols, through experience and constant repetition, but certainly not many. I can understand quite a few words, including most of the things Alex says to me and some of the things that others say to her — if they speak slowly enough — but much of what other people say to each other is a mystery to me unless I can look into their eyes while they are speaking.

I don't know why eye contact is important, but it seems to have something to do with my ability to sense thoughts and feelings. My sister and I became so good at this, as puppies, that we could carry on simple conversations with each other, supplemented and punctuated by the noises we could make with our mouths and throats.

As Alex and I walked into the thick of the crowd, I tried to ignore the sights and smells and focus on my other senses. As I did, it seemed to me that some people were there for a reason. I couldn't tell what they were thinking, but I sensed that there was a purpose to their thoughts. Other people seemed to be almost aimlessly walking about, being carried along with the rest of the crowd without necessarily knowing what it was all about. I even got the clear sense, from the occasional person, that they were actually wondering what it was all about.

We didn't have much trouble mingling with the people in the crowd. I'm not a small dog, and I've heard many people remark on how much they think I look like a large wolf. Although that pleases me, it means that some people are instinctively afraid, or at least wary, of me. As a result, the crowd didn't press against me too much.

Since Alex was able to look ahead better than I could, I was simply walking beside her and following wherever she led until my senses were struck by something new and I stopped to look around in an attempt to identify the source. Alex sensed this immediately and stopped.

"What is it Silver?" she asked. "Smell something?"

I gave a low whine in acknowledgement, as I continued to sweep my head this way and that. Something didn't seem right.

Then, I had it. There was something... that way! I tugged at the leash and led us sharply off to the left. Alex was willing to follow along, and let me lead into a different part of the crowd.

At first, I had to weave back and forth a bit trying to find the source, but eventually the sense I'd picked up became sharper and I could approach it more or less directly. When we were close enough to be able to see the cause, I stopped and stared.

The disconcerting sense I'd picked up had been new and confusing, but now I knew why. There were two overlapping thought patterns, but I could now separate them and identify their sources.

Standing not far away, with their backs to us, were two human males. One quite large, and the other quite average. They were speaking to each other, but in low tones such that I couldn't identify many specific words.

Alex crouched down to one knee, so she could place her head near mine. She had immediately sensed that that the fur was rising on the back of my neck, and I knew that with her hand on my back she could feel the tension in my body.

"Something wrong? Is it those two men?"

"Grrruph," I said, in acknowledgement, but not loudly.

Looking her straight in the eyes, I tried to project the sense of evil I was picking up. Not danger, precisely. Not imminent danger, anyway.

I sensed a dark kind of purposefulness in the thoughts of the larger man. In the 'average' man's mind, I sensed utter blackness — and evil. Only once before had I had sensed such blackness and evil in the mind of a human. It was in the mind of the human called Jim that had killed my former master[14].

"Let's move to one side," she said, "and see if we can get a better look."

I understood the essence of her words, and we tried working our way further left and forward. As we did, I realized that she wanted to be able to see what the two men looked like from the front.

Most of the crowd had stopped flowing by this time, and had become a large number of people standing or milling around, as if waiting for something.

That made it easier for us to change position, and we had just about flanked them when one of the men strode off towards the large fire that was burning inside a circle of box-shaped rocks.

***

I was surprised to see Silver pick up a scent, or perhaps a sense, of something that concerned him. Although he had many other skills and qualities, he had been specifically trained to detect explosives. The front lawn of the Parliament Buildings seemed like an unlikely place for someone to be carrying explosives, but with so many people crowded together it wouldn't take much of an explosion to do a lot of harm, so I gave him his head and followed along, trying to look everywhere at once.

Having worked his way through the crowd and focused in on what was concerning him, he eventually came to a complete standstill and just stood there. He seemed to be staring at two men that were just ahead of us. One was quite large, with a shock of rather unruly-looking dark hair and the other quite ordinary – about medium height and medium build - in fact, the only really distinguishing feature of the second man was that he had blond hair.

I could see that the fur on the back of Silver's neck was standing up and I thought I detected a quiver in his body, so I knelt down for a closer look.

"Something wrong?" I asked, quietly. "Is it those two men?"

"Grrruph," he said, in acknowledgement, but quietly – as if not wanting to be overheard.

This was unusual. If he had smelled explosives, or even the

chemical precursors used to make explosives, he would have simply walked up to the source, sat down on his haunches, and looked up at me to signal his find. But he hadn't done any of those things.... Something else then, but what?

Then I looked into his eyes and got a sense of *darkness*, it seemed like, and *menace*, and I could feel his body shaking. I'd only seen him react like this one other time – when he'd met Jim Dumont, a hunting and fishing guide in northern Saskatchewan. I hadn't known how to interpret Silver's reaction then, but Jim had turned out to be a murderer and thief! I wasn't about to discount Silver's instincts a second time.

Silver and I moved to one side and worked our way around, trying to get a view from the front so I could see what the two men's faces looked like.

We just had a glimpse, before the larger man stepped away, strode purposefully up to the Centennial Flame and hopped up on the low stone wall that surrounded it. He had a bullhorn in his hand.

Quickly slipping my daypack off, I took out my camera and looked at it. Not much of a surveillance camera, I thought. The only camera I owned at that time was the Kodak Pocket Instamatic camera I'd purchased as a university student. Its virtues had been its low price, small size, and the fact that I could afford to buy the Ikelite underwater housing for it that allowed me to take pictures while SCUBA diving. The small, cheap lens and '110' roll film it used didn't lend themselves to high-resolution photographs, but they produced acceptable slide transparencies and 4 x 6" prints.

In this case, it did look like the kind of camera an impoverished university student might own, so I used it to take a picture of the man with the bullhorn. Then, edging closer to the Centennial Flame, as if eager to hear what the man had to say, I kept an eye on the blond-haired man, watching for a chance to see him from the front.

When there was a gap and I could see his face, I snapped as many pictures as I could while holding the camera at chest height, hoping that if spotted I would look like I was waiting for the right moment to take another picture of the speaker.

When the crowd settled, the man with the bullhorn began to speak. Between the garbled sound of his amplified voice and his tendency to swing the bullhorn back and forth, right and left, it wasn't easy to understand everything he said but I could pick out the sense of it. He was arguing for an end to seal hunting in Canada's northern and eastern coasts, and calling for people to step up and demand action from the federal government. I had seen a number of people carrying banners and signs. Now they brandished them above their heads. Some of them had graphic colour pictures of Harp Seal pups, lying dead and bleeding on the snow and ice, with words like '**Stop the Murder**,' and so on.

That helped explain the location for the crowd's gathering: right in front of the Parliament Buildings.

Watching Silver, I tried to figure out which of the two men was the focus of his attention, but I got a surprise. It was both of them. His body would stiffen, as would the fur on the back of his neck, when he looked at 'bullhorn man,' and also when he looked at 'blond-haired man.' The only difference was that he'd sometimes give a low growl when gazing at the blond-haired man.

I decided to look for a better vantage point and signalled to Silver that we should continue moving to our left. As we did so, the bullhorn man seemed to wrap-up his remarks and, with an ever-increasing note of hysteria in his voice, called for the crowd to march on and make their voices heard.

Heard by whom? I wondered.

As the crowd shifted, Silver and I went with the flow for a while. While the bullhorn man was leading the crowd out the main gate and back onto Wellington Street, the people near us seemed to know where he was heading, and we were swept past the West Block of the Parliament Buildings, and eastward towards the Chateau Laurier Hotel.

Walking down the street with the crowd we found ourselves, for a moment, at the head of the crowd. This happened because those around us had slowed down to wait for their leader, with the bullhorn, and the advance guard of banner and protest sign bearers, to catch up and take the lead.

Taking a moment to look around, it was only then that I saw the police line!

Perhaps 30 or 40 metres (30–40 yards) away, a police line stretched from just before the Chateau Laurier, to our left, all the way across Wellington Street, to the Government Conference Centre[23] on the other side. Two things immediately flashed into my mind. One was that there were some kind of high-level meetings going on between the Prime Minister and the Provincial Premiers, and their respective entourages of Cabinet Ministers and senior civil servants. The meetings were being held in the conference centre and the out-of-town politicians and civil servants were staying at the Chateau Laurier. That explained the timing and focal point of the protestors.

The second thing that imposed itself on my mind was the police line. A mixture of RCMP and Ottawa City Police officers were assembled, but this was no ordinary police line with rolls of yellow tape instructing people not to cross. This was a huge turnout. It stretched out all the way across one of Wellington Street's broadest intersections, and was at least six officers deep at any point. Furthermore, the front line of officers, facing towards the advancing protestors, were fully outfitted in riot gear.

I have to admit that my first reaction was fascination, as I assessed the deployment of the police resources to my left and then the sheer size of noisy protesters heading towards me from the right.

My fascination was heightened even further when I heard the throaty-engine sounds of a very large diesel engine approaching.

What in the world? I wondered.

The engine noise sounded louder and louder as something mechanical approached from behind the police line. Then, just as I heard the sound of the engine changing gears, I saw a long nozzle appear above the police line, which blurred for a moment as officers in the centre of the line shuffled aside to make room. Then the rest of it appeared.

They had brought in one of the huge greenish-yellow-coloured, crash-tender fire-engines from the Ottawa Airport!

Only then did it dawn on me that Silver and I were not standing in a smart place to be. The police line was clearly well staffed, well equipped, and bracing for violence. They certainly weren't going to need help from us.

Looking them over, I could see that they were prepared to elevate their response according to the "use of force" doctrine[8]. This means employing only the amount of force necessary to achieve the specific mission. When applied to riots, this would proceed as follows:

1. A show of force,

2. The use of riot control formations to halt or drive a mob, and/or to split it into manageable groups,
3. The use of high-pressure water to disperse the mob,
4. The use of riot control agents, like tear gas[24], to disperse the mob,
5. Fire by sharpshooters to render the mob's leadership ineffective, and
6. The use of full-unit firepower when all else has failed.

The police line in front of us had implemented the first two of these, the presence of the fire truck meant they were prepared to deploy number three, and they would certainly have come prepared to advance, if necessary, to number four. Number five had been rarely used in North America, although most people still remembered the 1970 Vietnam War protests in which protesting students were either shot or bayonetted by troops.

In the demonstration I was facing, the protestors were resolutely, and noisily, advancing – being egged-on by bullhorn man and their own rising adrenaline. They were showing no signs of being intimidated by the police line, much less their obvious show of willingness to turn a high-pressure water cannon on them.

As I belatedly realized that we were going to be caught dead centre between two resolute forces, I decided that we should make our way out while we could, and certainly before the police starting firing tear gas and smoke cannisters!

Fortunately, the people near us were still waiting for the leaders to catch up, and Silver and I were able to get off of the street, back up onto the Parliament Hill Grounds, and then make our exit along the front of the East Block.

So much for our Sunday 'walk in the park.'

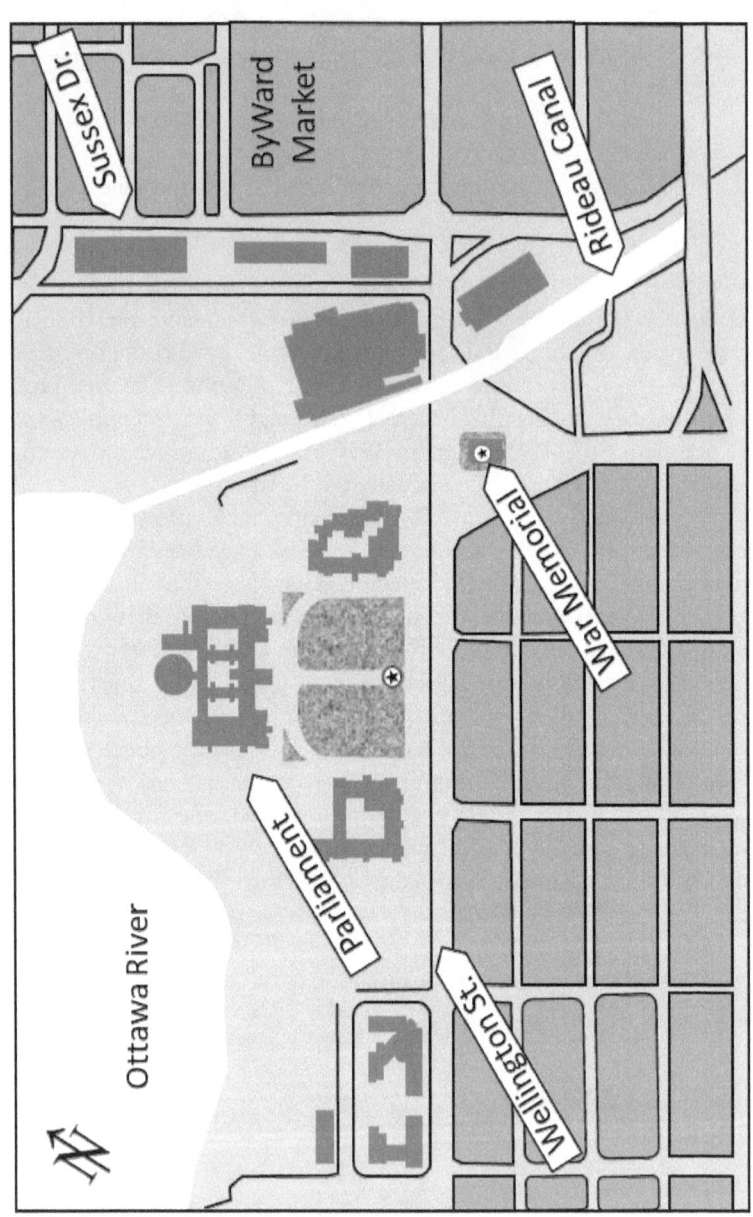

The rioter has changed from the hurler of brickbats to the thrower of dynamite bombs.

Unknown Military Author
20ᵗʰ Century

Back at work, the next morning, I related my story of finding myself between the protesters and the riot squad to my boss, Staff Sergeant Bob Simpson. He was naturally interested in our mystery person, citing concerns that violent agitators seemed to be infiltrating the seal hunt protesters who were otherwise peacefully demonstrating with occasional lapses into mild civil disobedience.

"We're not concerned with the law-abiding protesters," he said, "and any minor transgressions are for the local police to deal with, but the violent ones are a concern for two reasons: one, for the damage they can do, and two, because their actions can encourage others that might normally be peaceful and law-abiding but get caught up in the heat of the moment and follow the example set by the instigators. In the worst cases, it can lead to outright riots."

"Who are the instigators then?" I asked, "anarchists?"

"Sometimes, yes, people that want to bring down all of society's organized systems to make room for a new kind of society."

"I've always wondered what anarchists would do if they succeeded. Would they then shift to rebelling against whatever kind of new government and society came next?" I asked.

"I really don't know," said Bob, "anarchists have always struck me as short-term thinkers. I can understand their frustrations and anger, but it's *naïve* to think that you can bring a system down and not have some kind of new one grow-up in its place. Sometimes I think they're like dogs chasing cars: the chase is all well and good but what would a dog do with a car once it caught it?

"Anyway, there are several other types of violent instigators beside anarchists: foreign agents attempting to undermine our political system, for example, and *provocateurs* hired by a third party."

"Hired?"

"Sure. Remember the student protests in the United States during the Vietnam War?"

"Yes. I met a few American students in university that had fled here to avoid the draft. Some of them had been beaten by the police for simply being part of a crowd of demonstrators. Between their anger at the war and their disenchantment at being attacked by their own police, they'd come to Canada vowing never to return to the U.S."

"Well, the FBI think that some of the more violent clashes between the students and police were incited by *provocateurs* that had been hired to goad the police and national guard into retaliating with excessive force, causing the demonstrators to respond with violence - leading to injuries, property destruction, intense media coverage, and even deaths."

This was a new thought for me. "Who would do that... and why?"

"I don't know, but it wasn't just American students that were against the war. There were many others that were against it but unwilling to be seen to disagree publicly, some of them quite wealthy. The FBI think that there may have been people that felt that if the student demonstrations could be turned into violent confrontations, especially if there were injuries and deaths, then the horror of seeing government forces acting against their own citizens would lead to further demonstrations, and that eventually the general public would turn against the war, causing the government to pull its troops out of Vietnam."

That triggered memories. "Four students were killed at Kent State...."

"In 1970, yes, and nine others were shot and injured. Within a week, nearly a dozen students were bayonetted at demonstration at the University of New Mexico, and within a week of that more students were killed or injured at Jackson State University[25]."

"And you think that the more violent clashes were triggered by these *provocateurs*?"

"I don't know. Neither does the FBI, they just have suspicions. Even if their general suspicions are correct, the instigators could just as easily have been foreign agents. North Vietnam, China, and the Soviet Union would all have wanted to see the American public turn against the war."

"And now you think Silver and I might have accidentally come across one of these *provocateurs* yesterday?"

"The thought crossed my mind, that's all," said Bob. "Maybe

we got a lucky break.... Let's wait and see whether any of your pictures turned out. If so, we'll have a search done and see if anything comes up. In the meantime, why don't you do some reading up on the seal hunt protests. We might want you and Silver to go sniff around a few more of their protests – but carefully."

I'd noticed that since being promoted to Corporal[26], Bob seemed to be giving me more latitude to follow my own instincts and choose, or even suggest, some of the cases that I took on. This was the latest example. It meant shouldering more responsibility, but it felt good.

After my talk with Bob, it was time to do some research, so I headed over to the library at Carleton University to see what I could dig up. After an afternoon's poring through a dozen articles and a half dozen books, I'd learned that seal hunting in the eastern Arctic region predates the arrival of Viking and European explorers, and that it originally provided food and clothing for the Inuit peoples in the far northeast. It became a source of revenue when the European Sealing Fleets arrived in the 1700s. By the 1800s, it was a major industry, particularly in Newfoundland and Labrador. Modern-era, commercial sealing began in the 1930s, when Norwegian sealers began arriving, and these were soon joined by Canadian commercial sealers. The commercial sealers were mostly after the seals' pelts, and prized among these were the pure white pelts of each season's young harp seal pups – 'whitecoats.' Although the Canadian Government began regulating the hunts in the 1950s, this did nothing to satisfy the people that wanted to see an outright ban on commercial seal hunting.

In the 1960s, came the first wave of protests sponsored by organized animal and environmental conservation groups, who also began to directly lobby politicians regarding their opposition to the seal hunts in Canada[27] (and Norway). Their major weapons in such campaigns were explicit, colour photographs and documentary films showing cute, white seal pups being clubbed to death by commercial sealers interested only in their pelts.

All of the above tended to be well covered by the media, particularly the newspapers and television. It was television, in fact, that led to the first wave of public reaction. In 1964, the CBC French network aired a documentary film that contained particularly graphic scenes of violence against the seals, including one that showed a seal being skinned alive[28]. Although the hunter concerned latter admitted to being paid to stage the scene precisely to create a horrifying image, the documentary was very effective at stimulating public outrage.

I also found some magazine and newspaper articles about the protest movements themselves. Not long after the CBC documentary film was aired, the International Alliance for Animal Protection[29] (IAAP) was founded, based in Fredericton, NB. Although generally opposed to the killing or inhumane treatment of any animals, limited resources forced them to focus on only a few specific initiatives at any one time. Of these, the annual seal hunts quickly became a priority for action. Most of the initial activities involved advertising to raise public awareness and lobbying of governments and industries, all using the opportunities presented by the graphic photographs and films which could so easily be shown as direct evidence on placards and mailers, and in newspapers and television.

In particular, IAAP focused on large-vessel sealing operations. The efforts of IAAP, and similar organizations had an impact. By the mid-1970s, the Canadian government had brought in new regulations, including setting quotas, licensing of sealers and their vessels, and prohibiting the skinning of live seals. The organizations, and a significant fraction of the international public, weren't satisfied, however, with the extent of the regulations and the perceived lack of enforcement of them. These concerns were only compounded when a government appointed Committee on Seals and Sealing called for a phase-out of the Canadian and Norwegian seal hunts by 1974[30], but their recommendation was ignored.

Meanwhile, the proliferation of colour television in households across the country provided an ideal medium to show graphic, heart-rending pictures and movie clips of the bloody seal hunts to a broad audience. This fueled increased public interest and outrage with another wave of protests surging in the mid-1970s. The protests themselves were boosted by the participation of movie stars. In March 1977, activists had been able to fly-in French actress Brigitte Bardot, and the cover of the next edition of *Paris Match* featured a picture of her hugging a whitecoat seal pup[31]. This helped the controversy spread to Europe.

When I next met with Bob to discuss what I'd learned, we

talked about the police-related aspects of the protests.

"The organized protests, for the most part, have been conducted legally as legitimate expressions of public opinion," he explained. "In these cases, the only matters of concern to us are the minority of protesters that step 'over the line' into illegal activities… and it's not just the protesters," he pointed out. "We've had cases of counter-protesters that just as angrily condemn the protesters and sometimes they cross the line too."

Counter-protesters, in the case of sealing, were usually made up of the sealers themselves, plus members of their families and/or residents of communities that were dependent on the seal hunt. There were already instances in which some of these had taken violent exception to what they viewed as the protesters threatening their livelihoods.

"That raises another concern," continued Bob, "which is that if violence breaks out on both sides. Things could escalate into a riot.

"The real concerns for us, though, are the activist protesters who, as the name implies, are not content with public awareness and diplomacy, and who turn to more direct ways to accomplish the changes they want. Although some of these people confine themselves to perfectly legal means, such as protest marches, we've seen others purposely tread 'across the line' into barricades and even physical disruption of the seal hunts. We suspect that even the larger organizations, like the IAAP, are becoming dissatisfied with what they perceive to be an almost complete lack of progress with government, and may be considering ways to impede the sealing operations directly."

"Aren't they doing that already?" I asked. "I thought I read somewhere that one of these groups recently took a ship right onto the ice pack and had a bunch of protesters rush out onto the ice a spray the seal pups with coloured dye, hoping to save them by making their pelts useless for making clothing."

"Yes, but we're worried that they might get impatient enough to create even more media attention by hiring professional agitators to incite and inflame things."

"Ah hah. Like our mystery man from the Parliament Hill protest march."

"Exactly."

I'd read a bit about this too. Generally unknown to the media or the public at large, there had been disturbing indications of the involvement of professional agitators in some mass demonstrations of the 1960s and 1970s.

"What kind of people are these professional agitators?" I asked.

"Mercenaries. Usually, they are ex-military or ex-police that have been dishonourably discharged or otherwise weeded out, but who have found that their lack of ethics combined with their military or police training are in demand. They bring with them the tools of professional anarchy: fighting tactics, weapons, and explosives."

I must have made a face, as I was thinking about Bob's words, because he next spoke a bit more sharply.

"Don't underestimate these people Alex. They lack integrity, and maybe even humanity, but they are generally well trained, experienced, and motivated. Within the context of what they're hired to do, some of them are quite intelligent and even professional. Others are deranged but very cunning.... Some of them are killers."

"Riiiiight," I said. *Nasty*, I thought.

I had an unsettling feeling that the mystery man Silver and I had encountered might be one of these professional agitators. Now, I would have to try digging deeper...

***

The next development was with the pictures I'd taken (no pun intended). As predicted, the 4 x 6" prints from my small camera were anything but high-resolution. Nevertheless, one shot of bullhorn man was very clear and several of the head-and-shoulders shots of the blond-haired man were very good.

It wasn't long before Bob, had news about them.

"The man with the bullhorn has been identified as the President, and one of the founders, of the International Alliance for Animal Protection and he lives in Fredericton, where the IAAP has their main office. His name is Arne Kristiansen. He's well known in the animal rights movements internationally, and pops up in the news media now and again. IAAP is a legitimate not-for-profit organization, and as far as we know both IAAP and Kristiansen have been law abiding and not a police concern. It was the IAAP that organized the demonstration you two walked into."

"How about the blond-haired man?"

"Your other man is a bit of a mystery. We tried running his photo through CPIC[32] but no match came up...." Bob gave his Cheshire Cat smile.

"And?" I prompted. I could tell there was more coming.

"Well, as you know, CPIC is linked to the U.S. National Crime Information Center."

"Right, NCIC."

"Mm hmm. Do you remember Deputy Director Jonathan Wheeler, of the FBI?"

"Sure, I met him after the Aleutian Islands incident[20] and then again after Soviet satellite incident[18]."

"Right. Well the U.S. system passed a null response back to CPIC, but I received a phone call from Jon Wheeler the next day. Turns out our query did match one of their records, but the record is classified Top Secret. Even though we didn't get a useful response from the computer system, the fact that there was a query and a match raised a flag that was sent to the FBI."

"Wow. OK, so he's known to the Americans but they're protecting his identity because of some kind of security concern. Did he tell you what it is?"

"Nope. He wanted to know why we were interested, and when I explained he said they were very interested but he wouldn't tell me why. Not even over a STEW phone[33]."

"Has that ever happened before?"

"Not to my knowledge. If you've stumbled onto something so hot that they won't even trust a secure telephone, then they're seriously worried about something."

"So that's it then – we've hit a brick wall?"

"Oh no, not at all. Jon wouldn't talk about it over the phone, but he's sending Vivian up to meet with you. They'd like to hear your story firsthand, and in return she'll brief you on what they know and why they're interested." His Cheshire smile returned. "I don't think they're protecting him at all.... I think they're trying to find him."

***

A few days later, Special Agent Vivian Rule flew in on a commercial flight. Silver and I went to meet her at the Ottawa airport. I was in uniform, as Silver and I had just been outside the city helping with a search for a lost child (fortunately, it turned out to be a false alarm).

"Where are you staying?" I asked, while we waited for her luggage to be delivered to the carousel.

"Some hotel downtown," she replied, "I'll have to look up the reservation."

"Why not cancel it and come stay with Silver and me? It will be more comfortable and easier for us to talk. I'd like to hear all about what you've been up to lately."

"Thank you, yes, that sounds great," she replied, "I'd like to hear how things are coming along with you too, and how you got the corporal's stripes I see on your sleeve."

Vivian is about my age, and was one of the first two women to become Special Agents in the FBI. She's brunette, fairly tall, slender, and has wonderful, large brown eyes. We'd found, on previous assignments, that we worked well together, and we'd become friends as well.

Settled in at my place, we only chatted about things like what each of us had been doing outside of work in the month – *had it only been a month?* - since we'd worked together in the Northwest Territories[60], above the Arctic Circle. Vivian had just come back from an exciting vacation in Europe, and wanted to know how things had been going with my boyfriend Don, who was in military intelligence and a colleague of ours.

After dinner, we sat out on my back porch watching one of Ottawa's classic evening thunderstorms roll across the sky. The cracks of lightning followed by rolls of thunder provided a perfect backdrop for Vivian's story.

"We've been watching a pattern lately that has emerged from quite a few of the big demonstrations in our larger cities," she began.

"You mean like the anti-war protests?"

"Yes those, but also demonstrations for women's rights, human rights generally, and even animal rights – like anti-whaling for example. Activist demonstrations are becoming normal now, which is fine as far as free speech and all that. The local police have to deal with crowd control and the rowdy fringe elements - and we sometimes get called in to investigate hate crimes – but something new has emerged.

"Tensions can run high, of course, with demonstrators

throwing bricks and bottles and such at the police, and the police hurling tear gas at the protestors. The strange thing is that at some demonstrations, just when the tensions on both sides are right at the tipping point – where one small thing could tip the balance between calming the crowd or a full-fledged riot, there's a gunshot that causes an immediate reaction from the police and surge of rioting from the demonstrators."

"You mean like when an officer gets carried away and fires into the crowd?"

"That has certainly happened before, and more than once, but I'm talking about cases where the shot came from the demonstrators' side. The first couple of times it happened, we thought they were just random incidences of armed hotheads getting carried away, but we have a forensic psychologist on staff that specializes in crowd psychology and riots. She's been looking at the demonstrations that weren't exactly peaceful, but weren't expected to turn into riots. Her goal is to come up with ways to de-escalate crowd violence before the police have to resort to water cannons, tear gas, and rubber bullets. She's the one that found this pattern, and she thinks that there's someone out there doing the exact opposite."

"You mean watching a crowd, judging the critical moment, and doing something to escalate the violence?"

"Exactly. I can see from your expression that you find it hard to believe."

"Well, it seems like a stretch. How sure are you that it's not just a series of coincidences?"

"We aren't sure, but let me lay out a few things. The demonstrations that unexpectedly turned into riots seem to have begun with the anti-war demonstrations at Kent State University in May 1970."

"That's the one where four students were killed."

"Right, and it led to violent clashes at other universities in the following weeks[25]. That was eight years ago. Since the war ended, we've had six other demonstrations, for other causes, but that seem to fit the same pattern."

"OK," I said, thinking about it, "and you and your psychologist think that some person or some organization is inciting the shifts to violence.... It still sounds a bit crazy to me. If these demonstrations have been for different causes then what's the common factor? You think it's anarchists?"

"Not exactly. There's a second part of the pattern, and this takes us to the really secret part of my story."

"Ah hah, let me refill your wine glass," I said, topping up our glasses.

Suitably restored with a sip of wine, Vivian continued. "After each of the seven demonstrations we've identified in the U.S. that fit the pattern, the police or security people have found a particular kind of gun left at the scene. In each case the gun was found lying close to what would have been the front line of the crowd of demonstrators."

"What kind of gun?"

"It's called a Deer Gun. Here, I'll show you." Getting up, Vivian went into the house to get her briefcase. Bringing it outside, she opened it and withdrew a glossy black and white photograph of a rather ugly looking little pistol.

"Home-made?" I asked.

"Not home-made. Cheaply made. It's a single-shot pistol, although it's made to carry extra rounds in the grip, and they're designed to be used once then thrown away."

"A disposable pistol. OK, why?"

Vivian sighed. "They were made for the CIA in the 1960s. I gather the idea was to provide them to guerrilla or revolutionary forces that the U.S. might be supporting in overseas countries. The soldiers there would use them to kill enemy troops and then arm themselves with the enemy's weapons. The CIA codenamed them Deer Guns, and they were cheap to make – mostly aluminum and plastic, and costing about $4 each!"

"Are they easy to get? I mean like on the black market or whatever."

"Actually no, they aren't. That's another strange thing. There were only a thousand of them ever made. 150 of them were sent to South Vietnam during the war and then the program was abruptly halted and all of them were ordered destroyed. The CIA says they are confident that the 850 that were never deployed were properly destroyed, but it's a little less certain that all of the 150 in Vietnam were destroyed."

"Why's that?"

"They had been sent to the army's Special Forces. We were able to check the army's disposal records, which contain a receipt showing that all 150 of them were sent for destruction. The signature on the receipt shows that the guns were received by a Major Davy Jones...." She paused for effect.

"*CRACK!*" There was a loud crack of lightning, almost immediately followed by a roar of thunder and it started to rain. There was a roof over my deck, so we didn't have to move but it certainly happened at the right time to add some drama to Vivian's story.

"Major David Jones, U.S. Special Forces was the cover name for a CIA officer operating in South Vietnam, but he had been listed as MIA[34] after a battle with the North Vietnamese several months earlier. It was thought that he died in a helicopter crash, although no body was ever found. Neither was the helicopter."

"Who was it then? No, let me guess. Major Jones was still alive and it was the CIA that quietly took them back."

"Maybe. The CIA aren't prone to giving up their secrets, even to the FBI, so it's difficult to be sure about anything. But in this case, we suspect that the man known as Major Jones caused his own disappearance and struck out on his own as a mercenary, taking the guns with him and probably the helicopter too."

"And you think he was hired as a professional agitator for the demonstrations you listed, and that each time he used one of these Deer Guns and then left it behind as a kind of calling card."

"That's exactly what we think. The guns are untraceable, and our forensic psychologist thinks it's some kind of ego thing for him to leave them behind. Taunting us, if you like. Challenging us to find and catch him, even."

"OK then, don't take this the wrong way, but why haven't you caught him then? I assume he must have been seen at some of the demonstrations?"

"First of all, if you piece together all the eyewitness accounts you might conclude that it was a different person each time. Different heights, different builds, different clothes. But it could have been the same person in each case, wearing disguises. He wouldn't be able to artificially lower his height, but he could easily raise it. The rest could be done with wigs, makeup, and different clothes and accessories."

"So, he's good with disguises."

"Better than good. Did you happen to read about the women's

rights demonstration in downtown Toronto back in March of this year?"

"The one where the police fired on the crowd and were hammered in the press for shooting at unarmed mothers and grandmothers?"

"That's the one. Apparently, things only got out of hand when someone threw two Molotov Cocktails into the police ranks. Except they weren't your everyday, spur of the moment Molotovs. According to the forensic report, they were a pretty fancy self-igniting kind – no need to do anything obvious like light the wicks, and they had been disguised as ordinary beer bottles. Several of the demonstrators told the police that they had seen a grey-haired woman take a beer bottle out of a large purse or shoulder bag and throw it over the police line. Part of the reason it stuck in their memories was that the woman had such a strong throwing arm!"

"And was there a shot from the crowd?"

"There was. A single shot was heard by the same people that remembered the grey-haired woman, and a police officer was struck in the leg by a slug from a 9 mm gun."

"I suppose the Deer Guns fired 9 mm rounds?"

"Right again, and a Deer Gun was found lying on the ground less than ten feet from the front of the police line in Toronto."

"You obviously suspect your Major Jones."

"Yes. Same MO[35], same results, same kind of gun. The only new twist was the Molotovs, but even those were the work of someone with specialized knowledge. From the witness reports, our mystery person was tall enough and stocky enough. Add the wig and glasses, put on a full-length dress - you know, she even wore a shawl! - and there you have our man in disguise rather than someone's grandmother."

"So, the Toronto demonstration gives you eight that fit your pattern?"

"That we know of. He's a killer, Alex. A couple of Deer Guns have also been found near the scene of assassinations in third-world countries. It's possible that they're not connected, but we think it's the same person and that he's sometimes hired himself out as a paid assassin." She sighed, and then changed the subject. "How about telling me about your Ottawa demonstration?"

I told Vivian about Silver's and my experience at the Ottawa demonstration, and the photos I'd taken.

"Can I see the photos?" she asked.

"Sure, I have copies for you," and I went to get them for her.

When I returned, I explained that the one I thought of as bullhorn man had been identified, but it was the other one that had her full attention.

"I think he's finally made a mistake," she said thoughtfully.

Going back to her briefcase, she withdrew a different file folder and opened it. Taped onto the inside cover of the folder was an old, faded colour-photograph of a man wearing jungle camouflage and holding an automatic rifle. Attached to his backpack shoulder straps, where they came over his shoulders and upper chest, were a large sheath knife (mounted upside down) and a grenade. In the background was jungle. "This is him, taken in Vietnam in 1963."

"It's not very clear," I said, doubtfully, as I looked at it.

"No, but look at the hair."

The man in the picture had his hair cut short, but it was blond.

"Could be a coincidence?" I suggested.

"Sure, but maybe not. His size and age seem about right too. A young Major could have been 32 in 1963, which would make him about 47 now. Maybe he was at your demonstration to meet your bullhorn man and talk about a future job. They may have thought that meeting in the middle of a large crowd would be enough to avoid attention. If it's our elusive Major Jones then I'm sure he's travelling under a false name and passport, and probably feels quite safe and anonymous. Like 'hiding in plain sight.' That could explain why he wasn't in disguise."

"So, what's next?"

"Feel like going undercover again?"

"Maybe. What do you have in mind?"

"Well, up until now, we've only learned things about him after he's long gone. Maybe we can get ahead of him with this IAAP organization."

"You mean get inside and wait for a big demonstration that might turn violent, then try to spot him?"

"Basically. Yes."

"I don't know, Vivian. The next sealing season isn't until next March or April. I'll have to talk to Bob about it. Can I tell him what you've told me?"

"Bob yes, but no one else – and nothing in writing. OK?"

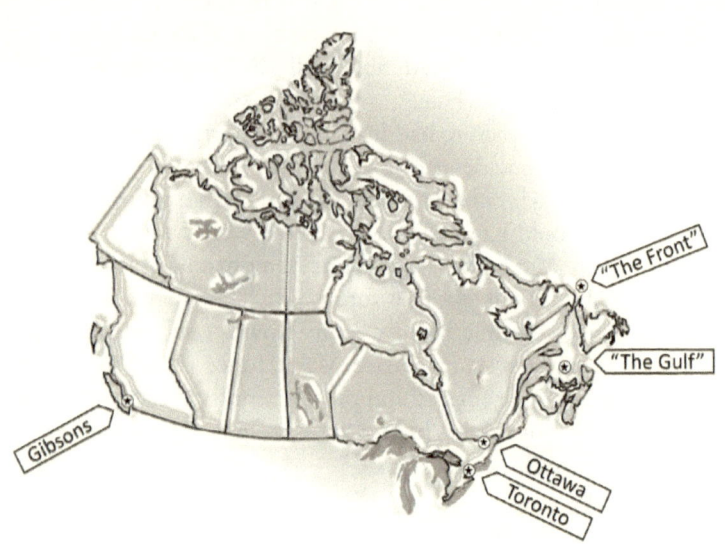

4 THE ACTRESS

July 21, 1978
Gibsons, British Columbia

Having wrapped up an unrelated case in Vancouver, Silver and I had boarded a B.C. Ferry at Horseshoe Bay, in West Vancouver, and made a very enjoyable 40-minute crossing of the Strait of Georgia. Since he is a police dog, the ship's crew allowed him to stay with me, rather than remain cooped up in the truck on the vehicle deck, so he was able to enjoy the crossing as well. It never ceases to amaze me how Silver can hate the water so much and yet enjoying boating so much – even in rough water – but he does.

Once across the strait, we drove off the ferry and into the small village of Langdale. A quick left turn took us a short distance along Marine Drive to Gibsons, a small town of a few thousand people whose current claim to fame was that it was the home setting for the popular CBC-television series *The Beachcombers*[36].

The series focused on the lives and adventures of several characters that made their living boating up and down the British Columbia coastline salvaging logs that had slipped away from logging-industry barges and booms. The hometown of the central characters in the series was this same town of Gibsons, although several of the series' buildings were studio sets, not real buildings.

The network was in the process of filming new segments, and Silver and I were there to meet one of the show's stars, a drop-dead-gorgeous blond actress and sex-symbol named Ginger

Brandt. I'd never met a movie star before and was looking forward to it.

The trailers for the actors and staff were set up in a compound on the edge of town, right near the edge of the water. This put them within easy walking distance of the town and gave them a fantastic view of the sheltered waters of the Strait of Georgia. Not wanting to disclose my occupation to these people, I only identified myself by showing my driver's licence to the guard at the security gate. Having consulted a list to verify that I was expected, the guard showed me where to park and waved in the general direction I should walk.

"Trailer number five," he said, "ask anyone if you get lost."

Each trailer had a large number taped conspicuously to its front, and they were actually arranged more or less in numerical order, so we had no trouble finding number five. It had a doorbell, and was quite promptly opened by a blond, blue-eyed woman of about my own age. It was Ginger Brandt all right.

"Yes?" she said, looking a bit stern and aloof.

"My name is Alex Houston. I have an appointment to see you."

"You're Alex Houston?" she asked. "And you're a Mountie?"

"That's right, Corporal Alexandra Houston, and this is my partner Silver."

"Really? He's a Mountie too?"

"Well, he's an RCMP police service dog, so yes, I guess he is. I never quite thought of it quite that way."

"I love animals. Can I say hi to him?"

"Sure."

Bending down on one knee, she very formally said "Hello Silver, my name's Ginger," and stretched her hand out for him to sniff.

"See how he looks into my eyes," she said, without taking her gaze away. "It's like he can see right inside my head."

"You'll think I'm crazy, but that's not far off. He's unusually perceptive, and picks up more of human conversations than any animal I've ever heard of."

"Nothing is crazier than the movie business. Well, Silver if you look deep inside, you'll see what I'm really like."

After a long look, Silver broke his gaze, took a step forward and gave her a lick on the chin.

"That's a high compliment coming from him," I said.

Ginger's demeanor had changed radically during our introductions, and now she started laughing. "Come in. Come in, and let me explain why I was a bit surprised by your appearance."

As she stepped back to wave us in, we entered a beautifully laid-out room that was a combination living room, kitchen and dining room. It was also very bright and cheerful with almost the entire ceiling having been taken over by large skylights which nourished an amazing assortment of plants.

"Like it?" she said, observing my reactions.

"I love it," I said. "It's beautiful. Like being in a conservatory."

"It's two trailers put together, actually. The second half has a bedroom, *en suite*, and an office. Behind that is a deck. Let me get you something to drink and I'll show you. What would you like?"

"Anything cold would be great. Water's fine."

"How about a Perrier for you and plain water for Silver? I'll join you."

Going to the kitchen, she extracted two large glasses and two bottles of Perrier, which she handed to me. Then, she filled a bowl with water, motioned with a nod of her head and led me out to her back deck.

The deck was quite private, having solid walls on each side and a translucent roof. The view was fantastic. We were just high enough to have an unobstructed view of the ocean and, across the straight to the eastern coast of Vancouver Island.

"Pretty great view, huh?" she said, watching me closely.

"It's amazing. I love being on the coast. Either coast."

As we settled into comfortable deck loungers, she brought the conversation back to business.

"Bob didn't tell me he was sending a woman to see me, he just said it would be one of his people, name of Alex Houston...."

"Yes, my formal name is Alexandra but everyone calls me Alex. I hope you will too."

"And you really work for Bob Simpson?"

I nodded. "You know what he does for a living, right?"

"Yes, but I didn't know the RCMP was letting women in."

"There aren't many of us yet. They started with me as a single-woman pilot project in 1974, then an entire troop of women in 1975, and now there are more and more each year."

"So you were the first! That must have been hard."

"There have been a few rough spots, but not as many as you

might think. Not for me anyway. Between my undercover work and being a dog handler, I get a lot of independence, which I love, and I think that by not being in any of the larger detachments or sub-divisions I haven't really been seen as a challenge to anyone."

"Well good for you. I like to see women get ahead and not just because of their looks." She looked at me knowingly. "I imagine you're wondering how I know Bob."

"You know, I was actually wondering how it is that Bob knows a movie star."

"Well, that part's easy. He's my uncle – on my mother's side. He called and said he needed my help and it would be for a cause I believe in. He said he'd be sending two of his best officers, and that they would explain...." Then, she laughed. "Call me out of touch, but I expected to see two men, not a woman and a dog."

"Yes, that sounds like Bob's sense of humour. Here's the thing, we're after a killer that hires himself out as a professional agitator. He'll slip into a group of angry demonstrators, wait until tensions between them and the police are near the boiling point and then initiate the first moves of real violence."

"Initiate how?"

"In many cases, he uses disposable guns to shoot someone like a police officer. Sometime he uses explosives. Then when things on both sides tip out of control he slips away, leaving behind one of his disposable guns as a kind of calling card."

"You said 'he.' Do you know who he is?"

"Not for sure, and it could be a woman, but the methods this person uses match those of an ex-CIA officer gone rogue that the FBI have been after for years now. One of the trademark guns was found after a women's-rights demonstration in Toronto that turned violent. Whomever it is, they seem to be a master of disguise. Silver and I got involved in this because we were bystanders at a 'save the seals' demonstration in Ottawa earlier in the month. Silver reacted so strongly to the presence of two men that we followed them for a few minutes and I was able to unobtrusively take their pictures. One of them turned out to look like the man that the FBI thinks is the one they're after."

"What do you mean Silver reacted?"

"Ah. That's hard to explain. I mentioned that he's unusually perceptive. Well, several times now he's reacted strongly to people that later turned out to be evil, killers even. I didn't understand it, or even believe it, at first but it's happened too many times for me to ignore. When he reacted to the two men we saw in Ottawa, I followed his lead. One man is the one we were talking about. The other is the head of an organization called IAAP. That stands for International..."

"Alliance for Animal Protection, I know. You're talking about Arne Kristiansen."

"That's right. Do you know him?"

"No, but I know of him. It's becoming common for movie stars to support 'causes' and I'm no exception. In my case, the causes are animal rights: everything from prevention of cruelty to animals in general, to saving the whales, to saving the seals. I've been a supporter of IAAP for quite a while now.... I think I'm starting to see what Bob has come up with in that devious little mind of his. You want me to get attached to one of these animal rights demonstrations and help you find this bad guy, right?"

I must have looked as nonplussed as I felt, because she continued right on.

"You're surprised to find out that I have a brain, aren't you? No, don't bother to deny it. It's a very natural reaction. I know how people look at me: 'All boobs and no brains,' they think. If I do a great job of acting, hardly anyone notices, and if I do a lousy job no one cares all that much as long as I look good. It's my own fault for building a career playing roles that call for an empty-headed piece of sexy eye-candy."

I couldn't help but ask "Why do it then?"

"Well, money at first. When I started modelling it was just a job. I didn't like it though, so when I got a chance to try acting in a TV series, I jumped at it. The TV series led to movies, which are all right, but acting in a TV series turned out to be something I really love doing. In *The Beachcombers*, the director is fantastic, the cast and crew are great, and because we work together so much, we've become kind of a second family. Have you ever watched it?"

"Sure."

"OK, then you know that the character I play is 'thick as a post,' as the saying goes. That's OK, because I love the work, and it's starting to bring me opportunities to play better roles, and I'm hoping to branch out a bit. My agent is negotiating a guest appearance on *Charlie's Angels*[37] that would cast me playing a private detective that looks like a 'dumb blonde' but isn't."

"Sounds great. I hope you get it."

"Thanks, but we seem to have wandered from the point of your visit. Why don't we have lunch, and then you can tell me what it is that you and Bob want me to do?"

"Sounds great to me." I agreed.

"OK then, I'll ask my assistant to get us something. The Crafty Table makes food and snacks available for the cast and crew all day." Reaching for an extension phone that was on a nearby table she called her assistant. "Brittany, would you be a dear and pick up some lunch from the Crafty for my guests and I? I'll have my usual salad," she placed her hand over the mouthpiece and turned to me. "What would you like? They'll have salads, sandwiches, hot dogs, chips, …"

"A sandwich and some kind of diet pop would be great for me."

"How about for Silver?"

"He used to be a sled dog, so he can eat almost anything, but he loves hot dogs."

"OK. Brittany? My guest would like a sandwich and diet pop. Would you pick out a couple of kinds of each for her? And she has a dog. He'd like a couple of hot dogs, OK? We'll have them out on the deck. Thanks!"

"There you go, Brittany will bring it all over for us." Then she looked at me expectantly.

"We think that the IAAP is likely to be planning a major demonstration against the seal hunt," I began. "We know that they haven't been as successful as they'd hoped at stopping the hunting of baby harp seals. They've tried going out and dying the fur of the seal pups to destroy its commercial value, but that's been mostly a symbolic gesture as they can't dye all of the pups before being stopped by the hunters or the police. Similarly, the demonstration that Silver and I accidentally encountered in Ottawa recently got them some publicity but no real action from the federal government."

"What do you think they're going to try next then?"

"Something more dramatic. Maybe even something drastic. If we're right that this ex-CIA mercenary was meeting with the head of the IAAP in Ottawa, then it was probably about hiring him to catalyze violence."

"Where do I come in?"

"Well, I'd like to try joining the IAAP under cover and going out with them on the next protest demonstration, which we think will be in the spring during the main seal hunting season. The IAAP seem to have formed some kind of alliance with the Ocean Saviour Society, so they can use their ship – the *MV Ocean Saviour* – to get out to the ice pack off the Labrador coast."

"Ah ha! You want me to volunteer to join the protest. They'll want me to come along as a publicity stunt, and you would be able to come along as my assistant – right?"

"That's our idea exactly. What do you think?"

"I like it. I'm always looking for new things to do to contribute to the animal rights movements and this one sounds like fun. It's a natural extension of things I've done before, so it won't look suspicious. I'll get my agent to contact them about it, and if they press him, he can tell them that it will be as much a publicity stunt for me as it will for them."

"Will you be able to bring me along as your assistant?"

"Of course. We stars are so spoiled and helpless that we can't be expected to function without our personal assistants." She flashed a brilliant smile. "And naturally we'll make them pay all of our expenses. It's the least they can do."

"Ah, there is one more thing...."

"You want to bring Silver along, don't you?"

"I do. Besides being my partner, it was he that identified this dangerous fellow in the first place, and even a master of disguises won't be able to fool Silver."

At this point, she surprised me by turning to face Silver. "What about you Silver. Do you want to come with us to help save the baby seals?"

"Grrruph!" he said, looking directly into her eyes.

"How much of this does he understand?" she asked in amazement.

"I really don't know, but he knows some of the words and he has the most amazing ability to sense the essence of what people are thinking, especially when you can make direct eye contact."

"Right then, Silver comes too."

"Just like that?" I asked, somewhat unbelievingly.

"If you want to be a star, you have to act like a star," she said, pontifically. "People expect stars to be eccentric. You wouldn't believe some of the things that actors get written into their contracts." She flashed her brilliant smile again. "My contracts, for example, specify that the producers have to keep my trailer supplied with Canadian snacks, like Smarties™ and Cheezies™. That's easy here in Canada, but you wouldn't believe how hard they are to get in the U.S. Anyway, what we'll do is have my agent say that I'm willing to join their spring crusade to Labrador, that I'll be bringing my personal assistant and her dog, and that we'll each need our own accommodations. If they put up a fuss, I'll throw a movie-star-quality tantrum and refuse to go, but they won't put up a fuss – you'll see."

"This is very good of you Ginger.... I have to tell you though, that there could be some danger. This fellow we're after is dangerous, and if violence breaks out between the protesters and the sealers, people can get hurt – even innocent by-standers."

"Thanks for the warning, but I grew up as quite the tomboy, and I'm not as helpless as I look. Besides, you and Silver will look out for me, right?"

"We'll do our best."

We were interrupted then, by Ginger's assistant Brittany who arrived with a large box from which lunch was dispensed.

As we ate, I commented on the gorgeous view.

"Yes, it's beautiful here. That's another attraction of working on this show. When we're shooting on location, I get to wake up to this view every morning. I like to sit here with my coffee at first light and watch the boats. Gibson's is the gateway to the Sunshine Coast, so there's always a stream of boats travelling up and down the Inside Passage."

"The food's great here too. How do you manage to stay so slender?"

"Salads!" she sighed. "I get as much exercise as I can fit in, but that's not much so my only other option is to watch the calories. That means lots of salads for me, and just the occasional treat of Smarties or Cheezies."

Silver's hot dogs, of course, disappeared in an instant and it didn't take long for us to eat our light lunch. It was Ginger that brought the conversation back to work.

"Bringing Silver along won't be a problem. Can I tell Brittany about you? She's going to have a lot of questions if I suddenly hire a new assistant without consulting her."

"Yes, I think you'll have to but please just say that it's a favour for your uncle, and please don't tell her until just before you leave for the East Coast. Will she be OK with being left behind for this trip?"

"Oh yes. She gets seasick, even on the car ferry! So, she'll be relieved not to have to go out on a real ship in the open ocean."

"And what, by the way, does an actor's personal assistant do exactly?"

She laughed. "That's easy. Anything the actor wants of course! But don't worry. It's menial work but it's easy work. Besides, I can take care of myself if I have to. We'll just have me send you off on some trivial errands from time to time for appearances sake."

We only had a few more minutes for small talk, before Brittany called to remind Ginger that she was due for makeup shortly. As we took our leave, I thanked her for everything: her hospitality, and her willingness to go along with our plan. "Especially since it might come to nothing. Our mystery person might not show up!"

"That's OK, it will be fun," she insisted. "A chance to do some good, a trip to Labrador, a hint of danger, and my agent's going to love the publicity angle! When he gets a response from the IAAP, I'll let you know."

As Silver and I drove back to the ferry terminal, I reflected on our meeting. Not only was it successful, I'd found Ginger to be intelligent and surprisingly nice and down-to-earth. I really liked her.

Now we just had to wait.

***

July 29, 1978
Darlington Nuclear Generating Station, Ontario

Silver and I did try attending a couple more demonstrations in hopes of spotting our quarry, but without success. Near the end of the month, for example, an anti-nuclear demonstration had been advertised for the construction site of the future Darlington Nuclear Generating Station.

The Darlington site is on the north shore of Lake Ontario, about 70 km northeast of Toronto. Although the site had been cleared and fenced, construction of the four CANDU nuclear reactors themselves hadn't even begun yet (and wouldn't officially begin until 1981). Nevertheless, Greenpeace had organized the demonstration to call for a halt to the construction on the logical assumption that there would be a better chance of stopping a nuclear power plant before construction had begun in earnest than it would when the facility was half built, let alone completed and up and running.

They chose a Saturday, and were rewarded with a clear, sunny day as over a thousand demonstrators marched on the site[38]. Silver and I simply joined the throng and let it carry us along.

There was quite a mix of people – lots of students of course, but also young families, some middle-aged people, and lots of seniors. They were quite energized, with many carrying signs and banners with slogans like "**Save our Environment**," "**Support Project No Nuc**," and "**Stop Darlington**." Some of the slogans were quite creative too. My favourite one read: "**Better Active Today than Radioactive Tomorrow**." I was also struck by the mood: this wasn't an angry crowd - not yet, anyway – it was more like a bunch of people heading off to a Sunday picnic in a park. Some people were honking horns, others chanting and clapping their hands, and one person was even playing bagpipes.

In another tactic I'd never seen at a protest demonstration before, a number of the organizers – identified by conspicuous green 'Greenpeace' armbands – mingled through the crowd, effectively policing their own protesters to keep things orderly and peaceful. It worked too. There was no violence, no angry confrontations with police or security people, and only a couple of pre-planned acts of civil disobedience.

The disobedience, for the most part, was limited to trespassing on the nuclear station's construction site. In the first of these, three demonstrators staged an aerial sit-in by climbing halfway up a 56 m (185 ft) electrical transmission tower at the site, and then hung large signs and banners from their perch bearing slogans like "No Nukes," and "Stop Darlington." Although they initially vowed that they wouldn't leave until the provincial government agreed to conduct a full environmental assessment on nuclear energy and a moratorium on construction at Darlington, after a 36-hour vigil they did climb down, leaving their signs and banners on display. The three were charged with trespassing and released with a summons to appear in a local court at a later date, and seemed well content with their bargain.

In another eye-catching stunt, five demonstrators parachuted onto the site, more or less, with one parachutist getting temporarily caught-up on one of the unfinished transmission towers. Here again, the demonstrators were charged with trespassing, released with court summons, and were able to walk away with only minor injuries.

Finally, at about the same time as the parachuting a sub-group of about 60 scaled the fence and held a sit-down protest. After giving them some time to make their point and ensure that the TV crews got some good news footage of them, the police calmly moved in, arrested them, and later charged them with trespassing too.

All in all, the demonstrators, security personnel, and police officers were the most peaceful and professional that I have ever seen at a protest demonstration. Although Silver and I did our best to mingle through the whole crowd, it wasn't practical for us to get close to everyone there and neither I spotted, nor Silver smelled or sensed our quarry. Either he wasn't there, or the two sides were too calm and well-behaved for him to incite or catalyze anything violent.

At the end of the afternoon, with the vast majority of the demonstrators leaving, I decided we'd done what we could and Silver and I left as well.

That's one of the things about what people call 'good old-fashioned police work,' a lot of one's time is spent being methodical and checking for evidence, clues, and even just insights. The exciting parts, when they come, tend to be intense, sometimes even spectacular, but relatively brief.

It was quite some time before our next opportunity arose.

Laurie Schramm

5 THE ACTIVISTS CONTINUE

August 27, 1978
Sydney, Australia

A crowd had gathered for the latest protest against police intervention and actions at a Mardi Gras Parade that had been organized by Sydney's GLBTQ[39] communities as part of world-wide International Gay Solidarity Day, June 24, 1978. Although the authorities had given prior approval for the event, which included a march followed by speeches, the state police had intervened to stop the parade, confiscated the public address system, and ordered the protesters to disperse. None of these actions being well received, the protesters kept on parading and the police called in reinforcements. Eventually tensions erupted, leading to bad behaviour on both sides. Some of the 1,000 protesters shifted from singing and dancing to throwing bottles, cans, and other debris at the police. Some of the police took off their identification numbers and waded into the crowd swinging their batons at everyone they could reach. The ensuing riot lasted two hours and culminated in over fifty arrests.

Over the next two months, a series of demonstrations were held around Australia not just to appeal for sexual equality under the law but also in protest over the actions of the police. The numbers involved were large, as the GLBTQ communities were increasingly supported by other citizens and several civil liberties groups. The demonstrations in Adelaide, Melbourne, and Sydney involved more police interventions, more conflict, received broad radio and television coverage, and became a major embarrassment for the New South Wales government which had claimed to be a strong upholder of civil rights[40].

Now, two months after the original Mardi Gras Parade and demonstration, things were heating up yet again as the protesters learned that the government was debating whether to change the laws in favour of sexual equality. One more large protest might be enough to tip the scales, it was thought, and more than a thousand people had already turned out to begin a march, with more likely to join along the way. Their mood was still one of brooding anger.

As the march began, so did the chants. As the crowd passed downtown bars, the chants changed to "Come out of the bars and join the march!" Many people did. When they reached Hyde Park for the speeches, the police had barricaded it and denied them entry. When, on top of this, the police ordered the crowd to disperse, the brooding anger and pent-up energy of the crowd resolved themselves into a defiant, continued march through the streets of the city. The chants were resumed as well, beginning with one of the classic anthems of the civil rights movement, '*We Shall Overcome.*'

As the crowd continued to increase in numbers, so did the size of the police presence with seemingly endless streams of paddy wagons arriving on nearby streets. Among the police reinforcements was a man wearing the uniform of the New South Wales police force, but with no badge or identification number. It was the former Major Jones. Beyond the uniform, his only other elements of disguise were that his short hair had been dyed brown, and the addition of a false moustache of matching colour.

As evening set in, from the centre of one of the police lines, Jones closely watched both the demonstrators and police, waiting for the pivotal moment. Finally, it came. A particularly raucous burst of yelling and rock-throwing shifted the balance of pushing and pulling and several police officers waded into the crowd, swinging their batons with intent to injure. Major Jones waded in with them, yelling and swinging his baton even more violently than the others.

Many of the protesters fought back, of course, which soon led to numerous people falling or being pushed and the scene became one of chaos. As the riot, which was what the encounter had now become, escalated the confusion was compounded by the semi-darkness. Projectiles thrown by the demonstrators were now as likely to strike other demonstrators as they were the police. At this point, Major Jones took out his Deer Gun and, concealing it close to his body, shot the police officer immediately to his right.

"Over there! The shot came from over there!" he yelled, pointing towards his left.

As the nearby police officers surged to the left, more aggressively than ever before, Major Jones judged that it was time for him to fade away. As he began to do so, however, he was struck by a forceful blow to the back of one shoulder that drove him to his knees. Recognizing that remaining low to the ground made him vulnerable to worse injuries, he struggled to get back on his feet but a helping hand from a nearby police officer was countered by another demonstrator who hit him on the side of the head with a sizeable rock.

Dazed and lying on the ground now, he was alternately kicked and simply walked over by any number of people. In the darkness, it was hard to tell whether he was being trod upon by demonstrators or police officers. It didn't matter. All he knew was that he needed to get up, clear a space, and get away – but he couldn't.

He thought he was finished, when one of the largest policemen he'd ever seen in his life lifted him up with a single arm, hoisted him over his shoulder, and simply bulled his way out of the rioting chaos and towards the rear of what was left of the nearest police line. Once there he simply said "Stay quiet mate, and wait for the medicos to get around to you," and then plunged back into the rioting mass.

Major Jones forced himself to lurch to his feet and slowly limped off to the rear of the police line, and along the rows of paddy wagons. When he reached the last one in line, he got in, verified that the keys had been left in the ignition, started it up and put it into reverse. When there was enough space in front of him, he shifted it to forward gear, turned around and accelerated away, turning on its flashing blue lights as he did so.

That was too close, he thought to himself, *maybe I'm getting too old for this sort of thing.* It had been a bizarre job as well. He was used to being hired by shadowy forces on one side or the other of demonstrations but this time he'd been hired by a shell-company that he strongly suspected was working for one of the ultra-conservative organized religions. Being hired by the church to break multiple commandments was a new one for him.

Maybe just one more, he thought, as he continued to drive away along empty, dark streets. *Just that last job I agreed to do in Labrador and I'll finally retire.*

The abandoned paddy wagon was found the next day, near the dockyards. The discarded Deer Gun was found near the epicentre of the worst of the previous night's rioting, and was an unusual enough discovery that it was brought to the attention of the Australian Federal Police (AFP), who in turn contacted the FBI to see if it could be identified.

It was.

***

27 August 1978
Somewhere off the New England Coast, U.S.A.

Coincidentally, the same day that Major Jones waded into the gay rights demonstrations in Sydney Australia, some ten thousand miles away, Captain Mickey Webb was preparing his ship, the *MV Ocean Saviour*, for a dangerous manoeuver off the United States' New England coast.

It was nearing the end of the whaling season for North Atlantic Right Whales and, having been stymied all season long in his attempts to inhibit the illegal hunting of Right Whales, Webb was frustrated and out of patience. He'd resolved to 'make a difference' one way or another, and had decided to tackle the pirate whaler *Sierra* head-on – literally. A source in a Washington-based conservation organization had provided Webb with the *Sierra's* approximate location, and it had taken a few days patrolling to actually find it. *But they had found it*, Webb thought, with satisfaction.

As the *Sierra* completed a refueling and reprovisioning stop and left port, heading for the open sea, the *Ocean Saviour* was lying in wait. The skipper of the *Sierra* was probably not very concerned. They had tangled with the *Ocean Saviour* before, and were well used to its usual tactics of sending Zodiacs out to buzz around and make their hunting difficult. On this occasion, however, the bridge watch reported no Zodiacs being deployed, which was curious. Yet the ship kept on sailing directly towards them. *A game of chicken, perhaps,* the shipper of the Sierra thought to himself.

On the *Ocean Saviour,* Webb decided it was time. Soon, the skipper of the other ship would realize something was up and take evasive action.

"Full speed ahead. Steer for just before the bow," Webb ordered the helmsman, as he picked up a handset to call the various departments of his ship and warn them that a collision was imminent.

For his part, and as soon as the skipper of the other ship saw the
Ocean Saviour increase speed but not change course, he ordered his helmsman to increase speed and steer hard to starboard. As a result, the *Ocean Saviour,* which had been attempting to use its

reinforced bow to destroy the *Sierra's* harpoon gun, was only able to strike a glancing blow. The *Sierra* was forced to slow down and check for damage, however, which allowed Webb to bring the *Ocean Saviour* around and take another run at her.

The second ramming struck the *Sierra* amidships and left a sizeable hole in its hull. Secure in the knowledge that the *Sierra* would be out of commission for a long time, Webb left it to limp back towards the nearest port[41] while the *Ocean Saviour* headed for Fredericton, New Brunswick.

The surviving mother whales would now be able to continue their journey south, to the waters off Florida, to calve.

Captain Mickey Webb

> "*Anyone who makes his living from the torture, trauma, and death of animals is less than scum, should be squashed underfoot and then roasted, slowly and painfully, upon arriving in Hell.*"
>
> An opponent of the seal hunt.

Captain Webb pulled the letter[42] from his typewriter, signed it with a purposefully indecipherable script. Folding the letter, he sealed it into a previously addressed and stamped envelope, then tossed it into his out-basket with the rest. *Another letter-to-the-editor to another newspaper, from another seal-hugger*, he thought, smiling grimly.

Done with whalers for a while, and having returned to the *Ocean Saviour*'s home port of Fredericton, Captain Webb had turned his attention to the annual seal hunt. He was in the middle of typing another copy of the form letter when a crew member knocked on his door.

"Someone here to see you, Captain."

"Arne Kristiansen from IAAP?"

"I think so. That's what he said his name was, anyway."

"Fine. Show him up would you please?"

"Arne!" he said, when his visitor was shown to his cabin, which also served as his office, "have a seat."

"How are you Mickey? Any luck with the whalers this time?"

"I'm fine, but we had so little success with those damn whalers that I lost my cool and deliberately rammed the pirate ship *Sierra* off the New England coast."

"Good for you," was the prompt reply. "Sunk her, I hope?"

"No, but we rammed her twice. Couldn't get to her harpoon gun, so on the second run we put a good-sized hole in her hull amidships. Left her limping for port when we last saw her. She's a dockyard job now – should be out of commission for next year too."

"Well done, Mickey. Are the police after you?"

"That's the funny thing. No one chased us out, and my sources tell me that no notices have been put out about us either. I think that's because it's a foreign-registered pirate with murky ownership. The Americans don't like ships that register in small Caribbean countries so they can pay low wages, avoid most fees, and ignore international regulations. One of my sources told me that, off the record, the port authorities are pleased with us, and that they're looking forward to finally getting some money out of her for dockage and repairs."

"Well I'll be dammed. Like I said, good for you.... Now then, what do we do about the seal hunt next year?"

"I'll tell you right off, Arne, that I'm frustrated with our lack of progress so far. The demonstrations aren't making enough of a difference. No matter what the quotas are, and no matter what our protesters do, the hunters still take about 160 thousand seals each season. Demonstrating in Ottawa, demonstrating in Newfoundland, demonstrating on the ice itself isn't doing it for us. Even last Spring, when we went out and sprayed the pups' fur with green dye, we didn't save very many seals because we couldn't spray enough of them before the sealers and the police arrived."

"I agree. So, I take it you want to try something different next year?"

"I do. We need something that will generate more media-coverage. Prime-time, coast-to-coast coverage, at a minimum. Overseas coverage if we can get it. We need to reach more people to have any chance of fueling a larger anti-sealing movement."

"How about using the *Ocean Saviour* to blockade the St. John's harbor for a couple of weeks to bottle-up the sealing ships[43]? The Narrows there is well named: it's narrow enough for a single ship to block."

"Maybe, but I'm not sure we'd get enough publicity out of it and I wouldn't put it past the Coast Guard to bring in police and tugs to push us out of the way. I still think we should try some kind of publicity stunt."

"Hmmm. Headline news... How about if we bring along a famous actor? A woman, preferably, that we could photograph cuddling a baby seal in a protective, motherly embrace. That sort of thing?"

"I like it. Can we afford it?"

"By 'we' I take it you mean the IAAP? You're usually lucky if you can pay your fuel and dockage costs, not to mention your crew... Wait a minute, let me think.... When that French actress, Brigitte Bardot came over a few years ago, it made big headlines in Europe. She was expensive though. Maybe if we could find another actress that is very well known, is a supporter of animal rights causes, but is still rising in her career. A combination of sympathy and the extra publicity it would bring for her might be enough to bring her fee down to something we could afford."

"Do you know anyone like that?" asked Mickey, getting interested now.

"Maybe, there are a couple of actresses I can think of. It would be even better – and cheaper - if we can find a well-known but rising Canadian actress. Hmmm... you ever watch *The Beachcombers* on TV when you're in port?"

"Sure. You're not thinking of the blonde?"

"That's right. Ginger Brandt. Former beauty contest winner, former Playboy model, one of the stars of *The Beachcombers*. Someone who's on her way up in Hollywood too from what I read. Best of all, she's a member of IAAP!" he concluded with a flourish.

"You're kidding."

"Not at all. Signed up last year, with a nice contribution, too. Turns out she's a supporter of Greenpeace and few other outfits as well, but her passion is animal rights."

"Can we get her?"

"I don't know, but if you agree I'll see what I can do. I'll call a few agents, put out some feelers, that sort of thing, just to keep our options open. But I'll make a special plea to Ginger Brandt's agent... wine-and-dine, the whole shebang."

"If you can get Ginger, the local media will fall all over themselves to cover us. Imagine if we can film her out on the ice hugging a whitecoat and holding off a horde of ugly, bloodthirsty sealers!"

"Now you're talking, Mickey. So, let's plan this whole thing out. We'll need a more detailed plan than usual if we're going to get a horde of media out in St. John's, and a decent sized group to commit to a few days at sea and on the ice with us when March comes around."

The planning went on for several hours, but when it was concluded they had the outline of a workable plan and schedule, and both men felt well satisfied that they'd have better success in the 1979 season.

Laurie Schramm

St. John's Harbour and the Narrows

6 CALM BEFORE THE STORM

January 8, 1979
Ottawa, ON

It was a Monday, one week after New Year's Day, when I received a call from Ginger.

"Happy New Year Alex, it's Ginger Brandt. Remember me?"

"Of course, I do. Happy New Year to you too."

"My agent got a call from the IAAP. They want me to join them in early March for a trip on the *Ocean Saviour*. There will be sealing protests and a documentary movie filmed. We said yes, and that I'll be bringing an assistant along with me."

"Great. Do you know where they're going?"

"Somewhere called 'The Front' off the coast of Labrador. Can you get to St. John's by March 9?"

"Sure."

"OK then. My assistant here will send you an itinerary, the same background information they'll be sending me, and we'll have a hotel room booked for you. Apparently, the ice conditions are good so far, and they're expecting the seal pups to be born sometime in the following two weeks. The plan is to stick around St. John's until they get word about the pups, then sail on the *Ocean Saviour* up to the ice pack and make a big fuss over the pups for the cameras. You and Silver will have your own cabin, right next to mine, same as at the hotel. OK?"

"Sounds good. We'll drive to North Sydney, Nova Scotia and take the ferry to Port aux Basques. That should get us there by mid-afternoon."

"Great. Keep your receipts. Everything's being paid for by IAAP and the Ocean Saviour Foundation. My assistant will also send you some contact names and phone numbers you can call if you have any questions or problems later. I'll be down in Hollywood filming a new movie, but either my assistant or my agent will be able to get messages to me. I'll be in St. John's by March the ninth."

"Thank you Ginger. We'll see you then!"

"OK. Got to run now. Bye!"

And that was that, we'd have another chance to spot the elusive ex-CIA guy... maybe... if he was even going to show up. *Oh, well,* I thought, *it should be a nice relaxing trip if nothing else.*

I was wrong, of course.

Other than letting my boss, Bob, and my boyfriend, Don, know what I was going to be getting up to next, my only other preliminary was to phone Vivian at her FBI office. I gave her the same information I'd received and told her that I would be posing as Ginger's assistant and bringing Silver along with me. She said she'd try to join our expedition as well and that she'd come up with something for a cover story.

As I told Ginger, I had planned to drive from Ottawa to Cape Breton Island, Nova Scotia and then take the ferry to Newfoundland from North Sydney. When I tried to make a ferry booking, however, I discovered that the ferry to Argentia, which is fairly close to St. John's, only runs from mid-June to late September. The other ferry option, to Port aux Basques, runs year-round but involves a 7-hour crossing followed by a 9-hour drive.

I decided we should fly, but since I wasn't willing to put Silver through the ordeal of travelling in the baggage hold, we'd have to travel officially so he'd be allowed into the passenger cabin with me. Although I wasn't going to travel in uniform, I'd have to identify the two of us to the airport authorities and the airline and hope that the other passengers simply assumed that he was accompanying me as a service dog. To further reduce the risk, I decided that we would fly out a few days early. That would also give us a chance to walk around St. John's and maybe learn how the locals felt about the seal hunt.

March 7, 1979

When early March arrived, and we went to the airport, I identified Silver and myself to CP Air[44] at check-in. They took everything in stride – even my desire to be inconspicuous and let people assume that Silver was some kind of service dog – and they even moved me to a new seat that was beside an unoccupied one, so that Silver would have more room to lie on the floor. When we changed planes in Halifax for the flight to St. John's, they were one step ahead of us, and had given me another seat beside an empty one. The extra seating made a big difference, and the flight attendants made such a fuss over Silver with water and snacks that he radiated contentment. I told him that I thought he was being spoiled, even though I didn't expect him to understand the word spoiled but, as always, he correctly interpreted my thought and managed to look rather smug.

Knowing that I might need an easy way to get around St. John's, whether related to my mission or to running errands for Ginger, I picked up a rental vehicle at the airport – a 1980 Ford Bronco SUV[45]. This had lots of room for Silver and I, and we were soon driving into St. John's and following the long sloping turns that would take us downhill to the harbour. I'd booked a room at The Battery Hotel[46], which was located partway up the famous Signal Hill but still very close to the downtown core and the harbour-front. As we started up the hill, we soon came to the turnoff for the hotel grounds and passed between two vintage, cast-iron muzzle-loading cannons that were positioned like sentinels. I found out later than they had been recovered from a shipwreck in Placentia Bay, on Newfoundland's southeast coast.

Ginger's assistant had booked us a beautiful suite that had a fantastic view of the St. John's harbour and downtown core. Once we'd settled in, I was doubly glad that we'd arrived early as it would give me a chance to absorb some of the rich history of the area. We started this almost right away, as there was time for a walk before supper. For our first walk we did Signal Hill, which is a marvel on its own. From sea level, it rises some 167 metres (nearly 550 feet) and is capped by old fortifications and the famous Cabot Tower. Near the summit, the challenge is whether to focus on the rich history or the stunning, panoramic views. Naturally, I did both.

I learned that Signal Hill has been the pinnacle of St. John's harbour defences from the wars of the 17th century right through the First- and Second World Wars. Along the way, it was also the site at which Marconi received the world's first transatlantic wireless signal, sent by Morse Code in 1901.

At one of the many scenic viewpoints, Queen's Battery, nine large cannons, still mounted on their gun carriages, still crouched behind the fortifications from which they defended the harbour from enemy ships in the 18th and 19th centuries. I made a mental note to remember to tease Vivian, if she succeeded in joining me, with the fact that the last major modernization of the Queen's Battery cannons was in 1862, when the British sent additional troops and artillery to protect St. John's from the Union Navy.

The next day, Silver and I took a longish walk along the harbour-front docks, all the way from Battery Road, at the base of Signal Hill, past the downtown core to the containership pier at the south end[47]. After turning around to walk back, we strolled up a block to Water Street to get a cup of coffee for me and then headed back down to the docks to find a place to just sit and a look out at the inner harbour. I had worn a daypack with water and a bowl for Silver, and I was just pouring the water for him when a man came up and sat down beside us.

My clothes must have marked me as being 'from away[48]' because his first word was "Visiting?" as he filled and lighted a pipe.

"Yes, I'm from Ontario but I sure enjoy every chance I get to visit Newfoundland."

"Lived here all my life," he said, contentedly, and in between puffs from his pipe. "Been a fisherman since I was old enough to stand up and keep my balance in a boat."

"Do you still fish?" I asked.

"Yes b'y. My boats' right over there across the harbour."

"I think I read somewhere that the fishing fleets are taking in more fish each year. Is that right?"

"You're right there, but you have to look a bit deeper. The fish stocks used to be growing but now they've passed the peak and the numbers are decreasing each year."

I noticed that he had the Newfoundland habit of saying 'fish' when he specifically meant cod. Taking his pipe out of his mouth, he continued. "There's two things that have been going on. First," he waved his pipe stem in the air, "new technology lets us fish a bigger area, trawl deeper, and stay out on the water for longer at a time. But the new technology is a curse in disguise because it's given us the ability to take fish out faster than they can breed and get replenished.

"Second," he waved his pipe stem in the air again, "a few years ago – 1976 it was - the government moved the exclusive fishing zone out to 200 miles offshore. The idea was to fix the decreasing fish stocks by kicking the foreign fishing boats out."

"Didn't that help?" I asked.

"It looked like it at first, but then the government increased the quotas for Canadian and American trawlers so nothing really changed and the fish stock just keeps on dropping."

"Won't they reduce the cod quotas then?"

"Doesn't look like it. Seems like the politicians and bureaucrats are afraid to admit they made a mistake, so they keep arguing that the fish are there but we fishermen are too incompetent to find them. Hah! We spend our lives out there on the water. The fish stocks are dropping all right. That's why I'm against the seal hunt."

That caught my full attention. "What? The seal hunt? I thought everyone here supported the seal hunt."

"Well, it's just one more thing on top of the overfishing. See, the seals eat fish that eat baby fish."

"I don't understand."

"Sorry, there's fish and then there's fish. Let me try it again. The seals eat fish that eat baby cod. That's good for the fishery. But, if the seal population drops due to their being hunted, then there's more predatory fish available to eat the baby cod. One more thing taking the cod population down is one more thing we don't need – right?"

"I see. I guess I didn't think about the predator-prey relationships."

"There you go. Everything's connected, the fish – I mean cod – the other fish, the seals, even the plankton. That's why the government messes things up every time it steps in and makes a new regulation. It's because they only change one thing and don't take into account the way the whole system works. It's stupid, but they do it over and over again."

"What's the answer then?"

"Simple." Out came his pipe again to punctuate each point. "We fishermen have been fishing these waters for generations and the older the crab, the tougher its claws[49], as they say. We know all too well when the area is being overfished. The government needs to tackle the whole problem, not just the little pieces: keep the foreign fishing fleets out - the Americans included - reduce the fishing quotas, and restrict the seal hunt to the Inuit people that need it to survive. Then the fish will come back[50]."

We sat in companionable silence for the next while, enjoying the view, the weather, and the boat activity in the harbour. "Well, time for us to continue our walk," I said, eventually. "Nice talking to you."

"Fair weather to you[51]," was his reply.

Since we had another day free before Ginger's arrival, I decided we should spend it sightseeing. An easy drive took us through the downtown core and then overland until we reached Cape Spear, where two lighthouses perch at the edge of a rugged cliff that marks the most easterly point in North America. One of the lighthouses was built in 1836, and rises right up out of the roof of the lightkeeper's residence. No longer active, it was retired in 1955 when the second, more modern lighthouse was commissioned. The newer light house is of the familiar octagonal-tower-with-balcony design that can be seen in many other parts of Atlantic Canada.

Among the short walks at Cape Spear is a winding path that leads down and around the point to Fort Cape Spear, which still houses the twin, 10-inch guns that formed part of the St. John's harbour defenses during the Second World War.

I was standing on the edge of the fortifications, looking out at the open sea and enjoying the brisk wind and smell of ocean air, when I noticed another visitor stroll up beside us. It was an older but vigorous-looking man of about my own age who was also walking a dog and sightseeing. The typical reactions of our dogs, that had them cautiously circling and sniffing each other, prompted a brief conversation. A few light remarks led the conversation to how much we each enjoyed Canada's ocean coastlines, which happened to remind him of the TV series *The Beachcombers*.

"Did you know that Ginger Brandt, one of the stars is supposed to be coming here to help protest the seal hunt?"

"Yes, I read that in the paper this morning," I replied. "Are you a fan?"

"I'm a big fan! I watch the show every week. In fact, I'm planning to go see her arrival at the airport tomorrow, so I can see what she's like in person."

"Sounds interesting, but I don't like crowds very much."

We drifted on to other topics before I moved on, using the excuse of getting a bit chilled from the cold offshore wind. As we walked away, it occurred to me that he was about the age and build of our ex-CIA quarry, the elusive Major Jones, master of disguises. *Could that have been him?* I wondered, as a second chill struck me – one that had nothing to do with the weather. I decided that it was improbable, since Silver hadn't reacted to him at all, and decided that I was letting my imagination run away with me. *All the same*, I thought, it was a good reminder that we were hunting a dangerous killer and I would need to remain vigilant.

Ginger arrived the next day, and Silver and I did go to the airport to observe her arrival even though we didn't plan to meet until she was settled into the hotel.

Naturally, the media had been alerted in advance and they were there in force to greet her. As she entered the main terminal building, there was complete mayhem as a wave of reporters pressed forward, many of them yelling questions at her – so many, in fact, that it was almost impossible for me to understand what the questions were – and all amid a blaze of light from the television camera crews and the almost continuous flashes of brilliant light from still cameras.

It was interesting to see how well Ginger handled things. None of the lights, noise, crowd, or shouted questions seemed to faze her in the least. Stopping for only a moment to size-up the audience, she then quickly made her way to a baggage carousel and stepped up onto it so that everyone, including the cameras would have a good view of her. Then she held her hands up for the crowd to quiet down and waited patiently for the noise to subside, which it did, almost immediately.

"Thank you for coming to see me. I'll be happy to take questions," she said, "but one at a time please, so I can hear them." Then she pointed at one of the reporters in the crowd and said, "Let's start with you," and then she methodically worked the crowd, picking out reporter after reporter.

Was it true that she was there to protest against the seal hunt? "Of course," she said, "I abhor cruelty to animals, and this seal hunt is barbaric. They're planning to kill 200,000 poor, defenseless seals this year including baby seal pups! It's horrible and it needs to stop."

What was she hoping to achieve there? "I want the Canadian government to stop protecting and subsidizing the seal hunt and all other governments to prohibit all imports of sealskin."

Was she going to speak to the government directly? "I don't know. I hope so. I have asked for meetings with the Premier of Newfoundland and with the Prime Minister, but their offices always say they are too busy.... Too busy, can you believe it? How can they be too busy to talk about the torture and killing of defenseless animals, I'd like to know."

Not all the questions were as friendly and leading as these, but she handled them all with ease. For example, a reporter asked whether she wasn't simply out to gain publicity for her TV series and her upcoming new movie. "Look," she replied, "an actress needs all the publicity she can get, but when I'm out for publicity I go to the big cities like New York and Hollywood because I get more bang for the buck there. But when I come to Newfoundland, it's either for a cause or a vacation – because I love the people, and the ocean, and the beautiful scenery you have here. In this case, I'm here for a cause – the cause of the Harp Seals."

That was a pretty good reply, I thought, but it led to another difficult question. If she loves the people, she was asked, then what about the local communities that need the money from the seal hunts, especially when there is no other income outside of the fishing seasons?

Uh oh, I thought, *that's a tough one*. But I needn't have worried, she was ready for that one too.

"I understand that people need to work and earn money so they can look after themselves and their families," she replied, "but killing these poor defenseless seals for their skins is a barbarous practice that should have been retired long ago.

"If the Canadian government took the subsidies that they currently throw at the seal hunt, and instead put them into factories that can easily make perfectly good synthetic fur products, it would provide good, year-round jobs and money for people here in Newfoundland and Labrador. Locally produced synthetic fur products could be sold all over the world. I'd wear them myself, and I'm willing to volunteer right now to helping to promote them."

What about the fishermen who need work outside of the fishing season? "Ecotourism," she fired back. "This is one of the most beautiful places on earth. Marine ecotourism, including seal and whale watching, would be a great option for fishermen and their boats, and can bring in far more money than seal hunting."

Surprisingly, those last few answers turned the tide and the next few questions focused on smaller things like how long she planned to stay, whether she was going to tour around the province while she was there, Hollywood gossip, and so on. Sensing that the impromptu media scrum had peaked, she quickly switched gears, thanked everyone for coming out to see her, and promised that there would be other opportunities to ask questions in coming days.

With that, she jumped down from the baggage carousel, and strode through the terminal. Although several reporters followed her, shouting questions and snapping more pictures, I was able to get into her line of sight long enough for her to see me and wave. "See you at the hotel" she mouthed, just before reaching the curb outside and stepping into a waiting limousine that was strategically placed, bore a large sign with her name on it, and had its rear door already open for her. With another wave, she was gone.

Wow, I thought, *like a whirlwind*. But a whirlwind with purpose. She'd been in complete control the entire time. I was impressed.

Ginger had taken a morning flight from somewhere, and had arrived in St. John's shortly after lunchtime. I knew that we'd been booked adjacent suites, and I guessed that it wouldn't be long after Silver and I had returned to the hotel that I'd hear from her, so I wasn't surprised when there was a knock on the connecting door between our suites. I was however, completely taken aback by the woman standing in the doorway when I opened the door on my side.

"Elizabeth Peterson," said the woman as Silver padded up to her, gave her hand a lick and received an ear rub in return.

After a double-take, I got a grip on myself and said "Ginger?"

The answer came first in the form of a brilliant smile. I knew that smile.

"It is you! But what a transformation." The woman standing in front of me appeared to be two or three inches shorter than the Ginger I'd met in BC, had hazel-coloured eyes (previously blue), lustrous, medium-brown hair cut short, wore no makeup, and had glasses.

"What do you think?" she said, giving a bit of a pirouette as she strolled into the room.

"I'm amazed," I replied, truthfully, and then as my brain started processing again: "I take it this is your way of avoiding fans and the media when you need to?"

"That's right. I told you before I'm a very private person in real life, and the only way I can achieve balance is to be able to leave the movie-star world now and again and just be the real me in the real world."

"So, you made up your own character?"

"Not exactly. Ginger Brandt is my stage name; Elizabeth Peterson is my original name. As for my appearance, this is the real me. The only made-up part, is that the Elizabeth Peterson that you see before you often pretends to be Ginger Brandt's personal assistant. That way, people can see her going in and out of my room without giving it another thought.

"The Ginger Brandt you saw at the airport yesterday was wearing high heels, blue contact lenses, a blond wig, and full makeup."

"And your..." I pantomimed cupping my hands below my breasts.

"Oh yes. Another marvel of modern engineering. Ginger wears bras that enhance the appearance of her breasts, while Elizabeth wears bras that diminish their appearance."

"I'm amazed," I said, for the second time, "and so simple."

"Like magic, in fact. Any magician will tell you that all their illusions are simple once you know their secrets. Some time when we're not on this adventure, I'll come see you in Ottawa and we'll do the reverse for you."

She looked me over appraisingly, which made me feel quite self-conscious and even a bit nervous. "You have fantastic red hair and green eyes," she said, "I'd add a wig of the same colour to give it more body and length, makeup to bring out your eyes... I bet you don't wear skirts or dresses, do you?"

"No, not really. Not for a very long time anyway."

"So, a long silky gown, high heels to show your legs off, a push-up bra to focus people's attention, and you'll be the talk of the town. What do you say?"

"I'd say I'm skeptical, but what the hell, let's give it a try some time."

"Do you have a boyfriend?"

"Yes. His name's Don, but I'm not sharing him!"

"That's OK, when I'm done with you, we'll knock his eyes out! By the way, you figured me out pretty quickly when I walked in here. What gave me away?"

"It wasn't anything you did, it was Silver. He walked right up to you like he knew you and licked your hand. That was my clue. He doesn't do that with strangers, but he picked up on two things you didn't change: your scent and the sound of your voice."

"Smart boy, Silver. Good for you," she said to him. To me, she added: "Feel like a walk? I need some fresh air and exercise after that flight."

"Sounds great. Have you ever been to St. John's before?"

"Only once or twice."

"Well, one of my favourite things to do here is just walk along the harbour-front. How about that?"

"Let's do it, and by the way, please call me Liz when you're with the real me, OK?"

"Deal."

Since we were both already dressed in casual clothes, all we needed to do was to grab light jackets and sun hats, and off we went. As we exited from my room, I noticed that there were a couple of photographers hovering in the hallway and keeping a close eye on the door to her suite. Of us, they took no notice whatsoever. Once we were alone in the elevator, with the door closed, she turned to me and said "See, safely anonymous."

Unbelieveable, I thought.

The three of us did essentially the same walk that Silver and I had done two days previously, the only difference being that it was an overcast, grey day. When we neared the southern end of the accessible part of the harbour-front, there were two tour boats tied up, each with advertising stands set up nearby. One of them the *Scademia*[52], which was billed as being the last old-school-type, two-masted schooner to have been built in Newfoundland, the kind that used to sail around Newfoundland as a fishing boat in a

565

previous era.

"Would you like to try a short boat tour Liz?" I asked. "I went out on the *Scademia* the last time I was in St. John's and really enjoyed it. They do a run through the harbour, go out through the Narrows into the open ocean, and then over to see Cape Spear, before coming back. It only takes about two hours, so depending on when the next sailing is, we could still be back in time for supper."

"Sounds great," she replied.

"The only thing is, I don't know whether they'll let me take Silver on board. Last time I was here, was before Silver and I had even met."

Walking up to the display booth for the *Scademia*, I was pleasantly surprised to recognize the man standing there as the Captain of the schooner the last time I'd been on it. I asked when the next sailing was and whether or not we could take Silver on board with us.

"We don't normally allow pets on board, which is a bit of a contradiction because you'll see my Newfoundland dog come on the trip with us, but there won't be many people coming along since we're so far ahead of tourist season. As long as he's on a leash, you're welcome to bring him along. Next trip leaves in 20 minutes."

Thanking him, I bought two tickets for Ginger and myself – he refused to charge me for Silver – and we continued our stroll to kill time before the sailing. When we returned to the boat 15 minutes later, we were welcomed by the sounds of traditional Newfoundland music being performed by two local musicians who were sitting in the stern, one playing an electric violin and the other an accordion.

As we handed over our tickets to a crew member, the Captain was on hand to tell her that we could bring Silver on board with us. When we did, he personally led us to the stern to meet his Newfoundland dog who, we were amused to learn, was named Ginger. After suitable circling and sniffing, the two dogs decided they liked each other and remained close together for the entire trip. They made an unusual pair as Silver is a large dog, over two feet tall at his shoulder and about 85 pounds, but Ginger the dog was in a class all her own at about the same height but (according to the Captain) 120 pounds!

The boat cruise, of course, was great. To the sounds of rousing, Celtic Sea tunes, the schooner did a circuit of the harbour then took us past old gun batteries and through the Narrows – the only passage into and out of the harbour, bounded by steep rocky cliffs, and only about 60 m (200 ft) wide at its narrowest. The schooner, under the power of its twin 100-horsepower engines, had no trouble navigating the channel, but I wondered at the skill that would be required to navigate a container ship through or, in days long past, ships that had only their sails to propel them through.

As we entered the open ocean, the musicians took a break from their singing and playing to become bartenders. This was our cue to get a couple of traditional Screech[53]-and-Cokes as the schooner plowed through the waves, heading for Cape Spear. This gave us time to sit, enjoy the journey, and chat while Silver was companionably stretched out beside Ginger, the Newfoundland dog.

Besides the dogs, we pretty much had the open deck to ourselves as the small number of other sightseers had quickly made their way into one of the two glassed-in, heated cabins. It was 10 °C, quite warm for March, but others seemed to find it quite cold. In fact, I was surprised that Ginger seemed fine with the cold, and asked her about it.

"I was born in Calgary and spent a lot of time in the Rocky Mountains. When you go there, you have to be prepared for all kinds of weather, and in any season. I remember camping near the Columbia Icefields Parkway one year, and getting snowed on in the middle of summer! Anyway, you learn to adapt and I've always loved being outdoors, no matter the weather.... This is Liz talking, mind you," she laughed. "Ginger would be freezing to death and worrying that the wind would mess up her hair."

Since there were no other ears around, we traded growing-up stories while the schooner made its way slowly but surely towards Cape Spear.

We were far too early for either the iceberg-watching (April – June) or whale-watching (May – Sept.) seasons, but it was still a fun trip that provided a unique view of Cape Spear's two lighthouses and lower fortifications. Even just getting out on the open ocean was enough for me.

On our return, the Captain put on a traditional Screech-In Ceremony by telling a couple of probably-fictitious (but certainly amusing) stories in an exaggerated Newfoundland accent and using so many colloquialisms that it was impossible to understand at times. After the stories, he asked us "Is yer screechers?" He'd already coached us on the correct answer, so everyone was able to respond "Indeed I is, me old cock, and long may your big jib draw," the latter phrase meaning "may there always be wind in your sail," or "good luck." In the second part of the ritual, the crew passed out samples of smoked cod to try.

In the third part, we were invited to "kiss the cod." On shore, such ceremonies usually involved being handed a frozen cod to kiss. On the schooner, it was an actual stuffed cod (that is, a real cod - taxidermically 'mounted' - not a plush, toy cod). Lord knows how old it was, or how many people had previously kissed it but, unhygienic or not, the stuffed cod was passed around for each person to kiss.

In the fourth part of the ritual, they gave us each a small glass of Screech to drink. The Captain then explained that because each of us had spoken, eaten, kissed, and drunk something 'Newfoundland,' we were entitled to a small scroll that proclaimed us to be honourary Newfoundlanders.

After the *Scademia* docked and we disembarked, we strolled up from Harbour Drive to Water Street, then one more street higher to Duckworth where there were quite a few restaurants.

"What do you feel like eating?" asked Liz.

"Seafood. How about you?"

"Anything! I'm famished."

In the end, we found a nice little restaurant with an outside patio where dogs were allowed. 'On leash,' of course. I knew Silver wouldn't mind too much as long as he got 'people food.' The restaurant people hadn't been planning to serve outdoors (it being only 10°C after all), but the tables and chairs were all there and our server kindly said "Why not?" and took it all in stride.

When we'd been served a pair of glasses of Chardonnay, and a bowl of water for Silver, we looked at each other for a moment. "That was great Alex. I felt free. Thank you," said Liz, contentedly sipping her wine.

"I really enjoyed it too. The wind, and the ocean, and the live music. It felt exciting through the narrows, and I especially liked the wild feeling of being out on the open ocean.... Did you enjoy just being 'Liz' for a while?"

"I love my job and my work, but I can't tell you how wonderful it is to be just me for a few hours and to have been able to spend it with a friend – a new friend."

I raised my glass in acknowledgement: "Cheers."

She raised her glass in return and, with an absolutely straight face said "Long may your big jib draw."

We both giggled, and relaxed even more as she continued. "The *Ocean Saviour's* due to come in tomorrow, so plain old Elizabeth will have to go back to being Ginger the actress."

"Well, I like you both," I asserted, "and for tonight you can still be Liz."

"Deal," she agreed.

It was a little chilly out there on the deck after all, but we persevered and had a nice quiet dinner. All by ourselves.

The Daily News

Saturday, March 10, 1979

Ginger Brandt to Protest Sealing
Famous Actress Turns Activist

When we met in her suite for breakfast the next morning, Ginger was energized and well-pleased with the Saturday morning newspaper and the earlier radio coverage that she'd received. She had also received a message that the *Ocean Saviour* ship had come in overnight, and was tied up along the dock on the edge of downtown.

To avoid the media, Ginger, Silver, and I went aboard very early to meet the Captain. As we approached the ship, we stopped for a moment to look up and take it all in. I suppose it wasn't huge compared with some commercial ocean-going vessels, like tankers and container ships, but it certainly appeared large from the point of view of someone standing on the wharf beside it. The *MV Ocean Saviour* was nearly 200 feet in length and had a beam of more than 30 feet. It had the word 'RESCUE,' in bold eight-foot-tall red letters, stenciled on its side, and there was a small helicopter secured to a landing flatform near the stern.

The gangway wasn't roped off, so we went up and were met at the top by a crew member who introduced himself by saying "Everybody calls me 'Red.' I guess you can tell why," he said, looking pointedly at my own red hair.

I laughed and said, "Yes, but I try not to let anybody get away with it!"

Chuckling, he escorted us to the Captain's cabin.

When we got there, and were announced, the Captain bounded up from his desk to greet us. "Mickey Webb, glad to meet you. Please have a seat," he said to Ginger, waving towards his one good visitor chair and sparing only the briefest of glances at Silver and I before continuing. "I think you already know Arne Kristiansen, President of IAAP. He'll be coming out with us."

"Hi Ginger, said Kristiansen, who was sitting perched on the Captain's bunk. "Nice to meet you in person. Thank you for agreeing to join us." Silver and I only merited a glance from him as well. Clearly, we were to be treated as lowly 'staff.' That was OK, as I didn't want to attract attention anyway. Silver and I simply stood quietly by the cabin door and watched and listened.

It was interesting to watch, as the two men treated Ginger like visiting royalty while she, for her part, accepted their fawning as if it was an everyday occurrence – *which for her it probably was*, I reflected – and yet she somehow still managed to convey the sense of empty-headed, wide-eyed innocence of the *Beachcombers* character that had helped make her famous.

While they chatted, it gave me time to size-up the two men. Kristiansen, I had had previously seen as the Ottawa protest leader the previous July. Up close, he seemed even larger than he had before, and still had a shock of rather unruly-looking dark hair. In Ottawa, he'd been the man with the megaphone but his normal voice was quite booming in the confines of the Captain's cabin, as he talked about the sealers and the need to stop them, pounding with a meaty hand on the wooden sides of the Captain's bunk to emphasize his points. *Like a bull in a china shop*, I thought to myself. Even his normal speaking manner suggested latent violence.

In contrast, Captain Webb wasn't physically imposing, and his manner was friendly and easy-going. He was of medium height, with a medium build, thick, sandy-coloured hair that was just long enough to look unruly, and he had the stereotypical sailor's clear blue eyes. He didn't add much content to the discussion, seeming content to make small jokes here and there, as if to take the rough edges off of Kristiansen's rather harsh and angry assertions. *This one's all smiles*, I thought to myself, and yet I sensed an underlying character that I though was probably different entirely. Those eyes were very watchful and I suspected that they didn't miss much. I wondered whether his easy-going exterior masked a mind of intelligence and cunning. Whereas my new impression of Kristiansen was of someone that would impulsively come and challenge a person or situation directly, Captain Webb would be more strategic, develop a plan first, and come at his quarry by stealth. Both men would bear watching, I decided.

I was jolted out of these thoughts when Ginger deftly turned the conversation to lighter matters, beginning with asking about the ship. "It seems so very large," she said, with a shockingly wide-eyed, vapid expression that very nearly made me laugh out loud. As it was, I had to deflect my surprise into a pretend coughing fit that earned me dark looks from both men. Apparently 'staff' were to be seen but not heard.

It was the right approach to make to the Captain though, as he smiled even more brightly than before and sat up straighter in his chair.

"We were lucky to find it," he said proudly. "It's classified as a research and survey vessel and used to be used for marine meteorological and oceanographic research. That made it well suited for our purposes. We haven't had it long. It was purchased in 1978 by the Ocean Saviour Foundation, and the only real modifications we had to make were to strengthen the hull to make her more ice-worthy."

"So, it's like an ice-breaker?" Ginger almost gushed.

"Well, I don't think I'd go that far..." He paused, as if

judiciously considering the question. "We can ram our way through one- or two-season ice, but not the really thick multi-season ice like the Coast Guard icebreakers can."

"You must have an awful lot of responsibility, with so large a ship. How many people will there be?"

Ginger had clearly found the source of his pride – his ship and everything on it. If anything, his chest swelled out even further than it had before. "For this sailing, we'll have about 45. That includes the crew, staff and volunteers from the Ocean Saviour Foundation. And, of course, the media." He went on to describe something of what it took to run a ship of the *Ocean Saviour's* size, and the nature of the volunteers that would form the main body of the protest demonstration on the ice pack. That led, of course, to the plan for the trip.

"We'll need two more days for supplies and minor repairs. You might want to move your things onto the ship on Monday and sleep here that night. We'll be sailing at high tide the next day."

"How exciting," said Ginger, in a breathless kind of voice. "How long will it take us to get to where the seals are?"

The Captain sat back in his chair and shifted into a pontificating manner. "Well now, we have to wait for the birthing to be well underway – almost over, in fact. That's what the sealers will be waiting for too, because they particularly want to go after the white-coated seal pups...." He steepled the fingers of his two hands at this point, and went on in a professorial tone to explain that once we got to the 'Front,' the ice pack off the southeast Labrador coast, they'd use the ship's helicopter to scout for the main parts of the herd and watch for the seal pups.

As for the time to sail from St. John's to the Front, he first looked up at the ceiling for a moment, as if considering the question. Then he shrugged. "Well, it's over 300 nautical miles and we'll most likely be cruising at about 13 knots so we're looking at around 42 hours just to get into the right area." He leaned forward at this point, and adopted a concerned tone. "A lot depends on how rough the seas are, of course. We'll get there a bit sooner if we have calm water, later if it's rough. Have you ever sailed on a ship before?"

"Oh no," she exclaimed. "Only those little boats that you see on our TV show... and the car ferries, of course," she added as an afterthought.

"Well, if you see the ship's doctor when you come back aboard, he'll give you something to help with seasickness. It's better to take the medicine before you need it, than to wait until you're not feeling well."

"Oh, thank you for being so kind," Ginger gushed again. "I'm sure everything will be just fine with you looking after us!"

"All part of the service," purred the Captain, charmingly. "I'll have someone show you your cabins, so you'll know what to expect when you next come aboard." Lifting a telephone-style handset, he pushed a button and spoke briefly, then replaced it and got up. "It was a pleasure to meet you in person Miss Brandt, and I'm looking forward to having you with us for the trip."

"It was my pleasure, I'm sure, and please call me Ginger," she purred.

Kristiansen had also risen by this time and put his hand out to shake. "Thank you again for agreeing to come with us on this trip Ginger. Once the world media see our documentary and the pictures of you helping us saving the baby seals, we'll be a big step closer to shutting down this despicable seal hunt."

"I'm looking forward to it!" she said.

There was a knock on the door, which opened to show a rather weather-beaten, tough-looking man that I judged to be in his mid-fifties. "This is Sam Hynes," explained Captain Webb. "He'll be looking after you while you're with us. He's been with this ship since it was commissioned and knows it like the back of his hand. Anything you need, just ask Sam."

"How do you do Sam?' said Ginger, holding out her hand and giving him a dazzling smile.

"Just you follow me, ma'am," was all he said, before turning to head down the passageway. But I had seen the look in his eyes before he turned. In only five seconds, Ginger had already hooked another fan.

Sam led us to the Boat Deck, which was below the Bridge Deck (where the Captain's cabin was), and just above the Upper Deck (the main deck, which ran the full length of the ship – from bow to stern). On the Boat Deck, we'd been assigned two adjacent, 'outside' cabins that would have been originally designed to house research scientists. Each cabin contained a double berth (bunkbed), a closet with pull-out drawers, and a desk unit. The two cabins shared a head (bathroom). Since the head had two sliding interior doors, one leading to each of our cabins, our cabins were essentially interconnected. The cabins were not huge, but since each was designed for double occupancy, they weren't tiny either and they were fitted with decent-sized rectangular-porthole windows as well.

Sam also gave us a partial tour of the ship, which still retained many of its original nameplates, like "Officers' and Scientists' Saloon" (meaning dining room), "Officers' and Scientists' Lounge" (and bar), "Library and Conference Room," "Hospital," "Laundry," and so on. It seemed pretty nice for a former research/survey vessel, and even had a sauna on the Tween Deck (which, as the name suggests, was between the Upper Deck and the Lower Deck).

After thanking Sam and leaving the ship, I couldn't resist telling Ginger how amazed I was at her performance.

"What do you mean?" she asked, with an air of innocence.

"Hah!" I said, "I already know you well enough not to fall for that wide-eyed, 'dumb and innocent' act you seem to be able to turn on and off like a switch. But the two men went for your performance hook, line, and sinker. It was unbelievable. They were lapping it up like starving kittens at a fresh bowl of cream, while I was constantly struggling to stay quiet and keep a straight face."

Ginger giggled. "Well, I am an actress after all.... To be completely honest though, all I had to do was give them what they expected. They already thought of me as if I'm the character I play on TV, so all I had to do was play along and not disappoint them."

"I still think you're a wonder, Ginger."

She giggled again and took my arm. "You know, I'm going to enjoy having a friend along that also knows the real me."

"I'm looking forward to this trip myself," I admitted. "Just please try to remember that it won't be all fun and games. Don't forget, I'm after a killer, so while you're playing games with all the men as Ginger, please make sure your inner Liz stays sharp and keeps her wits about her."

"I promise," said Ginger, instantly sober, "but we still have the rest of today and all of tomorrow before things get complicated – right?"

"Right," I agreed. "What would you like to do next?"

"Let's trade," she suggested. "I'll pick something for this afternoon and you pick something for tomorrow afternoon, OK?"

"What about tomorrow morning?" my analytical mind wanted to know.

"Tomorrow morning, we sleep in," she said with a firm tone. "It might be our last chance for a few days."

"OK then, it's a deal," I said, laughing. "So, what do you pick for this afternoon?"

"How about a hike? The hotel's front desk gave me a brochure that describes some short hikes around Signal Hill. I thought we could do the North Head Trail and then the Ladies Lookout Trail."

"Those are great hikes, I did them the last time I was in St. John's. There's something irresistible about them. The views are fantastic."

So, that's what we did – with Ginger back in her 'Liz' persona. Having found a nice spot for an early lunch on the way back to the hotel, with an outside deck of course, we slipped back to our rooms to grab our raincoats – just in case – and some bottles of water, then went walking.

It was a fairly typical spring day in St. John's: partly cloudy, with a moderate onshore breeze. Since the Battery Hotel was itself partly up the side of Signal Hill, we had to first walk down to get to Battery Road, which led us through a small community known – appropriately enough – as The Battery. Although known as an artistic/fishing community, one's first impression is inescapably the kaleidoscopic collection of brightly-coloured homes. Our second impression was one of wonder, that the beginning of the North Head Trail was also the front deck of someone's house. Being big-city people, our first instinct was to conclude that we must have gotten our directions mixed up, because surely a public trail wouldn't cross someone's front deck – would it? But we were reassured by a two small signs, one proclaiming the deck to be the trailhead and the second, which simply said, "Public Entrance."

Tentatively, we mounted the stairs and crossed the deck, all the while feeling that we must be doing something wrong. "Only in Canada," said Liz, with a chuckle.

As we left the houses behind, the terrain became rougher and we found ourselves circumnavigating the steep-rock side of Signal Hill. As we did, we passed Second-World-War-era bunkers and a range of sights, from the sea and the Narrows below us, to a clear view along the length of the harbourfront behind and to one side, and a narrow path along the steep, rocky wall that lie ahead. In fact, portions of the path were so narrow and rough that some sections were provided with a heavy steel chain secured by eye-bolts that had been driven into the rock, while others were covered with wooden boardwalks and railings.

One of my favourite pictures of Liz is one that I took of her standing on the narrow path with both hands clinging onto the heavy chain, with the vertical, rocky face of the hill to one side and the open vista of the sea to the other. In the picture, she manages to look like she's timid and hanging-on for dear life, but in fact she took all of the hikes' challenges in stride, even when later we had to do some significant uphill stretches and, much later, when we had to contend with the final climb up a seemingly never-ending staircase up another almost vertical side of Signal Hill. It wasn't never-ending, of course, but it did have more than 1,000 stairs. Liz and I were both in pretty good physical condition, but we agreed that the 150 m (500 ft) ascent had earned Parks Canada's rating as "strenuous." Silver, for his part, seemed unfazed by the climb although even he seemed happy to have a few moments to rest and pant when we reached the top of the climb. He looked quite happy with his mouth open and his tongue drooping out to one side in a kind of wolfish smile.

Once we'd caught our breath, it was still only mid-afternoon, so we continued on to the trailhead for the Ladies' Lookout Trail, which wasn't far away.

The Ladies' Lookout Trail basically sticks to the 'backbone' of Signal Hill and, while it only has a modest elevation gain on its way to the summit, it is a much more rugged route than our previous hike had been. It had scenery though!

"Beautiful!" Liz would stop and exclaim every once in a while, as we reached yet another ocean vista. We'd been fortunate to pick a day that was neither rainy nor foggy, so the blue-grey ocean seemed to stretch out forever, until it was lost in the thin line that marked the horizon. Other than a few clouds and seabirds, it was all rock and ocean.

The summit, of course, was the "Ladies' Lookout" from which the trail gets its name. Our trail brochure explained that, in days past, women would go there in hopes of a first sighting of returning ships carrying their "husbands and lovers."

"I wonder how often their husbands and their lovers were travelling on the same ship?" said the irreverent Liz.

It was distinctly windy and chilly at the summit, so it wasn't very long before we decided it was time to head back. By the time we'd made our way down Signal Hill to our hotel, we'd been walking and sightseeing for nearly three hours.

The next day was Monday, our last day of freedom before joining the ship. It was my turn to pick an activity, and I chose another personal favourite.

"There's a group of small islands that are protected as a bird sanctuary near a fishing village called Bay Bulls. It doesn't sound like much, but it's a nice boat ride out and you have to see the birds and the islands to believe them."

"Sounds great! Let's do it," exclaimed Liz.

"OK. Bay Bulls is south of here, about half an hour's drive along the coast. Since we're not in the tourist season, we'll have to check around and see if we can persuade one of the tour boat operators to take us out. If that doesn't work, we might be able to hire a fisherman to take us out."

"Let's try it," said Liz. "I have a feeling we'll be lucky today."

So, we piled into my rental SUV about mid-morning and made the drive to Bay Bulls. When we got there, we parked and strolled down to the docks where quite a few tour- and fishing boats were tied up. Several of them sported signs of human activity, mostly people cleaning, repairing, or even painting parts of their precious boats.

Even though there were no signs or pictures painted on it, one of the boats looked like the kind that did fishing and whale-watching charters. It was a Cape Islander[54], probably about 40 feet in length, and instead of being full of fishing gear it had an open stern fitted with benches, a generous main cabin behind the wheelhouse, and there was an additional viewing deck on the roof of the main cabin. There was a man working on something in the boat's stern section, so that's where we headed first.

After saying 'good morning' to him, we explained that we were hoping to charter a boat to take us out to see the bird sanctuary at Gull Island[55]. "I took one of the tours there when I was last here, a few years ago. My friend hasn't seen much of Newfoundland, and I thought she should see more of it."

"Well," he said, scratching his chin thoughtfully, "you're a bit early. We're not into the main season yet, and the birds won't all be there."

Seeing out disappointed looks, he continued on a bit more encouragingly. "Don't get me wrong, now. The birds have been flying in pretty steadily the past few weeks, but there's more on the way that will be arriving over the next couple of weeks. I can take you out if you want – I just don't want you to be disappointed."

"We'll be fine," I assured him. "Even just getting out on the water and touring around a bit will be good for me." Liz nodded her agreement.

He smiled. "I think we can do better than that.... Now then, I'd have to charge you more than the tourist season rate to take just the two of you out. This old boat of mine eats fuel like you wouldn't believe."

"Can Silver come with us too?" I asked, pointing to Silver. "He's used to being on boats."

"Sure can, I only meant that I wouldn't charge for him."

"How much would it be?" asked Liz. This was a very different persona from the Ginger that had been on the *Ocean Saviour* the previous day. As Liz, she sounded like a businesswoman preparing to negotiate.

"The normal rate would be $45 per person, but with just two passengers – plus your dog – I'd need to charge you double that."

"So, $90 each then," said Liz. He nodded.

At this point Liz unleashed one of Ginger's trade-mark, brilliant smiles and said "OK then, I'll tell you what. How about if we pay you $200 and you throw in some sandwiches and something to drink. I'm starving!"

"No, no," he replied. "You're both visitors here, and I'm not going to let you get cheated. I'll take the $180, only, and if you'll give me a few minutes I'll go get my son and we'll pack some food and drink to bring along. OK?"

"There's just no negotiating with you is there?" This, accompanied by another brilliant smile. "My name's Liz, my friend here is Alex, and you've already met her dog Silver."

"My name's George O'Dell," he said, climbing up out of the boat, onto the dock, and holding his hand out to shake. "My house is just by the shore over there. Why don't you wander around the village here a bit and you'll see us when my son Jimmy and I come back to the boat."

We readily agreed, went for a stroll around the village, then made our way back to the docks and prowled them – looking at all the different boats that were tied up there. In what seemed like no time at all, we spotted George walking towards us, accompanied by a tall, gangling teenager who turned out to be Jimmy, his son. Soon, we were established in the stern of the boat while the O'Dells piloted us out of their small, well-protected bay and onto the open ocean. Before long, we were far from shore and cruising towards our destination. The wind was up a bit, and the sea was choppy, but being down low and behind the main cabin gave us some partial protection.

After taking in the scenery for a while, Jimmy came to let us know that lunch was available in the main cabin, where we found comfortable bench seats and two tables. Lunch turned out to be sandwiches and whatever we wanted from the bar, plus bowls of smoked fish (i.e., cod) and water. Silver particularly liked the smoked cod.

While we were eating, we noticed that an animated discussion, in hushed tones, seemed to be underway between the skipper, who was standing at the helm, and his son.

Uh oh, I thought. But I needn't have been concerned. Eventually, the skipper came back to where we were sitting and said, "Excuse me. Sorry to interrupt, but my son insists that you're Ginger Brandt from *The Beachcombers*, but he's too shy to come and ask you himself."

"Guilty as charged," replied Liz, reverting back to her Ginger persona and waving Jimmy over with a smile.

In between bites of her sandwich, Ginger fielded questions from Jimmy, who stood near our table, and George, who had resumed his position at the wheel.

Jimmy's first question was "Aren't you going to get sick, like you always do on the boats in *The Beachcombers*?"

"...and like you told Captain Webb," I murmured, *sotto voce*.

"No," she laughed. "In real life, I love the ocean and I only get seasick when it's really rough."

"You'll be fine today then," he said, knowledgeably. "It shouldn.t get any worse today than it is right now. It might even ease up a bit after we've gone round the islands."

After a few more questions, it was inevitable that they'd ask for a picture with her. She graciously agreed, which led to Ginger, George, and Jimmy crowding into the wheelhouse, with Ginger at the wheel, all of them smiling back at me in the main cabin, where

I'd been given the job of photographer.

"There you go," she said, after I'd taken several shots. "I hope one of them turns out for you."

"Can we put a copy up on the wall inside the main cabin?" asked George, hopefully. "It would help promote our business!"

"Put them up wherever you like," she said, "and if you send me a print, I'll autograph it for you and ship it back. Here, let me write out my address in Gibson's. If it arrives when we're not there filming, someone will forward it to me."

Well, she was their heroine for the day after that.

The bird sanctuary islands themselves were not huge, but they did rise impressively – and almost vertically – out of the sea. As we approached Gull Island, we moved up to the viewing deck that was the roof of the main cabin. Nearing the island, we could eventually see that what at first appeared to be roughness in the steep, rock faces was actually thousands and thousands of bird nests in every imaginable nook and cranny, and forming tier, after tier, after tier of nests. Even without the full complement of birds having arrived yet it was stunningly impressive.

"Like an apartment building for birds," I mused, "and they're all out sitting on their balconies."

"This is the spring home for the largest Atlantic Puffin colony in North America," explained George, who had slowed the engine and taken us in quite close so we could see the birds coming and going from their nests. With the engine noise much reduced, he was able to lean out of the wheelhouse door, point out the sights, and explain them to us. "In a few weeks, there'll be half a million puffins here."

As we made appreciative noises, George explained that Atlantic Puffins mostly live at sea, and that their parrot-like beaks only get their characteristically bright colours in mating season. "Quick! Watch right there," he exclaimed, pointing to a spot on the rock face where a puffin had wobbled to the very edge of one of the tiers.

No sooner had we identified the bird he meant, than it threw itself off of its perch and plummeted straight down towards the sea, with its stubby wings flapping for all they were worth. As Ginger gasped, it curved out of its fall at the last minute, barely avoided getting dunked, and flew off, skimming just above the waves, with its little wings flapping madly and occasionally even touching the water – sending up small splashes.

"My God," exclaimed Ginger. "I thought it was going to drown, and look how it's barely able to stay out of the water as it flies away even now.... Do they do that all the time?"

"Oh yes," said George. "He's gone off to hunt for small fish. If you keep watching, you'll see that they can actually kind of swim using their wing motions to paddle and their webbed-feet to steer."

Although we were fascinated by the antics of Newfoundland and Labrador's official bird, the islands provided nesting sites to more than just puffins. As we continued to slowly circumnavigate the four islands, George handed us each a set of binoculars and pointed out many other species of bird, including the one that outnumbered even the puffins. "Leach's Storm-Petrel," he said, pointing out several nearby examples of the smallish dark birds with white stripes running across their wings and tails. Whereas the puffins would occasionally dive underwater to fish, the petrels would grab plankton from the surface.

Each island was similarly congested with birds already, making it difficult to imagine what it would be like when all of the birds had returned to nest. "All told, there'll be upwards of 4 million birds here by next month," George said. "It'll be like permanent 'rush-hour' during the daytime, when they're all here."

When at last we had to say goodbye to the birds and head back to Bay Bulls, George offered to do a Screech-In Ceremony with us, but we explained that we'd done one just two days earlier.

"We'll take the Screeches though, if you're offering," said the irrepressible Ginger, and as we took our drinks onto the lower, stern deck to get out of the wind, George put some traditional Newfoundland music on the sound system.

All the way back to port Ginger and I sat back, enjoying the ocean, the rugged coastline, the Celtic-influenced seafaring music as we chatted away. It was heavenly, and it was only when we were in sight of the harbour entrance at Bay Bulls that we were brought back down to earth in remembrance of the next trip we'd be taking.

As we thanked George and Jimmy for our wonderful trip, Ginger reminded them to send a print of the picture I'd taken, so she could sign it, and insisted on paying for the whole excursion herself.

Laurie Schramm

7 THE CALL OF THE NORTH ATLANTIC

March 12, 1979
The *Ocean Saviour*

It was time to board the *Ocean Saviour*, which we did fairly early in the morning. Ginger and I were both interested in meeting our fellow voyagers, Ginger because she was excited about the adventure and the cause itself, and me because I hoped Silver would be able to help me identify the mysterious Major Jones.

At various times during the day, media people boarded the ship. These turned out to be of two types. There was the documentary film maker and his cameraman, who turned out to be from the BBC. The rest were reporter/writers from different print media. A woman from the IAAP was there to write media releases, and also to write a story for their quarterly newsletter to supporters and other stakeholders. Another woman was a reporter doing a feature story for *Macleans* magazine. One man was a freelance journalist, and another was a reporter from CBC's St. John's office. Finally, and one of the last to board the ship, was a reporter for *The New Yorker*, Vivian Rule.

The one thing all of these people had in common was that they all wanted to have an exclusive interview with Ginger. To each such request, Ginger would breathlessly exclaim that she would be happy to give them an exclusive and then airily say, "Just arrange something with my assistant." In other words, me. I say that as if it were a complaint, but I didn't really mind as it cemented my cover story and it also gave me a chance to meet and get initial impressions of each of them.

The interview with the BBC people was arranged for that very afternoon, in the Library and Conference Room. It was a good setting for a filmed interview. I noticed that when Ginger entered, she instinctively sized up the room and went directly to a chair at one end of the conference table where she would have a row of glass-fronted bookcases behind her, and a large window forward and to one side of her. This provided excellent lighting and a professional looking backdrop. The cameraman, meanwhile was able to set up his camera at a suitable distance away, from which he could pan and zoom as needed. As she took her seat, she immediately breathed, "Do you think this would be all right?" as if it were the purest accident that she had selected to best location in the room.

I was fascinated to be the fly on the wall, observing the whole process by which she remained in control of the entire interview while at the same time allowing the male interviewer and camera operator to feel like they were in charge. I will admit that I can sometimes be a bit devious myself, but here I was in the presence of greatness.

The interviewer began with some soft questions about her personal causes, which allowed her to explain the various animal rights causes and organizations she'd been supporting.

"Oh! I just can't abide cruelty to animals of any kind.... Can you?" she began, and then went into a lengthy answer.

Next, the questions shifted to the seal hunts in particular.

"Well," she explained, "this is another horrible example of humans being cruel. Every year, the hunters come here and go out on the ice to kill as many baby seals as they can. The poor little creatures are so trusting that they just lie there while the cruel hunters beat them to death and then skin them for their pelts." Already, at this point, there were tears in her eyes. "These hunts have been condemned all around the world, and they have to be stopped."

"What about this trip in particular?" the interviewer asked.

"I was asked by the IAAP to come along and observe the seal hunt and IAAP's protest of the killings, especially those of the poor little baby seals... and I am happy to be able to come along."

After this, the questions got a bit tougher. "Some people say that killing the seals is no different than killing cows, and pigs, and chicken. How would you respond to that? You do eat meat, don't you?"

"Of course I eat meat, but that is to survive. But the skins of baby seals don't keep anyone alive. Their pelts aren't even needed to make coats and jackets warm. They're only used to make clothes look fashionable." She sniffed, at this point, as if to imply that fashion was a poor excuse for wearing or doing anything.

"You realize that it's your famous name that they really want?" the interviewer continued.

"Oh! Do you really think so? How nice!" She paused for effect. "Well, if it helps with the cause, then that's OK isn't it, because sometimes it's hard to get people's attention when you want to talk about serious things, don't you think?"

The interviewer was forced to agree that yes, he thought that was probably the case, but undeterred, he went on. "What would you say to the people that say you're only here because of the publicity that you will get out of this? I mean all this media attention will be good for your career too, won't it?"

Ouch, I thought, but Ginger was ready for this too.

"Oh! I think that's so mean," she said, with a frown. "I think that if people want to check, they'll see that I've been supporting animal rights as much as I can for years now. My favourite charity is the SPCA, but as I told you before, I've done things with the Save-the-Whales people, and I've worked with IAAP before to try to save the seals."

"Well, what about money then? You must be getting paid a lot of money to come on this trip. What are people going to think about that?"

Just for a second, I thought I saw her eyes flash. *There's steel in there*, I thought. She only hesitated for that one second, though.

"Oh, do you really think they would have paid for me to come?" she asked, and then made another dramatic pause. "They didn't offer to pay me, except my travel expenses of course. It's very nice to think that they would have been willing to pay for me to come." Gushing again now. "I thought that only famous people got paid to do things like this."

"But Ginger, you are famous. That's why we're all lining up to interview you, and when the pictures and films of you trying to save the seals get broadcast, they'll go all around the world and part of the reason will be because of you."

"Oh, so you're so nice." Eyes very wide open now. "That's such a nice thing to say to me.... Well, all I can say is that if having little Ginger Brandt along helps gets the message out about the horrible things being done here, then I'll be able to die happy knowing that I did at least one good thing in my life."

The interviewer surrendered at this point, and moved to gentler topics, a few of which seemed to be aimed at producing comments from Ginger that could later be laid over filming that would be done out at the hunt itself and the accompanying protest.

The interview with the other two men, the freelance journalist and the CBC reporter went similarly, but not on such a grand scale. The two men certainly seemed like fans but not quite as susceptible to either Ginger's performance or the protest venture itself. *Just another assignment for them*, I thought to myself. They went through the routine, but I had the impression that's all it was – routine. Their lack of enthusiasm did make me wonder whether they were really reporters, but neither matched the appearance of Major Jones and neither produced any kind of reaction in Silver.

We came to a halt after the third interview, having scheduled the interviews with the three women reporters for the next day.

"What did you think?" asked Ginger, when we were back in her cabin, alone.

"I'm impressed," I said, frankly. "I didn't realize how demanding interviews would be, or how you always have to be ready for a penetrating question to leap out at you after a few easy ones. But you had them eating out of your hands the whole time. The tough questions didn't throw you off topic one little bit, and I think they went out believing that you have a heart of gold but are dumb as a post."

"What do you mean?" she asked, sounding perfectly innocent.

"You don't fool me. How about when he asked you a very simple question and you said 'What's that?' and put on the most vacuous, wide-eyed expression I've ever seen in my life?"

"I did not," she retorted.

"You did too!" I replied, just as strongly, "and it was so amazing, it threw them off completely."

"Yes, I did, didn't I?" she laughed, which got us both laughing. "Well, no one said I couldn't have fun on this trip, and besides, it's important to maintain the illusion of my character. It's also good practice."

With a bit of time to kill before supper, I looked in on the group of protesters that had boarded. This was mostly a younger crowd – a party crowd. Many seemed to be in their late teens and early twenties. They were easy to find, as they had almost immediately commandeered the Officers' and Scientists' Lounge, and I strongly suspected that the rock and roll music, which was already turned up loud and echoing down the steel passageways, would be a fixture for the duration of the voyage.

It was far too noisy in there to do more than look around, smile, and wave so I made a mental note to try to approach some of them individually when the ship was underway.

Our first shipboard supper was memorable, as the cooks welcomed everyone onboard with local favourites. The appetizers were cod tongue, which I didn't care for, and cod cheeks, which I loved. The main course was Jiggs' Dinner with Figgy Duff. The former is common throughout Atlantic Canada, and is a boiled dish made with salted meat (usually beef, or pork, or turkey), vegetables, and cabbage.

I'd never heard of Figgy Duff before. It is a bag-pudding dish, served for dessert. The name is misleading, as it contains raisins rather than figs, figgy being an old Cornish word for raisin. Filled, as it was, with molasses, brown sugar, and butter, it made for a tasty and hearty finish that seemed very appropriate on a ship about to venture into the North-Atlantic Ocean.

Over dinner, Vivian (in her guise as a reporter-at-large for *The New Yorker*) asked whether she could meet with me to get some background prior to her interview with Ginger, which was scheduled for the following day, and we agreed to meet in the Library and Conference Room.

"Well, here we are. Together again," said Vivian, closing the door and taking a seat. "how are you liking your role as personal assistant to a movie star?"

"So far, so good," I replied. "In real life, she's actually very nice. Intelligent too. That dumb and shallow act of hers is just that, an act. How about you? Any news on our elusive Major Jones?"

"Nothing recent. We did hear a strange story through

INTERPOL though. Apparently, he was involved in a gay-rights protest, that turned into a riot, in Sydney, Australia last August. The New South Wales police discovered another of the Deer Guns at the scene where one of their officers was shot and killed. The way they've reconstructed events, they think Jones must have been dressed as one of their own officers. He even stole one of their paddy wagons to make his getaway."

"Wow. Is that the first time he's killed someone?"

"Maybe. We really don't know. The Australian police are understandably mad as hornets, to the point of applying diplomatic pressure for us to find him and get him out of circulation. They're basically saying that a CIA Officer gone rogue is a U.S. problem, and that we should fix it, pronto."

"Ouch. I guess they have a point, though."

"They do.... One more thing. Apparently, he was beaten-up pretty badly in the riot. That's according to an officer that rescued him from the crowd."

"Badly enough to put him out of action?"

"No one knows. Maybe he's incapacitated, maybe a few serious injuries were enough to persuade him to retire? Who knows? I somehow doubt it though. I take it that you and Silver haven't spotted him either?"

"No." I told her about there being no signs of him at the Darlington Nuclear Station protest the previous July, and that we hadn't seen or sensed any sign of him on the *Ocean Saviour*. "Not yet anyway," I concluded, "do you think we're on another wild goose chase?"

"Could be, but we always knew we would just be playing the odds to come along on this trip." Vivian paused in thought. "My father was in the Marines and he used to repeat that old military phrase, 'They also serve, who only stand and wait[56]' I guess that's all we can do – wait and see."

"And be vigilant."

"Very vigilant. He's a trained killer. If he's around, he's dangerous."

"Well, I'm glad you're here."

"Likewise."

The next day was to be sailing day, but not until just before high tide, which was going to be at 7:39 pm. In the morning, while the ship's crew were busy loading the last of the supplies and running around making sure everything else was ready, Ginger did the remaining interviews. Once again, she was convincing and handled all of the reporters' questions with style and ease.

The last of them was Vivian. I had agreed not to expose Vivian's true identity, not because we didn't feel Ginger was trustworthy but because we didn't want to risk a chance comment or even a manner that might suggest Ginger and Vivian knew each other.

As far as the interview went, I thought Vivian did a convincing job as a reporter. She had obviously done her homework and asked a range of good questions about Ginger, her work, and her interests in animal rights.

When we finally left dock in the evening, there was a beautiful full moon. It seemed like a good omen.

For me, the highlight was sailing out of the harbour and through the Narrows. We had a great view from the Monkey Island deck, which was a small deck immediately above the Navigation Bridge, and which held the ship's searchlights, the main standard magnetic compass, among other things. It was a great vantage point for sightseeing and I couldn't believe how close the ship had to sail to the channel markers on each side, even at high tide. As we went through, the steep cliffside of Signal Hill loomed over us on the portside, while to the right we had a great view of Fort Amherst and its lighthouse and Second World War battery and fortifications.

After that, it was the open sea and the ship began to move around a bit more as the wind and swell increased.

"Sensible hat," remarked a passing crew member. I was wearing a bright reddish-orange, navy-divers-style toque of the kind that was popular among SCUBA divers at the time[57]. Whereas most Canadians refer to such hats as toques, people in Newfoundland (and Nunavut) often refer to them as simply hats. Ginger thought my toque funny, and to this day she still teases me about it.

Eventually, there was just the roll of the ship, reflections of light from the full moon, and little specks of light from lighthouses and the occasional other boat or ship. When the cold wind got us shivering, we abandoned the open deck for the warmth of our cabins.

Fort Amherst

That first night out, the sea became considerably rougher. Although the ship was stable in the rough water, it was not a gentle ride. Captain Webb explained that the originally fitted external stabilizers had been removed when the ship was modified to enhance its ice-breaking capabilities. Although he was reassuring, as the evening wore on the ship rocked more and more, occasionally violently, which didn't help any of us landlubbers get a good night's sleep.

The next day was to be a full day at sea, although there were not many early risers. This was partly because most of the passengers hadn't had a very sound sleep on their first night at sea. I hadn't had a great night myself, but I was an early riser by nature and one of the few that showed up for breakfast. Even so, the cook remarked that "the ones that are up are all crooked," a term some Newfoundlanders use for what the rest of us would call cranky.

After breakfast, Silver and I went up on deck again to look out at the rolling sea. It was quite chilly, especially with the sea breeze, so I had my red toque on again. This produced some interesting reactions. The ship's crew was comprised of several nationalities, mostly British and Canadian, with some Norwegians, Swedes, Americans, and Australians. My toque was a hit with the Scandinavians and Australians, wasn't even worth comment from the Canadians, and was a source of amusement to the Americans.

At lunch, as was the case with all of our meals on the ship, Ginger was very gracious about accommodating people's natural desire to want to sit with us at meals. As a result, we got to know quite a few of the people onboard through our mealtime conversations, and it allowed me to cement my role as Ginger's assistant. I was somewhat surprised to note how many people jumped to the conclusion that Silver was along as a kind of canine security guard for Ginger, which seemed to further deflect attention away from me, an added bonus.

That afternoon, Ginger did some further interviews with the various journalists, but for the most part everyone was waiting for the adventure to come, out on the icepack. As a result, we had most of the afternoon to ourselves.

I did manage to find a few minutes alone with Vivian, out on one of the open decks, and away from other ears, but we too had only a few bits of news to share.

We already knew that there were American warrants out for Jones' arrest. I told Vivian that there was now a Canadian warrant out as a result of the Toronto shooting. Vivian explained that the FBI had learned that Jones had spent some of the previous six months causing trouble in Europe, where his signature guns were found in the aftermath of violent political demonstrations in a number of East-European countries. Each of these exacted a heavy toll of injuries and deaths among both police and demonstrators.

Vivian added that there was also an Australian warrant for impersonating a police officer and for murdering a police officer. Her final bit of news was that at the request of the U.S., Australia, and Canada, INTERPOL had issued a Red Notice[58] concerning Jones.

Supper provided a welcome change of pace. This time, with everyone on board fairly well acquainted with each other, the dinnertime discussions were warmer and the topics more varied.

In the evening, Silver and I walked every deck and passageway we could find, partly for exercise and partly keeping an eye on things, but our walks were uneventful as well. Like most of the passengers, we turned-in early, in hopes of catching up on some the sleep we'd lost the night before.

The next morning brought us our second full day at sea. There were more early risers at breakfast, and everyone seemed to be in better spirits and eagerly anticipating the first sight of the icepack. It took much of the day but eventually, as if following the Captain's initial estimate, there was an announcement on the ship's loudspeakers at 2 pm – some forty-two and a half hours since leaving St. John's. "Welcome to The Front ladies and gentlemen!" crackled a metallic version of the Captain's voice.

When Ginger and I hurried to up the Monkey Island deck, we couldn't see anything but waves, with their white foamy tips as they crested and broke over and over again. Fortunately, a thoughtful crew member arrived with a pair of binoculars for us to use. When it was my turn to look through them it took some practice to keep the horizon in view against the rolling of the ship but when I finally got the hang of it, I could just make out a thin ridge of ice between the ocean and sky.

The next thing we heard was the sound of the helicopter's engine starting, followed by the sweeping sounds of the rotors as they began to turn and then spin faster and faster. Although the ship's helicopter was small, it was noisy when heard up-close, and it was soon too noisy for us to talk. We all knew that the helicopter was heading off to search for the seals, and especially to see whether large clusters of seal pups had been whelped yet. This created a heightened sense of anticipation among everyone on board.

It was nearly supper time when the helicopter returned, but the first order of business was to cram into the library for a briefing from the pilot and the spotter that had accompanied him. It was good news. Captain Webb and Arne Kristiansen had timed the voyage well, as lots of seals and pups had been observed on the ice, in several large clusters. Basically, the plan was to go the edge of the ice pack in the morning, and try to get the bulk of the documentary movie filming and picture taking done before the sealers arrived.

"Are the sealers close?" Someone asked.

"There was no sign of them from the air," replied the spotter.

"Maybe not, but they can't be far away," said Captain Webb. "We've been listening to them on the VHF radio. The fleet is out, and they're probably no more than half a day's sailing behind us. We'll use the helicopter to get a fix on them in the morning."

***

Earlier that same day.

In the wheelhouse of the fishing boat *Jonah's Escape*, Major Jones rested his coffee mug on the narrow shelf that ran along the lower length of the glass windscreen. Lifting a pair of binoculars to his eyes, he adjusted the focus and resumed his lookout. "There's no sign of the protesters and no sign of the icepack. Nothing but water," he said to the boat's skipper.

The skipper picked up his own pair of binoculars and took a long look in the indicated direction. "You're an impatient man, I see. They're probably half a day ahead of us, maybe more," he grunted. "I suppose this is as good a time as any to find out whether the police are on their way to help us or not."

"You don't know?" asked Jones, surprised.

"I don't know a damn thing. We knew the protesters would be going out to the Front. We complained to the police that they'd be trying to disrupt the hunt, and we asked them to keep the protesters off our backs. All I could get out of them was that the matter was under active consideration.... Active consideration! Sounds like government-speak for doing nothing."

Reaching for the VHF radio that was mounted overhead, just above and to the left of his shoulder, he changed the frequency from the inter-ship one he'd been using to keep the sealing fleet together, to the Canadian Coast Guard Channel, number 22A. The nearest station was located at St. Anthony, near the northernmost tip of Newfoundland, with call sign VCM. *Jonah's Escape's* call sign was VO1 ORZ.

"St. Anthony Coast Guard, St. Anthony Coast Guard, St. Anthony Coast Guard, Victor, Charlie, Mike, this is Jonah's Escape, Jonah's Escape, Jonah's Escape, Victor Oscar One Oscar Romeo Zulu. Over."

There was a delay of several minutes.

"Why don't they answer?" asked Jones.

"They will," replied the skipper. "This channel is continuously monitored. They'll be looking for an open channel for us to continue on." The radio was silent for a few more minutes, enough to start Jones fidgeting but he had the sense to remain quiet. Finally, there was a response.

"Jonah's Escape, Jonah's Escape, this is St. Anthony Coast Guard, St. Anthony Coast Guard, Victor, Charlie, Mike. Go to channel seven one. I say again, seven one. Over."

"St. Anthony Coast Guard, St. Anthony Coast Guard, this is Jonah's Escape. Roger, switching to seven one."

The skipper switched the radio channel to 71.

"St. Anthony Coast Guard, this is Jonah's Escape. Over."

When the Coast Guard operator responded, the skipper asked to make a radiotelephone call to the St. John's RCMP. When that connection was made, it took him some time to explain who he was and why he was calling, but he was eventually referred to someone that seemed to know about the sealers' request for help.

"The CO approved sending a squad to keep the peace and we have requested the Coast Guard supply the transport. Over."

"Well, we're half a day's sailing from the Front now, and in the morning, I expect to see the *Ocean Saviour* run up on the ice right in front of us. So, where the hell are your people? Over."

"What is your position? Over."

As the skipper provided their position, Jones left the wheelhouse for the open stern of the boat, where he could have a smoke and prepare himself. When he retuned, fifteen minutes later, the skipper was just wrapping up his call.

"Roger. Jonah's Escape, Victor Oscar One Oscar Romeo Zulu. Out," the skipper said, switching the radio back to the general channel for monitoring and alerts, channel 16.

"Any luck?" Jones asked.

"Well, for once, they listened to us. The Mounties have sent a squad. They're on the Coast Guard ship *John A. Macdonald*, and they're only about 30 nautical miles behind us. We'll be at the Front before noon tomorrow."

***

March 15, 1979
The Front, southeast of Labrador

Sure enough, in the morning sunrise, some 60 hours after having left St. John's, we arrived within sight of the ice pack.

From the Monkey Island deck, using binoculars we could just make out some of the seals. As we approached the icepack, several things happened in fairly rapid succession. First, the ship's small helicopter was launched to check the position of the sealing fleet.

Not long after that, we were overflown by a Canadian Coast Guard Grumman S-2 Tracker. This was a rather squat-looking, twin engine aircraft of the kind used by the Royal Canadian Navy for anti-submarine warfare[59].

Someone said, "Well, they certainly know where we are now."

After the plane had passed, Captain Webb came on the ship's intercom to say that the sealing fleet had been spotted about four hours behind us, that the Coast Guard plane meant that the police were probably not far behind the sealers. He added that we would shortly be driving our ship into the icepack, so everyone was to get ready to get out onto the ice.

A few minutes later, Ginger and I were in our cabins gathering our boots and parkas when Captain Webb came back on the intercom saying "Sound the collision alarm."

Moments later, we heard one of the bridge crew say "Brace for collision!" over the intercom. This was immediately followed by the sound of the ship's general alarm: an impossible-to-ignore seven short blasts followed by one long blast.

"I'm glad we got off the Monkey Bridge before that alarm went off, or we'd be hard-of-hearing for a while," I commented to Ginger.

The general alarm sent all crew members to their designated muster stations, while the rest of us braced ourselves as best we could.

The tension mounted as our ship sailed straight at the icepack, but we didn't have long to wait before the ship began to shudder and we could hear a grinding noise. This only lasted for a few minutes, before the ship's motion stopped completely, the engines were shifted down to idle, and everything went silent.

Our ship had been driven partway into the ice.

When we returned to our favourite viewing positions atop the Monkey Bridge, we watched as the crew pushed out a ramp from a lower cargo hatch. With the ramp in place, a small cascade of snowmobiles and trailers were driven down the ramp and onto the ice.

"Looks like no dog-sleds on this trip," I said to Silver, who looked disappointed. I explained to Ginger that several of our northern adventures of the previous few years had involved travelling by dogsled, and that as a former sled-dog himself, he probably missed it.

As we continued to watch, the ship's crew and some of the staff from the Ocean Saviour Foundation busied themselves setting-up tents for the staging of media equipment and installing stoves that would be needed later to warm-up protesters and media alike.

Although we had enjoyed cool springtime temperatures in St. John's, at the Front it was freezing – literally. The overnight low had been -21 °C (-6 °F) and the forecast high for the day was -9 °C (+15 °F). Being on the ocean, it was a humid cold, making it harder to block, and it was windy. And if that wasn't enough, the sky was completely overcast and there was a possibility of snow later in the afternoon.

Having grown up in Ontario, I was well used to cold, high-humidity winters and had brought suitable clothing. Silver, of course, was probably going to enjoy the cold, I thought, having grown-up in Alaska and being genetically well adapted to cold and snow. Vivian, I knew, was used to the warmer climates of the continental United States, but we had recently shared an adventure in the Northwest Territories[60] above the Arctic Circle, in the dead of winter, and I knew she could take care of herself.

Ginger I wasn't so sure about, not so much because of the stereotypes about spoiled movie stars but because I knew she was used to the warmer Pacific Coast climates of southern British Columbia and California. My fears were heightened when she came into my cabin fully decked-out, saying "How do I look?"

She was wearing new and expensive-looking jacket, ski-pants, and boots. "You look great," I said, and then closed in for a closer look. I needn't have worried, however. The jacket and pants were simply stylish (and expensive) models of a top-ranked ski clothing brand, and hidden under the flared cuffs of her ski pants was a pair of top quality felt-pack boots that would keep her feet warm in far colder temperatures than we were about to encounter.

Seeing me relax, she started teasing me immediately.

"Satisfied? Or is your naïve and spoiled movie star completely out of tune with where we are and where we're going?"

"Sorry," I said sheepishly, "I should know you better by now, but when you put on your famous actress persona I still get taken in sometimes."

"That's OK," she laughed. "I'm glad you care, but don't worry about me, I grew up in sight of the Rockies – remember? I was skiing in the mountains by the time I was eight."

"Right. Sorry," I repeated. "But seriously, don't forget who I'm looking for out there. If we find him, I want you to promise me that you'll keep out of the way and let Silver and I deal with him. There may be fighting among the protesters and the sealers too, and I want you to be careful to steer clear of that too... You promise?"

"I promise, I promise, but they'll be dangerous for you too, won't they?"

"Yes, but we're trained for this, and it's our job.... Besides, we're dangerous too."

"Yes," she said, looking at me thoughtfully, "somehow I don't doubt that. And armed too, I'll bet, hmmm?"

"Absolutely," I confirmed, patting my left arm under which I had a snub-nosed Smith & Wesson '.38 Special' revolver in a shoulder holster. I also had a few other things with me that I didn't mention.

"It's time," I said, having checked my watch. "You're due in the larger tent for a quick interview with the documentary producers, then they're taking us out to one of the groups of seals so they can try to get some footage of you with a seal pup."

"Sounds like fun," she said, and we made our way down to the opened hatch and ramp, and from there down onto the icepack itself.

Several tents, and even a flagpole and flag, had already been set up.

After everything it had taken to get ourselves onto the trip and then out to the Labrador icepack, standing there for a moment before going into the larger tent felt like an anticlimax. We were standing on ice and snow, under an overcast sky, in the cold with an icy breeze blowing, and for a moment I felt like we could just as easily have been in any of a million other locations in Canada's winter. *Oh well*, I thought, before following Ginger into the tent for a preliminary interview.

The documentary people just wanted to get some footage of Ginger reiterating her feelings about the seals and the hunt, before going out to mingle with them in person. That didn't take long, and soon we were whisked away by several snowmobile-sled combinations.

Suddenly, there we were, and it seemed like there were seals everywhere. In among the adults, were the seal pups with the beautiful white fur. We waited for a moment, while the documentary people got set up, and then Silver and I stayed back while Ginger was filmed walking up to one of the baby seals. When she did, the cameraman moved in close to catch the baby looking up with its big, trusting, brown eyes. Then, Ginger dropped to her knees and took it up in her arms. The producer was ecstatic when she leaned over and, with tears in her eyes, kissed the baby seal on the nose.

After that the other reporters asked Ginger to give them some poses with the seal pups for their still cameras. It was about -12 °C (+10 °F), so most of the pictures were close-up showing Ginger with her hood up, holding a seal pup in her arms, and her breath freezing into tiny droplets and crystals when she exhaled. There would be no mistaking that she was out in the cold, and not in some artificial movie set.

Most of the protestors next took up cans of red or green spray paint and made sure that the media recorded them saving a hundred seal pups by spraying them, making their pelts commercially valueless.

When the picture-taking was finished, that pretty much concluded phase one of the on-ice events.

As if on cue, we heard a shout and saw much pointing of fingers back towards the ship.

The sealing fleet had arrived.

8 CONFRONTATION

As the sealing fleet prepared to moor its boats, the protesters began to get ready. This mostly involved each being issued a large placard mounted on a stick so they could hold it high and wave it around. They were then organized into a line, roughly two people deep, which stretched across the ice a short distance from one of the larger groupings of seal pups.

I couldn't help noticing the nature of the sticks that were being used to hold up the placards. Every one of them seemed to be made from a hockey stick that had its blade cut off. That meant that not only were the sticks more than strong enough to support the placards, they were strong enough to be used as weapons.

In my university years, I had often played a game called floor hockey. It was played indoors, usually on a basketball court, and in our case the puck was an open, weighted ring. The sticks we used were hockey sticks that had the blade sawed off and the exposed end wrapped with hockey tape. We played with much less padding than is used in ice hockey, usually just hockey gloves and helmets with plexiglass visors. In university, at least, the officiating was generally loose enough that the games could get quite violent and I knew from personal experience what it felt like to be struck with a hockey stick on an unprotected part of the body.

Remembering my floor hockey experiences gave me a bad feeling about a group of nearly 40 protesters and ship's crew that were armed with virtually unbreakable hockey sticks and about to encounter a bunch of angry sealers that would no doubt be armed with their own traditional wooden clubs. Seal-hunting regulations, I knew, specified that a sealer use a hardwood club, 24 to 30 inches in length, because that was considered to be the quickest way to 'humanely' kill a seal.

The media people, for their part, set themselves up in two clusters, one each in front of and to the side of the protesters' line. From these vantage points they would be able to get dramatic shots of the sealers approaching, the protesters blocking, and whatever might come next.

By the time the protesters were set up, the sealers had moored their boats to the edge of the icepack using long lines attached to steel rods or spikes that they hammered into the ice. There were a lot of them, and they divided themselves into three groups. At our particular location on a large sheet of ice, there were three main groups of seals each of which had whelped a large number of pups. Each group of sealers headed for one of these, which meant that two of the groups would be able to immediately begin the killing, while the third would confront the protesters. It might have been my imagination, but it seemed to me that the group making its way toward the line of protesters may have comprised the larger, more heavily built sealers.

Spotting Arne Kristiansen talking to some of the reporters, I went over and asked that he assign someone to take one of the snowmobiles and get Ginger back to the ship where she would be safe. He didn't want to, and it occurred to me that he may have been hoping to place Ginger out in front of the protesters to see what would happen. I was in no mood to waste time arguing with him, and I wasn't ready to break my cover yet so, playing my role as Ginger's assistant I meekly acquiesced and turned away. Then, taking Ginger's arm I guided her over to where Vivian was checking her camera.

"Vivian, I'm going to grab one of those snowmobiles and get Ginger back on the ship. After that, I'll come and join you. OK?"

"Right," she said. "I'll be here."

Steering Ginger towards a cluster of snowmobiles that were standing a little way away, I said "We're heading back to the ship. If I can get one of these things started, get on behind me and we'll drive back."

"But I'd like to stay here and help," she said.

"It's too dangerous. The protesters have come prepared for a fight, and those sealers are going to be angry enough to give them one. I think they'll start out by yelling and swearing at each other, but before long some idiot will lose their temper and throw something, or rush the line, and the fighting will break out. There are nearly forty protesters here and that looks like almost the same number of sealers heading straight for them. If things turn violent, the only way I can protect you from that many people is to get you away from them."

"But the protesters know me now, and the sealers wouldn't hurt me, would they?"

"Not normally, no. But when people lose their temper and fights break out anything can happen. Sometimes people start swinging at anything within reach. The safest place for you right now is on the ship. OK?"

"OK, I guess."

"Besides, it's your inner Liz that wants to stay. No one will expect your Ginger persona to hang around."

Fortunately, the snowmobiles had been left with the keys in their ignitions so all I had to do was start one, check the fuel status, make sure Ginger was holding on to me, and go. Steering the machine in a wide arc, we quickly left the protesters and drove well away from all the groups of people. Only then did I make a turn and steer a broad arc towards the *Ocean Saviour.* I didn't have to worry about Silver, he simply let me break a trail with the snowmobile and ran along behind us on the packed track in the snow.

When we reached the ship, I jogged up the ramp and asked the crewmember that was standing guard to call for Sam. When he arrived at the cargo hatchway, I took another close look at him.

"Sam, you have the look of a navy man about you. Were you in the service?"

He straightened up just that little bit before answering. "Royal Canadian Navy ma'am. Petty officer, first class. Served 25 years before 'retiring' so to speak."

"I thought so. You have the manner of an experienced seaman and the tattoos on your biceps aren't completely faded yet." I took out my wallet and showed him my badge and ID. "I need your help PO. There's a fight brewing out there on the ice and I need to go back there, but we need to keep Miss Brandt here safe, that's why I brought her back to the ship."

"Don't you worry, Corporal, she'll be safe here with me." He looked over at Ginger, who flashed him a look that made him stand up even straighter, if that were possible.

"Please just keep calling me Alex. Besides, I'd like to keep my real identity secret just a little bit longer, OK?"

"Your secret is safe with me ma'am... Alex."

"OK then. Ginger, promise me you'll stay with Sam OK? That way, I'll be able to go do what I have to do without worrying about you the whole time."

"I promise, Alex," she said. "But you have to tell me all about it later."

"Count on it," I said, as I ran back down the ramp.

"Come on Silver, we've got work to do."

"*Grrruph!*" said Silver, standing in readiness while I turned the snowmobile ignition over and pressed the throttle.

When I arrived back where the sealers had been advancing on the protesters, it looked like something out of a Hollywood movie. The two groups were arranged more or less face-to-face, with much yelling, swearing, hand-waving, and brandishing of wooden sticks – hockey stick handles in the case of the protesters, and long clubs in the case of the sealers. The protest placards, I noticed, were rapidly disappearing leaving the hockey sticks looking like what they had become: weapons. Meanwhile, the documentary film crew had their camera set up on a large tripod and were busily filming everything, and the reporters were equally busy taking still photographs and/or brandishing microphones attached to shoulder-slung tape recorders.

Leaving the snowmobile parked some distance from the crowd, I took the precaution of removing and pocketing the key – I thought I might need that snowmobile before long – and set out to search for Vivian.

I found her hovering at the edge of one of the media groups.

"Any sign of Major Jones?" I asked.

"Not yet," she replied.

"How about if we try walking just behind the lines of sealers. If you can hold your camera up and make it look like you're just taking pictures, I'll scan the sealers and we can see if Silver can pick up his scent."

"Ok", she replied, "But here, pin this to your parka. This should keep them from attacking us." She handed me a large laminated white card bearing the word PRESS in large black letters. It had a pin attached to the back, which I used to attach it to the front of my parka.

The scene was rapidly becoming chaotic. While I'd gone to the ship and back, the sealers had advanced on the protesters and, while the media cameras clicked and rolled, the confrontation followed a predictable pattern. First there were exchanges of angry words and calls for the other side to disperse and "go home." This led to even harsher words, and then the pushing and shoving began. From there it was a short step to someone throwing the first punch, and a scattering of fist fights broke out.

Silver, Vivian, and I had been walking several feet behind the rearmost ranks of the sealers during this escalation, but none of us saw or sensed any one matching the description of Major Jones. Vivian and I didn't actually expect to see anything useful, as we assumed that if he were there it would be in disguise. It was Silver's nose that we were counting on.

As several fights broke out, what began as two well-defined lines facing each other disintegrated into a dynamic mass of small clusters. In some clusters, the two sides remained in exchanges of heated words, while in others the physical violence continued. Fortunately, the latter was so far restrained to an ebb and flow of fists and sticks.

It was only as we approached one of the last clusters that Silver tensed, his hackles went up, and he gave a low but menacing growl deep in his throat.

I immediately went down on one knee beside him and tried to make out which man (the sealers all seemed to be male) he was looking at.

"I think it's got to be one of the men right in front of us," I said to Vivian.

"Let's get closer," she replied.

As we moved closer, Silver stayed with me while Vivian moved several steps away and to one side. Silver was continuing to growl, but I couldn't yet make out which man had attracted his attention.

Then one of the men turned to look at us briefly, looked away, then turned his head again and took a closer look. We were just close enough for me to see his expression harden. He immediately pushed himself further into the cluster of sealers and protesters and I lost sight of him.

"He's the one wearing an old army parka!" I called to Vivian, pointing at his last position. "He ducked into the middle of the fray."

Just as I saw her nod, three of the clusters merged into a single mass, and we heard the sharp crack of a small gun. Rather than dispersing the mass of people, this seemed to simply add to the confusion and spur more fighting.

***

Major Jones had joined the sealers in their march toward the protesters, but held himself to the rear so he could watch the engagement and its escalation.

When tensions and anger spilled beyond words and into violence, and as the two lines broke up into clusters, he selected one of the clusters in which the sticks had been turned into weapons and again stayed close, but at the rear – observing the ebb and flow of the emotions and actions that surrounded him.

It was just when he was considering moving in to escalate things further that he happened to look back and spot two people and a dog approaching. Mentally classifying them as reporters, he dismissed them and turned back but... *was there something about that dog?*

He turned back for another, more careful, tactical look. Now he saw what he should have seen the first time. One of the figures was moving sideways, as if to begin a flanking movement. The other stayed with the dog and was clearly in control of it. The dog was looking directly at him and looked angry.

Trouble, he thought. *Time to move.* He immediately turned back and pushed his way into the centre of the cluster of angry people and selected a sealer-and-protester pair that seemed to be acting particularly out of control. He sidled up beside them. From a pocket, he withdrew a Deer Gun. Holding the gun close to his body, and at hip level where it was unlikely to be seen, he aimed a shot right between the two struggling people.

There was a sharp crack, and someone on the other side fell, screaming that they'd been shot. It might have been a sealer or it might, equally, have been a protester. He didn't care, but he did add his voice to the confusion.

"One of them has a gun!" he yelled. "Get them before they can shoot again!"

In another situation, the gunshot and accompanying yells might have caused people to step back in shock and assess what was going on, but in this case, Jones had judged his moment well. What actually happened was that the fighting intensified and bodies jammed in even more closely than they had before. Any semblance of a line had long since been lost. It was now just a mass of sealer-and-protester pairs faced off against each other, rather like happens when a brawl breaks out in a hockey game, except that in this case the use of fists was increasingly giving way to the use of the stout sticks everyone was carrying.

Somewhere in the mass, the person that had been shot must have been lying, bleeding on the ice. Even that was difficult to judge, however, as the stick-swinging had already begun to produce its own casualties, leading to other shapes that were down, huddled on the ice.

Jones, for his part, was slipping through the crowd, his eyes everywhere as he tried to judge whether to risk reloading and taking another shot. He was feeling tempted to do just that, when he heard the roar of medium-sized helicopter approaching. His trained ear told him that the sound wasn't right for the protesters' small spotting helicopter, this was something a bit larger. Then he saw it: a bright red helicopter bearing a diagonal white stripe.

The Coast Guard had arrived, he realized.

Time to leave, thought Jones, correctly guessing that the helicopter was ferrying police officers to the scene of the fighting. With that, he immediately shed his faded army-surplus parka and dropped it onto the ice where it disappeared underneath the jostling fighters. Underneath the parka, he'd been wearing a trendy, bright-red down jacket of the sort that a university-age protester might wear. From one pocket of his insulated pants he brought out a blond wig. Ducking low for a moment, he removed the dark, oil-stained baseball cap he had been wearing and replaced it with the wig. From the other pants pocket he took out the Deer Gun and simply allowed it to fall from his gloved hand as he resumed slithering through the crowd, looking for a way out. He wasn't worried about the loss of the gun; he had brought a second one.

Jones had not forgotten about the suspicious people with the dog. When he exited the large cluster of fighters, he was purposely on the opposite side from them. He began walking away from the crowd and towards the protesters' snowmobiles. As he did so, he heard the blasts of two ships' horns. Looking over towards the *Ocean Saviour*, he saw two Coast Guard ice breakers approaching. That explained the helicopter.

Well back from the crowd now, he was able to observe the side door of the landed helicopter slide open. Out scrambled four Mounties, after which the helicopter immediately took off and headed back towards one of the icebreakers.

Going back for more, thought Jones. *Definitely time to be gone.*

Forcing himself to maintain a walking pace, he continued towards the parked snowmobiles, started one and drove off.

Although disguised like a protester now, he was not headed for the *Ocean Saviour.*

***

Since the gunshot somehow had the effect of compressing the fighters, rather than dispersing them, I could see that there was no way Silver and I were going to be able to get inside the crowd and accomplish anything useful. Motioning to Vivian, I tried to indicate that we were going to try working our way around the outside.

She nodded, and motioned that she was going to work her way around the other side.

As we each skirted the crowd from our own side, I first heard and then saw a Coast Guard helicopter approach and land somewhere near one of the other crowds of fighting people. *Reinforcements*, I thought, wondering whether they would spook our quarry.

Eventually, Silver and I made our way to the far side of the cluster from where we had started, where we met up with Vivian.

"Anything?" she asked.

"No, nothing at all. Let's try going around the side you came from." We did this, and completed the rest of the circle without Silver sensing anything.

"Damn. We've lost him. He's either in the middle somewhere where Silver can't sense him or he's not in this group anymore."

It was only when the noise from the helicopter, returning to one of the icebreakers, faded that Vivian turned her head, saying "Hear that?"

"Hear what?" I asked.

"Sounds like a snowmobile," she said, walking further away from the crowd. After a few moments, she beckoned me with a wave and pointed back toward the ships. "See it?"

Squinting, I could make out two specks in the distance. "A snowmobile and trailer," I said.

"Right. One of the protesters' machines, but it's not heading for the *Ocean Saviour*."

"No, it's not," I agreed. "Where's it going then?"

"What do you want to bet it's Major Jones, heading for the spot where the sealers tied-up their fishing boats?"

"I know better than to bet against you. We'll never catch him before he grabs a boat and casts off, let's go see if the Coast Guard will help us."

As we walked over to where I had parked 'our' snowmobile, we could hear, and then see, the Coast Guard returning to drop off four more police officers. That made eight on the ice so far, which was enough for them to begin dispersing the first cluster of fighters while the helicopter returned to the ship for more.

When we got to our snowmobile, we took off for the icebreakers as fast as we could. As we approached, we could see that one icebreaker had drawn itself up into the ice and right alongside the *Ocean Saviour*, while the other icebreaker had stationed itself broadside against the latter's stern.

The *Ocean Saviour*, at least, wasn't going anywhere for a while.

I steered for the icebreaker that had rammed its way into the icepack.

Laurie Schramm

9 THE CHASE

"Once is happenstance. Twice is coincidence.
The third time it's enemy action."
Auric Goldfinger in:
I. Fleming, *Goldfinger*, 1959

As we approached the icebreaker that had run itself into the ice alongside the *Ocean Saviour*, we could make out the name inscribed on the bow, *John A. Macdonald*[61]. Seen up close, it was huge; twice as long and twice as wide as the *Ocean Saviour*. A ramp had been set up by an open cargo door amidships, so that's where we headed.

Leaving the snowmobile parked to one side, we walked up to the ramp and identified ourselves to the sailor and the officer on duty. They seemed surprised, but didn't question the credentials we showed them, and telephoned our request to see the Captain. It was granted, and the sailor escorted us into the ship and up to the bridge.

When we arrived, a surprisingly young-looking, sandy-haired, blue-eyed man of medium height and build came over to greet us. He was wearing a Lieutenant Commander's epaulettes, and the sailor introduced him to us as Captain Stanford.

Being in plain clothes, I didn't salute him but I introduced Vivian and we both showed him our badges and identification cards.

"So. What brings an undercover Mountie and FBI agent to the coast of Labrador? Something to do with all the fighting that's been going on ashore?"

"Not quite, Sir," I responded. "We came aboard the *Ocean Saviour* looking for a wanted murderer. He wasn't among the ship's crew or passengers, but we did spot him among the sealers so he must have come on one of the fishing boats. Just after we spotted him, there was a shot and he disappeared in the confusion. By the time we spotted him again, he had taken a snowmobile and was headed for the fishing boats. He had too much of a lead on us for us to catch him, so we came here instead. We're hoping you can help us."

"I see," said the Captain, scratching his head. "Well, as you've probably noticed, we're a bit busy right now. We're still ferrying the last of your colleagues over to the scene of the fighting. We brought 15 of them along and the last are going out right now." He pointed to the helicopter, which had just taken off from the flight deck and was heading towards the mass of struggling figures on the ice. "Once they get everyone settled down out there, they'll be making arrests and seizing the protesters' ship[62]. Our mission is to support your colleagues and then tow the ship back to St. John's," he concluded. "That means we need both of our ships right here, for the time being."

"How about your helicopter then? Can you have it take us out so we can at least find the fishing boat and figure out where it's headed?"

While he considered for a moment, Vivian interjected. "Captain, these people out here have broken a few rules, and there's probably going to be some assault charges for people on both sides of the conflict out there on the ice, but this fellow we're after is a murderer. He's already shot people in four countries and killed at least one, maybe more. Now, we think he's shot someone out there on the ice today already. We need to stop him before he strikes again."

"I hear you, Agent Rule, and I'm not against helping you." He sighed, and came to a decision. "Tell you what. We'll have to call this in and get authorization."

"Would it help if my boss in Ottawa called your boss and made an official, high-level request?"

"It might."

"Can I make a radiotelephone call?"

The Captain nodded, took a step back and motioned to one of the bridge crew. "Give him the number you want, and he'll put you through."

The number I gave him was constantly monitored, 24 hours per day, and I gave the duty officer my rank, name, regimental number, and asked for my boss, Staff Sergeant Bob Simpson. "Top priority. I'll hold."

It seemed to take forever, but was probably only five minutes before the duty officer came back on to say, "connecting you now."

When Bob came on the line, I quickly summarized what had happened, where we were, and what we needed. He seemed completely unsurprised and simply asked me to pass the handset to the Captain. The Captain took the handset and moved a few feet away from us. Taking this as a sign that he didn't want to be overheard, we stepped away ourselves and spent a few moments looking out at the trapped *Ocean Saviour* and the mass of figures on the ice, the latter of which seemed to have stopped fighting.

When the Captain hung up the handset, he came over to us. "You forgot to mention that you're with the Security Service."

"I didn't think it was important. Would it have made a difference?" I asked.

"Probably not." He smiled. "Your boss is going to have his Assistant Commissioner call my Assistant Commissioner in St. John's and make a formal request. I'm pretty sure it will be granted." He looked out one of the bridge windows. "Our helicopter is on its way back now. While it's refueling, I'll have you escorted down to the pilots' ready room where you can tell them what you want. Assuming I get a call granting the authorization, I'll have the pilots do whatever you want short of endangering the helicopter or its crew. OK?"

"Thank you, Captain. Much appreciated."

He motioned for one of the bridge crew to escort us, then put out his hand to shake, saying "Good luck."

Just before leaving, I turned back. "Captain, could I make one more request, please?"

He raised an inquisitive eyebrow, then nodded.

"Could we possibly make a quick stop on the *Ocean Saviour*. There's something there I need to bring with us."

He thought for a moment. "The ship hasn't been impounded yet, and it's a police matter in any case, so it's fine with me." He nodded to the bridge officer, saying "See to it."

We were led down two decks to where a ramp had been extended and lowered to the deck of the *Ocean Saviour*. The bridge officer said he'd wait at the ramp for our return and left us to cross on our own.

When we did, I asked the first crewmember we encountered where we could find Sam Hynes. "Officers' and Scientists' Lounge," we were told. As we made our way there, Vivian asked what on earth I'd come back for. "You'll see," I said, mysteriously.

When we reached the lounge, Sam wasn't actually there, but I'd found what I was looking for.

"Alex!" said Ginger. "What's going on? Everyone is so tense and nervous!"

"There's been fighting. Our quarry was there and shot someone, but he got away. By the time we spotted him again, he was about to grab a fishing boat and get away. We couldn't get to him in time, so we came here, and we're going to go after him in a Coast Guard helicopter. Do you want to come with us?"

"What? ... Yes, of course."

I put a hand up. "Not so fast. You need to understand your options first. If you stay here it will be safer, but the other police are going to impound the ship and tow it back to port. The Captain and crew are certainly going to be arrested, and maybe some of the protesters, media, and sealers too. It's an offence just to observe the seal hunt this close without a permit, so they might arrest you too. It's possible there could be violence when the arrests begin.

"On the other hand, we're chasing a murderer and I don't know what's going to happen. We might not find him, or we might find him and simply alert other people so they can close in on him. On the other hand, we might end up going after him ourselves. It could be dangerous for you if you come with us."

"So, it could be dangerous either way," she said. I nodded, and watched her face as she thought for a moment, her actress persona momentarily discarded. "I take it you're not really a reporter?" she asked Vivian.

"No. FBI. I couldn't tell you before... sorry."

Ginger just nodded again, then came to a decision. "I want to come with you," she said in a firm voice.

"OK?" I said to Vivian. She knew what I was really asking. Bringing a civilian along could complicate things for us.

"OK with me," she said.

"OK then, put some warm clothes on," I continued. "If you have anything valuable with you here, you can bring it if it will fit in your pockets."

Sam caught up with us when we were at Vivian's stateroom getting her outer clothing and boots, and I briefly explained what we were doing.

He wasn't one for small talk. "Good luck then," he said, "come visit me in jail sometime."

"You're practically a bystander here. At worst, the judge will give you a fine and send you on your way. Thank you, Sam, for looking after us."

Once Ginger had offered her thanks as well, we went back to the coast guard ship.

As we went up the ramp to the *John A Macdonald*, the bridge officer looked surprised to see Ginger with us but didn't say anything. "She's coming with us," I said. "Could you take us to the pilots' ready room please?"

"Yes Ma'am," was all he said, and he led us there.

Along the way, Vivian sidled up to me and said, in a low voice, "You trying to keep her safe, or keep her from being arrested?"

"Both," I whispered back. "She stuck her neck out to help us and I don't want anything to happen to her. You OK with that?"

"Oh, sure. Just curious."

When we reached the ready room, the helicopter had obviously returned, as the pilots were there waiting for us.

After introductions had been made, we briefly explained what we were doing. "If the Captain gets the authorization he needs, then we'd like your help finding the fishing boat without him spotting us, figuring out where he's heading, and then get there before he does, also without being spotted. Can you do that?"

They both nodded, then one of the pilots explained that the helicopter had a bench seat with places for three people, in the cabin behind the pilot and copilot seats.

"What about Silver?" I asked, nodding to where he was sitting patiently.

"No problem. He can lie on the deck at your feet."

Meanwhile, the other pilot had pulled out a chart of the area, and spread it out on a table. "OK," he said, "we are here, about 50 nautical miles east Labrador's southeastern coast. That's about 57 road miles."

"You already know how long it takes to sail here from St. John's," said the other pilot. "If your guy is in a hurry, he'll head for something a lot closer. The nearest options for him are to head WNW to Mary's Harbour in Labrador, though he'll have to go around the ice." He pointed to its location. "That's about 65 nautical miles away. If he can make 13 knots, he'll be there in 5 hours."

"Is there much there?" I asked.

"It's a town of several hundred people. They have an airport and there's a highway. If he can steal or rent a plane he can fly almost anywhere. If he gets a vehicle, it would be a 25-hour drive to Sept-Iles, Quebec, or else he could drive south and take the ferry to Brig Bay, then continue down either coast, but it's a long way to St. John's – 12 to 13 hours at least."

"OK. What else?"

"Well, he could be heading WSW to St. Anthony in Newfoundland. That's over here on the map, about 60 nautical miles away. If he goes there, he'll be just under 5 hours. St. Anthony is a larger town of more than a thousand people. It's a main service and supply centre for northern Newfoundland and southern Labrador, and it has an airport too.

"Or, he could go SW to Cook's Harbour. That's here. It's actually a bit closer, less than 60 nautical miles away. If he goes there, he'll be about four and a half hours, but it's much smaller, maybe a hundred people or so and no airport."

"So, it sounds like the most likely spots are St. Anthony or Mary's Harbour," I suggested.

"Can he fly an aircraft?" asked one of the pilots. I looked to Vivian.

"We know he can fly a helicopter, even a big one. I don't know whether he can fly a fixed-wing or not, but I wouldn't bet against it."

"He really could take the boat anywhere down the coast," said one of the pilots. They wouldn't have come all the way from St. John's without enough fuel to get back."

"That's right, but we have to start somewhere," said Vivian.

"Can you take us up and look for the boat?" I asked.

"If the Captain says so, we can. I'll check," said one of the pilots, and then to the other pilot added, "While I'm doing that, why don't you take them to see what's on the radar."

"Radar?"

"Sure. If your guy has taken a boat, the radar will have at least shown us his initial heading. That should help. Come on."

Back up on the bridge, the pilot led us to one of the radar screens and asked the operator if she'd seen one of the fishing boats leave.

"I did," she replied. "There's been no other traffic besides the helicopter and one of the boats. I reported it to the Captain, but I'd understood that we weren't worried about the fishing boats. I mostly watched its trace because there's so little else to watch right now."

"What direction was it headed?" asked the pilot.

"South, but then it pretty much has to either go north or south to get around the icepack. Look here, I'll show you." She pointed to a dot on the screen. "That's your boat right there, about six nautical miles south of our position."

Thanking her, we left the bridge and headed for the helideck where we were met by the other pilot.

"You ladies seem to have some pull in high places," he announced. "We're to give you all possible assistance short of endangering the helicopter or the people in it."

"Great," I said. "Let's go find him."

"We're not fully fueled up yet, so why don't you go grab a cup of coffee and we'll let you know when we can take off."

A crewmember was assigned to show us to the main galley, where the three of us were able to get coffee, and a bowl of water for Silver. Twenty minutes later one of the pilots came to get us. They were ready to go.

When we reached the helicopter, he said, "Let's get you settled in. I brought you the chart we were looking at. We have our own in the cockpit. Once we've found him, this will make it easier for us to discuss what to do after that."

With that, we were guided to the helicopter, which they called a Bo 105[63]. Once we were all buckled in (except for Silver, of course) we were given headsets with boom microphones, and soon we had lifted off and left the three ships far behind.

Although Major Jones had about an hour and a half's head start on us, the pilots had estimated the fishing boat's speed at about 13 knots, whereas the helicopter's cruising speed was 110 knots. As a result, it only took about 25 minutes for the pilots to find the fishing boat.

"There he is," the co-pilot's voice crackled over the intercom. He was looking through binoculars. "Right where he's supposed to be."

"We'll keep well back so he doesn't hear us. I'm going to veer off and circle for a little while. Any minute now, he'll be turning west if he's heading for any of the nearby ports. If not, he'll keep heading more or less south."

It was hard to be patient while the helicopter turned back and flew in a broad circle. Vivian and I, at the windows, kept looking out as if trying to spot the boat. We both knew that we were flying the wrong way, and in any case the pilots were keeping us well back, but there was really nothing else for us to do.

Finally, we had closed the circle and the co-pilot was scanning the horizon with his binoculars again.

"There," he said, pointing to our right. "He's heading due west.

He could be trying to make for St. Anthony. That'll be about 50 nautical miles."

So, nearly four hours, I estimated. "Are you OK with us hanging around in the background until we're sure of his destination?"

"As long as we have fuel, we can," answered the pilot. "Fuel status gives us another three hours. After that, we'll have to land at St. Anthony for fuel, whether your target is going there or not."

"OK, thanks. Can we make a radiotelephone call from here?"

"Sure. Who do you want to call?"

"The RCMP detachment at St. Anthony."

"All right, Stand by."

Looking across at Vivian, I said, "This will make their day."

When the connection was made, I identified myself, gave a brief summary of what was going on, and concluded with a request for assistance. Fortunately, the NCO[64] in Charge of the detachment was there, so I was able to get a rapid confirmation that there would be backup waiting for us at the airport in two hours, and that they would wait for us for at least another hour after that.

The pilots, who had been listening in on the call agreed to keep circling behind the fishing boat – close enough to observe its course but far enough away to be out of hearing. Since every fishing boat would be equipped with binoculars, we would have to take a chance on Jones not being able to scan the skies well enough to spot us. The odds were in our favour, since the circling would ensure that there would only be brief intervals in which we would be distinguishable through binoculars.

For the next two and a half hours Ginger and Silver were very patient, with Ginger seeming to enjoy the views. Vivian and I, for our parts, were getting pretty uncomfortable between the waiting, the noise and vibrations, and the poorly padded bench seating. On the other hand, every close of a circle confirmed that Jones was heading for either Cook's Harbour or St. Anthony. Even if Jones somehow guessed that he was being followed, Vivian and I both felt that he would make for an airport where he could hire or steal something to fly him out of the area.

"He's changed heading since our last sweep," reported the co-pilot, "he's now heading north. That means he's probably intending to bypass Cook's Harbour. The next nearest harbour is St. Anthony. That's less than 20 nautical miles from his current position. All he has to do is cross the head and then turn southwest."

"OK, can you head for St. Anthony without him seeing us?"

"Can do. We can head due west, cross overland, then turn north and be there in 30 minutes."

"Great. Let's do it, please."

The pilot's response was a sharp banking turn to the left and an acceleration back up to cruising speed. Ten minutes later, we could see the Newfoundland coast. We actually flew right past Cook's Harbour, and then the pilot turned more or less north and we got a good view of Newfoundland's most northern terrain as we headed straight for St. Anthony.

When we landed, three police vehicles pulled up to the helicopter: two highway patrol cars and a Chevy Suburban SUV. When we climbed out of the helicopter, we had just a moment to stretch before the NCO from the detachment, a Sergeant, came forward to meet us.

"Alex Houston," I said, reaching out my hand to shake.

"Al Donaldson," he responded, with a firm handshake. "Welcome to St. Anthony."

I introduced Vivian, Ginger, and Silver.

He was polite to each, but his voice increased in warmth when he recognized Ginger.

"How did you get involved in all of this Miss Brandt?" he asked.

"I'll tell you everything later, but basically it was me that snuck Alex aboard the *Ocean Saviour* as my assistant. Silver too, of course. Alex's boss in Ottawa is my uncle. It was all his idea."

"Staff Sergeant Bob Simpson," I supplied.

"This is starting to sound like a scene out of a movie script," said Al, but he smiled to show he was amused, not irritated. "By the way," he said, turning back to me, "I've heard about you."

"You have?" I asked, surprised.

"We have a friend in common, Mike Morrison – we trained together and still keep in touch. It's a small world in The Force, right? Anyway, he's told me a lot about you.... He's a Sergeant now."

"That's great news, I'll send him a note. He was my supervisor on my very first posting[14]. I learned a lot from him, and we became friends too."

Al smiled. "We'll have to compare notes later too. How much time do we have before your suspect arrives?"

I looked at my watch. "According to the pilots, almost exactly one hour."

"So, how do you want to do it?"

I took a deep breath. "I'll tell you what I was thinking, but you know the local layout, so please pitch in here…. If he doesn't think we're on to him, then I imagine he'll just pull up at one of your main docks and then look for a vehicle or aircraft. If he suspects we're following him then he'll try something tricky. He's a former CIA-officer turned mercenary *provocateur*, and he's good at disguises. How much help can we have?"

"This is a small detachment, just me and four constables. One is off sick and one is on a case out of town. That leaves three of us. We could place one man in a car at the lighthouse that overlooks the entrance to the harbour. He can then describe by radio every boat that comes into the harbour. If your timing is right, there won't be many boats coming in at that time of day. Then, you and Constable Ross here could cover the Municipal Dock, which is the most likely, and Agent Rule and I could cover the Ministry of Transport (MOT) Dock, which is the next most likely."

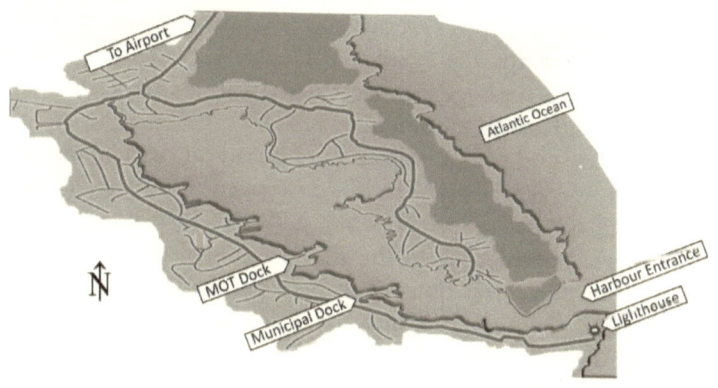

St. Anthony Harbour

Vivian and I agreed to this, so we all went for a quick cup of coffee, over which we described the boat as best we could. "It's a fishing boat. All we could see from a distance, was that it has a white cabin with a blue hull, it's probably 50 to 60 feet in length, and it has one trolling boom on each side.... I know that's not a very unique description."

Donaldson nodded. "It'll be enough."

We didn't linger over coffee, as we wanted to be in position well before our estimate of the time Major Jones might reach the harbour.

The Municipal Dock was the first major docking area for boats entering the harbour. When Constable Ross, Silver and I reached it, we agreed that Silver and I would wait in the car until we received a radio message that a boat matching our description was entering the harbour. Then, Silver and I would stroll out on the dock and pretend we were just out for a casual walk. Constable Ross, who was in uniform, would stay out of sight and watch for my signal. If I put my arm up and straightened my hair twice in a row, that would be the signal that Jones was indeed on the boat. He would then call all the rest in to back us up.

It was a long 45 minutes before the radio crackled and the constable at the lighthouse reported a boat matching our description approaching the mouth of the harbour. After another 15 minutes, the constable radioed again to say that the white and blue boat had entered the harbour and was motoring close to its southern side, towards the Municipal Dock. Sergeant Donaldson acknowledged the message, and instructed the constable to stay where he was and watch for other boats.

It was breezy and cold, as Silver and I began our walk along the dock. When we reached its end, we stopped for a while and watched until we could see the white and blue boat coming our way. Then, we walked back to the shore. I was planning to stroll the dock once more, but only when the boat was lining itself up alongside. Then Silver and I would just 'happen' to be strolling along when Major Jones hopped out to tie it up.

Things went approximately according to plan, at first. The boat slowed as it approached, then turned to come alongside the dock and manoeuvered back and forth a bit to get into position. Silver and I had strolled quite close to the boat when a figure hopped off with a mooring line in hand and went to tie it to a bollard on the dock. It was a male, but something wasn't right. I could only see him from the back, but he seemed too thin to be Major Jones, and his movements seemed more like those of a very young man, or teenager, than those of a fiftyish-year-old man. Whomever he was, Silver wasn't reacting to him at all. Making a conscious effort not to raise either arm, I decided to wait and watch.

When he had secured the bow line, the man jumped back up onto the boat and then hopped off again, this time with a stern line in hand, and he went and secured it to another bollard. Silver and I strolled closer, but I kept my distance from the boat itself and made sure I remained in clear view of Constable Ross. If this was some stranger, then it seemed probable that the Major was still on board the boat.

When the figure finished securing the stern line, rose and turned, it was a teenager I'd never seen before.

I was close enough to speak without raising my voice. "Good afternoon," I said, with a smile. "Was it rough out on the water today?"

"Not really, but it was still a bit of an adventure."

"Oh really, why?"

"I'm really sorry, ma'am. I know it's not polite, but I can't stay and talk to you – I need to go ashore and call the police."

"Really!" I said, "what's wrong?"

"You won't believe it, but I was hijacked. A man with a gun, hijacked the boat and made me bring him here."

"My goodness, what a strange thing to do. Is he on the boat then? Are we in danger right now?"

"Oh no," he replied. "The man left just as we were entering the harbour. That's why I have to go call the police right now."

As he moved to go past me, I said. "Hang on just a moment, please, the police are already here. I dug into one pocket and took out my badge and ID to show him. "Corporal Houston, RCMP," I said. "You were out at the Front, right?"

That stopped him, and his jaw dropped for a moment.

"Right" he said, when he'd recovered himself. "I was left behind to mind the boat and do some small repairs. Then, out of nowhere, this man came on board and threatened me with a gun!"

"Can you describe the man?"

"Well, he's about my height, say five foot nine, not as skinny as I am but not a heavy build either. He has blond hair and blue eyes. When he came on board the boat he had long, blond hair and he was wearing a fancy bright red jacket, but the long hair was a wig.

He tossed it overboard and his hair is still blond but cut short. He left the red jacket on the boat and took one of ours – kind of a dark brown work coat."

"That's a good description. Thank you. What did he say?"

"Only that he wouldn't hurt me if I did what he told me. He wanted me to bring him to the closest decent-sized town with a real airport. Then, he said, he'd leave the boat and I could go wherever I wanted after that. I knew that St. Anthony was the business centre for this area, and I figured it would have the largest airport, so I came here."

"And he didn't hurt you?"

"No, but he broke our radio. Wanted to make sure I couldn't call for help later, I guess."

"OK. Now, how and where did he leave the boat?"

"He made me slow down and stop just after we entered the harbour. Then I had to help him lower our dingy over the side and he took off in it. After he left, I came straight here, to the closest pier I could find, so I could call the police."

"And there's no one else on the boat?"

"No ma'am."

"Ok then, would you please come with me so we can call this in. The others may have more questions for you."

He agreed and the three of us walked back to the police SUV where Constable Ross was waiting. As we walked, I asked him for his name, it was James MacDonald.

When we all got in the SUV, I got on the radio and explained what had happened and what I'd learned, so that everyone involved could hear the same story at once.

"What does the dingy look like?" asked Sergeant Donaldson.

"It's a 15-foot Zodiac, red, with a black, 30 hp Mercury motor," said James.

"Standby," said Sergeant Donaldson. "I brought binoculars with me." There was a pause as he scanned the harbour, which fortunately was quite narrow so it was easy for him to see the northern shore from his position.

"Got it!" he said, with satisfaction. "Red Zodiac with black Mercury motor. It's heading west along the northern shore."

"I bet he'll put in somewhere, grab a vehicle and make for the airport," I said. "James said he specifically wanted to be landed somewhere with a reasonable sized airport."

"Agreed," said Sergeant Donaldson. Addressing the constable at the lighthouse, he instructed him to drive to the junction of East Street (leading out of the town's business district) with North Street (the road Jones would have to take to get to Highway 430 and the airport, which led northward out of town, before turning westward to the airport). "When you get there, park somewhere out of sight and stay on the radio."

"We're going to take a quick look on board then we'll join you," I added.

"No offense," I said to James, "but I have to be absolutely sure that this guy didn't force you to tell us a fairy-tale while he stayed in hiding on the boat. Would you be willing to come back with me and show me around?"

"Sure," he said. "No problem."

"I'll join you," said Constable Ross. I knew that he meant that he was coming along 'just in case,' and I nodded in appreciation.

As it turned out, my extra caution was unnecessary.

When we reached the boat, I looked Silver directly in the eyes and asked him to search for the 'evil man' just like I had when we were out on the icepack. I know it sounds a bit silly, but he knew what I wanted.

With Silver in the lead, James and I followed. Constable Ross followed too, but kept himself several yards behind us at all times.

Silver sniffed around everywhere, pausing only for James to reach out and open bulkhead doors for him. The only thing he found was the red jacket, which had been stuffed down, out of sight, between a mattress and the ship's hull.

I apologized again to James if I'd seemed to doubt his story, and asked whether we could take the red jacket with us. He agreed, and Constable Ross asked him to wait for us at a nearby restaurant until someone could return later, to take an official statement from him.

"Do you have any money?" I asked.

"No!" he said, surprised. "I forgot to tell you. He made me give him all the money I had."

"OK. Here's enough so you can have dinner while you're waiting. OK?" I asked, taking some bills out of my wallet.

"Yes. Thank you," he said, seeming surprised that we would help him out that way.

"All part of the service," I quipped, as we thanked him for his help and got back into the police SUV.

A quick radio check brought the news that, while we'd been searching the boat, the Zodiac had been run ashore almost directly across the harbour from Sergeant Donaldson's position. A man matching Jones' description had disembarked and was walking westbound along East Street.

"I think he's hitch-hiking," said the sergeant.

The radio was silent for the few minutes it took us to drive up to where Sergeant Donaldson and Vivian had parked the highway patrol car. We had no sooner pulled up behind them when the radio crackled again. It was Sergeant Donaldson. "Someone's stopped. A late model pickup truck. White, two-door. Looks like nets or something similar sticking up out of the box.... It's moving again and the man... is not in sight. I think the truck picked him up."

The sergeant then instructed the constable at the road junction to watch for the white pickup truck and report which way it was heading. "We're coming to your position now," he concluded.

We were almost in sight of the parked highway patrol car, when the constable on surveillance came on the radio. "White pickup truck matching your description just turned right onto North Street. Two people in the truck. They may be heading for the highway."

"Roger. Follow them but remain out of sight. We're right behind you." Then, to me, he said "What do you think? If we try to stop them now, he'll have a hostage and he may force a chase on the highway rather than stopping. If we let him get to the airport, we may be able to catch him out in the open."

"I'd say try to get him out in the open. Vivian, if he thinks he's surrounded with no chance of escape, can we get him to surrender?"

"As long as we give him time to think it through, yes. He may even think that he has enough leverage or 'friends in high places' to get off scot-free," she replied.

"I think we should warn the pilots of the Coast Guard helicopter though," I suggested.

"Do you know their callsign?"

I provided it, and Sergeant Donaldson asked his dispatcher to contact the helicopter and warn them that the man we were chasing might try to hijack their machine.

The drive to the airport took a little over half an hour. About halfway there, Sergeant Donaldson slowed his car so we could pass in the SUV, explaining, "We're well back, but if he's been watching he'll now see a truck behind him now instead of a car."

As we turned off the highway, I could see that there was a main terminal building, with several hangars spaced out on each side of it. The pickup truck had turned towards a cluster of three buildings to the right of the terminal. As soon as it was out of sight, Sergeant Donaldson radioed his two constables to say that he would join Vivian and I behind the centre building, and that they should go and park behind each of the other two. If the white truck passed either of them, they were to stop it, make sure there was only one person in it, make sure they were OK, get their name and the truck's licence plate number and let it go. Otherwise, they were to stay close to their vehicles and their radios.

For our part, we agreed that Vivian, Silver, and I would go after Jones, while the sergeant would stay back out of sight, and that Ginger was to stay in the police SUV and not get out under any circumstances. Ginger didn't like it, but she agreed.

Jogging to the front of the centre hangar, Vivian and I stopped for a look around. Sure enough, the white pickup truck was stopped not far ahead of us on the tarmac and just beside it was a small, fixed-wing airplane. Major Jones was standing by the airplane, and appeared to be pointing a gun at another person who was climbing down, out of the plane. As we watched, the person from the plane was waved over to the truck, got in, and the truck drove off. Jones then walked around the front of the plane and bent down to remove the wheel chock from the wheel that was furthest away from us.

"Let's go," said Vivian, "we'll never get a better chance than this."

"Right," I agreed, and turned to motion to Sergeant Donaldson that we were going to approach Jones.

As we walked toward the airplane, Vivian and I moved apart by about ten feet, and I told and motioned Silver to sweep out to one side so he could approach from one flank. We had done this manoeuver so many times before that he immediately knew what to do.

As he rose from his crouch, holding a wheel chock in one hand, Major Jones immediately saw us. Tossing the chock to one side, he quickly went to pull the chock from the second wheel, which he also tossed to one side.

By this time, Vivian and I were close enough to call out to him without having to yell.

"Major Jones!" I called out.

He stopped and looked at me, his hand reaching into a pocket, from which he withdrew a pistol.

"Corporal Houston, RCMP," I explained, "and this is Special Agent Rule, FBI."

"What do you want?" he asked calmly.

"I'm afraid this is the end of the line for you. I need you to drop your gun and surrender," I responded, drawing my own gun at the same time.

"I saw you, just for a moment, out on the icepack. How'd you get ahead of me?"

"Coast Guard helicopter from the icebreaker. It's over on the other side of the airport but it hasn't refueled yet, just so you know."

"He nodded. I thought it might not have been refueled, that's why I came for this plane instead.... How'd you know I'd be at the Front in the first place?"

"We didn't. We just started staking out organized protests, playing the odds that you'd eventually show up at one."

"You've been at this for a while then."

I knew he was buying time to think, but that was alright. I wanted him to be calm and rational. "Yes. Quite a while, and between us, Agent Rule and I followed a lot of blind alleys before spotting you this morning."

"And you think I'm just going to surrender to you now? To just one Mountie?"

"And one FBI agent," said Vivian, brandishing a pistol of her own.

"And there are uniformed officers out of sight... You're surrounded, you see."

"Maybe," he said, "maybe not. I only see the two of you."

"OK. Even if you don't believe me about the backup, Agent Rule and I are both armed, as you see, and we're both pretty good shots at this range. I know you have the training and experience to make good tactical decisions. How do you see this one? We're well enough separated to keep you from jumping both of us, we can each fire multiple rounds without stopping to reload, and... I see that you have another of your Deer Guns there."

He flinched, startled that I'd seen that.

"According to my friend here, that's a single shot weapon. If you shoot one of us, the other won't give you time to reload."

"Maybe I'll take my chances," he said, pointing his gun straight at me. Vivian and I had continued to walk towards him while this discussion was taking place, and we were now close enough that none of us was likely to miss if any shooting started.

I was debating what to say next, when Jones' attention shifted to something behind Vivian and I. As I turned my head slightly to see what he was looking at, I expected that it would be Sergeant Donaldson. He had, in fact, made an appearance in the front of the hanger, but that wasn't the focus of Jones' attention — it was Ginger.

"Ginger Brandt?" he said. "What's she doing here?"

I didn't answer him. Instead, I gave a specific hand signal to Silver, who had crept up close to Jones from one side, and just out of his line of sight.

Without making a sound, Silver sprang into action. He took three large bounds and jumped at Jones, closing his mouth on Jones' gun hand and letting his weight drag Jones down on one knee.

I had started running forward as soon as Silver had clamped his jaws on Jones, so that I was able to quickly close the distance between us.

"Drop the gun Major. He's strong enough to tear your hand apart if you don't, and if you try to hurt him..." Jones had raised his other arm, his hand balled into a fist. "Then I'll shoot you myself."

He took a close look at me, decided I was serious - which I was - and then exhaled sharply, lowered his raised arm, and dropped the gun.

"Silver. Grab the gun," I ordered. Silver released his grip, took up the Deer Gun in his jaws and came over to stand beside me.

"Good boy, Silver. Well done," I praised, as Vivian walked over to see about bandaging Jones' bleeding hand with a handkerchief.

Sergeant Donaldson and Ginger had both run up to us by this time, as I was saying "Major Jones, I arrest you for assault with a weapon. You need not say anything. You have nothing to hope from any promise or favour, and nothing to fear from any threat, whether or not you say anything. Anything you do or say may be used as evidence against you at your trial."

"Trial," he snorted. "There'll be no trial. You mentioned military tactics earlier. I may be surrendering now but I have friends in high places. They'll get me off, and they'll get me home."

10 EPILOGUE

Sergeant Donaldson had promptly radioed his other two constables when the action had started, so Jones was quickly searched, handcuffed, and placed in the back of one of the highway patrol cars.

Ginger had rushed up to give me a big hug.

"You promised to stay behind in the SUV," I admonished.

"Yes, but I was worried about you, and then I worried even more when it looked like he was going to shoot you. So, I thought if I could distract him for just a moment, that you'd find a way to get the upper hand on him – and I was right!"

"Yes, and thank you. But you took an awful risk. What you did was brave and foolish. Vivian and I, and the Sergeant and his men, were perfectly capable of handling him."

"Sure, with you maybe getting shot in the deal! I don't care about this Jones guy. I care about you."

"Well, thank you Ginger. As it turned out, you were a big help. He forgot all about Silver for a moment, and didn't see him coming until it was too late."

Sergeant Donaldson had heard some of our conversation, as he walked up to us.

"I agree with what they said about being brave but foolish Miss Brandt, but boy did you distract him! You're not like your TV character at all!"

"Not dumb and helpless, you mean Sergeant? Well, if you want to do me a favour then keep it to yourself, please. I don't want my fans to suspect that I'm anything else and, if you can, please keep my name out of the papers as much as you can, OK? And please, call me Ginger."

"Whatever you say, Miss Ginger. The reporters will probably find out you were here today, and they can sensationalize that all they want I guess, but we'll keep the details of your involvement quiet if that's the way you want it."

Vivian had taken possession of the Deer Gun, and showed it to us before handing it over to the sergeant for evidence.

"It's a nasty-looking thing alright," said the sergeant, looking at the gun, which looked even smaller in his large hand. "How many of these things did he have? Must be quite a few to be able to leave them everywhere as calling cards."

"We'll probably never know for sure," said Vivian, "but he probably got all or most of the 150 of them that went missing in Vietnam, and only seven or eight have turned up at crime scenes so far as I know. Our government will be filing an extradition request so we can get him home after your courts are done with him. We'll see what we can pry out of him."

As the police car with Jones in the back drove off, that was the last I ever saw of him. He was placed in cells in the St. Anthony Detachment pending orders on when and where to transport him for a court appearance.

Vivian and I thanked Sergeant Donaldson and his people for their help, and we took some pictures of the sergeant and the remaining constable posing with Ginger, which she promised to sign and return once they were printed. I'm told that the signed and framed photograph she sent them still hangs in the detachment office.

The two Coast Guard pilots, having seen the excitement and recognized us, came over to check on us (when it was safe) and offered to take us back to St. John's once their refueling was complete. That was good of them, as it probably involved stretching their original orders a bit, and we thanked them warmly and accepted.

It was getting late in the day by the time the helicopter took off, and with our adrenaline coming back down a blanket of weariness settled on us. For my part, however, I slept soundly almost all the way to St. John's, the helicopter's noise and vibrations notwithstanding. I'm pretty sure Silver did too. There was one small event that happened just before I fell asleep. We were well out over the ocean when Vivian suddenly leaned forward from her seat, opened a small window that was inset in the side door, and tossed her gun out.

"What was that?" I asked, rhetorically, because I knew very well what it was.

"Oh, nothing important," she said.

"So, tell me, hypothetically speaking of course. If an FBI agent was coming to Canada to work undercover on a dangerous mission, and she felt that it was prudent to have a gun, for self-defense if nothing else, what would she do?"

"You mean if there hadn't been time to get special permits and she didn't want to risk being caught with a gun when she crossed the border into Canada?"

"Exactly."

"Well, I suppose that our hypothetical agent would just innocently cross the border and then go buy one when she was here."

"Yes, but where the hell did you... I mean, where would she even get a gun without a permit, and so quickly too."

"Ah. Well, that part's easy. Our resourceful agent would probably drive to a small-town gun show, scope it out, maybe stand for a few drinks in the local bar, and find out who at the gun show might quietly sell a gun and a box of rounds, for cash, out of the trunk of their vehicle. That kind of thing happens every day in the States, but it happens here too, just not as blatantly."

"And then when the danger has passed?"

"Oh, well then, when the action's past and it's time for the agent to go home, she probably doesn't want to risk crossing the border with it on her then either. She wouldn't want it to fall in the wrong hands, of course, so she'd probably try to dispose of it somewhere no one would ever find it."

"Like at the bottom of the ocean, for example?"

"That would be a good place, don't you think? Even in the one-in-a-million chance that someone found it, as long as it wasn't right away, it would have rusted into uselessness." She gave me a wide-eyed innocent look.

"Remind me never to play poker with you," I said, and went to sleep.

Meanwhile back at the Front, the officers there had established order at the scene of the fighting, and charged several protesters and several sealers with assault. They were later all convicted and fined accordingly. Captain Webb, his entire crew of 24, and the ship's complement of protesters were all charged with being unlawfully within a half mile of the seal hunt. All of them were eventually convicted and fined as well. The media people on the ship were initially charged, but the Crown Prosecutor later dropped their charges. Ginger was never charged, having been judged to have only been there in her capacity of helping the police.

The next day after the return ride in the helicopter, back in St. John's, we said our goodbyes to Vivian, who flew back to the U.S.

That same day, Staff Sergeant Bob Simpson flew in from Ottawa. It was his practice to meet me for a debriefing after each assignment and, in this case, his niece Ginger's presence gave him an added incentive. He followed the whole story with careful attention and, predictably, had a few words for both of us on the subject of taking reasonable but not excessive risks. He was clearly proud of both of us, though, so we knew we weren't in too much trouble, and I knew that he was partly speaking out of his own guilt for having thought up the idea of Ginger's role in the first place. For Silver, of course, he had unequivocal praise, which Silver lapped up like dog treats.

***

Much later, I heard from Ginger that the IAAP paid all the fines for Captain Webb, his crew, Arne Kristiansen, and the protesters and even for the release of the *Ocean Saviour* from impoundment. Ginger told me that, while she had had enough of such protests, the IAAP people were well satisfied with the media exposure they received from the documentary film and news articles, and that they felt the whole adventure had taken them one step closer to ending the seal hunt, or at least the end of the killing of the seal pups.

Perhaps they were right. Although the Canadian government remained slow to make changes, the protests eventually did sway public opinion in Europe. Several years later, in 1983, the European Union banned the sale of whitecoat pelts, and for the first time in the history of the Canadian seal hunt, the kill fell below 100,000 seals. In 1987, the Canadian Government finally halted the commercial hunt for 'whitecoat' harp seal pups.

***

And Major Jones?

The day after his arrest a black, sleek-looking private helicopter landed at the airport in St. Anthony. A man in a three-piece business suit disembarked and took a taxi to the RCMP Detachment where he identified himself as Major Jones' lawyer. The man met with Jones for an hour and a half, then returned to the helicopter and left. The helicopter was later found to have flown under a fictitious registration. Its flight plans were from and to Dulles Airport, Washington, DC.

The next morning, Jones was found dead in his cell. The pathology report cited death due to saxitoxin, a potent neurotoxin known to be used by the CIA.

It seems that Jones' friends in high places took note of his activities, but not with the results that he'd had in mind.

Laurie Schramm

... Alex and Silver will return,
in *An Intimate Mountie.*

Laurie Schramm

BOOK 8 ENDNOTES

1. The Civilian Irregular Defense Group (CIDG) was a covert CIA program that established and supported paramilitary South Vietnamese units for which training and advice were supplied by U.S. Army Special Forces personnel. The main purpose of the CIDGs (at least initially) was to counter insurgency into South Vietnam by the Viet Cong. Boun Enao was the first of many CIDG villages. See E.C. Piasecki, "Civilian Irregular Defense Group: The First Years: 1961-1967," *Veritas - Journal of Army Special Operations History*, **5** (*4*) 2009, pp. 1-10.

2. The CIA Deer gun was made of cast aluminum and carried no identifying markings. It is five inches long and just over four inches tall. The barrel unscrewed for loading of a single 9mm round. After reattaching the barrel, a striker would be cocked to prepare it for firing. A simple, insertable plastic clip served as a safety. The pistol grip was hollow, and could store three rounds plus a metal rod that was used to clear the barrel of a spent case. They were designed to be delivered by airdrop, and were packaged in polystyrene boxes together with three cartridges and pictorial instructions. Although 1,000 Deer Guns were manufactured (in 1964), only about 150 were sent

to South Vietnam "for field testing." All 1,000 of them were supposed to have been destroyed but some examples have survived. The name 'Deer Gun' is thought to have been a codename.

3. "Yards" was a U.S. Army Special Forces nickname for the Montagnard Tribes that formed the first CIDGs. It was meant affectionately. See the reference in endnote #1.

4. U.S. Military Assistance Command, Vietnam (MACV), which by this time had taken over command of the Special Forces-led paramilitary activities from the CIA.

5. Much of this account is fictional, of course, but in real life the Ohio National Guard later claimed that a sniper had fired on them. Whether or not this was true remains a topic of debate.

6. The famous refrain "Four Dead in Ohio" appears in the protest song *"Ohio"* written by Neil Young and recorded by the group Crosby, Stills, Nash & Young on May 21, 1970 – just 17 days after the shootings at Kent State.

7. The United States eventually withdraw their forces in 1973, but the war continued on and was won by North Vietnam in 1975, thus consolidating the North and the South into the present-day country of Vietnam.

8. J.K. Stoner, "Riot Control Doctrine," *Military Review*, **45** *(2)* 40-44, 1965.

9. In real life, such direct-action campaigns were carried out by the Canadian and Hawaiian Greenpeace organizations between 1975 and 1977.

10. 'Zodiac' is a famous brand of small, rigid-hulled inflatable boats (RIBs) that are prized for their seaworthiness, speed (30 knots or more), and manoeuverability. Although there are other brands, the term Zodiac is frequently colloquially applied to any RIB.

11. Years later, protests such as this would be considered to be part of the 'second-wave of feminism.' Demonstrations and related activities in this period, spanning the 1960s - 1980s, focused on women's cultural and political inequalities in

society.

12. In March 1978, women workers at Fleck Manufacturing went on strike to protest against poor working conditions. They also challenged the (male-dominated) labour movement to support them. The strike was organized and led by women, but it gained the support of the United Auto Workers Union (now Unifor) and the feminist group, Organized Working Women. Eventually, following a bitter strike that shut the plant down and generated national-level media coverage, a settlement was reached with the company. Thereafter, the UAW began to bargain generally for women's issues such as maternity leave, harassment protection, and affirmative action. After numerous bitter strikes at other companies, the Ontario government finally made landmark changes to Ontario labour law. See: M. Landsberg, "Fleck Women Put Fire Back into Feminism," *Toronto Star*, 16 May 1978.

13. Potassium chlorate is a strong oxidizing agent and sugar is very easy to oxidize. When they are exposed to concentrated sulphuric acid, there is an immediate, vigorous reaction that produces heat, purple-tinted flame, and smoke.

14. See *An Inconvenient Mountie* (ISBN: 978-1-9994940-0-1).

15. At this point in time, it was still part of the RCMP Years later, in 1984, the Security Service was spun-out to create the present-day Canadian Security Intelligence Service (C.S.I.S.).

16. See *An Inconspicuous Mountie* (ISBN: 978-1-9994940-2-5).

17. See *An International Mountie* (ISBN: 978-1-9994940-6-3).

18. See *An Indispensable Mountie* (ISBN: 978-1-7772424-2-8).

19. See *An Indestructible Mountie* (ISBN: 978-1-9994940-4-9).

20. See *An Inseparable Mountie* (ISBN: 978-1-7772424-0-4).

21. See *An Inexorable Mountie* (ISBN: 978-1-7772424-4-2).

22. Ottawa's professional football team. At the time, the Ottawa Rough Riders was still in its heyday as a dominant force in the Canadian Football League. It lost its momentum in the 1980s, however, and was wound-up in the 1990s. Ottawa's modern

replacement, the Redblacks, was launched in 2014.

23. Formerly Ottawa's central train station, until the 1960s, this building was the Government Conference Centre, until being turned into a temporary home for Canada's Senate in 2018.

24. The most common type of tear gas is a cyanocarbon called o-chlorobenzylidene, or "CS gas." It isn't actually a gas but is deployed as an aerosol. The CS agent causes tearing and a burning sensation in the eyes, and burning irritation in the nose, mouth and throat. The results are that an affected person has to close their eyes, experiences coughing and difficulty breathing, and becomes disoriented. It has been available since the 1960s.

25. On May 4, 1970, 13 unarmed students were shot by the Ohio National Guard during a peace rally at Kent State University. Four days later, 11 people were bayonetted by the New Mexico National Guard at a University of New Mexico rally. On May 14, two students were killed and many more were wounded by police at a Jackson State University rally.

26. See *An Inexorable Mountie* (ISBN: 978-1-7772424-4-2).

27. See D. Barry, *Icy Battleground. Canada, the International Fund for Animal Welfare, and the Seal Hunt*, Breakwater Books: St. John's, NL, 2005.

28. S. Deyglun, *Les Grands Phoques de la Banquise (The Great Ice Seals)* aired on CBC French, on 17 May 1964.

29. The name International Alliance for Animal Protection and its acronym, IAAP, are entirely fictitious, and are used here as such.

30. Ronald, K. (Chair), "Interim Report to the Minister of Environment from the Committee on Seals and Sealing," 18 January 1972.

31. See *Paris Match*, Issue 1453, 1 April 1977 (cover).

32. The Canadian Police Information Centre (CPIC) is a central police database maintained by the RCMP at its 'HQ' Division in Ottawa. It was launched in 1972 and contains investigative,

identification, intelligence, and ancillary databases which are made available to law enforcement organizations across Canada. Some, but not all, information is also shared with the U.S. National Crime Information Center.

33. 'STEW phone' is reference to a secure telephone capable of providing secure voice communication over non-secure analogue telephone networks. In this case, it was a reference to the STU-I secure telephone unit which was developed in the 1970s by the U.S. National Security Agency. Special variants were provided to selected allies, including Canada.

34. Missing in action (MIA) and presumed dead.

35. *Modus operandi* (MO), meaning a person's method of operation.

36. *The Beachcombers* was a very popular CBC Television series that was originally broadcast from 1972 through 1990.

37. *Charlie's Angels* was an ABC television, crime-drama series that was originally broadcast from 1976 through 1981.

38. The real demonstration calling for a halt to the construction of Ontario's Darlington nuclear generating station was held on 2 June 1979, almost a year later than I have placed in in this story. See D. Fairey, "Nuclear Protesters Invade Hydro Site," *The Canadian Statesman*, Bowmanville, ON, 6 June 1979, pp. 1-2, and S1-S2.

39. In 1978, GLBTQ referred to gay, lesbian, bisexual, transgender, and queer/questioning people. A more current acronym would be LGBTQ+, referring to lesbian, gay, bisexual, transgender, questioning and 'plus,' to represent other sexual identities such as pansexual, asexual, and omnisexual.

40. In the case of the real-life demonstrations, the New South Wales government eventually made legislative changes. In May 1979, the Summary Offences Act was repealed. It had been under the authority of this act that the police had been able to intervene in the demonstrations. Later, in 1984, homosexuality was decriminalized.

41. A somewhat similar series of incidents actually happened in

1979, except that it was the conservation ship *Sea Shepherd* that caught up with the pirate whaler *Sierra* off the Portugese coast. The *Sea Shepherd* rammed the *Sierra,* causing serious damage. Later, when repairs to the *Sierra* were nearly complete, unknown saboteurs used magnetic limpet mines to sink her in Lisbon's harbor.

42. Paraphrased from actual letters written by citizen-opponents of the northwest-Arctic seal hunt. See R. Joyce, "More than One Way to Skin a Seal Hunt," *Maclean's Magazine,* **95** (*12*) 1982, pp. 93-94.

43. This was actually tried in 1983, when the *Sea Shepherd II* blockaded the harbor for two weeks.

44. CP Air (formerly Canadian Pacific Air Lines) flew until 1987, at which time it was bought by Pacific Western Airlines and then absorbed into Canadian Airlines International.

45. Sport utility vehicle.

46. Most of the building remains standing but it's no longer a hotel. In 2013 Memorial University purchased the landmark Battery Hotel and renovated it into a multi-purpose facility that includes a conference centre and graduate student housing.

47. You can't do that walk any more. Many years later (after '9/11' 2001), the city fenced off the best parts of the harbour-walk to provide secure moorage for cruise- and other commercial ships.

48. The expression 'come-from-away' (or 'from away') refers to people that were born outside of Atlantic Canada, and is sometimes used to refer to people born outside of a specific Atlantic Canadian province.

49. An expression meaning 'It's hard to fool a person that's older and wiser.'

50. As it turned out not much actually happened until 1992, by which time the cod stock had dwindled to about 1% of its previous levels. This led to the government declaring a moratorium on the Northern Cod fishery.

51. An expression meaning 'Good luck on your way.'

52. In real life, the 90-foot, 44-gross ton schooner *Scademia* wasn't yet operating in 1979. It was actually built in 1981, and was used for boat tours in and out of the St. John's harbour between 1986 and 2006.

53. Screech is brand of rum originating in Newfoundland and Labrador. Originally a Demerara rum from Guyana, it is now made in Jamaica. At one time, trading ships would take salt-cod south to the Caribbean and bring back barrels of Screech.

54. A classic style of lobster-fishing boat, commonly seen in the Atlantic Provinces. It has a distinctively high bow, from which the gunwales curve down towards a low, flat deck at the stern. Cape Islanders have a reputation for being stable in rough seas.

55. The Witless Bay Seabird Sanctuary comprises four islands in close proximity: Gull Island, Green Island, Great Island, and Pee Pee Island. They were designated as a Wildlife Reserve in 1964, and then re-established under new legislation as a Seabird Ecological Reserve in 1983.

56. This is actually the last line of John Milton's poem "On His Blindness," published in 1673.

57. Sometimes known as a diver's toque, the bright red or reddish-orange knitted-cap was originally a trademark of commercial divers, who wore them under their large brass helmets in the 1800s and early 1900s. When SCUBA diving was brought into broad, non-commercial use by Jacques Yves Cousteau, and others, he and his crew members were often photographed wearing the same bright red toques. As a result, many sport divers picked up the habit as well.

58. An INTERPOL Red Notice is a request to law enforcement worldwide to locate and provisionally arrest a person pending extradition, surrender, or similar legal action.

59. In Canada, most of the Grumman S-2 Trackers were operated by the navy, and were gradually phased out between 1978 and 1990. Many of them, however, were repurposed as Conair Firecat fire-fighting aircraft, in which a large (3,296 litre) fire-

retardant-tank was positioned in the torpedo bay. This allowed them to live on through the early 2000s.

60. See *An Indispensable Mountie* (ISBN: 978-1-7772424-2-8).

61. The *CCGS John A. Macdonald* was classified as a heavy icebreaker, and was named for Canada's first Prime Minister. She was originally commissioned in 1960, as a Department of Transport ship, transferred to the Coast Guard in 1962, and served until 1991, at which time it was decommissioned.

62. The police confrontation with seal-hunt protesters in this story was inspired by a somewhat similar, real-life-incident that occurred in March 1983. The protest-ship *Sea Shepherd II* first blockaded the St. John's harbor, delaying the departure of the sealing fleet by two weeks, then moved into the Gulf of St. Lawrence where it forced several sealing ships away from the harp seal nursery. Two Coast Guard icebreakers carrying 15 RCMP officers blocked and boarded the *Sea Shepherd II*, arresting the captain and 19 crewmembers, all of whom were charged with conspiracy to violate the Seal Protection Act (approaching within a half-mile of a seal hunt and interfering with seal-killing). One of the Coast Guard ships was the *CCGS John A. Macdonald*. See: "Our History," Sea Shepherd Conservation Society, Alexandria, VA, 2017, https://seashepherd.org/our-history/

63. The Messerschmitt-Bölkow-Blohm Bo 105 is a fairly light, twin-engine helicopter. It was introduced into service in 1970. The Canadian Coast Guard Bo 105s were all retired in 2016, but others remain in service in many other countries around the world.

64. Non-Commissioned Officer.

BOOK 5 – 8 SUMMARIES

An Inseparable Mountie (**Book 5**). Called away from vacation in Alaska, Constable Alexandra Houston, the RCMP's first woman Mountie, and Silver, her best friend and police-dog partner, are inserted into an unfolding mystery in northwest British Columbia. Second World War artillery shells seem to be washing up on a beach and having disturbing effects on the kids that find them. These catch the attention of Military Intelligence as well, and Alex and Silver join Canadian Forces Lieutenant Don Harrison in a search that will take them into danger once more.

An Indispensable Mountie (**Book 6**). The year is 1978. When a Soviet nuclear-powered spy satellite veers off course and enters earth's atmosphere, NORAD goes on high alert. When it explodes over Canada's extreme north, a large military search operation is launched to recover the potentially highly-radioactive pieces. But there is a search within the search. RCMP Constable Alex Houston, her dog Silver, and colleagues from military intelligence and the FBI are sent in undercover to discover whether one of the satellite's top-secret components may have survived. As they search a virtually uninhabited wasteland, they soon discover that aircraft malfunctions and the Arctic cold are the least of their problems.

An Inexorable Mountie (**Book 7**). RCMP Constable Alexandra Houston sets out on a cross-Canada train journey to look for security vulnerabilities in advance of an upcoming VIP trip. At least, that's her cover assignment. In reality, Alex, Silver – her police-service-dog partner – and colleague Const. Jack McDonald, are after bigger game. Against a backdrop of beautiful, constantly-changing countryside, Alex notices some strange behaviours on the part of several of her fellow passengers. As her journey continues from Canada's Atlantic Provinces, through Central Canada, and then westward across the Prairies, the behaviours resolve into break-ins, intrigue, and a growing certainty that quite a few people on the train besides herself are not who they seem to be.

An Intrepid Mountie (**Book 8**). When RCMP Corporal Alexandra Houston and her partner Silver experience a chance encounter with two suspicious characters on the front lawn of Canada's Parliament Buildings, Alex decides to do a little digging. The results take them from the Pacific coast of British Columbia to the Atlantic coasts of Newfoundland and Labrador, on the trail of a professional agitator whose appearances at organized protest events seem to coincide with a trail of violence, injuries, and death.

ABOUT THE AUTHOR

Laurie Schramm comes from an RCMP family, grew up while living in the RCMP Barracks (Depot Division) in Regina, Saskatchewan, and spent several summers working as a civilian for the RCMP while in high school and university. Early personal influences included not only the real-life RCMP culture but also Hollywood's versions via such classics as Rose Marie, and Susannah of the Mounties. Many of the events described in this novel are based on the author's real life, although not necessarily within an RCMP context.

For more information, see Laurier L. Schramm on **Linked** in

and:

www.laurieschramm.ca

or

www.facebook.com/LaurieSchrammBooks

Laurie Schramm

ADVENTURES OF THE FIRST WOMAN MOUNTIE

Book 1: *An Inconvenient Mountie*
Book 2: *An Inconspicuous Mountie*
Book 3: *An Indestructible Mountie*
Book 4: *An International Mountie*
Book 5: *An Inseparable Mountie*
Book 6: *An Indispensable Mountie*
Book 7: *An Inexorable Mountie*
Book 8: *An Intrepid Mountie*
Book 9: *An Intimate Mountie*

Adventures of the First Woman Mountie.
Omnibus Volume 1 (Books 1 – 4)

Adventures of the First Woman Mountie II.
The Second Omnibus (Books 5 – 8)

www.laurieschramm.ca

www.facebook.com/LaurieSchrammBooks

Laurie Schramm

Adventures of the First
Woman Mountie

Laurie Schramm

www.ingramcontent.com/pod-product-compliance
Lightning Source LLC
Chambersburg PA
CBHW020241030726
47499CB00001B/16